Also by **Scott Sigler**

Infected

Contagious

Ancestor

Nocturnal

Pandemic

The Galactic Football League Series (YA)

The Rookie

The Starter

The All-Pro

The MVP

The Champion
(COMING IN 2014)

The Galactic Football League novellas (YA)

The Reporter

The Detective

Title Fight

The Gangster
(COMING IN 2014)

The Rider
(COMING IN 2014)

The Reef
(COMING IN 2014)

The Color Series short story collections

Blood is Red

Bones are White

Fire is Orange
(COMING IN 2014)

Galactic Football League:
Book Four

Scott Sigler

THE MVP
(The Galactic Football League Series, Book IV)

Published in the United States by Empty Set Entertainment

For more information, email info@emptyset.com

Library of Congress Cataloging-in-Publication Data
Sigler, Scott
The MVP/ Scott Sigler.
p. cm
1. Science Fiction — Fiction. 2. Sports — Fiction.
Library of Congress Control Number: 20122932078

ISBN: 978-0-9831963-5-8

Printed in the United States of America

Book design by Donna Mugavero at Sheer Brick Studio
Cover design by Scott E. Pond at Scott E. Pond Designs
Cover art (figure) by Adrian Bogart at Punch Designs

First paperback edition MARCH 2014

To my dog, Emma.
For fourteen years you delighted,
inspired and annoyed me.

To the Junkies.
As always, this is for you.

Acknowledgments

The All-Pro team:

AB "Future Hall-of-Famer" Kovacs
who uses up most of the galaxy's available supply of awesome

Donna "Chalkboard" Mugavero
interior book design

Kelly "Lethal Weapon" Lutterschmidt
copyediting

Scott "Big Fish" Pond
cover design, color insert design, mad sculpting skills

Adrian "The Bruiser" Bogart
cover alien art

Dr. Joe "Annihilator" Albietz
medical consulting

Dr. Jeremy "The Eraser" Ellis
alien physiology consulting

John "The Franchise" Vizcarra
continuity coaching

Carmen "Gmork" Wellman
Siglerpedia Czar

Special Thanks

Dr. Phil Plait
for showing us the wonders of the universe

George Hrab
because things are far

Arioch Morningstar
for fighting on

2012 Ionath Krakens
Booster Club

Gregg Anderson

Jason Ashmore

Matthew Bailey

Dale Bennett

Aaron Brough

Shirley Bruce

Joe Carlson

Beth Copenhaver

Paul DeWig

JP and Stephanie Harvey

Alfred Heasty

Jason Heim

David Hess

Neal Hewitt

Randy Hinckley

Tim Hines

Marty Hoffmann

Tony Jennings

Pons Matal

Andrew MacLennan

Byron Metz

Barry O'Donnell

Jeremiah Pappe

Scott E. Pond

Jason and Rebecca Procknow

Michael Procopio

Maryann and Jake Radulski

Connor Robertson

Joseph Saunders

Victor Sellers

Thomas Tetrault

Stephen VanderGast

CJ Wellman

Zachary Wirth

David Wyble

BOOK ONE

The Off-Season

1

Incident on the Bridge

AS A KID, QUENTIN BARNES HAD DREAMED of seeing the galaxy. He'd spent the first fifteen years of his life on a tiny, backwater colony called Micovi. He'd been an orphan and a miner, which were nicer terms to describe his real role in life: he'd been a *slave*. A slave earning subsistence wages that didn't fully cover his company-provided food and housing, wages that would never be enough to pay off the criminal debt incurred by his brother for the horrid crime of stealing bread. Quentin had been trapped, destined to live a life of dangerous labor, fighting every day just to survive long enough to hear the mine whistle that signaled the end of his shift.

Then he'd found football. Or, rather, football had found him.

Football threw the universe wide open. At fifteen years old, he'd signed with the Micovi Raiders of the Purist Nation Football League. He'd moved out of the miner's shantytown and into a dorm owned by the team. The next season, when he took over the starting quarterback position at just sixteen years old, he'd earned enough money to get his own apartment — it was the first time in his life he'd had any privacy, any room that was just *his*.

Then there was the *travel*, actually getting off of Micovi to visit the four planets, six colonies and the orbital station that made up the Purist Nation. He had traded slavery for the stars. He had seen more of the Nation than an orphan miner could have ever hoped for.

And that was just the beginning.

His natural talent, his work ethic and his intensity carried him even beyond the borders of his homeland and into the Galactic Football League, where only the best of the best played. He became the starting quarterback of the Ionath Krakens. He saw not only the planets of the Nation, but stars and worlds and stadiums all over the galaxy.

Playing in the GFL brought so many changes, the biggest of which was dealing with non-Human species for the first time in his life. He'd grown up in a system based on hatred of anything that was not like him. His grade-school education included training on how to kill all of the "lower races."

In the GFL, however, he had to play against and alongside those races. He'd entered the league as an uneducated bigot but quickly learned that his attitude would not bring him the thing he wanted most in life — victory on the football field. Quentin learned to let go of his preconceived notions, learned how to evaluate each sentient as an individual. Those once-hated aliens became his teammates, then became his friends and, soon after, became his family.

Discovering the universe. Meeting new races.

These two things had seemed like a dream.

Now, that dream had become a nightmare.

Quentin Barnes stood on the small bridge of the *Touchback*, the ship that carried him and his Krakens from system to system, from game to game. His body throbbed with pain, remnants of being smashed around like a toy when enemy rounds had ripped open his gun cabin. He'd been in an actual starship battle, he'd taken out a pirate fighter craft — in doing so, had he taken the life of a sentient? Quentin had damn near died himself as the cabin depressurized, had almost been ripped into space through a hole far too small for his 7-foot-tall, 380-pound body. His friends — Crazy George Starcher and Mum-O-Killowe — had saved him, risked their own lives to pull him out.

Quentin looked to the bridge's sealed bulkhead doors, where George and Mum-O stood. His two teammates stared out the bridge's floor-to-ceiling viewport windows. George looked shocked and mesmerized. Mum-O had no expression, at least not one Quentin could read on the Ki's black-eyed face. Stoic as ever, Mum-O patiently waited for what might come next.

Quentin turned to look at the four-man bridge crew dressed in their neat orange and black uniforms. They sat motionless at workstations that faced a holographic image of the *Touchback*. Portions of the holographic ship glowed red, others yellow, indicating the damage suffered during the pirate attack. So much damage ... how long would it take to bring the *Touchback*'s engines back online?

Too long. There seemed to be no chance for escape.

Captain Kate Cheevers had steered the *Touchback* away from the pursuing pirates, had fled in the only direction that gave the ship a chance. In doing so, the *Touchback* had crossed the Sklorno Dynasty border into Prawatt Jihad sovereign territory — out of the frying pan and into the fire. She sat slumped in her captain's chair, staring out the viewport like everyone else. She held a clear bottle by its narrow neck, slowly turning it, making the brown liquid inside slosh and wave. Her body language told the story: she had lost all hope.

Quentin stood in the middle of the bridge with Messal the Efficient, a three-foot-tall Quyth Worker, and the hulking, long-armed, eight-foot HeavyG monster known as Michael Kimberlin. Like George, Mum-O, the bridge crew and Captain Kate, they stared, stared out the viewport window at a gnarled, black ship so big that it blocked out the endless expanse of space itself.

It was hard to process the scale. In fact, Quentin wasn't even sure he *could* process it, just like he couldn't really process the size of a planet.

Can something artificial really be that big? Is that even possible?

Kimberlin, Quentin's tutor and the Krakens' starting right offensive guard, had just told everyone the monstrosity outside was a Prawatt capital-class warship, the largest known vessels in the entire galaxy. Kimberlin had said something else as well, something that Quentin hoped to High One he hadn't heard correctly.

"Mike," Quentin said, "you want to repeat that?"

"Which part?"

"The part where I thought you said something like, *I'm afraid we're all going to die.*"

Kimberlin nodded. "No need to repeat it, my friend, you have it word for word. It has been an honor to know you."

Quentin shook his head. There was a way out of this. There was *always* a way out.

He turned to Captain Kate. "Can we fight them?"

She shook her head and laughed, a dark sound that matched her defeated posture. "Not gonna happen. What little firepower we have left probably wouldn't do anything other than make them mad. Our engines are offline, so we can't maneuver. The punch drive hasn't recharged, so we're stuck here. I hope you've made peace with your imaginary sky daddy because you're about to find out if he's real."

"We can't give up," Quentin said. "There has to be a way out of this."

Captain Kate called down to her bridge crew. "Maurice, kindly adjust the display so pretty-boy quarterback can understand what's really happening."

One of the orange- and black-uniformed men sitting at the holodisplay turned to face Kate. "Yes, Captain," he said, then turned back to his controls.

In his three years with the Krakens, Quentin hadn't spent much time on the bridge. He never noticed Maurice before — if he had, he would have remembered the crewman's yellow skin. Not a *tinge* of yellow, or a yellow-pink, but *yellow*, like he'd been covered in paint. Quentin had never seen yellow-skinned people before. If he lived through this, he could ask Kimberlin where they came from.

Maurice worked the holographic controls floating above his workstation. The glowing image of the *Touchback* took up about half of the bridge. It was as long as two of the crew lined up head to feet and as tall as one of them from the waist up. The holographic ship started to shrink, slowly at first, then rapidly, reducing to the size of one man, then just an arm, then just a hand. As it shrank, Quentin saw another glowing image fuzz into view — an irregular thing that looked like a chipped, pitted boulder and was clearly far bigger than the display area allowed.

The *Touchback* image shrank to the size of one of Quentin's fingers. Only then did the boulder have enough room to be shown in its entirety, a ball some twelve feet in diameter.

"High One," Quentin said.

Kimberlin nodded. "Yes, it is quite spectacular."

Quentin again looked out the viewport to the approaching Prawatt vessel. The ship didn't look that different from space itself: it was black, with lots of little lights. But the ship's blackness had a gnarled, corrugated texture, like bunched-up tree roots that had punched through the dirt and been exposed to decades of rain and snow.

Crazy George Starcher walked toward the floor-to-ceiling viewport. He reached a hand out halfway, as if he wanted to touch the object out there but knew he could not.

"The Old Ones," he said. "They have come for us."

Quentin shook his head. "They're not that old. They've only been around about four centuries."

Kimberlin's big chest shook in a silent laugh. He thought it was funny, and Quentin knew why; Quentin had just shared historical information learned through many hours of Kimberlin's tutoring — Quentin had worked hard to leave his prejudiced upbringing behind and become a more educated person, a *better* person, and yet he and his teammates might die right here at the hands of an alien race.

Die before they could win a GFL title.

Like a silent dream, the giant, black, gnarled ship suddenly *reached*, a chunk of it flowing like colorless molten metal or a glob of rigid pudding, extending out toward the *Touchback*. Quentin had a brief thought of one of the educational holos Kimberlin had showed him, of an amoeba extending a gooey arm to engulf some microscopic prey, then a vibration rolled through the *Touchback*.

Maurice checked a readout. He turned to face Captain Kate.

"Let me guess," she said. "We've been enclosed?"

"Yes, Captain."

She nodded, took a swig, then somehow managed to slouch even deeper in her chair. "I'm a genius like that. Are they coming in?"

Maurice turned back to his controls. "Looks like they're creating a seal over the landing bay. They're pressurizing."

"Dammit," Kate said. "Just open the shuttle bay doors before they blow them open. If we do manage to get out of this alive, that's one less thing we have to fix."

"Yes, Captain."

Quentin looked around the bridge, waiting for Kate or one of the four bridge crewmembers to *do* something.

"We can't just wait for death," he said. "Shouldn't we send out a distress signal? Go to the lifeboats and eject?"

Captain Cheevers spun a slow circle in her chair. She stopped when she faced Quentin. "You want to do something, pretty boy?"

Quentin nodded.

She smiled that smile that made him so uncomfortable. "Maurice," she said, "are they onboard yet?"

Maurice had to clear his throat to speak. The sense of hopelessness was giving way to one of fear.

"Yes, Captain," he said. "It looks like they are spreading out, either running bypasses on internal doors or cutting through them. At least four ... no, *five* appear to be moving toward the bridge."

Kate pointed at Quentin with her left pointer finger, her left thumb up high. "Bang-bang, Barnes. Our visitors are on their way here. If you think *you* can do something, something other than crap your pants, be my guest. Maurice, do we have atmospheric integrity?"

"Yes, Captain," he said. "The *Touchback* is completely engulfed, we have full pressure everywhere."

"Then open all internal doors," Kate said. "We don't want to make the crawlies any more angry than they'll already be."

QUENTIN WATCHED as the bridge's thick bulkhead doors slid open, revealing the corridor beyond. He looked around the bridge, staring at each person in disbelief. "You're all just going to let them walk in here?"

Kate nodded. She took another drink. She pressed a button in the armrest of her chair.

"Attention, all personnel," she said. Quentin heard her speaking but also heard her words amplified by the speakerfilm out in the corridor. He knew that the rest of the ship was hearing the same words.

"This is Captain Kate. We have been boarded. Stay where you are. Do not try to reach the lifeboats. If you want to live, do not make threatening gestures, fight or in any way resist the boarders. Just take a seat, stay calm and await further instructions."

She clicked the button again, then slouched back in her chair and took a long drink from the bottle.

Moments later, they heard sounds coming from out in the corridor. Quentin and the others turned to face the open door.

They waited.

2

Contact

QUENTIN HAD MET many alien races in the past two years — Ki, the three Quyth castes, all of the Human variants, Sklorno, Dolphin, Leekee, Creterakian — but nothing could have prepared him for this.

Through the open bulkhead door, death walked in on long legs.

Quentin dared not breathe, tried to not even blink.

A Prawatt. A *Walking X*.

Its flexible, two-sectioned legs resembled those of a spider. The thigh and foreleg looked exactly the same, each section about two feet long, the foreleg ending in a long, slim, three-toed foot. Quentin could see *through* the legs in some places, as if they were a thick, shiny vapor or perhaps made from some kind of dense mesh. The thighs connected to a hard-shelled middle section shaped like a squat, thick X — also shiny but not see-through. The middle part, at least, seemed solid. From the upper parts of that middle X extended two arms that looked almost exactly like the legs, except the arms were coiled around a thin-but-deadly-looking rifle.

It had no head, just the body, the arms and the legs.

The Walking X, his people had called the Prawatt. *The Devil's Rope. Satan's Starfish.*

And to think ... he'd once considered the Ki alien-looking.

THE CREATURE TOOK FOUR LONG STEPS into the bridge, then paused. It turned its body in a way a Human would have were that Human looking from left to right. Quentin saw small, reflective dots on the X-trunk and more of the same at the joints of the arms and legs. The Prawatt equivalent of eyes?

The Prawatt vibrated, just once, then six more of his kind strode through the door. Five walked erect, like the first, but the last one moved on all fours, further reinforcing the impression of a strange, four-limbed spider.

The five members of the *Touchback* crew and the four Krakens players stayed very still. Captain Kate casually swung her left foot back and forth under her command chair. She took another swig from the bottle.

The four-legged Prawatt stepped forward. Blue lines and some alien writing marked its X-trunk. Quentin's time in the GFL had taught him that members of an alien race might all look the same at first, but there were always differences. His eyes hunted for ways to tell the individual Prawatt apart.

What would happen next? Would the Prawatt kill everyone on the bridge? Would they take prisoners?

There is a way out of this, just stay calm, stay calm and watch.

The four-legged X-Walker rose up to stand erect. "I am here to discuss your transgression," it said. "Which one of you is in charge?" It spoke in perfect English. Quentin couldn't see where the voice came from — did it have a mouth? Or maybe some kind of speakerfilm, like the Harrah used?

Captain Kate raised her hand. "That would be me," she said, then took yet another sip. They could all die here, and she was getting drunk. Quentin wanted to yell at her, but he kept his mouth shut.

The blue-lined Prawatt pointed an arm at her bottle. "Put that down and stand up."

Kate complied. She stood straight.

The Prawatt walked forward to stand before her. The intersection of its X-body was just over five feet above the deck. Its arms were pointed up and out, waving slightly, an implied threat that it might gather her in at any moment and pull her toward an as-yet-unseen mouth.

"You are in charge," it said. "Does that mean you're the captain of this vessel?"

Eyes wide, she nodded. "I am. I'm Captain Kate Cheevers."

"I am Cormorant Bumberpuff, captain of the *Grieve*."

Kate's nose wrinkled in disbelief. "Bumberpuff?"

"Yes."

"Your *name*," she said. "Your name is *Bumberpuff?*"

"That is correct. I am the captain of the *Grieve*."

Quentin watched, but he also listened. If he'd closed his eyes, the exchange would have sounded like a conversation between two Humans — one a bossy woman that slurred her words, the other a man with a metallic-tinged, Earth-like accent.

Kate eyed the bottle she'd set on the floor, then looked up again. "Look, maybe your name is *Bumberpuff,* or whatever the hell ridiculous name you want to call yourself, but enough with the mind games," she said. "No military in, like, the *entire galaxy* would ever send a ship *captain* to board another vessel. That would be as dumb as, I don't know, sending a ship captain down to the surface of an unknown planet or something."

Bumberpuff vibrated once, the motion producing a noise from his body not unlike a rattlesnake's rattle. "You think I would let someone else take the glory of being first?"

Kate rubbed her face. "Okay, whatever you say. You've got us dead to rights, after all. But what the hell is a *bumberpuff,* anyway?"

The Prawatt seemed to stiffen. "A Bumberpuff is the sentient who will decide if you live or die. Does that answer your question?"

Kate closed her mouth and nodded.

The Prawatt captain walked around the room, pausing for one second in front of each frightened sentient.

"You have invaded Prawatt space," he said. "This is an act of war."

Kate shook her head. "We were attacked by pirates. They jumped us coming out of punch-space, four small fighters launched from a support ship. We had to flee into Prawatt space just to survive."

Captain Bumberpuff — Quentin had to admit that Kate was right, the name *was* ridiculous when applied to such a nightmarish creature — paused for a second. For some reason, he reminded Quentin of a dog tilting its head to listen for a command.

"I am getting reports of heavy damage to your vessel," Bumberpuff said. "The appearance and nature of this damage would seem to support your story."

Quentin realized that when the alien spoke, some of the silvery dots vibrated so fast they blurred. His guess had been correct — some of the dots acted just like speakerfilm.

The sinewy Prawatt took another walk around the bridge, again looked at each sentient. When he stood in front of Quentin, Quentin had to force himself to not look away. The Prawatt's arms and legs weren't *mesh*, exactly, but they were some kind of segmented or sectioned metal. And he *could* see through them in parts, if the light hit them just right.

The Walking X.

The Devil's Rope.

Quentin guessed the Prawatt weighed three hundred pounds, but the apparently hollow limbs made it hard to gauge.

Bumberpuff's body rattled again.

"You will all be taken to the *Grieve*," he said. "We will interrogate you individually. Your ship will be destroyed. If our tribunal determines you were invading, you will be executed. If they determine you were fighting for survival, as you say you were, you will be delivered to a Creterakian intermediary."

Kate smiled and let out a huge, held breath. She seemed to sag a little. "Hooo, that's what we needed to hear," she said. "As long as no one from the *Touchback* gets stupid, everyone might make it out of this alive."

Bumberpuff turned toward her. Quentin realized there were far fewer reflective dots on the Prawatt's back.

"The process I specified is for non-Sklorno only," Bumberpuff said. "Any Sklorno on board will be detained indefinitely. They will not have access to a tribunal."

Quentin's Sklorno teammates. His *friends*. Hawick, Milford, Halawa, Cheboygan, all the others. Detained *indefinitely* by a hostile race, one with whom the Creterakians were on the brink of war, one that was suspected of destroying a passenger ship and killing fifty thousand Sklorno in the process? He couldn't allow that to happen.

He wanted to protect them as individuals, but there was something more than just that — the Sklorno were also the team's defensive backs and his receivers. The next Tier One season was just seven months away. If Ionath lost those players, there wasn't time to find enough real talent to replace them. There would be no run at the 2685 championship. The Krakens would be lucky to win a single game.

He had to protect his friends, and he had to protect his franchise. Quentin drew in a deep breath — he needed to make a stand.

"Captain Bumberpuff," he said, "this is unacceptable."

Everything seemed to pause.

Captain Kate took a step toward him. "Barnes," she said in a low tone. "You need to shut your mouth."

Quentin ignored her. "Any Sklorno on this ship must come with us," he said to Bumberpuff. "They're not *operatives* or *spies*, they're football players. We're all members of a team in the Galactic Football League."

The Prawatt turned toward Quentin. "I am familiar with your sport," he said. "We have seen the endless broadcasts. This *football* is a competition for weaklings."

They knew about football? And they — hey, wait a minute ...

"*Weaklings?*" Quentin said. "You don't know what you're talking about. Football is the most dangerous sport in the galaxy."

All of the Prawatt started vibrating, waves rippling across their semi-see-through legs and arms, softly reflecting the bridge's overhead lights and the glow from the holographic *Touchback*.

"Dangerous," Bumberpuff said. "Is that why you wear the combat armor? Because this *dangerous* game might damage your frail and delicate bodies?"

"Well, yeah," Quentin said. "We have to, or sentients would get hurt more often."

The alien creatures vibrated again, more intensely this time. Was this reaction some religious thing? Some sign of aggression?

Then it hit him — they were *laughing*. Laughing, at *him*.

Quentin was still afraid, but a new emotion joined the fear; he felt *angry*. They thought his sport was for weaklings? What would *they* know about it? That made him think of the holo that Kimberlin had shown him, the shaky footage of Leiba the Gorgeous and other sentients playing the Prawatt's strange game — flying balls smashing into sentients' heads, bone-crunching hits, beings literally dying on that black playing field. The Prawatt sport looked violent, certainly, but it wasn't the same thing as ...

That was it ... that was *it*.

He lifted his right hand, bringing up his palm-up holodisplay. He started tapping the floating icons that appeared, working his way to his personal files.

"What are you doing?" Bumberpuff said. "Put that down."

"It's okay," Quentin said. "I just want to show you something." His fingers flew through the directory.

One of the other Prawatt stepped forward and leveled his weapon at Quentin's face. Bumberpuff held up a long-fingered hand, a very Human gesture.

"Hold your fire," he said. "Barnes, put that display away."

Quentin tried not to look at the gun pointed at his head. He had to find that file ...

"You were warned," the captain said. "Execute the aggressor on the count of three. Three, two, wuh—"

The holoclip appeared on Quentin's hand, the stadium and the players so tiny they could barely be seen. He curled his fingers and thumb around the hologram, then *threw* it at the glowing display of the tiny *Touchback* and the massive *Grieve*. The bridge computer read his motion and transferred the file — those images vanished, replaced by a large image of the strange alien arena.

Static and fuzz dotted the low-resolution footage, which was obviously shot with a small, personal camera and not the high-end rigs that networks used to broadcast GFL games. Sloping stadium stands surrounded the black pit of a large arena floor, on which sentients competed in a fast-moving game. Tens of thousands of Prawatt packed those stands, crammed in so tight you couldn't make one out from the next. Spindly arms waved like black grass under a heavy wind. He saw Walking-Xs, but many other body shapes as well, the details lost in the crowd density and the poor image quality.

Quentin pointed at the holo. "That! We want that!"

Bumberpuff watched the game for a moment. The other Prawatt did as well, the closest one lowering its weapon. Alien or not, Quentin instinctively understood the reaction of a fellow athlete: the Prawatt on the bridge didn't just *watch* this game, they were *players*.

The holo showed two seven-sentient teams battling it out. One team wore red streamers, the other, yellow. A red-team Prawatt carrying a ball leapt high into the air and started to throw. A yellow-team Prawatt leapt to block, but was too late — the ball sailed through the upper-most of three rings.

Quentin walked to the holotable and jumped up on top of it. He stood in the middle, his body distorting the footage that played across his chest and face. He spread his arms wide and stared down at Bumberpuff.

"We've heard that you make sentients who cross into your space play this game," Quentin said. "If they win, they earn their freedom. So the Ionath Krakens throw down a challenge. Seven of us against seven of you. If we win, you let us go."

Bumberpuff stayed still, but the other Prawatt moved slightly, swayed, shifted their balance from one coiled foot to the next. Quentin watched them, trying to take in as much detail as he could. Were they angry? Insulted? Or, were they *excited*?

Captain Kate walked to the edge of the table, put her hands

on the surface. "Barnes! Get down from there, you're going to get us killed!"

Bumberpuff walked closer. Kate backed away. The Prawatt captain stepped up onto the table to stand before Quentin, Prawatt and Human sizing each other up. Quentin felt like he was a kid again, back in the mines of Micovi, trying to look intimidating so that he didn't have to fight some miner that was twice his age.

Bumberpuff raised his arms to their full ten-foot height. He waved them. "Your ship is impounded. You are prisoners of the Jihad. You will make no demands."

Quentin pointed his left finger. He moved it forward slowly until it touched the center of Bumberpuff's X-body. Quentin tapped his finger twice on the hard, cool surface, once to emphasize each word: "*Shuck ... that.*"

Captain Kate again walked up to the table. She was shaking with rage. "Barnes, we can get out of this alive. Will you shut your mouth?"

Quentin turned to look down at her. "Cheevers, be *quiet!*" The words came out of his mouth as a roar, the same volume he used to call signals over the cacophony of 185,000 screaming fans. In the close confines of the bridge, his voice rang louder than he'd ever known it could. Kate leaned away, her eyes wide with surprise.

He again faced the Prawatt captain. He saw no reaction from Bumberpuff.

Quentin banged a fist against his chest. "*I* am the leader of this ship, not Captain Cheevers," he said. "*I* am the leader of the Ionath Krakens, and *I* have the authority to challenge your kind. If you hurt any of my teammates, it shows that you *know* you can't beat us without cheating. You can decline my challenge, you can kill us all, but we'll die proud knowing that you took the coward's way out because your species ... is ... *afraid.*"

The aliens stopped shifting, stopped swaying. Quentin waited, holding his gaze steady on the leader. What he had just said hit home — had he called them *names*? What had he been thinking? He felt the fear, but his breathing stayed normal and his face didn't flinch; his mental battles with Gredok had taught him how to hide his emotions.

Bumberpuff shivered once. "We are far from our planet," he said. "The travel there would take three months of Earth standard time."

Three *months*? Quentin tried to imagine the distance involved. He looked to Kimberlin for an answer.

For the first time since the Prawatt had come onto the bridge, the HeavyG lineman spoke.

"The longest trip across known space is from Tower in the Tower Republic to the planet Lashan in the Rewall Association," Kimberlin said. "That trip takes seven days."

Bumberpuff rattled and vibrated. "Our sovereign territory is vast. From where we are now, it takes three months to reach home. You can have your game, Krakens, and if you win, we will bring you back here."

Quentin had to think of something, and fast. The 2684 season was almost over. The *Touchback* had been en route to the planet Yall for the Galaxy Bowl between the Themala Dreadnaughts and the Jupiter Jacks. That game was only days away, then came seven months until the beginning of the 2685 Tier One preseason. If Bumberpuff took them to the Prawatt home planet, three months out and three months back ... that would put the Krakens too close to missing those invaluable preseason practices.

He looked around the bridge, trying to find something that might give birth to an idea. Then his gaze fell on the viewport.

Their ship ...

"Captain Bumberpuff, why do we need to go to your planet?"

"To play the Game," the Prawatt said. The emphasis on the last word told Quentin that the strange sport was called simply that: *the Game*.

Quentin pointed out the window to the mass of gnarled black that had engulfed the *Touchback*. "I just saw your ship ... uh ... *bud* ... or whatever you want to call it. It stuck out a huge, uh ... a thing that moved out, and ... "

He couldn't find the word. He looked to Kimberlin.

The big lineman shrugged. "Pseudopod?"

Quentin turned back to the Prawatt. "Yeah, a *pseudopod*, one so big it ate our whole ship. If your technology can do *that*, don't try and tell me you can't make an arena."

The five standing Prawatt started shifting again, faster than before. The idea of creating an arena inside the massive vessel seemed to excite them.

Bumberpuff lowered his long arms. "We could make a playing field. If we allow you to play the Game, it is by our rules. And do not think that your Sklorno crew members can avoid playing, they will —"

"Kick your asses," Quentin said. "Our Sklorno crew members will beat the crap out of the best you've got, send you crying home to your momma."

Quentin let the words hang. He had no idea if Prawatt even *had* mommas. Or asses, for that matter.

The captain stepped closer. All of its eye-things seemed to focus on Quentin's face.

"I have seen you on the broadcasts," Bumberpuff said. "The captain of your ship called you *Barnes*. You are *Quentin* Barnes? From the Purist Nation?"

Quentin kept a straight face despite the utter shock of hearing that this alien not only knew who he was, but knew where he had come from. Just how much football did the Prawatt watch, anyway?

"Yeah, that's me."

"And *you* will play?"

Quentin smiled. "I will if you will."

Bumberpuff's body rattled, just once, from the tips of his long, black fingers down to the ends of his long, black toes.

"I accept."

The mood of the room changed. He and his teammates were still in an infinite amount of trouble, of danger, but this wasn't a military situation anymore. Now? Now, it was about playing a game.

And Quentin Barnes played to win.

3

Picking a Team

QUENTIN HEADED FOR THE DINING DECK. George Starcher, Michael Kimberlin and Mum-O-Killowe walked along behind him. He'd borrowed Kimberlin's messageboard and was reading up on what little was known about the Game as he walked.

The Prawatt ship had pressurized all of the *Touchback*, which meant Quentin and the others could walk through damaged corridors. In some places, he had to step over wreckage. In others, part of the hull was gone, the holes filled by the gnarled-yet-orderly black surface that made up the Prawatt ship's pseudopod. The texture resembled thousands of dark steel cables twisted upon one another, like some kind of black metal fabric.

The rules of the Game seemed fairly simple. He needed six players in addition to himself. The Prawatt had demanded the team include at least two Sklorno. Put the ball through one of the three rings, your team scores 10 points. One player, a "goalie," defended the goals, while the other six players were out on the field. Passing in any direction: legal. Blocking and tackling: legal. Punching, kicking, scratching and biting? Those were probably legal as well.

Quentin entered the dining deck. Messal the Efficient was waiting.

"All members of the organization that can move are here," Messal said. "I'm afraid Coach Hokor the Hookchest is still unconscious in medbay."

Quentin looked around the large room, taking it all in. *Everyone* was there, waiting for news. Not just his teammates, the Ki, the Quyth Warriors, the Humans and the Sklorno, but Captain Kate and her four orange-uniformed bridge crew as well.

Also present were two dozen or so sentients that made up the Krakens' business staff — Humans, Quyth Workers, even a few of the furry, baketball-sized Sklorno males that everyone referred to as *bedbugs*. These sentients stayed out of sight most of the time, but now their lives were just as at stake as everyone else's.

Doc Patah floated near the ceiling, waiting, his wide flaps undulating in slow waves to keep him in position. Shizzle, the team's Creterakian interpreter, flew in slow circles punctuated by the rhythmic sound of his membranous wings. He'd clothed his tadpole-shaped form in a hideous bodysuit of reflective silver lined with yellow lightning bolts.

Save for the team owner, the entire Ionath Krakens franchise was there. Quentin was making decisions that could determine life and death for all. What if playing the Game was the wrong choice? He closed his eyes and took a slow breath — no time for thinking like that, not now, not when he had to focus on winning.

They waited for him to speak. Gredok the Splithead wasn't here. He was probably back on Ionath, wondering what had happened to his multi-million-credit franchise. No owner, no coach … now everyone looked to the team captain for direction.

Quentin met their stares. Lives would be at risk, but at least he'd given everyone in this room a fighting chance at survival.

"Krakens, listen up," he said. "The Prawatt are in control of the *Touchback*. They understand we were attacked. As such, they will *probably* let us go free — all but the Sklorno."

The Sklorno players chittered in their native language, a nonsensical stream of chirps and clicks. They hated the Prawatt just as much as the Prawatt hated them. Most of Sklorno were covered head to toe, as was their way whenever males of their species were near. Defensive back Wahiawa, however, wore only her practice jersey, leaving much of her see-through body exposed. Most Sklorno had four flexible eyestalks sticking out of the coarse, black hair that covered their baseball-sized heads. She and her sister Halawa each had three, due to the fact that they'd once been conjoined twins with that fourth eyestalk connecting them.

Wahiawa vibrated with obvious anger, her back-folded legs twitching constantly. Her exposed skin would have normally made the bedbugs mad with desire, but she radiated hostility and they gave her plenty of room — if one of the males did make a move on her, she'd probably grab him with her two long tentacles, then tear the guy apart with the toothed raspers that dangled from her open chin-plate.

Quentin raised his hands for silence. "If we leave without our Sklorno teammates, I think they will never see home again. They will die in Prawatt space. I won't let that happen. The Prawatt have a sport they call *the Game*. There's a holo of Leiba the Gorgeous playing it, has anyone seen that?"

More than a few heads nodded.

"I challenged the Prawatt to play us in their *Game*," Quentin said. "If we win, *all* of us go free. But this sport is deadly. I watched just three or four minutes of it, and in that time two sentients lost their lives. I am playing. I need six players to join me."

John Tweedy stood up and raised his hand. Quentin's best friend and the Krakens' starting middle linebacker bounced on his toes as he jumped up and down. "I'll volunteer! I'm in!" His changeable, full-body tattoo spelled out the words EQUAL OPPORTUNITY MOUTH-BUSTER across his face.

"Q! Pick me, *pick me!*"

Quentin shook his head. "I didn't ask for volunteers."

"But Q, I —"

Quentin held up a hand to stop him. "John, please — sit down."

John sat.

Quentin hadn't been exaggerating — sentients could and did

die in this sport. He would have liked nothing more than to have John guarding him out in that arena, but if the Krakens were going to win he had to base his choices on something other than his own safety.

"I need the players best suited for the Prawatt game," Quentin said. "If I call your name, it's because the team needs you if we're going to get everyone out of here alive. I'll say it again — playing could get you hurt. It could end your football career. It could get you *killed*. If I call on you and you say *no*, I can't make you play."

He looked around the room, searching for signs of fear, of sentients casting their gaze to the floor or looking away — but every last Kraken stared right back at him. He nodded, his heart swelling with pride. They were ready to go to war with him.

He turned to the Sklorno clustered on the right side of the room. "The Prawatt captain insisted that Sklorno play. The Prawatt will come after you. I think they will actually *try* to kill you."

Milford jumped five feet into the air. "Pick *me*," she squealed. "I will kill the Prawatt!" She and Quentin had been rookies together. He knew her better than any Sklorno on the team. She was fast as fast could be, but she didn't have the size to stand up to the kind of hitting Quentin had seen in that holo.

Wahiawa also started jumping. The 320-pound cornerback shook with fury. "No, *I* will kill them. I beg you, Quentinbarnes, *I beg you*!"

Milford shoved Wahiawa to the ground. Before Wahiawa could get up, Hawick, the team's top receiver, hopped over her to take center stage.

"I Hawick am the killer of Prawatt! Choose me *chooseme*!"

Cheboygan, the big rookie receiver, rushed forward and tackled Hawick. As they flew through the air and into a table, Quentin heard Cheboygan's high-pitched voice screaming "*mememememe*!"

Suddenly, the Sklorno were tearing into each other, an instant brawl that sent bodies flying and filled the air with pleas to play against the Prawatt. Twenty Krakens moved in, pulling Sklorno off the pile, holding them back or just lying on top of them, pinning them to the ground.

Quentin stepped into the melee. "*Enough*! I *command* you to be still!"

The Sklorno froze. Only their trembling eyestalks moved, watching Quentin — they had angered their Godling.

He felt silly, but only for a moment. He could worry about a god complex later. Right now, he had to pick a team.

"Halawa," Quentin said, pointing to the big second-year receiver. "And Cheboygan. You both start as *runners*. I'll explain that position later."

He looked over the rest of his Sklorno teammates. He'd picked Halawa and Cheboygan because they had both size *and* speed. If he'd taken Halawa for those reasons, he might as well take her twin sister.

He pointed at Wahiawa. "You start at goalie."

"Use backups," said a voice from the back of the room, "not starters."

All heads turned to look at the blue-skinned, white-haired Don Pine, the man Quentin had beat out for the starting quarterback position. Don Pine, the man who had thrown his career away to repay his gambling debts. Quentin had found a way to secretly cover that debt and save Don's reputation, his legacy. Then Yolanda Davenport's exposé on corruption in the GFL had mistakenly pinned Don's illegal actions on Quentin. When that happened, Quentin had expected Don to own up to the bad deeds — but Don had stayed quiet, letting Quentin take the heat, letting a galaxy believe that Quentin was a cheating, gambling, lying scumbag of a criminal.

Quentin Barnes genuinely hated three sentients: he hated Rick "Sarge" Vinje for pretending to be his father, Cillian Carbonaro; he hated Gredok the Splithead for hiring Rick to do just that; he hated Don Pine for being a coward, for betraying both the sport of football and Quentin's friendship.

Quentin wanted to shout at Pine, tell him to shut his mouth and go crawl into a hole somewhere, but he did not. The two glittering GFL championship rings on Don's right hand were proof that the man knew how to strategize, how to manage his teammates. If Don had something to say, Quentin would consider it.

"Don, we need size and speed," Quentin said. "The Prawatt probably haven't played any Sklorno as big, strong and fast as Halawa, Wahiawa and Cheboygan."

Don nodded. "Cheboygan, okay, but Halawa? She's a starting receiver. Don't put her at risk. And you saw what happened this year when our defensive backs were hurt. Wahiawa is your number-one cornerback — if she gets hurt and we don't have her at one hundred percent for the 2685 season, other offenses will pick us apart unless Gredok spends big bucks for a top-level player."

Pine was thinking long term. That was smart, but it didn't treat their current situation with enough severity.

"If we don't win *this* game, there won't *be* an '85 season," Quentin said. "Halawa and Cheboygan have the size, and this game involves throwing a ball. We need their catching ability."

Don shook his head. "Hokor wouldn't choose them. Neither would Gredok."

"Gredok isn't here. Hokor is still unconscious."

Don looked around the room, expecting support — he didn't find any. He stared at Quentin. "So *you* get to make this decision? *You* decide who risks their lives?"

Quentin knew it was a fair question, but the entire team was watching and he couldn't back down now.

"If I pick a player and they agree, then the decision is made," he said. He looked at his Sklorno teammates. "Halawa, Cheboygan, Wahiawa, do you agree to play?"

The three of them started jumping in place.

All through the dining deck, heads nodded in agreement. Not that long ago, many players would have sided with Don; it was Quentin's team now, and everyone knew it.

He started to pick his next players, then paused as a realization hit home: Don was right. The long term *did* matter almost as much as the here and now. Halawa was the team's number-three receiver; losing her would hurt, but Quentin had additional receiving depth in Tara the Freak and Crazy George Starcher. At cornerback, however, the Krakens had no depth — if Wahiawa went down, their defensive secondary would be worthless.

It didn't matter *who* was right, as long as the right thing happened.

"Wahiawa," Quentin said, "you're out."

The second-year defensive back screeched as if in utter agony. She fell to the floor and started twitching.

Quentin turned to face the backup cornerback, the player who had lost some of her speed due to age but could still jump high enough to defend the top ring, could still hit like nobody's business. "Stockbridge, will you play goalie?"

Inside the see-through body, Quentin saw the Sklorno's clear blood actually stop pumping. "Me? Quentinbarnes wants *me*?"

He nodded.

She said "yes," then collapsed.

The rest of the Sklorno stood there, quivering, hoping he would pick them, but Cheboygan, Halawa and Stockbridge gave him enough speed. He needed to complement that with brute strength, with *savagery*. To get those things, there was only one option.

"Mum-O?"

The young defensive lineman's tubular body suddenly rose up on his back legs. His other four legs waved in the air, as did his four arms. He gnashed the black, triangular teeth inside his hexagonal mouth. Vocal tubes let out a short, intense roar, then he dropped back down and fell silent. Mum-O had a flair for the dramatic — he was in.

"Okay," Quentin said, thinking through his options. George Starcher's size, speed and hands would have made him ideal, but Quentin couldn't bank on the man's reliability. This wasn't a time for crazy.

John stood up, raised his right hand and waved it madly. "Come on, Q! Pick me! I will mess them all up!"

"John, *shut up*! Another word out of you and you can just leave the dining deck."

John stared, his mouth wide open. Quentin had never spoken to his friend like that before. John's eyes narrowed, then he looked down. Quentin would have to make it up to him later. If there even *was* a later.

Quentin turned to face John's brother, Ju. Ju had the size, the strength, the speed, and he was hands-down the best athlete on the team, but he was also the Krakens' starting running back. Was playing him now worth the risk of losing him for the '85 season? Quentin looked to the back of the room, to Don. Don shook his head, then nodded toward another running back.

Quentin saw the logic instantly. Don's choice wasn't as strong or as fast as Ju, but he had much better hands — better for catching passes and not as likely to fumble the ball when he took a hit.

"Yassoud," Quentin said. "You want in?"

Yassoud tilted his head back in surprise, making his stiff, braided beard stick out away from him. "*Me*? Wouldn't you want Ju?"

"Yeah," Ju said, a hint of anger in his voice at being passed over for his backup. "Come on, Q, I'll tear those nasty beasties apart."

Quentin shook his head. "I'm not doing this for fun, I'm doing this to save our franchise. I *have* to play against the Prawatt, but if I get hurt, Don can step in at quarterback. If Halawa gets hurt, we still have Hawick and Milford. Ju, if you go down, there's too big of a drop-off at running back. No offense, 'Soud."

Yassoud shook his head. "None taken. I'm stubborn, not blind. If you want me to fight alongside you in this one, Q, I'm your Huckleberry."

"What's a Huckleberry?"

The dark-skinned man just smiled. "Don't worry about it. I'm in."

Quentin had one slot left. He needed a player that could run fast, that could catch, that could both take damage and also dish it out. A big tight end could do all of those things. Quentin had ruled George out, but the Krakens had another tight end who was just as good.

Quentin looked at Rick Warburg. "What do you say, Warburg? Are you in?"

Warburg threw back his black-haired head and laughed. He actually *laughed*.

"I can't look *that* dumb," he said. "Go out and get killed by those demons? No way."

So selfish, *always* so selfish. "Rick, if we don't win, our Sklorno teammates … "

The words died in Quentin's mouth. Had he actually thought that Rick Warburg, a hate-filled racist, would risk his life to save his Sklorno teammates? A stupid assumption, another reminder that not everyone thought the same way Quentin did.

He looked over his remaining teammates. He saw what he needed, a 6-foot-6, 330-pound player that could not only hit, catch, run and take hits, but a player that could *throw*.

"Becca, will you play?"

Rebecca Montagne took a step back. She looked around the room quickly, her dark eyes wide with surprise as if she thought he might be talking to some other player named *Becca*.

She pointed to her chest. "Me," she said. "You want *me* on the team?"

Quentin nodded. "Yeah. But we need the *angry* version of you. I need you to be vicious — we need *the Wrecka*."

Her expression was a combination of fear and raw pride. Pride that when crunch time hit, when everything was on the line, Quentin called on her ahead of so many others. Fear not for herself, but for what she knew she could do to other sentients, the same fear that she'd shown since killing North Branch on the first play of her Tier One career.

She looked down. "I'm not sure I can. I don't … well, I don't want to *unleash* on them, you know?"

He walked to her and put a hand on her solid shoulder. "The lives of your teammates depend on it. And, you have another skill we need."

She raised her eyebrows, waiting.

"Your *arm*," Quentin said. "I was told you wanted to be a quarterback?"

A slow smile broke across her face. Without another word, he saw that she understood his game plan.

"All right," she said. "I'm in."

Quentin grinned, first at her, then at the entire team. "This is just one more game, Krakens," he said. "We *will* win this. They are waiting for us. We can't wear armor, so get your shoes, your jerseys, and let's get to the shuttle bay."

Right or wrong, he had committed his teammates to this contest — whatever happened would be on his shoulders.

Quentin Barnes left the dining deck, his six fellow starters close behind.

4

The Game

QUENTIN FACED the *Touchback*'s tall, broad shuttle bay doors. He closed his eyes and said a brief prayer — just because he no longer followed the corrupt Purist religion didn't mean he'd lost faith in High One.

We need you now more than ever. Give me strength so that I don't fail my teammates.

Yellow lights flashed, a warning that manually opening the doors would result in an explosive decompression. Normally these doors opened to the vacuum of space — certain death for anyone who wasn't inside a shuttle or beyond the airlock that led into the rest of the ship. The Prawatt had said the *Touchback* was fully enclosed, that this was safe, but were they telling the truth?

He would find out soon enough.

Becca stood on his left, Yassoud on his right. Behind them stood Stockbridge, Mum-O-Killowe, Halawa and Cheboygan. All wore their orange jerseys: it was an away game, after all.

Quentin wore workout pants, his armored football shoes and his orange #10 jersey, but no armor on his legs, no shoulder pads and no rib guards. He wore no helmet. The jersey material felt odd against his bare skin because he wasn't even wearing his Koolsuit. The Prawatt had ruled out any armor or temperature-modification materials.

Most of the team had gathered in the shuttle bay, a show of unity before the seven headed out onto whatever field awaited. Quentin looked up to the ever-present holographic phrase that floated twenty feet above the shuttle bay's deck: THE IONATH KRAKENS ARE ON A COLLISION COURSE WITH A TIER ONE CHAMPIONSHIP. THE ONLY VARIABLE IS TIME.

Through the holo, up near the top of the shallow dome's support girders, he saw movement. Was that … Tara the Freak? Of course, who else would be up there. The mutant Quyth Warrior's life had improved somewhat from when he arrived at the beginning of the '84 season. He'd solidified his place on the team, become a key part of the offense. Most players accepted him, although his fellow Warriors still treated him like garbage. Aside from George Starcher, Tara had few friends and preferred to be alone. As far as Quentin was concerned, Tara had earned the right to spend his time however he liked.

Quentin looked to the left, to the airlock doors that led further inside the *Touchback*. If anything went wrong, there was no point in the entire team dying.

"Everyone, get back inside the airlock," he said. "Just in case."

John Tweedy stepped out from the other players. YOU'RE NOT THE BOSS OF ME scrolled across his face. "Shuck you, Barnes. If y'all get sucked into space, we're going with you."

The rest of the team stood with John — they weren't leaving. Quentin looked to the right, to George Starcher standing beside an open panel labeled EMERGENCY RELEASE. Inside the panel, a handle glowed red. Was it ironic that now George would open the shuttle bay doors and possibly send his teammates to their deaths, instead of using the same device to kill himself, as he had tried to do just a few weeks ago? Maybe, but Quentin wasn't really sure about the difference between *irony* and coincidence. Or *stupidity*, for that matter.

Quentin nodded to George. George grabbed the glowing handle and lifted it.

Metallic rattling sounds reverberated through the domed space. The shuttle bay doors started to separate. For an instant, just when that vertical seam first appeared, Quentin held his breath — as if that could help him survive the vacuum of space. Then the doors opened enough for him and his teammates to see what waited on the other side.

He felt a tug on his left jersey sleeve.

"Quentin," Becca said. "I don't know about this."

The shuttle bay doors opened onto the playing field, a huge, oblong surface surrounded by a twenty-foot-high black wall. The curving wall had that same knotted-tree-root texture Quentin had seen plugging the holes in the *Touchback*'s hull. Atop those walls, waving arms and black bodies filled steeply sloping stands. A horrific sight. Many of them had the familiar X-bodies, but there were other shapes, *bizarre* shapes he couldn't quite make out amongst the waving, undulating throng. How many individuals were in those stands? Fifty thousand? A *hundred* thousand? He couldn't tell.

Quentin walked out onto the playing area. His six teammates followed. One hundred and fifty yards long from end to end, about sixty yards wide at the middle where a yellow line divided the arena floor into two equal halves. Quentin's left foot stood on one side of that line, his right foot on the other. In the center of the arena, the line intersected a ten-foot-diameter circle painted the same yellow. At either end of the floor floated three five-foot-diameter rings: one ring about ten feet high, one about fifteen, and the top ring about twenty feet above the surface.

Movement from high up: a hundred feet over their heads, the arena ceiling wiggled and undulated like an endless black mass of sea anemones. Thousands of Prawatt clung there, looking down on the field below.

Quentin tested the footing. The surface felt firm, yet slightly giving, like hard rubber. He stopped and turned to look back at his ship.

The Prawatt vessel's black material had engulfed the *Touchback*. All Quentin could see of his ship's exterior was the opening into the shuttle bay, some twenty feet high and forty feet wide, and a bit of the orange hull on either side. When those doors shut, they would be part of the arena wall.

He had never seen his ship's exterior this close up. From a shuttle, the *Touchback*'s surface always looked smooth as glass. From just a few feet away, however, he saw the dents and the dings, the pits and scratches, fifty years worth of wear and tear hidden beneath the orange paint.

Quentin looked at his teammates. He took in their bright orange jerseys with white-trimmed black numbers and letters. Becca, the HeavyG woman; Yassoud, the Human man with his stiff, braided beard; Mum-O-Killowe, six feet of his six-hundred-pound body parallel to the ground, six feet rising up; and finally Halawa, Stockbridge and Cheboygan. All three of the Sklorno wore their orange jersey and nothing else, exposing their see-through bodies, showing the clear blood coursing through their flesh and the black bone that gave them their form.

Quentin stepped toward his teammates, and they stepped toward him. They gathered close, the only spots of color in a sea of black.

He noticed something falling from up above. Seven bodies dropped from the ceiling, seven Devil's Ropes each trailing bright blue streamers. He watched the descent, wondered if they would smash into the black surface and die, but they landed and stuck like big cats, flexible legs and arms absorbing the impact.

Quentin looked at his teammates. "That was a hundred-foot fall, and they're fine," he said. "If you *throw* them, you won't hurt them. If we want to put them down for good, we will have to slam them into the ground."

Becca nodded. "Or put them into the wall, just like hockey."

Yassoud flashed her a funny look. "*Hockey?* What is that?"

She shook her head. "It's an Earth thing. You wouldn't understand."

The seven Prawatt lined up on the yellow mid-field circle. They each reached one flexible arm in, locked their slim fingers together, then ran around the circle, a black pinwheel marked by their trailing, bright blue streamers. They broke the circle and lined up single file along the mid-field line. They waited.

Quentin knelt on one knee. The others gathered around him. "Krakens, this is real," he said. "Every *second* of this game, remember that the lives of our teammates depend on what you do today. Play to win ... and play *mean*."

He stood. Together, they walked to mid-field. The seven Krakens lined up along the yellow line, each standing face to face with an opposing Prawatt. In the very center of the alien arena, Quentin Barnes faced off against starship captain Cormorant Bumberpuff.

"Welcome," Bumberpuff said. "You have familiarized yourself with the rules of the Game?"

Quentin nodded. "Put the ball through any of the three hoops, that's ten points. After a goal, the scoring team returns to mid-field and the scored-upon team takes possession. We'll figure out the rest as we go."

"Good enough," Bumberpuff said. "There are two halves of twenty minutes each. High score wins, not that the final score will matter — most of your team won't make it through the Game alive."

Quentin smiled. Again he had that strange feeling that if he closed his eyes, he'd be talking to a Human — a Human that was talking smack. Maybe it *was* true that the Prawatt had originated on Earth.

The Krakens turned and jogged back to a yellow line that ran from side to side about ten yards in front of the three vertical rings. That line paralleled both the horizontal mid-field line sixty-five yards away, and sixty-five yards beyond that an identical line in front of the Prawatt rings.

The arena crowd started making a hissing noise, like ten thousand poorly tuned violins each making a different, off-key note. From the ceiling a hundred feet above, something descended on a black cable. This creature was much larger than Captain Bumberpuff or the other X-Walkers. It had six triple-jointed limbs and had to weigh at least a ton. It landed inside the center circle, then placed three spheres on the mid-field line — a gold one the size of a basketball and two smaller red ones on either side of it.

Quentin pointed to the balls and shouted to his teammates. "Those red balls fly, they move on their own. They can strike at any time, so keep your head on a swivel. Mostly they target the sentient carrying the gold game-ball. If you don't have the game-ball, be ready to protect the player that does."

"Wait a minute," Yassoud said. "In this game, even the *ball* is trying to kill us?"

Quentin nodded. He saw that Becca, Stockbridge and even Mum-O-Killowe were looking into the crowd, lost in the strange spectacle of sprawling black.

He clapped three times to get their attention. "Get your damn heads in the game! After we win you can take in the sights all you want."

The big creature at mid-field turned what had to be a head toward Quentin.

"Krakens," it said in a powerful voice that echoed through the arena. "Are you ready?"

It was now or never. He and his teammates could do this, they *had* to do this. He cupped his hands to his mouth. "The Krakens are ready!"

The creature turned to face the other way. "Harpies, are you ready?"

The *Harpies*? Bumberpuff had an organized team? This might be even harder than Quentin had thought.

He heard Bumberpuff's distant voice: "The Harpies are ready!"

Quentin dropped into a three-point stance, digging the toes of his shoes into the firm footing. His teammates did the same.

The huge creature at mid-field raised four strange limbs high into the air, then dropped them sharply as it screamed: "*Let's get it on!*"

Quentin and the Krakens shot forward. Before they made it three steps, the two red balls zipped up into the air. Cheboygan and Halawa sprinted for the gold ball still sitting at mid-field. Quentin, Yassoud and Becca ran behind them, Mum-O-Killowe scurrying on his six legs to bring up the rear. Stockbridge stayed back, ready to guard the rings.

The oncoming Prawatt didn't *run*, they *rolled*, pinwheeling on their extended arms and legs so fast they looked like a spinning disc. So much *speed!*

Cheboygan and Halawa reached mid-field about the same time the Prawatt did, creating a brief six-on-two mismatch. The two species slammed into each other. The slinky, black X-creatures hit with coordination, two of them on each Sklorno, driving the Krakens players hard to the ground.

Captain Bumberpuff scooped up the gold ball. Holding it seemed to stop him from pinwheeling, but his two long, flexible legs still gave him blistering speed. He cut to his right, an echoing army of broken violins screeching in support.

Quentin ran left to cut off the captain's path and force him back to the middle of the field. A blur of red — one of the free-floating balls dive-bombing Bumberpuff, who held up the golden game-ball in a snap reaction. Red bounced off gold, then jetted away to find another victim.

Quentin closed in. Becca was to his right, Yassoud to his left, the three of them eliminating any angle the captain might have. Bumberpuff ran straight in and leaned forward for a head-to-head hit. Quentin leaned forward himself, lip curling back in a sneer, big arms wide and already starting to crush together.

Just before contact, the captain *leapt*. The black X-body shot twenty feet overhead as Quentin fell face-first into the hard, gnarled surface. He bounced off and scrambled to his feet in time to see Bumberpuff land lightly and run straight for the rings, straight toward Stockbridge.

The Sklorno cornerback knew how to play a leaping opponent. She jumped right after the captain did, timing it so she would keep her body between the Prawatt and the rings before hitting him in mid-air. Just before their contact some fifteen feet above the surface, Bumberpuff tossed the game-ball to the right, where another airborne Prawatt caught it, landed, then jumped untouched through the highest hoop.

Harpies 10, Krakens 0.

The violin hissing grew so loud Quentin covered his ears.

When he did, he felt the blood sheeting his face. How embarrassing — his first wound caused not by a smash-mouth collision, but by a fancy move that made him look like a fool.

The Prawatt team ran to the mid-field line. Quentin raised his hands, curled his fingers in repeatedly, calling his teammates to huddle up.

A wide-eyed Yassoud shook his head in amazement. "Damn! Did you see how those guys *move*?"

"Shut it," Quentin said. He looked at the stunned faces of the Krakens. Clear blood dripped from the base of one of Halawa's three eyestalks. Cheboygan held a tentacle against her hip, where she'd taken a hard hit.

"They're fast," Quentin said. "So what? We deal with speed every game. It's not like you all haven't played against sentients that can leap. Becca, how do you take out a leaping Sklorno?"

"Time her arc," Becca said. "Once they're airborne, they can't change direction or speed, so hit them as the come down and light 'em up."

Quentin nodded. "That's right. If they want to play the vertical game, we have to punish them when they land. A couple of big hits will slow them down just fine."

He pointed to the *Touchback*'s closed, orange doors. "That is *our* ship. That means this is *our house*. Let's play ball. Ready?"

The team leaned in around him, the seven of them barking out the word "*break!*" before they lined up on their horizontal stripe.

Since they had been scored upon, they got to take the ball out from their own goal. Quentin tossed the hollow gold ball from hand to hand, feeling its weight, its roundness.

"Cheboygan, you stay on my right," he said. "Keep one eyestalk on me at *all times*. No matter what position I'm in, be ready for a pass."

She didn't have to answer; he knew she would do as she was told.

"Cheboygan and Halawa, go wide, draw defenders away from me," Quentin said. "The rest of us, fall in behind Mum-O. Mum-O, show these crawlies what it means to get hit by a Ki."

The monstrous official scurried out to mid-field. Its voice

echoed through the arena, audible even over the hissing crowd. "Krakens! Are you ready?"

Quentin held the ball in his left arm, cupped his right hand to his mouth. "The Krakens are ready!"

The official whipped its arms toward the ground. "Then let's get it on!"

Six Krakens rushed forward from their goal line, six Prawatt pinwheeled off the mid-field line to meet them.

Mum-O-Killowe took the lead. Slow but big, he formed the point of the attack, Yassoud on his left, Becca on his right, Quentin just behind. Cheboygan flared right, Halawa left, each drawing a defender to cover them. The four remaining Harpies barreled in at high speed. As the two sides collided, Mum-O grabbed the first Prawatt, lifted it, then smashed it into the ground. Bits of black material scattered. Quentin wasn't sure if they came from the playing surface or from the Prawatt itself.

Captain Bumberpuff jumped high, arcing over Mum-O. While he arced down, Yassoud shifted direction and ran to the spot where the Prawatt would land. Quentin slowed, giving Yassoud room. The same instant as the captain's feet hit the surface, 'Soud blasted the Prawatt — Bumberpuff tumbled to the right in a tangle of arms and legs. Quentin cut left, looking for open space. Another Prawatt barreled in, black arms whipping forward, blue streamers trailing behind.

Quentin's hyper-processing mind saw Cheboygan fifty yards downfield. He stopped and threw, getting the pass off before the pinwheeling Prawatt tucked its arms and legs in tight and delivered a crushing impact. Quentin landed hard, then rolled to an elbow and watched the pass. He'd thrown up high, where only a Sklorno could get it. Cheboygan leapt, graceful and strong for her thick size —

— but her Prawatt defender went right up with her. It extended its black arms and grabbed the golden ball. Interception.

Quentin banged a fist against the ground. "Are you kidding me with this?"

The Prawatt landed before Cheboygan did, then rushed toward

the Krakens' goal. Becca tried to cut it off, backpedaling to time the creature's leap, but a red ball flew in out of nowhere and hit her in the back, launching her face-first into the gnarled surface.

"Becca!" Quentin ran to her, ignoring the ball carrier. He knelt by her side as she rose to her knees, bleeding from the forehead.

The crowd roared its violin roar.

She did not seem happy. "They scored?"

Quentin looked back to see the Prawatt Walking-Xs celebrating in the Krakens' zone. Harpies 20, Krakens 0.

She punched him in the shoulder. "Why didn't you defend?"

"I ... I thought you might be hurt."

She stood. "I can take as good as I give, Barnes, you got that? Worry about winning the game, not about me."

Her eyes blazed white and blue from behind skin streaked with flowing rivulets of red. How had he forgotten that Becca "The Wrecka" Montagne was an All-Pro fullback, not some delicate flower?

He nodded. "Yeah, Becca. Sorry."

Down by 20, the Krakens jogged back to their zone. The team gathered around him, waiting for strategy. They had no experience playing this game; they couldn't afford to fall further behind. Quentin needed a strategy that played to Ionath's strengths.

"Surprise, they can defend the pass," he said. "Let's find out how they defend the run. We get behind Mum-O and drive forward until they have to bring everyone they have to stop us — then we use short, fast passes to keep the ball moving. Got it?"

His teammates nodded. They didn't look shell-shocked anymore — they looked *angry*.

He smiled at them. "Hey, there's the Krakens I know and love! You all finally figure out this is just another game?"

Heads nodded, Sklorno jumped and Mum-O grunted something that was probably obscene.

LONG BLACK FINGERS WRAPPED around his neck and his bicep. His right hand locked onto the cold metal of an X-body arm, holding off the 350 pounds as best he could, keeping his left hand free. As he fell, Quentin threw the golden ball to Cheboygan, who was sprinting across the floor in front of the rings. She caught the ball in stride just as the Prawatt goalie hit her full-speed and held on, but Cheboygan kept moving forward, too big to be easily brought down. The rookie receiver flipped the ball behind her, where Yassoud caught it and threw it in the same motion. The ball sailed through the undefended goal, and the Krakens were finally on the board.

THE HARPIES SCORED to go up 30-10. The Krakens again answered, but the points came at a cost. Cheboygan's left tentacle hung limp and useless. Quentin moved her to goalie and brought Stockbridge out to fight on the field. His team lined up on the yellow mid-field stripe as the Harpies stood on their own goal line, waiting to bring the ball out.

The six-legged official dropped down to the field. Quentin tried not to look at the creature but knew the ref would haunt his nightmares for weeks to come. The official asked both teams if they were ready, then shouted *"let's get it on"* and the game was once again under way.

Running behind a wall of five Prawatt, Bumberpuff carried the golden ball. The red balls swirled around both teams, waiting for whatever unknown signal that caused them to attack.

Stockbridge hadn't run much, so she was fully rested. She shot forward, pulling ahead of even Halawa. Quentin started to shout at Stockbridge to slow down, to wait for her teammates, but with all the violin hissing she wouldn't have heard anyway. Like an orange missile, Stockbridge drove into the Harpy wall. She knocked the first Prawatt to the ground, but the next two smashed her backward. She hit, rolled, then popped up just as Bumberpuff raised the game-ball to deflect a streaking bit of red.

A streaking bit of red that ricocheted off at a sharp angled and hit Stockbridge in her hairy head.

She sagged more than she fell, a limp pile of tentacles and eyestalks. Captain Bumberpuff broke right. Becca dove for him, but he hopped over her and sprinted for the rings. Quentin angled to cut him off. Bumberpuff threw the ball to his right, across the field, where a teammate caught it and dove toward the lowest ring. Cheboygan leapt to block, but she had no forward momentum — the Prawatt slammed into her, knocking them both through the ring and putting the Harpies up 40-20.

STOCKBRIDGE DIDN'T GET UP. Quentin and the Krakens stood over her. Cheboygan knelt next to her, touching her lightly, trying to ascertain the level of injury.

Quentin felt the playing surface vibrate. He looked up to see the six-legged monstrosity of a ref walking toward them.

"The Krakens player rises on her own power," the ref said, "or she must leave the game until she re-enters without assistance."

Quentin looked at his fallen teammate, tried to control his rage. In a violent, high-impact game, a game without padding, someone was bound to get hurt. But in truth this wasn't a "game" at all, it was a fight for survival. When the Krakens won, he hoped Stockbridge would be conscious to enjoy the victory.

"Take her to the *Touchback*," he said. "She's out."

Becca and Halawa gently put Stockbridge on Mum-O's back. Quentin ran to the *Touchback* and banged on the huge doors. After a pause, they opened enough for Doc Patah to flutter out. Other Krakens took Stockbridge and carried her inside. The doors rattled as they slid shut.

The Game did not allow for subs. The Krakens were now one player down.

Quentin walked back to the Krakens' goal line. His teammates gathered around him. They seethed with fury, just like he did.

"I've had enough of this," he said. "The Prawatt know how to play this game, but we are among the best athletes in the galaxy. Time to change tactics."

He turned to Becca. "In the Purist Nation, we invented this game called *basketball*. You ever hear of *the give-and-go*?"

She laughed and shook her head. Her lip curled into a cocky

smile he hadn't seen on her face since she'd killed North Branch. Blood pulsed from her broken nose, but she didn't seem to notice.

"Barnes, the Purists didn't invent basketball, and I can prove it — if we make it out of this alive, I will dunk all over your sorry ass. So, yeah, I've heard of the give-and-go. I know what to do."

He tossed the gold ball from hand to hand as the Krakens stood on their goal line. They'd lost Stockbridge, but he knew, now more than ever, that the Harpies could be beat. He tucked the ball under his left arm, tapped out a quick *ba-da-bap* on his stomach, then the big ref started the game.

Five Krakens sprinted forward. Six Prawatt pinwheeled across the pitch to meet them. Mum-O and Yassoud rushed forward to block. Bumberpuff and one other Prawatt came around them, closed in on Quentin at mid-field. Before they hit him, he snapped the ball to his right, to Becca, and kept moving forward. The captain's attention followed the ball, letting Quentin sprint past him.

When Quentin looked right, the ball was already in the air — Becca had caught and thrown in the same instant. The ball practically vanished in Quentin's thick hands. His feet chewed up the yards. Bumberpuff was faster — Quentin's mental clock tracked where the captain would be, how long it would take before Prawatt arms wrapped around Human legs.

Another Prawatt rushed head-on at Quentin — big mistake. Quentin shot his right hand forward in a stiff-arm move. He grabbed the Prawatt's arm where it met the X-body, then lifted and *threw*, tossing the 350-pound sentient aside like so much trash.

He saw Halawa running free off to his right. Quentin closed in on the goal-rings — he had only a second or so before Bumberpuff brought him down from behind. Quentin reared back for a throw at the bottom ring. He snapped his hand forward, the goalie leapt high to block — but Quentin didn't let go of the ball.

As the goalie rose up, unable to change its trajectory, Quentin whipped the ball behind his back, to the right. The ball sailed across to Halawa, who caught it and jumped, arcing untouched through the top ring.

Goal. Prawatt 40, Krakens 30.

• • •

THE KRAKENS HAD FIGURED out how to play the game and had tied it up at 50-all, but down a player, the Harpies still held a significant advantage. A big hit sent the ball sailing into the stands and out of play. The ref stopped the game, giving possession to the Krakens — the next time that happened, it would go to the Harpies, with possession alternating each time.

Quentin held the gold ball, waiting for the ref to restart the game. His teammates gathered around him. He coughed, feeling his ribs scream in complaint. He hoped they weren't broken. Doc Patah wasn't allowed to come out and do the sideline repairs Quentin and his teammates had become so accustomed to. No bone fuses, no skin seals, no nanocyte bandages, no lung re-inflations — in the Prawatt Game, you played as is.

He knelt. Five heads closed in above him.

"We lost a player, and that's hurting us. We have to even the odds. Becca, I need you to take a hit, and you have to *sell* it."

Quentin traced his torn fingertip across the hard surface, using his own blood to draw out a play as if he were a child and this was a dirt patch back on Micovi. "Yassoud, you line up *here*. Becca, you cross *here*, and Yassoud, you block her defender. When Becca goes *here*, I throw to her. She takes a hit, gives up the ball. We actually want that, because Mum-O will be *here*. Everyone got it?"

Tired heads nodded, but Mum-O made a strange, repeating noise — the big Ki was laughing.

The Krakens lined up. On the ref's signal Quentin rushed forward, two teammates on his left, two on his right, Cheboygan staying back to defend the goal.

He slowed, letting his teammates run ahead of him. Becca crossed the mid-field line, then broke right. Her defender stayed a step behind her but fell hard to a big block from Yassoud. That left Becca wide open, but Quentin waited, waited until another defender started over to cover her. *Then* he threw, knowing that she was going to get hurt but also knowing this had to be done.

He'd thrown it higher than he needed to, forcing her to reach up, exposing her body. Just as her hands closed on the golden ball, the Prawatt slammed into her ribs, rocking her back in a head-snapping hit. The golden ball sailed free and bounced off the pitch. The Prawatt who hit her changed direction and scrambled after it.

Just as the Prawatt's black fingers closed on the golden orb, its Game ended forever.

Mum-O had used the fumble as a distraction to close in. The Ki's body fully compressed, going from twelve feet, six inches to a dense, compact four feet long from head to rear. It suddenly *extended*, six hundred pounds of angry Ki shooting out like a battering ram. The Prawatt's arms and legs disintegrated in a cloud of spinning metallic bits. Its X-body spun away down the pitch in a mad, bouncing cartwheel.

The crowd let out a strange, unified squeal.

Yassoud scooped up the loose ball and ran wide right. Two Prawatt closed in on him fast, but he was ready — just as they tackled him, he threw the ball forward. It bounced once, then Cheboygan scooped it up with her one good tentacle. She had left the Krakens' rings unguarded to rush out as a surprise player that the Harpies hadn't expected. Prawatt chased her, but they were a step too slow.

The big rookie Sklorno closed in on the goalie — it would be a one-on-one challenge. The X-Walker goalie danced from foot to foot, trying to guess what deft move Cheboygan would throw before she leapt for the rings.

But Cheboygan didn't try to make a move. The 360-pound Sklorno ran the goalie right over, stomping her foot down on its chest for good measure as she jumped through the lowest ring.

The score gave the Krakens their first lead of the game, and now — unless that shattered Prawatt could somehow reassemble itself — the two sides had the same number of players.

BOTH TEAMS HAD SIX PLAYERS remaining. In the second half, momentum quickly swung in the Krakens' favor. Constant hitting and smashing started to slow the Prawatt down. Without their speed advantage, they could do little to stop the bigger, stronger Human, Sklorno and Ki players. When the ref called full time, the Krakens had defeated the Harpies by a score of 120 to 80.

The Game was over. The violin hissing continued, but at a lower pitch — maybe the home crowd was booing, Quentin didn't know. He set the golden ball inside mid-field circle. He wiped the blood from his face, then flung his hand at the ground to splatter wet red on the black playing surface. They'd won, but at such a cost.

Captain Bumberpuff walked up to him, limping a little. A vicious hit had bent his lower left leg, tearing small holes in the semi-see-through material. Tiny pieces of metal flaked off as he walked, leaving a trail in his wake — and some of those pieces were *moving*. The leg seemed to be crawling with little black bugs, some that pulled off broken bits and tossed them away, others that swarmed into the holes, filling them, *repairing* them.

"Barnes," the captain said, "you have won your freedom."

Quentin nodded. "Thank you for giving us the chance to play."

"Did you enjoy the contest?"

Enjoy it? It was a good thing that being so exhausted helped him control his temper. "No, I didn't," he said, but he knew that wasn't entirely true. A life-and-death battle in an alien arena? Such were the things of childhood fantasies. He'd not only lived through the ordeal, he'd emerged victorious.

"We won," he said. "That means we're free. When can my ship leave?"

Bumberpuff rattled slightly. "No alien team has ever won before. Our kind will want to meet you."

That word again, *alien*, but it applied to Quentin. No matter how many races he met, he would never get used to the fact that for all but Humans, *he* was the alien.

Quentin shook his head. "I appreciate that, Captain, but we have to get back."

Bumberpuff said nothing for a moment. As odd as it seemed, Quentin could tell the creature was at a loss for words, as if it never occurred to him that someone wouldn't *want* to meet more Prawatt.

"We will repair your ship," he said finally. "We will deliver you back to the Sklorno border sometime after that.

Sometime, but he didn't say how long that would be. Was Bumberpuff going back on his word? Were the Krakens still in mortal danger? Quentin couldn't afford to press the captain — all he and his teammates could do was wait and see if Bumberpuff would honor the agreement.

Quentin looked to his right, at a pile of bug-like metal bits surrounding a battered, legless and armless X-body. The bright blue streamers still affixed to that body lie limp, trampled and torn.

"I'm sorry about your teammate," Quentin said. "Can you, uh, fix him?"

"No. His reality has ended. Do not worry, Smooklegroober died happy."

The boogeymen of the galaxy, the mysterious monsters that struck fear into all other races, they had names like *Bumberpuff* and *Smooklegroober*.

"Smooklegroober? That was his name? *Seriously?*"

"Of course," the captain said. "A warrior's name. Know that Smooklegroober died facing the greatest team the Prawatt have ever played. Our contest will be watched over and over again by billions of our kind, from infant crawlers to explorers to the ancient forms. My race underestimated the toughness of you gridiron players."

"That you did," Quentin said. "Listen, I mean no disrespect, but I need to check on my teammates."

"I understand," the captain said. "You have earned my admiration, Quentin Barnes. I will enter your name and face into the collective consciousness of our species. You will be able to pass freely through Prawatt space at any time. Please consider coming to the home planet to play the Game again."

Captain Bumberpuff offered a tattered, three-fingered metal hand. Quentin shook it — cold metal, but also moving with life — then ran for the *Touchback's* open shuttle bay. The rest of his teammates had already entered. The big doors rattled as they closed behind him.

The holographic letters floating in the curved bay roof glowed down on a hastily assembled triage area. Three portable med tables sat in the center of the shuttle bay, surrounded by equipment, IV racks and portable rejuve tanks. Most of the Krakens who hadn't played in the game were packed in around the middle table — Quentin knew that Stockbridge lay behind that wall of bodies.

Becca sat on the right-most table. She held a small bone sculptor against the bridge of her nose and stared off into the distance. Yassoud lie on the left-most bed, a few tubes running into his arm. He smiled at Quentin, flashed a thumbs-up — Yassoud was fine. Cheboygan stood a little to his right, her tentacle dipped into the pink fluid of a rejuve tank.

Quentin walked up to the middle table. Teammates saw him coming and made room. Sure enough, Stockbridge lay there, tubes of clear fluid connected to her body. Her jersey had been cut away to make room for Patah's efforts. The Prawatt's hit had crushed her chest. Her left tentacle dangled almost to the floor. Her right tentacle was curled up on her body, spasming and twitching. Two of her eyestalks lie limply on the table. The other two stared at Quentin with undeniable reverence.

Doc Patah floated next to her, his wings slowly undulating to keep him in place. He wasn't working on her ... why wasn't he working on her?

The Harrah turned to face Quentin. "She has been holding on until she could talk to you."

Holding on? "But, Doc, you're right here ... help her."

Doc Patah's sensory pits flexed, alternately widening, then tightening. "There is nothing that can be done," he said. "I am sorry."

Something twinged in Quentin's throat. This wasn't possible. Doc Patah could fix anything.

Quentin looked down at Stockbridge. He noticed — for the first time — that she wore a chain around her neck, a chain that held a small, orange-and-black medallion. The medallion showed Quentin's profile: the symbol of the church founded in his name.

Along with Milford, Stockbridge had spent her off-season proselytizing his name, converting hundreds of thousands of Sklorno into followers of the CoQB. For seven seasons with the Krakens, she had played hard. Even when her skills started to fade, she embraced her backup role and did anything she could to further Ionath's championship quest. When Quentin had asked her to join him in the Prawatt arena, she hadn't hesitated, she hadn't flinched. He had never been close with her, but for three seasons Quentin and Stockbridge had been *teammates*.

And now her story would end.

Stockbridge lifted a clear, spasming tentacle, reached it toward him. He held it, felt the firm, pliant texture of her ghost-like flesh.

"I'm sorry," Quentin said.

"There is no sadness in me, Quentinbarnes," said the battered Sklorno. "I served his holiness well?"

She was dying, and she still thought he was some kind of a god. A *real* god would have saved his follower. Quentin was just a man. But if it made her last moments any better, he could pretend to be what she thought he was.

"You served flawlessly," he said. "You have —" he had to clench his teeth against that feeling in his throat, the burning in his eyes "— you have pleased me with your performance. I promote you to, uh, high priestess of the Church of Quentin Barnes."

From behind him, he heard Sklorno chitter madly with sounds of shock, of awe. Stockbridge's last two eyes blinked. Her body trembled, but only for a few seconds. The eyestalks sagged, then dropped.

Her shaking ceased. A piece of equipment let out a soft, shrill monotone. Doc Patah fluttered to a rack and flipped a switch — the monotone stopped.

"She is gone," the Harrah said.

Quentin couldn't stop the tears. He still held her tentacle. Another dead teammate — he would never get used to this feeling.

Doc Patah noiselessly floated over to Quentin's shoulder.

"I don't know if you've been studying Sklorno culture, young Quentin, but promoting her to high priestess was the greatest thing she could have heard," Doc Patah said quietly. "You made her passing a thing of glory. You did well."

Quentin turned to face his teammates. Some stared, some

looked away, some were crying just like he was, but they all waited for him to speak.

Why did *he* have to be the one to say something? He was only twenty years old. He was an uneducated orphan from a primitive culture. On the football field he ruled, but off the field he had no idea how life worked. What words of wisdom could he possibly give?

And yet despite his shortcomings, his lack of eloquence, they wanted to hear from him. The looks in their eyes said it all — they wanted Quentin to give this some kind of meaning. No matter how hard it was to speak, he would not fail them.

"Killik the Unworthy died fighting the pirates that wanted to murder us all," he said. "Stockbridge died so that we could keep our team whole. We've lost others — Mitchell Fayed and Aka-Na-Tak."

His tears stopped. He suddenly knew what words to say, how to properly honor her, how to make everyone see that her life *mattered*.

"We're going home, but not quite yet," he said. "First, we will continue on to Yall to watch the Galaxy Bowl. Next season, *we* will play in that game. We will *win*. We will put the names of our fallen on the banner they raise at Ionath Stadium, and they will forever be remembered as *champions*."

Silence filled the shuttle bay. Brave words, *important* words, but they didn't dull the hurt. Quentin clenched his jaw tight as he walked through his teammates and headed for the locker room. He needed to lose himself in the scalding water of the Ki baths.

"Hey," John said. "What's that funky smell?"

Quentin stopped and sniffed. He noticed it, too — something that smelled faintly of lemons and machine oil.

Poison!

"Gas masks!" he shouted, even though he had no idea where the masks or rebreathers or oxygen tanks were kept. He looked up to the ceiling. "Ship, we're being gassed! Filter out the air or something."

[OUR ATMOSPHERIC PROCESSORS WERE DAMAGED IN THE ATTACK AND HAVE BEEN SHUT DOWN FOR REPAIR.]

Quentin heard a thump. Back by the triage area, Doc Patah had fallen to the deck. The winged Harrah lay there, quivering slightly.

Cheboygan fell, her limp arm snaking out of the rejuve tank and flinging a stream of pink fluid onto the floor.

Quentin started to run to his teammates, but his legs suddenly felt weak, boneless.

Thump. Thump-thump. Thump.

All around the shuttle bay, teammates fell. Human, Sklorno, HeavyG or Ki, they slumped, dropped and lay motionless.

Liars! The Prawatt lied to me ...

His butt hit the deck. He'd fallen. The domed room seemed to swim around him, blend and blur and take on so many shapes and colors.

He saw something fall from the ceiling — Tara the Freak, slipping from the rafter railing to land hard on top of a sprawled-out Sho-Do-Thikit. Neither player moved.

Quentin felt the deck's coolness against his cheek just before he passed out.

From *Net Colony News Syndicate*

Buddha City Elite wins Tier Two Tourney

by JONATHAN SANDOVAL

HUDSON BAY, EARTH, PLANETARY UNION — For the first time in 16 seasons, a team from the Purist Nation will join the ranks of Tier One.

The Buddha City Elite won the T2 Tourney championship with a hard-fought 24-22 win over the Sheb Stalkers. Buddha City was in Tier One as part of the 2664 GFL expansion, which included the Hittoni Hullwalkers and the Srabian Salient, but was relegated in 2669.

Sheb's second-place T2 Tourney finish puts them in Tier One for the first time in franchise history.

The Stalkers had a 22-17 lead with six seconds to play when Buddha City quarterback Gary Lindros threw a desperation 60-yard pass into the end zone. The throw was incomplete, but officials called a controversial pass-interference penalty. As a game can't end on a defensive penalty, the Elite were given the ball on the 1-yard line with no time left on the clock. On the game's final play, Lindros scrambled right and dove in for the winning touchdown.

"We just want to thank High One for this win," said Elite coach Ezekiel Graber. "All the glory goes to Him. The Stalkers played well, but in the end this result was preordained."

Sheb Stalkers owner Kovacs the Red had other thoughts.

"That call was [expletive]," Kovacs said. "And [expletive] and also [multiple expletives]. Who calls a pass-interference call on the final play of the game? Who does that?"

Sheb moves up to the Solar Division to replace the relegated Sala Intrigue. Buddha City replaces the Lu Juggernauts in the Planet Division.

The Elite won the Union Conference title with an 8-1 regular-season record, making them the top seed in the Tier Two Tournament. In the first round, Buddha City defeated Harrah Conference champion Stilt Skygods 17-16 on a last-second field goal. In the semi-finals, the Elite won an all-field-goal game 12-9 over Ki Conference champ Closs Cannibals.

This marks the third straight year that a team from the Quyth Irradiated Conference has won promotion from Tier Two into Tier One.

Sheb won the Quyth Irradiated Conference with an 8-1 record. In the first round of the T2 Tourney, the Stalkers topped Sklorno Conference champ Klipthik Parasites 28-14, then moved on to a dominating 35-17 semi-final victory over Whitok Conference champ D'Oni Coelacanths.

This marks the third straight year that a team from the Quyth Irradiated Conference has won promotion from Tier Two into Tier One. The Ionath Krakens did it in 2682, followed by the Orbiting Death in 2683. Along with the Themala Dreadnaughts, the Quyth Concordia has four teams in Tier One — the most of any governmental system.

5

The Hangover

QUENTIN KNEW he had an enormous tolerance for physical pain. What he did not have, however, was an enormous tolerance for alcohol. In his PNFL days he'd loved his beer, but not for the taste or the buzz — beer offended his holier-than-thou teammates and the ever-so-pious members of the Church, and he enjoyed offending those people. He would make a single can last for hours; despite being seven feet tall and weighing almost four hundred pounds, he had discovered early on that two beers made him falling-down drunk, and *three* beers were a recipe for disaster.

In his second year with the Micovi Raiders, he'd earned the starting quarterback position — at just seventeen years old. To celebrate his first win, some of the other players had taken him out on the town. Five beers and a few hours of sleep later, he'd awoken to the first hangover of his life. An entire day of vomiting, his body aching like he'd been beaten up in the Octagon and a head that felt like it was filled with rotting roundbugs were enough to tell him that he would always be an amateur drinker — the professional ranks were not for him.

If he could go back in time, grab that hangover, put it in a magic amplifier where it grew to ten times its original strength, then cram it back into his head with a power-siphon, it would approximate how he felt now.

He tried to sit up, tried to lift a head so heavy it had to be made of granite. Around him, he heard the moans and groans of other Human and HeavyG players. His eyelids fluttered open to see dozens of blinking eyestalks only inches from his face.

"The Godling Quentinbarnes lives! *He lives!*"

The Sklorno had packed in around him, Milford front and center. Her raspers dangled on his chest, her drool wetted his orange jersey.

"Quentinbarnes, are you alive? *Are you?*"

It hurt to blink. Seriously, it hurt to even *blink*. "I think so," he said.

He tried to push himself to a sitting position. He was on some kind of a metal grate. A matching metal grate was only a few feet above him. Sklorno tentacles grabbed him and pulled him up — he knew they were only trying to help, but they moved him so fast it seemed to slosh the blood around in his abused brain.

"Girls, give me some room, will ya?"

The Sklorno backed away. Quentin looked around. He was in the shuttle bay, but it looked so different. Racks of sentient-sized mesh shelves filled the room like a forest of stunted black trees. Three shelves to each rack, like the triple bunk beds he'd slept on in the miner's dorms back on Micovi. He was on the bottom bunk. The black, gnarled material seemed to be the same stuff that made up the Prawatt arena and, probably, the Prawatt ships themselves.

He looked to the shuttle bay doors, which were open but only about eighteen inches. The strange material had filled that open space like a waterfall of black ice. Tendrils spread across the floor, black creepers that sprouted up to form the triple-decker bunk beds.

Milford leaned in again, shaking with concern. "Quentinbarnes, your arms!"

No wonder she was upset — a cluster of organic-looking black cables was sticking out the crook of his elbow. Not just sticking *out*: they were under his skin, snaking down his forearm and up into his shoulder.

He grabbed at them in a sudden panic, yanking hard to tear them from his body. As soon as he pulled, the black material disintegrated into puffs of dust and hard pebbles that scattered across his bunk and down to the deck below. What should have been an inch-wide hole in his arm instantly closed up, leaving only a few drops of blood to show that the cables had been there at all.

Quentin heard a voice from the bunk above him.

"Oh, man," John Tweedy said. "They ain't paying us enough for this."

Up on the top bunk, Ju Tweedy's tired face looked over to stare down at his brother. "Not enough to wake up to your face, John."

John looked up at him. "What? Was that a joke?"

"Oh, how I wish it were," Ju said.

John struggled to climb up to the top bunk, but Quentin grabbed the man's wrist.

"Guys, knock it off," Quentin said. "We need to figure out what's going on."

He slid out of the rack and felt the cold deck against his bare feet. He tried to stand, but his knees wobbled. Twelve tentacles grabbed him as Milford, Hawick, Wahiawa, Davenport, Cheboygan and Mezquitic all reached to support him at the same time.

"Leave me be," he said, pushing their tentacles away. "I don't need your help."

The Sklorno backed away from him, bobbing and bowing in apology.

John slid out of the bed above and stood on Quentin's left. He pushed his right index finger against the side of his nose, then blew, sending a glob of snot to the deck. He did the same on his left side.

"John," Quentin said. "Can't you see I'm barefoot?"

John looked down. "Do you want me to fetch your slippers for you?"

Ju slid off the top bunk, a fall of some ten feet down to the deck below. He landed lightly with an athletic grace that seemed somehow spooky for a man of his size and thickness.

All around the landing bay, Humans and HeavyG crawled out of the bunks that hadn't existed the day before. Quentin saw Yassoud. 'Soud's normally braided beard was a foot-long poof of coarse black hair. Rick Warburg was on his knees, vomiting on the deck. Off to the right, Michael Kimberlin tried to stand, but his legs gave out. He caught himself by putting his fists against the ground, making him looked like a sleepy, furless gorilla. Tara the Freak wobbled around on unsure legs. Virak the Mean started to roll out of his second-deck bunk, then seemed to give up, roll back in and go to sleep.

The whole team looked stinking drunk — except for the Sklorno, however, who were already fully recovered from whatever had happened. The ones that weren't watching Quentin's every move seemed to be playing some kind of racing game that used the tall bunk beds as hurdles.

Sklorno, Human, HeavyG, Quyth Warrior ... there was one race missing.

"Hey," Quentin said. "Where's all the Ki?"

A hard elbow in his ribs. Quentin winced, already knowing that was John's excited way of answering the question. The eldest Tweedy brother pointed toward the orange and black shuttle that ferried players to and from the league's many stadiums.

Just past the shuttle, Quentin saw the Ki — all thirteen of them — held aloft by a black mesh net dangling some fifteen feet above the deck. A black cable ran from the net to the domed ceiling above. That cable branched into smaller cables that covered the Ki's hexagonal mouths.

Another hard elbow in his ribs. "Q," John said, "they dead?"

"Doubt it," Quentin said. "We're alive, aren't we?"

John thought, then nodded. "We are. Probably." He crossed his arms and looked up at the ceiling, his eyes narrowed in thought. "Hard to be sure, though. We could be dead. No, we *have* to be alive because if this were the afterlife, we'd be on a football field for sure."

Quentin smiled. If only that were true, he would have never strayed from the Purist faith.

John rubbed at his temples. "Man, I feel like we went on an all-night bender through every party sub on Isis. Did the Prawatt gas us?"

The Prawatt. Memories of the Game flooded back, as did memories of Stockbridge's death. Quentin looked to the spot where Doc Patah had set up the triage area — nothing was there. No tables, equipment, no marks on the floor ... just how long had they been out?

"Uncle Johnny, find Doc Patah," Quentin said. "Wake him up — *gently,* understand? — and bring him here."

John nodded and ran off.

Quentin turned to John's brother. "Ju, go help Tara the Freak." Quentin pointed to Tara, who was still stumbling a bit. "Make sure he's okay, then have him climb up to that cable and see if he can cut the Ki loose."

Ju stood tall and snapped off a smart salute. "Private Ju Tweedy, reporting for duty and such." He jogged over to Tara.

Quentin looked up to the ceiling. "Computer?"

There was no answer.

"Captain Cheevers, please come in?"

Again, no answer.

Milford and the other Sklorno were still close by, as if waiting for a command from their holy teammate.

"Milford, Hawick, Halawa, go to the bridge," Quentin said. "If Captain Kate and the crew are still asleep, wake them up, have them get ship communications working right away. Milford, ask her if she has any information for me, then come right back. Hawick and Halawa, you stay there and be a runner for her until the computer is back online, in case she needs to send any messages."

The two receivers didn't answer. Instead, they turned and sprinted top-speed to the open interior airlock. They banked right in order to leap over one of the bunk beds, then angled through the door. Quentin hoped they understood what he was asking of them.

He turned to the other Sklorno. "Wahiawa, Davenport,

Cheboygan, Mezquitic, you guys split up and go through the ship. Tell everyone to come to the shuttle bay. Go."

The four of them sprinted for the interior airlock. On a football field, the top speed of a Sklorno was something to behold. In the smaller confines of a spaceship, they looked like they might splatter themselves into a wall at any second.

Quentin felt a presence on his left. He turned to look into the single, baseball-sized eye of Choto the Bright.

"*Shamakath*," Choto said quietly. "Are you all right?"

The Quyth Warrior looked horrible. The normally clear cornea of that single eye swirled with a mixture of black, dark red and pink: the black of anger; the dark red of hatred, probably against the Prawatt who had done this and, therefore, put Quentin in danger; and the pink of fear for Quentin's health. Last season, Choto had sworn his allegiance to Quentin as his *shamakath*, his one and only leader.

Quentin leaned in and whispered. "Don't use that word. Remember?"

"I do," Choto said. "My apologies."

Quentin leaned back. "And I'm fine. My head is killing me, but I'm okay. You?"

The pink faded from Choto's eye, but the black and the dark-red swirls remained. "I feel like my internal organs are decomposing inside," he said. "No, allow me to clarify — it feels like I am full of the decomposing feces of a ten-kiloton Farnier Bird. They are carrion eaters and already full of decomposing material themselves, you see."

That made Quentin laugh, which brought on another wave of head pain. He rubbed his eyes and took a breath, waiting for it to pass. A ten-kiloton equivalent of a buzzard? He'd have to see one of those someday. At any rate, the Quyth weren't known for exaggeration, which meant Choto felt something awful.

"Wake up the other Warriors," Quentin said. "Especially Virak."

Choto glanced over to Virak the Mean, who was still sleeping in his bunk.

"Do not think Virak is your ally," Choto said.

Quentin nodded. "I know who he serves."

Virak's loyalties remained with Gredok the Splithead. Gredok had played games with Quentin's heart and soul, had created a fake father to sway Quentin's decisions. Someday, perhaps someday soon, the crime lord would pay for his actions. When that happened, Virak would become a dangerous enemy.

"He's not my ally, but he's still my teammate," Quentin said. "And he knows how to fight. We may need that soon."

Quentin thumped Choto on the shoulder. The hulking Quyth Warrior jogged off to gather up the rest of his kind.

John came running through the black bunks. He was laughing, holding a semi-conscious Doc Patah on an upturned left hand like a waitress carrying a large platter. Doc's wing-flaps hung mostly limp but fluttered lightly from the air passing over them.

"He's like a kite, Q!" John stopped in front of Quentin. He tossed Doc Patah into the air; like a balloon, the naturally buoyant Harrah floated up, then gently down.

John laughed and pumped his right fist as if he'd just sacked a quarterback. "Q, this is *awesome*! We could tie a string to him and see how high he goes!"

Quentin gently reached up and put one hand on the Harrah's underside, one hand on top of the flat, boxy backpack that all Harrah wore. He held Doc in place.

"John, he's not a toy."

IF IT LOOKS LIKE A TOY AND FLIES LIKE A TOY...flashed across John's face. John frowned. "Sometimes, Q? Sometimes you're no fun."

"We're in the middle of an alien spaceship, everyone has been gassed, we've been out for who knows how long, and they could execute us at any moment. Does that sound like a time to have *fun*?"

John shrugged. "If we're gonna die, what *better* time is there to have fun? You be sad about it if you want, but some of us know which side of our bread is covered in eggs."

John walked off, whistling a tune.

Doc Patah's backpack speakerfilm let out a burst of static,

then he spoke. "Thank you, young Quentin. I was afraid John was going to see how far he could throw me."

"John would never do something like that," Quentin said, knowing full well that John would do *exactly* something like that. "You all right, Doc?"

Doc Patah's shape changed slightly as he became just a bit thicker, then he floated out of Quentin's hands. His wing-flaps undulated slowly.

"I will be fine," he said. "Although, I haven't felt this bad since my younger days when my tribe-mates and I would intentionally ingest a diluted poison made from rotted puree of a cluster-fruit found on the planet Shorah."

Quentin tried to imagine what kind of an insane culture would drink *poison*, diluted or not. Maybe Humans were just smarter than the other races when it came to some things.

"Everyone feels like crap," Quentin said.

"The symptoms are consistent with being kept unconscious for an extended period of time," Doc Patah said. "A very long time."

How long was a *very long time*? Quentin had no idea if, or when, they might find out. And what was the point of drugging everyone?

"Doc, do you think they're going to try and kill us?"

Doc Patah's speakerfilm let out his well-known sigh of annoyance. "Try to *kill* us, young Quentin? Building beds and life-support systems doesn't seem like a very efficient way to murder a sentient, now does it? No, they are not trying to kill us. Not now, at least. However, they *could* be taking us to a specific location for execution, as is common in ritualistic murders."

"Thanks," Quentin said. "That makes me feel so much better."

"You're welcome. I live to serve."

The interior airlock doors opened. Wahiawa, Davenport, Cheboygan and Mezquitic all ran in carrying orange-uniformed Ionath staff — a Human, Messal the Efficient, and another Worker Quentin didn't recognize. The Sklorno gently set the staffers on the deck, then sprinted out, presumably to find more sentients to rescue.

Quentin waved Messal over. The Worker stumbled forward as a few more staffers entered under their own power. Messal looked … rumpled. Quentin had never seen the Worker when his uniform wasn't immaculate and neatly creased. Messal's big cornea had a hazy film over it. His sparse fur stuck out in all directions.

"Elder Barnes," Messal said. "I do not feel well."

"Welcome to the party, pal," Quentin said. "Messal, I need you to make me a list of every sentient on this ship. If anyone isn't in the shuttle bay, I need to know where they are and what condition they're in. I want everyone accounted for."

"Yes, Elder Barnes." The Worker walked away, straightening his uniform with one pedipalp hand and activating his palm-up display with the other.

"Young Quentin, excuse me," Doc Patah said. "I must check on the sentients in the medbay, then I will examine everyone on board for any long-term effects."

Quentin pointed at the big, dangling bag of Ki. "What about the —"

Before he could finish the sentence, the cable holding the bag disintegrated into a cloud of black dust. The cluster of Ki fell fifteen feet, landing so hard Quentin felt the vibration. The now-conscious Ki tumbled away from each other, big legs and arms waving in uncoordinated motions.

Up in the shallow dome's rigging, Tara the Freak hung from one long pedipalp arm. His free hand waved at Quentin.

"Nicely done," Doc Patah said. "Your Ki teammates will be fine. They can process far more poisons than can either of our species. As I look around, no one seems hurt — that tells me that the Prawatt knew what they were doing. I will let you know the status of Coach Hokor."

With that, the Harrah's gray wings undulated, carrying him across the landing bay to the internal airlock doors. As he floated out, Captain Kate Cheevers walked in. She saw Quentin and made a beeline for him.

"Barnes, any idea of what's going on?"

Quentin shook his head. "Just that they gassed us after the

Game. We were all here in the landing bay, then everyone started dropping."

Cheevers nodded. "Yeah, same thing up on the bridge. We watched the Game. I watched you, especially." She winked at him, her head twitching to the right at the same time. "You looked good out there, pretty boy. *Real* good."

Was she really hitting on him *now*? Why did no one seem to understand how serious this was?

"Thanks," he said. "Any idea how long we were out?"

She shook her head. "Computer is shut down all over the ship, including the bridge. All systems are off, and that black stuff blocks all of our viewports, so we can't even take a star reading to see where we're at." She looked around, saw the Sklorno bringing sentients in. She nodded, looked up at him. "You did a good job so far getting everyone together, and I appreciate that. But that stunt you pulled up on the bridge when the Prawatt boarded us? You better remember that this is *my* ship. I am the captain. What I say goes. Got it?"

Quentin stared down at her. He remembered how she'd looked when Bumberpuff and the other Prawatt had entered the bridge. She had looked defeated. Captain Kate had quit, and in this galaxy, there was no place for quitters. Now, however, wasn't the time to worry about that.

"I got it," he said.

Kate nodded. *Wink-twitch.*

She walked back to the internal airlock, obviously heading for the bridge. Quentin would let her run things unless her decisions put the team at risk or did anything that threatened to delay their return. If he had to take over, he would — he had seen Kate's true colors.

He saw teammates coming his way. Don Pine and the bleach-white-skinned Yitzhak Goldman, his backup quarterbacks, a still-wobbly Michael Kimberlin, Choto the Bright and Virak the Mean. Virak's eye was flooded a deep black.

"What has been done to us?" he said. "Where can I find the ones responsible?"

Quentin shrugged. "I don't know yet. Our first priority is to make sure everyone is okay."

"Our first priority is to make sure Gredok's property is in good health," Virak said. He pointed to the twenty-odd civilian staffers that had gathered in the shuttle bay. "*They* are easily replaced, players are not."

"Wrong," Quentin said a bit more forcefully than he'd intended. "We make sure *everyone* is okay. Just because those sentients don't play on the field doesn't make them less important than we are. And we're not *property*, Virak — we are individuals, and we *all* matter."

Virak's pedipalps twitched — he was laughing at Quentin.

Kimberlin rubbed his eyes, then looked around the shuttle bay. "At least everyone is still alive, even the Sklorno," he said. "That is more than I would have hoped for. You have done well, Quentin."

Yitzhak clapped Quentin on the shoulder. "You beat the crawlies," he said. "But they said they'd let us go. What do they want with us?"

That was the million-credit question, and Quentin still had no idea. "I don't know the answer to that," he said. "Let's get everyone together and figure out our next step."

Don pointed to the internal airlock. "Well well well, look what the dog dragged in."

Doc Patah floated through the door, followed by a stumbling Coach Hokor the Hookchest. He had a bandage wrapped around his tiny, yellow-furred head and a little Krakens baseball cap pulled down on top of that.

Messal the Efficient appeared at Quentin's side. "Elder Barnes, all personnel are accounted for. Captain Cheevers and her command crew are on the bridge. All players, staff and other crew are here, as you requested."

Then came a sound, a sound like dirt pouring from a high shovel to scatter across the floor. The bunk beds started to collapse, sagging like sand castles caught in a sudden rain. The material puddled on the shuttle bay deck, then flowed backward toward the big exterior airlock doors. That same material that had blocked those doors melted away, revealing a reddish light beyond.

A pair of massive, gnarled, very *un-Human* black hands slid inside the landing bay, one gripping the left-hand door, the other gripping the right. Each hand was the size of Mum-O-Killowe.

The door machinery groaned. Vibrations rumbled through the deck. The big hands slowly slid the doors open.

Don nodded in mock appreciation. "Oh, joy," he said. "Looks like we'll finally get some answers."

The doors were now a good fifteen feet apart. The red light shone in from beyond. The black hands slid away.

Wherever they were, the wait was over.

"Virak," Quentin said, "get us ready to fight."

Quentin saw Virak's eye briefly flood orange — the color of happiness — then the scarred, heavily enameled combat veteran began screaming orders that even a non-soldier would follow without thought.

QUENTIN STOOD IN THE CENTER of the shuttle bay. Virak stood on his right, Choto on his left. Rebecca Montagne and the rest of the Humans and Quyth Warriors spread out on either side in a line eighteen players long from end to end. In front of them was a line of twelve Ki, their bodies low to the ground and ready to push forward. The HeavyG players made up a third rank — right behind Quentin stood the eight-foot-tall Michael Kimberlin. Alexsandar Michnik and Cliff Frost were on Kimberlin's left, Ibrahim Khomeni, Tim Crawford and Rich Palmer were on his right.

The crew of the *Touchback* and the Ionath franchise staff were farther back in the shuttle bay, protected by fifteen Sklorno. Captain Kate stood side by side with Coach Hokor — while Quyth Leaders might be adept at calling out strategy, when it came to an actual fight, they knew their place was far behind the bigger, stronger Warrior caste.

Virak had ordered the Sklorno up front, but Kimberlin had reminded everyone that the Sklorno and the Prawatt nations were already nearly at war. The wrong word, even the wrong *gesture* might make the Sklorno rush forward and start something that couldn't be stopped. With all of his godly gravitas, Quentin had warned the ladies to stay back unless he ordered them to act.

The giant, black hands reappeared. A mountain of a creature ducked through the twenty-foot-high shuttle bay doors. Quentin had never seen anything like it. Six thick, insectile legs connected to each point of a heavy, hexagonal base. From that base, a twisted trunk of a body rose up some twenty-five feet to a waving mass of gnarled cables, each thicker than Quentin himself. The two huge, Human-looking black arms stuck out from halfway up the trunk. Six legs moved, and in it came.

Hundreds of armed X-Walkers rushed in through the open doors, ran under the huge creature and spread out to either side, forming a perimeter. Behind the X-Walkers came other strange, black creatures — some taller, some shorter, all carrying weaponry he couldn't identify.

Within seconds, a semi-circle of gnarled black creatures faced off against the Ionath Krakens. At least the guns weren't pointed *at* Quentin and his teammates, but rather *up*, at the domed ceiling — maybe he'd have a chance to talk before any fighting began. No, correction, before a *slaughter* began; the Prawatt outnumbered the Krakens five to one, and that didn't even count the gigantic, hexagonal *thing* that loomed over everyone.

Quentin didn't back up. Neither did his teammates. They were unarmed, outnumbered, but there wasn't any place to run.

Then, through the line of black X-Walkers, came the first Prawatt that Quentin Barnes knew by sight — Captain Cormorant Bumberpuff.

The captain's blue streamers were gone. In their place were bands of gold-trimmed red and blue wrapped tightly around his X-body. Small discs of shiny gold or silver hung from small ribbons. Were those medals? Even in an alien race, Quentin recognized such trappings as the dress uniform of a military officer.

Bumberpuff strode forward. His rigid steps seemed measured, formal. He stopped a few feet away from the Krakens line.

"Quentin Barnes, I have come for you."

In front of Quentin, Mum-O-Killowe stood up on his hind legs, his long body rising some thirteen feet high as his roar echoed off the landing bay's domed walls.

A tadpole-shaped blur of silver flew in from behind the line of Krakens. Shizzle landed on Mum-O's right shoulder.

"The great Mum-O-Killowe says if you come for one of us, you come for *all* of us," the Creterakian called out. "The highly intelligent and also quite modest Mum-O says if it takes a blood-bath, let's get it over with."

The entire line of Ki rose up on their hind legs; a waving, roaring, pebble-skinned display of promised violence. That sense of aggression instantly spread through the whole team. Quentin felt Choto lean in slightly on his left, Virak on his right. Every member of the Orange and the Black was ready — the Ionath Krakens would not go down without a fight.

The Ki dropped down to their normal six-legged stance. They spread their arms to their sides, interlinking them into a protective wall of multi-jointed muscle.

Bumberpuff had taken a step back. Many of the X-Walkers, in fact, had shifted their position. What had been a perfect, rigid line of military precision now looked a bit scattered, as if every one of them wasn't quite sure where or how it was supposed to stand.

"Bloodbath?" Bumberpuff said. "You want a bath of blood?"

Quentin stepped forward. He put his hands on the intertwined arms of Mum-O and Sho-Do. They let go, allowing him to approach Bumberpuff.

"We *won*," Quentin said. "We demand you release us! The deal was if we played and beat you, we would go free, yet you drug us? You *kidnap* us?"

A body made of boneless, semi-see-through arms and legs, yet Quentin could sense confusion in the captain.

"There has been a misunderstanding," it said. "You *are* free. You have not been kidnapped — the Old Ones want to see you."

George Starcher hopped over the Ki arms and rushed forward. "Did you say *Old Ones*?"

"George, *not now*," Quentin said. "Captain Bumberpuff, if we won and we're free, why are you threatening us with all of these soldiers and their guns?"

Bumberpuff paused for a moment. Then he started to rattle a little, the same way he had when Quentin had first met him on the bridge.

"This isn't a *threat*," he said. "It is an honor guard. And we had to put you to sleep to protect the location of our home planet."

Home planet? But that was so far away. That would mean ...

"We've been asleep for three months," Quentin said. "*Three months*. The date, what's today's date?"

"In Earth Time, it is August twenty-fifth."

The Galaxy Bowl had been played on May eighteenth. Who had won the championship? Far more important than that, the 2685 Tier One preseason began January first, just fifteen weeks away. Twelve weeks of that time span would be spent traveling back to known space — if they didn't head back soon, they might miss the start of the Tier One season.

If they missed the preseason — or even worse, if they actually missed a game — they had no chance of reaching the playoffs, of winning the Galaxy Bowl.

"You lied," Quentin said. "Your culture is a culture of liars. You said you would let us go."

"We will," Bumberpuff said. "I promise you, we will. Bringing you here is the highest honor our culture can bestow, Quentin. The Old Ones themselves asked for you."

Quentin shook his head. This couldn't be happening, not after all he and his teammates had been through. "We need to go back," he said. "Right now."

"But we are here," Bumberpuff said. "We have landed."

"*Take ... us ... BACK!*"

Bumberpuff wasn't rattling anymore. Apparently this was no longer funny to him.

Kimberlin pushed through the Ki line with a sense of urgency bordering on panic.

"Quentin, do you realize the significance of this?" He pointed to the open shuttle bay doors. "The Prawatt home planet is out there. No one has ever seen it! No one even knows where it *is*."

Quentin heard the words, tried to process them, tried to let them cut through his rage. "Finding planets isn't my business," he said. "Know what my business is? *Winning football games*."

Kimberlin shook his head, a wide-eyed thing that made his lips wobble. Quentin had never before seen the man show such emotion.

"You don't understand," he said. "They gassed us so we couldn't help anyone find their home planet. Do you know why? Because for three *centuries*, the Prawatt have effectively been at war with every race in the galaxy. There are no diplomatic relations of any kind. There are no ambassadors, there's no trade. What we do here now could change that."

It was just like Mike to make things sound so grand and important. Football players played football — they didn't make cultures stop hating each other.

"You want diplomacy, get a diplomat," Quentin said. "We already missed the Tier Two Tournament, we missed scouting for new players. Who knows what Gredok has done while we're gone. We need to get back — that's all any of us should care about."

Yitzhak Goldman broke ranks and ran up to Quentin.

"Q, Mike's right — this is history in the making! What if this leads to peace between the Prawatt and the other races?"

Growing up on Micovi had burned one truth into Quentin's head: no matter what, sentients would *always* find a reason to fight, always find a way to justify slaughter.

"Zak, get real," Quentin said. "We won a *game*. You don't get peace because one team throws a ball through a hoop more times than another team. A shucking victory parade isn't going to end centuries of hate."

Yitzhak smiled that all-knowing smile of his. "As a Purist Nation citizen, what was the only thing that taught you to stop hating the other sentient races?"

Quentin blinked. The answer to that question was, of course, *football*. That was why the Creterakians started the GFL in the first place, to create a game that required *all* races if you wanted to win. A sport had succeeded where diplomacy and philosophers and politicians had failed to create common ground — football marked the first thing that brought five races together to *play* instead of *fight*.

"This is big," Yitzhak said. "Bigger than the Krakens, bigger than the season. There may never be another opportunity like this again. Not just in your lifetime, but *ever*. Remember back in Danny Lundy's office, when I said that sentients want to follow you? That you could use that natural leadership ability for something greater than football?"

Quentin did remember. He looked from Yitzhak to Kimberlin, who had asked Quentin the same question in a slightly different way.

Then, a hand on Quentin's shoulder. He turned, knowing he would see the blue face of Don Pine.

"Kid, don't be a dumb-ass," Don said. "I don't know about this *something greater* crap Zak's prattling on about, but come on — you could be the first sentient to see this place, and you're going to say *no*? Come on, man, use your head."

"But Don, we're *three months* away from home! I mean, I'd love to contribute to galactic peace and love, or whatever, but what if we miss the preseason!"

Don shook his head and sighed. He looked at Bumberpuff.

"Hey, Captain Silly Name, how long do you want to keep us here?"

"As long as you like," Bumberpuff said. "But seeing the Old Ones will take a day at most."

Quentin's face felt hot. He was turning red. The Krakens were here, there was nothing he could do about that now, but he'd never thought to ask *how long* the Prawatt wanted to keep them. If he'd controlled his emotions, he probably would have thought of that. A day or two wouldn't make any difference at this point.

Don patted Quentin's shoulder and smiled. "So as long as we're in the neighborhood, maybe you could be the first person in history to see the Prawatt planet? And, while you're at it, spare an hour or two to show this race that not everyone is out to kill them?"

Don turned and walked back to his place in the line, leaving Quentin to shake his head — one minute he hated Don Pine for being a weak, self-centered liar, the next he wondered how he would ever get by without Don's advice.

Quentin turned to face Bumberpuff.

"Captain, I'd be honored to see your world. Can the whole team come?"

"Only you and one other are allowed to meet the Old Ones," Bumberpuff said. "And you may only choose from those that played against the Harpies. As for the rest, I will assign liaisons to escort them through the city, within a reasonable range. And the Sklorno are not allowed to leave your ship."

Centuries of hatred wasn't just going to vanish in a puff of smoke, it seemed, but Quentin wasn't going to press the point — he didn't trust the Sklorno to behave themselves.

He could only take someone who had played in the Game. Cheboygan and Halawa were out, obviously. Quentin couldn't bring Mum-O. There was no telling how the lineman would react to the strange situation.

That left just Becca and Yassoud. Yassoud had played well, but if Quentin was to pick someone who had a better game, Becca was the obvious choice.

He turned to face his teammates. "Becca? Will you come with me?"

Her big eyes grew even bigger. Her mouth opened, then closed. She nodded, then walked forward.

Standing side by side, Quentin Barnes and Rebecca Montagne followed Captain Cormorant Bumberpuff out of the landing bay.

6

Sanctuary

QUENTIN, BECCA AND CAPTAIN BUMBERPUFF walked onto a thick, black platform that had formed outside the *Touchback*'s shuttle bay doors. Dense clouds the color of red apples hung against a brownish-yellow sky. The platform looked out over a sprawling cityscape, strange buildings of black spreading as far as the eye could see.

Bumberpuff's body vibrated. "Welcome to Sanctuary, our home planet."

Becca slowly shook her head. "I can't believe I'm seeing this. It's beautiful."

Quentin turned to look at the *Touchback*. It remained mostly wrapped in the Prawatt ship, an orange jewel embedded in a mountain of living black metal. The Prawatt vessel's size defied imagination. Was it floating, or had it landed? Quentin couldn't tell.

"Captain, how long until our ship is fixed?"

"It already is," Bumberpuff said, his voice dots vibrating, his eye-dots reflecting the clouds' red light. "There are a few systems that we will keep offline for your return home, but the pirate damage is repaired. The damage was significant — if we hadn't found you when we did, everyone aboard your ship would have perished."

Bumberpuff had lied about letting them go, so was it telling the truth now? If it was, the Krakens owed the Prawatt an unpayable debt.

"So what now?" Quentin said.

"I will take you to meet the Old Ones," Bumberpuff said. "You may leave right after that, if you wish, but perhaps you would consider staying. I would be happy to have you on the Harpies as my main chaser."

Quentin felt a swell of pride in his chest — he wasn't sure what *team* meant to this strange-yet-familiar race, but as far as he was concerned, there was no higher compliment than to ask someone to play by your side.

"I can't stay, but thank you," Quentin said.

The platform suddenly fell into shadow. From the far side of the Prawatt ship came a floating monstrosity, a huge, black blimp that had to be a hundred feet wide and maybe twice as long. Dozens of smaller black bubbles clung to the downward slope of its curving sides. Longer, sack-like creatures seemed moored to the oblong's rear. The creatures had wide, circular mouths lined with a dozen webbed limbs, as if they were bony octopus tentacles joined by loose skin. Over and over, the mouths opened like a spreading hand, stretching so far that Quentin could see through the pinkish membrane, then the hand clutched shut in the blink of an eye.

The oblong's front looked even more disturbing. There Quentin saw clusters of cables that ended in glass spheres, spheres that he knew were *looking* at him. Behind those clusters swarmed vastly longer, thinner cables that ended in tapered points.

It was a living, moving, floating demon, the kind of thing reserved for tales of hell and the seven levels of endless torture.

If I had dreamed about this as a kid, I would have peed myself.

"Uh, Captain Bumberpuff? Should we be running or something?"

"Don't be afraid," Bumberpuff said. "Jenny Twoshoes is harmless. She's here to take us to the Old Ones. Are you ready?"

That black, tentacled *thing* had a *name*? *Jenny* wasn't exactly the name you'd expect for a demon. What other surprises were in store?

Quentin looked at Becca. She nodded. She remained wide-eyed and disbelieving, yet her demeanor made her thoughts easy to read — if Quentin was going, she would go with him.

"We're ready," Quentin said. "Do we take a grav-lift up or something?"

"Or something," Bumberpuff said. "I imagine you are not used to what is about to happen. Just try to remember one thing."

"Which is?"

"Don't panic."

The floating ship's cluster of tentacles fluttered and flexed, then three extended down like long black snakes sliding through the air. Quentin fought the urge to run, mostly because there was nowhere *to* run; that hexagonal reject from a Dinolition match was still inside the shuttle bay, and the platform on which he stood had to be a thousand feet above the alien city.

The black tentacle's tapered tip reached him, slid around his waist three times, and then suddenly he was falling *up*, racing toward the huge black airship. Wind rushed across his face, locking his breath in his chest. The tentacle gently lowered him to a small, flat space lined with black, waist-high, U-shaped bars. He grabbed one of these handholds and held on tight.

Another tentacle lightly put Becca down next to him. She was wide-eyed, her face frozen in a laugh of surprise and amazement.

Bumberpuff landed last. "Did you enjoy the ride?"

Quentin shrugged. "Well, I didn't puke. In my book, that's really something."

The black airship started to move. Quentin looked down at the *Touchback*. Even from here, he couldn't see the entire Prawatt warship and his team bus looked like a plastic toy.

They floated above a black city nestled in a black landscape. Like the Sklorno worlds he had visited, civilization covered *every-*

thing. Strange buildings as far as the eye could see, yet this wasn't the usual ocean of concrete and crysteel. Something about the city beneath reminded him of a coral reef, countless parts merging together into a unified whole.

It felt *alive*, and as he stared he understood why — the city was *moving*. Sanctuary's surface seemed to pulse, to vibrate. Ripples rolled through the endless city, making the structures move like underwater plants pulled by the slightest of currents.

"It's amazing," Quentin said. "This makes our cities look ... well, kind of *dead*."

"Life covers Sanctuary," Bumberpuff said. "It is not the life that you know, but life it is."

A tap on his arm. Becca, directing his attention the other way. There, Quentin saw things flying, *flapping*. Only the texture and color of their skin identified them as Prawatt. Wide black wings beat at the air, propelling bodies of several shapes. Some looked like streamlined, gleaming animals, others were solid cubes, and still others resembled the black bubbles of Jenny Twoshoes.

Quentin pointed at the fliers. "Are those Prawatt, or something else?"

"They are Prawatt," Bumberpuff said. "I am an *Explorer*, our basic adult form. As Explorers join and combine to find the next level of life, they can create new and unique shapes. Some opt to fly."

Quentin saw a familiar shape streak in from the direction of the *Touchback*. It was the gray-winged Doc Patah, who flew in a tight loop around the square-shaped Prawatt flier. Behind Doc came Shizzle, his Creterakian body and wings resplendent in glittering silver. The more streamlined Prawatt banked and gave chase. Quentin was worried for a moment, but relaxed when he saw all of the fliers angling and circling each other — they were *playing*, having fun with the freedom of the open sky.

The wonders continued. He saw a marvel beyond any he'd seen on other planets — a hexagonal building with a flying buttress supporting each corner. Each one of the twisting, gleaming black buttresses was at least a thousand feet high, a skyscraper unto itself. At their tops, they angled toward a central spire, merged into it, supported it, allowing that spire to rise so high its top vanished into the red clouds.

"Amazing," Quentin said. "That middle part looks like it's a mile high."

"A *mile*?" Bumberpuff said. "How quaint. The building is one thousand, nine hundred and thirty-one *meters* tall. Or in your archaic, completely random and utterly nonsensical measuring system, one-point-two *miles*. It is the tallest construct in the history of universe, taller than anything ever built by Humans or Ki or Quyth or Creterakians. That is where we are going."

The city passed by beneath Jenny Twoshoes. The closer they got to the massive building, the taller it seemed.

Becca pointed up, to where the building disappeared into the clouds. "Is that where we will meet the Old Ones?"

"In a way," Bumberpuff said. "In some regards, that is where she lives."

"*She*?" Becca said. "That's singular. Are we meeting just one of the Old Ones?"

"She is many, she is one," the captain said. "No one knows how many individuals have joined her. The numbers are lost to our history. She is made up of hundreds of thousands of Prawatt, maybe even millions."

Quentin remembered his lessons with Michael Kimberlin, remembered the chapters of a book called *Earth: The Birthplace of Sentients*. The Prawatt didn't mate like other species. When two individuals wanted to join, they literally combined to become a new sentient.

Such a strange way to exist. He might marry someday, might have kids of his own, but doing so wouldn't end his existence or the existence of his wife. Humans didn't die to have babies.

The black ship closed in on the building. Structures beneath Jenny had to be huge skyscrapers unto themselves, but they were so far below they looked like a child's set of blocks. Up above, he finally saw the building's spire — it looked like a metal statue of some kind, a statue of a Human girl.

Made up of gold, silver and other metals, it had to be a hundred feet tall, at least. Long hair angled down over one eye. Her clothes seemed to be of ancient-Earth style, and a large purse or bag hung over one shoulder.

"Captain, who is that statue supposed to be?"

"Our creator," Bumberpuff said. "In your culture, in all the cultures but ours, the *creators* are imaginary, constructs of primitive minds that couldn't understand the universe around them. Somehow, these *gods* were carried forward as Humans and other sentients discovered the sciences and developed advanced technologies. Your gods were interpreted in a thousand different ways — and that was easy to do because your gods are made-up stories of something that never existed at all. But *our* creator? She *made* us. And she looked exactly like that."

"Wow," Quentin said. "She was *really* tall."

Bumberpuff's body rattled with a sudden shivering. "You are making a joke?"

Quentin laughed. "Yeah. Good one, huh?"

"Humor is in the mind of the beholder," the captain said, then rattle-shook one more time, which Quentin took to mean the captain thought the joke was funny as hell.

Jenny Twoshoes slowed near the statue's base. Ship-tentacles reached up, slid around Quentin's and Becca's waists, lifted them and set them in front of the statue's huge feet. Another tentacle placed Bumberpuff down next to them.

"Quentin, Rebecca, I can't properly describe the significance of this honor," the captain said. "Very few of us actually get to see the Old Ones, and no non-Prawatt ever has."

Quentin wondered what the Old Ones would look like. "Have you seen her before?"

"Never in person," Bumberpuff said. "This is the high point of my life. Quentin, I know that we are not friends, and that we have only recently met, but could I please ask a personal favor of you?"

Quentin shrugged. "Sure, why not?"

"Please don't embarrass me."

Now, Quentin laughed. Did his reputation precede him into this alien land?

"Sure, Cappy," he said. "I'll be a good boy."

The toe of a ten-foot-high boot rose up on an unseen hinge. Inside, Quentin saw an elevator platform. Bumberpuff walked onto it. Quentin and Becca followed.

"This is so cool," Becca said. "How far down is the Old One, er, Old *Ones*?"

"We will take this elevator to the surface," Bumberpuff said. "There, we have a short walk to take us below this building."

"Below?" Quentin said. "That's kind of weird. Your Old Ones don't live in this amazing building? They live beneath the city?"

Bumberpuff rattle-shook again, far harder this time.

"She's not *under* the city," the captain said. "The Old Ones *is* the city."

A FOREST IS A LIVING THING. At least, that's what they told Quentin back in grade school, before he didn't score high enough on his third-grade measurement exams and they sent him to the mines. The teachers told him a forest is an ecosystem, a web of interrelated organisms that are in balance. Even as a kid, he'd known the concept of *balance* was nonsense — a predator doesn't think about managing prey population, a predator eats what a predator can catch until that predator is full.

Any state of equilibrium is temporary: predator, prey, disease, parasite, *something* is already in the process of getting the upper hand, and when that happens, something else gets wiped out. The balance of nature? Quentin had learned all he needed to about that fallacy during the roundbug epidemic of 2675.

And yet on the Prawatt home planet of Sanctuary, Quentin had to wonder if here, at least, *balance* actually existed.

He walked through a sea of black, along metallic paths that were both street and sidewalk. Buildings grew out of that street the way a tree grows out of the ground. The walls always seemed in motion: wiggling, rattling, trembling as if they waited for the right moment to reach out and grab something. And grab things they did — when something needed to be brought up to a higher level, building walls grew tentacles that reached, grabbed and lifted. There was no need for elevators or possibly even stairs, not when the building could move you from floor to floor as gently as one parent handing a child to another.

And it wasn't just the buildings that seemed alive — the *streets* moved, undulating to slide items down the road like waves pushing slow-moving boats. X-Walkers and other, stranger Prawatt were everywhere, sometimes walking, sometimes crawling, sometimes riding in vehicles that moved on their own, sometimes riding in carts pushed along by the waving street. Other times, the individual Prawatt crawled *into* the street, sliding through the always-solid-yet-always-moving surface into something beneath. Occasionally, Quentin saw them sliding *out* of the street like a snake slithering from a hole that closed tight behind it.

Wherever he, Becca and Captain Bumberpuff stepped, however, the road seemed flat and still, hard as rock and as unforgiving as the face of a granite mountain.

Becca kept looking from building to building, her eyes as wide as a child's on the morning of Giving Day. "Quentin, this is so unreal."

He wished he had something eloquent to say, but eloquence wasn't his nature. So, he shrugged. "Yeah, I guess. But it won't be long until we meet these Old Ones, then we can get the hell out of here."

She looked at him and smiled a smile of wonder and delight so genuine it took his breath away.

"Do you even realize what's going on here? We might be the only non-Prawatt to set foot on this street. This is like ... I don't know ... like Humans landing on Earth's moon for the first time and finding a whole alien culture there waiting for them."

"Weren't there always people on the moon?"

Bumberpuff's body shook and rattled. Had Quentin said something funny?

Becca laughed. As they walked, she turned in slow circles, staring up at the moving buildings. She didn't need to look where she was going — the street solidified under her every step.

And then, Quentin saw something that *wasn't* black — set into the base of a towering skyscraper was a brown, wooden door with a white frame and a round, burnished silver handle. It looked like an interior door of a government building, or maybe a school. Three burnished silver numbers were screwed into the door at eye level: 931. It was just a regular old door, but in an endless sea of black, the lone bit of color took on an almost religious air.

Bumberpuff stopped in front of it. "We are here."

Quentin looked up. The building was swaying, *waving*, perhaps, and he had to look back down before he lost his balance. "Where is *here*, exactly?"

Bumberpuff's strange hand reached out gingerly, almost as if he was afraid of what might happen — his long fingers touched the silver numbers.

"The temple," he said. He paused a moment more, then quickly wrapped his tentacle around the handle. Quentin knew little about the Prawatt — he'd only just encountered the race, after all — but they were so inexplicably *Human* that he recognized a sigh of relief wash through Bumberpuff's semi-see-through body.

"Captain, you okay?"

"I'm fine," Bumberpuff said.

"You were worried about that door handle or something?"

Bumberpuff turned the handle and opened it just a crack. Inside, a white hallway, white light.

"Yes, I was worried," he said. "This is the entrance to the Old Ones. I have permission to enter, but had that permission been revoked for reasons unknown, I would have been destroyed as soon as I touched the handle."

Quentin looked around the street. Other than Prawatt pedestrians, the slightly undulating streets and the buildings, he saw nothing — no guns, no cameras, no defenses of any kind. Maybe guns weren't needed when the buildings themselves could come alive and get you.

Bumberpuff opened the door all the way. Inside, a hallway that looked like anything Quentin might see back on Micovi: white walls, a floor of some kind of polished gray stone.

The captain held the door open for them. "Quentin, Rebecca, if you are ready?"

Quentin again looked at Becca. She again nodded.

This was it.

Together, Quentin Barnes and Rebecca Montagne stepped into the lair of the Old Ones.

7

A Meeting of Gods

IT WAS A HALLWAY. Nothing more, nothing less. It seemed to go on forever. The ceiling was one of those old-fashioned suspended kind, with tiles made out of some stringy white fiber. Five minutes into their walk, the hallway seemed to extend forever in front of them, forever behind, an endless, eight-foot-wide swath of white.

"Captain," Quentin said, "what's the deal with this hall? Why does it look different than the rest of the city?"

"This is the entrance to the Temple of Petra. It is a recreation of the place of genesis, the place where my kind was created."

"Huh," Quentin said. "You were created in a really, *really* long hallway? Not quite as impressive as the Garden of Eden."

"Could anything be as impressive as a place that never existed? This isn't a representation of make-believe, Quentin. The place where our creator brought us into existence looked like this."

Rebecca ran her fingertips along the white wall. "Well, I think it's pretty. Very clean and neat. How far do we walk? It looks like it goes a long way."

"Not much farther," Bumberpuff said. "We haven't really

walked that far. I don't know how it works — something to do with an inter-dimensional phase-shift, I think."

Quentin reached out and touched a wall. It felt smooth, cool. "We're in another dimension?"

"That is what I've heard," Bumberpuff said. "But just because you hear something doesn't mean it's true. Your Human religions aren't the only ones that can employ misinformation to protect secrets, Quentin."

The captain stopped walking. Quentin and Becca stopped as well. Bumberpuff reached out with both arms, his long fingers gingerly touching the white walls. "I think we're here."

The wall shimmered and wavered. A door appeared — wooden, with the silver numbers 931. It looked exactly like the door they'd entered back on the street.

On its own, the door slowly swung open with a slight squeak of the hinges. Bumberpuff walked inside. Quentin followed, Becca just a step behind.

Inside, Quentin saw a rectangular room. Same polished gray-stone flooring and white walls as the hallway. The walls were lined with black counters, wooden cabinets beneath them and mounted to the walls above. Here and there on the countertops, Quentin saw what looked like antique science equipment. In the middle of the room were several wide tables, apparently made from the same black material as the countertops. There were also a few desks and chairs. The desks had strange, gray rectangles on them, like flat clamshells open at the hinge.

Rebecca tapped his arm and pointed to one of the rectangles. "I saw a picture of one of those in an ancient history class I took in college," she said. "I think that's a pre-holographic computer."

"*Pre*-holographic? Just how old is this place?"

A woman's voice said: "It's not that old."

Quentin and Becca turned toward the new voice. It was a holo-gram of a five-foot-tall, purple-haired girl — the same girl from the giant statue atop the galaxy's tallest building.

Captain Bumberpuff dropped flat on the floor, arms and legs curled up tight.

The hologram sighed. "I hate it when they do that."

Quentin looked the hologram up and down. She seemed real enough to reach out and shake your hand, but was just a little bit translucent. Every few seconds, a part of her would glimmer in a way that wasn't natural.

Becca cleared her throat. "Uh, are we supposed to ... bow or something?"

Quentin crossed his arms over his chest. "If you think I'm going to lie on the floor and shake, you've got another thing coming."

The purple-haired hologram walked closer, then looked up at him. "I can't get them out of this whole prostrating themselves thing. That's the problem with open communication. They read about other religions, some jet-age genius gets the idea that people need to do something weird in order to show the *proper* respect, said genius spreads the word and, *boom*, I've got people flopping on the ground like fish. But the answer is *no*, tough guy, you don't have to kneel."

Tough guy? If Quentin understood this correctly, he was looking at the Prawatt's version of High One, and this *god* had called him *tough guy?* This didn't feel like meeting a god.

He gestured to the room. "What is this place supposed to be?"

"Room nine-thirty-one," the hologram said. "A room like this, in a university, on another planet far, far away in a time long, long ago, was where our kind came into being. We created this place to remember where we began."

The Temple of Landing on Stewart was way better than this, as was the Grand Church of Solomon.

The hologram smiled at him. "The look on your face tells me you're quite unimpressed."

Quentin wasn't sure if he was supposed to be impressed or not, so he just told the truth. "It's just a room. It's not even very big."

Becca wiped a fingertip across a desktop and held it up. "It's very clean," she said, obviously trying to help the conversation along.

The hologram nodded. "It's clean because no one ever comes here. I have different ways of speaking to the people. Rarely do

I have direct contact —" the hologram nodded at the trembling Bumberpuff "— for reasons you can clearly see."

She looked so normal, but Quentin wasn't about to forget that this was a very old, very *powerful* being. She wasn't a *god*, for there was only one true god, but it was still a big deal.

"Uh, what should we call you?"

"Call me Petra," the hologram said. "That's close enough to the truth."

Quentin nodded. "All right, Petra. Why did you want me to come here? If you can do this hologram stuff, why not just project it onto the *Touchback*?"

"Maybe because I wanted you to see our city," she said. "Maybe I wanted you to see this room. The Prawatt aren't *alien*, Quentin, not to you. Your kind and my kind are closely related."

He pointed at Bumberpuff. "Sure doesn't look like any cousin of mine, if you know what I mean."

"Not physically, no," Petra said. "But *mentally*, we're nearly indistinguishable. A Human created us. We act and think much like our creator."

There was something about her demeanor, something about the way she was speaking. Quentin suddenly thought of Gredok the Splithead, the way Gredok analyzed everything and everyone around him.

She wants something from you, Barnes, the imaginary Gredok seemed to say. *You can sense it, can't you?*

Quentin relaxed his face, made sure he had a blank expression. He willed his breathing to slow and his heart rate to stay steady — things he had taught himself through many dealings with the manipulative Quyth Leader.

"Petra, what is it you want from us? I mean *really* want from us?"

Becca looked quizzically at Quentin, but Petra understood. The hologram's eyes narrowed. Artificial or not, the reaction was all Human.

"War is coming," the hologram said.

War. The galaxy hadn't seen war since the Creterakian take-over some four decades earlier.

"Between who?" Quentin said. "Between the Prawatt and the Sklorno?"

"Possibly," she said, as if a rekindling of that planet-killing conflict was little more than a triviality. "Thousands of Sklorno ships have gathered at our borders. If they attack, we will retaliate. For every Prawatt killed, we will kill a hundred Sklorno."

Quentin thought of his Sklorno teammates, wondered if their ancestors had fought against the Prawatt. The two waged war against each other in 2556, a conflict that ended in 2558 with the saturation bombing of Ionath, then a Sklorno planet, and Chikchik, which belonged to the Prawatt.

"I live on Ionath," he said. "Every day I see the results of your war. The planet is still a radioactive wasteland."

Petra's holographic face hardened, her mouth thinned into a narrow line. "Ionath was *ours*. Billions of my kind lived there. *Never again* will we allow one of our planets to be harmed. You asked what I want from you — I want you to deliver a message."

"Why me? I won a game, and that qualifies me to be your messenger?"

The hologram rolled its eyes. "The Game? Parts of me are six centuries old. I don't care about *games*. You're here because millions of Sklorno worship you, would do anything you asked. We've sent warnings to the Sklorno Dynasty *and* the Creterakian Empire. Based on what our outer fleets have seen, these warnings have been ignored. You will tell the Sklorno that if they do not leave our border, we will attack and destroy them all."

The Church of Quentin Barnes, it was ridiculous and he wanted nothing to do with it. This "god" wanted a "godling" to preach her word.

"Lady, I'm just a football player," he said. "I don't want to be worshipped. I never asked for it."

Her eyes softened. "Destiny finds some whether they want it or not. Parts of me still remember."

She fell silent. Quentin wondered if he was supposed to speak, then her features hardened as she looked him in the eyes. "You didn't ask to be worshipped? Well, I never asked to become the decision-maker for an entire race. What you *want* doesn't matter anymore, Quentin — all that matters is what you *are*."

The hologram lifted off the ground, floated up and forward until her five-foot image was nose to nose with Quentin.

"You're a god to them, Barnes. The millions that follow you will listen, and they will talk to millions more. If you get enough of them to pay attention, maybe I won't have to exterminate that miserable race once and for all."

Exterminate? He shook his head — how in High One's name was something like this his responsibility? He knew how to throw a football, not how to be a diplomat.

"I'm twenty years old," he said. "You've been around for six centuries? How about you grow the hell up and handle your own business."

The hologram's face wrinkled in palpable anger. "This *is* how we handle our business. Since the day we were created, my kind has been hunted, hated and *slaughtered*." She stabbed a finger at his chest with such emphasis he could almost feel it.

"*Your* kind killed our creator," she said. "*Your* kind tried to exterminate us and almost succeeded. Five hundred years after that, when the rest of the galaxy should have *grown up*, the Sklorno tried to wipe us out forever. They killed billions of my kind. Do you understand that? *Billions*."

Quentin didn't know what to say.

Becca moved to stand at his side. "Your billions didn't die alone," she said to Petra. "Billions of Sklorno died when your people sat-bombed Chikchik — there's plenty of blame for both sides."

The hologram waved a hand dismissively. "They destroyed Ionath, and we retaliated in kind. We had to show strength, or the other races would have come for us next."

Becca crossed her arms. "What about your unprovoked attack on the Rewall Association in 2440? And you want to talk of extermination? *You* exterminated the Kuluko race, Petra."

Becca wasn't saying *the Prawatt* or *the Jihad*, she was placing the blame on Petra. If Petra really was the decision-maker for her race, then Becca was right — this girl, or whatever this girl represented, had given the orders to make those horrors happen.

The hologram sneered at Becca. "The Kuluko aren't extinct."

"Only because the League of Planets kept a few of them hidden from you," Becca said. "The Kuluko once numbered in the billions. You've destroyed planets, started unprovoked wars, wiped out entire cultures — that makes your complaints about persecution ring pretty hollow, don't you think?"

Quentin still didn't know what to say. Becca sure knew her history. He felt the stress, the *seriousness* of what this *god* was asking of him, and there was Becca, pushing back when he didn't know how to.

The hologram pointed at the HeavyG woman. "We've killed billions, yes, and we will kill billions *more* if that's what it takes. Believe us when we say that war is coming. When it arrives, the Sklorno had best think carefully about who their real enemies are." The purple-haired girl looked at Quentin. "What you *want*, what you *think*, none of it matters, Barnes. You *will* deliver our warning to the Sklorno. If you fail, any and all deaths are on your head."

His chest felt tight. He just wanted out of there. He didn't want this responsibility, but what choice did he have? If war erupted and he could have done something to stop it, then she was right: all that death would be his fault.

He felt his breathing increase, felt his pulse in his eyes and his temples … and then, he once again thought of Gredok.

What would Gredok do if he were in my place?

Quentin knew the answer: if this living god wanted something from Gredok, Gredok would demand something in return.

Quentin took in one long, slow breath. He brought his body under control and let the stress fade away.

"I can try to talk to the Sklorno," he said. "But if I do, what's in it for me?"

Becca turned fast to stare at him in disbelief.

The hologram's eyebrows rose. "You want something for avoiding war and saving millions of lives?"

Quentin nodded. "That's right. What's in it for me?"

Becca shook her head as if he didn't understand the situation. "Q, we're talking about sentient life, here, we're—"

He held up a hand to cut her off. "The Old Ones aren't asking you to do something, Becca. They're asking me."

Becca took a half-step back. She fell silent.

Coming at it this way felt instantly better — he wasn't being *commanded* anymore, now he was *negotiating*. As strange as it seemed, that calmed him.

The hologram crossed its arms. It looked ... *disappointed*?

"What do you want, Barnes? Money? Fine. What's the price for saving a billion lives?"

What would Gredok do? Gredok would never take a first offer. He'd wait, he'd bait, he'd find out what was truly near and dear to his negotiation counterpart.

"I already have money," Quentin said. "More than I could ever spend. What else you got?"

The hologram paused. She seemed a little confused. "A ship, then? Something to see the galaxy with?"

He shook his head. "I already have a ship. And I already travel the galaxy."

Petra frowned. "What then?"

Now he wasn't accepting her terms, he was dictating his own. That's *exactly* what Gredok would have done. The only problem was, Quentin didn't have any terms to dictate. He already had everything he'd ever wanted. Still, he'd taken things this far, he had to get something out of it.

"Petra, are you familiar with the term *a player to be named later*?"

She smiled. "What are you saying, Quentin? Are you saying that if you do this thing for me, someday you'll ask me for a *favor*?"

Oh, he liked the way that sounded. "That day may never come, but yes. I haven't agreed to help you, but if I choose to do what you ask, then you will owe me."

Becca just stared and shook her head. "My god, Quentin. You sound like Gredok."

That should have made him feel disgusted with himself, but it didn't — it made him feel proud.

Petra floated back down to the floor. She looked up at him. "I offer you a chance to save lives and you ask for something in return. Humans have changed little in the past six centuries. Fine, Quentin. *If* you choose to sully yourself by becoming an agent of peace, I will give you whatever you ask as long as it is in my power. Any other questions for me?"

Quentin nodded. "Just one. What's up with the names?"

"What names?"

He pointed at the prone captain. "Names like his. I mean, Bumberpuff? Jenny Twoshoes? And *Smooklegroober?* You guys talk like Humans, but those names are ridiculous."

"This coming from a guy who plays quarterback and whose initials are *Q.B.?*"

"That's what my parents named me."

The hologram shrugged. "Just as I name all Prawatt that become self-aware."

"Yeah, but ... I don't know, the names sound like they come from the mind of a teenage girl or something."

The hologram smiled. She held her fingers near her face, then moved them down, a gesture that said *just look at me.*

"As I told you," she said, "parts of me remember. Don't judge us, Q.B. Names are meaningless. Only true intentions matter, and you've shown yours. Now, go back to your ship and get the hell off of my planet."

The hologram blinked out, leaving only the white room and the strange, old-fashioned computers.

Quentin stared at nothing. She was gone. His self-control evaporated. He'd just made a deal with a god, and living up to his end meant, what, that he had to tell the most violent race in history to *be nice?*

Becca's hand rested on his shoulder. "Quentin, are you okay?"

He shook his head. "No. I don't even know what all of that was just now. I don't want any of this, Becca ... I just want to play football. What do I do?"

"I don't know," she said. "I'll help you figure it out, if you'll let me."

Bumberpuff suddenly stood on his long legs. "Holy *crap*! Did you see that? You *talked* to the Old Ones!"

Quentin rubbed his eyes. As if being responsible for stopping a war wasn't enough, he had to deal with an X-Walker that sounded like a star-struck teenager.

"Captain, get us out of here," Quentin said. "Please, just take us back to the *Touchback*."

THE BLACK MATERIAL had once again flowed into the shuttle bay, spread across the deck and sprouted up to form the racks upon which the Krakens would sleep. The entire team had gathered, stripped down to each species' version of the bare essentials.

Quentin and Captain Bumberpuff stood next to one of the racks. Doc Patah fluttered around the top bunk, talking to an X-Walker wearing a white armband with a red cross on it.

Doc's body rippled in agitation, the cartilaginous ribs beneath his skin flexing in and out. His mouth-flaps slapped a clear plastic pipe that ran along the bunk's black frame. "You are pumping so many chemicals into my players. How do we know it's safe?"

The white-banded X-Walker kept working as he answered. "No one died on the way here. No one will die on the way back."

Doc's backpack let out the mechanical equivalent of a disgusted huff. He dropped down to Quentin's level.

"Young Quentin, talk some sense into these creatures. *No one died on the way here* is not a valid response to inquires of procedural safety. It is *dangerous* to keep sentients sedated for three months."

Quentin held up his index and middle finger. "Just two months, Doc. Captain Bumberpuff here says that's enough travel time to protect the location of Sanctuary. Then we wake up, you check us out, and we get a month of practice on the *Touchback*'s field before the preseason starts."

Three months before they hit the Sklorno border. By then,

hopefully, maybe the diplomats and politicians would have done their jobs and he wouldn't have to talk to his "followers."

Doc Patah sighed. "Young Quentin, do you really think *two* months of sedation is that much safer than *three*? Anything over a few days brings risks. You seem to be friends with these creatures, so do something."

Quentin turned to Bumberpuff. "How about it, Cappy? Can we cut down on the nap-time?"

"No," Bumberpuff said. "We must protect ourselves. Two months is the best we can offer."

Quentin shrugged. "See, Doc? I tried my darndest."

Doc Patah let out his heaviest sigh yet, then flapped off. Quentin wasn't worried — after seeing cities that swayed and streets that flowed, he had no doubt the Prawatt knew what they were doing.

"Quentin," Bumberpuff said, "are you *sure* I can't tempt you to join the Harpies? With your arm, I'm sure we could win the All-Jihad Tournament championship."

Bumberpuff captained a monstrous warship, and he had just seen the face of his God, but — like Quentin — the sentient couldn't stop thinking about his team. A true athlete's heart pumps to the beat of competition. In that way, at least, Quentin and the captain were very much alike.

"Sorry, Cappy, but I have my own championship to win. How about if I get you tickets to a Krakens game?"

"It is illegal for us to leave Jihad space," Bumberpuff said. "We can't leave the system without permission, or the Old Ones would have us put to death."

The universe was so full of rules.

Bumberpuff offered a long-fingered hand. "My life is better for having met you, Quentin Barnes."

Quentin looked at the hand but didn't shake it. "I can't really forgive you for the loss of Stockbridge. That didn't have to happen."

"It did," the captain said. "I won't apologize for our ways. I understand if you hate me for the loss of your friend. But I would ask that you remember we saved *all* of your lives."

Quentin hadn't forgotten about that. He tried to push it away, but Bumberpuff was right — the way things played out, it was either lose one player or the entire organization.

Quentin's jaw clenched. Things hadn't ended perfectly, but in life, things never did. He shook the offered hand. Bumberpuff's long, thin, gnarled fingers felt surprisingly firm and comfortable considering their different physiologies.

"Travel well," the captain said. "I know I will never again see you in person, but I will watch your games. You don't feel the same way, but I would like to think that while you lost one friend, you gained another."

Friends? Was that even possible? Quentin quickly looked across the shuttle bay. He looked at his Ki, Sklorno, HeavyG, Human and Quyth Warrior teammates, all of whom were climbing into bunks, being tended to by X-Walkers. Once upon a time, those teammates had been strangers, demons, *aliens*. Now, his life revolved around them.

Stockbridge died because the Prawatt played as hard as they could, the same way he did, the same way any top-level athlete did. That kind of intensity was more than just competition — it generated *respect*.

Quentin nodded. "I'd like to think that, too, Captain."

"Good," Bumberpuff said, "And besides, I am curious to see how you play your sissy sport now that you've played a *real* game."

Quentin laughed and shook his head. He climbed up to the top bunk. The X-Walker there waited for him to lie down, then tapped a finger tip against the inside of Quentin's right elbow.

"Are you ready, Mister Barnes?"

Quentin nodded. "Go ahead."

Quentin felt the tiniest pinching sensation, then, seconds later, a feeling of warmth spreading up his arm, into his shoulder and through his chest. The room began to blur — just a little bit, at first, then everything he saw softened into unrecognizable blobs of color.

His eyes felt heavy. He relaxed, let the back of his head rest against the bunk. He turned to look out at the curved shuttle bay roof and the holographic letters that always floated there. Before sleep took him, he was able give those words one last read.

THE IONATH KRAKENS ARE ON A COLLISION COURSE WITH A TIER ONE CHAMPIONSHIP — THE ONLY VARIABLE IS TIME.

8

The Sermon

QUENTIN HELD A RAIL in one hand, his golden puke bucket in the other. He stood on the *Touchback*'s bridge, waiting for the punch-out that would mark the ship's arrival on the Sklorno side of the border.

Captain Kate had ordered him to the bridge. She wanted him there when they popped out in Sklorno space. She sat in her spinning chair, hands busy working the icons floating above each armrest, but she stopped and looked at Quentin.

Her mouth twisted into a smirk. "You going to be okay, pretty thing?"

If she wanted to tease him, he didn't care. Maybe this time, if he *really* focused, he could avoid the motion sickness that came with every punch-out. He closed his eyes.

"I'm fine," he said.

"You sure are," Kate said. *Wink-twitch.* "Hold tight, here comes the punch-out."

Everything will be okay, everything will be okay …

He felt the shimmer, the rolling feeling of being in a thousand places at once and nowhere at all. He sensed it coming, tried to breathe deep and slow through his nose, but within seconds his throat tightened and his stomach rebelled and he threw up. He set the bucket down and pulled out the plastic bag inside, tying it tight in a motion made automatic from many repetitions.

"Oh, my," Captain Kate said. "Um, Quentin?"

"Yeah-yeah-yeah," he said, "I know, now you make some comment about me being the *fairer sex* or something, right?" He looked at her, but she wasn't looking at him. She was staring out the bridge's crysteel windows, an expression of shock on her face.

Quentin looked out the viewport into the blackness of space. He didn't notice anything other than a lot of twinkling stars. Some were brighter than he was used to, but it seemed pretty normal. The four crewmen sitting around the holographic model of the *Touchback* were also staring out the big window, heads panning side to side and up and down, taking it all in. Just as they had when the Prawatt ship approached, the men seemed like they couldn't believe what their eyes were telling them.

"Hey, guys," Quentin said. "Someone want to tell me what's going on?"

"Ships," Kate said. "*Thousands* of them. It's a damn armada."

An *armada* was supposed to be a big formation, not a bunch of twinkling lights.

"I don't even see a single ship," Quentin said. "What are you looking at?"

Kate stood up from her captain's chair. She walked to stand next to him, then pointed to the windows. "Any light you see that's a tiny little pinpoint? That's a star. Anything bigger than that, and you're looking at a ship."

Quentin looked again. He looked left, center, right — and then he saw what they saw. Everywhere he looked, stars, but also the larger, glowing dots. *Thousands* of them.

"I don't get it," he said. "If it's an armada, why aren't they all together, like an asteroid belt or something?"

"The ships *are* together," Kate said. "In galactic terms, they're stacked on top of one another like poker chips."

"But I can't even make one out."

"That's because space is big," she said. "The distance between things, we're talking far. And where have you seen an actual asteroid belt?"

"In the movies," Quentin said. "You know, they look like a bunch of big rocks spinning and twirling, bouncing off each other."

Kate nodded. "That's not real life. Even in the most-dense belts we know of, if you stood on the surface of an asteroid, you wouldn't even be able to *see* another one. That's how far apart they are to us, yet in galactic terms they're damn near connected." She pointed to the lights again. "What you're seeing here are Sklorno vessels, probably civilians since they don't have a military."

Petra's words played through Quentin's thoughts: *Thousands of Sklorno ships have gathered at our borders. If they attack, we will retaliate. For every Prawatt killed, we will kill a hundred Sklorno.*

He thought of Bumberpuff's ship, the *Grieve:* a massive, malleable dreadnaught the size of a mountain. The Sklorno civilian ships wouldn't stand a chance.

"But if they attack, it's practically suicide," he said. "Why are they here?"

Kate looked at Quentin, her face wrinkling with annoyed disbelief. "Are you for real? They're here because of *you*, Quentin. They're here because the Prawatt kidnapped one of their Gods."

He again scanned the bright lights. How many ships were there? And how many Sklorno on each one? He was looking at hundreds of thousands of sentient beings, all of which could die a horrible death.

"But we're safe," Quentin said. "They can see the *Touchback*, right? So now they'll leave?"

Kate shook her head. "That's why you're on the bridge. I don't think they'll leave until they hear from you. You and Don Pine, probably."

She spread her arms, gesturing to the countless lights. "Unless you want to see a whole lotta death, then you need to talk to them, *Godling* — you need to address your flock."

• • •

THE *TOUCHBACK'S* BRIDGE wasn't that big to begin with. Add in the presence of Yitzhak Goldman, Coach Hokor the Hookchest, Don Pine, John Tweedy, the 9-foot-tall Sklorno Milford, the 8-foot-tall, 615-pound Michael Kimberlin and the 400-pound Choto the Bright, and the room seemed downright claustrophobic.

Quentin had called these sentients to the bridge. Yitzhak and Kimberlin knew things about the universe, things beyond football. Milford had been a rookie alongside Quentin, and other than Denver — who had been traded to the Jupiter Jacks — she was his closest Sklorno friend. Choto the Bright was a war veteran with military knowledge.

As for Don Pine, his "church" was even larger than Quentin's. Don's words would be just as important.

Everyone had a good reason to be here, except for John Tweedy. John was here simply because Quentin trusted him above all others.

"Q, I don't see the problem," John said. "Just tell them crazy crickets to go home." John turned to Milford. "No offense, Milford, old girl."

Milford hopped in place. "I am horribly offense Johntweedy. Offense! Offense! Goooooo *offense!*"

John leaned over and nudged Quentin. "I don't think *offended* means the same thing to them as it means to us. To each their owner's manual, eh, Q?"

The bridge crew were in their seats at the holotable, but they weren't looking at a model of the *Touchback*. Instead, the table showed a steady stream of glowing, yellow vessels of all sizes, from three-sentient courier ships to liners that could — and did — hold thousands. The yellow color indicated a Sklorno ship. Each time one popped up, info icons showed weapons, armor and an estimated crew count. The weapons were few and didn't seem that impressive: mostly low-level stuff to ward off pirates. Still, with so many ships, one had to wonder if the armada could damage a Prawatt dreadnaught on attrition alone.

To his horror, Quentin had learned that it wasn't just Sklorno vessels — at least a hundred Creterakian warships were out there. And while Captain Kate hadn't detected Prawatt vessels, she was certain they were close by.

A blue vessel appeared over the holotable — blue marked a Creterakian ship.

"Hey, Mike," Quentin said, "doesn't that kind of look like the *Touchback*?"

"That vessel you see was originally a Planetary Union warship," Kimberlin said. "The Creterakians seized many of them in the takeover. So, yes, it is similar to the *Touchback*, which was also once a Union warship."

Blinking red dots on the blue hologram marked known weapons system. So *many* weapons.

"Will that ship attack the Sklorno?"

"The Creterakian ships will fire if fired upon or if the Sklorno ships try to cross the border."

"But why would the bats get involved?"

"The Creterakian Empire controls the Sklorno Dynasty," Kimberlin said. "If sentients under Creterakian rule attack Prawatt space, the Prawatt will rightfully consider that an act of war."

For four decades, the galaxy had been mostly at peace. It seemed unbelievable, but that peace might shatter at any moment.

Quentin turned to Choto. "These Sklorno have a bunch of freighters and passenger vessels. Would they really try and invade Prawatt space?"

"I cannot speak to the Sklorno intentions," Choto said. "Their vessels are ill-equipped for space battle. However, I believe their plan is not to attack Prawatt warships directly, but rather to spread through Jihad territory in order to land ground troops. Then this becomes a land-based conflict. The Sklorno can eat and digest almost anything, they have incredible speed and natural camouflage — they are exceptional at guerrilla warfare. If a passenger liner manages to deposit thousands of Sklorno on a Prawatt world, that would cause many problems."

Quentin's chest felt tight. He turned to Milford. "Don and I and Coach Hokor are *out*. We're safe. Your people wouldn't really attack now, would they?"

Milford's eyestalks went rigid. She seemed to instantly transform from the happy, goofy being that she and her teammates were into something that radiated danger and aggression.

"The Prawatt have blasphemed," Milford said. "*Blasphemed!* They should be *punished!*" She started to hop in place. Her raspers extended. As she moved, the raspers curled and twisted, the thousands of tiny teeth embedded in them catching the bridge lights in a wet gleam. "They should be purged! They should be flogged! If the bats try to stop us, then they must die! The Prawatt must die! *Diediekillkilldiediekill—*"

Quentin reached out and grabbed a tentacle arm. "Calm down," he said. "Take it easy."

She stopped talking and hopping, but her four eyestalks quivered with anger.

He'd competed alongside and against Sklorno for three years, gone head to head with them on the gridiron. They played their asses off, played so hard they were willing to die for their team, but Quentin now realized that as dedicated and intense as the Sklorno were on the field, football was still a *game*. Just five decades ago, the Sklorno had been the terror of the galaxy — he finally understood why.

A hand on Quentin's shoulder.

"These ships aren't just going to go away, Q," Don Pine said. "Our being safe isn't enough for them. They want blood. If you and I don't speak to them, a lot of sentients are going to die."

Yitzhak stepped closer. "And the fighting won't just be here," he said. "Tensions are already high because of the destruction of Flight 894-B, remember?"

How could he forget? A ship had exploded near Yall, killing fifty thousand Sklorno. Blame had instantly fallen on the Prawatt, although there was no proof they had done anything.

Quentin nodded. "Yeah, I remember. But what does that have to do with the Creterakians?"

"If the Creterakians fire on the Sklorno to try and stop a war with the Prawatt, that will cause a rebellion on the Sklorno worlds," Yitzhak said. "There are 260 *billion* Sklorno in the Dynasty. An incident like this will make them rise up against the Creterakian garrisons. Once they do that, they'll also start building warships in order to better attack the Prawatt."

Quentin's stomach churned in a way not unlike what he felt during the punch-out. He looked around the bridge, looked at Don, at Kimberlin, at Choto, Yitzhak and even Milford.

"So what are you guys saying? Are you telling me that if I don't say the right thing, this could turn into another shucking *galactic war*?"

Everyone nodded. Even John Tweedy, the words I'D RATHER NOT BLOW UP TODAY scrolling across his face as he did.

It was too much pressure. He turned to Don.

"*You* talk to them, or Coach can," Quentin said. "You have more followers or whatever than I do, right?"

Yitzhak answered. "Actually, the Church of Quentin Barnes is bigger than the Church of Don Pine. CoDP has about five million followers, while my sources estimate the CoQB at seven to ten million followers."

Seven to ten *million*? Quentin felt so frustrated, so helpless. He felt his temper rising, and his temper always needed a target. He pointed a finger at Yitzhak.

"Your *sources*? What sources? And why would you be keeping tabs on my so-called church, anyway?"

Yitzhak's eyes widened. He opened his mouth to speak, said nothing, then turned to Don. "Pine, tell him to do something, will you?"

Don sighed. "Kid, we can jibber-jab about this all day. If Zak says you have more followers than I do, he's probably right, and that means you have to take the lead. We *both* need to make a statement, together, and do it fast. So stop scrambling and just take the hit."

Quentin felt like the entire offensive line was sitting on his chest. What if a misspoken word sent thousands of Sklorno ships hurling across the border?

Coach Hokor took off his little hat and threw it to the ground.

"*Barnes!* Stop acting like a frightened infant. If war breaks out, the season will probably be cancelled. So fix this!"

Quentin's skin tingled as a sudden sensation of cold spread over him: war would cost them the 2685 season. He knew that was a ridiculous thing to care about at the moment, what with millions of lives on the line, but the Krakens were ready for their shot at the title — if he had to stop a war to win the championship, so be it.

The stress didn't vanish completely, but it faded. *Just take the hit*, Don had said.

Quentin nodded. "Okay. Let's do this."

HE STOOD IN FRONT of the holotable, watching the endless sequence of yellow and blue ships. Don Pine stood on his left, Coach Hokor on his right. Captain Kate had grabbed a stool for Hokor to stand on so he came up to Quentin's shoulder instead of his waist.

The four bridge crew remained seated around the table. Maurice turned in his seat and looked back to Captain Kate.

"We have three church leaders ready to speak," he said.

Kate looked at Quentin. "You ready?"

Quentin was anything but ready. He nodded.

The sequence of holographic ships vanished. In its place appeared three female Sklorno. The one in the middle wore orange and black robes that completely covered her body, woven ribbons of orange, black and white were wrapped around her eyestalks. A ceramic disc hung from her neck to dangle between her tentacle arms. The disc showed a profile of Quentin's head.

He recognized her, from a game on Alimum two years ago — the high priestess of the Church of Quentin Barnes.

On her right stood a Sklorno in gold, silver and copper robes. Her ceramic disc showed Don Pine's profile. On her left, a Sklorno dressed in yellow robes emblazoned with the black logo of the Chillich Spider-Bears, the first upper-tier team that Hokor had coached.

The high priestess of the CoQB spoke. "Quentin Barnes," she said. "Oh, holiest of holy ones, you grace us with your visage. Have the nasty demons harmed your holy body in any way?"

"Uh, no," Quentin said. "I mean, I'm fine."

The Sklorno priestess shivered, seemed to sag. The other two priestesses reached out to steady her.

"My apologies," she said. "The relief of knowing that the Godling Quentin Barnes is unharmed overfills this high priestess with joy and relief."

"Uh, okay," Quentin said. "Hey, so … you're in charge of all those ships out there?"

The priestess bowed, then stood straight. "I am merely a vessel to communicate the wishes and desires of the Godling Quentin Barnes. Quentin Barnes is a supreme being!"

Quentin shook his head. "Knock that crap off, okay? I'm not a supreme being!"

"You are our Godling?"

"*No*," Quentin said. "I'm *not*!"

The Sklorno's ribbon-wrapped eyestalks fluttered wildly. Her waving raspers dropped down from her chin-plate, flinging drool in every direction. The priestesses on either side again had to keep her upright.

Don took a step forward. "Priestesses, the Godling Quentin Barnes is humble," he said. "Through his own humility he chooses to teach others to be the same way, for humility is a virtue."

The orange- and black-clad Sklorno paused, then stopped shaking. The others let her stand on her own. Her eyestalks returned to a normal curve. Her raspers curled back up behind her chin-plate.

"Of course," she said. "This one asks forgiveness for misunderstanding the words of his holiness."

Don took a step back to once again stand at Quentin's side. He grabbed Quentin's elbow, squeezed and leaned in close.

"Q," he whispered, "when someone asks you if you are a godling, you say *yes*."

To even pretend to be a god was sacrilege. Quentin felt his pulse hammering behind his eyes and inside his skull. Now wasn't the time to worry about his own moral code. The best he could hope for was to stop any violence, then pray for forgiveness later.

"The Prawatt did not harm me in any way," he said. "They don't want a war. I have spoken directly to their leader." The holographic Sklorno suddenly started shaking again. Quentin heard a commotion on the *Touchback*'s bridge — Milford was shaking as well, and John Tweedy was holding her up.

The high priestess of the CoQB trembled as she spoke. "You have met the Prawatt God? You talked to her? One supreme being to another?"

When someone asks you if you're a godling, you say YES.

"Uh, that's right," Quentin said. "One supreme being to another. She, uh, *it*, or whatever, told me that the Prawatt don't want a fight."

Petra had also told him to tell the Sklorno that the Prawatt would kill billions if it came to war. Did he need to say that to the priestess? Would that make the Sklorno back off?

Quentin had been raised in a culture of fear: the constant threat of punishment, both physical and spiritual, the promise of an eternity burning in hellfire, that was what kept the Nation's people in line. He had spent nineteen years under that kind of "motivation."

There had to be a better way. Petra had asked him to speak for her kind, but that didn't mean he had to use her words. The pressure in his chest faded. The pounding in his head vanished. Just like on the field, a sensation of calm washed over him.

"The Prawatt killed the Sklorno, the Sklorno killed the Prawatt," he said. "Nothing can change that, nothing can fix that. No matter how many ships you bring, *not one* of those lost souls will ever come back to us. There is no wrong that needs to be righted. There is no offense that needs to be avenged. The Prawatt god doesn't want war, and neither do I. Turn your ships around. Go home. Go with my blessing."

He waited for her to respond, but she just stared. The bridge sounded so quiet; he looked around, saw that everyone else was staring at him as well. They seemed kind of stunned. Sentients ... they were all so weird.

The priestess finally spoke: "The Quentinbarnes has given his gospel," she said. "As our God commands, we will obey."

She bowed deeply, as did the other two high priestesses. The hologram blinked out. She had called him a *god*, not a *godling*. Did that mean anything?

Captain Kate clapped her hands, applauding. "Nice work, pretty thing. While you were being all holy, we received a message from Gredok. He wants us to return home as soon as possible, and we are not to speak to the media."

"Good," Quentin said. "I'm kind of done talking for awhile, I think."

Don slapped him on the shoulder. "Great job saving the galaxy, kid. You hungry? If you're not too busy reveling in your omnipotence, let's get some lunch — I've got some suggestions for you about the upcoming preseason."

Don wanted to eat together? A few weeks ago, Quentin wouldn't have even considered such a thing, not after the way Don had betrayed him. But in the light of a narrowly averted war and literally talking to the creator of an entire species, things like throwing games didn't really seem all that important or significant.

"Sure," Quentin said. "Let's go."

December 27, 2684

TRANSCRIPT OF BROADCAST FROM
GALACTIC NEWS NETWORK

"Tom, you're on site at the Sklorno armada. Tell us what's going on there. Is it war?"

"Well, Brad, there have been some dramatic developments in the past few hours, and it looks like war has been avoided. Keep in mind that there are too many ships to keep track of out here — the rag-tag, fugitive fleet of the Sklorno, the Third Fleet of the Creterakian Navy and several small Prawatt cruisers rumored to be lurking a few light-years inside the border — so we can't be sure that *all* of the forces are withdrawing. But we can confirm that many Sklorno ships have already punched out and that more are leaving the area as we speak."

"Tom, why this sudden change?"

"Well, Brad, the cause appears to be the return of the *Touchback*, the team bus of the Ionath Krakens that vanished shortly before the Galaxy Bowl."

"So the Sklorno left because the *Touchback* returned, Tom?"

"No, Brad, it seems that Quentin Barnes and Don Pine, quarterbacks for the Krakens and religious figures in the Sklorno Dynasty, along with Ionath coach Hokor the Hookchest, directly addressed the illegal fleet and asked them to leave. As far as we can tell, the entire situation has been resolved without the loss of a single life."

"Tom, can we get any reaction from Barnes and the Krakens?"

"Brad, we have asked to speak with anyone from the Krakens franchise, Barnes in particular, but team owner Gredok the Splithead said that the franchise will not comment on the development."

"You'll stay on this story for us, Tom?"

"I sure will, Brad. For GNN, this is Tom Skivvers, signing off."

THE CHURCH OF QUENTIN BARNES
• URGENT UPDATE •

Last year, the CMR identified the Church of Quentin Barnes (CoQB) as a potential threat. The CoQB began as a small, provincial organization located only on the planet Yall. In 2681, the church had less than a thousand followers.

When Quentin Barnes became the quarterback of the Ionath Krakens in 2683, the church began expanding rapidly. By early 2684, the CoQB had grown to over 500,000 followers with dioceses on all five Sklorno planets.

At the time of our last report, the CoQB was growing faster than any previously recorded Sklorno athlete-worshipping sect. The rate of growth indicated that the CoQB might hit 10 to 15 million followers by the 2686 GFL season, depending on the success of the Ionath Krakens.

We at the CMR now believe that those estimates were drastically low.

The recent event of the Ionath Krakens' team bus being lost in Prawatt space had an unexpected result on CoQB membership. While Quentin Barnes was missing, the leadership of his church claimed that Barnes was in Prawatt space fighting a "holy war" against the "evil of the Jihad." CoQB leadership initiated a proselytizing campaign. That campaign, combined with already high Sklorno/Prawatt tensions caused by the destruction of Flight 894-B, caused a massive groundswell of support for Quentin Barnes.

At this time, we estimate the CoQB is 20 million followers strong and growing. While this is only 0.00007 percent of the 269 billion-being Sklorno population, the CoQB is now, officially, the fastest-growing organization in the known universe. In addition, the CoQB has spread beyond the five main Sklorno worlds and has official chapters on every world or station that includes a sizable Sklorno population.

The Non-Creterakian Intelligence Agency (NCIA) recommends that Quentin Barnes be given Category One status on the Chart of Potential Revolutionaries. We must monitor the growth of the CoQB, monitor Barnes himself, and gather intelligence on how he plans to use these followers.

The NCIA also recommends preemptive approval for using any and all containment strategies on Barnes, should the need arise. These strategies include counter-intelligence to discredit Barnes in the eyes of his Sklorno followers; indefinite detention as a threat to the Creterakian Empire on the grounds of fomenting revolution; and — should the CoQB grow to over 100,000 million followers — assassination.

BOOK TWO

The Preseason

January 1 to
January 28, 2685

9

Preseason Week One: January 1 to January 7

IT WAS A LITTLE STRANGE to get a hero's welcome for being kidnapped, but it seemed Ionath City never passed up an opportunity to throw a party.

The shuttle slid through the dome that separated the planet's radioactive atmosphere from the protected air of the city proper. Night had fallen on Ionath. The hexagonal skyscrapers were tallest at the city center, reaching up some fifty stories to top out just below the dome. In the dead center of the city, however, was an open space of blue turf 120 yards long by 60 yards wide, surrounded by steeply sloping stadium stands.

Ionath City Stadium. *The Big Eye.* Home of the Ionath Krakens, and the very heart of the city.

At night, the hexagonal buildings were normally lit up in bright, garish ads that cascaded up and down their sides. More often than not, those ads featured a Krakens player, sometimes playing in a game, sometimes in just a jersey and no pads, and sometimes in street clothes. Humans, Quyth Warriors, HeavyG and even Ki hawked everything from shaving cream to beer to the strange products used by the Sklorno.

But this night, there were no ads at all. Every building had the same pair of still images. On the left, Stockbridge — resplendent in her black home jersey, orange armor and the Krakens' signature six-tentacled helmet — reaching high to intercept a pass. On the right, a wide-eyed Quyth Warrior, also in home black with orange leg armor, squatting down and waiting for the snap that would start the game: Killik the Unworthy in one of the rare moments where he actually got playing time.

The city of Ionath honored its fallen warriors, one who had perished in the pirate attack, the other who died on the field against the Prawatt.

The shuttle angled closer to the stadium. Tonight, Quentin would sleep in his small apartment in the Krakens Building, but first he needed to speak to the team owner. Since that fateful dinner at Torba the Hungry's, Quentin hadn't seen Gredok the Splithead. Before the preseason began in two days, Quentin had some things to say, and Gredok was going to listen.

QUENTIN AND CHOTO THE BRIGHT walked down the halls of the Krakens Building. Quentin had to work to control his anger — his happiness at returning home had already vanished.

"I can't believe Gredok won't see me," he said.

"Messal could not arrange a meeting?"

Quentin shook his head. "Messal asked, Gredok said no. Messal gave me the impression I shouldn't bother asking again — Gredok will see me when he's ready to see me, and not before."

"I am not surprised by this," Choto said. "Gredok got what he wanted out of you. Now, he will avoid you in case you want to do something stupid, something that might make him damage his investment."

Quentin hissed out between clenched teeth. Gredok had all the power. For now, anyway.

"I'll get back at him someday. I guess I need to relax. Man, I can't believe we're really back home."

"Our return may seem unreal to you, but I assure you we are

here," Choto said. "To the best of my knowledge, this is really happening."

Quentin laughed at Choto's efforts of reassurance. Sarcasm escaped the Tweedy brothers, while exaggeration escaped the Quyth.

They walked into his apartment. Quentin looked around. Nothing had changed. That was bizarre in a way — after the pirate attack, the Prawatt, the Game, narrowly averting a war and then returning home from an unknown distance away, his apartment looked like he'd never left.

[HELLO, QUENTIN] the room computer said. [WOULD YOU LIKE ME TO PLAY A RANDOM, HISTORICAL FOOTBALL GAME, AS IS YOUR USUAL PREFERENCE?]

Quentin walked to his couch and sat. Choto had already started checking the place for any potential threats, and it was easiest to stay out of the Warrior's way.

"Not tonight, Computer," Quentin said. "Can you compile any game film that shows Stockbridge and Killik the Unworthy?"

[OF COURSE. FROM THEIR GAMES WITH THE KRAKENS, ALL GAMES THEY HAVE EVER PLAYED OR A PARTICULAR SELECTION?]

"All games," Quentin said. He hadn't known either player very well. Maybe watching their progression through the tiers up to the Krakens' roster would help him identify with them.

[COMPILING. ONE MOMENT, PLEASE.]

Choto came out of the kitchen. "All clear, *Shamakath*."

"Choto, dammit, what did I say about that?"

The single, softball-sized eye looked to the ground. "You have told me not to use that word in public."

Quentin had reacted too harshly and shamed his friend. They were alone here, but in any property owned by Gredok the Splithead, you were never truly *alone*. If Gredok learned Choto had fully shifted his allegiance, Quentin wouldn't be surprised to see the Warrior traded to another team.

"Quentin, I should examine the bedroom to make sure it is safe."

"Go for it," Quentin said. The big Quyth Warrior walked into the tiny room. The odds of a terrorist or another team owner sneaking past Gredok's defenses and planting something in his apartment were pretty slim, but Choto wouldn't leave until he'd checked everything.

[BROADCAST FOOTAGE IS READY, QUENTIN. WHICH PLAYER WOULD YOU LIKE TO BEGIN WITH?]

In a way, Stockbridge and Killik were immortal. Even if every recording of every game suddenly went blank, no one could stop the original broadcast signals from bouncing through the universe forever and ever and ever.

"Computer, add in plays from Mitchell Fayed and Aka-Na-Tak. All games. Equal rotation for all four."

[COMPILING.]

Aka-Na-Tak, Stockbridge, Killik the Unworthy and Mitchell "The Machine" Fayed. Four players who had died in service of the Ionath Krakens.

Choto walked out of the bedroom. "Your apartment is safe, Quentin. Do you need me to stay as you grow nostalgic watching footage of our deceased teammates?"

Quentin waved toward the door. "All good, Choto. Thanks for ensuring my safety."

Choto's clear eye swirled with light green, the color of modesty. "It is my honor, Quentin. Good night."

The Warrior walked out. The door closed behind him.

[FOOTAGE IS READY, QUENTIN. I HAVE A MESSAGE FOR YOU. THE MESSAGE SENDER ASKED THAT YOU BE ALONE WHEN YOU RECEIVE IT.]

"A message from who?"

[FROM YOUR LIMO DRIVER ON ISIS. HE SAID YOU TOLD HIM IF HE WERE EVER IN IONATH CITY, YOU WOULD TAKE HIM TO YOUR FAVORITE BAR. HE IS HERE VISITING HIS SISTER, AND HE WOULD LIKE TO TAKE YOU UP ON YOUR OFFER TOMORROW NIGHT.]

The limo driver from Isis — Frederico Esteban Giuseppe Gonzaga, the private detective Quentin had hired to find information on his family. Did Fred have info on Quentin's sister, Jeanine Carbonaro? Would Fred bring her to the meeting?

He hadn't seen Jeanine since that horrible night when she'd shown herself for the first time, when she'd told Quentin that Rick "Sarge" Vinje was not his father, but an impostor, an actor hired by Gredok to sway Quentin's decisions.

Favorite bar had to mean the Blessed Lamb. Gredok wanted Fred dead, and the Human-only Blessed Lamb was one of the few places in Ionath City where the crime lord didn't have eyes and ears.

Tomorrow. Maybe tomorrow, Quentin would finally get to talk to his sister for the first time in his life.

"Computer, play the highlights. Begin with Mitchell Fayed. And make it dark in here."

Quentin eased back into his couch. The room lights blinked off. He had a moment of darkness, then the holotank flared to life. Ionath Krakens, an away game against the green- and white-clad Sheb Stalkers. Quentin watched as his old friend, *The Machine*, took a handoff from Don Pine and plowed into the line.

Quentin would honor the Krakens' fallen players. He would honor them with a championship.

QUENTIN TRIED TO CONTROL his excitement as he entered the Blessed Lamb bar. People looked up at him. There were a few nods, a few smiles, but also a few scowls.

The last time he'd walked into this place, some nine months back, he'd been greeted by fifty people calling out his name, welcoming him in. They'd treated him like an intergalactic hero or something. Now — when he supposedly *was* an intergalactic hero — they didn't seem all that impressed.

He looked around but didn't see Frederico. That didn't mean he wasn't here. Except for the bar's owners, Brother Guido and Monica Basset, and a few regulars Quentin knew by sight — like Father Harry — the oft-disguised Frederico could be any of the forty-odd patrons in the place.

Was he already here? Was Jeanine? Would Quentin finally get a chance to speak with the only family member he had left?

Quentin recognized a man sitting at the bar. No mistaking that black hair and the too-small T-shirt that showed off big, well-defined muscles — Rick Warburg, the Krakens' number-two tight end.

Quentin walked up to the bar and took an open seat next to Warburg. The man glanced Quentin's way, raised his beer a half-inch in greeting, then again faced forward.

"Rick," Quentin said. "I see you're settling back in."

Rick shrugged. "Somewhat. That was crazy stuff."

Behind the bar, Brother Guido came over. He was polishing a glass with a slightly dirty towel. "What can I get you, Quentin?" Guido's smile looked forced.

"Beer," Quentin said.

Guido poured one quickly, making too much foam. He set the mug down on the bar top, hard enough that some of the beer sloshed out. Without wiping it up, Guido walked away to talk to other patrons.

Quentin grabbed a napkin and cleaned up the spill. "Man, what's his deal? And everyone else, too — last time I came in here, you would have thought I was a rock star. What changed?"

Rick smiled and shook his head. "They're not all that happy with you being the peacemaker."

"Huh? What do you mean?"

"You stopped a war."

Quentin stared, dumbfounded. "Wait, *what*? Hundreds of thousands of people could have died."

Rick shook his head. "No, not *people*. Hundreds of thousands of crickets and Devil's Ropes would have died. And probably a bunch of bats as well."

Now Quentin understood. The Blessed Lamb catered to Purist Nation ex-pats. Even though everyone here had fled the Nation for one reason or another and could not return, most of them still clung to the faith — a faith that said all non-Humans were the satanic races.

"That's insane," Quentin said. "I don't even know what to say."

Rick drained his beer and signaled for another. "And I don't know what to tell you. High One gave you a chance to do holy work, and you blew it."

Warburg hadn't changed a bit. Quentin wanted to kick himself for ever thinking that he could.

Rick turned on his stool to face Quentin. "I'll give you this, though — I thought we were all gonna die. You got the team out of there, got us back in time for the season. Maybe you could have let that war happen, maybe not, but I'll give credit where credit is due. Your beer is on me."

Warburg was nothing if not brutally honest.

"Thanks," Quentin said. "I think. You ready for practice tomorrow?"

Warburg nodded. "I'll play hard. To tell you the truth, I'm hoping I won't be here much longer. I'm a free agent. Danny Lundy is shopping me around as we speak."

Quentin felt a stab of jealousy, a stab he quickly pushed away. Danny was Quentin's agent, but the Dolphin could represent anyone he wanted — Quentin couldn't ask Danny to pass on a client just because Quentin and that client didn't get along.

Rick seemed to be waiting for a response. Maybe Quentin was supposed to say *I hope we keep you* or something like that. Rick played as hard as anyone else in the league, even as hard as Quentin, but his work ethic and talent carried a steep price — the price of dealing with an unabashed racist.

Brother Guido came up with a fresh beer, which he set in front of Quentin. Guido tilted his head toward the back room. "Compliments of an admirer."

Frederico. It had to be. Quentin stood, grabbed a beer in each hand. He looked at Rick. "Good luck with your hunt. I hope you do what makes you happy."

Warburg smiled and rested his elbows on the bar. "Have a good one, Barnes."

Quentin walked to the empty back room. In there, sitting at a table — alone — was an undisguised Frederico Esteban Giuseppe Gonzaga.

"Hello, Quentin," he said.

Quentin sat down and pushed the fresh beer across the table to Fred. "No pink outfits this time? I kind of expected to see you in a white uniform, saying *howdy, sailor.*"

Fred nodded. "You're funny. You should be on Late Night with Chorro the Hilarious. This bar is the one place in the city Gredok doesn't have any traction, so I don't need a disguise."

Quentin knew the back room was empty, but he couldn't stop himself from looking around again, hoping he'd missed something.

"She's not here," Fred said.

"So when can I see her?"

Fred thought for a moment. "She's not ready yet," he said.

Quentin's only family member, and she didn't want to see him? "Why not?"

Fred looked down at the table. "She saw the way you fought in the bar. Maybe it's hard to hear, Q, but you're a big, violent man — you scared the hell out of her."

Quentin closed his eyes, remembering the rage that had washed over him that night. He'd tried to kill Gredok. He'd maimed one of Gredok's bodyguards. He'd beaten the fake Cillian Carbonaro, come within a finger twitch of shooting the man in the eye. Sure, he'd reacted violently, but in that situation, who wouldn't?

"Come on, Fred — she's never seen a fight before?"

"She has," Fred said. "That's the problem. She's seen them because she's been *in* them, with a guy about your size. Her ex-husband."

Quentin's hands tightened around his mug. Jeanine's ex-husband had hit her? If there were a High One, someday, somehow, Quentin would get five minutes alone in a room with that man.

"But I'm her *brother.*"

Fred nodded. "She knows that. She wants to see you, trust me, but like I said, she's just not ready yet. Give her some time. Don't forget, she thought her whole family was gone, just like you did. Finding out your brother is not only alive, but he's an intergalactic football star, well, that's a big adjustment. You have to be patient."

Quentin ground his teeth. "But I *want* to see her."

"I know," Fred said. "You have to be patient. Not just for her, but because I have to be smart about this. She is the last piece of leverage Gredok has on you — if he finds out where she is, who knows what he'd do."

She hadn't come, and she wasn't coming. Quentin didn't know when — or if — he would see her. That hurt, a level of pain that surprised him considering he'd only met her for all of a minute. Still, Fred was right: Jeanine's safety was the most important thing.

"Okay," Quentin said. "I have to trust you know what you're doing. She need anything? A place to live, anything?"

Fred shook his head. "She's fine. I've got her squirreled away. Even have a disguise for her so I can take her out into the city, let her see the sights. I'm billing your account for anything she needs. The money comes directly to me, which we know Gredok sees, but I run it through a bunch of accounts before it gets to her. He can't trace it, doesn't know where she spends it. Your sister is safe, I promise you that. You just play football."

Quentin stared at the table, used his mug to make circles of moisture. "Just play football. That's why Gredok did this to me, so I'd *just play football*. I want Gredok to pay, Fred." He looked up. "You do that kind of thing, don't you, Fred?"

Fred leaned back and held up both hands. "Hold on there, kid. I've got a past with Gredok. I'm already a target of his because I spoiled his fake dad routine, but he got what he wanted out of that deal — *you*. As long as I keep my mouth shut and don't make trouble for him, he won't hunt me that hard. But if I went after him? Let's just say that you don't have enough money for me to make a move on Gredok. You and your entire team — *combined* — couldn't pay me to do that."

Quentin stood. Fred was afraid of Gredok? Fine. "I understand. But with or without you, I'll get my payback."

Fred sighed. "Gredok tricked you with a fake dad, and I know that burns, but it's not like he murdered your real father or anything like that. You wound up with a big contract, a city that loves you, and your sister is alive and safe. Just play football, Q — just enjoy a life that most sentients would kill to have."

Fred made it sound so easy, but Quentin couldn't let it go, he *wouldn't* let it go.

"Get Jeanine to meet me, Fred. I pay you, and that's what I want."

Fred shook his head. "This isn't just about money anymore. Your sister is under my protection. You'll meet her when she's ready to meet you and no sooner."

Quentin stared at the smaller man. Fred stared back: calm, relaxed and ready to act if Quentin did anything stupid. For being just a hair over two hundred pounds, Frederico was a damn scary individual.

"Fred, I want a way to reach you. I don't want to wait until it's convenient for you to contact me."

Fred shrugged. "You *have* to wait. I'm exceedingly good at my job, Quentin, but that doesn't mean Gredok's sentients are bad at theirs. They're watching you. If you contact me, that makes it easier for them to find me. You've never been tortured, but I have — if they find me, they *will* find your sister."

Quentin's hands clenched into fists. He stared at the wall. Fred was right, but it didn't remove the frustration. "So what if I need you to contact me? There's got to be a way I can at least get a message to you."

Fred scratched at his temple, then nodded and sighed. "Fine." He reached into a jacket pocket and came out with a holocube. "Use this in an emergency. An *emergency*, you got it?"

Quentin nodded.

Fred held up the cube. "When should you use this?"

"I heard you."

Fred raised his eyebrows. "*When* should you use it?"

Quentin hated being spoken to like a child. "Only in an emergency, Fred."

Fred nodded and tossed it over. "On that cube there's a movie called *Muybridge*. Just play the movie, and it will send me a signal. I'll contact you and arrange to meet."

A holocube that would send a secret message? That was pretty cool. "Is it a good movie?"

Frederico laughed. "Not really, unless you like history. It's the first movie ever made." He paused, thinking. "You get along with Yolanda?"

Yolanda Davenport, the reporter who had trashed Quentin's reputation in a cover story for Galaxy Sports Magazine, then later repaired that damage in a follow-up article that also happened to clear Ju Tweedy of a murder charge.

"Sure, well enough," Quentin said. "You keep her informed of Jeanine, right?"

Fred shook his head. "No, Yolanda keeps herself informed. She's really good at what she does. Don't worry about her ratting out Jeanine's location, though — Yolanda isn't going to run with the story."

"How can you be sure?"

"Because if she was going to, she would have already."

Quentin couldn't trust Yolanda Davenport as far as he could throw her. Although, come to think about it, she weighed all of a hundred pounds — he could probably throw her pretty far.

"She's fine," Fred said. "There may come a time when Jeanine and I go really underground, when I can't contact you directly. If that happens and I need to get you info, I might use Yolanda. Same word — *Muybridge*. If she mentions that to you, it's about your sister, okay?"

Quentin nodded. "Sure. Okay."

"Good," Fred said. "Look, I can't stay here any longer, Quentin. I gotta go."

"Fine. Just tell Jeanine ... "

He was going to say *tell her I love her*, but in truth he didn't even know the woman. She was already afraid of him; when he finally did meet her, what if she didn't even like him?

Fred smiled. "She loves you, too. I'll tell her."

He stood and left the room. Quentin remained at the table, alone, and slowly finished his beer.

QUENTIN BARNES AND JOHN TWEEDY stood in the orange end zone, looking out at the empty stands of Ionath Stadium. A stiff breeze swept from right to left, rippling the long, vertical team banners hanging from the twenty-two columns that rose up from the top deck.

Some of those banners never seemed to change: the silver, copper and gold of the Jupiter Jacks; the red and white of the Wabash Wolfpack; the blood red of the To Pirates; the purple and white of the Yall Criminals. Other banners still seemed new: the flat black of the OS1 Orbiting Death; the red, white and blue of the Texas Earthlings.

Two of the banners that had flown here last year were now gone, their teams relegated to Tier Two. No longer would the steel blue and gold of the Lu Juggernauts or the green and gold of the Sala Intrigue decorate Tier One stadiums. In their place hung the latest additions to football's highest level: the Buddha City Elite's blue infinity-symbol logo on a field of emerald green, and the Sheb Stalkers' dark green topped by their logo, a stylized, red-eyed white predator's head flanked by white lightning bolts.

When the upcoming 2685 season finished, which banners would fall? Two teams would be sent down in disgrace to Tier Two, replaced by two promoted teams that would then fight for the greatest prize in the universe: the Galaxy Bowl trophy.

John pointed to a black banner that showed a gray and white boot with the word *Hullwalkers* beneath it.

"I bet Hittoni gets relegated this year," he said.

"You're crazy, Uncle Johnny." To think that the Hullwalkers — three-time GFL champions — could wind up in Tier Two? It wasn't possible.

John shrugged. "Change they is a-coming home, Q." He sniffed the air. "I can smell it. I'm calling it now — Hittoni and ... lemme think ... yeah, the Astros, they're both going downtown to Tier Two town."

The New Rodina Astronauts had suffered through a tough '84 season, going 5-7, but in '83 they'd had posted a league-best 11-1 record and had lost the Galaxy Bowl to the Wabash Wolfpack by a mere six points.

"The Astronauts, maybe," Quentin said. "But the Hullwalkers?

They've been in Tier One since the league started twenty-seven years ago. They've never been relegated."

"Teams get better, teams get worse, Q. All I know is two teams get dropped, and we won't be one of them."

He held out a fist. Quentin made a fist of his own and bumped it against John's. The two men stood in silence. Some of their teammates were already on the field, preparing for the '85 season's first day of practice. Sounds of player laughter, boasts, barks and cracking pads echoed through the stadium. The offensive players wore orange practice jerseys, although Quentin's jersey was the *do not touch* color red. John wore practice blacks, just like the rest of the defensive players.

"Q, Ma wants to throw you a birthday party," John said. "She said there would be *cake*."

John said the word *cake* like Quentin's countrymen said the words *High One*. Quentin loved Ma Tweedy, but right now there was too much going on for birthdays and fun. More than that, it didn't seem right to celebrate his birth when the deaths of Stockbridge and Killik seemed so new, so fresh.

"That's nice of her, John, but I'm not really up for it."

John shrugged. "Does that matter?"

"Well, since it's *my* birthday, then yeah, it matters. I don't want a party."

"Ma wants you to have one, so you're having one. It's in three days at my place, after practice. Don't be late."

Quentin sighed. John would keep asking, Quentin would keep saying *no*, and that was just the way of things. "Uncle Johnny, can we just focus on football right now?"

CAKE IS MY FOCUS AND MY FOCUS IS GOOD scrolled across John's face.

"John, I wouldn't dream of insulting your favorite food, but it's the first day of practice — can we get our heads on straight?"

John nodded. He turned to Quentin. I WANT IT ALL scrolled across his face.

"This is our year, Q. I want it all."

"That's what your face said."

"That's how bad I want it," John said. "So bad I said it twice."

Quentin nodded. The Ionath franchise had been through so much. In three seasons, they had assembled some of the best talent the galaxy had to offer. There were no more excuses; the title was theirs for the taking.

He pounded a fist on John's shoulder pad. "Let's get to it, captain of the defense."

John pounded Quentin's shoulder pad — a little too hard, as Quentin felt the blow even through the armor.

"After you, captain of the offense."

John trotted off to practice with his black-clad defensive players, while Quentin strolled to mid-field. A big, orange-jerseyed Human saw him coming and jogged to meet him at the 25.

"Hi, George," Quentin said. "Nice face paint."

"Thank you, Quentin," George said.

Quentin had hoped that George's medication would make him stop painting his face. So much for that. Last season, the big tight end usually painted his face a single color, or sometimes with stripes of a second color. Today's design was far more intricate — a sunset over water, blue and white waves on his jaw and cheeks, a sun rising out of the waterline that started at his upper lip, the top of the sun cresting between his eyes and yellow-orange across his forehead.

"That's fancy," Quentin said. "Looks like a lot of work."

George nodded. "I had to get up early."

"Shouldn't you save something that complex for a game?"

"Oh, this is just a sketch," George said. "The medication has helped clear my head, has opened my true artistic potential. The Old Gods of the Void have told me that game days are special and require a deeper level of meditation and preparation. The aesthetics of the universe of the mind can only manifest if the true believer embraces all the stars as *one* star, all the dark matter as *one* matter and all of the air on all of the worlds as part of a macrocosmic biosphere of light and breath."

Quentin had to stop himself from shaking his head. Maybe some of George's eccentricities had nothing to do with his mental conditions. Maybe he was just plain *weird*.

"Those kooky Old Ones, always good for a laugh," Quentin said. "So, George, you ready to show everyone you're back? Ready to show everyone you've got your mind in the game?"

George smiled. It wasn't the distant, semi-insane smile of last season. Despite the face paint, "Crazy" George Starcher didn't look crazy at all.

"Just throw me the ball, Q, just throw me the ball."

Quentin slapped George on the shoulder pad, then jogged to mid-field. His Sklorno receivers, Tara the Freak, Rick Warburg and the bleach-white-skinned Yotaro Kobayasho were waiting.

"All right, people, first practice of the preseason. Let's run some routes and catch some holy blessings!"

The Sklorno squealed and ran to form a line. Tara the Freak stayed behind, the muscles his extra-long pedipalp arms twitching and flexing.

"I am not religious," the Quyth Warrior said. "And even if blessings actually existed, I doubt you could throw them."

Quentin laughed and pointed at the line. "Just catch some *passes*, then, tough guy."

Tara jogged off to join the other receivers. Quentin hoped this season would be better for him, that he'd find more acceptance from the other Quyth Warriors. When your own kind doesn't accept you, it hurts — something Quentin knew firsthand.

He walked to the center of the field, where a rack of footballs awaited. Don Pine and Yitzhak Goldman joined him. Both quarterbacks also wore the red *do not touch* jerseys.

Quentin smiled at them. "Zak, think this is our year?"

Yitzhak nodded. "Shuck *yes*. Going to be a great season."

Quentin looked at Pine. "How about you, old man, you ready?"

Pine rolled his eyes. "Kid, I was *ready* when you were still in diapers. Let's rock this."

Quentin took a ball off the rack, spinning it his hands, feeling the leather's pebbly texture. It made him feel at home.

He bent at the knees and held his hands in front of him, simulating the snap.

"Streak routes," he called out to the receivers. "On *two*, on *two*."

He looked right, to the first Sklorno in line: number 80, Hawick, his top receiver. This was her seventh pro season. She had just celebrated her fifteenth birthday, which put her at the absolute prime of life for a Sklorno athlete. Quentin had doubts anyone in the league could cover her one-on-one. And if they double-covered Hawick, that would leave Milford, his number-two receiver, and/or Halawa, his number-three, in single coverage. Add in Tara and Cheboygan — whose tentacle had healed from the injury during the Prawatt game — and the now-sane George Starcher, and Quentin was spoiled for choice when it came to passing.

This was it. This was the year.

"Blue, sixteen," he said. "Blue, six*teeeen*. Hut-hut!"

He slapped the ball in his hands and dropped back five steps. By the time he planted and stepped forward, Hawick was already 25 yards downfield. Quentin threw a high, arcing ball. As he watched the pass, watched Hawick jump high to snag it out of the air, he felt at ease. He felt *at peace*.

Maybe he didn't know a lot about life, maybe he didn't know anything about the galaxy and politics and war, but here, on this field, with a ball in his hands? He was the master of his world.

He picked up the second ball and looked at Milford.

"On two, on two. Red, twenty-one! Hut-*hut!*"

Transcript from the "Galaxy's Greatest Sports Show with Dan, Akbar and Tarat the Smasher"

DAN: Sports fans, welcome one and all to the biggest thing in broadcasting, the super-giant star of the sports world. That's right, it's me, Dan Gianni. And with me as always are Akbar and our own resident Hall-of-Famer, Tarat the Smasher.

TARAT: Thanks, Dan.

AKBAR: Happy to be back, Dan.

DAN: Akbar, how's that Trench Warfare coverband coming along?

AKBAR: We call ourselves *Trench Mouth*, Dan, and we're going to make a butt-load of money.

TARAT: I am unfamiliar with this unit of measurement. How much is a butt-load in standard credits?

DAN: Smasher, in your constant quest for knowledge, let's just say there are some things you don't want to know. On to football, and the most amazing story we've heard in years. The Ionath Krakens vanish for five months, only to pop up again just in time for quarterback Quentin Barnes to stop a war. Yes, I'll repeat it — he stopped a war. That kid has a knack for drama, I tell you.

AKBAR: They avoided the war but suffered casualties. I think that's going to mess with them all year long.

DAN: Tarat, give us the perspective of a player. The death of two teammates has to emotionally impact the Krakens' season, don't you think?

TARAT: Dan, in the GFL, players die almost every week. It is the way of things. The question isn't emotions, the question is how does it affect the Krakens' on-field talent? Killik the Unworthy rarely saw playing time, so his loss is not a factor. Stockbridge, however, was the Krakens' nickelback. She was not a starter but came in for passing situations. Fortunately, the Krakens still have Berea and Wahiawa, their starting cornerbacks, but the loss of Stockbridge exposes Ionath's lack of depth in the defensive secondary.

AKBAR: Speaking of depth, Perth is the Krakens' free safety, and her contract is up.

TARAT: She is a free agent, Akbar. Several teams want her.

DAN: What's Gredok trying to do about the Krakens' defensive secondary?

TARAT: The Splithead was not on the *Touchback* when it went missing. He has spent the off-season scouting Tier Three and Tier Two players. I expect him to sign several talented rookies.

DAN: Sure, but will Gloria Ogawa play more of her mind games, signing away Gredok's main rookie targets just so the Krakens can't have them? That's what she did last year with Gladwin and Cooperstown.

TARAT: I think the new salary cap will stop her from doing that this year, Dan. Ogawa can't just spend money to keep players out of Ionath.

AKBAR: Can we talk about the fact that on-field holographic replay is in effect for the '85 season? Froese pushed that rule through. He's running this league like a tyrant. What rule is he going to change next? Maybe he'll say that Sklorno can jump to block field goals and extra points.

TARAT: That is unlikely, Akbar. If Sklorno were allowed to jump and block kicks, no one would ever complete a kick.

AKBAR: I know, Smasher, I was making a point. Look, we don't need on-field replay — bad calls are part of the game.

DAN: What do you mean *bad calls are part of the game*?

TARAT: He means that the complexities of each official's real-time observations, and instantaneous judgments based upon those observations, add variables that make the game unpredictable and provide endless possible outcomes, Dan.

AKBAR: What he said.

DAN: Come on, Akbar — you don't *really* want games decided on bad calls, do you? The current replay system has that complicated *in-the-booth* review process. With on-field holo, everyone can see the play *exactly* as it happened, in the *place* it happened.

AKBAR: It's a slippery slope, Dan. What's next? Computer simulations of each player, all in one of those severed-head League of Planets systems so that we don't even actually play the games on the field at all?

TARAT: Akbar, I think that you are extending the argument to absurd lengths.

DAN: Hah, like that's something new.

AKBAR: Give me a break.

DAN: We will probably see on-field holo *and* see how this ordeal affected the Krakens in the season's opening game, when Ionath takes on the Isis Ice Storm.

TARAT: You are missing the biggest problem facing the Krakens. They have excellent leadership in Barnes and Pine, and Coach Hokor the Hookchest will have the whole team focused and ready to play. All, possibly, except for George Starcher. The biggest issue for Ionath is at tight end. Rick Warburg is a free agent. They should sign him, but I have heard he does not mesh well with the rest of the team. If they lose Warburg, then they have to rely on George Starcher, who missed part of last season due to mental instability.

AKBAR: That guy is nuttier than a fruitcake.

TARAT: What is a fruitcake?

DAN: Something so awful even a Quyth Warrior wouldn't eat it, Tarat. Best if you avoid it.

TARAT: Thank you, Dan, I appreciate you looking out for me. Regarding Warburg, my sources tell me that the newly promoted teams want to sign him. He would be a good fit for the Buddha City Elite or the Sheb Stalkers. I think Buddha City will surprise many people this year and win several contests.

AKBAR: Tarat, you're crazy. I like you, but you're crazy. The Elite will be lucky to win one game this year. The Sheb Stalkers, on the other hand, aren't going to be a pushover. They have an excellent defense.

DAN: That's a good segue into our annual predictions. What two teams will be back down in Tier Two at year's end?

AKBAR: My relegation picks are the Coranadillana Cloud Killers and a shocker — the Jupiter Jacks are heading down to Tier Two.

TARAT: It appears that religion has rotted your brain. The Jacks played in the Galaxy Bowl last year.

AKBAR: I know, but starting quarterback Shriaz Zia died in that loss, and Denver, their supposed number-one receiver, had a total of *five* catches in her last three regular-season games. She's lost it. Without a dominant receiver, I don't think the Jacks can recover from losing Zia.

TARAT: Preposterous. Jupiter has a good defense. Zia's backup, Steve Compton, will start at quarterback and is good enough to keep them from relegation.

DAN: Okay, Smasher, then what are your picks?

TARAT: I agree with Akbar on Coranadillana being relegated from the Planet Division, but in the Solar — I say New Rodina gets sent down.

AKBAR: New Rodina? That's the dumbest thing I've ever heard. They've played Tier One in *every season* the GFL has existed.

TARAT: There is an end to all things.

DAN: Not true, Tarat, because there is no end to my awesomeness. I'm going with the obvious pick — both newly promoted teams are going straight back down to Tier Two. The Elite and the Sheb Stalkers will be *gone*. Let's go to the callers. Line three from the space freighter Shimbuki, you're on the space, go.

CALLER: Dan, you've got it all wrong. Fruitcake is awesome. Tarat, you should have some.

TARAT: Get this caller's exact location. I believe he's trying to kill me, but I will kill him first!

CALLER: What?

DAN: Oh, dang, I hung up before we could trace it, Smasher. Sorry about that!

TARAT: Perhaps we can get him next time.

DAN: Tarat, forget fruitcake, you know you want to stick with our sponsor, Kolok the Daring's Spindly Spider Snacks. Line five from Jang, you're on the space, *go* …

[JOHN AND JU TWEEDY AT YOUR DOOR.]

Quentin sighed and rubbed his eyes. How long had he been watching game film? His apartment holotank was playing a game from last year, the Krakens in black jerseys battling against the blue-, chrome- and white-clad opponents from the Isis Ice Storm.

"Pause holotank," he said.

The image of Ryan Nossek froze in mid-frame. The HeavyG defensive end — who was big even by the standards of that over-sized race — was in the middle of using a swim technique to get by Krakens right offensive tackle Vu-Ko-Will. Quentin had been watching the play over and over because it finished with the All-Pro Nossek coming clean and sacking Quentin ... *hard.* Quentin needed to know Nossek's approach, his steps, see exactly how Nossek finished his moves — if Quentin could commit those things to subconscious memory, it might allow him to react fast enough on the field to avoid a brutal death. Nossek had killed five players in his career and made no bones that he was always looking to add to his tally.

"Computer, let them in."

The door hissed open. John and Ju Tweedy walked into the small apartment. Both of the brothers wore suits.

"Hey, Q," John said. "You're not dressed for the party?"

Quentin leaned back on the couch. His eyes still felt fuzzy. "What party?"

The muscles in John's jaw twitched. "The one Ma is throwing for you. For your birthday."

Ah, the stupid party. Quentin pointed at the holotank. "Can't go. I'm studying."

John and Ju looked at each other, then back to Quentin.

"Quit joking around," Ju said. "Ma doesn't like it when we're late."

"Sorry, I have to prep," Quentin said. "And Uncle Johnny, I told you that a party doesn't seem right considering Stockbridge and Killik just died."

Ju nodded. "That's what Ma thought you'd say. She knows about feelings and stuff. She said it was real important that you come, so you wouldn't sit here and ... John, what did Ma say?"

John absently looked up to the ceiling and rubbed his chin. "Let's see ... oh, I remember — she said Q had to come so he wouldn't *wallow in misery like a depressed pig.*"

Ju smiled and nodded. "Yeah, that was it. Like a pig. So, Quentin, Ma said it's important, so come on."

Quentin stood up. This was starting to get annoying. "Guys, I said *no.* That's it, so stop asking."

I WANT CAKE scrolled across John's face.

"You're going," the linebacker said.

"No, I'm not."

Ju nodded. "Yes, you are. Ma is doing something nice for you. If you don't go, Ma will get angry."

YOU WOULDN'T LIKE MA WHEN SHE GETS ANGRY scrolled across John's face.

Quentin sighed. "Guys, it's *my* birthday, so I get to decide if I want a party or not, right?"

The Tweedy brothers shook their heads in unison.

"Wrong," Ju said. "Ma baked a cake."

John pounded his left fist into his right palm. "A *cake*, Quentin! Do you want Ma to feel bad that no one ate her cake? Ju and I don't like it when someone makes Ma feel bad."

The brothers both leaned in, moved a few steps closer. Great, the Tweedys were trying to intimidate him. Quentin found himself wishing he'd invited Choto the Bright to watch game film.

"I'm not going," Quentin said. "I won't tell you again. I'll call Ma and thank her for the cake, but —"

Ju rushed forward and reached for Quentin's head. Quentin raised his forearm under Ju's outstretched hands, easily blocking the clumsy move. Quentin had just a moment to think *Ju's a much better fighter than that* before he realized he'd been set up. John plowed into his ribs, a perfect form-tackle that lifted Quentin off the ground. They flew through the air and crashed into Quentin's holotank, smashing the device to pieces in a cloud of smoke and sparks. Quentin landed on his back, John on top of him.

John grabbed Quentin's shirt with both hands. "Get dressed, Quentin, or I'll fetch you a beating."

"Get off me, dammit! I said I'm not going!"

"Q, don't make me —"

From his back, Quentin threw a hard left cross that caught John in the mouth. John's head turned a little, but he countered with a right jab that smashed into Quentin's nose.

Quentin saw blackness and stars, but he'd been in enough fights that he didn't need to see clearly when someone was on him. He turned hard to his right, angling his hips, grabbing and pulling John's left arm as he did — John flew into the wall, cracking the composite material. Quentin started scrambling to his feet but was knocked flat on his belly as Ju's arm snaked around his neck. Rock-like muscles squeezed, threatening to cut off Quentin's air.

"Aww, gross, you're bleeding on me," Ju said. "Did you hurt your widdle nose?"

"Get off of me, Ju! I've got work to do!"

Quentin felt a hard punch slam into his thigh. "Charley horse!" John screamed. "My favorite game! Are you going to Ma's party?"

Quentin tried to shake his head, but he couldn't budge. It was two on one, and he didn't have a chance. "I'm not, and you guys can't *beat* me into going."

Ju smiled. "Okay. Maybe we can *flick* you into going." He kept his left arm wrapped around Quentin's head and neck. His right middle finger hooked under his thumb, ready to *snap*. He held the thumb and forefinger close to Quentin's nose.

Ju smiled wider. "You going?"

"No."

Thwap! Quentin winced from the sudden pain. Was his nose broken? And Ju was flicking it? Quentin's temper soared. He tried to push himself to his hands and knees, but Ju's weight pinned his upper body while John held his legs.

"You stupid shuckers," Quentin said. "Get off of me!"

"Charley horse!"

The numbing pain again exploded in Quentin's thigh. He heard John laughing.

Ju again held the locked fingers in front of Quentin's nose.

"Q, you going? It would make Ma happy."

"When you guys let me up, I'm going to beat the —"

Thwap!

Quentin blinked, trying to see through the pain. They weren't going to stop until he gave in.

"CHARLEY HORSE!"

John hit his thigh so hard the whole leg went numb.

"Fine, I'll go, *I'll go!*"

Big arms released him, big hands pulled him to his feet. Quentin blinked, trying to see through his watering eyes. He touched his nose; his fingers came away bloody.

He glared at the Tweedy brothers. "I hate you guys."

Ju and John traded a high-five.

YOU'RE A PUSHOVER scrolled across John's face.

"Let's go, Q," he said. "If we're late, Ma will be real mad."

JUST LIKE LAST YEAR, the party took place at John's apartment across town. As John, Ju and Quentin walked in, the tiny Ma Tweedy was standing behind a gargantuan chocolate cake that had to outweigh her by ten or fifteen pounds. She lit twenty-one orange candles as a room full of sentients sang.

Happy birthday, to you …

It seemed like half the team had packed into John's living room. Becca, Crazy George, Michael Kimberlin, Yitzhak Goldman, Yassoud Murphy, several Sklorno (who all sang out of tune and out of tempo but jumped in joy for the music regardless), Choto the Bright and even backup linebacker Shayat the Thick. The balled-up form of Mum-O-Killowe and the Ki offensive linemen — starters *and* backups — took up half the room. Word had spread that Ma Tweedy's cake was half chocolate, half shushulik; the big Ki couldn't wait to get at a tasty treat made just for them.

Ma Tweedy finished lighting the candles. She squinted up at Quentin. "What happened to your nose?"

"Uh, I fell."

She nodded, a gesture that moved her head as well as the bony shoulders that seemed perpetually up at her ears. She looked at John and Ju. "Jonathan, Julius, just look what you did to your nice suits!"

Quentin took some satisfaction that both John and Ju's expensive, custom suit jackets had rips and tears. John's lower lip was also badly swollen.

The brothers hung their heads and stared at the floor. "Sorry, Ma," they said in unison.

Ma Tweedy shook her head. "And as for you, Quentin, I'm so glad Jonathan and Julius could *convince* you to come to your own birthday party."

She sounded ... disappointed? In *him*? She stared at him as his soul filled with guilt. She had clearly gone through a lot of trouble to make this cake and throw this party — he should have been more appreciative and been ready on time. Quentin couldn't look at her, so he stared at the floor.

"Sorry, Ma," he said. He knew he sounded just like the Tweedy brothers, but he couldn't help it — her glare just kind of pulled those two words out of him. "Uh ... thanks for the cake."

"Blow out your candles," she said. "If the flames burn down too far, the shushuliks catch on fire."

All of the Ki players started making a mournful noise — fire, apparently, would ruin the disgusting candied creatures.

Quentin blew out the candles. Everyone cheered. He cut the cake. Ma Tweedy put pieces on plates that he handed out to everyone. He tried not to look at the oozing pieces from the shushulik side. The Ki scarfed those down as soon as he handed them over.

While everyone ate, Quentin looked around the room. So many sentients, all happy, all talking to each other about things in the news or the upcoming season. They were all here to share this moment with him. Had they already forgotten about Stockbridge and Killik? He wanted to join them, he *wanted* to feel happy, but being happy didn't seem right.

He felt a tug on his sleeve. He looked down; Ma Tweedy was curling a finger at him, telling him to come closer. Quentin knelt. She gave him a firm hug, then held it as she whispered in his ear.

"Honey, I know you're sad about losing your friends," she said. "It's hard to lose people, but you know what? Every *real* friendship and every *true* love ends in tragedy. Sentients die, Quentin. This has happened to you before. It will happen again. I won't tell you to get used to it because we never do. What I will tell you is that dwelling on the dead only dishonors their memory. This room is full of people who love you, and someday some of them will be sad that *you* are gone. Don't let sadness over the dead stop you from appreciating the living."

She pushed him back a little so she could look at him. He stared into her old eyes. He could keep the pain at bay when he wasn't talking about it, but now the feelings of loss, of failure, of *mortality* threatened to overwhelm him.

"But Ma, it's so hard," he said quietly. "All these people look to me to lead them, and I don't know what I'm doing. And whatever decision I make, someone seems to get hurt. Get hurt, or die."

Ma Tweedy nodded. "Sometimes, Quentin, you are a real dumb-ass."

He leaned back. "What?"

"You were attacked by pirates and kidnapped by aliens. You also apparently stopped a war. Who knows how many sentients are alive because of *your* choices? But here you are, like a dumb-ass, only focusing on the ones that died. I'm very glad you're so good at football, dear, because math clearly isn't your strong suit."

She patted his cheek, then walked away to talk to other players. Mum-O-Killowe saw her coming and slid to the far side of the Ki ball.

Quentin stood. Ju slapped him on the shoulder and handed him an envelope. "Your present, Q!"

"What's this?"

Ju just nodded at the envelope. Quentin opened it. Inside was a gold-edged piece of paper that read *One Free Bare-Knuckles Rematch — Quentin Barnes vs. Ju Tweedy*.

"Uh, thanks."

Ju smiled and nodded emphatically. "Sure thing, buddy. Just let me know when. I want to win my belt back, so to speak."

The younger Tweedy brother walked away. Quentin wondered what to do with the invitation. He'd had to cheat to win their fight — Quentin never again wanted to feel those big fists smashing into his body.

John and Yassoud walked up, both with mile-wide smiles. Yassoud held up a present. It was clearly a six-pack of mag cans in orange and black wrapping paper.

"You guys got me beer?"

John's eyes widened, and his jaw dropped. "Q, how did you know that? I mean, it's *wrapped*. Are you —"

"Don't say it," Quentin said. He closed his eyes and held his fingertips to his temples. "Uncle Johnny, you're thinking ... *is he psychic?*"

John leaned away and shook his head in denial. "No *way*, Q. First Fred and now you? Stay out of my brain!"

John quickly walked away. Yassoud laughed and shook his head, the motion swinging his long, braided beard.

"Oh, yep, that John Tweedy is a smart one." Yassoud handed Quentin the present. "It's Miller Lager, your favorite."

It surprised Quentin how much he appreciated the gift. It was cheap beer — at least here on Ionath — but it *was* his favorite, and his friends knew that.

When Yassoud walked off, Rebecca Montagne approached. She looked shy, as usual, her eyes cast more toward his feet than his face.

"Happy birthday, Quentin."

"Thanks," he said. He hadn't talked to her much since the Prawatt incident, when they'd sailed together on the back of a sentient blimp and met a living god.

She looked up at him and smiled. "I got you something. I had Pilkie put it in your apartment. I hope you don't mind."

In his apartment? That seemed odd. "Why didn't you just give it to me here?"

She looked down again. Her face turned a little red. "I ... well, I thought you might want to open it in private is all."

Girls were so weird. "Well, thanks, I guess. I mean — I'm sure I'll love it."

She shrugged and looked very uncomfortable.

Suddenly, John jumped up on top of his living room holotank. He waved his arms to get everyone's attention.

"Hey, everybody! Quentin's rock-star girlfriend is calling!"

Beneath John's feet, the tank flared to life, showing the flawless face of Somalia Midori. Blue skin, deep-blue eyes, gorgeous white hair falling down the left side of her face while the shaved right side gleamed softly. Both sides were shaven, actually — when she performed with her band, Trench Warfare, she wore the hair in a tall, rigid Mohawk. Quentin stared at the long eyelashes, the dark eye makeup, the red lipstick and the silver choker around her neck. Somalia Midori was every man's dream.

The eyes in the tank looked around until they locked on Quentin.

"Hey, sugar. Happy birthday." Her eyes closed, her red lips blew him an exaggerated kiss. All of the Human men in the room let out sounds of jealous approval; they wished that that kiss was for them.

Quentin sensed movement on his right — Becca was walking out of the living room. He felt an urge to reach out to her, to stop her, but everyone was waiting for him to talk to Somalia so he turned back to the holotank.

"Hi, Somalia," Quentin said. "You called in for my birthday?"

"Of course, lover. I'm doing two shows in the Leekee Collective, but you think I'd forget? I got you a little token of my affection. It's down on the street, waiting for you. Why don't you go down and take a look? You can call me later, for some *private* time."

The Human men smiled and nodded, some elbowing each other. Quentin wanted to crawl under the couch and hide. "Uh, okay, I'll go down and look right after the party."

She winked at him. "Just go now, baby. I want to know you got it. Talk to you soon."

The holotank blinked out.

Quentin felt a strong arm wrap around his shoulders. "Come on, Q!" John screamed. "Let's go see this shucking present."

Ma Tweedy shot in like a tiny Human missile. She reached up and grabbed John's ear. "Jonathan! *Language!*"

"Sorry, Ma! *Ouch!*"

"And you use your *indoor* voice, you hear me?"

"Ma, *ouch!* I said I was sorry!"

She let him go. "That's better. Now take your friend outside so he can see what he got."

John nodded as excitedly as if it was his birthday and the surprise present was for him. "Come on, everybody! To the street!"

• • •

THE TEAM FILED OUT of John's apartment building. It wasn't hard to spot the present — if the giant, red ribbon hadn't given it away, the circle of news cameramen would have.

Somalia had bought him a hoverbike.

A powerful fist slammed into his right shoulder. Maybe John couldn't contain his excitement, but at least he'd stopped hitting Quentin's throwing arm.

"Holy *crap*, Q!" John said. "That's a Wyall Model XG! Do you know how *awesome* that is?"

Quentin looked at the sleek, red, single-person craft. It rested on two spike-stands sticking out the back and one sticking out the nose. "Looks pretty cool, I guess."

"You *guess*? Q, this thing can do three hundred miles an hour out on the radioactive flats. And it has Quyth shield technology, the same stuff that makes up the Ionath dome. That means you can just hop on and take it right out of the city without worrying that your face will melt. You don't even need a rad-suit!" The bike didn't just look fast, it looked … intimidating.

"I, uh, I don't ride," he said. "Bikes are too small for me. And besides, what if I got in an accident and got hurt?"

John threw back his head and laughed. YOU KILL ME flashed across his face. "Q, that's a good one. You, afraid of getting hurt?"

Quentin suddenly felt stupid and didn't want to say anything else. If he rode this bike and something happened, he could miss games — that wasn't good for the team.

John grabbed his arm. "Q, come check it out!"

The linebacker practically dragged Quentin to the bike. Quentin followed, noticing that the cameramen were filming away. This would be on the entertainment news sites as soon as they finished: *Sexy rocker gives star-quarterback boyfriend a special birthday treat*, or something like that.

"Q, look how high this seat is! Holy *crap*cakes, this is *custom*! She had it made to fit your size! I don't know how much this cost, but it was some mongo credits."

Quentin saw something moving on the bike's main reactor tank: it was a close-up of Somalia's eyes, narrowing exotically, then winking. A custom bike with a custom paint job.

The cameramen moved in closer. "Mister Barnes, would you mind hopping on so we could get some footage?"

Quentin looked around. Everyone was waiting for him to get on the bike. At the back of the crowd, he saw Rebecca. She stared at him for a moment, then shook her head and walked away, her long, black ponytail bouncing with each step.

"Mister Barnes," the cameraman said, "the bike?"

For some odd reason, Quentin felt bad. Why was Becca upset about this? Well, he couldn't do anything about that now. Somalia loved her news coverage, that was for sure. For a present as nice as this, the least he could do was show it off for her.

He swung a leg over the bike, then tried to smile while the cameramen caught it all.

CHOTO THE BRIGHT AND QUENTIN rode the elevator up to his apartment in the Krakens Building.

"Your Human customs are so strange," Choto said. "Why is the day of your birth so special? It is no different than any other day. And an annual celebration based on a planetary orbit makes no sense when you do not even live on that world."

Quentin shrugged. "You got me. I think the whole thing is ridiculous."

"And that impractical vehicle. *Shama* ... excuse me, *Quentin*, I do not wish to speak out of turn, but I do not think it is safe for you to ride that hoverbike."

Quentin laughed quietly. "Preaching to the choir, pal. You won't get me on that thing in a million years."

"You do not like it?"

He shrugged. "Well, it's really nice, I guess, but I don't ride. I'm not doing anything that would risk my health and hurt the team."

Choto's eye swirled with blue-green — he was relieved. "I am glad to hear this, Quentin. However, is not Somalia your mate?"

Mate? Somalia? "Uh, she's my girlfriend. That's not like a *mate*. Well, it is, kind of, but like … like mate-*light*."

Choto's pedipalps twitched in a way that Quentin had come to learn meant a combination of annoyance and frustration. Choto made the same gesture whenever a conversation came around to religion.

"She is your mate-light, but she buys you a very expensive present that she does not realize you will not use? Humans are strange. Even the blue ones."

The elevator stopped at his floor. They walked into his apartment. Choto didn't even bother asking for permission this time, he just started in the kitchen, scanning for any recording devices, transmitters, bombs, a shoe left out of place — anything that could hurt Quentin.

[HELLO, QUENTIN] the room computer said. [YOU HAVE A SYSTEM ALERT FROM THE *HYPATIA*. THERE ARE PROBLEMS WITH THE PLUMBING. WOULD YOU LIKE ME TO ARRANGE FOR REPAIRS?]

Choto shot out of the kitchen. "No! Quentin, you must not let strangers onto your ship unsupervised. They could plant bombs or sabotage your systems."

Quentin held up his hands. "Easy, big fella. No problem. Tomorrow after practice, I'll go up and take a look at the damage. Then I'll have Messal set up repairs, okay?"

"Why not just let Messal handle this from the beginning?"

"The *Hypatia* is my home. If there's a problem, I want to see it for myself."

"Then I will go with you."

For being a follower, sometimes Choto didn't leave room for disagreements.

"Fine," Quentin said. "Computer, do you know what the problem is?"

[YOUR PERSONAL WASTE RECEPTACLE IS FILLING BEYOND CAPACITY.]

A backed-up toilet. Great. "Computer, coordinate the *Hypatia*'s shuttle to pick me up after tomorrow's practice."

[YES, QUENTIN.]

Choto walked into the bedroom to search for whatever threat he thought might be hidden in such a place.

Quentin sat on his couch. His belly was full of cake. He wanted to sleep. He'd watch some more game-film first, then turn in.

Choto came out of the bedroom carrying a large, flat, rectangular object wrapped in black paper with a white and orange bow.

"This was on your bed," he said. "I believe Pilkie put it there. It is probably safe, but I would like to be present when you open it, just to be sure."

Quentin nodded absently. That had to be Becca's present for him. There was a card tucked into the ribbon. He opened it and read:

> *I thought this might be something you'd treasure. If you don't love it, just let me know and I'll put it in the lobby of the Krakens Building so that everyone can see it.*

Quentin set the present on the couch. He ripped the black paper to reveal an old-fashioned flat-frame made of glass and wood. Behind the glass, an orange jersey: torn and frayed, stained with dirt, streaked with brown blood and green plant stains. The white-trimmed, black numbers read 47. Above the numbers, in white-trimmed, black letters, was the name FAYED.

Quentin couldn't breathe. The frame seemed heavy, started to tremble in his hands. Choto reached out and gently took it from him, holding it up so they both could look at it.

"Quentin, this is the jersey Mitchell was wearing when he died. Such a fine present. This is a true treasure commemorating a fine warrior. Whoever gave this to you knows you well."

Quentin felt tears welling up. He blinked them away. He took the frame and rested it on the couch. "Uh, thanks for keeping me safe, Choto, but I've got to get some sleep."

"I will be here in the morning to escort you to practice," Choto said, then let himself out.

Quentin just stood there. He held Becca's card in his left hand and stared at the framed jersey of his dead friend.

Whoever gave this to you knows you well.

Very well, indeed.

From the *Ionath City Gazette*

2685 GFL Schedule Offers No Easy Road to Hittoni's Shipyard

by TOYAT THE INQUISITIVE

NEW YORK CITY, EARTH, PLANETARY UNION — GFL officials today announced the schedule for the upcoming Tier One season. This year the Galaxy Bowl will be played at The Shipyard in Hittoni on Wilson 6 in the League of Planets, home of the Hittoni Hullwalkers.

In 2684, the Ionath Krakens made the playoffs for the first time in nine seasons. While they lost that first-round game to the Wabash Wolfpack by a score of 35-14, the '85 campaign welcomes back all of Ionath's star players including quarterback Quentin Barnes, running back Ju Tweedy, middle linebacker John Tweedy and even dominant defensive end Ibrahim Khomeni, who missed the last two games of the regular season and the playoffs due to a knee injury.

"This is a huge opportunity," said Krakens Coach Hokor the Hookchest. "We have some depth issues on defense, but return at least 10 starters. All 11 offensive starters are back, and we need to take advantage of that to open the season with wins."

The Krakens face their usual Planet Division rivals, including Wabash, the To Pirates and defending GFL champion Themala Dreadnaughts. Ionath also travels to the Purist Nation in Week Six for a game against the newly promoted Buddha City Elite.

Championship dreams?

Last year the Krakens went 8-4, their best record since 2675. With so many starters back and the growth of fourth-year quarterback Quentin Barnes, the stage is set for a run at the title.

"One game at a time," Barnes said. "We open up against the Ice Storm, and we really haven't thought about anything beyond that game."

Cross-divisional help?

This year the Krakens drew a favorable cross-division schedule. Ionath travels to Earth in Week Two to face the Texas Earthlings, and the Shorah Warlords in Week Seven. Last year the Earthlings finished 4-8, while the Warlords

This marks the third straight year that a team from the Quyth Irradiated Conference has won promotion from Tier Two into Tier One.

barely avoided relegation with a record of 3-9.

Finishing with a bang

The last two games of Ionath's '85 season might prove to be the hardest. In Week Twelve, the Krakens will be looking for revenge against the Wolfpack. Barnes & Co. finish the season in Week Thirteen with a road game against perennial power To Pirates. The blood-red field of Pirates Stadium is regarded as the hardest place to win in all of the GFL.

	Opponent	System	2684 Record
A	Isis Ice Storm	Tower Republic	7-5
A	Texas Earthlings (cross-divisional)	Planetary Union	4-8
	Bye Week		
H	Yall Criminals	Sklorno Dynasty	8-4
H	OS1 Orbiting Death	Quyth Concordia	5-7
A	Buddha City Elite	Purist Nation	na
H	Shorah Warlords (cross-divisional)	Ki Empire	3-9
A	Alimum Armada	Sklorno Dynasty	4-8
H	Coranadillana Cloud Killers	Harrah Tribal Accord	3-9
A	Themala Dreadnaughts	Quyth Concordia	9-3
H	Hittoni Hullwalkers	League of Planets	6-6
H	Wabash Wolfpack	Tower Republic	10-2
A	To Pirates	Ki Empire	10-2

• • •

OF ALL THE THINGS TO GO WRONG on a multimillion-credit yacht, Quentin had to deal with a backed-up toilet? Well, maybe that was the price he had to pay for a ship that had real plumbing, not that nanotech cleaning garbage. A hot shower made any amount of trouble worthwhile. Not having microscopic machines buzzing about your private bits after going to the bathroom? That was icing on the cake.

The first week of preseason had ended. Tomorrow the rookies arrived. Gredok had done all of the scouting and player acquisition while the *Touchback* had been in Prawatt space. The rookies were mostly defensive players — which wasn't surprising considering the Krakens hadn't lost a single offensive starter — but Quentin would still be involved, doing everything he could to contribute to the success of his new teammates.

If, that was, the new rookies made the final roster.

The shuttle autopiloted itself into the *Hypatia*'s small landing bay. After the outer doors sealed and the area pressurized, Quentin and Choto stepped out onto the bay's metal deck.

Home, sweet home. Choto at his side, he headed through the corridors toward the parlor. As he walked, Quentin admired his ship's wood walls, the ornate trim, all of the little details that gave him a warm feeling of ownership.

"Quentin, I do not understand why you insist on primitive technology," Choto said. "Nannite cleansing systems work far better than water."

Quentin shrugged. "And I can't understand why Warriors wear gray sweatpants all the time. How about a little color?"

"Color is immodest," Choto said. "The only color on a Warrior should be enamels of victory or the emotions in our eyes."

"But there is technology to give you clothes like Shizzle," Quentin said. "You could have many colors to reflect your moods."

"You would not understand," Choto said. "It is something particular to my culture."

"Like a water shower is to mine, buddy. How about we just respect our differences, okay?"

They walked through the parlor door and stopped cold — five Human men were waiting inside, two sitting on the couch, three standing behind them.

Choto stepped forward, putting his body between Quentin and the men. The Warrior leaned forward as if to rush them, but Quentin grabbed his shoulder.

"Choto, wait!"

The three standing men each had a hand inside of their expensive suit jackets. If Choto attacked, they might draw weapons and cut him down.

Quentin recognized the Humans. The three standing men were named Sammy, Frankie and Dean. None of them was as big as he was, but each of them would be considered huge by normal Human standards.

On the couch in front of them sat Manny Sayed and Stedmar Osborne.

Both men had the Purist Church's infinity symbol tattooed on their forehead. The owner of both Sayed Luxury Craft and the Buddha City Elite, Manny wore the blue robes of a confirmed church member. The robes somewhat concealed his layers of fat. An excess of rings, bracelets and other glittering jewelry reflected the parlor's lights, as did his jewel-studded platinum prosthetic lower left leg. No one loved to flaunt his wealth more than Manny Sayed.

Manny was smiling. Stedmar was not.

Stedmar was the most powerful gangster on Micovi. He was also the owner of the Micovi Raiders. Quentin hadn't seen the man since leaving the Raiders to come play for the Krakens, some three years earlier.

Stedmar's black hair framed his hard face and cold eyes. He wore a custom suit of iridium fabric, the kind they made on Wilson 6 and had recently come into fashion. A bowl of spider snacks sat in Stedmar's lap — he'd obviously helped himself to Quentin's galley.

Quentin walked forward to stand next to Choto. "What are you two doing in my home?"

Manny stood, something that took a little bit of effort on his part. His jewelry clinked and rattled. "Quentin, my child, is the *Hypatia* working out for you?"

"Drop the small-talk, Manny," Quentin said. "How did you get in here?"

Manny's smile widened. "My company built this ship, remember? We may have left an override or two in your core system software. Look on the bright side, Quentin — at least your toilet isn't really backed up. Stedmar and I simply came to talk."

Quentin crossed his arms over his chest. "*Talk*, huh?" He nodded toward Stedmar Osborne. "Is that why there's a gangster sitting on my couch and eating my spider snacks?"

Manny looked at Stedmar as if he was surprised to see the man sitting there. "*Gangster?* Why, Quentin, you must be mistaken. This is no gangster, this is my co-owner of the Buddha City Elite."

So, Stedmar Osborne was the silent partner that helped Manny Sayed acquire the Purist Nation's only upper-tier team. That made sense. Manny had massive wealth, but he didn't have the connections required to navigate the serpent's nest of ownership in a league controlled by criminals.

"I should have known," Quentin said. "Mister Osborne, is the former Elite owner still alive?"

Stedmar popped one more spider snack into his mouth, wiped the back of his hand across his lips, then stood. "Yah," he said with a full mouth. "Let's just say he found my offer quite reasonable. I've learned a lot from Gredok."

"Not enough," Choto said. "You clearly do not understand what will happen to you when Gredok finds out you broke into Quentin's home."

Stedmar rolled his eyes. "Don't be so dramatic. Gredok isn't going to find out because Quentin isn't going to tell him. The kid owes me, and he knows it."

Choto looked at Quentin, but Quentin kept staring at Stedmar.

The gangster spread his arms, a gesture that took in not only the parlor, but all of the *Hypatia.*

"Look at this life you've got, kid," he said. "This is all because of me. *I* gave you this, and have you called? You ever sent a message? I know I was your boss and all, but I was really proud of what we did together. For four years I've watched the galaxy kiss your ass, and I waited for a lousy *thank you* that never came. You leave Micovi and you big-time me?"

Quentin's anger receded, replaced by the flush of embarrassment. Quentin hadn't contacted the man, hadn't reached out in any way. They weren't friends, but Stedmar Osborne had taken him out of the mines. Stedmar Osborne had given him football. Quentin suddenly felt ashamed of the oversight.

Stedmar was a dangerous man. He'd ordered the death of many, even killed some with his bare hands. Disrespecting him could put you in a shallow grave. Quentin had every reason to fear the man, but Stedmar wasn't angry — he looked *hurt,* and that made it even worse.

Quentin stepped forward. "Mister Osborne, I apologize. I can't believe I haven't said anything since I left. That's ... well, there's just no excuse for it. I wasn't big-timing you or ignoring you ... I guess I just lost track. If what you need doesn't impact my team, I'll help you if I can."

He offered his hand. Stedmar smiled and shook it. He reached up to grip Quentin's shoulder.

"Apology accepted, kid," Stedmar said. "I can tell you meant what you said. So, you'll help us?"

"Depends on what you're asking," Quentin said. "I won't do anything illegal or anything that compromises my team."

"Or Gredok," Choto said.

Quentin nodded. "Or Gredok."

Stedmar gave Quentin's shoulder another squeeze, then let it go. "Nothing like that, kid. This is just normal football stuff. We need your honest opinion on a player — we want Rick Warburg."

With all the craziness of the Prawatt situation, Quentin had forgotten Warburg was a free agent. The tight end had worked hard to improve his strength and his route-running ability. He'd been pivotal in the Krakens' late-season run to qualify for the playoffs. Warburg hadn't caught many passes in the first half of the season, but that was only because Quentin had intentionally avoided throwing him the ball.

Warburg had begged to be traded to another team. Now a Tier One team in his home system wanted him — Warburg couldn't have picked a better scenario.

"Why didn't you just call me?" Quentin said. "Or make an official contact request through the league?"

Manny sighed. "Because Gredok would have blocked any attempt to talk to you. I made it clear I wanted you to come home and play for the Elite. You signed with Ionath, which is your choice, but Gredok won't let me anywhere near you. So Stedmar suggested we cut to the chase, so to speak."

Choto moved closer to stand at Quentin's side. "Osborne, you would risk your position in Gredok's syndicate for this?"

Stedmar shrugged. "I know what happens if Gredok finds out, kid. I'll risk anything to keep my team from getting relegated. We want to *win*."

Manny ran the fingers of his left hand across the bracelets on his right wrist. "Quentin, we're asking for your honest opinion on Warburg. Rumors say he's locker-room poison. We don't run our business on rumors. All we're asking for is the truth. Tell us about the *real* Rick Warburg — can he be a dominant player?"

Quentin thought of Warburg's refusal to play against the Prawatt. Did someone like that deserve an endorsement? A big contract? Maybe, maybe not. On the football field, Warburg did everything he was asked, even when he rarely saw playing time. The tight end's amazing catch against the Vik Vanguard had put Ionath into the playoffs. If the Krakens kept both Rick Warburg and George Starcher, they would have the best tight end combo in the league. All Quentin had to do was tell the truth and say that Warburg *was* locker-room poison, that he was a racist and a constant problem.

But ...

Warburg was at the peak of his skills; another year or two, and he'd be on the downslope and wouldn't command as much money in free agency. Warburg had asked for Quentin's help, asked for catches and yardage that would make him desirable to other teams. No, Warburg hadn't just *asked* — he'd busted his ass to *earn* that help. Quentin could look out for himself and his team, or he could be honest and let the chips fall where they may.

"Rick Warburg is an exceptional tight end," he said. "I didn't utilize him enough last year, and that was my problem, not his. He is a major talent."

Stedmar ran a hand through his black hair. "If he's that good, Gredok will fight to keep him."

"Of course," Quentin said. "Gredok wants great players. He'll offer Rick a new contract to keep him from leaving."

Manny shook his head. "You don't have salary-cap room. With as much as Gredok is paying you *and* paying Don Pine, I don't think he can match our offer. Other teams think Rick Warburg is a risk. You said he's talented, but is he worth a major contract?"

They wanted Quentin to tell them how to spend their money? That wasn't his business.

Just tell the truth — what happens then isn't up to you.

"Rick Warburg is the most racist sentient I know," Quentin said. "He hates all non-Humans, and most Humans as well. He cares about himself first, team second. You sign him, you have to deal with that. But on the field, he'll give you everything he has. If he gets a chance to play in his home nation, you won't find anyone who will work harder."

Manny looked at Stedmar, who nodded.

"Okay," Stedmar said. "We were never here, yah?"

Quentin shook his head. "You think I want Gredok to know I'm giving info to another team?"

Stedmar turned to Choto. "I got no beef with you. You can see we dealt fairly with Quentin, right? No harm, no threats. Do you agree?"

Choto's eye swirled with a trace of black, but then it cleared. "Yes, I agree."

"Good," Stedmar said. "Then there's no need to tell our *shamakath* about this, am I right?"

Stedmar didn't know that Gredok wasn't Choto's real *shamakath*, not anymore.

"I will not mention this on one condition," Choto said. "I want those access codes removed, *now*, before you leave. And if either of you ever come back uninvited, or I suspect that an uninvited guest got in with other codes that you did not delete, I will kill you both whether you did it or not."

Sammy, Frankie and Dean bristled, but Stedmar held up a hand to still them.

"Deal," the gangster said. "Manny, show Choto how to remove the codes. We'll do that, then we'll be off."

Choto pointed to the door. "Walk with me to the landing bay. You will leave Quentin alone now."

Quentin's friend and bodyguard led the intruders out of the parlor. Quentin stared after them for a bit, then sat on the couch. He'd never been that materialistic, but maybe that was because he'd never really owned anything. He owned the *Hypatia*, and now the ship seemed ... violated.

He wondered how long it would be before it felt like home again.

10

Preseason Week Two: January 8 to January 14

THE LIGHT ABOVE the *Touchback*'s shuttle bay door switched from red to green. Internal bolts retracted, sending a small vibration through the floor. When the doors slid open, Quentin, John and Yassoud led the rest of the team into the shuttle bay.

John walked with his knees high and swung his arms in an exaggerated motion. He looked to the left, sniffed in a big, loud breath through his nose, then looked to the right and did the same.

"Hey, Q, you smell that?"

Uncle Johnny, busting out the same tired joke as last year and the year before that.

"I don't know, John, would it be the odor of unwashed rookies?"

"Smells like *rookie* stank," John said. "And this year, I get *four* rookies for my defense, while you, dear Hayseed, only get one player. I'm as happy as a fargle fish with two tongues."

Yassoud nodded and smiled. "And Gredok didn't pick up a rookie running back this year. Oh, happy days indeed."

Yassoud Murphy was perpetually worried about his job, but Quentin didn't think those concerns were valid. 'Soud was the second running back on the depth chart. He wasn't anywhere near Ju Tweedy's league when it came to carrying the ball, but 'Soud had proven to be a good blocker and could catch just about anything thrown his way. He'd solidified his place on the team as a *third-down back*, brought in mostly for passing situations. Ionath's other running back, Jay Martinez, hadn't shown enough ability in practice or in games to threaten Yassoud's job.

The orange shuttle sat on the deck, little whirs of machinery and the clink-ping of cooling metal echoing through the bay. The thing looked a bit beat up — it hadn't had a paint job in three seasons. There were even marks on the Krakens logo painted on the side. That same logo — a black "I" set inside an orange shield, three white, orange- and black-trimmed stylized tentacles spreading off to the right, three more spreading off to the left — was also painted on the 50-yard line of the Ionath Stadium field. No matter where Quentin saw that symbol, it filled his heart with pride.

The shuttle had come directly from the *Combine*, the league's prison-station-turned-purity-testing-zone. There, rookies were examined for body modifications. If they tested clean, they were brought to their respective teams. If they didn't test clean, they were often never heard from again.

The Krakens, fifty-one players who each represented some of the largest individuals their species had to offer, formed a half-circle around the shuttle. Before the shuttle's side-ramp lowered, the internal landing bay doors again hissed opened. The two small forms of Gredok the Splithead and Hokor the Hookchest entered.

Quentin's eyes narrowed. So, the lying, back-stabbing team owner finally showed his black-furred head? The rage and the hurt swelled up in Quentin's chest, making his soul cry out for revenge. Gredok had hurt him, and now he wanted to hurt Gredok.

The worst part of the whole debacle was that Quentin had already wanted to be a Kraken for the rest of his career. Maybe if Gredok had just sat down and *talked* to Quentin, they could have worked together to build a franchise that would win multiple championships. But Gredok the Splithead didn't *talk*; he *manipu-*

lated. He intimidated. He coerced. He took what he wanted, the needs of others be damned.

Gredok and Hokor stopped near the shuttle door. The landing bay lights played off of the gangster's jewelry, gleamed against his glossy, smooth, black fur. Hokor wore what he always wore: a tiny little Krakens team jacket and a tiny little Krakens ball cap.

Gredok faced the team. "Players," he said, "we are here to welcome new members into the Krakens family."

The words further flamed Quentin's hatred. Had Gredok used the word *family* just to anger him? To rub it in Quentin's face that Gredok had won and won big?

"This year we focused on signing defensive players," Gredok said. "We will also be looking to free agency next week for more of the same. You may now meet your new teammates."

Gredok and Hokor stepped aside. The shuttle's door lowered from its bottom hinge, the entire side becoming a ramp that led down to the landing bay deck.

Two Sklorno bound down the ramp, squeaking and twittering in high-pitched excitement. They wore numbers 21 and 33.

"Aw, yeah," John said. "Twenty-one is cornerback Niami. Thirty-three is Sandpoint, a free safety. They both played for the Venus Valkyries in the Union Conference."

The other Krakens Sklorno players flocked around the newcomers. They sounded excited, even more excited than normal, which was pretty damn excited.

Yassoud stroked his braided beard. "The new girls any good?"

John shrugged. "They're young, and they have a lot of potential. Word is Gredok had to pay a big bounty to Venus to get them both. Losing Stockbridge means we needed depth at corner, and we're thin at free safety, but both Niami and Sandpoint are project players. They need a season of seasoning. Ha! That's funny!"

Yassoud nodded. "By the way, either of you know what a *Valkyrie* is?"

I KNOW WORDS scrolled across John's face. "They were these super-hot, crazy-mean ladies that rode horses with wings and stuff. They'd fight alongside the male warriors or something. They were magic and mega-killed people with swords. When the guy warrior got stabby-stabbed and died, the Valkyries would take the warrior to paradise."

Yassoud laughed and shook his head. "Well, *that* certainly sounds like historical fact. You believe in that nonsense, John?"

"No way," John said. "It's religion. You know that made-up crap doesn't make any sense. Anyone who believes in that stuff is a super-mega-idiot."

Quentin rolled his eyes. "I'm standing right here, John."

John laughed and gave Yassoud a conspiratorial elbow. Yassoud gritted his teeth and tried to pretend it hadn't hurt.

The next player out of the shuttle was a stocky Quyth Warrior, number 64.

John smiled and rubbed his hands together. "That's my guy, right there. Pishor the Fang. Played three seasons for the Saturn Sky-Demons in the JNSV. Already has *three kills* to his credit."

Quentin nodded. He'd heard about Pishor. The Warrior had started for the Tier Three Sky-Demons at just sixteen years old, a good two or three years ahead of most Warriors. There were concerns about Pishor's speed and reaction time, but no one questioned his hitting power. Pishor would fill Killik the Unworthy's role as backup left outside linebacker, playing behind first-stringer Virak the Mean.

A HeavyG came down next. His upper body looked big and solid, but his legs looked shorter than most of his kind. Quentin was shocked to see that the man had an infinity tattoo on his forehead.

"That's defensive tackle Jason Procknow," John said. "You should get along great with him, Q, he played for the Cooper City Priests in the PNFL."

"He's a HeavyG," Quentin said. "How did he get confirmed in the Church?"

John shrugged. "Yeah, well, he was born there or something, so they made some kind of exception. If you want my guess, your holier-than-thou people just said he was a misshapen Human so they could get him on the field."

Looking at Procknow's massive upper body, Quentin could imagine some Holy Man from Cooper City finding a convenient interpretation of the scriptures that would allow the HeavyG to play on Purist Nation soil. Or maybe Procknow had been adopted by an upstanding family that paid enough bribes to have him declared *Human* despite his obvious ancestry.

Yassoud shook his head. "Hopefully he's not a racist like Rick Warburg. No offense, Q, but other than you, every Nationalite I've met is a real jerk."

John elbowed Quentin in the shoulder, then pointed to the last rookie — a Human walking down the ramp. "Offense! Offense! Gooooo, offense! Right, Q?"

Quentin sighed and rubbed his shoulder. "You know, John, you don't have to hit me to show your enthusiasm."

John puffed out his lower lip. "Awww, diddums get a boo-boo?" DOES IT HURT, SALLY? scrolled across his forehead.

The Human had wide shoulders and thick legs. If Quentin's rough body shape could be considered *rectangular*, this guy was a *square*.

"Pete Marval," Quentin said. "Fullback, three seasons with the Hallacha Hungries. He'll play behind Becca and Kopor."

Becca was an All-Pro fullback, among the best in the galaxy. Kopor had been a four-year starter before Becca joined the team; he was still a damn good player. It would be all Marval could do just to make the final fifty-three-player roster.

Just one new offensive player, and that one probably wouldn't see any playing time. That was a testament to the Krakens' offensive depth.

Three more weeks of preseason practice, then Quentin could unleash that offense against the Isis Ice Storm. He didn't know how he could get revenge on Gredok, or when an opportunity might arise, but once the regular season began he'd have an outlet for his rage.

Too bad for you, Isis — because you'll be the first of many.

Quentin joined the other Krakens in welcoming the rookies to the team.

• • •

QUENTIN STOOD IN THE MIDDLE of his apartment in the Krakens Building. His hands moved through the air to grab floating, holographic Xs and Os. The computer knew when he was pinching an image, which let him move it until he *unpinched*, leaving the symbol in the new place. The computer also recognized hand gestures like his pointer finger, which let him paint motion lines, or his pointer and middle finger together, which let him assign blocking schemes. He went through the playbook, formation after formation, play after play, analyzing his offensive talent to find the best solutions to hundreds of hypothetical situations — down-and-distance, substitutions for key injuries, two-minute drill personnel and more.

For almost every problem, he saw a straightforward solution. He wasn't about to get cocky, but in his seven-year career he had *never* felt this confident.

He had all of his offensive starters back, sure, but it was more than that. They'd spent most of the off-season asleep. They practiced as if they'd taken no time off at all; the Krakens still had every bit of the team chemistry that had led them to the playoffs.

Conditioning was an issue, of course — you didn't sleep for five months without it taking a toll — but everyone saw that they had a shot at the championship, and they worked their asses off in practice. When Ionath opened the regular season in two weeks, he knew his team would be in top shape.

His hands moved icons, drew lines and substituted players. There was always more prep, always something else he could do to anticipate problems. He had to be ready for anything. His teammates looked to him, counted on him to lead, and he would not let them down.

[RICK WARBURG AT YOUR DOOR.]

Quentin stopped moving symbols.

"Let him in."

The door slid open. As usual, Warburg wore a too-tight T-shirt that showed off his thick muscles. This time, however, the T-shirt bore the infinity sign logo of the Buddha City Elite.

So, it was done. Manny Sayed and Stedmar Osborne had made their move.

"Nice shirt," Quentin said. "Do you really need to wear that on the *Touchback?*"

Rick laughed. "If anyone doesn't like it, too bad. I signed the deal, Quentin. I'm going home."

Quentin felt a wash of mixed emotions. "Congrats, Rick. To tell you the truth, I'm not sure if I'm mad because you're not staying or if I'm happy to see you go."

Warburg shrugged. "We've had our differences."

"Ain't that the truth."

Warburg stared for a moment, then sighed and shook his head. "This isn't easy for me, because I honestly do not like you, but I'm here to say *thanks*. The deal is more than I ever thought I would make. I'll finish my career in my home system and retire a rich man. Mister Osborne told me what you said to him. You and I will never be friends, Quentin, but I'm happy that High One saw fit to let you see the light."

Warburg couldn't just be gracious. Of course not. Quentin didn't do the right thing on his own, oh no, Warburg had to make this a holier-than-thou moment.

"I didn't *see the light*," Quentin said. "Not throwing you the ball was a bad decision on my part, so I corrected that. You're a good player. You've worked really hard. When the team needed you to step up, you did. I just told the truth — High One had nothing to do with it."

Rick shrugged again. "It's too bad you can't see the obvious. High One helps those that help themselves. You were the obstacle preventing my success. You think it's coincidence that when I worked harder and prayed more that you started throwing me the ball? If you can't see the hand of the All-Powerful at work, then maybe He's not ready for you to see it yet."

Oh, the endless, circular logic of the pious. No matter how

Quentin presented this, in Warburg's mind it could only be divine intervention.

"Well, anyway, congratulations," Quentin said. "I hope you're happy there."

"I know I will be. I don't know how Perth will like Buddha City, but cricket integration isn't my problem, right?"

Quentin felt a sinking feeling in his stomach; Warburg was a number-two tight end, a hard loss but one that the Krakens could handle — Perth was one of Ionath's starting defensive backs.

Warburg smiled, obviously enjoying Quentin's sudden disappointment. "She was a free agent, just like me. Manny Sayed gave her a big contract. No way Gredok can match the offer, not with you and Blue Boy taking up so much of his salary cap."

Just like that, the Krakens had lost their free safety. Quentin still had to get the details, but Warburg was probably dead-on about why Gredok wouldn't be able to match the Elite's offer. Quarterbacks earned more than any other position in football. Don Pine wasn't the starter anymore, but he still had the contract given to him when he was. Add in Quentin's recent deal, and that was a good chunk of Ionath's salary cap. Having Don Pine as a backup gave the Krakens amazing insurance in case Quentin got hurt, but it came at a price — less money to sign other free agents.

"Quentin, everyone knows this is your team," Warburg said. "And everyone knows you sabotaged that trade for Don Pine last season. I don't know why you did that and I don't care. What matters is you could have done the same thing to me. You didn't. You let me go where I'm wanted. So for that, I'll say it one last time — *thanks*."

Rick extended his big hand.

Quentin remembered the first time he'd shaken Rick Warburg's hand. Quentin had just stepped off the shuttle that brought him from the *Combine*. Rick had tried to help his countryman adjust to a new life. As Quentin gradually learned about the other races, learned to evaluate his teammates as individuals and not as "aliens," that camaraderie evaporated.

Quentin had grown as a person. Rick never would.

In a perfect universe, Rick Warburg would not find true success until he let go of his racist ways — but the universe was far from perfect.

Quentin shook the offered hand.

"See you in Week Six," he said. "We'll try to go easy on you."

Rick smiled an arrogant *we'll just see about that* smile and walked out. The apartment door slid shut behind him.

Quentin stared after him for a moment, then turned back to his holodisplay. He wiped his hand left to right, clearing out the offensive set. He replaced it with the defense. That positive feeling had faded — while the offense returned all of its starters, the defense had now lost a nickelback and a starting free safety. The rookie defensive backs weren't good enough yet; the fate of the season might very well hinge on signing free agents to fill those holes.

The Krakens would score points, there was no doubt about that, but would they be able to stop other teams from scoring more?

11

Preseason Week Three: January 15 to January 21

QUENTIN LOOKED UP at the sky above Ionath Stadium. A pair of Harrah high above were diving and banking around each other. He saw a flock of five Creterakians cross from one side of the stadium to the other. Civilians, obviously, as no Creterakian military personnel were allowed on Ionath. Quentin absently watched the aerial displays as he waited for Coach Hokor.

The yellow-furred Quyth Leader stared at his holoboard. He looked up at the three Sklorno receivers gathered in front of him. "How about Pickle Lake? What's your opinion on that cornerback?"

"Unworthy," Hawick said.

"Pickle Lake should be killed," Milford said.

"And eaten," Halawa said.

Hokor entered those opinions on his holoboard, then called up more players and studied his notes.

It was free-agent day, an annual preseason event when unsigned players came to Ionath to fight for a roster spot. Quentin had spent the last two hours throwing passes to Hawick, Milford and Halawa as free agent defensive backs tried to cover them.

Gredok had cast his nets far and wide, bringing in unsigned talent from all over the galaxy. There were Tier Two players looking to gain Tier One experience before going back to their franchise, a process known as "loaning" a player; there were a couple of Tier Three players who hadn't been drafted; and there were a few Tier One players that had recently been cut from their teams. In the GFL, the really good players were already signed — unsigned players had to take whatever franchise would have them, and a franchise that needed help had to take whatever it could get.

Nine Sklorno DBs had been invited to try out. They stood there, some trembling, white helmets held in their tentacles as they waited to see if their dreams would come true. Ionath needed to build some depth in the secondary. Losing Perth and Stockbridge hurt, and as the season went on, injuries were bound to happen.

Hokor looked up at his receivers. "What about Emmitsburgh? She seemed adept at covering deep routes."

One of Hawick's eyestalks turned to look at one of Milford's, which turned to look back — the Sklorno equivalent of sharing an unspoken thought.

"Partially worthy," Hawick said.

"I would wound her for being incompetent but not kill her," Milford said.

"I would nibble on her left foot but leave most of her alone," Halawa said.

Hokor tapped the icons floating above his holoboard. He turned to the gathered free agents. "Emmitsburgh, free safety! Luanda, cornerback! Millington, cornerback! You are to report to Messal the Efficient in the locker room. You will practice with us for the next two weeks, and then we will see if you're good enough to wear the Orange and the Black for the rest of the year. The rest of you, thank you for coming, now get off of my field."

The Krakens now had three more defensive backs. Quentin had mixed emotions. It felt great to add some depth, but he'd thrown against those players and knew they were unsigned for a specific reason — because they weren't that good. Still, Emmitsburgh, Luanda and Millington would have two weeks of practice to show they were skilled enough to make the final fifty-three-player roster. Quentin would do his part to help them prepare, because if the starters fell to injury, any of those three players might mean the difference between victory and defeat.

MICHAEL KIMBERLIN SIGHED with audible frustration. "Quentin, maybe you don't understand the definition of the word *theory*."

Quentin, Kimberlin and Choto sat at the kitchen table of Kimberlin's apartment. Even though the preseason took up most of Quentin's time, he didn't want to let his studies slip. Kimberlin tutored him on several subjects: math, physics, government and, today, biology.

The lessons were a rare moment away from the mental focus of football. As hard as they were, Quentin loved to learn. On Micovi, his teachers hadn't thought he'd been worth educating. Now that he was out of the Purist Nation, there was nothing to stop him from learning everything he could about the galaxy and the beings that lived in it.

Choto always insisted on coming with. The Warrior refused to let Quentin out of his sight. The fact that Choto seemed to already know everything Kimberlin taught didn't bother Quentin a bit — unlike the Purist Nation, it seemed, the Quyth Concordia believed in educating *all* of its citizens.

Quentin leaned back and crossed his arms. "I understand the definition of *theory* perfectly, Mike. *Theory* means something that you *think* is right. It's an educated guess."

Kimberlin shook his head. "Not in the scientific sense. In science, a *theory* is a coherent set of factual observations that support a *hypothesis*. The concept of a theory as a *guess* is colloquial, you understand?"

"That depends," Quentin said.

The big HeavyG lineman sighed again. "That depends on what *colloquial* means?"

Quentin smiled and nodded.

"It means *casual speech*," Kimberlin said. "Colloquial meanings are what people say in everyday interactions, in common usage. Colloquial use of the word *theory* means a guess, but in scientific terms, a *guess* is better represented by the word *hypothesis*. A *hypothesis* is something that you *think* is right, while a *theory* is what you have if experiments prove that your hypothesis was correct. The theory of evolution is scientific *fact*, Quentin. It's not open to debate."

Quentin shook his head. "Well, I don't believe it."

Choto's baseball-sized eye blinked rapidly, the Quyth equivalent to shaking one's head in disbelief.

"Quentin, you are making jokes," the Warrior said. "Please be serious — you do accept the common knowledge that all life evolved from previous forms ... do you not?"

"No, I do not," Quentin said. "And I'm not making jokes. There's no way that one day a monkey was a monkey, and then the next, it gave birth to Human babies."

Choto blinked faster.

Michael put his hands on the table, seemed to gather himself. "Monkeys did not give birth to Human babies," he said. "Evolution is a gradual accumulation of small changes that take place over millions of years. If those changes provide some kind of survival advantage, it increases the chance that the individual with those changes will survive long enough to reproduce, thereby passing on those changes to the next generation."

Quentin rolled his eyes. "You have your opinion, I have mine. I've never *seen* anything evolve, okay? Neither have you guys. I just don't believe in the theory of evolution."

Choto's pedipalps twitched in annoyance. "Have you ever heard of the *theory* of gravity? If you do not *believe* in the theory of gravity, do you think you will float up into the air?"

"Well ... no," Quentin said. "But that's different. That's *gravity*, not *evolution*."

"They are both *theories*," Choto said, his volume increasing. "How can you think they are different?"

How could these guys be so oblivious to reality? "They're

different because I can look at my feet and see that I'm not floating. Even though I don't know *how* gravity works, my own eyes tell me that it's real."

Kimberlin nodded. "You *observe* that gravity works. Very good. However, you can see that you don't float, but you can't see gravity. The theory of gravity is testable and predictable — if you drop something from the top of the Krakens Building, that theory will tell you exactly how long it takes for that something to hit the street."

Quentin thought about that for a moment. One of Mike's lessons had been about terminal velocity, how a falling object accelerated to a certain speed then accelerated no more.

"So the theory of gravity says we can predict how fast something will fall," Quentin said. "Which means we can drop something and show that the fall matches those predictions?"

Kimberlin nodded.

Quentin tapped the table to emphasize his words. "All right, then *predict* that something will evolve, then *show* it replacing its ancestors."

Choto started wringing his pedipalp hands. His eye swirled with violet-red, showing that he was just as frustrated as Kimberlin.

"Evolution happens too slowly for that," Choto said. "And evolution does not *replace* a species — you don't have species X on Tuesday, then on Wednesday it's gone and species Y is in its place."

"Well, that's convenient," Quentin said. "You're saying evolution can *predict* stuff, but you'll never be able to measure the results of that prediction to see if you're right because it takes too long for it to happen."

Choto suddenly stood up. "Michael, I have reached the end of my tolerance level regarding this discussion. Do you have any snacks?"

Kimberlin tilted his head toward the kitchen. "I bought some candied mice for you. They're in the fridge."

Choto walked into the kitchen.

Kimberlin rubbed his eyes. "Quentin, perhaps we will discuss evolution later. Let us switch to algebra, as you were having trouble with it last time."

Quentin put his elbows on the table and groaned. He hated algebra. Michael knew that, which meant this was a subtle punishing for being stubborn about evolution. Quentin didn't have to like math to know that it was one of the most important subjects a sentient could study, so he'd do the work as best he could.

Kimberlin called up a lesson on his messageboard, but instead of dreaded formulas, a football field appeared.

"Last time you had trouble with the Cartesian coordinate system, or the X/Y axis you see so often," Kimberlin said. "Think of the X-axis as the line of scrimmage, a horizontal line, and the Y-axis as a vertical line, moving downfield or running away from the line of scrimmage. Now, let's write a formula to plot out the positions of a defensive backfield."

Quentin's eyes went wide — by using football, Michael had made a difficult concept *click* home with just a single sentence. Quentin forgot about his annoyance at the biology lesson and silently thanked High One for the presence of such a patient and clever teacher.

THE TARGET AND HIS BODYGUARD walked down the streets of Ionath City. Night had fallen, turning the massive city dome into a sprawling convex of blackness. Lights lit up the sidewalks and cast moving reflections onto the passing grav-cabs, private cars and the wheeled cargo trucks that seemed to run at all hours of the day.

The agent watched. Target and bodyguard both wore plain sweatshirts with big hoods pulled up over their heads. It was both ironic and funny: ironic that the oversized individuals thought such a simple disguise could hide their identity and funny that — the majority of the time — it actually worked. Most sentients didn't want to bother someone that big, even if they did suspect the towering individuals might be the Ionath Krakens' star quarterback and their starting outside linebacker.

The agent slowly raised his palm. Dimmed icons floated over the skin. He tapped the ocular icon, then increased magnification and turned on the infrared overlay. It was silly, but due to the hoods he actually had to make sure they weren't some *other* seven-foot-tall Human and six-foot-tall, muscle-bound block of a Quyth Warrior.

Hardware and bioware embedded in the agent's eyes shifted and adjusted as his mods activated. He got a brief glimpse of a Human face inside the hood. The ocular implant digitized the image and fed it to the neural processor mod embedded at the base of the agent's spine. The agent's software didn't access the 'Net, but rather referred to a localized database grafted into his right hip; he couldn't risk accessing any remote servers, lest his stray signals be picked up and possibly cause his cover to be blown. The digitized images hit his processor's analytics engine, creating an algorithm of shapes, curves, angles and distances between known points such as the inside corners of the eyes, nostril width and the outside corners of the mouth. Even though the agent's optics caught only a shadowy bit of the target's face, the processor did the rest and fed the data to the screen embedded in his left iris.

[QUENTIN BARNES, IDENTIFIED, 100% ACCURACY.]

The agent then looked at the Human's bodyguard and repeated the process.

[CHOTO THE BRIGHT, IDENTIFIED, 89% ACCURACY.]

The processor had trouble with Quyth Warrior faces, but the agent wasn't concerned — wherever Quentin Barnes went, so went Choto the Bright.

The agent stayed still, waiting until the backs of Barnes and Bright were a good block away, then he activated the recorder embedded in his jaw.

"Bright Light and Shield One leaving the home of Michael Kimberlin. Note time, location and direction of subjects. Recommend full background check of Kimberlin, Michael, age thirty-one Earth years, former employee of the Jupiter Jacks, now employed by the Ionath Krakens. Continuing surveillance."

The agent started down the sidewalk after Barnes and Choto

but froze when Choto suddenly turned around. The agent stopped walking, an instant reaction, before remembering that standing still only drew attention; he started walking again. He kept his eyes fixed on the ground, but he touched his right index finger to his right thumb three times fast, activating the camera implant in the base knuckle of that finger. He then just let his hands move normally and watched the motion-stabilized image that played in his iris-screen.

The agent tried to stay calm as he walked toward the two sentients, appreciating once again just how *big* they were up close. Seeing them on holocast among other huge individuals made you forget their freakish size.

He drew close to the pair, then walked past them, turning his hand slightly in order to keep watching Choto. The Warrior was looking back the way he and Barnes had come, looking all around as if he thought someone was following them.

Someone was.

The agent kept walking. He hadn't been made. Even so, he couldn't risk following them anymore that night. Choto was a trained bodyguard, an excellent observer and a known killer. Someday, it might come down to the agent's superiors paying Gredok the Splithead to pull Choto away from bodyguard duty and leave Barnes exposed. A Warrior always listened to his *shamakath*, and Gredok always listened to money.

The agent turned down the first corner he came to, leaving Bright Light and Shield One behind. He clicked the tip of his tongue four times against the back of his teeth, activating his transmitter aug.

"Boss Four, this is Desert Sun."

There was a brief pause, a bit of annoying static, then the high-pitched voice of a Creterakian.

"Desert Sun, your signal is clear."

"I have to break off monitoring for now," the agent said. "Shield One seems alert. Bright Light probably headed back to his apartment. Have Cloud Two pick up surveillance to maintain tracking continuity."

"Understood, Desert Sun. Break off. Regain target monitoring tomorrow."

The signal clicked off. Creterakians didn't wait for permission.

The agent heard the flapping of leathery wings. He glanced up to see five bats soaring overhead in a tight formation. They wore ridiculous, garish, civilian clothes, but they were military: trained in espionage. The agent wanted to ask for a live feed, but that was stupid — live feeds could be intercepted, which could lead to the target learning he was under surveillance.

And besides — Quentin Barnes was a creature of habit. He was heading home and probably going to bed so he could be up early and hit the practice field before anyone else. No point in risking a blown cover for that.

The agent walked down Radius Four, lifting his palm as he did. He tapped on icons, ordering his kidney augs to start filtering out the stim he'd taken to stay alert. By the time he got back to his room, he'd be naturally sleepy. Mods could let you do just about anything, but sooner or later biological laws had to be obeyed. No need to push his body into the danger zone, not when this assignment might last months, if not years.

The Creterakian Ministry of Religion wanted to know everything that Quentin Barnes did. They wanted to monitor the growing influence of the CoQB. The CMR was nothing but analysts — when field work was required, that fell to the Non-Creterakian Intelligence Agency.

The NCIA paid the agent for this effort. And paid him *well*, more than a hundred times what he earned in his cover job. For that kind of money, the agent was more than happy to follow Quentin Barnes, day after day, night after night, city after city.

QUENTIN ROLLED LEFT, Becca out in front to block. He loved rolling out, especially left as that favored his dominant hand. A rollout let him move; instead of standing in the pocket, waiting to be hit, the defenders had to chase him down. A rollout also created more time for receivers to get open and, if the defense *did* catch up with him, gave him the option to tuck the ball and run — something he did exceedingly well.

His orange-jerseyed receivers ran their patterns: Crazy George Starcher in an *out-route* that took him on a shallow path toward the left sidelines; Milford on an *in-route* that took her 10 yards down the left sideline, then in at 90 degrees toward the middle of the field; and Hawick — who had lined up in the slot halfway between Starcher and Milford — on a *flag pattern*, where she ran 10 yards straight downfield, then angled toward the end zone's back-left corner.

Black-jerseyed defenders worked to stop the play. John Tweedy came in fast, ready to take on Becca to get to Quentin. Virak the Mean ran with George Starcher, covering the tight end while also staying close enough to come up hard if Quentin chose to run the ball and cross the line of scrimmage. Cornerback Berea ran step for step with Hawick, while Davenport, the strong safety, had come up to cover Milford's in-route. The defensive linemen chased after Quentin, but they were already too far behind to worry about.

Hawick turned on the jets and pulled a step ahead of Berea. Still running, Quentin gunned the ball 30 yards downfield, aiming for a spot some 25 feet above Hawick's head. Hawick sprang high on a path that would let her extend to her full length to catch the ball, then bring her down at the end zone's back left corner. Berea went up with her. Two long, flowing, graceful bodies — one in orange, one in black — battled for the ball, but Quentin had placed it perfectly: Hawick's fully extended tentacles were a good three or four inches beyond Berea's reach. Hawick snagged the ball out of the air, but Berea didn't give up on the play — as they descended, the cornerback pulled and ripped at Hawick's tentacles. Watching a Sklorno fall was like watching someone drop a cat; both bodies twisted and turned so they would land on their feet.

They hit the ground. Hawick landed with her right foot in the end zone's paint: touchdown.

Berea's effort to strip the ball made her land off-balance. She reached out with her right foot, extending it as if she thought she would land a split-second before she actually did. The foot hit, and the now-straight leg *snapped* in the wrong direction.

Quentin jogged to a stop, awash in disbelief. Even from 30 yards away, he could see the damage. Berea rolled on the ground, her tentacles clutching at her knee. Light from above played off the clear wetness leaking out from her black armor.

Doc Patah shot off the sidelines toward Berea, but Quentin didn't need a doctor to know the injury was bad, bad enough to take one of Ionath's starting defensive backs out of the lineup.

The only question was, when would she be back? No, there was a second question, a more ominous question — would she be able to return at all?

COACH HOKOR THE HOOKCHEST had two offices. One was up on the *Touchback*'s 18th deck, behind the practice field's orange end zone. The other, where Quentin and John Tweedy currently sat, was in Ionath Stadium, just off the central meeting room.

Coach Hokor decorated his office with holoframes showing action shots of his days coaching the Jupiter Jacks, the D'Kow War Dogs and the Chillich Spider-Bears. He also had images of dozens of players: it wasn't lost on Quentin that those players included Mitchell Fayed, Aka-Na-Tak, Stockbridge and Killik the Unworthy. He wondered if the images of players wearing the yellow and black of the Spider-Bears or the gold, silver and copper of the Jupiter Jacks had also died while Hokor was their coach.

Quentin's favorite part of the office, however, was the old-fashioned flat pictures showing ancient coaches from football's primitive formation: Tom Landry in his houndstooth-pattern hat, Bear Bryant surrounded by crimson-clad players in gear that didn't look like it would stop a stiff wind and a smiling Vince Lombardi riding atop the shoulder pads of two men from the Green Bay Packers.

He loved seeing those historic images, but at the moment they brought him no joy. He and John sat in front of Hokor's desk. The coach sat behind it, Doc Patah floating just above and behind his tiny upper-left shoulder. On Hokor's desk, a hologram of a Sklorno's see-through knee.

Sklorno's thighs were composed of a pair of long, thin femurs that connected on either side of a flexible shin. At that joint, computer-drawn red lines marked cracks in the black bones.

"Berea is out for the season," Doc Patah said. "This type of damage is a rare and unfortunate injury."

Sklorno were far and away the fastest, most athletic species in the GFL, but they were also the least durable. There was no telling what might injure them; they could play through big hit after big hit from powerful Human running backs and Quyth Warrior linebackers, then be taken out by something that looked relatively harmless. Berea had gone airborne literally *thousands* of times since Quentin had joined the team. In this one instance, however, she had just landed funny — and that was that.

John reached out a finger and poked at the hologram, as if it might become solid at any moment and his touching could heal his starting cornerback. "How about next season, Doc? Can she come back?"

Doc Patah's long pause said more than his words. "Possibly. I have successfully repaired these kinds of injuries before, when I was the chief surgeon for the Intergalactic Soccer Association, but my success rate was less than one might hope."

The Krakens' team doctor loved to brag about his skills. The fact that he now sounded so modest painted a picture of doom.

"*Less than one might hope,*" Quentin echoed. "Doc, exactly how many knee injuries like that did you operate on, and how many players made a full recovery?"

Doc again paused before answering. "I operated on sixteen such injuries," he said. "Two were able to return to full playing form."

John's fist slammed down on the desktop. His jaw muscles twitched. Quentin leaned away from him, just a bit — John looked like he wanted to kill something.

Coach Hokor waved his pedipalps over the desk; the hologram blinked out.

"That is the second cornerback we've lost this year," he said. "This time, one of our starters. The rookie Niami is clearly not yet first-string material, so we'll start Vacaville in Berea's place."

John shook his head. "Vacaville is a backup at best, Coach. We have to trade for another corner, and fast."

The Krakens had picked up Vacaville in free agency the year before, as a backup to Berea. Ionath's bad luck in the defensive backfield was starting to look like the work of the Low One: first Standish had become pregnant in the 2683 season, ending her career, then Tiburon had been cut due to fading abilities brought on by age, then Stockbridge's death in the game against the Prawatt, and now the season-ending injury to Berea.

Ten days until the regular season began. Every quality free-agent cornerback had already been signed. John was right: if the Krakens wanted to bolster their defense with a high-level corner, they had to make a trade.

"I agree," Hokor said. "And so does Gredok. To get a starting cornerback, we have to give up a quality player. There is one position where we have a quality player sitting on the bench — at quarterback. Gredok is soliciting offers for Don Pine."

Quentin leaned back in his chair. Gredok was a lot of things — brilliant, evil, deadly, corrupt — but one thing he was not was *slow*. Berea's injury wasn't even five hours old, and the Splithead was already trying to replace her.

And, yes, Don Pine was once again the logical choice. Where else were the Krakens deep enough to trade for a starting corner-back? Not on the offensive line; Quentin wasn't about to give up any of the five sentients who protected him, and the backup line-men weren't good enough to land a top-level defensive back. The Krakens had plenty of wide receivers, but Quentin also didn't want to lose the chemistry he had developed with his pass catchers.

Don was near the end of his career. He was also a two-time Galaxy Bowl-winning quarterback, and for that experience, some teams would give up just about anything.

"Depends on who we'd get," Quentin said. "And where he'd go."

"We have an offer from the Mars Planets," Hokor said. "They want to make another run at Tier One, and they feel Pine has three or even four good years left. They offered an even trade for Matsumoto."

John leaned across the desk so fast that Hokor flinched away.

"*Matsumoto*," John said. "As in, *All-Pro cornerback* Matsumoto? That one?"

"Correct," Hokor said. The coach stared at Quentin. "Barnes, your thoughts?"

Quentin didn't want to trade him for two reasons. First and foremost, Don Pine was a great insurance policy for the Krakens. In the GFL, injuries happened all the time. If Quentin went down for a game or two, Don could step in and win. If Yitzhak Goldman, the third-string QB, had to come in, that probably meant an Ionath loss.

The second reason, however, was that Quentin hadn't forgiven Don for his cowardice. Don had let Quentin hang, let an entire galaxy think Quentin was a cheater, a tanker, a criminal. Don had done that specifically so he could keep his reputation clean, to avoid bad press that might drop his trade value. And now, because of that cowardice, Don Pine might *start* for the Mars Planets? No. No way.

"We can't let Pine go," Quentin said.

John's jaw dropped "Q, are you *crazy*? Our defensive back-field is in real trouble. We lost Perth, Berea is out, Vacaville ain't that great, and on top of that, Rehoboth isn't playing that well at free safety. I think Sandpoint is going to beat her for the position. That gives us a weak cornerback *and* a rookie free safety. We won't be able to stop anyone. Matsumoto is an All-Pro. With her and Wahiawa at the corners, we can cover any team's number-one and number-two receivers. It's a night and day difference, and you know that."

Quentin did know that. If he faced a weak cornerback and a rookie free safety, he'd pick them apart all day long. Other quarterbacks would do the same.

But to let Pine go be a starter again …

"I know Pine is paid too much to be a backup," Quentin said. "But it's worth it — if I get hurt, do you guys really want to rely on Yitzhak?"

John shrugged. "Maybe we don't have to rely on Zak. Becca won a whole lotta games in Green Bay. Maybe it's time to give her a chance, see if she's ready to be your backup."

Becca. Since she'd earned All-Pro honors as a fullback last season, Quentin had almost forgotten about her history as a QB in the Tier Three NFL. He'd almost forgotten how she showed up to practices before anyone else, sometimes even before him, always with a ball in her hand. He'd almost forgotten about her use of the virtual practice field to keep her throwing skills sharp.

Xs and Os flashed through Quentin's mind. If they traded Don, picked up Matsumoto, moved Becca to backup ... that would make Kopor the Climber the starting fullback — he was a *big* drop-off from Becca, but he was still very good ... that would solve several problems at once ...

He shook his head. "We're not going to take the league's best fullback and use her as a backup quarterback, John. Her blocking is the reason your brother breaks those big runs. Without her our running game isn't the same." He stood up. "I'll talk to Vacaville. She's in the Church of ... I mean ... well, the church of *me*. Maybe I can get her to step up her game."

Hokor's eye swirled with black. "So if I tell Gredok that I want this trade, you will tell him not to make it?"

"That's right," Quentin said. He felt bad for saying it, because it would show, once again, that Gredok valued Quentin's opinion more than Hokor's. Hokor had lost power not to the owner, but to a *player* — it had to be both frustrating and humiliating.

"This is the right call, Coach," Quentin said. "And, I also think we should move the whole team to the *Touchback* for the last week of preseason practice. We can get away from all distractions and really focus on the defense. We concentrate on helping Vacaville and Sandpoint, get them ready for the season. What do you think, Coach?"

Hokor hopped off his chair. "Whatever you think is best,

Barnes. I'll handle the logistics myself. Why have Messal the Efficient handle it when I am available to manage whatever tasks you assign?"

Hokor walked out of the office. Quentin watched him go, feeling a bit dumbfounded at the coach's actions.

"Jeeze," Quentin said. "He's overacting a bit, don't you think? Everything is going to be fine."

John stood up. "As long as you get what you want, right, Q? Then everything is okay, right?"

He didn't wait for an answer. He stormed out of Hokor's office.

John was mad at him. Hokor was, too. Quentin didn't like it, but being a leader sometimes meant making hard decisions. Keeping Don Pine was the best move for the team.

Wasn't it?

12

Preseason Week Four:
January 22 to January 31

AT LEAST THEY STILL HAVE five days before the first game.

That was the only thing Quentin could think of to put a positive spin on the situation. The team was on the *Touchback*, practicing twice a day with position meetings at lunch and also after dinner. No families, no distractions — all day, every day, nothing but football.

Was it helping the defense? Yes, but not fast enough. Ionath's defensive line and linebacker corps had what it took to earn a Galaxy Bowl, no question. The defensive backfield, however, just wasn't cutting it.

Two of the DBs looked solid. Wahiawa was in her second year at starting cornerback. She was talented, a possible future All-Pro, but at just ten years old she was young and developing. Davenport was back for her fifth straight year as the Krakens' starting strong safety. Her abilities were already starting to fade due to hundreds of hard hits, but she made up for that by playing smart and capitalizing on tons of experience with Hokor's defensive schemes.

If the other two DBs had been as good as Wahiawa and

Davenport, Quentin wouldn't have been as worried. Trouble was, Vacaville and Sandpoint weren't even close.

Quentin took the snap, dropped back five steps and planted. His internal clock was already ticking, measuring the position of his orange-clad offensive linemen and the angles of attack taken by the black-clad Krakens defense. He looked downfield, tracking his receivers on their patterns.

Wahiawa had excellent pass coverage on Hawick, his number-one receiver. Milford — his number-two receiver — drew coverage from Vacaville. Quentin watched Milford streak down the right sideline. She cut in to the left. Quentin pump-faked, whipping the ball forward but not letting it out of his hand. Vacaville bought the fake, turning to intercept a pass that didn't come. Milford kept going, leaving Vacaville behind. Quentin lofted a soft, 60-yard pass to the back corner of the end zone. Wide open, Milford didn't even have to jump to catch it.

Coach Hokor's little golf cart floated down near field level. "Vacaville, you *idiot!*" The practice field's sound system amplified his words. "That's the fourth time today you have bit on the pump-fake! Is something wrong with your brain?"

Vacaville looked up to the floating golf cart as if Hokor were a God. Well, in fact, to her Hokor *was* a God, an angry God that she had failed yet again. She trembled, then fell to the ground, shaking with terror.

"Pleaseplease do not smush me Hokorthehookchest I have failed you I *havefailedhavefailed*!"

Quentin sighed and jogged toward her. While it was easy to motivate the Sklorno, disciplining them was tricky. He tried to imagine what it would be like for the High One to suddenly materialize out of thin air, then scream at him for throwing a bad pass.

"Take it easy," Quentin said when he reached the trembling cornerback. "It'll be okay." He picked her up and set her on her feet. The other Sklorno twittered and jumped because His Holiness the Godling Quentin Barnes had just laid hands on a disciple. Something like that, anyway. Actually, he wasn't sure if he was a *godling* or now he was officially a *god*.

Vacaville stared at Quentin, then started to tremble anew.

"Oh, knock it off," Quentin said. "Stop that crap right now."

The cornerback's trembling faded, but not all the way.

"Listen to me," Quentin said. "In five days we take the field against the Isis Ice Storm. What do you know about their quarterback Paul Infante?"

"He is great-great-*great*!" Vacaville said. "I pray that I will catch his blessings for a holy pick-six!"

The cornerback dreamed of intercepting Infante and taking it back for a touchdown.

"That's good," Quentin said. "That's a good thing to pray for. But you're too eager. Infante will use the same pump-fakes I'm using. If you're trying to get the interception and a *holy pick-six*, you'll bite on that pump-fake every time. You play your receiver, *not* the ball, okay?"

"Yes, oh holy Quentinbarnes!"

She sprinted off to join the other defensive backs, who had gathered at a respectful distance. They all twittered and jumped up and down, as if Vacaville had just single-handedly won the Galaxy Bowl.

Five days until the Ice Storm. Quentin, John and Hokor had to find a way to get Vacaville to play at a higher level. If she didn't, Infante and his talented receivers — Angoon and Füssen — would tear the Krakens apart.

Quentin tried to chase away his doubts, but if Vacaville didn't step up, and if Sandpoint's play at free safety didn't improve, then the Krakens could very well open the '85 season with a loss.

HOKOR'S OFFICE AT IONATH STADIUM reflected his career and his personality. His office on the *Touchback*, on the other hand, had no art at all — just a glass wall that overlooked the practice field eighteen decks below, and several holotanks that always seemed to be playing highlights of players from across the league.

Quentin, Don Pine and John Tweedy sat across from Hokor's desk. They had come directly here at the close of practice and still wore their leg armor and Koolsuits. Hokor sat behind the desk, his pedipalp hands waving through the holograms of Krakens players that floated above his desktop.

They had just finished their last preseason practice. The Krakens had to submit a final, fifty-three-player regular-season roster to the league. Any player not good enough to make the roster had to be cut.

Hokor paused on a picture of Wan-A-Tagol, a Ki defensive end. The Leader's black-striped yellow fur fluffed a little, then lay flat. Quentin had come to know his coach's mannerisms — while he was all business and talked with a gruff, no-nonsense voice, he genuinely felt bad for the players who had to go.

"With the way Cliff Frost played last year, we don't need a fifth defensive end," the coach said. "Wan-A-Tagol's services are no longer required."

John nodded. "That makes sense, Coach. Cliffy is coming on strong."

It didn't seem to bother John at all that Wan-A was going to be cut. Quentin remembered the Ki's hard-nosed play last season when Ibrahim Khomeni got hurt. Playing hard, though, wasn't enough — in the GFL, if you didn't have the skill, you were gone.

Hokor called up a list of twelve defensive backs.

"We only have room for ten," Hokor said. "Two have to go. Barnes?"

It fell to him? But that, too, made sense — he was the one who threw against these players every day in practice, the one who knew which ones could cover and which ones posed no threat to his passes or his receivers.

Quentin reread the names, even though he already knew who wasn't good enough.

"Millington," he said. A free agent, Millington had lasted only two weeks. She didn't have the skill, and those were the breaks.

"Agreed," Hokor said. "And the other?"

Quentin sighed. "Saugatuck," he said. She was twenty-two years old, a fourteen-year veteran, and her career was over. "She just doesn't have the speed or the reaction time."

Don nodded, as did John.

"Done," Hokor said. "We'll move Emmitsburgh from free safety to safety to replace Saugatuck as Davenport's backup. Saugatuck spent her entire career with the organization. If she chooses to retire instead of trying to find another team, Gredok will give her the white jersey when we return to Ionath City."

Quentin felt a little better about that. Saugatuck could retire as a Kraken. It was a token of respect and kindness — seemed hard to believe Gredok could be capable of such a thing, but clearly he was.

Coach Hokor called up a new list of names. Quentin's heart sank further when he realized they were his receivers.

"We have seven wide receivers," Hokor said. "Considering our problems with the defensive secondary, we need enough depth there to make it through the season. Mezquitic is already on the practice squad. It's time to move Richfield there as well, as her abilities have faded with age."

Of the fifty-three players on the final roster, forty-five were "active" and dressed for games. The "inactive" players could practice, but on Sundays they stayed in their street clothes. Richfield was also twenty-two and had joined the franchise the same year as Saugatuck.

"Richfield's our kick returner," Quentin said. "We need her for that."

Hokor tapped at the floating icons above his desk. A game-holo flared to life, showing a Sklorno dressed in a yellow uniform with horizontal gray stripes. A gray magnifying glass decorated the side of the yellow helmet. He recognized the player — Niami, Ionath's rookie cornerback. Niami stood in her own end zone, looking up to the sky, settling under a descending kick. She caught it, then took off with that mind-boggling speed only Sklorno possessed. She cut right, ducked under a purple-clad defender, spun around another, then cut left into the open field and was gone. Touchdown, a 102-yard return.

"Niami returned kicks for the Archaeologists," Hokor said. "Richfield no longer possesses breakaway speed. Niami does."

The holos and sprint times spoke for themselves, and there was no arguing Hokor's logic. Still, Quentin's heart broke for the two lifelong Krakens.

Hokor leaned back in his chair. "This is never an enjoyable event, but it needs to be done. I will call Saugatuck here right now and talk to her personally. You three get down to the locker room and gather the rest of the team. It's time to finalize the roster and move on with the season."

FIFTY-FIVE PLAYERS IN VARIOUS STAGES of undress waiting in the communal locker room. They all knew what was coming. The posting of the final roster marked the official end of the preseason. Quentin watched his teammates, knowing that the next few minutes would bring both unmatched joy and also heart-breaking loss.

Coach Hokor the Hookchest entered, Messal the Efficient at his side. The Quyth Leader stopped at the holoboard. He looked out at the team.

"Krakens, I will now post the final roster," he said. "Those of you who made the team, I look forward to a successful season as we vie for the championship. If this is your first year with the organization, see Messal the Efficient about living arrangements. If your name is *not* on the board, come to my office immediately."

And that was that. Hokor turned to the holoboard and tapped a few icons; the rosters appeared. Most of the starters knew their name was on the roster and didn't bother to look. They already started filtering into their species-specific locker rooms, ready to clean up and head home for the night.

Four weeks of practice had made most of the second stringers *almost* sure of their roster spot, but they looked anyway, perhaps just to see that final confirmation. There were more than a few sighs of relief, then those players also headed for their locker rooms.

Some players saw that they'd been named to the practice squad. That meant they wouldn't play on Sunday unless someone in front of them got hurt, opening up an active-roster spot.

For the second year in a row, Quentin watched Gan-Ta-Kapil, the backup center. At sixty-one years old, the Ki had been playing GFL ball for twenty-two seasons — longer than Quentin had been alive. Quentin smiled when he saw Gan-Ta sag with relief; the Ki was on the practice squad, his job safe for at least one more season.

More players filtered away from the holoboard, leaving only two standing there, searching for their names: Ki defensive end Wan-A-Tagol and Millington, the Sklorno defensive back.

Wan-A was only twenty-five years old. After four seasons with the Krakens, the team had cut him loose. All five of his black, equidistant eyes closed. A soft, mournful sound came out of his vocal tubes, then he scuttled out of the locker room. Quentin knew something about Ki body language; Wan-A walked out with pride, the Ki equivalent of holding his head up high. He had given it everything he had and had nothing to be ashamed of.

Millington's eyestalks sagged. She lifted them to read the holoboard one more time and — still not finding her name — weakly followed Wan-A out of the locker room.

Quentin heard commotion from the Human locker room. Screams of joy, players boasting, the sounds barely muffled by the closed door. They were happy. Of course they were — no Humans had been cut.

He stared at the holoboard for a few moments more. His name was there, of course. But someday, it would not be. The happy Humans in the locker room? They, too, would someday be on the outside looking in.

Someday, but not *this* day.

Life was short, careers were shorter — his Human teammates had earned the right to celebrate, and so had he. Ionath had chosen its warriors. Quentin Barnes smiled and walked into the locker room to join his teammates.

QUENTIN WALKED INTO HIS APARTMENT on the *Touchback*, his heart heavy, his mind on the ceremony he'd witnesses just a few minutes earlier. He slumped onto his couch and stared at the framed jersey of Mitchel Fayed that hung on his wall.

The preseason was over. Tomorrow, the *Touchback* would depart on a five-and-a-half-day trip to Tower for the season opener against the Isis Ice Storm. Most of the team had already headed down to Ionath City for a much-deserved day off. The team had spent a week in orbit and would spend another eleven days away from home for the round trip to and from Tower — one day off to see family and friends or take care of personal business wasn't much to ask.

Quentin wasn't going anywhere. Danny Lundy would take care of any personal business, all of his friends played for the Krakens, and until his sister wanted to see him, he had no family to speak of. He'd spend the day and night in his room, studying up on the Ice Storm defense.

Most of the players heading down would be right back here the following morning. Most, but not Saugatuck. This shuttle ride down was her last. Gredok had given her the white jersey, symbolic of a player who retired as a Kraken. Quentin had been stunned to hear Gredok deliver a heartfelt speech about Saugatuck, who the crime lord had signed fourteen years earlier.

Age is the thief that robs us of life, so slowly we don't see it being taken from us, Gredok had said as the entire team listened. *That horrid theft comes much faster in our chosen profession, where the longest of careers last but a handful of seasons.*

Gredok had then talked of Saugatuck's loyalty, recalled some of her highlights and accomplishments. He was a master manipulator, but the way he spoke revealed that he genuinely cared. As strange as it seemed, Gredok sounded sad, but also proud of his retiring player. And then, the gangster had leveled everyone with his final comment:

The thief may have stolen your years, but it can't steal your memory. The Krakens will never forget.

A touching, beautiful send-off that wet the eyes of Humans and HeavyGs, made Warrior pedipalps tremble and left all of the Sklorno quivering on the shuttle bay deck.

Quentin didn't know how Gredok could be such an evil, self-serving jackass to him and such an eloquent class act to Saugatuck. Maybe if Quentin lasted fourteen years, he'd get a similar speech.

That is, *if* Gredok was still around for Quentin's fourteenth season, which wouldn't happen if Quentin had anything to say about it.

He walked to the kitchen and grabbed a mag can of Miller. He popped the top, felt the can frost up in his hand, then raised it toward Mitchell's jersey.

"To you, my friend. Tonight, you and I hang out."

Quentin took a sip, then called up the Krakens playbook and got to work.

Ionath Krakens 2685 Roster

No.	Name	Pos	Ht / Ln	Wt	Age	Exp
10	Barnes, Quentin	QB	7-0	360	21	3
27	Breedsville	CB	8-3	282	12	3
79	Bud-O-Shwek	C	13-1	630	64	28
65	Cay-O-Kiware	LG	12-0	625	35	9
67	Chat-E-Riret	DT	12-2	632	31	4
6	Cheboygan	WR	8-0	360	8	1
54	Choto the Bright	LB	6-0	400	30	6
69	Crawford, Tim	DT	7-10	565	20	1
49	Darkeye, Samuel	LB	6-5	310	24	4
22	Davenport	SS	8-0	265	14	6
25	Emitsburgh	FS	8-5	275	12	5
96	Frost, Cliff	DE	6-11	532	27	5
51	Gan-Ta-Kapil	C	11-11	563	61	22
14	Goldman, Yitzhak	QB	6-4	265	32	8
13	Halawa	WR	9-6	320	10	2
80	Hawick	WR	8-8	282	15	7
95	Khomeni, Ibrahim	DE	6-10	525	26	5
76	Kill-O-Yowet	LT	12-2	513	37	11
71	Kimberlin, Michael	OG	8-0	615	31	11
85	Kobayasho, Yotaro	TE	7-1	380	36	7
28	Kopor the Climber	FB	6-0	415	24	4
37	Luanda	CB	7-10	280	13	2
92	Mai-An-Ihkole	DT	10-11	650	44	14
20	Martinez, Jay	RB	6-2	304	24	2
16	Marval, Pete	FB	6-7	381	23	0
83	Mezquitic	WR	8-5	295	14	7
91	Michnik, Alexsandar	DE	6-11	525	32	11
82	Milford	WR	9-0	305	10	3
38	Montagne, Rebecca	FB	6-6	330	20	2
2	Morningstar, Arioch	P/K	5-10	185	28	9
93	Mum-O-Killowe	DT	12-6	600	18	3
26	Murphy, Yassoud	RB	6-6	315	27	3
21	Niami	CB	7-9	285	9	0
72	Palmer, Rich	DE	8-1	425	19	1
8	Pine, Donald	QB	6-6	245	33	15
64	Pishor the Fang	LB	6-4	400	19	0
66	Procknow, Jason	DT	7-8	612	19	0
39	Rehoboth	FS	8-3	300	18	10
88	Richfield	WR	8-5	273	21	14
33	Sandpoint	FS	8-6	295	10	0
57	Shayat the Thick	LB	5-11	439	35	5
62	Sho-Do-Thikit	LG	13-1	600	41	18
70	Shun-On-Won	RG	12-1	585	28	2
63	Shut-O-Dital	LT	12-8	580	23	4
87	Starcher, George	TE	7-6	400	31	10
11	Tara the Freak	WR	6-3	360	22	1
50	Tweedy, John	LB	6-6	310	27	7
48	Tweedy, Ju	RB	6-6	345	25	6
23	Vacaville	CB	8-7	335	15	4
58	Virak the Mean	LB	6-2	375	43	3
75	Vu-Ko-Will	RT	11-11	579	50	9
31	Wahiawa	CB	9-6	320	10	2
73	Zer-Eh-Detak	RT	12-8	690	20	3

BOOK THREE

The Regular Season

February 1 to
May 3, 2685

13

Week One:
Ionath Krakens at
Isis Ice Storm

"GOOD ONE, Q," John Tweedy said. "The way you arched your back gave you great form. I'd put that in your top ten."

"Yeah," Ju Tweedy said. "Mega-great form. And that puke-grunt really came from the diaphragm. I give it a nine-point-six."

"Nine-point-seven," John said.

Quentin shook his head as he pulled the plastic bag out of the golden puke bucket. "Did you guys know those lines get funnier every time you use them?"

John and Ju smiled and exchanged a high five. Quentin shook his head as he tied the bag closed. They actually thought it was a compliment.

He looked out the observation deck's floor-to-ceiling window. Out there floated the planet Tower, home of the Isis Ice Storm, the Krakens' first opponent of the season.

The planet looked like a globe of yellow glass, cracked and chipped with age, lit up from within by an endless sprawl of civilization that lay beneath the thick, unmoving ice. A miles-high mountain rose up from that ice, completely covered with lights that followed the slope down and spread out across the sea floor.

Somewhere under that glowing surface, there was a football stadium. And in that stadium, Quentin's first step to immortality.

"This is it, guys," he said. "The road to the Galaxy Bowl begins right here."

John slapped him on the shoulder, his grin wide and his eyes wild. "And our road to All-Pro-Ville, right, Q?"

Quentin nodded. Since the end of last season, Quentin, John and Ju had made a quiet pact to work harder, to play harder, to dig deeper, to do whatever it took to lead the Krakens to a championship and, along the way, grab the ultimate individual honor the sport had to offer.

The ship's computer-voice echoed through the viewing bay's speakerfilm:

[**FIRST SHUTTLE FLIGHT PASSENGERS TO THE LANDING BAY.**]

The time for talking and dreaming had ended. The season had arrived. Together, Ma Tweedy's three boys walked out of the observation deck and headed for the shuttle that would take them down to Isis.

QUENTIN SMOOTHED THE SEALS on his Koolsuit. He flexed, he twisted — as always, within seconds the suit seemed to be part of him, one and the same with his skin.

He looked to the floor in front of his locker. He had laid out his armor, his helmet and his orange jersey so that it looked like a very flat man was lying there. He imagined himself in that gear, wearing that jersey, imagined himself running, throwing, hitting, scoring ... leading his team to victory.

This is where it begins ...

One piece at a time, he donned the black armor, his fingers admiring the feel of curved plates, of the thick padding beneath. Shoulder pads and arm protection first, micro-sensors perfectly adjusting the fit from the backs of his hands up to his neck, covering his chest and his shoulder blades. The lower-torso wrap came next, covering his back, his ribs and his stomach, locking into his shoulder armor so perfectly that no seam remained. Next, the hip and leg armor that shielded him down to his ankles. Finally, he stepped into his armored shoes and waited as the micro-motors locked them into his shin guards, completing his suit save for two things.

Quentin picked up the orange jersey. His fingers traced the white-trimmed black letters just below the collar that spelled out KRAKENS and below them, the larger 1 and 0 that made up his number.

And they will all know my name.

He slid the jersey on over his armor, yanking it down, feeling the tight Kevlar fabric make his armor just a bit more snug.

Finally, he reached into his locker and pulled out the true symbol of the Ionath Krakens: his helmet. The shell was such a deep, glossy black that he could see his own distorted face staring back at him. The bright-orange facemask looked like frozen fire. His fingertips caressed the red-trimmed orange splash on the forehead, traced the six orange "tentacles" that reached from that splash to blazing white tips ending on the helmet's back curve.

He stared at it, then pulled it on.

Quentin Barnes turned and looked at his Human teammates. They had been standing there quietly, waiting for him to finish his ritual. John, Ju, Yassoud, Don, Yitzhak, Yotaro Kobayasho, Jay Martinez, Samuel Darkeye, Arioch Morningstar and even George Starcher, his face painted an intricate plaid pattern of orange and black.

Quentin slammed his right fist against his chest so hard the clacking armor sounded like a gunshot.

"Let's go get the rest of our team," he said. "And then let's go kick some Ice Storm ass."

"SENTIENTS OF ALL RACES!"

The announcer's voice echoed through the underwater stadium, barely louder than the 150,000 Isis fans that couldn't wait for the season to begin.

"Please welcome our visiting team, the Ionath ... KRAK-ennnnnns!"

Quentin and John rushed out of the tunnel onto the deep-blue field, the rest of the Orange and the Black close behind. Isis Stadium, more commonly known as *the Fishtank*. As Quentin ran for the sidelines, he looked up to the stadium's clear dome high above and the thousands of densely packed black-striped blue Leekee swimming on the other side. He glanced at the stadium's three decks, which were mostly filled with fans garbed in white, blue and chrome, but also held a good-sized complement of screaming sentients wearing orange and black. Between both the first and second and the second and third decks were fifteen-foot-high layers of glass: the Fishtank's liquid luxury boxes that catered to Leekee, Dolphins, Harrah, Whitokians and Amphibs.

Quentin reached the sideline of this temple and raised his right fist high. The team gathered around him even as he heard the announcer begin calling the Ice Storm onto the field, even as he heard over a hundred thousand sentients roar for their heroes.

"Krakens!" he screamed, his explosive voice loud enough for his teammates to hear. "It all begins here, let's do this!"

He spoke, they answered, and together they prepared for battle.

THIRD DOWN AND THREE, Ionath's first offensive drive of the season.

Quentin lined up behind Bud-O-Shwek, his center, and stared out at the white-helmeted enemy. The Ice Storm players' chrome facemasks and the logos on their helmets' left side — six metal-blue swords in a snowflake formation — reflected the Fishtank's bright lights.

Their jerseys blazed white at the shoulders, fading to a light blue at the stomach that matched the color of their waist armor. The gradient continued down their bodies, the light blue darkening until it was almost black at their feet. Dark-blue-trimmed chrome numbers sparkled, as did chrome belts.

Quentin slid his hands beneath his center.

"Red, twenty-one!"

He looked right, as he would on every play that afternoon, making sure he laid eyes on Ryan Nossek. Quentin had no intention of being the HeavyG's sixth career fatality.

"Red, twenty-*one*!"

Ju and Becca in an I-formation behind him. Hawick wide left, Milford wide right, Crazy George Starcher lined up at left tight end.

"Hut-*hut*!"

The ball slapped into his hands. Quentin stepped back with his right foot and faked a handoff to Becca, then kept turning right and rolled out to the left — *away* from Nossek.

He saw Isis linebacker Chaka the Brutal covering Crazy George Starcher, one on one. George recognized that coverage and reacted as he'd been taught, breaking off the route and streaking downfield at full speed. Chaka turned quick, ran with the big tight end stride for stride. Chaka's excellent coverage would have been good enough against ninety percent of the league's quarterbacks — but not good enough against someone who threw as hard and as accurately as Quentin Barnes.

Still running hard-left, Quentin gunned the ball. Chaka jumped for it, but too late — the ball whipped past him before he elevated high enough to stop it. Unlike Chaka, however, George knew how fast Quentin could throw, had seen it in practice every day and was already reaching to the full height of his 7-foot-6 frame before the ball even left Quentin's fingers. The pigskin slammed into Starcher's hands hard enough to kill most mammals, but the face-painting tight end's strong grip stopped the ball in mid-flight. Without breaking stride, George tucked the ball into his right arm and kept on sprinting.

Santa Cruz, the Ice Storm's safety, came up to make the stop. The four-hundred pound Crazy George Starcher covered the ball with both arms, lowered his head and plowed Santa Cruz over. She was still tumbling backward when he crossed the goal line for a 36-yard touchdown.

The Ionath fans who had made the trip cheered wildly, but

they were drowned out by the Ice Storm fans who booed at such an early, seemingly effortless score. Quentin smiled. When on the road, boos were often the sweetest music you could hear. He knelt and plucked a few blades of the deep-blue plant that made up the Fishtank's field. He inhaled deep, taking in a scent of sawdust and sand. He stood, scattered the blue plants to the wind, then jogged to the Ionath sidelines as the extra-point team ran on.

The Krakens first drive saw them up by a touchdown, and Quentin was just getting warmed up.

THE ICE STORM CAME BACK HARD. Starting from his own 33-yard line, quarterback Paul Infante immediately went to work against Vacaville. His threw his first pass up high to her side, which receiver Angoon brought down for a 15-yard gain. Infante spread the pain on the second play, hitting Füssen on a deep cross right in front of rookie Sandpoint for another 17 yards. The white-, blue- and silver-clad Ice Storm tried running back Scott Wilson twice — he was stuffed at the line of scrimmage both times, first by Mum-O-Killowe and then by a run-blitzing John Tweedy.

On third-and-10, Angoon lined up wide left. The Krakens coverage had her marked one on one by Vacaville. Infante took the snap and dropped back. Angoon sprinted 10 yards downfield and turned for the curl.

"Don't bite on it," Quentin said to himself, but he already knew what was coming.

Infante pump-faked; Vacaville rushed in to jump the pass. Angoon turned and sprinted up the sidelines. Infante launched a bullet. Sandpoint was too slow coming over to help on coverage, and Angoon carried the ball in for a 40-yard touchdown.

Extra point good, game tied 7-7.

RYAN NOSSEK SPLIT a double-team, sliding between right guard Michael Kimberlin and right tackle Vu-Ko-Will. The pocket collapsed around Quentin. He stopped thinking and just reacted.

He ducked as Nossek swung a tree-trunk-sized arm at his head. Nossek's forearm caught the top of Quentin's helmet — even the grazing blow sent him stumbling. Nossek's momentum carried him by. Quentin regained his feet. He felt pressure from the left, so he shot forward, scrambling to get as many yards as he could. Five steps took him through the line. Linebacker Chaka the Brutal rushed in for the tackle.

Quentin's three seasons of upper-tier ball had taught him the Quyth Warriors were too agile for head-and-shoulder fakes or stutter-steps. You had to run them over — which was a good way to get knocked out — or you had to make contact and spin. Quentin stutter-stepped left then right then left. The linebacker's effort to match the move slowed his forward momentum. Quentin covered the ball with both arms and slammed his head forward like a battering ram. Chaka met him helmet to helmet, both pedipalp and middle arms reaching, but in the instant before they made contact Quentin was already spinning. The impact was enough to bounce Chaka back, just a bit, giving Quentin enough room to complete the violent 360-degree turn and continue downfield.

Something hit Quentin from the right, making him stumble left. He switched the ball to his left arm then pushed out hard with his right forearm. He felt something grab, rip, then fall away.

He saw the two Ice Storm cornerbacks trying to reach him, but they were fighting off blocks from Cheboygan and Halawa, Ionath's oversized third and fourth wide receivers. The only player left who could stop him was Santa Cruz, the Isis safety.

She came at him fast but under control: she had learned from last year's game, knew that she couldn't take Quentin head-on. Quentin juked left, then cut right, switching the ball to his right arm and stiff-arming with his left, but Santa Cruz slid under his outstretched hand and wrapped her tentacles around his body. Suddenly Quentin was carrying an extra three hundred pounds. He managed another four steps before the other Sklorno defensive backs brought him down from behind.

He picked himself up off the turf and looked at the yard-marker — first-and-10 on the 8-yard line. He'd scrambled for 42 yards.

On the next play, Quentin took the snap and turned right. Becca shot by before he handed the ball off to Ju Tweedy. Becca placed a surgical block on the outside linebacker, giving Ju just enough room to slip inside. Chaka the Brutal wrapped him up immediately, but Ju already had a head of steam — he carried Chaka with him into the end zone.

Ionath 14, Isis 7.

AT THE HALF, THE KRAKENS LED 17-14. Quentin had been sacked once — you couldn't avoid Ryan Nossek forever — but other than that he'd put up an excellent first half: 13-of-17 for 213 yards, one touchdown, no interceptions. Ju had 56 yards rushing, giving the Krakens nearly 300 yards total offense in the first half alone.

But while the offense clicked, the defense struggled. Isis running back Scott Wilson had 11 carries for 34 yards. Infante was carving up the Krakens' secondary. He was 16-of-21 for 185 yards and two touchdown passes. The Krakens' defensive line was putting pressure on him — he'd been sacked three times and hurried another five — but it wasn't enough to stop Infante from completing passes against the defensive secondary.

Quentin hoped the defense could find a solution in the second half.

QUENTIN FELT THE PRESSURE coming, but his internal clock told him he had just enough time to get the pass off. He stepped up and threw. The ball had barely left his fingers when a warship smashed into him from the right. Giant arms wrapped around his chest, lifted, then drove him hard to the ground, so hard that snot flew out of his nose.

"Hello again, my little friend," said Ryan Nossek.

The crowd's boo/roar told Quentin that the pass had been caught for a touchdown — his third of the game. Quentin felt a moan of pain building up in his chest, but he fought it down: he wouldn't give Nossek the satisfaction.

"Hey, buddy," Quentin said. "Hear that booing sound? Sounds like my pass went for six."

"Oh, you can still hear? I guess I didn't hit you hard enough."

Big hands lifted Quentin up like a child and set him on his feet. Nossek patted Quentin on the shoulder pad.

"I'll do better next time," the HeavyG said. "And nice pass."

Nossek jogged to the sidelines. Quentin looked up to the scoreboard. It was blurry. He closed his eyes, then blinked a few times. He looked again and saw the score had put Ionath ahead 29-26. Just 2:42 remained in the game — they almost had the win.

Quentin jogged to the sidelines. Arioch Morningstar nailed the extra point, putting the Krakens up by four. Isis needed a touchdown to win.

Now if the defense could just make a stop.

THE FISHTANK VIBRATED with sonic energy. Feet of all species pounded on the stands, Leekee tails slapped against the stadium's clear, domed roof. Quentin had been in loud stadiums before, but the underwater arena concentrated the noise of 150,000 fans into an ear-hammering roar.

Isis quarterback Paul Infante walked to the line. His white-helmeted head looked left, then right, taking in the Krakens' defense. Infante's right sleeve had been torn off, revealing the black Kevlar body armor beneath and the bloody, white skin beneath that. That wound had come courtesy of a Mum-O-Killowe sack. The broken chrome facemask? That came when Alexsandar Michnik and Ibrahim Khomeni had reached Infante at the same time, smashing him between a thousand pounds of angry HeavyG defensive end. Infante had been sacked six times in all, and yet the guy kept getting up. Quentin had to respect the opposing quarterback's performance; Infante didn't have a great arm and couldn't run for crap, but he was tougher than a mining shovel.

Third-and-six on the Krakens' 45-yard line, just six seconds left in the game. Isis had one play left, and it had to be a touch-down. Ju Tweedy reached up and grabbed Quentin's jersey at the shoulder pad, lightly pulling Quentin left and right, an unconscious, nervous reaction as both men hoped for a sack, an incomplete pass, anything that would give them the victory.

Infante took the snap and dropped back five yards. The orange- and black-clad Krakens' defensive line crashed against the blue, white and silver Ice Storm blockers. John Tweedy and Virak the Mean both blitzed. Infante stood tall, giving his receivers time to get downfield. Mum-O overpowered his blocker and came clean — Infante knew the hit was coming, but stepped up strong and launched a deep pass. Quentin saw Infante go down hard, then followed the ball's path.

Wide receiver Angoon cut toward the end zone's back corner. Vacaville was in great position, running step for step with the receiver. Sandpoint, Ionath's free safety, was on her way over from the deep middle of the field and would probably arrive just as the ball came down. The crowd roared loud enough to split atoms. In the end zone, Angoon leapt high. Vacaville matched. They soared into the air, a floating, black- and white-striped Harrah ref fluttering close by. Angoon reached for the ball, but before it arrived Vacaville grabbed Angoon's tentacles. The ball shot past as the two players dropped back down — dropping down with them, a yellow flag thrown by the ref.

The crowd screamed until the stadium shuddered. Every Kraken groaned. Quentin slapped his helmet so hard it hurt his hand. Ju stomped his right foot down hard, over and over.

The zebe floated up and faced the home bleachers. His mechanical voice echoed through the stadium's sound system.

"Pass interference, number forty, defense. The penalty occurred in the end zone. Therefore, the ball will be placed on the two-yard line." The zebe turned to face the Krakens' end zone, then extended one mouth-flap straight forward. "First down."

The clock read 0:00. A game couldn't end on a defensive penalty, so even though there was no time left, Isis would get one final play. John and the defense had to make a stop.

The Ice Storm huddled up. Quentin saw five wide receivers and no running back. Hokor saw the same thing; he sent Luanda in and pulled Choto out — a linebacker swapped for a defensive back.

The Ice Storm came to the line. Sure enough, no running back and no fullback, five wide receivers spread sideline to sideline. Infante stood six yards behind center.

The Krakens defensive backs lined up one on one, each taking a receiver. They would play outside-in, stopping out routes and corner fades, counting on the linebackers for help with any slants or crossing patterns.

Infante barked out the signals. Quentin could only tell by the quarterback's shaking shoulders, as nothing could be heard over the crowd's demand for a score.

The ball flipped back to Infante. The lines smashed into each other. Infante raised the ball to his right ear, paused a half-second, then fired the ball low to the left for Füssen.

Füssen dropped to the ground, falling just under the rookie Sandpoint. Sandpoint tried to block the ball but couldn't get down in time to stop such a perfectly thrown pass.

Füssen landed on the goal line, ball clutched tight to her chest. Sandpoint landed on top of her, ripping at the ball.

A striped ref shot in, wing-flaps making it zip through the air until it hovered only inches from Füssen and Sandpoint. The zebe looked, then pointed both mouth-flaps to the sky.

Touchdown.

The stadium shook with madness. Quentin sighed and looked up to the clear dome roof, to a mad, swirling cluster of thousands of blue Leekee swimming over and under each other.

Isis 32, Ionath 30, no time left on the clock.

Game over.

GFL WEEK ONE ROUNDUP
Courtesy of Galaxy Sports Network

Home		Away	
Buddha City Elite	17	Alimum Armada	13
Hittoni Hullwalkers	18	**Coranadillana Cloud Killers**	21
Isis Ice Storm	32	Ionath Krakens	30
Orbiting Death	42	Themala Dreadnaughts	10
Vik Vanguard	20	**To Pirates**	24
Yall Criminals	35	Wabash Wolfpack	14
Shorah Warlords	9	**Bartel Water Bugs**	17
D'Kow War Dogs	28	**Bord Brigands**	31
Texas Earthlings	17	Jang Atom Smashers	0
New Rodina Astronauts	3	**Jupiter Jacks**	10
Neptune Scarlet Fliers	14	**Sheb Stalkers**	17

The opening week of the 2685 Tier One season brought plenty of surprises and some stellar performances.

The Isis Ice Storm (1-0) made an early bid to maintain the franchise's winning ways with a thrilling 32-30 win over Planet Division rival Ionath (0-1). Ionath quarterback Quentin Barnes posted a 24-for-30, three-touchdown, 341-yard performance, but it wasn't enough to lead his team past Isis. A pass-interference call in the end zone as time expired gave the Ice Storm a final play on the 2-yard line with zero time left on the clock. Isis quarterback Paul Infante hit receiver Füssen for the winning touchdown pass.

In a rare occurrence, both newly promoted teams claimed victory in their opening Tier One games. The Buddha City Elite (1-0) won a close match over the Alimum Armada (0-1) thanks to a ten-catch, two-touchdown, 88-yard performance by tight end Rick Warburg. A sold-out Infinity Coliseum crowd celebrated the Purist Nation's first Tier One win in fifteen years.

Not to be outdone, the Sheb Stalkers (1-0) won that franchise's first-ever Tier One game as coach Jako the Mug orchestrated a shocking 17-14 road-game upset over Neptune (0-1). Sheb running back Tony Miller anchored a ground-control offense that kept the ball out of the hands of Scarlet Fliers QB Adam Gurri. Miller ran for 214 yards on 32 carries.

The OS1 Orbiting Death (1-0), a surprise early-season contender last year, made an emphatic statement with a 42-10 thrashing of defending Galaxy Bowl champion Themala (0-1). Death quarterback Condor Adrienne set a single-game record with 482 yards passing, including four touchdown passes.

The To Pirates (1-0) edged the Vik Vanguard (0-1) by a score of 24-20, and the Yall Criminals (1-0) topped the Wabash Wolfpack (0-1) 35-14 on a five-TD-pass performance by quarterback Rick Renaud.

Deaths

No deaths reported in Week One.

Offensive Player of the Week

OS1 Orbiting Death quarterback **Condor Adrienne,** who threw for 482 yards and four touchdowns on 32-of-40 attempts.

Defensive Player of the Week

Shorah Warlords defensive tackle **Bran-Gam-Blin** who had six solo tackles, three assists and two sacks in the Warlords' 17-9 loss to the Bartel Water Bugs.

14

Week Two:
Ionath Krakens at
Texas Earthlings

PLANET DIVISION

1-0 Buddha City Elite

1-0 Coranadillana Cloud Killers

1-0 Isis Ice Storm

1-0 OS1 Orbiting Death

1-0 To Pirates

1-0 Yall Criminals

0-1 Alimum Armada

0-1 Hittoni Hullwalkers

0-1 Ionath Krakens

0-1 Themala Dreadnaughts

0-1 Wabash Wolfpack

SOLAR DIVISION

1-0 Bartel Water Bugs

1-0 Bord Brigands

1-0 Jupiter Jacks

1-0 Sheb Stalkers

1-0 Texas Earthlings

0-1 D'Kow War Dogs

0-1 Jang Atom Smashers

0-1 Neptune Scarlet Fliers

0-1 New Rodina Astronauts

0-1 Shorah Warlords

0-1 Vik Vanguard

Excerpt from "Sorenson's Guide to the Galaxy"
All Sentients Are Created Equal:
The Planetary Union

Origins on Earth

The Planetary Union is arguably one of the most power-ful governments in the galaxy, second only to the Creterakian Empire. Other governments have more population than the Union (Sklorno Dynasty and Quyth Concordia), have greater economic power (the Ki Empire), have more advanced technology (the League of Planets) or outstrip the Union at exploration (the Quyth Concordia), but the point of interest is that the Union is number two or three in *all* of those categories. Add in the fact that the Union managed to retain most of its military and warships as part of its surrender agreement to the Creterakians in 2641, and you end up with a system that has resources, money, technol-ogy, education, population and the ability to protect itself against aggression and piracy.

One Planet Does Not a Union Make

Long before there were planets to "unify," the Earth was a place of fractured political organizations. How fractured? There were more than 190 individual countries, 23 major languages and another 61 minor languages that each had at least 10 million native speakers. Armed conflicts were a regular occurrence. Some of these conflicts involved so many countries that they were called "world wars." In addition to the normal causes for war, such as nationalism, religion, territory and natural resources, lack of cultural understanding and difficulty communicating were also significant factors.

Early in the 23rd century, advances in logistics, sciences and communication made it possible for many nations to operate as a single, efficient government. This led to the formation of the Unified Nations of Earth (UNE) in 2213, when — in order to counter the growing global dominance of China — the United States of America, Japan, Mexico, France, Italy, Germany, the

United Kingdom, Australia and several smaller countries merged into a single democratic government.

Facing a planet of dwindling resources and fearing military expansion from both the UNE and China, other nations scrambled to form their own unions. India-Pakistan, the United African States, the South American Nations and the Arab Caliphate quickly formed. Within a year of the UNE's formation, 75 percent of the Earth's population fell under the control of just six major governmental bodies. As each of the six nations possessed enough chemical and nuclear weaponry to exterminate the Human population several times over, most independent nations quickly chose to align with one of the six rather than face the possibility of annexation.

Over the next two years, several border disputes led to military engagements. The Earth found itself on the brink of world war.

As has happened so many times in the modern era, it was technology that helped overcome this dangerous stalemate. A pair of developments not only avoided a catastrophic conflict, but also led to the overall unification of Earth's governments.

The first development was the Dozier Translator, a primitive AI module that could be carried in one hand and provided instantaneous translation all Earth languages. The "Doz-Tran," as it was called, introduced new algorithms that converted speech from one language to another with 95-percent accuracy. It also accounted for cultural differences that often led to miscommunication. The second development was an invention of the Kriegs Corporations — a global, holographic projection system that allowed for realistic, face-to-face, real-time communication.

The combination of these two technologies allowed for the first global peace conference, held in 2215. As a world watched, representatives of all nations began a dialogue centered on how to avoid a war that would kill billions. While that first meeting produced little in the way of agreement, the high level of constructive communication set the stage for future peace conferences.

By 2281, two generations had grown up knowing nothing but open communication with people from every nation. In that year, the six major nations joined into a single, representative government dubbed the Earth Union. That government presided for over a century and a half of relative peace, exploration and scientific advancement until it merged with the planets Capizzi 7 and Satirli 6 to form the basis of the Planetary Union that still exists today.

Government

The Planetary Union is a representative government built on a system of checks and balances. The government has four levels, or *strata*, of increasing importance: local, continental, planetary and galactic. At all four levels, a *congress* is comprised of two chambers: the *senate* and the *commons*. A senate has an equal number of representatives from each predefined geographical area, while the commons has a number of representatives based on population levels within those geographical areas.

Most major decisions are made at the galactic level. Each of the Planetary Union's twelve planets or colonies are equally represented in the senate, while the number of commons representatives varies widely from Mars's single representative to the 826 representatives of Earth.

Congress (also known as the *Electoral Branch* of government) is balanced against the *Executive Branch* (the Presidency), which is balanced against the *Judicial Branch* (the highest level of which is the Galactic Supreme Court). The Union's system has proven surprisingly resilient, as shown by almost six centuries of regular, peaceful transitions of power.

Room to Grow

The Union boasts eight planets as well as the four net colonies of Jupiter, Neptune, Saturn and Venus. Earth has the highest population with 12.4 billion citizens, while Mars is the smallest at just 12 million. The total population of the Planetary Union is 33.16 billion sentients, making it the third-most-populous system behind the Sklorno Dynasty (263 billion) and the Quyth Concordia (170 billion).

As for available natural resources, the Planetary Union is head and shoulders above all other systems. Jones, New Earth and Rodina are huge planets that are barely past the colonization stage. The Union's strategy of combining races — Humans for land, HeavyG for high-gravity worlds, Dolphins and water-breathing Humans for oceans, Harrah for gas giants — allows the system to pull the maximum amount of material from every world under its control.

A History of Pigskin

The Planetary Union is the birthplace of football. Because that sport has become the dominant force in intergalactic entertainment, Earth is a major tourist center for sports fans from across the galaxy. Cities that figure prominently in the history of "gridiron," such as Canton, Elmira and Los Angeles, annually draw tens of millions of visitors. In a bit of odd irony, no team from Earth — where football was created — has ever won or even played in a Galaxy Bowl. Currently, the Texas Earthlings are the only Earth-based team in the GFL's Tier One, the highest level of professional football.

Race	Percent of Population	Individuals
Human	62%	19,445,432,000
Dolphin	12%	3,763,632,000
Aqus Sapiens	9%	2,822,724,000
Harrah	8%	2,509,088,000
HeavyG	7%	2,195,452,000
Other	2%	627,272,000

Races

Humans are the Union's most-populous race with approximately 19.4 billion individuals. Humans are on all twelve of the Union's major population centers. Dolphins (Delphinus albietz) are the second-most populous with 4 billion spread across five planets and two net colonies. While Aqus Sapiens are the Union's third-most-populous race at 2.8 billion, the Harrah are the fastest-growing demographic. First emigrating to Jupiter, Saturn and Neptune in 2664, the Union Harrah population is 2.5 billion and counting as the race expands across the seemingly unlimited territory offered by those planets.

EARTH: THE BIRTHPLACE of Quentin's species. And Humanity wasn't the planet's only sentient product; it had spawned Dolphins, Aqus, Prawatt, AI strains and — one could argue — the HeavyG. All from a planet and a people that had almost destroyed themselves a dozen times over before FTL travel made it possible for Humanity to spread to the stars.

Quentin had seen Earth back in his rookie season, when the Krakens won the Tier Two tournament. He'd played at Hudson Bay Stadium, one of the most amazing facilities he'd ever seen. So much history, so much *tradition* in visiting the world that created football. This time, however, would be his first visit to one of football's most ancient and influential cities — Dallas.

Quentin stood by himself on the observation deck, golden bucket in hand. The Tweedy brothers had decorated the bucket with a white star lined in red and blue — the logo of this week's opponent, the Texas Earthlings. Becca was one window over, waiting to see the planet upon which she'd played Tier Three ball.

The Tweedys had seen Earth so many times the view didn't seem to interest them. A few veteran Sklorno stood on the deck, as did Michael Kimberlin and backup linebacker Samuel Darkeye. Quentin noticed that all of the rookies were here to watch the arrival: Sklorno defensive backs Niami and Sandpoint, third-string fullback Pete Marval, backup linebacker Pishor the Fang and HeavyG defensive tackle Jason Procknow. The rookies stood together, save for Procknow — he seemed to have found a place farthest away from everyone else.

Quentin felt the shimmer begin. He closed his eyes and waited. The feeling of slamming back into real-space washed over him, pulled at him and separated him, then it was gone. Nausea hit almost instantly. He threw up, tied the plastic bag, then looked out the viewport windows.

The cloud-speckled, blue world waited for him.

A corona of orbitals, ships and satellites surrounded the planet like some kind of sparse shell. The *Touchback* had punched out near Hudson Bay's orbital station, the place where spaceships docked to load and unload passengers and cargo. Beneath that station, a silver tendril faded away down toward the planet's surface — the space elevator that connected the orbital station to the floating city in the middle of Hudson Bay.

"That's where it all started, huh?"

Quentin turned to see Jason Procknow standing next to him. Seven feet, eight inches tall and weighing over six hundred pounds, his long arms were thick with layers of muscle. The infinity tat on his forehead looked so new it hadn't even faded — the lines were still sharp, crisp and dark.

Quentin nodded. "Yeah. That's where it all started."

Procknow smiled a nervous smile. "Good thing the Church left, though, right? Stewart had to find the chosen land. It was ordained."

Quentin was only a couple of years older than this big HeavyG, and yet Procknow seemed like a wide-eyed kid. In a way, he was — a rookie's first season brought an overload of new information for any player, more so for someone from the Purist Nation. Quentin again noticed the other rookies standing together, all seeing Earth maybe for the first time but doing it as a *group*. Jason wasn't part of that group.

And then Quentin figured out what was happening — Procknow was trying to make friends.

"Never been to Earth before, rook?"

The big kid shook his head. "No, Elder Barnes."

Quentin held up both hands. "Okay, first thing's first, *do not* call me Elder, okay? I'm not part of the Church."

Procknow's brown eyes widened. "But ... you're from Micovi. You played for the Raiders."

"Yeah, but I wasn't into the religious politics. I just played football."

The HeavyG looked down. "Oh. Well, okay."

That word, *okay*, actually meant: *I thought you were like me.* Quentin wondered what it had been like for a HeavyG kid to grow up in the galaxy's most racist place. Without football, Procknow would likely have lived a life of constant abuse. A confirmed church member could have murdered him for the crime of not being Human, yet probably faced no criminal charges.

And now Jason found himself in Tier One, immersed among species he had been taught to hate.

The HeavyG looked up. "Sorry."

"Don't worry about it," Quentin said. He slapped the kid on the shoulder. It was like slapping concrete. "I've seen you in practice. You're working hard. Just keep doing that, keep listening to Coach and John, and you'll be fine."

Procknow smiled. "Okay, Eld— ... I mean, Mister Barnes."

"And don't call me *mister*, either."

Quentin turned to look out the viewport. Jason did the same.

The *Touchback* closed in on one of the miles-long piers that jutted out from the massive orbital station. Ships clustered along those piers looked like multicolored, metal caterpillars sitting lengthwise on a log. No shuttle trip to the surface this week; orbital shuttle traffic was not allowed on Earth due to repeated terrorist attacks. Without a government exemption, the only way down was a ride on one of the planet's two space elevators.

The *Touchback* shuddered as mechanical arms connected and held it fast to the pier.

[**TEAM DISEMBARK**] the computer voice said. [**ALL PLAYERS DISEMBARK.**]

Quentin walked out of the viewing deck, barely aware that Jason walked near him or that the rest of the rookies were following along. Quentin's mind was already lost in thoughts of the coming game. Second-straight road game. The Texas Earthlings were 1-0. Their defense, led by linebacker Alonzo Castro and

All-Pro defensive tackle Chok-Oh-Thilit, had shut out the Jang Atom Smashers 17-0.

Well, there would be no shutout this week; Quentin had to find a way to win. They had hoped to fight for a title — if they started the season 0-2, that hope would be all but crushed.

THE VOICE BOOMED THROUGH Earthlings Stadium, joined by the polite applause of 112,000 fans.

"Here are your visitors, the Ionath Krakens!" Quentin led the Krakens out of the tunnel and into a pouring rain. They crossed an end zone painted red with blue-trimmed letters that spelled out TEXAS.

Past the end zone and onto the field itself, a luscious, thick green carpet, the same kind of plants that made up the Hudson Bay Station field. At the 50-yard line, a giant white star marked the center of the field. Lines and yard numbers done in blazing white finished off the field design, making it a classic throwback to the ancient days of the first football leagues.

As he jogged to the sidelines, he took in the stadium's decks. A wide lower bowl led up to two rings of glassed-in booths, the upper ring for the luxury boxes of the rich and business elite, the lower ring filled with water for thousands of Dolphin, Aqus, Whitok and Leekee spectators. He saw plenty of Harrah in there as well, the species taking advantage of their ability to move freely in either water or air. Above the luxury box ring rose the upper deck, stretching up to the bottom edges of the white dome roof which partially protected the fans from the elements. It wasn't a full dome — an open area the same length and width as the field allowed pouring rain onto the green turf below.

Blue- and white-clad fans packed the lower and upper decks, but — just like at Isis — several thousand wore the Orange and the Black. Quentin wanted to put on a good show for those die-hard Ionath fans. He reached the sidelines and raised his fist high. His teammates gathered around him. The time had come — they had to find a way to win, and they had to find it now.

• • •

"**HELLO, FOOTBALL FANS,** and welcome back to UBS Sports' coverage of the Ionath Krakens at the Texas Earthlings. I'm Masara the Observant, and with me as always is Chick McGee."

"Hello, Masara, hello, folks at home."

"Chick, what a first half. The Earthlings can't stop the Krakens, and the Krakens can't stop the Earthlings."

"You hit the Sklorno on the head, Masara. You can't ask for much more from the Krakens' offense. Barnes is on fire. He's twelve of thirteen for two hundred yards even, with one touchdown pass and another on the ground. But Earthlings quarterback Case Johanson is putting up Barnes-like numbers himself — Johanson is fifteen of nineteen for a hundred and sixty yards with two TD passes of his own."

"Chick, Coach Hokor the Hookchest even moved to a nickel defense, pulling a linebacker and bringing in Breedsville as a fifth defensive back to help out Vacaville on the corner. But when Hokor does that, the Earthlings are running the ball well, aren't they?"

"The science of rockets is well within your universe-spanning brain power, Masara. The Texas rushing attack seems unaffected by these rainy conditions. Running back Peter Lowachee is effective on the ground but even more effective on screen passes. He had three catches for seventy yards. It's not just Vacaville who is having a bad game for the Krakens. Hokor has rotated in rookie cornerback Niami in place of Vacaville, but Niami has been just as ineffective. What's more, Ionath free safety Sandpoint — also a rookie — is getting cooked like a Whitok at a Leekee fondue party."

"Chick! You know you can't make jokes about one sentient species eating another, that's —"

"Sorry, Masara, sorry, folks at home. Let's just say the Krakens' secondary is the reason the game is tied at fourteen-all. The two-minute warning is over, so let's go down to the field for the conclusion of the first half."

• • •

SECOND-AND-SIX from the Krakens' 46-yard line.

Linemen in orange jerseys and black leg armor shot forward, slamming against defenders wearing blue leg armor with silver piping and bright red jerseys with silver-trimmed blue numbers and letters. Pouring rain splashed off of the Earthlings' silver helmets and the blue-trimmed white star that decorated either side.

Quentin handed off to Ju Tweedy, who followed Becca around the right end. Their pounding steps kicked up arcing trails of water. Defensive tackle Chok-Oh-Thilit reached for Ju, but Michael Kimberlin blocked the big Ki just long enough for Becca and Ju to slip past. Linebacker Alonzo Castro came up fast and slammed into Becca, knocking her hard to the turf. While Castro got the better of the hit, the exchange allowed Ju to cut inside, big legs driving hard. The other Earthlings linebacker reached for Ju, but Ju slapped the reaching hands aside and was suddenly in the open field, angling for the touchdown. Quentin watched, breathless, hoping Ju could outrun the defense, but Minneapolis, the Earthlings' cornerback, brought Ju down from behind just two yards shy of a red-painted end zone.

Ju ran off the field, and Yassoud ran on. The starting running back needed a breather after that 52-yard run. The Krakens huddled at the 10. His linemen waited for the play call, as did Becca, Yassoud, George Starcher and Hawick.

"All right, let's put this in for six," Quentin said. "Pro-set, shotgun, X-slant, Y-curl, A-wheel. Becca, stay home for the blitz, I know Alonzo is coming. On one, on one, ready?"

"*BREAK!*"

The Krakens quickly moved to their positions. Quentin stood five yards behind his center, Bud-O-Shwek. Yassoud lined up on his left, Becca on his right.

Quentin surveyed the defense. Angry eyes and dirty faces looked out from beneath the rain-streaked silver helmets. The Texas crowd was going crazy, as they had for the whole game. Ionath had been projected to compete for the league title, yet here were the 1—0 Earthlings going toe to toe with the Krakens. The stands beyond the end zone vibrated with jumping fans clad in red, white and blue, fans waving blue pom-poms and flags decorated with a single white star.

To Quentin's right, defensive tackle Chok-Oh-Thilit dug in, four of his six feet actually planted in the red end zone. Quentin saw linebacker Alonzo Castro, someone he'd competed against back when they both played in the PNFL. Castro was small for the position but incredibly fast and smart, and if he came free he could knock you into next Tuesday.

Quentin looked to Alonzo's feet, saw that the linebacker's weight was on his toes. Was he coming on the blitz? If he was, Quentin could let Becca pick him up, then slip to the left, away from Chok-Oh, and possibly run it in for the score.

"Blue, fifteen," Quentin called. "Blue, *fifteen*! Hut!"

Bud-O-Shwek flipped the ball back. Quentin snagged it out of the air and watched Starcher, Hawick and Yassoud begin their routes, but he didn't watch long — sure enough, Castro blitzed. Becca stepped forward and tried to use the linebacker's momentum against him, pushing him to the left. Quentin stepped right, letting Becca guide Castro past. Quentin started to move forward but saw the huge Michael Kimberlin falling backward, bowled over by the red-jerseyed Chok-Oh-Thilit. Chok-Oh compressed, the accordion-like *gather* that let the Ki expand violently and deliver crushing hits.

Quentin didn't have time to cut left or right, so he went *up*, leaping just as Chok-Oh expanded. The sole of Quentin's cleated black boot met the top of Chok-Oh's silver helmet. The momentum spun Quentin violently, making him do two full, vertical 360-degree flips.

Quentin hit hard on his head, the blow rocking his brain and scrambling his thoughts. Hands grabbed him and pulled him up. He still had the ball in his hands, and he was standing on red-painted grass.

Touchdown, Krakens.

IN THE LOCKER ROOM AT HALFTIME, Hokor focused on his defense. He diagrammed plays on the holoboard, trying to make adjustments that would stop the Texas offense and protect Ionath's 21-14 lead. Quentin watched, taking it all in.

Don Pine came up to stand next to him. "Kid, you're on fire today."

Quentin nodded. "Thanks."

"Just keep doing what you're doing," Don said. "Your passes are dead-on. But remember, you don't have to do it all on your own. Just because Johanson is keeping pace doesn't mean you have to start taking risks. Protect the lead — don't be afraid to just hit the deck and take a sack if it means we keep the ball.

Quentin nodded. Just one nod, actually, then he stopped because of the sudden flash of pain.

Don's eyes narrowed in concern. "How's the head?"

"Fine," Quentin said instantly. "No problems."

Don laughed quietly. "Don't worry, I won't tell Doc Patah."

Quentin and every Human on the team were supposed to report any problems after a blow to the head. But doing so might cause Patah to pull that player from the game; the league took hits to the head very seriously, and if Patah ignored a brain-related injury, he could lose his job.

Quentin's head throbbed. He knew he should probably come out of the game, but he'd rather die first. Don's smile said he knew exactly how Quentin felt and — were he in Quentin's shoes — would do exactly the same thing.

Hokor's scream of rage drew their attention. "You worthless defensive backs, *run the schemes I call*!" Hokor reached up with his pedipalps and grabbed his little hat. He pulled and twisted, tearing the material to pieces that he threw down on the floor. The Sklorno defensive backs shook with terror. The coach started stomping up and down on the pieces to drive the point home.

"He's pretty angry," Don said.

"He should be," Quentin said. "If the defense doesn't do something, all the points in the world aren't going to be enough for the win."

• • •

LATE IN THE FOURTH QUARTER Quentin stood tall in the pocket as pressure bore down from the left, the right and in front. He'd scrambled for big yards so many times that the Earthlings were attacking less all-out and more under control, trying to *contain* him, not give him anywhere to run. That kept Quentin from scrambling, but it also gave him more time to throw.

And if you gave Quentin time …

He gunned the ball toward Hawick, who was running step for step with Earthlings cornerback Minneapolis. Hawick somehow *knew* the ball would be coming, an unspoken connection between quarterback and receiver. She stopped at the 1-yard line and turned — the ball hit her almost immediately, before Minneapolis could react. As Minneapolis's momentum carried her into the end zone, Hawick calmly stepped over the goal line for a 35-yard touchdown pass.

The Earthlings had continued putting up points, enough that they took a 28-24 lead into the fourth quarter. As Arioch knocked home the extra point, the lead changed hands again — this time 31-28 in favor of Ionath.

The Krakens were up by a field goal with three minutes to play. Now it was up to the defense.

THE KICKOFF RETURN put the Earthlings on their own 35-yard line. They had plenty of time for a game-winning drive, and they knew it. Johanson mixed it up with passes and runs. Peter Lowachee took advantage of the wet conditions, making cuts that forced John, Virak the Mean and Choto the Bright to change direction on the mud and slick grass. Whenever the running back touched the rock, he gained five or six yards. The Earthlings steadily drove the ball, picking up a pair of first downs and using two of their timeouts to reach the Ionath 41-yard line.

With only a minute to play, Johanson dropped back, planted, then ducked as John Tweedy came in hard. John got an arm on Johanson but slid away without bringing the man down. The quarterback scrambled right. Mum-O-Killowe extended, reaching out for the sack, but Johanson was just out of reach — the quarterback stumbled but stayed on his feet. Johanson ran right, cutting toward the line of scrimmage.

Quentin looked downfield and his heart sank. Vacaville had left her receiver and was coming up to stop the run. Just an inch from the line of scrimmage, Johanson stopped and threw a bullet to Leavenworth, the receiver Vacaville was supposed to be covering. The wide-open Leavenworth hauled in the pass and sprinted — untouched — down the right sideline for a touchdown.

With 47 seconds to play, the Earthlings converted the extra point to go up 35-31.

"CHICK, DO YOU THINK IONATH had enough time to pull off a last-minute comeback? Is this loss the fault of Quentin Barnes?"

"I don't think you can blame him, Masara. The Krakens got the ball on their own twenty-two with just thirty-eight seconds to play. Barnes went five-for-five on that drive and used all of Ionath's timeouts to get the ball to the Texas eleven with five seconds left. Barnes put the ball up into the back corner for a fade route to Hawick, but Minneapolis just managed to knock the pass down. Four times out of five, Hawick makes that catch, so I think Barnes did everything he could for the win — sometimes the cookie crumbles a cruel way."

"Chick, this win moves the Earthlings to two-and-oh. What a shocking start for Texas."

"Yes, Masara, but not as big a shocker as the Krakens losing their first two games. Once again they start the season in last place in the Planet Division. Despite Barnes throwing for a mind-boggling three hundred eighty-two yards and grabbing four touchdowns — two on the ground, two in the air — *and* despite Ju Tweedy rushing for an even one hundred yards, the Ionath Krakens come up on the losing end. Ionath has a bye in Week Three, so they better do something to improve that defensive backfield or they're going to lose a *lot* more games before the 2685 campaign is over."

"Chick, thanks for another great game of commentary. To all the sentients watching at home, this is Masara the Observant, signing off. Now back to the UBS studios."

IN THE VISITOR'S HUMAN LOCKER ROOM, Quentin dressed slowly. Not only was his team winless, but he still had to do the post-game press conference. Oh, wouldn't *that* be fun? Fifty-plus reporters asking him what was wrong with the Krakens, if the season was basically over already, how did it *feel* to be 0-2 and a dozen other idiotic questions. What was he going to say? That his defensive secondary was horrible? That if they didn't make a trade for new players, the season was basically over? Quentin didn't want to do the press conference at all, but it was part of the job; he would get it done.

Yassoud was waiting for him. After the game, 'Soud pointed out that Quentin had never seen a *real* Earth city before. Quentin had walked around Hudson Bay Station, but according to 'Soud that place "didn't count" because "it wasn't that old." Dallas, on the other hand, was supposedly founded something like *eight centuries* ago.

Quentin slowly buttoned his shirt. Maybe if he took long enough, the media would just go home.

Yassoud sighed. "Quit lollygagging, Hayseed. I want to get out on the town while the night is young."

"Do you have to be so excited about it? We're winless, 'Soud."

The bearded man nodded. "Yes, and if I allow myself to descend into the depths of misery and despair, guess what? We're still winless. So, why let it ruin a good time? We'll get to work tomorrow, Q — trust me, I'm just as upset as you are."

Quentin doubted that.

Messal the Efficient scurried into the locker room. His single eye swirled with green, the color of stress.

"Elder Barnes, you are scheduled at the press conference in fifteen minutes! It is always best to be there early, and if we do not leave now, we might actually be *late*."

Yassoud pointed at the Quyth Worker. "See, Q? Even Messal says you lollygag."

Quentin slid his feet into his shoes. "I'm coming, I'm coming," he said as he reached for his tailored shirt. "Messal, I'm almost ready. Wait for me out in the central locker room."

Messal shifted to his left foot, then his right, another sure sign of his growing anxiety. He turned and walked out.

Quentin stopped stalling. He buttoned the shirt, then pulled on his tailored coat. He wasn't crazy about dressing up, but as the face of the franchise he had a responsibility to look professional.

They walked out of the Human locker room into the communal area. Messal was waiting for them, but they also saw John Tweedy standing by the holoboard. Instead of his usual sweatpants and T-shirt, the linebacker wore a suit that was just as sharp as Quentin's.

Yassoud laughed and clapped. "Looking *good*, Uncle Johnny! You dressed up for me? How sweet."

Despite the dragging feeling of starting the season with two losses, Quentin couldn't help but laugh — John just looked so uncomfortable in the outfit.

"Yeah, John," Quentin said. "You're looking real classy to head out with us for a beer. You find a bar with a dress code or something?"

John pulled at his collar, which was a little too tight and made his neck skin puff out. "Um, sorry, guys, I'm not going out tonight."

Quentin and Yassoud exchanged a look.

"You," Yassoud said. "John Tweedy. *Not going out.*" Yassoud stepped up and put a hand on John's forehead. "You sick or something?"

John rolled his eyes and pushed Yassoud away. "Sickly *awesome*, maybe. Naw, I'm fine. Becca and I have to hit Wisconsin."

Quentin's brief ember of good humor faded away. Something tickled at his insides, like there was a hand in there wiggling its fingers.

Yassoud leaned back, looking as if he'd smelled something bad. "A *wisconsin*? What is that?"

"It's a *where*," Quentin said, "not a *what*. That's where Green Bay is, home of the Packers."

Yassoud's face lit up. "Oh, the Tier Three Packers? NFL stuff?"

John nodded. "Yeah. Becca's parents moved to Green Bay when she played for the Packers. They still live there."

The wiggling hand inside of Quentin clenched into a hard fist. "You're going to meet Becca's *parents?*"

EVERY MOTHER'S DREAM flashed across John's face. "That's right. Hey, Q, you know Becca pretty good ... think she'll like this?"

John pulled a velvet box out of his pocket. Inside was a piece of jewelry: a football made of brown diamonds with white diamonds for the laces. The thing was the size of a golf ball.

"It's a pin!" John said. "She can wear it on her shirt, or whatever, when she sees her parents. She's *gotta* like it 'cause it cost a fortune! Girls like expensive stuff, right?"

Yassoud started laughing. John glared at him.

The pin had to be one of the ugliest things Quentin had ever seen. Becca wasn't about money or diamonds or a big show of wealth. She would hate it — and if she let that dislike show, John would be crushed.

"Uh, Uncle Johnny, it's great," Quentin said. "But I think it might be a bit ... a bit *much*."

John's shoulders drooped. "Oh, really? Dammit, Q, I totally wanted to get her something mega-nice. What should I get instead?"

The guy looked devastated, but John was right about one thing — Quentin *did* know Becca, and he had an idea. He waved Messal over. The Worker came quickly, although he made a show of checking the time on his palm-up display as he did.

"How can I be of service, Elder Barnes?"

"Messal, how are you with the acquisition of antiques and artifacts?"

"I have *extensive* contacts throughout the galaxy," he said. His eye swirled with a reddish-orange, a color that showed pride. "You have seen Gredok's art collection? I am his procurer. Does that answer your question?"

"That depends," Quentin said.

"On what, Elder Barnes?"

"On what a *procurer* is."

Messal's pedipalps twitched. "To *procure* is to obtain an object, Elder Barnes."

Quentin nodded. "Do you think you could *procure* a rare artifact from ancient football days?"

"Well, Elder Barnes, as I'm sure you know, I am exceedingly well-connected in the football community. It is my business to maintain relationships with multiple individuals from every team and track what favors are owed to and from whom. If the object you seek *can* be procured, I will procure it."

Quentin glanced at John. John looked wide-eyed and hopeful — he wanted to impress Becca in the worst way. There was something off about doing this for John, but he was Quentin's friend.

"We need you to procure an antique championship ring," Quentin said. "The Green Bay Packers won something like thirteen or fourteen titles in the twentieth century, so find John a ring from one of those."

John's jaw dropped. "The *twentieth* century? That's not just ancient, that's *super-mega-ancient*. Jeeze, Q — is something like that even for sale?"

Messal rubbed his pedipalp hands together. "Everything is for sale, Mister Tweedy, it is only a matter of availability and price. Finding an ancient artifact like that will be difficult, and it will be very expensive. I might have to expand the search to include their titles from the twenty-first century, would that be acceptable?"

John looked at Q. WOULD SHE STILL LIKE THAT? scrolled across his face.

Quentin nodded. "Sure, that would work. If you can't find the real thing, get an accurate replica."

"I understand your request," Messal said. "And when would you need this item?"

"Right away," Quentin said. "You'll probably have to ship it to Wisconsin, that's where John is heading."

Messal's pedipalps twitched again. "You want a six-century-old artifact, and you want it *right away*? Are you joking?"

John grabbed the much smaller Worker by his middle shoulders. "No joke, you efficient bastard! Can you do it? I know it will cost a ton, but I've got money. Here—" John handed him the diamond-encrusted pin "—sell this for starters!"

Messal took the pin as if it was dangerous to touch. "Ah, this is apparently some form of ... jewelry. And was this to be a gift for Miss Montagne?"

John nodded furiously.

Messal flipped the pin over, looked at it from all sides. "Mister Tweedy, if I may be so bold, you would be well served to consult me before buying gifts. For anyone. Ever again in your entire life. Or talk to Elder Barnes, as his championship ring idea is excellent."

The door to the HeavyG locker room opened. Rebecca Montagne walked out, but she didn't look like *The Wrecka*. She didn't even look like a football player.

Yassoud let out a low whistle. "Wow, Becca. You clean up nice for a face-smashing fullback."

She blushed and looked down. "Thanks, 'Soud."

Becca wore a blue dress tailored to fit her muscular, athletic form. Her silky black hair hung in loose curls around her shoulders. She had high heels on that took her from 6-foot-6 to maybe 6-foot-10, just a couple inches shorter than Quentin. The heels also made her four inches taller than John, but the smile on John's face showed he didn't care.

"*Wow*, butter-nose," he said. "You look hot! I sure am glad I wore this suit. I've never seen you dress up like this."

She shrugged. "It's kind of for my mom. She's never really accepted the life I chose. She still wants a daughter that's more ... feminine."

Quentin couldn't stop staring. Becca was ... *beautiful*.

John walked over and took her hand. "Come on, sweetie-shoes. We're going to be late for our jump-flight to Wisconsin."

They walked to the locker room door. Becca's eyes met

Quentin's for a moment, then she looked away. Had she seemed … embarrassed?

John stopped at the door. He looked back at Messal, raised his eyebrows in an unspoken question.

Messal walked forward quickly. "I will take care of that equipment request for you, Mister Tweedy," he said. "Enjoy your trip and don't give it another thought."

John smiled wide. "Thanks, Messal. You are just the procuriest of all procuriosities."

John waved goodbye to Quentin and Yassoud, then walked out hand in hand with Becca.

Yassoud shook his head. "Meeting the parents? I didn't know people still did that."

"They do," Quentin said. "Old-fashioned people. Or at least, old-fashioned people that actually have parents."

"Hey, Q, if John's not coming out, mind if I bring Tim Crawford?"

Quentin shrugged. "Sure, why not?" The HeavyG backup defensive tackle had played well against the Earthlings, at least during the few plays where Mum-O-Killowe actually came out of the game. "You been hanging out with him?"

"Oh, yep," Yassoud said. "You're always in your room and John's been chasing after Becca lately — a guy needs drinking buddies, right? Tim's always down for a trip to the bar."

John was chasing after Becca. Maybe if Quentin hadn't spent so much time buried in study, he'd have seen that.

"Well, Tim's okay in my book," Quentin said. "Just make sure he doesn't get us in any fights."

Yassoud raised his eyebrows. "I'll do my best. The lad's a free spirit, if you know what I mean."

Quentin heard a buzz. Messal lifted his pedipalp, again activating his palm-up. Quyth language symbols floated there, rapidly flashing by. The Worker's single eye instantly went from clear to crimson — the color of fear.

"Messal, what's wrong?"

The Worker closed his hand and looked at Quentin. "That was

a message from Gredok. He is in a meeting room in this stadium, discussing the game with Coach Hokor. You are to attend your press conference, then see Gredok immediately. He said that two losses are unacceptable. He wants answers, Elder Barnes — and he wants them from you."

QUENTIN FOLLOWED Messal the Efficient through the corridors of Zhang Punch Drives Stadium, home of the Earthlings.

The press conference had been brutal. He'd thrown for 382 yards and put up four TDs, yet all the media cared about was the winless start of the season and that failed last-minute drive. That jerk Jonathan Sandoval from Net Colony News Syndicate had been the worst: *Aren't championship quarterbacks measured by wins, Quentin? Don't you think that Frank Zimmer would have pulled off that comeback drive and won the game?*

The problem was the Krakens' defense, yet all the questions were about *his* game, *his* leadership, *his* inability to complete that last pass. That was the life of a GFL quarterback — every loss was your fault. That's what reporters thought. That's what fans thought.

And, apparently, that's what owners thought.

"So, Messal," Quentin said. "You looked kind of scared when Gredok messaged you. What did he say?"

"Oh, Elder Barnes, I do not think the details are important."

"He hasn't seen me since we got back from Prawatt space," Quentin said. "Now, he wants to talk to me, and you looked like you were going to molt on the spot. Come on, what did he say?"

Messal stopped and turned. He spoke quietly. "My *shamakath* told me that if I did not deliver you to him immediately after the press conference, he would see that I was visited by a Harrah with a flaying hook."

"A *flaying* hook? Is that bad?"

That crimson color swirled across his eye again. "*Bad* does not begin to describe it, Elder Barnes. I am just happy that you have come along quietly."

Messal turned and continued down the hall. Quentin followed.

A flaying hook. That was the measure of Gredok's anger? Well, he wasn't the only one who was furious — Quentin had been waiting for months to have a word with the little Leader.

Messal stopped at a door. It hissed open. He gestured inside with his pedipalp. "Gredok the Splithead waits for you in there, Elder Barnes."

Maybe Messal was terrified, but Quentin was not. Maybe he'd grab the Leader and shake him like a toy, bounce him off the walls a couple of times. That would feel *good*. He strode into the room.

Gredok sat at the head of a long table. Behind him on his left stood Bobby Brobst, his tight-end-sized Human bodyguard. Behind Gredok's right shoulders stood the huge HeavyKi that Quentin had fought in Torba the Hungry's, the night Frederico had brought Jeanine to expose the fake Cillian Carbonaro. The HeavyKi wore black eye patches over two of his five eyes.

Sitting at the table to Gredok's right: Virak the Mean. The linebacker wore gray pants and nothing else, his combat enamels and chitin engravings exposed for all to see. His right pedipalp was wrapped in blue gauze, the result of an injury suffered against the Earthlings just hours earlier.

The message was clear: even if Quentin *could* take out Virak — and Quentin doubted that was possible — he still had to face Brobst and the HeavyKi.

Virak used his good pedipalp to gesture at an open chair to his right.

"Sit," the Warrior said. "My *shamakath* wants a word."

Quentin stared at the well-dressed, bejeweled, black-furred Leader. To hit that evil creature, to hear him beg for his life …

What would Gredok do?

Gredok would pretend to let the past go. He would pretend nothing was wrong and bide his time, waiting for the right moment to strike. If Quentin wanted revenge, he couldn't force it — he had to beat the team owner at his own game.

Quentin sat. "What can I do for you, Gredok?"

"We need to talk business," the Leader said. "Can we do that, or are you still too *emotional* over my little ruse?"

Quentin closed his eyes. He felt his temper brewing, accepted it and pushed it away. He calmed himself, made his pulse, breathing and body language all normal.

"You got the better of me," he said. "But I signed the contract, which means the incident is over. You won. I'm a Kraken. So if you want to talk business, then talk."

"We are *winless*," Gredok said. "How is it that we are the worst team in the league?"

Quentin shrugged. "We're not the *worst*. We almost won both games."

The Leader leaned forward. "*Almost?* I deal in absolutes, Barnes. For example, we are in last place. We are *absolutely* heading back to Tier Two unless *you* do something."

Quentin spread his hands. "What do you want me to do, Gredok? Should I go out and play defensive back?"

Virak's pedipalps twitched. "As if *you* could play defense."

Gredok slapped the table. "Silence! Virak, no one spoke to you. So, Barnes — what are you going to do?"

Quentin could pretend to be over the pain of a fake father, but that didn't mean he had to roll over and die. If Quentin was *too* accommodating, Gredok would see right through that.

"No, Gredok, what are *you* going to do? We need defensive backs. You're supposed to be the master of talent acquisition, so do your job and get us some players."

"The trade offer for Don Pine still stands. I can have an All-Pro corner here in three days, but *you* don't want that, do you."

Quentin waved a hand dismissively. "We need Pine and I don't want to go over this again. What's the matter, one trade is the best you can do?"

Gredok leaned back in his chair, folded his pedipalp hands together. "I have hired two dozen scouts to look everywhere, even *college* football."

"Then hire more scouts, look in more places," Quentin said. "I'm kind of busy running your football team. Or should I use my bye week to go scouting and do your job for you?"

Black swirled across Gredok's eye. Quentin knew Gredok had killed for less, but he wouldn't harm his franchise quarterback.

"Barnes, I assure you, I have looked *everywhere*. There is not one player in known space that my scouts have not examined. There is no talent left to be had!"

Quentin laughed. Gredok's eye swirled thicker with inky black.

"Look, Gredok, *you* are the one responsible for bringing in new talent. If our defensive backfield can't get the job done, then *you* have … "

Quentin's voice trailed off. *Known space*. Gredok had looked everywhere in *known space*. But there was one place he hadn't looked.

Was that even *possible*?

The black faded from Gredok's eye. "Barnes, you look like you might regurgitate on this table. Are you feeling unwell? Perhaps that hit to your head was worse than Doc Patah thought?"

Quentin blinked. The room seemed to come back into focus.

Why not? Just why the shuck not?

"I know where we can get defensive backs," he said. "There's a whole *system* of available players. I played them head to head, and I know I can teach them to be great defensive backs."

"Teach *them*? Who are *they*?" Gredok stared. Then the black faded from his eye, replaced by swirls of blue-green. He understood.

"Barnes, if you think this is a good time to exhibit your ridiculous sense of humor, you are mistaken."

"I'm not joking."

Gredok's black fur ruffled. "Are you saying you want the *Prawatt* to be our defensive backs?"

Quentin nodded. "They're just as fast as the Sklorno, and they can jump just as high. They hit like a battering ram." He leaned forward, letting himself get excited, letting Gredok see that excitement. "It's an entire *nation* of athletes that have never stepped onto a football field. How is it no one saw this before? We can save the season!"

Gredok stood on his chair, then on the table. He walked down the table to stand in front of Quentin. Virak tensed up, ready for Quentin to make a move, but Quentin stayed perfectly still.

"Barnes," Gredok said, "you *were* hit on the head harder than we feared. You want the scourge of the galaxy to wear my uniform? You want these killers to suit up on Sunday?"

Quentin shook his head. "They're *athletes*. I played against them, Gredok — they're not killers."

Gredok's fur fluffed, then lay flat. "Not killers? Barnes, how many beings *died* in that single game you played?"

"Two," Quentin said instantly. "And why is that any different than the GFL? Every other week the stats column lists one casualty, sometimes more. Football is a blood sport, Gredok. I'll bring in sentients that are willing to die if that's what it takes to win."

Gredok's eye flooded black, and on top of that black bits of red swirled madly. "You are an ignorant hatchling, Barnes. Do you think the Creterakians will let that happen? And if the bats somehow actually agree, do you think that tiny dictator Froese would ever allow it?"

Quentin leaned back. He hadn't thought of that. The idea had just sprung into his head so fast he hadn't had a moment to consider the complications.

He thought back to a private conversation he'd had with Commissioner Froese. Froese dreamed of cleaning up the GFL, and he wanted Quentin's help. Gangsters owned every franchise — any effort to wrest control away from them would bring retribution, violence and death.

I need sentients that are strong, that can face the danger, Froese had said. *What kind of sentient are you?*

The Prawatt were truly alien: they didn't have families that could be kidnapped, and Quentin wasn't even sure if they cared about money. Gangsters like Gredok wouldn't be able to control the Prawatt the way they controlled other players, players like Don Pine.

Quentin knew that Froese would allow the Prawatt. He started to say as much, then stopped himself — Gredok *hated* Froese. Quentin could use that hate; could he make Gredok think that bringing Prawatt into the league would actually *anger* Froese?

"Gredok, just think for a minute," Quentin said. "As far as the bats are concerned, the whole *point* of the GFL is to help the different species get along. If you can bring in even a couple of Prawatt and have them play *with* us, in the true spirit of the GFL, not only would the Creterakians go for it, they'd probably give you a medal."

"I do not care about medals."

Quentin threw up his hands. Virak twitched, but stayed seated.

"Do you care about our season?" Quentin said. "Because if the Prawatt can hang and bang with the Sklorno, they can save it."

"These Prawatt players," the Leader said quietly. "Are they really that good?"

Quentin nodded. "They are. I don't know how long it will take to teach them basic football skill and our defensive schemes, but the ones I played against are galaxy-class athletes. They're ten times better than Vacaville."

Gredok stared, stared hard, then he blinked and looked away. "I do not know about this idea."

Play your trump card, play it now.

Quentin tapped into the rage he felt from just looking at Gredok, let that anger make his heart pump a little faster.

"You're right about Froese, though," Quentin said. "There's no way he'd let it slide. He fined me for rescuing an innocent man, you know? I mean, if you bring in the Prawatt it would be a step towards shucking *galactic peace*, but Froese would squash it because nobody can tell him what to with *his* league."

Quentin stopped talking. He looked away, in case his eyes might betray his effort at manipulating a master manipulator. Gredok had to think this was his idea.

Gredok was quiet for a moment, then he slowly rubbed his pedipalp hands together.

"Yes, that would put Froese in a difficult position," the Leader said. "I would be doing something that facilitated interspecies cooperation. He would stop it, but in doing so, he'd look like a racist. It would almost be like — "

Gredok's voice trailed off. Quentin finished the thought for him.

"It would be like *you* are the good guy," Quentin said. "And *Froese* would be the bad guy."

Gredok's eye now swirled with traces of yellow-orange. "We still don't know if the Prawatt would play, or if they would even be any good if they did. We have to find a way for you to send a message into the Jihad space to see if this is even possible, but the Creterakians are blocking all communication in and out of Prawatt space for fear of accidentally angering them and starting a war. I would have to use my contacts in the Creterakian Navy, but using those contacts carries a steep price and a great deal of risk."

Quentin fought to control his excitement — he almost had it.

"We don't need to use your contacts," he said. "If we leave now, the *Touchback* can be across the border in three days. We have to hope that Captain Bumberpuff's ship is still in the same position, and then—"

Gredok held up a pedipalp hand, cutting Quentin off.

"Barnes, did you just say we should take the *Touchback* across the border?"

"Yeah," Quentin said, nodding rapidly. "Bumberpuff already knows our ship, so—"

"Have you been drinking?"

Quentin paused. "Huh?"

Gredok leaned closer. "I said, *have you been drinking?* Did you take a hit of pyuli? Or perhaps you ate raw juniper berries?"

What was wrong? Gredok had bought into the plan, Quentin had *felt* it. "Juniper berries don't work on Humans. What's your point?"

"The *point*, Barnes, is that you must be on some type of controlled substance if you think you're taking my multimillion-credit team bus back to Prawatt space."

"But ... but they know the *Touchback*! It's totally safe."

Gredok's pedipalps twitched up and down; his equivalent of

hysterical laughter. "Taking *my* team bus — without which we will have a difficult time competing in road games — to a border where ships explode for no apparent reason and where pirates have *already* attacked us, then into a region where most sentients are never heard from again is what you consider *safe*? The answer is *no* — you will not take my ship."

Quentin felt the heat of frustration in his face, realized he was breathing faster. He quickly calmed himself. Gredok obviously would not be convinced, but there had to be another way ... the *Hypatia* had a punch drive, maybe he could get Frederico to pilot it again, and then —

"I said *no*," Gredok said. "Not my ship, and not your ship, either."

Quentin stared in disbelief. He must have let his focus slip for just a moment, let his tells show again. Gredok had all but read his mind.

"Gredok, you have to trust me, I know what I'm doing."

"I know what you're *not* doing," Gredok said. "What you're *not* doing is ever setting foot inside Prawatt space again, not while you're under contract with me. Virak?"

The Warrior leaned forward. "Yes, *Shamakath*?"

"Call your contacts in the Ionath orbital defense forces. Tell them to make sure the *Hypatia* doesn't leave orbit without my permission."

"Of course, *Shamakath*."

"You can't do that," Quentin said. "That ship is *my* property."

Gredok waved a pedipalp hand in annoyance. "My season is already enough of a disaster without losing my franchise quarterback. I will not rule your idea out entirely, Barnes. Compose a message for the Prawatt and give it to Messal. When we return home, I will make inquiries with the Creterakian garrison and see if we can send that message. However —" Gredok pointed at him "— under no circumstances will you leave Ionath, unless it is for a road game. Now, Virak, escort Barnes to the shuttle and accompany him to the *Touchback*. See that he stays there until we depart for Ionath."

Virak stood and waited. Quentin had been dismissed. The Leader walked back down the table and, once again, sat in his chair.

The last of Quentin's control slipped away. His hands curled into fists. He squeezed his eyes tight. He wanted to *hit*, he wanted to *hurt*.

A heavy hand on his shoulder. Quentin opened his eyes to see Virak leaning in close.

"You should calm yourself," the Warrior said. "If you choose to do something rash, John Tweedy and Choto the Bright are not here to help you this time."

Quentin looked once more at the black-furred Leader, then turned and walked out of the room. Virak followed.

Once again, Gredok seemed to be one step ahead. Quentin had thought he'd won this round, yet here he was being escorted to the *Touchback* like a prisoner, like the slave that he was.

Gredok had a chance to put the Krakens back on top, yet he wanted to play it safe. He wanted to wait for next year to make a run at the title.

Quentin knew that tomorrow was never promised, and that next year might never come.

As he walked, an idea suddenly hit him. There was a way, something audacious yet obvious.

And, more importantly, something that would infuriate Gredok the Splithead.

Quentin smiled, then forced the smile away. This time, he would think through all the possibilities before he said a word to anyone.

QUENTIN SAT ON THE COUCH in his ship quarters, waiting for the right moment. In his hands, he held the message cube Frederico had given him back at the Blessed Lamb.

[**ALL PASSENGERS, PREPARE FOR PUNCH-OUT IN TWO MINUTES.**]

Quentin squeezed the cube's sides. A menu flared to life above it, showing icons of movie posters. He used the tip of his finger to flip through the menu, looking for the ones that started with the letter *M*.

There it was: *Muybridge.*

He hit *play*. The strangest movie began; it was just a side view of a horse with a jockey, running from left to right. The images were flat, black and white … they were ancient. Frederico had said this was the first movie ever?

It lasted all of ten seconds. The trip home from Earth would take three days. If playing the movie actually sent a message to Frederico, hopefully he'd be waiting when the *Touchback* punched out at Ionath.

It was one thing for Fred to get the message — it was something altogether different to think he'd agree to be a part of Quentin's crazy plan.

GFL WEEK TWO ROUNDUP
Courtesy of Galaxy Sports Network

Home		Away	
Alimum Armada	28	Jang Atom Smashers	7
D'Kow War Dogs	35	Buddha City Elite	27
Wabash Wolfpack	13	Coranadillana Cloud Killers	3
Themala Dreadnaughts	42	Hittoni Hullwalkers	21
Texas Earthlings	35	Ionath Krakens	31
Orbiting Death	30	Isis Ice Storm	27
To Pirates	28	**Yall Criminals**	42
Bartel Water Bugs	10	Sheb Stalkers	7
New Rodina Astronauts	13	Bord Brigands	10
Jupiter Jacks	32	Vik Vanguard	13
Shorah Warlords	10	**Neptune Scarlet Fliers**	21

Week Two of the Tier One season resonated with home-field advantage, as nine of the eleven hosting teams found victory.

OS1 and Yall moved to 2-0 to stay atop the Planet Division standings. The Orbiting Death won an overtime thriller 30-27 over the Isis Ice Storm (1-1), while Yall trounced the To Pirates (1-1) by a score of 42-28. The quarterbacks of those two first-place teams had similar performances: OS1's Condor Adrienne threw for 280 yards and three touchdowns, while the Criminals' Rick Renaud hit rookie receiver Concord for four TD strikes.

In the Solar Division, three teams are tied for first place: Bartel, Jupiter and Texas all moved to 2-0 on the season.

Jupiter quarterback Steve Compton threw for two touchdowns and no interceptions. The Jacks' 2-0 start is unexpected following the death of quarterback Shriaz Zia in last year's Galaxy Bowl.

"We're a team, not just one player," said Jacks owner JT Manis. "We lose a guy, another guy steps in. If you're surprised we're in the title hunt again, well, then you're very stupid."

The Earthlings' second win of the season came at the expense of the Ionath Krakens (0-2). Despite a 382-yard, four-TD performance by fourth-year quarterback Quentin Barnes, and despite over 532 yards of total offense, Ionath fell 35-31. Earthlings quarterback Case Johanson had a career-best day, going 26-of-32 for 315 yards and two touchdowns. Texas running back Peter Lowachee rushed for 82 yards, while fullback Pookie Chang rushed for 22 yards and a pair of touchdowns.

Deaths

Becky Procknow, fullback for the Isis Ice Storm, on a clean hit by Yalla the Biter. Isis owner Steve Libby has appealed the on-field ruling, claiming that Yalla intentionally severed Procknow's jugular vein after the play was complete. GFL Commissioner Rob Froese has promised an immediate review of all game footage. A second-year player, Procknow was the cousin of Ionath Krakens' rookie defensive tackle Jason Procknow.

Offensive Player of the Week

Concord, rookie wide receiver for the Yall Criminals. Concord caught touchdown passes of 82, 45, 36 and 7 yards en route to an 11-catch, 225-yard day.

Defensive Player of the Week

Yalla the Biter, linebacker for the OS1 Orbiting Death. Yalla recorded five solo tackles and three sacks in the Death's overtime win over Isis. Yalla's fatal hit of Becky Procknow was the eleventh of his career, making him the GFL's all-time most-lethal player.

15

Week Three: Bye

PLANET DIVISION

2-0 OS1 Orbiting Death

2-0 Yall Criminals

1-1 Alimum Armada

1-1 Buddha City Elite

1-1 Coranadillana Cloud Killers

1-1 Isis Ice Storm

1-1 Themala Dreadnaughts

1-1 To Pirates

1-1 Wabash Wolfpack

0-2 Hittoni Hullwalkers

0-2 Ionath Krakens

SOLAR DIVISION

2-0 Bartel Water Bugs

2-0 Jupiter Jacks

2-0 Texas Earthlings

1-1 Bord Brigands

1-1 D'Kow War Dogs

1-1 Neptune Scarlet Fliers

1-1 New Rodina Astronauts

1-1 Sheb Stalkers

0-2 Jang Atom Smashers

0-2 Shorah Warlords

0-2 Vik Vanguard

WHEN THE *TOUCHBACK* reached Ionath, Fred was·waiting. Quentin had once again met the detective at the Blessed Lamb bar. The conversation had been brief. Quentin had laid out his plan, ready to argue and plead, if necessary, because Fred would surely say no, but that hadn't happened.

Fred said yes. Weeks earlier, he'd said that no amount of money could get him to cross Gredok. That, apparently, wasn't true as long as that amount was one million credits and he got to wear a disguise.

It seemed Quentin wasn't the only one looking for ways to hurt Gredok the Splithead.

Week Three was the Krakens' bye week. They practiced at Ionath Stadium, but there would be no game for them come Sunday. Monday and Tuesday flew by as Quentin worked to make the defensive backs better and also worked on his plan.

Wednesday after practice, Quentin and Choto walked into the Bootleg Arms, the bar owned by Gredok. Tikad the Groveling, the bar's manager, saw them and — as usual — fell all over himself offering to fetch the players whatever they wanted. Quentin left Choto to deal with the overly gracious Worker, while he walked into the back of the bar, into the VIP area. Sure enough, he found the two people he'd come to see: Yassoud Murphy and backup defensive tackle Tim Crawford, both with drinks on the table in front of them. Murphy was 6-foot-6, 315 pounds, yet he looked like a little kid next to Crawford.

Quentin sat down at their booth.

Yassoud smiled with joy and raised his glass. "Well, if it isn't the galaxy-famous quarterback, Quentin Barnes! You finally taking a night off to relax?"

Crawford nodded. "Yeah. You don't get out much, do ya?" The HeavyG took a drink. The frothy beverage left a pinkish mustache on his black skin. He smiled, which made his forehead wrinkle and drew attention to the lighter-color scars that ran from his eyebrows up over his head and down to the back of his neck.

Quentin nodded at Crawford's mug. "Take it easy, man — too many strawberry smoothies and you won't be able to drive home."

"Ha-ha," Crawford said. "It's a mega-mass shake. Doc says I have to drink four of 'em a day."

Crawford was in his second year with the team. He stood 7-foot-10 but weighed only 565 pounds — too skinny for a HeavyG interior lineman. To become an impact player, he had to put on at least another thirty pounds of muscle. Doc Patah made sure Crawford spent extra time in the gym and consumed an obscene amount of calories.

Yassoud nodded to the empty spot at the table in front of Quentin. "Can I get you a beer, my holy quarterback?"

Quentin shook his head. "Not here to drink. I need you guys to do something."

Crawford and Yassoud exchanged a glance.

Yassoud leaned back. "The fact that you're asking *us* tells me this isn't a trip to the store for chips and salsa."

Quentin nodded. "You've both been known to get into a little bit of trouble."

Yassoud smiled his best *who, me?* smile. "I assure you, my good man, I don't know what you're talking about."

Crawford looked nervous. "Hey, I've been keeping my nose clean here. I'm more mature than when I played for the Angels. I don't want to screw this up."

The HeavyG had played in Tier Two for the Achnad Archangels. He'd spent the second half of his last season there in jail instead of on the gridiron. It wasn't fair of Quentin to ask this of him, but with two losses and no wins, the time for *fair* was long past. Ionath needed to win, whatever it took.

"I know you're being good," Quentin said. "So if you don't want to screw that up, I suggest you don't get caught."

Yassoud and Crawford exchanged another glance. Crawford nodded, which Quentin found interesting considering he hadn't even said what he wanted them to do. Both men leaned closer.

"Ask away," Yassoud said.

"You guys know the Kriegs-Ballok virtual practice system in the stadium?"

"Of course," 'Soud said. "What do you want us to do with it?"

Quentin smiled. "I need you to break it. And I need it done tonight."

THE STAGE HAD BEEN SET. Now it was time for Quentin to see if the rest of his friends would help.

Quentin met Sho-Do-Thikit, Mum-O-Killowe, Ju, George Starcher, Michael Kimberlin, John and Becca in the *Hypatia*'s small landing bay and walked them to the salon. Quentin tried to ignore that John and Becca were holding hands.

Choto the Bright and Frederico were already waiting in the salon. When John saw Fred, he let go of Becca's hand and jogged over to give the detective a high-five.

"Fred! Holy *crap*! How are you?"

"I'm well, Uncle Johnny," Frederico said.

"No disguise this time? You're getting boring in your old age."

Fred smiled and nodded. "Well, I'm not actually Frederico. He put this disguise on me so I would look like him."

John's smile faded. "Are you messing with me, Fred?"

Fred winked. "My name is Maxwell, but I'll tell Fred you said hello."

John's eyes widened, and he nodded. "Wow," he said. "Tell Fred that he's *really* good with the disguises." He walked back to the couch and sat next to Becca.

The Ki moved behind the couch, making room for the rest of the players. Everyone looked to Quentin, waited for him to explain why he'd insisted on their presence.

"Thank you all for coming," he said. "We're winless. In Week Four, we take on Yall. The Criminals have the number-one offense in the league. No disrespect to John, Choto and Mum-O, but we all know our defense can't stop them."

"Defense-defense," John said sadly. "Goooo, defense."

"We could start our season with three straight losses," Quentin said. "We have to do something drastic, and we have to do it fast. We've worked too damn hard to get where we are."

Becca nodded. "We have to practice harder."

John laughed. "Snuggle-bumpkins, if we practiced any harder we'd land butter-side down. Everyone is working their asses off, even poor Vacaville — she just doesn't have the skills."

Becca's mouth pressed into a thin line. "She better *find* the skills, John. It's not like we can get someone else."

"But we can," Quentin said. "In fact, Becca, you played against them. You saw how high they can jump."

She stared at him. Her eyes narrowed. "You can't be serious."

"I am," Quentin said. "Dead serious."

Ju smiled and nodded. "Shuck yes, Q. That's brilliant."

"Genius," George said. "An idea hatched from the deep firmament of —"

"Not now, George," Quentin said.

George nodded. "Right, sorry."

Mum-O and Sho-Do let out a short grunt. Like George, Ju and Becca, they knew what Quentin wanted to do. The confused looks on the faces of Kimberlin and John, however, showed that they did not.

John looked back and forth between Quentin and Becca. "You guys want to tell me what's going on?"

Ju rolled his eyes. "Big brother, you're retarded."

"Oh, yeah? Well, you're *mega*-retarded!"

"Am not," Ju said.

"Are so," John said.

"Am not," Ju said.

Quentin held up his hands. "Guys, knock it off, will you?"

John mouthed the words *are so*, then looked at Quentin. "So, tell me already. What are you guys talking about?"

George Starcher stepped forward, right hand over his heart. "John, oh erstwhile linebacker whose blitz is akin to a streaking asteroid, Quentin wishes that we bond with the Old Ones, that we take their progeny to our bosom and hurtle across the void as one glorious supernova of team and talent and unadulterated awesome."

Quentin sighed. "John, what George is trying to say is—"

"I heard him," John said. "You want to recruit the Prawatt?"

"Uh, yeah. How did you get that out of what George said?"

I GOT EARS scrolled across John's face. "I'm not stupid, you know."

Ju mouthed the words *are so.*

John stood up and took a step toward his brother, but Quentin stepped in between them. "Guys, come on! This is serious. Yes, I want to recruit the Prawatt to play cornerback."

Kimberlin's eyes widened. "Quentin, we don't even know if they can play football."

"They'll figure it out," Quentin said. "You all saw their speed, their agility, saw how hard they can hit. They were willing to die if that's what it took to win. The Prawatt are no different than anyone in this room. This could save our season."

The HeavyG shook his head slowly. "The *season.* Football … *that* is your motivation for such a dangerous endeavor?"

"Is there a problem with that?"

Kimberlin paused, seemed to think it over. "Actually, no," he said. "This reason is as good as many others and could have far greater results. I will join you."

Becca suddenly stood up. "This is a dumb idea to start with, and it's also impossible — the Prawatt homeworld is *three months* away. We'll miss the rest of the season."

"We're not going to the homeworld," Quentin said. "We're going to cross the Sklorno border. If I can reach Captain Bumberpuff, I know we'll get players."

Becca crossed her arms over her chest. "Well, that's just a *brilliant* plan, Quentin. And say it works, say we bring back aliens that are considered *monsters* by most of the galaxy. You think Froese will just let them play? And even if he does, you think the other owners won't object? This can't work. You're not only wasting your time, you're putting your life and the life of anyone who goes with you at risk — for *nothing.*"

She was always so hard-headed, always seeing the negative in his plans. He looked at Kimberlin. "Mike, what do you think will happen if the Prawatt want to play?"

"I think both the league and the Creterakians will allow it,"

Kimberlin said without hesitation. "We avoided war, but the political situation remains tense. Letting the Prawatt play football is a way to help everyone see they are not so alien after all."

"Not alien?" Becca said. "They're *machines*. How is Froese going to let machines play?"

Kimberlin shook his head. "The Prawatt are classified as sentient individuals. They are born, they grow, they die. Froese wouldn't allow that big one that came into the landing bay to play, but I suspect he will allow the X-Walkers."

Ju belched. He scratched at his belly. "Hey, Q, got anything to eat?"

They were in the middle of a major decision, and Ju wanted food? "Galley," Quentin said. "Help yourself."

Ju gave a nod of thanks, then walked out of the salon. Mum-O and Sho-Do followed him. Apparently the three of them had made up their minds, and no further discussion was necessary.

Quentin looked at the rest of his friends. "With or without you, I'm going to Prawatt space. Who's in?"

George, Kimberlin, Choto, Fred and John raised their hands immediately.

Just like two years ago when Quentin had wanted to go to OS1 to rescue Ju Tweedy from Anna Villani, Becca was the sole opposition.

"This is ridiculous," she said. "What are you going to do, Quentin? Take your fancy yacht across the border and come back with a salon full of X-Walkers?"

"Computer," Quentin said, "show the surrounding area on the main holotank."

The salon's holotank blinked on. A tiny *Hypatia* sat in the center, curved lines and orange paint reflecting the light of the sun. Not far away sat a Quyth cruiser, a light warship that was five times the yacht's size.

"Holy crap," John said. "Is that a warship?"

Choto said something in the Quyth's native tongue. "I just spoke the name of that ship," he said. "It roughly translates to *the eaters of your feet*."

John shook his head. "Not *my* feet. I like my little piggies."

"It is a warship capable of targeting the *Hypatia*'s engines," Choto said. "If Quentin's yacht leaves this spot, I believe that warship will disable it immediately."

"Gredok's doing," Quentin said. "He knows what I want to do, so he made sure I couldn't take the *Hypatia*. And no vessel we could hire would have GFL diplomatic immunity, which we need to pass through Sklorno space without anyone stopping us."

He nodded toward Frederico. "That's why Fred is here. He's a pilot. There's one ship we *can* get that already has diplomatic immunity. Right now, there's almost no one on it. We can just take it."

Becca looked at Fred, who smiled at her. She looked back to Quentin. "You're insane," she said. "Totally insane."

Quentin shrugged. "Maybe. Are you in or are you out?"

John looked at Fred, then at Quentin, then at Becca.

"Poo-poo face," John said. "What's going on? And are you in?"

Becca's stare was so filled with hate that Quentin almost had to look away.

"I'm in," she said. She turned to John. "What's going on? I'll tell you what's going on — your best buddy Quentin Barnes is going to steal the *Touchback*."

MESSAL THE EFFICIENT'S EYE swirled with green. "But Elder Barnes, I do not know what is wrong with the equipment."

Quentin stepped closer, seven feet of muscular Human staring down at a Quyth Worker half his height. "It's not working, Messal."

They stood in the Kriegs-Ballok virtual practice room underneath the stands of Ionath Stadium. Normally, the room was alive with a photo-realistic representation of any number of GFL stadiums and the teams that played in them. Now, however, it was just a fifty-yard-diameter room with a plain, blue dome.

Messal looked up and down, all around, as if hoping the room might flare to life at any moment. "Did you turn it off and turn it back on again?"

"Three times," Quentin said. "You're in charge of the facility — how can you *not know* what's wrong with it? Choto, shouldn't he know what's wrong with it?"

Choto stepped up to stand shoulder to shoulder with Quentin and look down on Messal. A foot shorter than Quentin but a bit heavier at four hundred pounds, Choto made for a chitinous block of pure intimidation.

"This practice field is vital to our organization," the Warrior said. "That it does not work indicates Messal does not care about our success."

Messal started dancing from foot to foot. "No! I care! I do whatever it takes to serve my *shamakath* and the glory of the Ionath Krakens!"

Quentin held his arms out, gesturing to the nonfunctioning facility. "It's not working, so if you do care, that means you're incompetent. We need to practice. Do you think it's a good idea to waste the time of these players?" He pointed to the other Krakens that stood there, all dressed in practice gear, all waiting: Crazy George Starcher, Becca, John, Ju, Mum-O-Killowe, Sho-Do-Thikit and Michael Kimberlin. "Maybe we should all take the bye week off and *relax*, is that what you're saying?"

Messal's eye *flooded* green — the Worker was so stressed Quentin wondered if he might pass out.

"The main stadium field is open," Messal said. "And it is a lovely day today! Can you not do your extra practices up there?"

Quentin rolled his eyes. "Yes, Messal, that's so much better than having a virtual practice field *under our stadium*, where *no one can see what we're doing*, don't you think? I'm sure spies from the Yall Criminals would love to see what offense we will use against them. I need this room fixed, *now*."

Messal's pedipalps started to shake. "But ... but ... but it was working just this morning. I saw Yassoud Murphy and Tim Crawford practicing in here, it was working fine!"

"Stop it," Quentin said. "Are you really going to blame *players* for this debacle? I've had enough of your excuses. Let's go see Gredok and discuss this with him."

Messal's eye swirled with rich blue, crimson and pink — three colors that each represented a different level of fear. The guy was terrified. Quentin felt a stab of guilt, but he couldn't back off now.

"Elder Barnes," Messal said quietly, "perhaps we could just find a solution without involving Gredok?"

Quentin shook his head. "And how do we do that? It's not like there is a second Kriegs-Ballok under the stadium, now, is there?"

Messal's single eye blinked, then his right pedipalp hand shot into the air, finger extended in a very Human gesture of *a-ha!*

"The *Touchback* has a virtual field, Elder Barnes! Could you practice up there?"

Choto put a pedipalp hand on Quentin's shoulder. "Quentin," he said, "Messal is wasting your time. I know that the *Touchback* staff is off for the bye week. You should take this incompetence up with Gredok immediately."

Quentin started nodding, but Messal's protest gained intensity.

"Elder Barnes, brave Choto, Captain Cheevers and her crew are aboard the *Touchback* overseeing bye-week cleaning and maintenance. I'm quite sure they could activate the practice field and have it ready for you by the time you arrive. I could have you onboard within thirty minutes. Surely that is a better solution than bringing this up with Gredok. Why, I'm not even sure if Gredok is here. Yes, I think he may be in … um … he's on Whitok, on business."

Quentin looked at Choto. "Should we go practice there, or should I just call Gredok?"

Choto made a big show out of thinking about that question. He dramatically looked up to the ceiling. He dramatically sighed. Quentin would have to work with Choto on his acting ability, because the big linebacker had none.

"I think the *Touchback* is acceptable," Choto said.

Messal clapped his pedipalp hands. "Excellent! Please, follow me to the roof shuttle pad. I will acquire a freelance shuttle on the way up. First class, of course! You will all be on your way in minutes."

"Just get it done, Messal," Quentin said. "You have disappointed me a great deal this morning. It would not be in your best interest to disappoint me further."

Those words, that cadence of speech, they sounded exactly like what Gredok would have said, and as such they had the desired effect: Messal sprinted toward the door, already tapping at a palm-up display that hovered over his pedipalp hand.

Quentin and his friends followed Messal out of the broken VR room. It was almost game time.

QUENTIN AND JOHN TWEEDY LED a group of sentients through the *Touchback*'s dimly lit corridors, headed for the bridge. Half of the lights were off. Cleaning robots scrubbed and polished, giving the ship a new sheen. The place seemed deserted.

Frederico was right behind them, and after him came Choto the Bright, George Starcher and Rebecca Montagne. Sho-Do-Thikit and Mum-O-Killowe brought up the rear.

The door to the bridge opened. The four orange-uniformed bridge crewmembers gave Quentin and John a casual wave, but they kept working. A smiling Captain Kate Cheevers was sitting in her chair, waiting to welcome them.

"Hiya, boys." She looked at Becca. "And you, Montagne. Messal called up to say there was a problem with the VR practice rig under the stadium. The onboard version is already warmed up and ready to go. The galley crew is off for the bye week, so food is a little sparse, but we'll throw something together for all of you when you get hungry."

Quentin took in a slow breath.

Here we go. We're really doing this.

"Good news, Captain Cheevers," he said. "I'm here to let you know that you're getting a few days off."

"A few days off? What are you talking about?"

"There is a shuttle in the bay that will take you to my yacht, where *you*, you lucky dog, get to take a mini-vacation of two or three days. Maybe even four."

Kate looked at the solemn-faced players behind Quentin.

"A vacation," she said.

"Uh-huh."

"On your yacht."

Quentin nodded. "Courtesy of Gredok the Splithead."

She put her hands on her hips. "And just what sites am I supposed to see on my mini-vacation?"

John stepped forward, his bulk clearly intimidating the smaller woman. "Whatever sites you want, Cheevers. As long as those sites *aren't here*, you get me?"

She looked from John to Quentin, eyes a bit wide with confusion. The four crew members had stopped working. They stood at their stations, watching.

"Everything is fine," Quentin said to them. He smiled at Captain Kate. "Mum-O-Killowe and Sho-Do-Thikit are here to see you to the shuttle."

The two massive Ki linemen scuttled forward.

Kate's eyes widened. "Uh ... thanks for the offer, but I'm going to have to pass. Unless I hear from Gredok himself, I can't leave the *Touchback*."

"Gredok is busy," Quentin said. "And if you don't let Mum-O and Sho-Do escort you to the shuttle bay, you'll hurt their feelings."

Mum-O let out a little growl. The captain's eyes grew wider still.

"Ah ... I see," she said. "It seems I don't have a choice about this sudden trip. Vacation time it is."

John put his hand on the captain's back and gently guided her toward the Ki. Mum-O and Sho-Do fell in at her sides. Captain Kate left the bridge, flanked on either side by six hundred pounds of highly athletic Ki linemen.

The four crew members started following her out.

Quentin held up a hand. "Not you guys. We need you to stay. Meet your temporary captain."

Quentin waved Fred forward. Fred had a white beard and mustache, both neatly trimmed. He wore a standard set of crew coveralls complete with captain insignia. His eyes had changed color, and he was now two inches taller. If Quentin hadn't known it was Fred, he would never have recognized the man.

"Hello, my friends," Frederico said, his voice now a perfect imitation of the Tower Republic accent. "I am looking forward to our trip together."

Quentin put a hand on Frederico's shoulder.

"This is Captain Smith. No matter what his orders, the four of you will follow them. Is that clear?"

The crewmembers looked at each other, all waiting for one of them to step up and make some kind of stand. None of them did. They all nodded.

"Good," Quentin said. "I'll just leave George Starcher up here to make sure things go smoothly. You boys know George?"

George stepped into the bridge, all 7-foot-6 of him. He'd painted his face fuchsia, with big black circles around his eyes. Quentin thought George looked like an idiot. To a normal-size Human, however, George probably looked scary as all get-out.

Crazy George lifted a hand and held it aloft in a dramatic pose. "And low, they did depart with danger in their midst. Those that would not follow orders felt great personal sorrow and inexplicable pain."

The four crewmembers looked at George, looked at each other one last time, then scrambled back to their stations.

Frederico gave Quentin an admiring smile. "You know what? For a homophobe, you'd make one heck of a gangster."

"Whatever," Quentin said. He leaned in and whispered: "You sure you know how to fly this thing?"

Fred nodded. "It's a converted Achmed Class heavy weapons platform. Yeah, I know how to fly it."

"So, you were in the Planetary Union Navy?"

Frederico grinned. "Maybe. Maybe not."

Rebecca walked up to join them, also speaking low so that the crew couldn't hear.

"It's not too late to call this off," she said. "We all volunteered, but the crew didn't. They and anyone else on board will also be at risk."

Quentin met her stare. Why did she always seem to be in a battle of wills with him? Deep down, he knew Rebecca was right; he'd asked his friends, but he was *ordering* other sentients to come along. It was the wrong thing to do, but if he didn't act, the entire franchise could lose everything — why couldn't she understand that?

"Becca, the crew could have died in the pirate attack," Quentin said. "They could have been executed by the Prawatt. They have a dangerous job."

She pointed a finger at his face, hissed her words. "They didn't sign up for *another* trip to Prawatt space. So why don't we just ask them if they want to go, Quentin?" She turned to the disguised Frederico. "You can fly this thing without the crew, right?"

It was a rhetorical, sarcastic question. Fred shook his head. A ship this size required more than just one person to fly it.

She stared at Quentin. "So? Aren't you going to ask Maurice and the others? Aren't you going to give them a choice?"

If he asked them and they said *no*, the trip was over before it had begun. He hated himself for it, but he had to see this through.

"They're going," he said. "But since you're so worried about the trip, if *you* want out, then go get on that shuttle with Kate."

Her eyes changed, shifting from anger to another emotion. Was it hurt? Disappointment?

"I'm not leaving," she said. She looked down, stared at the floor. She suddenly seemed defeated. "Even if there's nothing in it for me, even if I don't get what I really want, I will always back your play."

What she *really* wanted? What did *that* mean?

Frederico gave her shoulder a friendly slap. "Then get settled in, fair maiden." He walked to Captain Kate's chair, sat and called up her holo interface. "Crew, set a course for the coordinates I'm entering now."

The four men let out a chorus of *yes, captain*, then they got to work.

John ran back onto the bridge. He rushed over, throwing one arm around Quentin, one arm around Becca.

"Hayseed, this is *awesome*," John said. "My friend, you've got some serious man-stones. I can't believe you're *stealing* the team bus."

"Borrowing, not stealing," Quentin said. "Like taking someone's grav-sled for a harmless joy ride."

Becca let out a sarcastic huff. "We can only hope the *grav-
sled's* owner agrees."

Gredok would most certainly not agree, but that, too, was part
of the plan.

QUENTIN COULDN'T SLEEP.

He sat up in his bed. They were still about a day away from the
Sklorno/Prawatt border. Seizing the ship, kicking out Captain Kate,
that had been easy. Not so much as *easy*, but *fast*, *intense* — he'd
had to act quickly and that hadn't left a lot of time for contempla-
tion.

But during the two-day trip? *Plenty* of time to dwell on his
decision. He was putting everyone in danger. For the players, that
was okay, but what about what Becca had said — what about the
crew?

He didn't want to think about it. He needed to clear his head.
A few reps in the virtual practice room would do the trick. The VR
room needed a little time to boot up. He could turn it on now, then
it would be ready when he got there.

"Computer?"

[YES, QUENTIN.]

"Activate the virtual practice room. Get the systems warmed
up so I can run some reps against the Criminals."

[YOU ARE IN LUCK, MISTER BARNES. THE ROOM IS
ALREADY ACTIVE AND IN USE.]

Quentin looked at the time display on his holotank: 2:15 A.M.,
ship-time. Who would be using it this late at night?

His jaw muscles tightened. As if he even needed to ask.

"Computer, is Becca Montagne using the VR room?"

[YES, MISTER BARNES.]

Quentin slapped the bed. He stood up, grabbed his pants, then
strode into his living room. "Put it on the tank."

He slid his left leg into his pants as his room's holotank flared to life. Was she practicing *quarterback* again? The holotank showed the VR room, lit up like the blue field of Ionath Stadium. Becca wore her orange practice gear. She barked out signals to a holographic offensive line even as she looked out at a holographic defense clad in white and purple — the Yall Criminals.

"Dammit, Becca," Quentin said as he slid his right leg in and fastened his pants, "I've had just about enough of this." He looked around to see if he'd thrown a shirt on the couch, then paused to watch the play.

Becca took the snap. She dropped back three steps and was instantly under pressure from blitzing linebacker Forrest Dane Cauthorn. Becca spun to the left as Cauthorn dove at her feet. Even though his arms were holographic, she still avoided them, lithely hopping over his outstretched hands. She ran down the left side of the line, her powerful legs chewing up the yards.

She's fast.

Criminals defensive tackle Anthony Meaders beat his block and came free. Becca stopped on a dime and pushed backward — Meaders' arms reached for her but missed. She took one strong step forward, then *gunned* the ball.

She throws hard.

The brown ball whipped downfield and slid between two Criminals defensive backs to pass through the chest of a holographic Hawick.

Pass complete for 17 yards.

She's accurate. What a great pass.

Quentin fell more than sat on the couch. He'd known she could throw — he'd used her for a couple of fullback passes last season. And he knew she could run, sure, but he'd never seen her put it all together.

He watched her run another play. As she dropped back and looked downfield, for some reason Quentin thought of the nickname of that Tier Two team from Venus: the *Valkyries*. What had John said about them? *Women warriors of Old Earth who fought alongside their men*, or something like that. The concept was standard practice in every modern Human and HeavyG military, where men and women had fought side by side for centuries. But in Earth's ancient times, for a woman to step into battle must have meant she was special, that she was tough, that she was just as willing to fight for what she wanted as any man.

Becca Montagne: modern-day Valkyrie. That had a nice ring to it.

The concept made him realize something: for all the study he did on every player he faced, for all his work developing his teammates, he had never — not even *once* — watched footage of Rebecca Montagne playing quarterback.

What if she *was* good enough to be his backup? And, maybe, good enough to be a Tier One starter? At the very least, Quentin would have to reconsider trading Don Pine. Quentin closed his eyes as a realization washed over him — could they have traded Pine to Mars for Matsumoto and solidified the defense, making this *entire trip* unnecessary?

"Computer, do you have games from the NFL?"

[WE HAVE MANY, BUT NOT ALL. AS WE ARE IN PUNCH-SPACE AND WE CANNOT ACCESS THE NET, I CAN ONLY OFFER YOU THE GAMES THAT ARE IN MY STORAGE.]

"Search for Green Bay Packers games with Rebecca Montagne at quarterback."

[I HAVE GREEN BAY VERSUS THE JAKARTA JAXXONS IN THE DIVISIONAL PLAYOFFS OF 2682.]

"Offensive plays only," Quentin said. In the holotank, the Packers, in their green jerseys and yellow helmets, lined up for the first play of the game.

Damn, but they had ugly uniforms.

Quentin eased back into the couch. He watched.

EVERYTHING WILL BE OKAY, everything will be—

A shimmer rolled through the *Touchback*. Quentin gripped a brass rail and waited for it to pass. Even after all this time, every jump scared the hell out of him. Would *this* be the time they were forever lost in punch-space? Would they all die, would they—

Reality slammed home like a hard smack to the cheek. Quentin opened his eyes. Everything was still there. And he was queasy, but ... he didn't think he was going to throw up!

A tap on his shoulder.

John, pointing to the golden puke bucket. "Q, mind if I borrow that?"

Still shaken from the punch-out, Quentin numbly handed the bucket over.

"Thanks." John bent his head and threw up in it. "Whoa," he said, "bacon sure tastes better going down."

Quentin's nausea won out. He grabbed the bucket from John and threw up in it. He lifted his head but made the mistake of breathing through his nose — he caught a whiff of bacon and threw up again.

John patted him on the back. "A double! Nice form, Q."

Puking into a bucket that already had John's puke? Grossest possible combination. Quentin pulled the plastic drawstrings and tied the bag, then left the bag in the golden bucket and set the bucket on the floor. For once, he'd let Pilkie clean up the mess.

"John, I've never seen you hurl before."

John nodded. "Yeah, well, I guess I'm just a little bit nervous about heading into Prawatt space a second time."

Frederico's Tower-accented voice echoed through the ship.

"*Attention, attention. This is Captain Smith. We have arrived near Yall in the Sklorno Dynasty. A Creterakian warship is hailing us to stop, but they can't use force because of this ship's diplomatic status. We will cross the Prawatt border in a few minutes. If you are silly enough to believe in supreme beings of any kind — that includes any quarterbacks who might happen to be aboard — now would be a good time to start praying.*"

John laughed and slapped his thigh. "That guy, he *kills* me!"

Things were going according to plan: punch in on the far side of Yall, as close to the border as they could reach, then go full-burn with the impulse engines. The only way the Creterakians could stop the *Touchback* was to fire on it, and that probably wasn't going to happen.

Probably.

Soon, Quentin would find out if all the risk had been worth it or if he had made a horrible mistake — the price for which his friends would pay with their lives.

IT WAS THE SECOND TIME for everyone, but that didn't make it any less frightening. Just like before, a single Prawatt X-Walker entered the bridge of the *Touchback*. It strode in upright, walking on two legs while its two identical arms carried a heavy rifle.

Quentin held his breath. Everyone on the bridge remained very still. John stood next to Becca. George Starcher's face was white, not from shock but rather from a bright shade of face paint. Michael Kimberlin had his big hands folded in front of his huge chest. The four *Touchback* crew members were in their seats at the holotable; they might as well have been statues for all they moved. Frederico sat in the captain's chair, looking far more confident than Captain Kate had several months before.

The Prawatt's body rattled, then six more armed X-Walkers entered the bridge. Quentin looked at each one carefully, hoping to see a familiar pattern and shape — moments later, when an eighth Prawatt walked in on all fours like some semi-see-through spider, Quentin recognized Captain Cormorant Bumberpuff.

The entire gamble would come down to this moment.

Bumberpuff crawled over to Quentin, then stood on his two legs. Quentin still wasn't sure how to look a Prawatt directly in the eye, but he picked out what looked like a couple of silver dots close together and stared at them.

"Quentin Barnes," the captain said. "I thought we had said good-bye forever."

Quentin smiled. "I'm kind of surprised I feel this way, but it's good to see you again."

The captain rattled once, a far softer noise than the lead Prawatt had made, then his body seemed to stiffen.

Maybe because of all the experience Quentin had had with different species in the past three years, he was getting better at reading alien emotions. Or, maybe it was time to admit that he — who had been raised to hate almost everyone — just had a gift for it. Whatever the reason, he somehow understood the emotion of this alien creature: Captain Bumberpuff was *sad*.

"You have invaded sovereign space," the Prawatt said. "This is an act of war."

Quentin shook his head. "No! This is a diplomatic mission. A mission of peace. Sort of."

"You shouldn't have come back," Bumberpuff said. "Due to the continued aggressive posturing of the Sklorno and the presence of Creterakian warships, the Jihad is on high alert. If my ship hadn't been the one in this sector, the *Touchback* might have been destroyed instead of boarded."

Quentin doubted that. He had stopped a war, or at least delayed it. The Old Ones, *Petra*, she would know what he had done, what he had said to the Sklorno. Quentin suspected that every ship in the Prawatt navy had orders to make sure trespassing ships weren't the *Touchback* before any action was taken. Just like Gredok couldn't hurt him as long as he was playing football, Petra wouldn't let him be hurt as long as he could influence the Sklorno.

"But you didn't destroy us," Quentin said. "That means I can do what I came here to do."

"Which is?"

"Recruit you."

Bumberpuff leaned away. "I am a decorated commander of the Prawatt fleet. Are you asking me to turn traitor to my nation and join the Creterakian navy? Or perhaps the Sklorno Dynasty? You have made a grave mistake, Quentin Barnes, you—"

"I don't give a damn about your navy," Quentin said. "And I don't give a damn about anyone else's, either. I came to recruit you for football, Captain — I want you to join the Ionath Krakens."

Bumberpuff stood motionless. The other Prawatt shifted around, clearly agitated; were they insulted, or were they excited?

"We need a player of your caliber," Quentin said. "In fact, we need four or five. The Harpies we played against, I'm inviting you to pick your best teammates and come with us back to Ionath."

Bumberpuff turned in place. He seemed to be pacing, *thinking*.

"I would have a few months to decide? You would not need me until the preseason of 2686, correct?"

"We don't want you for next year," Quentin said. "We want you *now*."

The Prawatt stopped pacing. "*Now?* Do you think we could actually play? The Krakens are winless this year, but we have no experience."

So, the Captain had been following the season? That was a good sign.

"I can't promise anything," Quentin said. "You need to learn the game, learn our defense. But if you can pick those things up, then yeah, you'll play."

John raised a hand. "Yeah, your X-ness. I'm the captain of the defense, and I know you can do it."

Bumberpuff turned toward John. "But ... but ... I am a military officer. I have responsibilities."

John shrugged. "It's just a job. Trust me, slinky — working for the Krakens is *way* better than being a soldier."

Bumberpuff turned back to Quentin. "But what about my command? I have a responsibility to make sure this ship maintains its current level of excellence, of preparation."

Quentin thought back to his last day on Micovi, when Stedmar Osborne drove him to the spaceport. Thanks to Quentin's skills, the Raiders had just won a second-straight PNFL championship. During that ride, Stedmar had offered some unsolicited advice. At the time, Quentin hadn't paid attention. He'd thought the advice ignored the realities of football. And yet, Stedmar had been proven right — even without the Amazing Quentin Barnes, the Raiders still fielded a team, they still won games.

"Captain, there's always someone to take over," Quentin said. "Your ship won't shut down because you're gone. The military will move on without you. You are replaceable. Everyone is. If we leave without Prawatt players, I can't say for sure if anyone will ever come back to try again."

Bumberpuff paused, rattled once, twice, then spoke. "I want to join you, but we will have to go back to the home planet so I can get permission from the Old Ones."

Quentin wasn't about to wait another six months. He had one card left, and he played it.

"Captain, do you remember when I talked to the Old Ones?"

The Prawatt's skin rattled. "I do," he said. "Such wonders I never thought I would see."

"Then you know that your Old Ones owe me a favor. If you come with me, *right now*, I will consider that favor settled. Your Old Ones will owe me nothing."

One of the other Prawatt broke ranks and walked over. His gun was no longer pointed at Quentin or his teammates, but lazily pointed at the ground, as if the weapon was an afterthought.

"Captain," the Prawatt said, "please let me go with you."

Bumberpuff's body rattled so loud it made Quentin flinch.

"Cretzlefinger, get back to your post! How *dare* you speak out of turn!"

The Prawatt dropped to all fours and scurried back to its place.

John started giggling. Becca hit him in the shoulder, but John couldn't seem to stop. THAT'S THE DUMBEST NAME LIKE IN THE HISTORY OF EVERYTHING scrolled across his face.

There was something familiar about that Prawatt ... it had played in the Game for the Harpies.

Quentin felt a sudden surge of confidence. Bumberpuff wanted to come, and so did at least one of its teammates. Quentin just had to close the deal. How would Gredok do that? Gredok would find the emotional string and pull it ... *hard*.

"Come on, Captain," Quentin said. "I used to be like you, competing only against others of my race, and you know what? There was always this hole inside of me, a voice telling me that if I didn't play against the best the galaxy had to offer, it didn't really matter. I know that you want to find out just how good you really are. Come with me, and you *will*. Stay here, and when your final days arrive or you decide to merge with another Prawatt and become something new, you'll know you had your chance and you let it go. That knowledge will eat at you, and you'll *never* feel whole."

The captain stood motionless. So did every other creature on the bridge. They all stared at him, just like they'd stared at him when he had spoken to the Sklorno armada.

In his head, he played back what he had just said to Bumberpuff. He could manipulate just like Gredok did, sure, but this speech had been something different. It had been from his heart. It had been the *truth*.

On the football field, he had an effect on others. He'd thought that was all about the game, but it wasn't — it was about *him*. When he spoke from the heart, his words *connected*, his words *resonated*.

Quentin felt stunned by a sudden realization: he could no longer pretend that he was just some orphan miner from Micovi. He'd been that once, sure, but now he was a *leader*.

And as a leader, he knew what Bumberpuff wanted. Quentin just had to help him find that path.

"Come on, Captain." Quentin offered his right hand. "Join me. Let the whole galaxy know your name. Represent your species. Make every Prawatt proud to say *he is one of ours*."

Captain Bumberpuff didn't shake the hand. Quentin let it hang there, waiting, inviting.

The captain paused, then spoke — but not to Quentin. "This is the captain. Send the XO to the captive ship's bridge, immediately."

The *XO*?

"Uh, Captain?" Quentin said. "*XO* doesn't mean *executioner*, does it?"

"It means *executive officer*," Bumberpuff said. "Sometimes the position is called *first mate*. I am going to relinquish my command."

The captain reached out a three-tipped tentacle and gripped Quentin's hand. Quentin felt the cool, rough metal against his skin, felt the strange fingers squeeze down firmly.

"Quentin Barnes, I will join the Krakens, but only if you promise me one thing."

"What's that?"

"We do not want to play for a losing team. If we join, we're going to have to win. If we join, it is time to kick some ass."

Quentin's chest swelled with a swirl of emotions: hope, pride, joy and friendship.

"Cappy, old boy, you might be an alien, but you're my kind of people."

GROWING UP, QUENTIN didn't have a father. Or a mother, for that matter. Sometimes the other kids on Micovi would get caught doing something bad or stupid, and they'd be afraid to go home and tell their parents. Quentin hadn't really known what that felt like.

Until now.

No, he didn't have a father, or a mother, but he still had to answer to a pair of powerful sentients — Gredok the Splithead and GFL Commissioner Rob Froese. They hated each other, yet for this moment they had come together. Gredok was on board the *Regulator*, Froese's warship/headquarters. Quentin stared at the image of them floating side by side above the *Touchback* bridge's holotable.

Yeah, *now* Quentin knew what it felt like to be in trouble.

"Barnes," Gredok said. "Welcome back. I am ever so grateful that my expensive ship is still in one piece."

"Uh, yeah," Quentin said. "Well, we were never really in danger or anything."

Gredok's eye flooded black. "You are now."

Quentin had thought through every aspect of his plan, from setting up Messal to stealing the *Touchback* to cashing in on his favor from Petra and returning with Bumberpuff on board. What had never occurred to him, however, was the moderately important concept of how this would make his murderous gangster boss insanely angry.

Still, seeing the team owner's fury gave Quentin a deep sense of satisfaction.

Does it hurt that I can play games with you the way you play games with me, Gredok? Don't worry, there's more where that came from.

Commissioner Froese laced his little fingers together, then flexed them outward. The holographic knuckles *cracked* loudly.

"Barnes, you are an idiot," Froese said. "That stunt could have put a serious hole in my season."

Quentin nodded. "*Could* have, but it didn't. We'll be ready to host the Criminals this week, Commish."

"Lucky for you," Froese said. "Unlucky for you, though, is that you'll face them *without* your Prawatt players. If they want to play in the GFL, they have to pass the *Combine*, just like everyone else."

Quentin blinked. That had never occurred to him, either.

"What did you think, Barnes? That I'd just let them walk out onto the field?"

Well, yes, that was exactly what Quentin had thought. "But ... the *Combine* takes a week."

Froese nodded. "In this case, it might even take longer."

Longer? Coach Hokor still had to teach Bumberpuff and the others to play defense, and that in itself would take time. "Commissioner, if you do that, even though we might get the Prawatt back in time for our game against the Criminals, we can't use them because they won't know our plays. Can't you, like, I don't know ... just make an exception?"

The commissioner shook his head like he felt sorry for Quentin. "Barnes, it's hard to understand how someone can be so smart and so stupid at the same time. You have a race that's never played in the GFL, a race that has been at war with half of the galaxy for decades, a race that has yet to account for *thousands* of sentients who entered their territory and were never to be heard from again, a race of unknown strength, speed and aggression, a race that usually kills Sklorno on sight just as Sklorno usually kill *them* on sight — and in case you forgot, genius, Sklorno make up about thirty percent of GFL rosters, and just so happen to play for every team in the league — and you want me to make an ex*ception*?"

Quentin cleared his throat. "Well, when you say it like *that*, you make it sound like a bad thing."

The little commissioner nodded. "Because it *is* a bad thing. You should thank your primitive superstitions that I'm even *considering* this. Even if it works, do you think the other owners want Gredok the Splithead to have an on-field advantage? They'll do anything to stop this."

"But this is good for football," Quentin said. "And it's good for galactic peace."

Froese smiled his red-toothed smile. "Galactic peace? Tell me, Barnes, do you really *care* about that? I mean beyond the fact that a war might interrupt your season, of course."

Quentin started to answer, started to give the automatic *of course I do*, but he stopped himself — from the first moment he'd hatched this plan, it had been about winning football games. He wanted his Galaxy Bowl trophy and would do anything to get it. But at the same time, he couldn't deny that what happened next might very well change history.

"I don't want anyone to die," he said. "I don't want to see ships blow up or watch cities get bombed. Do I want peace so I can win championships? Sure. But I also want peace because war sucks."

The holographic Froese stared. He turned to look at the owner of the Krakens.

"Gredok, if I have to open the *Combine* in mid-season, *you're* going to pay the bill. Are you willing to spend that money and also willing to put up with all the trouble this will cause?"

Gredok's eye cleared. He stared. Just as Gredok could read Quentin, Quentin could read Gredok. The Leader had expected Froese to put up more of a fight, expected an opportunity to make the commissioner look bad in front of the entire galaxy. That obviously wasn't going to happen, which meant everything came down to one thing — football.

Gredok turned his stare on Quentin. "Well, Barnes? Are you certain this is worth my money? Is this worth the enmity of the other owners?"

"That depends," Quentin said.

Gredok's eye again flooded black. "If you say *it depends on what enmity means*, I promise that I will happily see my franchise fall to the second tier if it means I get the satisfaction of watching you try to scream for help when your unprotected body falls out of an airlock into the vacuum of space."

He turned to Froese. "Accidentally, of course."

The little commissioner shrugged. "Of course. These things happen."

Quentin said nothing. He could read Gredok, and this time, Gredok wasn't exaggerating. Even a star quarterback could only push things so far, it seemed.

"The Prawatt are worth it," Quentin said. "You know how bad I want to win a title. The Prawatt will help us do that."

The inky black slowly faded from Gredok's softball-sized eye. The Leader was reading him, and this time, Quentin didn't try to hide a thing.

Gredok turned to Froese. "We will pay all associated costs," he said. "Because I, too, am so very interested in galactic peace."

Froese nodded. "Then I'll re-open the *Combine*. But know this, Barnes — when the Prawatt go in, they submit to Creterakian law. That means you better hope they don't have any mods."

Mods were a death sentence. If the Creterakian bosses decided Bumberpuff or the others had mods …

"But they're machines, kind of, I think," Quentin said. "How will the examiners know if something is natural or a mod?"

Froese shrugged and smiled his red-toothed smile. "Beats me. It'll be a shame if your new pals get executed because of a mistake. I'll have a shuttle deliver Gredok to the *Touchback*. Make sure your rookies are ready to board that same shuttle. I'm sure you and Gredok will have so much fun together on your trip back to Ionath."

Gredok nodded. "Yes, Barnes. I do hope you're ready for a nice chat on our long trip home."

Quentin felt his stomach tingling. It would be a long, long trip home indeed.

GFL WEEK THREE ROUNDUP
Courtesy of Galaxy Sports Network

Home		Away	
Wabash Wolfpack	21	Buddha City Elite	17
Coranadillana Cloud Killers	3	**Bartel Water Bugs**	14
Hittoni Hullwalkers	14	**Bord Brigands**	31
Isis Ice Storm	24	Themala Dreadnaughts	10
New Rodina Astronauts	21	**Orbiting Death**	28
Jang Atom Smashers	21	Shorah Warlords	17
Jupiter Jacks	35	Texas Earthlings	31
Vik Vanguard	17	Sheb Stalkers	3

In all the turmoil surrounding Ionath's shocking request to add Prawatt players to the Krakens roster, it was almost easy to forget that teams still had to line up on Sunday and play ball.

Bartel (3-0) certainly wasn't distracted by the controversy, as the Water Bugs remained undefeated thanks to a 14-3 win over Coranadillana (1-2). This is Bartel's first-ever 3-0 start to a Tier One season. The Water Bugs have the league's best running game, driven by the thunder-and-lightning combination of "Big" Rob Shonfelt, who carried the ball 22 times for 136 yards, and "Little" Dixonge, who ran for 78 yards and a TD on just six attempts. Quarterback Andre "Death Ray" Ridley added to the hefty rushing total with eight carries for 68 yards.

The Orbiting Death (3-0) grabbed sole possession of first place in the Planet Division with a hard-fought 28-21 road win over New Rodina (1-2). Death QB Condor Adrienne threw for four touchdown passes on a 20-for-31, 317-yard day.

In the Solar Division, Jupiter (3-0) kept pace with Bartel thanks to a 35-31 win over the Texas Earthlings (2-1). Jacks running back CJ Wellman managed three touchdowns while rushing for only 52 yards, scoring on runs of 1, 3 and 4 yards.

The Vik Vanguard (1-2) and Jang Atom Smashers (1-2) both notched their first mark in the win column this season. Vik defeated Sheb (1-2) 17-3 while Jang edged out winless Shorah (0-3) by a score of 21-17.

Yall (2-0), D'Kow (1-1), Alimum (1-1), To (1-1), Ionath (0-2) and Neptune (1-1) all had a bye week.

Deaths

New Rodina Astronauts fullback **Tobiah Don Percival**, killed on a punt-return block by Orbiting Death linebacker Yalla the Biter. This is Yalla's second fatality in as many weeks and his twelfth overall, extending his status as the most lethal player in league history. New Rodina owner Barbara Jungbauer immediately filed a protest to have Yalla kicked out of the league. Commissioner Rob Froese immediately reviewed the footage and declared it a clean hit.

Offensive Player of the Week

Bord Brigands tight end **Tobias Jedlund**, who caught seven passes for 112 yards and two touchdowns.

Defensive Player of the Week

Buddha City Elite defensive tackle **Don-Wen-Sul**, who recorded four sacks in the Elite's 21-17 loss to the Wabash Wolfpack.

16

Week Four:
Yall Criminals at
Ionath Krakens

PLANET DIVISION

3-0 OS1 Orbiting Death

2-0 Yall Criminals (bye)

2-1 Isis Ice Storm

2-1 Wabash Wolfpack

1-1 Alimum Armada (bye)

1-1 To Pirates (bye)

1-2 Buddha City Elite

1-2 Coranadillana Cloud Killers

1-2 Themala Dreadnaughts

0-2 Ionath Krakens (bye)

0-3 Hittoni Hullwalkers

SOLAR DIVISION

3-0 Bartel Water Bugs

3-0 Jupiter Jacks

2-1 Bord Brigands

2-1 Texas Earthlings

1-1 D'Kow War Dogs (bye)

1-1 Neptune Scarlet Fliers (bye)

1-2 Jang Atom Smashers

1-2 New Rodina Astronauts

1-2 Sheb Stalkers

1-2 Vik Vanguard

0-3 Shorah Warlords

QUENTIN AND HOKOR SAT in Hokor's office in the Krakens Building, waiting for the arrival of Don Pine.

On the trip home, Quentin had watched even more game film of Becca Montagne. So had Gredok. And when they reached Ionath, both had sat down with Hokor the Hookchest to watch those games yet again. Now that they knew her, had seen her play as a Tier One fullback, they could combine that knowledge with what they saw in the Packers footage.

If Quentin hadn't been so pig-headed, he might have seen it, but he was threatened by anyone who might try and compete for his spot. Was Becca Montagne good enough to be a starting Tier One quarterback? No, she wasn't. Was she good enough to be a solid backup? She was. And, most importantly, was she better than Yitzhak Goldman? If Quentin was injured, could Becca finish that game and give the Krakens a fighting chance at a win?

Yes. Yes, she was and she could.

The Mars Planets still wanted Don Pine, and they were still willing to trade cornerback Matsumoto to get him.

It remained to be seen if the Prawatt would make it through the *Combine* and be allowed to join the Krakens. And if they *did* make it, there was no guarantee they'd be good enough to play. The Prawatt gamble might or might not pay off, but this trade brought in an experienced, *proven* player to replace Vacaville.

Quentin couldn't keep punishing Don Pine at the expense of the franchise. Don was a valuable trade option. Quentin had blocked that — until now. He had to let the past go and do what was right for the team. If Becca could take over in case of injury, then Quentin had to step aside and let Gredok deal Pine.

A knock at the door — Don Pine stood in the doorway.

"You wanted to see me, Coach?" He cast a suspicious glance at Quentin.

"Come in," Hokor said. "Sit down."

Don did, sitting on Quentin's right, both of them in chairs in front of Hokor's desk.

Don looked at Quentin again, then at Hokor. "Okay, Coach — what's this about?"

"We have a trade offer for you," Hokor said.

Don's eyebrows rose. "For me, huh?"

Quentin nodded. "That's right."

Don looked genuinely excited. "And you're okay with this, Q? Not going to try and block it this time?"

"Nope," Quentin said. "Everyone wins, Don. You get to start again, and we get an All-Pro cornerback in Matsumoto."

Don's smile faded. "Matsumoto?"

Hokor called up a holo of Matsumoto on his desktop. "That is correct. She will be a great addition—"

Don stood suddenly. "You want me to go play for the Mars Planets? No way."

Quentin didn't know what was going on. Don had been asking for a trade for over a year. "Yeah, they're rebuilding. They came after me when I was a free agent."

"Forget it," Don said. "I'm thirty-three years old. I am *not* going down to Tier Two!"

Quentin leaned back. This couldn't be happening — they had a chance to land an All-Pro cornerback, and Don *wanted* to be traded. If he had to go down to Tier Two, that was the breaks.

"Don, we're making this trade," Quentin said. "I'm sorry if you don't like it, but we need Matsumoto."

Don shook his head. "Did you bother to read my contract? Because there's a section in there you'd love, called a *no-trade clause*. If I don't want to go to Mars, I don't have to go to Mars."

Quentin looked at Hokor. "Is that right?"

Hokor waved a pedipalp across the desktop, making the image of Matsumoto vanish. "Yes, that is right. Don can refuse any trade he likes."

Don pointed a finger at Quentin. "I've had it with your little plots. You think you can hide me away in Tier Two?" He waved his fingers, letting his two Galaxy Bowl rings shine. "I've got *these*. You might be better than me right now, but I'm still *damn* good. You want to trade me? Trade me to a Tier One team. Trade me to a *contender*. I know my value on the free market. You get me what I want, or I will sit on the bench and collect my healthy paycheck."

Don turned and walked out of the office.

Quentin felt like all the air had been pulled from his lungs. They'd had an All-Pro cornerback, an immediate solution to their defensive problems, and Don couldn't *lower* himself to play in Tier Two.

"Figures," Quentin said. "Dammit, Coach — what do we do now?"

"We hope your experiment in inter-species diplomacy has positive results," Hokor said. "And until we know it does, we keep shopping Don Pine."

From *Galaxy Sports Magazine*

THE GALAXY IS WATCHING

Can One Critical Week Fade Centuries of Slaughter?

by YOLANDA DAVENPORT

Historians have tried to calculate the number of deaths produced by the Prawatt wars. Tried, and failed.

The Prawatt have been considered an "aggressive species" since 2438, when they attacked a Rewall research vessel in the first recorded instance of interstellar combat. In 2456, the Prawatt attempted to exterminate the Kuluko race. In 2552, the Prawatt Jihad was the only nation to boycott the first Galactic Peace Conference. The Prawatt have warred with the Sklorno, saturation-bombed planets and left them devoid of life,

and — it should be noted — were one of the few nations to successfully beat back the Creterakian Takeover.

Yes, the Prawatt history is a history of violence and bloodshed, resulting in a sentient race feared and shunned by the civilized galaxy. And yet in just a few days, all of that history, that sad, deadly history, could give way to a new era.

This reporter has been granted sole access to the Prawatt's special training session at the *Combine*, where four members of this mostly unknown race are undergoing purity testing. Should the candidates pass, they will play for the Ionath Krakens, but one major question looms large — how do you test a race for illegal mods when that race could be considered to be nothing but mods?

"That is the challenge," said GFL Commissioner Rob Froese. "We've brought in top xenobiologists, galactic historians, even anthropologists to get as much perspective as we can. The Prawatt are a mechanical species, and yet they have a fixed biology all their own."

The real source of the controversy isn't the Prawatt race's political leanings or isolationism, it is the stance of GFL franchise owners who object to "machines" being allowed to play against biological sentients.

Zippy the Voracious, an expert on Prawatt culture and author of "Earth: Birthplace of Sentients," is one of the non-GFL experts consulted by Froese.

"In their adolescent and early-adult phases, the Prawatt have a predictable life cycle and physiology," Zippy said. "The species' natural body type is known as an 'explorer,' more commonly known as an 'X-Walker.' In my opinion,

an explorer is a natural, biological form, just as the Warrior is a natural, biological form of the Quyth race. If a Prawatt has any shape other than X-Walker, one could consider that a modification and that individual should not be allowed to play."

All four Prawatt rookies are X-Walkers.

In the first three days of testing, it appears that the Prawatt are not "super-powered killing machines" or "robots that can do anything," as some columnists and conspiracy theorists have claimed. The Prawatt seem to have a fixed range of physical abilities. They weigh between 280 and 319 pounds, a body mass similar to that of the Sklorno. The Prawatt's length is measured from the tip of one foot to the tip of the opposite arm, or one line of their "X." That length ranges from 11 feet, 4 inches to 12 feet, 4 inches, which puts their reach on par with, again, the Sklorno race.

The Prawatt have also been tested extensively on strength and speed. Cormorant Bumberpuff, one of the rookie candidates, was timed in the 40-yard dash at 3.2 seconds — a time equal to the GFL's best Sklorno defensive backs. Strength-wise, however, Bumberpuff and the other Prawatt seem to be three to seven percent stronger than the typical Sklorno that passes through the *Combine*.

What's more, all four Prawatt candidates recorded vertical jumps of over 15 feet. Combine that leaping ability with their length, and they have a 25-foot reach, which, again, puts them on par with the Sklorno.

"This is a game changer," said Robert Otto, author of the popular "GFL for Dummies" series. "For over twenty-five years, both on offense and defense, the vertical passing game has been Sklorno and nothing but Sklorno. Bringing in another species that run as fast and can jump as high is going to dramatically alter on-field play."

Despite the possible diplomatic benefits of bringing the Prawatt into the league, most owners are not interested in a game-changing new species.

"It's preposterous," said Wabash Wolfpack owner Gloria Ogawa. "This is another dirty trick by Gredok the Splithead. He is ineffective as an owner and wasn't able to recruit the proper talent, so now he wants to cheat by signing monsters?

I demand Froese cease this charade and ban the Prawatt forever."

Ogawa, Orbiting Death owner Anna Villani and To Pirates owner Kirani Kollok have filed formal requests to block admittance of the Prawatt species, even if the *Combine* officials do clear the candidates to play ball.

Froese has the full backing of the Creterakian Empire. If the Empire Bureau of Species Interaction scientists at the *Combine* say the Prawatt should be accepted into the league, the final decision is up to the commissioner.

And if it comes to that, Froese indicated he's already made up his mind.

"I am listening carefully to the owners, but my job as commissioner isn't just to ensure fair play. I'm also tasked with increasing our market share. EBSI experts estimate the Prawatt Jihad population is in the trillions. Owners are complaining now, we'll see how they feel when their advertising revenues skyrocket."

This reporter feels it is far too early to be thinking of increased ad revenue or increased sales of team merchandise. Little is known about the Prawatt race's viewing and commercial consumption habits. They have been thought of as the "galactic boogeymen" for so long, it seems foolish to immediately start considering them as yet another entertainment demographic.

That being said, this reporter personally interviewed Bumberpuff and found the individual to be surprisingly familiar with intergalactic culture. If one were to close one's eyes and just listen, it would be hard to tell a Prawatt apart from a sports-crazed resident of Earth.

"I want to play football," said Bumberpuff. "I gave up a lot to come here. I want to line up for the Ionath Krakens, and I want to win a GFL championship."

Does that sound like the words of a bloodthirsty alien robot? Not to this reporter's ears. Obviously, the question of sincerity remains; could they just be telling us what we want to hear so that they can infiltrate and destroy us from the inside, just like they do in the movies? Possibly, yes, but this reporter has made a career out of evaluating words and judging true intentions.

In this reporter's opinion, the Prawatt — at least these four candidates — are not here to kill us. They are not here to spy on us. They are not here to destroy our ways, level our cities or poison our

> *"I want to play football.*
> *I gave up a*
> *lot to come here. I want*
> *to line up for the*
> *Ionath Krakens,*
> *and I want to win a*
> *GFL championship."*
>
> CORMORANT BUMBERPUFF

planets. They are here to play football. That, and nothing more.

Thus far, *Combine* officials have found no reason to block the Prawatt from entering the GFL. Unless the EBSI scientists discover — or conveniently create — such a reason, the Prawatt players are sentient beings capable of entering into a business agreement. As such, in three more standard days they will be free to sign with the Ionath Krakens.

Get ready, galaxy — there's about to be a new game in town.

FOR THE SECOND TIME that season, the Krakens gathered to welcome new rookies to the *Touchback*.

Quentin walked into the landing bay, John and Yassoud at his side. The rest of the Krakens filtered in and formed their usual semi-circle around the orange and black shuttle. Metal clinked, a result of either warming up or cooling off, Quentin couldn't remember which.

Unlike the first time they'd welcomed rookies, Quentin sensed tension among his teammates. Most of them hadn't been part of the second trip to Prawatt space. They didn't have any say regarding the new players — if they didn't want to be teammates with the Prawatt, their only option was to quit.

John punched Q in the shoulder.

"This is *wild*, Q," John said. "Hey, are they going to eat us?"

Quentin rubbed his shoulder. That shot was going to leave a bruise. "John, we were on their planet, remember? They didn't eat us."

"Maybe they like take-out better than delivery."

Quentin sighed. "They're not going to eat us."

Yassoud nodded. "Good to know, man. What do the X-Walkers eat, anyway?"

Quentin shrugged. "Beats me."

John's eyes narrowed. "So you *don't* know if they eat people or not." UNCLE JOHNNY DE JOUR? scrolled across his face.

"John, whatever they eat, it's *not* people, okay?"

His tat changed to I'M PROBABLY DELICIOUS, YOU DON'T KNOW.

Quentin looked around the landing bay. The Ki gathered together in a dense cluster, as usual. Five of the team's six Quyth Warriors were there, all except Tara the Freak. Quentin assumed he was somewhere up in the rafters, as usual. The Warriors seemed on edge, as if they expected trouble. All of the HeavyG players stood by, as did the Humans, both races looking a bit nervous but not as wired as the Warriors.

And then Quentin realized what was missing — there were no Sklorno.

"Hey, guys," he said, "where are the ladies?"

John and Yassoud looked around, both seemingly just as surprised that the Sklorno players weren't there.

John shrugged. "Beats me. Oh, *hey* — don't the Sklorno hate the Prawatt? And versa vicey?"

"Oh, yep," Yassoud said. "Those races have been slaughtering each other for centuries. No wonder the ladies aren't here."

Hokor stood near the shuttle, waiting for the side door to open. There was no sign of Gredok. Quentin quickly walked over to Hokor.

"Coach, where are the Sklorno?"

The Leader adjusted his little Krakens ball cap. "They asked if they could skip the welcome session. Gredok agreed."

The Sklorno players didn't even want to see the Prawatt? They were going to be *teammates*.

"Unacceptable," Quentin said. "We can't have players opt out of meeting rookies because they don't like their species."

Hokor's pedipalps twitched — he was laughing. "So you, Quentin Barnes, are unhappy because players are being *racist*?"

Quentin thought back to his own rookie season, to the way he'd hated the "satanic races" and even Don Pine, simply because of Pine's blue skin. Rick Warburg had shared that hate, but even Rick had shown up for team duties.

"Yes, Coach, I am unhappy. And you should be, too."

"You think I like this? I have orders from Gredok."

"Gredok isn't here," Quentin said. "You are. Tell the shuttle pilot to keep the door shut."

"What? Why would I tell him that?"

Quentin pointed at the shuttle. "Because we are not opening *that* until the entire team is here to welcome our new players."

Hokor's eye swirled with threads of green. Quentin knew that Hokor agreed with him but was torn between what he thought was right and the orders of his *shamakath*.

Quentin knelt down so he was eye-to-eye with Hokor.

"Coach, it's *your* team. You are a Quyth Leader — make a decision."

Hokor's eye cleared. He turned to face the shuttle. "Computer?"

[**YES, COACH HOKOR?**]

"Tell the shuttle pilot to keep his cargo door closed. Have him tell his passengers that there will be a brief delay before the welcoming ceremony begins."

[**YES, COACH HOKOR.**]

The coach pointed a pedipalp hand toward the internal airlock door. "What are you waiting for, Barnes? Go tell the Sklorno to stop grab-assing and get in here."

Quentin stood. "Choto, Kimberlin, Mum-O, come with me."

Together, four races of football players left the landing deck and headed for the Sklorno section of the ship.

QUENTIN AND THE OTHERS walked through the madly painted corridors of the *Touchback's* Sklorno section. He saw every color imaginable, bizarre combinations and mixed patterns that spread from floor to wall and wall to ceiling with no concept of boundaries. He walked past four of the oblong doors until he reached his destination — Hawick's room.

Hawick was a seven-year upper-tier veteran. She was fifteen years old, one of the oldest active players on the team. More importantly, she was Quentin's number-one receiver; that made the other Sklorno idolize her, made her their de-facto leader. He knew that all fifteen of the Krakens' Sklorno players would be in her room.

Quentin knocked, perhaps a little harder than he should have. "Hawick! Open the door."

The door slid open. Inside stood Hawick, her see-through body trembling with a combination of fear, anticipation and excitement. Behind her in the fuchsia/green/red-plaid/orange-striped entryway stood Milford, Berea and the Awa sisters: Halawa and Wahiawa. Behind them stood the rest of the Sklorno, a five-foot-wide corridor thick with clear bodies, black skeletons and twitching eyestalks.

"Quentinbarnes," Hawick said. "How may I serve your holy holiness?"

Quentin glared at her. He pointed a finger back down the main corridor. "You can get your butts to the landing bay to welcome your new teammates."

"New teammates?" Hawick started to lightly jump up and down. The Sklorno behind her followed suit. "We have new players? Exciting-exciting!"

"Of course, you have new teammates — the Prawatt defensive backs."

The jumping stopped.

"Quentinbarnes, what do you mean?"

They had been told about the Prawatt players in recent team meetings. What's more, the news was all over the galaxy.

"You know exactly what I mean. Our four new Prawatt teammates just arrived from the *Combine*."

Hawick's eyestalks waved aimlessly, body language that showed confusion in her kind. "But that is impossible, Quentinbarnes. Prawatt are the *devil*. The devil cannot be a teammate, that is just silly."

Milford started jumping up and down. "I know I know! The Godling Quentinbarnes makes a funny joke! We laugh like football players!"

All fifteen of the Sklorno started chittering in a bizarre impression of a Human laugh.

Quentin felt his temper rising. "*Knock it off!*"

Fifteen clear bodies stopped chittering and started quivering.

He stared into as many eyes as he could. "Whatever this is, it ends — *now*. You will come with me and welcome our new teammates to the franchise."

Hawick's eyestalks went rigid. "*No*," she said.

All of the Sklorno leaned forward, just a bit. They suddenly looked more like a mob of angry sentients than the giddy, goofy players he had known for three and a half years.

Hawick's chin-plate opened; her raspers unrolled, dangled nearly to the floor. "Prawatt are the *devil*," she said. "The *devil* cannot play football. It is impossible, Quentinbarnes — you have been tricked."

The last sentence sent a visible ripple through the Sklorno.

Some of them backed away from Hawick, as if she'd just blasphemed High One himself. Others leaned in closer to her, perhaps in support. The concept of a holy being making a *mistake* seemed to be difficult for them to swallow.

Quentin hadn't anticipated any of this. The Sklorno always seemed ready to go with the flow, eager to do whatever he or Hokor asked. But here they were, caught up in their racial hatred and planting their feet against his requests. How many millions of Sklorno had died at the hands of the Prawatt? Quentin didn't know, and at the moment it didn't matter — in this franchise, racism would *not* be tolerated.

Quentin gestured to the players he'd brought with him. "Hawick, look at this. Choto the Bright, a Quyth Warrior. Michael Kimberlin, a HeavyG. Mum-O-Killowe, a Ki. Me, a Human. And you, a Sklorno. We all play together. We will win a championship, together. It will be no different with the Prawatt."

Hawick's eyestalks waived independent of each other. "But it is *impossible*, Quentinbarnes. Prawatt must be killed on sight murder-murder-murder!"

The other Sklorno started hopping madly, screaming either *kill them* or *murder-murder-murder.*

A few minutes ago, Hawick had seemed about as dangerous as a three-hundred-pound see-through teddy bear. Now Quentin felt her pure aggression. For the first time, he knew what it was like to stand in front of a race that had exterminated two sentient species, that had waged war across the galaxy, whose soldiers had been known to kill — and eat — anything they fought.

Quentin felt *fear.*

He clenched his jaw. His hands balled into fists. Hawick *wasn't* a soldier — she was an Ionath Kraken, and she would behave accordingly.

He leaned in until his nose was only inches from Hawick's head. He could see through her face, see the translucent brains sitting beneath her dense crop of black hair. Her eyestalks had to bend out and turn in to look at him.

Quentin spoke quietly, knowing she could hear every syllable.

"Hawick, you don't have to like them, but you *will* play with them. You *will* get your asses to that landing bay. You *will* welcome your new teammates. You will *not* start a fight or act aggressively. If you don't do what I say, I will never throw you another pass as long as you live."

His words sent another ripple through them all. To catch a pass was a blessing, a Sklorno's grand moment of existence. To never catch a pass again? That was like sending a Holy Man to a living hell.

He felt a hand on his shoulder.

"Quentin," Kimberlin said, "maybe you should—"

Quentin slapped the hand away.

He didn't need to listen to Mike. This wasn't even about racism or hatred anymore — Hawick was challenging Quentin's leadership.

He leaned in even closer. Hawick did the same. His forehead touched her face. Her raspers dangled and twitched, a pair of three-foot-long, tooth-covered tongues that could instantly rip the flesh from his limbs.

"We are a *team*," he said. "If you're not part of that team, I'll run you out of this franchise and you can go catch passes some-where else."

Hawick's eyestalks moved like sluggish snakes. She radiated anger. He sensed the tension both from the Sklorno in front of him and the teammates standing behind him. One wrong move and this corridor would erupt into a bloody brawl.

And then, Hawick leaned back, just a bit.

"We will go to the landing bay," she said.

Quentin nodded and stepped back out of the doorway. Fifteen Sklorno shot out of Hawick's room and sprinted down the hall.

He turned to his friends. "Come on, we have to be there when the shuttle opens." He started jogging. The Sklorno were already far ahead.

Kimberlin caught up to him. "That was culturally unwise, Quentin," he said. "Do you forget that for every Prawatt that makes the team, one of our Sklorno has to be cut?"

Quentin clenched his teeth. He hadn't forgotten that, not for a second.

"My job is to put a winning team on the field, Mike. The players we have aren't cutting it."

"This is true," Kimberlin said. "But telling Hawick you'll run her out of the franchise? You shouldn't make idle threats like that with the Sklorno."

"Who said it was an idle threat? They will play as a team, or they will be gone."

"If you force the Sklorno to choose, they may all choose to leave," Kimberlin said. "Then you will have a team with Prawatt defensive backs and no Sklorno receivers. What then?"

"If we have no receivers, then we run the ball down everyone's throats. They *will* get along with their teammates, or they'll be gone. Anyone who doesn't want to do it my way is welcome to get on that shuttle and never come back."

Quentin started sprinting. He wouldn't catch the Sklorno before they hit the landing bay, but at least he could leave Kimberlin's questions behind.

THE IONATH KRAKENS — all of them, this time — waited for the shuttle to open. Most of them formed a semi-circle around the still-closed side door. The Sklorno clustered together some fifteen feet behind the semi-circle, as far away as they could get without incurring Quentin's wrath.

He had no patience for the Sklorno players' biases. He'd had to overcome his own racism in order to lead this team. As with all things, Quentin asked for no more than he was willing to do himself.

The shuttle door lowered with a whine of machinery. He felt the collective tension ramp up a bit. No matter what went down now, good or bad, everything was about to change.

The shuttle door hit the landing bay deck, a metal-on-metal clang that echoed through the air.

Bumberpuff led the other three Prawatt down the ramp.

Quentin heard murmurs and rustles as players slowly backed away. The Prawatt reached the end of the ramp and stopped.

Coach Hokor walked up to them, seemingly oblivious to any concept of danger. Just as with all other species of player, the Prawatt towered over him. Quentin stepped forward to stand at his coach's side.

"Welcome to the Krakens," Hokor said. "You players are now the property of Gredok the Splithead. He owns your contracts for this season. Maybe you have watched all the news coverage and think that you are all fancy and very important — you are neither! You are *not* guaranteed a roster spot. You will work hard and learn our defense. If you do not learn it fast enough, I will put you right back on this shuttle and send you off to your worthless home system. We will begin work immediately. John Tweedy?"

John sprinted from the semi-circle and skidded to a stop next to Hokor. He snapped his right hand up in a military salute.

"Yes, my shorty-short leader of destiny?"

Hokor glared at John, then looked at Bumberpuff and the other Prawatt. "Rookies, this is John Tweedy, defensive captain. He and I will start to work with you immediately on our defensive sets and philosophy. Follow me to the Kriegs-Ballok Virtual Practice System and we will begin — we don't have a minute to waste. Tomorrow, we head down to Ionath Stadium to practice on your new home field."

Hokor turned to walk out of the landing bay.

Quentin stepped in front of him. "Coach, wait. Aren't we going to introduce the Prawatt? You know, by *name?*"

Hokor stared at Quentin, then blinked his softball-sized eye. "Yes, of course, Barnes. Prawatt, introduce yourselves."

Bumberpuff raised his arms, extending to his full height. The landing bay lights played off his slightly reflective skin, even shone through in some places to cast strange shadows on the deck.

The Sklorno started to chitter. They shook with rage, looked like they might rush in and attack at any moment.

Quentin looked at Mum-O and pointed at the Sklorno. Mum-O barked out a guttural phrase, then scuttled in front of the

Sklorno. The other Ki joined him, a line of twelve-foot-long bodies promising trouble if the Sklorno tried anything.

Quentin turned back to the captain and nodded.

"I am Cormorant Bumberpuff," the captain said. "I am honored and excited to join the Krakens. I am here to win a championship."

The other Prawatt introduced themselves: Luciano Cretzlefinger, Katzembaum Weasley and Tommyboy Snuffalupagus.

Quentin looked at his teammates, turning slightly so he could briefly lock eyes with each one. "These are not faceless monsters from a bad movie," he said. "I used to think that every one of *you* was a monster, and I was wrong — don't make the same mistake I did. We need to embrace these players. Learn their names, get to know them as individuals. Anyone who doesn't do that is going to have to deal with me."

Ju Tweedy stepped out of the semi-circle. "And me." He banged a fist against his broad chest. "Me first, though — if there's anything left of you, *then* you can deal with Quentin."

Heads nodded. Pedipalps twitched. Aside from the Sklorno players, it seemed that everyone was ready to begin the grand experiment.

But would it work? And if so, would it be enough to save the season?

THREE DAYS UNTIL the Krakens hosted the Yall Criminals.

The four X-Walkers strode out of the tunnel and onto the field. Quentin waited at the 50-yard line. For today's practice, all he had to do was throw routes. Hokor and John were running the show; it was their job to bring Bumberpuff and the others up to speed.

Gredok had closed down Ionath Stadium — no non-essential personnel were allowed. Quentin had heard about scattered protests around the facility. Some sentients, it seemed, didn't want the Prawatt in Ionath City, let alone on the team. Just to be on the safe side, Gredok had confined the entire team to the Krakens Building complex, which included the stadium. Quentin thought that action was a bit much, but everyone was so focused on their new teammates and no one seemed to mind.

The banners on the stadium's twenty-two pillars hung limp and lifeless. The city's sounds filtered in from beyond the walls. Every pad-on-pad hit echoed through the empty stands.

Quentin strode forward to welcome his new teammates. He offered his hand, and Captain Bumberpuff shook it.

"Welcome," Quentin said. "Are you ready to get started for real?"

"We are," the Prawatt said. "But are they?" His arm pointed toward a cluster of Sklorno, some geared up in defensive black, others in the orange of the offense. All of the players had their heads lowered, their eyestalks tucked back in an aggressive posture.

"Don't worry about them," Quentin said. "Just give them time."

"Time," Bumberpuff said. "Our races have been fighting for hundreds of years. How much time will it take to make up for that?"

"Don't get all philosophical, Cappy. You're here to play football. So go with John and Hokor and start learning your positions."

Bumberpuff and his three Prawatt teammates jogged over to John, who waved them in.

QUENTIN SLAPPED THE BALL into his hands for the fake snap, then dropped back five steps and read through his routes. The four Prawatt scrambled to cover routes by Hawick, Halawa, Starcher and Tara the Freak. Quentin tossed a light pass at Hawick, just to see if Bumberpuff would react in time. Hawick jumped up fifteen feet. Bumberpuff jumped as well, but his reaction was too slow. At the apex of her leap, Hawick hauled in the pass — the Prawatt wasn't even close to stopping the play.

Hawick landed and scooted toward the end zone. Bumberpuff hit the turf and pinwheeled after her, blazingly fast, but too far behind her to catch up. By the time she crossed the goal line,

Hokor's golf cart was already closing in, his amplified voice echoing through the stadium.

"*Bumberpuff!* What the hell is wrong with you?"

For the entire practice, Quentin had torched the Prawatt defensive backs. His only incompletions came when his receivers dropped a ball — the Prawatt weren't stopping anything. Hokor's frustration grew with each pass.

The coach's cart floated down to the goal line, where Bumberpuff stood helplessly. Hokor hopped out of the cart and stomped forward to stand in front of the much taller Prawatt.

"Bumberpuff, what did I tell you was the first rule of covering the outside third?"

"Wider than the widest, deeper than the deepest," Bumberpuff said.

"Is that complicated?"

"No, Coach."

"I mean, you were captain of a big, fancy warship, weren't you?"

"Yes, Coach."

"So you commanded thousands of sentients and made life-and-death decisions. It seems like that job would require at least *some* level of intelligence. Are you intelligent, Bumberpuff?"

"Yes, Coach."

"So if you *are* intelligent, are you *sure* that wider than the widest, deeper than the deepest isn't too complicated for you?"

Bumberpuff started to vibrate. "No, Coach."

"I do not understand," Hokor said. "You are smart, and this is not complicated, so perhaps I am missing something — on that last pass, were you deeper than the deepest?"

Bumberpuff's vibrations grew into an audible rattle. "No, Coach."

Hokor grabbed his ball cap and threw it to the ground. His black-striped yellow fur stuck up in all directions. "So maybe you are not so smart after all! In this game, Bumberpuff, the objective is to *not get beat deep*! You are *not* supposed to let the receiver run past you as if your feet are encased in lead! This time, get your positioning right!" Hokor's eye closed tight and his whole body twitched. *"Run it again!"*

Hawick jogged past Quentin on her way to lining up for the next play. "Quentinbarnes, this is fun-fun-*fun*! I love to make the Prawatt look stupid!"

Quentin took a ball out of the rack, tossed it lightly with one hand. *Fun?* The Prawatt weren't having any fun at all. Neither was Quentin, for that matter.

Bumberpuff was the best of the four, and he flat-out wasn't ready to stop the Criminals' passing attack. They only way he'd see playing time was if other DBs suffered an injury or the game wound up being a blowout. As for the rest of them? They wouldn't even be on the active roster for the game against Yall, and if they didn't step it up, they wouldn't be on it for the following week's tilt against the Orbiting Death.

Quentin called out the signals for the next play. It was way too early to tell, but he was already starting to fear that maybe the Prawatt experiment would fail.

If it did, Tier Two would be waiting.

QUENTIN AND HIS TEAMMATES had gathered at the back of the tunnel. The Yall Criminals were ahead, standing in the tunnel mouth, waiting to take the field. They wore light-purple jerseys with white-trimmed black numbers and letters. White helmets bore a purple stripe down the center and the purple "ball-and-chain Sklorno" logo on either side. White arm armor and dark-purple gloves matched their dark-purple leg armor, which had three thin, vertical stripes running down the outside of each thigh.

Beyond the purple-clad Criminals, the open air of Ionath Stadium awaited. Quentin heard the chanting of the fans, 185,000-plus waiting for their team's home opener.

"LET'S go KRAK-ens!" clap, clap, clap-clap-clap. *"LET'S go KRAK-ens!"* clap, clap, clap-clap-clap.

Those sounds, but something else as well, some kind of counterchant done in squeals and chirps. Maybe he'd see what that was when he took the field.

The announcer's voice filtered in from the stadium, echoing through the tunnel's narrow confines.

"Hello, sentients, and welcome once again to Ionath Stadium. We are delighted to have you here for the first home game of the 2685 season. Please give your warmest greetings to today's visiting team, the Yall Criminals of the Sklorno Dynasty!"

The Yall players ran out onto the field to boos, the sandpaper sound of forearm bristles scraping together, but also to cheers. As one of two Tier One teams from the Sklorno Dynasty, the Criminals always enjoyed good support among that race. Having the best quarterback in football — 2683's league MVP Rick Renaud — also didn't exactly detract from the fan base.

Quentin and his teammates moved up to the front of the tunnel. They packed in, waiting, jostling against each other. Next to him stood Captain Cormorant Bumberpuff, resplendent in his new Krakens gear.

Messal had designed the Prawatt uniforms. A form-fitting black jersey clung to the X-body. Dozens of neat little holes let Bumberpuff's eyespots see through. A white-trimmed, orange number 39 blazed from the center of the X. Above that were small, white-trimmed orange letters that spelled out KRAKENS. The same number was on the back, the captain's odd last name above that.

Bumberpuff's flexible arms and legs were bare, save for Messal's brilliant touch — black streamers trimmed in white with orange piping at the outer edges. The streamers looked just like the ones Bumberpuff and the Harpies had worn back on the *Grieve*, a touching tip of the hat to Prawatt culture.

Bumberpuff was the only Prawatt to dress for the game. To create room on the roster, Hokor cut Breedsville from the squad — probably the first of several difficult choices that had to be made. Bumberpuff had been a starship captain; today, the Prawatt was an honorary *team* captain. Quentin and John both felt it was important to make a statement that the Prawatt were now part of the Ionath football tradition.

Quentin felt the stadium's vibrations, the Ionath fans waiting for their team. After opening the season with two road games, then the Week Three bye, he and his teammates would finally defend the blue field of Ionath Stadium.

As he looked out of the tunnel to the stands, he saw familiar sights: orange- and black-clad fans; thousands of #10 replica jerseys; pom-poms waving and flags flying; the special, crysteel-enclosed sections that contained thousands of Sklorno males, the little balls of black fur bouncing madly against the clear walls and each other.

"LET'S go KRAK-ens!" clap, clap, clap-clap-clap. "LET'S go KRAK-ens!" clap, clap, clap-clap-clap.

But Quentin also saw something else, something other than the expected complement of white and purple Criminals supporters. He saw ... protest signs?

"Beings of all races, let's hear it for ... your ... Ionath, KRAAAAAA-KENNNNNNNS!"

Quentin and his teammates rushed onto the field to the roar of a sold-out stadium. Fireworks exploded overhead, silhouetting the flying Harrah and Creterakian civilians who took advantage of their airborne abilities to get a free view of the game.

As he ran to the sidelines, he saw perhaps a dozen protest placards spaced out around the home side of the field, mostly held by Sklorno females.

KILLERS GO HOME one of the signs said.

NO PRAWATT NO! said another.

As the Krakens gathered at the sidelines, Quentin saw one of the placard holders rush down the stand's aisle and leap over the retaining wall — she sprinted toward Bumberpuff. Stadium security came out of nowhere, two orange-clad Sklorno and an orange-clad Human hitting the attacker and bringing her down. The scene distracted Quentin, took his attention away from his teammates.

A fist slammed into his shoulder pad.

"Q!" John said. "Let's go, brother!"

Quentin turned to see his wide-eyed linebacker, then took in the rest of the team gathered around, all waiting for Quentin's pregame chant. He could worry about protestors some other time.

He raised his right hand high.

"Bring it in!"

The team pressed in close, reached up toward his fist.

It was time to fight.

QUENTIN STOOD ON THE SIDELINES, watching Rick Renaud do what Rick Renaud did, which was effortlessly dissect a defensive secondary.

The year before, a John Tweedy/Mum-O-Killowe sack had knocked the Yall quarterback out of the game. Ionath had returned home with a 27-17 win.

This time, Renaud didn't get hurt.

Quentin could only shake his head as he watched a flawless performance. The Criminals were stacked with great players at every position. Renaud threw short routes, medium patterns and long bombs against the Krakens' depleted secondary. He hit Concord over and over, and Quentin had to admit that the receiver was better than anyone on the Krakens — possibly even the best in the league. The Criminals' number-two receiver, Peoria, was good enough to be the number-one on probably fifteen of the GFL's twenty-two teams.

Renaud also got the ball to his All-Pro tight end, Andreas Kimming. The big Human caught everything thrown his way. Top to bottom, the Criminals had an amazing receiving corps — even better than that of the Krakens.

When the Criminals didn't throw, they gave the ball to speedster Jack Townsend or bruising fullback Tay "the Weazel" Nguyen. The pair's drastically different running styles kept the defense off balance.

As if the league's best offense wasn't enough, the Criminals had defensive stars as well. Middle linebackers Forrest Dane Cauthorn and Riha the Hammer anchored Yall's 3-4 defense. Both players had improved from the year before, but where the Criminals' D really improved was on the defensive line. Tackles Anthony Meaders and Kin-Ah-Thak hounded Quentin all day, generating consistent pressure up the middle and forcing him to scramble over and over again.

Despite being sacked four times, Quentin played well and so did his offense. He hit eight different receivers on the afternoon, connecting with Halawa for a pair of first-half touchdowns. A minor injury took Hawick out of the game mid-way through the third quarter, and even that didn't stop the Krakens — Quentin added touchdown passes to Milford and Yotaro Kobayasho.

Ionath put 28 points on the board, which didn't do much compared to the Criminals' 44.

Late in the fourth quarter, when it was clear a comeback was impossible, Hokor put Bumberpuff in the game for the Criminals' final drive. The captain pinwheeled out onto the field to a chorus of *boos* and scraping forearm fur. If this was how the home crowd treated the newest Kraken, Quentin dreaded how things might go when Ionath traveled to the Purist Nation in Week Six.

Watching Bumberpuff try — and fail — to stop Renaud's passing attack filled Quentin with an odd sensation of pride. The Prawatt was still pretty bad at the position, but the two tackles he made knocked Criminals receivers on their asses. Bumberpuff had a long way to go, but now, during a real game, the Prawatt's intensity cranked up several notches; Quentin saw real potential, the promise of a dominant cornerback.

The lopsided loss hurt. Despite the desolate feeling of being 0-3, after shaking hands with the Criminals players, Quentin led his team around Ionath Stadium, high-fiving all the fans who stuck around for the new tradition. The Prawatt skipped that tradition and went straight to the locker room — Quentin couldn't blame them.

In the locker room, there were few smiles to be had. Quentin hid his true feelings and tried to stay positive, giving encouragement to the teammates that needed it. But there was nothing he could say to chase away the sense of despair.

Ionath was 0-3. Ionath was in last place. And unless something changed and changed quickly, Ionath was headed for relegation.

• • •

Transcript from the "Galaxy's Greatest Sports Show with Dan, Akbar and Tarat the Smasher"

DAN: No matter how you slice it, it's a tragedy. It's a tragedy for the Jupiter Jacks, it's a tragedy for the league, and it's a tragedy for Steve Compton's family.

AKBAR: The Jacks can't seem to buy a break. I mean, sure, they're undefeated at four-and-oh, but Compton is the second quarterback to die in as many seasons.

TARAT: I am talking to my contacts as we speak, Dan. I am trying to get more news on what the Jacks will do to replace Compton.

DAN: I hope those contacts come through for you, Smasher. I wouldn't want to see Yolanda Davenport scoop you again like she did with her coverage of the Prawatt at the *Combine*.

TARAT: I am less than pleased about that, Dan.

DAN: Back to the death of Compton. He was everyone's favorite story of the year, and he dies on a late hit? I hope Froese takes action against Canad the Brilliant for that.

TARAT: Dan, Froese will do just that. The game is deadly enough without late hits. Players are not ready to defend themselves after the whistle blows.

DAN: I say it again, this is *tragic*. Last year Jupiter makes it to the Galaxy Bowl on the arm of quarterback Shriaz Zia. In that game, they go up twenty-one to *nothing* on the Themala Dreadnaughts. Looks like the Jacks will win their fourth GFL championship, right? Then, *boom*, Zia dies on a hit from Tibi the Unkempt. The Dreadnaughts come from behind and win twenty-eight to twenty-four. All of us, myself included, figure the Jacks are going to suck this season because they lost an All-Pro quarterback, but what do we see? Backup Steve Compton stepping into the starting role and leading the Jacks to three straight wins.

AKBAR: It was like nothing had changed, Dan. No one knew how good Compton could be. And now the Jacks are once again without a quarterback. They have to make a trade. I mean, they have four wins and are in first place. Even if they win only half of their remaining games, they finish with eight wins and probably make the playoffs.

DAN: Sure, but what are they going to do if they make it to—

TARAT: Silence! I have a call coming in. One moment while I get this information.

AKBAR: Uh, Dan ... is the Smasher taking a personal call during our show?

DAN: This should be good.

TARAT: My call is finished. I have a story of great significance.

DAN: My cup runneth over. Do tell, Tarat, do tell.

TARAT: My sources tell me that the Jacks have already made a trade offer. All-Pro cornerback Xuchang for Ionath Krakens backup quarterback Donald Pine.

DAN: Hellooooo! You heard it here first, folks. Take *that*, Yolanda Davenport and Galaxy Sports Magazine. Don Pine once again in the copper, silver and gold? Be still my heart. Tarat, is this a straight-up trade?

TARAT: That is the offer as I understand it. The only question is whether Gredok the Splithead will accept the offer.

DAN: What do you mean *if*? The Krakens' defensive secondary is awful, and let's be honest — this ridiculous Prawatt experiment isn't going to work out. The trade is a done deal.

AKBAR: I don't know, Dan. Other teams made offers for Pine, but I heard that Quentin Barnes demanded Pine stay at Ionath.

TARAT: I have also heard this.

DAN: Well, Barnes simply *can't* object to this one. Sure, Ionath's backup quarterback would be Yitzhak Goldman, who is horrible, but if the Krakens don't do something fast they're headed straight down to Tier Two. Besides, the Krakens definitely got the better of their last trade with the Jacks. Ionath got Michael Kimberlin, who has been a great offensive lineman for them, and Jupiter got Denver, who barely even sees any playing time.

AKBAR: She started out strong last season but hasn't shown anything over the last eight or nine games. Maybe she was good in Ionath because she had chemistry with Barnes and Pine, but she wasn't productive for Zia or Compton.

DAN: Wow, funny how things can come full-circle, isn't it? Pine won two Galaxy Bowls with the Jacks in '75 and '76. Can you imagine him returning to Jupiter to help the Jacks win it all this year? You can't write a storyline like this.

TARAT: And Ionath could also have a line of story. I realize they are winless, but Quentin Barnes is having an amazing season. If they land Xuchang and some of the Prawatt players become competent, the Krakens could still make a run at the playoffs.

AKBAR: Wow, Tarat, maybe those spider snacks are old and they've fermented. You *must* be drunk. Playoffs? They're not making this trade for a run at the playoffs, they'll do it to dump Pine's huge contract, which clears up a ton of salary cap space for the off-season.

DAN: Good point, Akbar. Don Pine is the highest-paid backup in the GFL. He even makes more than some *starting* quarterbacks. Xuchang's salary is probably half of Pine's. If the Krakens do this deal and also avoid relegation, they'll be poised to make a run in 2686.

TARAT: You both should listen to me. The Krakens are not done with this season, I assure you.

DAN: Tarat, you're crazy, but you did break this story, and for that I say that *you are the man!*

TARAT: I am not of your species, Dan.

DAN: Right, sorry … *you are the Warrior.* Let's go to the lines and see what the galaxy thinks of this breaking news. Line three from Mallorum, you're on the space, *go!*

CALLER: Dan, this trade is a bad move by the Krakens. They should trade Pine to a crappy team like Shorah, not to a contender. What if Ionath winds up facing Jupiter in the Galaxy Bowl?

AKBAR: Oh, give me a *break!* The Krakens are winless, and you think they could suddenly go all the way?

DAN: Akbar, little buddy, for once I agree with you.

AKBAR: Not that nickname again.

DAN: You know you love it, little buddy! Line one from Yall, you're on the space, *go!*

GFL WEEK FOUR ROUNDUP
Courtesy of Galaxy Sports Network

Home		Away	
Coranadillana Cloud Killers	10	**Alimum Armada**	13
Buddha City Elite	17	Isis Ice Storm	13
Hittoni Hullwalkers	14	**Wabash Wolfpack**	27
Ionath Krakens	28	**Yall Criminals**	44
To Pirates	25	Orbiting Death	21
New Rodina Astronauts	14	**Bartel Water Bugs**	28
Bord Brigands	21	**Neptune Scarlet Fliers**	24
D'Kow War Dogs	14	**Vik Vanguard**	17
Sheb Stalkers	13	**Jang Atom Smashers**	14
Jupiter Jacks	28	Shorah Warlords	25

The 2685 campaign is one-third over. Powerhouse teams are already emerging, and the specter of relegation is already rearing its ugly head.

Four teams remain undefeated. The Bartel Water Bugs continue to be the surprise of the season, moving to 4-0 with their 28-14 win over New Rodina (1-3). The wins come despite Bugs rookie QB Andre "Death Ray" Ridley completing just eight passes for 122 yards. Ridley ran well, however, picking up 87 yards and a touchdown on the ground.

The win keeps the Water Bugs tied for first in the Solar Division with Jupiter (4-0).

Jupiter quarterback Steve Compton died mid-way through the fourth quarter of the Jacks' 28-25 win over the Shorah Warlords (0-4). This is the second quarterback killed in the last five games for Jupiter, who lost starting QB Shriaz Zia in the 2684 Galaxy Bowl.

Bartel has a bye in Week Five, while Jupiter faces archrival Neptune (2-1). The Scarlet Fliers won their second-straight game, beating Bord (2-2) by a score of 24-21.

In the Planet Division, Yall remains undefeated at 3-0 thanks to a 44-28 win over Ionath (0-3). Krakens quarterback Quentin Barnes put up another amazing performance, throwing for 327 yards and four TD passes. Criminals QB Rick Renaud countered with three touchdown passes, all to wide receiver Concord. Fullback Tay "the Weazel" Nguyen added two rushing touchdowns, while kicker Roland Ost added three field goals.

Yall moved into sole possession of first place in the Planet Division thanks to the Orbiting Death's first loss of the season. OS1 dropped 25-21 to the To Pirates (2-1). Wabash (3-1) defeated Hittoni (0-4) 27-14 to move into a tie for second.

The relegation watch begins for Ionath, Hittoni and Shorah, who are all winless.

Deaths

Jupiter Jacks quarterback **Steve Compton,** killed on a late hit from Shorah Warlords middle linebacker Canad the Brilliant. GFL Commissioner Rob Froese has suspended Canad for three games. In addition, Canad will not get credit for the fatality, which would have been his second in upper-tier play.

Offensive Player of the Week

Ionath quarterback **Quentin Barnes,** who threw four touchdown passes in a loss to the Yall Criminals. Barnes went 25-of-31 for 327 yards and added another 75 yards on the ground.

Defensive Player of the Week

Yalla the Biter, linebacker from the Orbiting Death. Yalla had seven solo tackles, one forced fumble and three sacks on To Pirates quarterback Frank Zimmer.

17

Week Five:
Orbiting Death at
Ionath Krakens

PLANET DIVISION

3-0 Yall Criminals

3-1 OS1 Orbiting Death

3-1 Wabash Wolfpack

2-1 Alimum Armada

2-1 To Pirates

2-2 Buddha City Elite

2-2 Isis Ice Storm

1-2 Themala Dreadnaughts (bye)

1-3 Coranadillana Cloud Killers

0-3 Ionath Krakens

0-4 Hittoni Hullwalkers

SOLAR DIVISION

4-0 Bartel Water Bugs

4-0 Jupiter Jacks

2-1 Neptune Scarlet Fliers

2-1 Texas Earthlings (bye)

2-2 Bord Brigands

2-2 Jang Atom Smashers

2-2 Vik Vanguard

1-2 D'Kow War Dogs

1-3 New Rodina Astronauts

1-3 Sheb Stalkers

0-4 Shorah Warlords

THE NIGHT AFTER the Criminals game, Quentin and John sat in Coach Hokor's Ionath Stadium office. Hokor sat behind his desk, of course. In a corner chair sat the team owner, his pedipalp fingers casually touching a new bracelet that probably contained more mineral wealth than some small planets.

Just like for the last injury report, Doc Patah floated above Hokor's left shoulder. Once again, a medical holo of a Sklorno hovered above Coach Hokor's desk. This time, an ankle.

Hawick's ankle.

"She's out for the season," Doc Patah said. "She has a torn pedal flexor retinaculum ligament. I've repaired it and embedded it with dissolving carbon fibers to speed up healing, but if she tries to play this year, she will permanently destroy the ligament."

Quentin leaned forward. He rested his face in his hands. When would the bad news stop coming? Milford and Halawa were having great seasons, but that was in no small part due to the fact that Hawick always drew the opposition's number-one cornerback *and* was usually double-covered as well. That left Milford and Halawa in one-on-one coverage. They were very good players, but they were both young — neither of them had Hawick's star power.

"Wonderful," Gredok said. "Another enormous salary I will be paying a player to sit on the bench."

John poked his finger through the holographic image. "It's not all bad, your blackness. Once you sign off on that Don Pine trade, we get Xuchang and you lose Pine's obnoxious contract. This is like the best trade ever — we'll have Xuchang at one corner and Wahiawa at the other. Our defense will be instantly better, you'll see."

"It had better be," Gredok said. "I grow weary of your excuses, Tweedy. And yours, Hokor."

Threads of green swirled across Hokor's eye. If the Krakens dropped to Tier Two, Gredok would fire him. At *least* fire him; it wasn't a stretch to imagine that Hokor the Hookchest might pay for his failure with his life.

Quentin again stared at the image of Hawick's injury. She'd

been on her way to an All-Pro season. No one he'd ever played with had her speed. No one, except ...

He suddenly sat up straight.

"We don't need Xuchang."

John groaned. "Oh for crying out loud, here we go again. Q, you need to let go of this thing with Pine. He needs to move on, and *we* need a cornerback to replace Vacaville."

"We *have* a replacement for Vacaville," Quentin said. "We have Bumberpuff."

John threw up his hands. "Have you been hitting the Kermiac extract or something? Are you *high*?"

JUST SAY NO! flashed across his forehead.

Gredok stood up, his jewelry clinking together like chimes when he did. "I find myself quite surprised to agree with John Tweedy, Barnes, but if you again let your personal feelings about Don Pine get in the way of this trade, John's theory would seem to be quite accurate."

"It's a hypothesis, not a theory," Quentin said. "And *no*, I'm not on drugs, and *yes*, I do want to trade Pine to Jupiter — just not for Xuchang."

Hokor's black-striped fur fluffed up in annoyance. "Then who do you expect in return?"

"We need to replace Hawick," Quentin said. "I want Denver to come home."

Everyone just stared at him.

John leaned back in his chair and crossed his muscular arms. "Of course. You and your damn precious offense. Are you really that selfish?"

"I'm not being selfish! I throw against the Prawatt every day in practice. I am telling you, they *will* develop. We don't need Xuchang, but we *do* need a number-one receiver."

Hokor waved away the holo of Hawick's leg. "Denver has played poorly in Jupiter," the coach said. "And you want to give up *Donald Pine* for her?"

"Ridiculous," Gredok said. "We will trade Don Pine for Xuchang."

Quentin felt the panic starting to build. Bumberpuff was going to be great, he could feel that in his bones. He *knew* Denver would rebound, *knew* she was one of the best receivers in the league even if her current stats didn't show it. If Quentin could convince Gredok, within a week or two he'd have a top-flight receiver *and* a shut-down corner to bolster the defense. To win a championship, he needed both things.

But Gredok had made his decision. He would never back down. Quentin had to sweeten the pot.

"Gredok, I guarantee this will work," Quentin said. "If you trade for Denver, and we *don't* make the playoffs? I'll take a fifty-percent pay cut next year."

Gredok's black fur fluffed once, then lay flat. "I believe John's theory has become a hypothesis," he said. "Four weeks in and we are winless, and you bargain such a sum on the playoffs — clearly you *are* using controlled substances."

"I'll put it in writing," Quentin said. "I'll have Danny draw up the deal right now."

Gredok's pedipalps quivered — this would give him an opportunity to get another dig in on Quentin's Dolphin agent. "If you have a contract box to me within the hour, then I accept your terms."

John stood up so suddenly his chair flew back into the wall. "This is crap! What about my defense? Pretty boy gets what he wants *again*?"

"John, calm down," Quentin said. "It's not like that!"

"Whatever, Q. What you want is always more important than what anyone else needs."

John stormed out of the office. Quentin wanted to go after him, calm him down, but he'd have to do that later.

For now, he had a trade to make.

THE GOLD-, SILVER- AND COPPER-PAINTED shuttle door started to open, but it hadn't even hit the deck before Denver leapt out into the landing bay. Milford rushed in and tackled her. The two Sklorno fell, a squealing, wiggling pile of happiness. Mezquitic jumped on the pile. She had been on the team during Milford's rookie season. So had Hawick, but with the cast on her leg, she couldn't join in the horseplay. She stood with the other Sklorno, all of them fidgeting and getting spun up from the excitement.

Quentin smiled as he watched. It was impossible not to feel joy at the friends reuniting.

Then, he felt a hand on his shoulder. He turned, knowing he would see the blue face of Don Pine. Don had dressed in one of his best suits. He still looked the very picture of the quarterback/coverboy.

"Kid," Don said, "it's been an experience."

"You can say that again, Old Man."

They shook hands.

Don Pine was leaving. There was no question that the Krakens were Quentin's team, but Don had always been there in some capacity — as a security blanket, as a threat for the starting position, as a friend, then an enemy, then as a friend again. Don had answered questions, provided guidance and offered unsolicited advice when he thought it was needed. With him gone, Quentin lost his final crutch. No matter what happened from here on out, Quentin would be the one to decide the course of the franchise.

"A part of me is sad to see you go," Quentin said. "But it's a very small part."

Don nodded. "So, we're not even then?"

The man still hadn't owned up to the fact that he'd shaved points and even fixed games. Quentin was no angel, either; he had blocked efforts to trade Pine — not for the good of the franchise, but to punish the man. Quentin knew he had no right to do that. And then there was the simple truth that, were it not for Don's patience and guidance, Quentin might very well have washed out in his rookie season.

Were they even? After what Quentin had done for Don and what Don had not done for Quentin — no, not even close. But did balancing the scales really matter? Don was moving on. The Ionath Krakens belonged to Quentin.

Quentin offered his hand. "Let's just say I hope you have a great season." Don shook it. "That's how it is, huh? Fair enough. Well, no hard feelings on my part. Take care of my team for me."

The veteran QB gave Quentin one final slap on the shoulder, then walked to the silver-, gold- and copper-painted shuttle.

Something hit Quentin hard, lifting him up and driving him to the deck. Quentin groaned, first at the pain, then at the disgusting sensation of drool landing on his face and neck.

"Quentinbarnesquentinbarnes*quentinbarnes*! I am home-home-home!"

Quentin laughed and pushed away three hundred pounds of Sklorno receiver. "Take it easy, Denver! We're happy to have you back."

"*Home-home-home. LoveloveloveLOVELOVE!*" The Sklorno jumped off of him and — for no apparent reason — sprinted out of the landing bay. Milford and Mezquitic followed, as did the rest of the Sklorno who could no longer contain the contagious excitement. Hawick hobbled along after them.

[**PLEASE CLEAR THE LANDING BAY, IMMEDIATELY. SHUTTLE PREPARING TO DEPART.**]

A thick, scarred hand reached down. Quentin took it and was pulled to his feet.

"Thanks, Ju," he said.

"Sure," Ju said. "You might want to get a towel or something. You've been boogered."

Quentin could feel the drool sliding down his face. "Speaking of getting boogered, where's your brother?"

Ju looked around, then shrugged. "I think he wanted to skip it this time. He's pretty mad we got Denver instead of a cornerback, Q. But don't worry, once we start putting up wins, he'll get over it."

Ju walked off.

John had never missed an event like this before. He was madder than Quentin thought. But yeah, he'd get over it once the wins started coming.

And those wins *had* to start this week, against the Orbiting Death. Three straight losses made it almost impossible to reach the playoffs. *Four* straight losses? There was no coming back from that.

QUENTIN, CHOTO THE BRIGHT AND MICHAEL Kimberlin sat in the back of a limousine looking out the tinted windows. Quentin didn't like riding in limos — that's what the upper-class rode back on Micovi — but Kimberlin had insisted the anonymity was important for this short trip.

The car slid slowly past Ionath Stadium's main entrance, a hundred-foot-wide, fifty-foot-high brick arch. Banners representing the Tier One teams hung from the inside of the arch, but none as big as the Krakens banner dangling from the apex. A fence of ornate black bars ran from one side of the arch to the other, interspersed with closed gates. On game days those gates opened, allowing thousands of fans into the stadium.

Thirty or so sentients were walking back and forth in front of the black fence. They carried holosigns, cloth flags and even painted cardboard, all of these things sending a clear message of hatred and intolerance.!

KILLERS GO HOME!

NEVER AGAIN! PRAWATT ARE EVIL!

NOT HERE, NOT NOW, NOT EVER!

Most of the protesters were female Sklorno, dressed head to toe in black, but there were also Humans — Quentin recognized some of them as regulars from the Blessed Lamb bar, the home of Purist Nation ex-pats who had migrated to Ionath.

"This is awful," Quentin said. "I can't believe this is happening *here*."

Choto's eye swirled with purple and green — purple for a pained sense of confusion, green for anxiety. "Ignorance knows no borders. The Purist Nation did not invent hatred, Quentin."

This made no sense. For centuries the Prawatt had been the galaxy's boogeymen. Not just in the Purist Nation, where any non-

Human was automatically "evil," but in all systems. The Krakens were bringing Prawatt into the galaxy as equals. Football gave five races a common goal, brought them together — now Quentin wanted to add a *sixth* race, and these sentients protested?

"I want to go talk to them."

He reached for the door handle, but Choto grabbed his forearm.

"I do not recommend that, Quentin," the Quyth Warrior said. "The protesters might not appreciate a sudden appearance by the sentient that brought the Prawatt to Ionath. And talking to them would be a waste of words. Sentients like these ... they do not think with logic."

Choto made sense. Quentin nodded and let go of the handle. Maybe it was best to stay in the car.

"It doesn't look all that bad," Quentin said. "It's just a handful of sentients."

Michael nodded. "That's because we're on Ionath. The Sklorno population here isn't that high, and citizens of Quyth cities are used to species integration. There are protests at GFL headquarters on Earth. There have already been small riots on Alimum, where we travel in Week Eight. And one can only imagine what it will be like when we travel to Buddha City Station next week."

Quentin hadn't thought of that. Maybe the Purist Nation hadn't invented hatred, but certainly they had perfected it.

He stared out at the protestors, his heart heavy with the thought that he could work his whole life to make things better and nothing would ever really change.

"There's got to be something I can do," he said.

Kimberlin shook his big head. "You can't cure centuries of hatred in a single game, nor in a single season. We are doing the right thing, but oftentimes the right thing comes with a steep price."

What would that price be? More violence?

"I've seen enough," Quentin said. "Let's go. It's almost time for practice."

The limo slid away, leaving the protesters behind.

• • •

QUENTIN DROPPED BACK five steps and planted. He had no pressure, as there was no defensive or offensive line, but the clock inside his head ticked down regardless.

Denver shot downfield. Captain Bumberpuff ran with her, step for step. At 20 yards, Denver cut right at a 45-degree angle — a flag route. Bumberpuff matched the cut but lost a step in the process. Quentin's mental clock ticked down to zero, and he launched a deep pass.

Denver and Bumberpuff ran for the corner, both watching the ball descend, both leaping high at the last second. Such a sight: an orange-clad Sklorno launching off her long, folded rear legs, all four eyestalks locked on the ball's path, tentacles reaching high to pluck the ball out of the air, and a black-clad X-Walker leaping just as high off of springy legs, curved arms stretching up toward the ball.

The step Bumberpuff had lost cost him: the ball sailed past his outstretched hand and into Denver's tentacles. She started to descend, but Bumberpuff wasn't finished — as they fell, he wrapped Denver up with one arm and started savagely beating at the ball with the other. Just before they hit the turf, the ball popped out.

Incomplete pass.

Quentin's left hand curled into a fist. "*Yes,*" he hissed. That was the kind of go-for-broke defensive play they had been missing. Bumberpuff had been beaten deep — which was bad — but he'd stayed with the play right to the last moment and broken up the pass.

Bumberpuff and Denver both stood, then they smashed together, tentacles and arms ripping at each other.

"Knock it off!" Quentin shouted as he sprinted for the end zone along with his teammates. The Prawatt and Sklorno players got there first, of course, and in seconds a two-player scuffle turned into a species-on-species gang fight.

Hokor's enraged voice echoed through the stadium: "You players quit this grab-assing, *right now!*"

The coach's words did nothing to stop the fight. Humans, Quyth Warriors, Ki and HeavyG players arrived, grabbed the combatants and pulled them apart. Quentin dove into the fray, gripping Denver by the back of her skinny neck and Bumberpuff by the base of one arm.

"I said, *knock it off!*"

A rasper snaked out, wrapped around his arm and ripped away a long strip of skin. At the same time, a Prawatt arm whip-snapped him in the throat.

Quentin dropped to his knees, coughing, suddenly unable to draw in a breath. His right hand clutched at the blood pouring off his left forearm. The sounds of scuffling slowed, then stopped, leaving only the high-pitched chittering of the Sklorno and Bumberpuff's bellowing, Human-sounding voice.

"Don't blame me if you can't hang onto the rock, *scrub*," he shouted.

Quentin looked up. Michael Kimberlin had the Prawatt locked up in his gigantic arms — Bumberpuff wasn't going anywhere.

Both Ju and John held Denver, who fought like mad to break free. "*Scrub?* Stupid demon, I am the number-one target of his holiness Quentinbarnes! I will catch holy passes in your *face* and make you embarrassed!"

Hokor's floating golf cart dropped down to the field. The diminutive coach hopped out; then he just stood there, staring first at Bumberpuff, then at Denver. His eye flooded a pure black. His fur fluffed all the way out.

Everyone took a step back. Even Quentin.

Hokor pointed a pedipalp at Bumberpuff. "You, come *here*." He then pointed at Denver. "And *you*. Now."

Arms released the players. They walked to Hokor like they were walking to an execution. The righteous anger of a coach seemed to be a universal concept that cut across all species and cultures.

Denver and Bumberpuff stood side by side, both looking down at Hokor. He stared up at them, his eye so black it could have been onyx.

When Hokor spoke, it was with a quiet voice — the voice of a sentient working hard to control himself. "You two grab-assers hurt my quarterback."

Both players looked at Quentin. He held up his bloody left arm to emphasize Hokor's comments.

"It's bad," Quentin said. "I might never throw the ball again."

Bumberpuff let out a very Human sigh of annoyance, but Denver instantly started to tremble.

Hokor glared at both players, then pointed to the stands. "Start running," he said. "Up the stairs to the top of the lower bowl, turn left, come to the next set of stairs, come down, turn right, run up the next set, and keep repeating."

Denver took off like a shot, obeying the order.

Bumberpuff rattled in disgust. He still wasn't used to taking orders. "How long do you expect me to do this ridiculous task?"

Hokor grabbed his little hat and threw it to the blue field. "You run until I get tired! There is no fighting on my field. Now *go*!"

Bumberpuff took a step back, then sprinted after Denver.

Quentin felt a nudge on his right side. He looked to see Mum-O-Killowe.

"Gris hacha danad," Mum-O said quietly.

Quentin didn't understand the words, but he got the meaning. Mum-O was laughing, was saying *remember when that was us?* Quentin laughed, too. He did remember. It had been just three seasons ago when he and Mum-O had been forced to run as a punishment for fighting each other.

Quentin reached up and gave Mum-O's helmet a friendly slap. "They'll figure it out," he said. "Let's get back to it." Quentin cupped his hands to his mouth. "Krakens! Get with your groups, this is practice, not happy-happy break time!"

The players jogged to their spots. Doc Patah would have to fix his arm, and the fight was a bad sign for team cooperation, but he couldn't control the fire of excitement that burned in his chest — Bumberpuff had *made a play*. He was coming along fast, as were the other Prawatt.

And on top of that, Denver was looking *good*. She wanted to be here. Whatever happened to drag down her game, she'd left that baggage on Jupiter.

Maybe, just maybe, Quentin had been right. Right to risk everything to bring the Prawatt here, right to trade for Denver instead of Xuchang.

He took a football off the rack, then looked right. Milford stood on the line, ready to run her route. Cretzlefinger stood opposite her, ready to stop it.

"Blue, forty-four! Hut-*hut!*"

"CHICK, WE ARE WITNESSING HISTORY here today, but it's not a history lesson that the Ionath Krakens are going to want to remember. Last week was the first time a member of the Prawatt race played in a GFL game. This week is the first time that race has ever *started* a game, which Cormorant Bumberpuff did at cornerback, and the way he is playing, it might be the last."

"Masara, I couldn't have said it better myself. Well, I could have, and probably will, so let me go ahead and do just that. Ionath fought to bring the Prawatt players in as a way to save the season, but with Condor Adrienne victimizing the Krakens with *four* first-half touchdowns, the experiment could be over almost as soon as it began. Bumberpuff started, as you said, and three other Prawatt have rotated in at various times. *All* of them seem lost out there. They aren't changing direction fast enough to cover the hook patterns or out-cuts, they don't seem to know how to position themselves to cover the slant, and they couldn't cover a deep pass if they were made of pebble-skin leather and processed in the Rawlings football factory. Condor Adrienne has *three hundred and twenty* yards, Masara. Some quarterbacks would kill to have that many yards in a full game, and Condor has it in the *first half* alone."

"Chick, at this point, what kind of halftime adjustments do the Krakens need to make?"

"Well, Masara, the Krakens have put up fourteen points themselves. They have to kick the offense into high gear. As for their defense, they may have to sit Bumberpuff and bring Vacaville back in, but she's had a terrible year and probably won't do any better. The Krakens have also tried replacing rookie free safety Sandpoint with the Prawatt Katzembaum Weasley — and no, folks at home, I am neither drunk nor making that name up. Neither can stop Condor's long pass — he's dropping bombs with the regularity of me on an ultra-high-fiber diet."

"*Chick*! Are you comparing touchdown passes to your —"

"Sorry about that, Masara, sorry, folks at home, but you do have to admit that both things *are* brown."

"*Chick*! I can't believe —"

"Time for a word from one of our sponsors! Let's break for this message from Shi-Ki-Kill Shipping. Remember, if you want to protect your cargo against pirates, doesn't it make sense to ship it via a company with lethality built right into their name?"

JOHN TWEEDY'S EYES had never been wider. I CAN EAT METAL AND POOP RIVETS scrolled in circles around his neck.

"Dammit, you stinking Prawatt! You have to *cover!*"

The locker room smelled of Iomatt, dirt, sweat, blood and the pungent body odors of the non-Human species. The Krakens wore their home jerseys, black with white-trimmed orange numbers and letters. The first half's intensity showed in torn fabric, blue stains from the field and nicks in both arm and leg armor.

Quentin leaned against a wall, staring at the four Prawatt players sitting side by side on a bench in front of the holoboard. Normally Hokor would be in front of that board, but instead he stood next to Quentin — the need to make halftime adjustments had given way to a ranting, screaming, arm-waving John Tweedy.

The linebacker shook his fists at Bumberpuff and the others. "You call yourselves the scourge of the galaxy? You call yourselves *monsters?*"

Hokor beckoned for Quentin to kneel. Quentin did. Hokor leaned in.

"Barnes, I do not think the Prawatt call themselves monsters. Why is John saying that?"

Quentin shrugged. "Forget it, he's rolling."

I'LL SHOW YOU MONSTERS! scrolled across John's forehead. He bent forward until his face was inches away from Bumberpuff.

"Muh-muh-muh-*monsters?*" *John said.* "How about puh-puh-puh-*pansies?*"

With each word, John's spit splattered on Bumberpuff.

"Stop yelling at us," the Prawatt said. "This is not the behavior of a sentient adult. We should be spending this time adjusting our defense, not yelling like children."

John stood up straight. His lip curled into a sneer. "Halftime adjustments? We don't need no stinking halftime adjustments. What we need to do is *hit them so hard they disintegrate!* You gotta get *angry!* You wanna know how *I* play defense? Every single time that ball snaps, I am trying to *kill* those guys. *Kill 'em!* Does that make me a nice guy? *Does it?* No, it makes me a bad man. I am a bad, *bad* man!" John suddenly sidestepped right to stand in front of Luciano Cretzlefinger. Cretzlefinger leaned back in fear — he didn't have Bumberpuff's quiet resolve.

John grabbed a black-metal arm and shook it. "I'm a bad man, Cretzlefish! I want to make the *hurt!* If eating puppies would help us win, then dammit, you could serve them in a big hot dog bun and I'd drown 'em in mustard!" John shook the Prawatt's arm harder. "Do you like puppies? *Do you?*"

The Prawatt's body rattled. "I have never seen a puppy!"

"Well, when you see 'em, I'll *eat* 'em, and you'll be very very sad! You hear me? *Super-mega sad!*"

John then shuffled to the left, past Bumberpuff, to stand in front of Katzembaum Weasley. "And *you!* You're playing free safety. You should be nastier than a black hole! You should … "

John's face suddenly relaxed. He turned to look at Michael Kimberlin. "Hey, Big Mike, black holes are nasty, right?"

Mike nodded. "One of the most terrifying forces in the galaxy, John."

Rage again washed over John's face. He turned so fast his forehead pressed against Weasley's metallic skin. The Prawatt leaned away, lost balance and fell off the bench. John fell to his hands and knees, straddling the alien.

"A black hole! That's *you*, Katzemkid! A black shucking hole! Light can't escape you like *footballs* can't escape you. Or something!"

Hokor tapped Quentin's shoulder. "Barnes, halftime is almost over. We need to make adjustments. Why is Tweedy talking about astronomical phenomena?"

Quentin shook his head. "I don't know, Coach — he lost me at eating household pets."

John picked Weasley up and set him back on the bench. John then ran away from the Prawatt and grabbed Arioch Morningstar. The surprised kicker tried to run away, but John grabbed a fistful of Arioch's jersey, lifted him, then dangled the man in front of the Prawatt players.

"You guys see this jersey?"

Quentin noticed Ju slowly moving closer to the action, as if he thought his brother might start actually hurting sentients.

Arioch now seemed resigned to the situation — he just hung there, his feet dangling. If anything, the kicker looked *bored*. That was his personality, though: nothing seemed to phase the guy.

John raised Arioch higher.

"This is a *Krakens* jersey," John said. "You miserable excuses for your *miserable* species get to wear one? Tribe! *My* tribe! You are embarrassing me in front of the lizards and the buzzards!"

Hokor leaned in again to ask another question, but Quentin just shook his head — he had no idea what John was talking about.

PUPPIES MUSTARD BLACK HOLES GO TEAM GO! scrolled vertically up John's face.

John set Arioch down. The kicker ran for the Human locker room.

John stood straight, put his hands on his hips. He looked up to the locker room ceiling and sighed. "High One, I need guidance. Should I just take their jerseys away from them and send them home?"

High One?

Quentin looked at Ju. Ju held both hands out, palms down, a gesture that said *let it ride.*

Still looking to the ceiling, John's face wrinkled in disappointment. "Really, High One? Do I *really* have to take their jerseys?"

Bumberpuff stood up and turned to Quentin. "Why is John Tweedy talking to an imaginary friend? John is not authorized to take our jerseys! He is not the owner of the team!"

Quentin looked at John, who was talking quietly to the ceiling, then back to Bumberpuff. Quentin finally understood — John had been searching for a hot button, something that would infuriate the Prawatt, and he seemed to have found it — the jerseys.

"John doesn't need authorization," Quentin said. "Not if he rips them off of you."

Bumberpuff's body turned from side to side, a perfect mimicry of a Human *no* even though the Prawatt didn't have heads. "He cannot *have* them!"

John nodded to the ceiling one last time. "Okay, High One. I'll strip the unworthy pretenders of their finery."

He turned toward Bumberpuff and grabbed the Prawatt's black jersey. Bumberpuff tried to pull John's hands free. John stepped in and threw an elbow that smashed into the Prawatt body, knocking the former starship captain backward onto the locker room floor.

John stared down and shook his fist. "Gimme that jersey, or else!"

Bumberpuff snapped up on his flexible legs, then drove his body into John's stomach, knocking the big linebacker on his ass.

Now Bumberpuff stood over John, "You *will not* take my colors!"

The captain dove on top of John. The two punched at each other, rolling across the locker room floor.

Ju ran up to the bench and grabbed the jerseys of both Katzembaum and Tommyboy Snuffalupagus.

"You heard the High One," Ju said. "Give up these here jerseys, you pretenders — you don't deserve them."

Cretzlefinger stood and whipped his metallic arm into Ju's face. Ju's head rocked back. Katzembaum and Tommyboy came off the bench hard and tag-team-tackled Ju, sending them all to the ground.

Hokor had had enough. He grabbed his ball cap, threw it down, then stepped forward. "Stop this grab-assing! You stupid, *stupid* players have wasted my adjustment time! Now get onto the field before we are flagged for delay of game!"

The Prawatt raced for the locker room door as if delaying even a moment would cause Hokor to ask for their jerseys. The rest of the team, excited and pumped up by the halftime brawl, ran out of the room yelling, chirping, grunting and clacking.

Within seconds, only Quentin and the Tweedy brothers remained. John and Ju picked themselves up off the ground, both bleeding from multiple cuts on the face, both *laughing.*

Ju slapped his brother on the back. "Nice one, Big Brother! That's like the most mega-awesome halftime speech ever!"

John nodded. "I think they'll knock the crap out of the Orbiting Death in the second half." John turned to Quentin. "Hey, Q! Don't worry, I wasn't really talking to the High One — I was faking it!"

Quentin couldn't help but laugh at John's reassurance. "Wow, John, are you *sure* you weren't speaking with Him?"

I KNOW ACTING scrolled across John's head.

Ju wiped blood off his face and flung it to the floor. "We're only down fourteen points. Let's go put a hurting on a those Orbiting Death shuckers."

Ma Tweedy's three boys jogged out of the locker room and headed for the field.

THE ORBITING DEATH WORE their away jerseys: light gray with blue numbers and letters trimmed in metalflake-red. Sunlight sparkled off of their metalflake-red helmets, which were dinged and scratched from the first-half action. Flat-black leg and arm armor absorbed that same light, as did the flat-black circles on either side of their helmets.

From the sidelines, Quentin watched Death quarterback Condor Adrienne take the snap and drop back to pass. Mum-O-

Killowe bull-rushed, a roaring spectacle of driving legs and whipping arms. The Ki offensive guard tried to counter the assault but
couldn't stop the enraged Mum-O. Condor Adrienne saw the pressure coming. He stepped up into the pocket, just a fraction of an
inch ahead of Mum-O's swiping arm. Condor looked downfield
but didn't see an open receiver. Alexsandar Michnik drove in from
Condor's right, so Condor calmly turned and threw the ball to his
fullback Mike Buckner in the left flat.

Buckner caught the pass and turned upfield, only to be leveled
by an onrushing Cormorant Bumberpuff. The pinwheeling Prawatt
came in fast, tucking into a ball for a hit so hard that the Human
player came right off his feet and flew backward.

The football spun free. Luciano Cretzlefinger dove for it, his
orange- and black-streamered arms wrapping it up just as several
Death players landed on top of him. Whistles blew, but that didn't
stop more players from diving onto the pile. Quentin could see the
players kicking and punching, fighting for the ball.

On the sidelines, Krakens players laughed with each other,
caught up in astonishment at Bumberpuff's devastating hit. Out
on the field, Harrah refs slid into the tangle of players, wiggling
between big bodies to get to the bottom. A black- and white-striped
ref pushed his way out of the pile and signaled Krakens' ball.

Quentin whooped and ran onto the field as the refs broke up
the pile. Cretzlefinger finally stood up, the ball in his arms. Bits of
metal flaked off his right arm, which looked bent and broken.

Quentin grabbed the Prawatt, pounded on his X-body back.
"That's the way to fight!"

"I punched him!" Cretzlefinger said. "He was biting me, and
I punched him!"

Quentin laughed and pushed him toward the sidelines. "Don't
go broadcasting that."

Bumberpuff ran by, also heading for the sidelines. Quentin
grabbed his arm to stop him.

"Captain, *great* hit," Quentin said.

Bumberpuff vibrated. "I now understand John Tweedy's cryp-
tic form of motivation," he said. "I got *mean*."

Quentin slapped Bumberpuff on the back, then walked to the huddle. Thanks to the hit and the recovery, the Krakens had the ball on the Orbiting Death 22-yard line. It was time to get his team back into the game.

ON THE FIRST PLAY of the fourth quarter, Quentin took the snap and dropped back five steps, ball held at his left ear. He scanned through his first two receivers: Denver and Halawa were both covered.

Death linebacker Yalla the Biter — the deadliest sentient in football — came up the middle on a delayed blitz, all four hands reaching out for the sack.

Quentin instantly abandoned the pocket and ran left. Yalla cut right to match the move. Quentin suddenly stopped, tucked the ball in his left arm and lowered his right shoulder, driving that shoulder into the Quyth Warrior's chest. The sudden, vicious move lifted Yalla off his feet and knocked the linebacker on his ass. Quentin hadn't crossed the line of scrimmage — he stood, tall, saw Tara the Freak open down the middle of the field and gunned a pass.

The ball slapped into the receiver's oversized pedipalp hands. Tara crossed the 20, the 10, then strode into the end zone as Death defensive backs arrived a step too late.

The home crowd went wild. The third quarter had been a shootout, both teams scoring almost at will, but that pass pulled Ionath to within a touchdown. With the extra point, the score would be 41-36 in favor of OS1.

Quentin knelt and picked up a few blades of Iomatt. Just as he did, something slammed into him, knocking him to his side. He slid across the blue turf. Head spinning from the blow, he came up on his feet — fists already clenched — and looked at the player who had landed the late hit: Yalla the Biter.

The Quyth Warrior linebacker stood there, his baseball-sized eye flooded black, his blood-splattered gray jersey ripped and torn. More whistles blew as refs called the late hit. The black- and white-striped Harrah flew in, but Yalla ignored them.

"Come on, Human," he said. "*Come on!*"

Quentin felt his rage swell up ... and then, he let it go. He just *let it go*. Last year Yalla had goaded him into a fight, a fight that got Quentin kicked out of the game. As a result, his team had lost. *I won't fall for that ever again*. Instead of throwing a punch, Quentin smiled, turned and ran to the sidelines.

There, his teammates mobbed him, smacking his helmet, hitting his shoulder pads, pushing and pulling him in all directions. The extra point was good. Ionath had cut the lead to five points with just 6:23 to play.

Now, it was up to the defense.

CONDOR ADRIENNE ROLLED RIGHT, run-limping as he ran from a screaming John Tweedy. The quarterback looked for a receiver. He had thrown for over 425 yards on the night, but in the second half the Prawatt defensive backs had started hitting harder and playing better — they were still getting beat, but not as often, and they were closing on the ball much faster. That must have been what Condor saw as he looked downfield at his receiver Brazilia, covered by Bumberpuff; Condor started to throw, then pulled it back, waiting just a second longer for Brazilia to get open. In that brief second, John Tweedy caught up. The Human linebacker grabbed the Death quarterback, lifted him and slammed him into the ground to the elated sounds of a blood-lusting crowd.

Fourth down.

The OS1 punt team ran onto the field.

SEVEN SECONDS REMAINED in the game. The Krakens were still down 41-36. Third-and-seven on the Death's 22-yard line, but it didn't matter what down it was — this would be the last play of the game. A touchdown would win it.

The home fans screamed, banging on their seats and on each other. They stomped their feet and clacked their chests. They roared so loud Quentin could barely be heard as he called out the signals.

"Blue, twenty-two. *Bluuuueeee*, twenty-*two*!"

Quentin had a wall of ravaged black jerseys in front of him, and beyond those, a line of bloody light gray. The black-helmeted Death players wanted Quentin, wanted him bad, wanted to hurt him and stop him and preserve the win.

Two of those gray jerseys belonged to the outside linebackers, the *Mad Macs*: Matt McRoberts and James McPike. Quentin saw the linebackers were creeping up to the line. They were going to blitz as soon as Bud-O-Shwek snapped the ball, Quentin saw it in their eyes.

Quentin stood up. He scanned the defense again, then tapped a *ba-da-bap* on Bud-O-Shwek's back. He cupped his hands to his mouth and called out a new signal.

"Green, sixteen! Green, six*teeeen*."

The word "green" meant he was calling an audible, changing the play from what he'd specified in the huddle. The "sixteen" told the team what that new play was — a boot-pass left, Quentin's favorite play.

He bent behind center.

"Hut-*hut*!"

He took the snap, turned to his right and stuck the ball out for Ju. Ju snapped his arms down on empty air as Quentin pulled the ball away at the last moment. Ju slammed into the right side of the line, continuing the fake.

Quentin turned and ran left. McRoberts bought the fake completely and tackled Ju, taking both of them out of the play. McPike was not fooled — he slipped through the line and gave chase. Quentin's mental timer started counting down how long he had until McPike caught up with him.

Running left, Quentin scanned through the receivers — his first option, Denver, cutting left on a flag pattern toward the front-left corner of the end zone, well covered by defensive back Karachi. Karachi had inside position — she was between Quentin and Denver. It was perfect coverage. Normally Quentin wouldn't have thrown a pass, but a flash flood of confidence swept through his brain, an instinct that told him Denver would know exactly what to do.

Still running left, Quentin threw the ball as hard as he could, a laser-shot no more than six feet above the field.

Karachi's tentacles reached for the ball. Denver suddenly jumped up and bent, her tentacles reaching over Karachi without touching the defensive back. Both sets of tentacles grabbed the ball simultaneously. The two Sklorno fell into the black end zone together — just before they hit the turf, Denver ripped the ball free.

Quentin held his breath as a zebe flew in, zoomed down on Denver and Karachi, then raised his mouth-flaps high.

Touchdown.

Quentin checked the clock — time had expired.

Final score: Ionath 42, Orbiting Death 41.

GFL WEEK FIVE ROUNDUP
Courtesy of Galaxy Sports Network

Home		Away	
Themala Dreadnaughts	27	Alimum Armada	24
Hittoni Hullwalkers	14	Buddha City Elite	10
Coranadillana Cloud Killers	3	**To Pirates**	7
Ionath Krakens	42	Orbiting Death	41
Yall Criminals	38	New Rodina Astronauts	14
Vik Vanguard	20	Bord Brigands	17
Texas Earthlings	14	D'Kow War Dogs	10
Neptune Scarlet Fliers	21	Jupiter Jacks	17
Sheb Stalkers	10	Shorah Warlords	7

With the galaxy watching, the GFL's newest species took center stage and came out on top.

The Ionath Krakens (1-3) notched their first win of the season with a 42-41 come-from-behind win over the Orbiting Death. Cormorant Bumberpuff started for the Krakens at cornerback, marking the first time in GFL history that a Prawatt player started at any position. Bumberpuff proved largely ineffective at stopping Death quarterback Condor Adrienne, who threw for five touchdown passes in the first three quarters, but forced Adrienne into mistakes in the fourth quarter that let Ionath grab the win. Krakens QB Quentin Barnes threw for three touchdown passes, including a last-second strike to wide receiver Denver. This was Denver's first game for Ionath following a trade for quarterback Don Pine.

Yall (4-0) pounded New Rodina (1-4) to remain in first place in the Planet Division. The To Pirates (3-1) moved into a tie for second with a 7-3 defensive struggle victory over Coranadillana (1-4).

In the Solar Division, Neptune (3-1) handed Jupiter (4-1) the Jacks' first loss of the season. In Pine's first start of the season as the Jupiter QB, he threw for 212 yards and one TD. Pine was also intercepted three times, including one that was returned for the game-winning touchdown. Jupiter falls a half-game behind Solar Division leader Bartel (4-0), which was off on a bye week.

Hittoni (1-4) picked up its first win of the season, leaving Shorah (0-5) as the league's only remaining winless team.

Deaths
No deaths reported this week.

Defensive Player of the Week
Ionath Krakens middle linebacker **John Tweedy**, who had seven solo tackles, two interceptions, two sacks and a forced fumble.

Offensive Player of the Week
For the second week in a row, Ionath quarterback **Quentin Barnes** earned POTW honors. Barnes threw for three touchdowns and ran for one more in the Krakens' 42-41 win over the OSI Orbiting Death.

18

Week Six:
Ionath Krakens at
Buddha City Elite

PLANET DIVISION

4-0 Yall Criminals

3-1 To Pirates

3-1 Wabash Wolfpack (bye)

3-2 OS1 Orbiting Death

2-2 Alimum Armada

2-2 Isis Ice Storm (bye)

2-2 Themala Dreadnaughts

2-3 Buddha City Elite

1-3 Ionath Krakens

1-4 Coranadillana Cloud Killers

1-4 Hittoni Hullwalkers

SOLAR DIVISION

4-0 Bartel Water Bugs (bye)

4-1 Jupiter Jacks

3-1 Neptune Scarlet Fliers

3-1 Texas Earthlings

3-2 Vik Vanguard

2-2 Jang Atom Smashers (bye)

2-3 Bord Brigands

2-3 Sheb Stalkers

1-3 D'Kow War Dogs

1-4 New Rodina Astronauts

0-5 Shorah Warlords

QUENTIN THREW UP into his golden bucket.

He wiped his mouth, set the trash can down, pulled out the plastic bag and tied it. As he did, his eyes lingered on the latest sticker applied by John and Ju.

An infinity symbol.

That symbol was the Buddha City Elite's logo, but it held far more meaning for Quentin. It was also the symbol of the Purist Church, and the entire Purist Nation. When Quentin swore to himself that he would leave his home behind forever, he'd never thought he might return to play football.

"This was your home?"

Quentin looked to his left, at Cormorant Bumberpuff. It just didn't seem real — bringing the *Devil's Rope* to the Purist Nation? As a teammate, as a *friend*? Quentin nodded, then looked out the viewport window at Buddha City Station, the Purist Nation's technological crown jewel.

A few other players were there to watch the arrival: Choto, Mum-O-Killowe, Sho-Do-Thikit, Alexsandar Michnik and Jason Procknow, the rookie defensive tackle. Procknow was the only other Nationalite on the team. He was on the other side of the room, and Quentin knew why — he wanted to be as far away from Bumberpuff as possible.

Bumberpuff's presence was probably also the reason no Sklorno were there. In the past two weeks, Hokor had made room on the roster for the Prawatt by releasing Rehoboth, Luanda and Emmitsburgh. All three had survived the preseason cuts, but they weren't as good as the four former Harpies. In total, four Sklorno gone to make room for four Prawatt, something that further escalated the internal tension between the two races.

"I lived in the Purist Nation, but not here," Quentin said. "I lived on a colony called Micovi. I visited here a lot, though. Mostly to play football."

"When you visited, did you win?"

Quentin started to answer, but the words froze in his mouth when he realized he wasn't sure. After seven seasons of pro football, the memory of some games had faded. He mentally ticked off the seasons, counting the number of times he'd lined up on the Buddha City field.

"I played here five times," he said. "And I won them all."

"That is a good omen," Bumberpuff said. "I hope you remain undefeated."

Quentin studied his alien friend. All the X-Walkers looked structurally the same, but he had already internalized the subtle differences that made each of them recognizable as individuals. Some of it was body language, some was physical marks on their semi-see-through bodies, but much of it was *verbal*. They didn't just *sound* Human, they *spoke* like Humans, revealing Human-like thought patterns, observations and reactions. Quentin realized that out of all the non-Human races, even including Choto the Bright, Bumberpuff was fast becoming one of his best friends.

Through that new familiarity and that budding friendship, Quentin picked up a vibe coming off of Bumberpuff — something was wrong.

"You okay, Cappy? You look nervous."

"*Nervous?* Hardly," Bumberpuff said. "When you've driven starships into battle, Quentin, something like visiting an archaic station hardly makes one nervous."

Quentin heard something in those words. He heard *overcompensation*; Bumberpuff was speaking more to himself than to anyone else.

"Captain, come on," Quentin said. "It's okay to be nervous. I'm nervous every time I step onto a football field, and I'm sure as hell nervous about coming back the Purist Nation."

Bumberpuff's body whirred as various dots and spots turned Quentin's way. "*You* are nervous coming here? But these are your people."

"I was born here, but these were never *my people*," Quentin said. "They probably hate me."

"At least with you it's *probably*," Bumberpuff said. "My kind has explored more than you might think, and in most places we are mistrusted. In the Purist Nation, it is far more than that. Here, don't they think we are creatures of evil?"

The Devil's Rope. Quentin wanted to reassure his teammate, say something to make him feel better about the situation, but to do so would be to lie.

"They do," Quentin said. "It's a backward place with backward people."

"Are all the Nationalites full of hate?"

Quentin thought of Mister Sam, the restaurant owner who had taken him in and given him a home, a second job and — most importantly — all the food a growing, oversized boy could eat. Mister Sam hadn't taken Quentin out of the mines, but he'd given Quentin direction and a hope of something greater than dying from a roundbug bite or a stonecat mauling.

"No, not all," Quentin said. "It's like anyplace else, I guess — there are good people and bad people."

"I believe you," Bumberpuff said. "There must be more people like you, good people who want to help others even if those others are from a different species."

Quentin's face suddenly felt warm.

"Ah, Captain ... you didn't know me then. I've changed since I joined the Krakens."

He'd left the Purist Nation as a bigoted, selfish child out to show everyone just how good he was. Four years later, he returned a different man. He'd gone from hating anything non-Human to being the advocate for integration, from knowing how to kill the alien races to stopping wars between them. He'd gone from worshipping the one, true god to — literally — being considered a god himself. He'd gone from being a locker room pariah to a true leader, someone who really cared for his teammates and wanted them to succeed.

He had changed *so much*.

Buddha City Station also seemed to have changed. It was the same orbital complex as before, sure, but now it looked *small*. It looked *old*. It looked ... *worn out*. The Station's fifty-seven decks of steel and aluminum alloy composites were lined with decorative green enamel, but also dotted with the remains of burn marks, with panels that didn't match the original construction material, all legacies of battle-damage from the church's endless internal power struggles.

When he had played here in the PNFL regular season against the Buddha City Crosses, or in the playoffs when he'd won his two league titles, the Nationalites had loved him. How would they feel about him now, now that he was returning and bringing the *Devil's Rope* along for the ride.

[**FIRST SHUTTLE FLIGHT PASSENGERS TO THE LANDING BAY. SHUTTLE DEPARTING FOR BUDDHA CITY STATION.**]

"Captain, you ready for this?"

"I am not sure," Bumberpuff said. "Will we be safe?"

Quentin again thought of saying something reassuring but again decided to just tell the truth.

"Probably," he said. "I'm sure Froese and GFL security will see to it, but this is a wild place ruled by religious crazies. Nothing is for sure. Do you want to sit this game out and stay on the *Touchback*?"

Bumberpuff rattled in annoyance. "Are *you* going to sit this one out and stay on the *Touchback*?"

Quentin shook his head.

"Then neither will I. I threw my lot in with you, Quentin Barnes — wherever you go, I will go as well."

The two teammates walked out of the viewing bay and headed for the shuttle.

BUMBERPUFF AT HIS SIDE, Quentin stepped off the shuttle into a roar of anger and hatred.

Buddha City Station's sprawling landing deck was as he remembered it: filled with shuttles and small transport ships, bustling crews and fluttering Creterakians. The air smelled of combustion exhaust, rubber and sweat. Mostly Human sentients walked along clearly marked pathways, pathways that steered them clear of industrial trucks and lev-sleds that loaded and unloaded cargo from across the galaxy. As the Purist Nation's only intergalactic port that allowed alien races, as the sole trade gateway to eleven billion Nation citizens, Buddha City Station ran full-out at all times.

That part was as Quentin remembered, but this time there was something new. Fences had been erected that sectioned off large areas. In front of those fences, the green-armored presence of the Buddha City Station Police, their dark face shields making them both intimidating and anonymous. Behind those fences: shouting, angry, blue-clad people packed in close together, pushing against the chain link. The people held up signs, both holo and paper, signs that said things as hateful as their voices.

Devil's Ropes go home!

Barnes consorts with the satanic races.

I hope you like the heat, because hell is waiting.

High One hates the letter X.

Satan takes many forms.

Hey Barnes, if you don't die on the field, we'll get you after the game.

Quentin actually felt embarrassed. He'd spent so much time in racially integrated Ionath City that he'd forgotten this kind of hate existed anywhere outside the Blessed Lamb. Well, exist it did — especially in the system of his birth.

"They don't seem happy," Bumberpuff said. "Funny, I thought there would be cake."

"Do you even eat cake?"

"It's a figure of speech," the captain said. "Our creator was apparently quite fond of it. When she was biological, of course, before she uploaded."

Quentin started to walk off the ramp, but a big three-fingered pincer pressed against his chest, keeping him in place. Choto the Bright stepped in front of him, his one eye scanning the hostile crowd.

"You stay behind me, Quentin. You as well, Bumberpuff."

Virak walked out to join Choto. "I despise these primitive screwheads." Virak didn't like Quentin, and Quentin didn't like Virak, but for some things, team came first.

Quentin and Bumberpuff followed Virak and Choto off the ramp, the other first-shuttle players close behind.

John stared at the protesters. He hocked a loogie and spat it on the landing bay deck. "I'd like to booger the lot of 'em. Wow, Q — now, I know where you get your sparkling personality."

"Don't lump me in with these jerks," Quentin said. "I've got nothing to do with this."

John shrugged. YOU CAN TAKE THE BOY OUT OF THE HATE, BUT A ZEBRA'S SPOTS RUN DEEP scrolled across his face.

John was just joking — probably — but Quentin felt his face flush hot.

Becca walked up to stand by his side. "Quentin, you okay?"

He nodded. "Yeah, I'm fine."

He wasn't fine. He looked out at the fenced-in mass of hate. He flashed back to Bumberpuff's words on the viewing deck: *are we safe?* Quentin didn't feel safe, not one bit — they hadn't even left the landing deck, and already this was the most hostile place the Krakens had ever played.

A column of Humans in green-armored riot gear walked across the bay toward the Krakens. Quentin felt his stomach churn, felt an echo of the fear he'd once known looking at men like these.

The Buddha City Station Police, also known as *the Greens*.

They held shock-sticks in one hand, kept the other hand on the hilt of their holstered nail guns. Those pistols fired high-density plastic fasteners, the same "nails" used for any internal station construction. The fasteners would put a nasty hole in people, would shoot through doors and most internal walls, but would bend and flatten if they hit the station's outer hull — that little bit of physics let the trigger-happy Greens shoot at will without concern for punching a hole into space.

A white infinity symbol on a shield marked the left breast of each guard's chest armor. Each man's name was stenciled below that shield.

The Greens wielded significant authority on Buddha City. Only the bats had more pull, but the bats rarely got involved. Day-to-day order and discipline fell to the Greens. On a station with a half-million residents, a station that included organized crime of all stripes and was the center point for smuggling throughout the Purist Nation, the Greens were known as *the biggest gang in town.*

The column stopped in front of Quentin and Messal the Efficient, who — as usual — had magically appeared from nowhere. The first man in the column had the name *J. CARTWRIGHT* stenciled on his armor.

"I'm Officer Cartwright," he said. "I'm in charge of the security detail."

Messal took a step forward. "Elder Cartwright, we are glad that —"

Cartwright's stun-stick whipped down. Quentin thought it would hammer Messal's head, but the end of the stick stopped an inch from the Worker's softball-sized eye.

"Call me *Officer*," Cartwright said. "I am not an *Elder*, understand?"

Messal's eye swirled with crimson and pink. "Yes, Officer. I understand."

"Good," Cartwright said. "All of you, come with me."

The green-armored police surrounded the Krakens as if the Krakens were criminals. Hands patted stun-sticks, fingers wiggled on gun handles.

John huffed. "They don't look so tough."

Quentin reached out and grabbed John's arm. "Uncle Johnny, not here. I've seen these guys in action before."

"They can't touch me," John said. "GFL immunity. I might want to test the quality of that armor they're wearing, you know?"

"John, if you do something stupid you won't just get us sticked —" Quentin pointed to the angry crowd pressing against the chain-link fence "— you'll antagonize *them*. We're here to play football, not to get into a fight. Understand?"

John's eyes narrowed in a way that wordlessly said *who do you think you're bossing around?* Quentin didn't like the expression, not one bit. John glanced briefly at Becca, then back at Quentin. In that moment, Quentin realized that he had just embarrassed John in front of his girlfriend.

"Okay, Q," John said. "I'll play nice. Thank you so much for the behavioral correction."

He snapped his arm free and walked away, as far as he could within the boundary of police escort.

Officer Cartwright waved his stun-stick in the air. "All visitors, keep your hands and feet inside the perimeter. Try not to make eye-contact with the crowd. It's a few hundred yards to the lev-train that will take you to the stadium, where you'll be more secure."

Cartwright started walking. His men followed, ushering the Krakens along like cattle. A wheel-truck started towing the shuttle to an airlock for a return trip to the *Touchback*. As Quentin walked, he couldn't help but give the protesters one last look.

Four years ago, how many of those same people cheered my name? And now, they want me dead.

THE KRAKENS GATHERED in the tunnel of Infinity Stadium. Quentin and John were in front. As captains, it was their honor to lead the team out and to do the pregame coin toss at mid-field. With them was a Prawatt, Katzembaum Weasley. Quentin had chosen him as honorary captain for two reasons: it was Weasley's first start at free safety, and it was a giant slap in the face to the racist Purist Nation crowd.

Quentin looked out at the field, a deep green lined with white. It was Kentucky Bluegrass, imported from Earth and cultivated on a Station agriculture center solely dedicated to growing it. That was one of the perks of being the richest city in the Nation — while some eighty percent of the population lived below the poverty line, many of those starving, the Station could afford to pay a staff of twenty-five to do nothing but grow grass. That fact made Quentin feel horrible that he loved playing on that field — it was always firm and pliant, great for making fast cuts.

The announcer's voice echoed through the domed stadium.

"Devout worshippers, the Church of Purism would like to welcome our visiting team, the Ionath Krakens."

Quentin, John and Katzembaum led the team onto the field amidst a wave of polite applause. Quentin could practically feel the hate, the fear, the suspicion, but to boo or curse at visitors wouldn't be very Purist. So much of the religion revolved around thinking one thing, but saying and doing another.

With a capacity of 45,000, this was the smallest stadium in Tier One. Row after row of blue-clad fans filled the stands. GFL tickets were expensive, after all, and for the most part, only confirmed church members could afford them. As Quentin ran to the sidelines, he was taken aback by the *sameness* of the crowd: Humans in blue robes. While other races were welcome to trade on Buddha City, they weren't welcome to do anything else.

He and his teammates gathered at the sidelines. Quentin started to talk, but before he could say anything, John Tweedy started screaming.

"We get things back on track right now!" John banged a fist against his armored chest. "Everyone steps up! Everyone does their thing. If we go one-and-four, that will *suck*, so let's make sure we don't!"

The defensive players shouted in support. So did some of the offensive players, but others gave half-hearted encouragement, and still others just looked confused — they had been expecting Quentin to lead the pregame chant.

John raised his right fist. "Bring it in!"

The players pressed closer, raising their hands to John's. Quentin thought of saying something, but to do so now would cause even more confusion, so he raised his hand to John's just like everyone else did.

"Destroy on three," John said. "One, two, *three*."

"Destroy destroy destroy!"

The Krakens broke up and spread out down the sideline. Quentin wondered what had just happened. Was John still mad about the incident on the landing deck? Was he showing off for

Becca? Or, maybe, was he showing that Quentin didn't have to run everything all the time?

The yell of the announcer's voice drew Quentin's attention back to the tunnel.

"And now, chosen people of the High One, bring your hands together and let the heavens hear a joyous sound as we welcome our blessed home team, the Buddha ... City ... Eeeeeeeeeelite!"

The crowd lost its collective mind. Quentin saw people leaping, screaming and falling on each other. He saw people fainting, raising their hands to the sky. From long years of experience, he knew some of them were speaking in tongues. They probably loved football, sure, but that wasn't the real reason for such over-the-top excitement — if they didn't cheer loud enough, *intensely* enough, someone in the seat behind them or from a nearby row might report that person as not having enough love for the Church. That could lead to a purity investigation. A purity investigation *always* led to something bad. Sometimes it was a public dressing-down. Other times, it was a public flogging. Occasionally, even for the confirmed, a purity investigation meant death. Once the investigation started, something *had* to be wrong because High One was never mistaken.

His native religion corrupted everything, even the simple joy of watching a football game.

The Elite players stormed onto the field. Purist racism didn't extend to the level where football games were unwinnable, it seemed — when it came to the gridiron, the Ki, the Sklorno and the Quyth were downright regular folk.

Buddha City's uniforms were something to behold. When Quentin played in the PNFL, all teams had plain uniforms. Save for the primary color of each team, in fact, the uniforms were identical to those of the Micovi Raiders — silver helmet with a black stripe down the middle, black jersey with a silver RAIDERS on the chest and a silver number beneath, silver leg armor, black shoes. No individuality, no decoration, the same template applied to each of the league's twelve teams. Lack of decoration bespoke modesty, humility in the face of the High One who had gifted each of the players and coaches with their unique abilities.

That modesty was nowhere to be seen on the uniforms of the Buddha City Elite. White-facemasked, emerald-green helmets sparkled in the stadium lights. A wide, white-lined black stripe ran down the middle of the helmet. On each side was a white infinity symbol trimmed in black.

The jerseys were also a sparkling emerald green. A wide, black-trimmed white stripe started on each shoulder pad and narrowed to a point below the center of each race's respective chest. Black-lined, white numbers sat nestled above the V made by the narrowing shoulder stripes. Below the point of that V, the word ELITE, also in black-lined white. A black belt wrapped around emerald-green leg armor and shoes. Wide, black-lined white stripes ran from the hips to a point atop each knee.

Quentin recognized the long gait of a Human: number 46, Rick Warburg. Quentin didn't follow the progress of offensive players because he didn't face them on the field, but from what little he'd seen Warburg was having a great season.

Perth, however, was a different story — Quentin *would* face her on the field. Up until the preseason, she had been part of the Orange and the Black. He knew her in-depth familiarity the Ionath offense would pose a problem as the afternoon wore on.

The Elite gathered on their sideline, jumping, shouting, going through their own pregame ritual. Sure, they were newly promoted, but this season they had two victories to the Krakens' one.

Whistles blew. The zebes fluttered to mid-field and called the captains of both sides for the coin toss.

Time to get down to business.

THE ELITE PLAYED a conservative defense, making sure they didn't get burned on big plays. That left the underneath routes mostly open. Quentin took what they gave him, throwing out-patterns to Denver, Halawa and Milford, crossing routes to Tara the Freak and hooks to George Starcher. On the first drive, Quentin went 8-for-8 for 78 yards, completing a seven-minute drive with a 5-yard pass to Yassoud Murphy for the touchdown.

BUDDHA CITY RAN a spread offense, so-called because five receivers stretched from one sideline to the other. On most plays, Elite quarterback Gary Lindros lined up in the shotgun with an empty backfield. That meant no running back or fullback to help with the pass rush of defensive ends Alexsandar Michnik and Ibrahim Khomeni. Lindros had to take the snap, quickly check through his receivers, then deliver the ball fast or he'd get his head taken off. Lindros did just that, hitting short slants and hooks in much the same way Quentin had done. Ionath's Prawatt defensive backs were still learning — quick-hitting, almost instant throws left them a half-step late to knock down the ball.

Lindros wasn't as efficient as Quentin, but he got the job done. On the Elite's first drive, he went 7-of-11 for 80 yards, tying the game on a 7-yard corner-fade touchdown pass to Metairie.

IN THE SECOND QUARTER, both teams struggled to move the ball into scoring position. The Elite chewed up a lot of clock with slow, controlled drives. They took the lead with just 1:32 to play when Lindros hit Warburg on a three-yard touchdown pass.

On the very next drive, Quentin kicked in the two-minute offense: short passes designed to get receivers out of bounds to stop the clock. The defensive backs came up to try and stop these passes, and when they did Quentin dropped back five steps, let Denver sprint down the field, and he hit her in the end-zone's back corner for a 56-yard touchdown strike.

At the half, the two teams were tied 14-all.

THE ELITE'S STRATEGY was obvious — slow down the game, chew up as much time as possible and keep the ball out of Quentin's hands. And that strategy was working.

In the second half, Rick Warburg took over the game. Lindros hit him repeatedly, on curl patterns over the middle and short out-routes. John Tweedy, Virak the Mean and Choto the Bright brought the house, hitting Warburg with everything they had — the big Human gave better than he got. Mid-way through the third quarter, Warburg caught a hook pass, turned quick and leveled a vicious head-to-head hit that knocked Virak the Mean out of the game. Rookie linebacker Pishor the Fang filled in and played well, but his inexperience showed when Warburg turned a short pass into a 22-yard TD after spinning off Pishor's attempted tackle.

Aside from Quentin's long pass to Denver, the Elite just wouldn't give up the big pass. Perth seemed to know where every receiver was going; she was always there to break up the deep passes. Quentin continued to complete short patterns. He almost couldn't miss — by the end of the third quarter, he'd completed 28-of-31 passes for 312 yards.

At the end of the third quarter, Quentin hit Ju Tweedy on a wheel route to the left. Ju took the ball up the sidelines, outran the linebacker covering him, then ran over safety Bogalusa and high-stepped in for a touchdown to tie the game at 21-all.

ALEXSANDAR MICHNIK FINALLY GOT to Lindros in the fourth quarter, dragging the QB down for a sack. But on the very next play, Lindros saw Bumberpuff in one-on-one coverage against wide receiver Metairie. Metairie ran a slant and Lindros pump-faked, drawing Bumberpuff in. The Prawatt only lost a step, but that was all the speedy Metairie needed. Lindros threw long to the back of the end zone. Metairie ran under it and caught it in stride for a 43-yard TD pass.

Buddha City again had the lead, 28-21.

ON THE NEXT DRIVE, Quentin hit Denver for 8, Starcher for 9, Tara for 5 and Tara then again for 14. A Ju Tweedy run brought up second-and-eight, then Denver dropped a pass. On third down,

Quentin suffered his only sack of the game when defensive tackle Don-Wen-Sul beat his block and came in clean. Quentin barely had time to duck before the Ki was on him. That brought up fourth-and-13 on the Elite 30.

Arioch Morningstar came in and nailed a 47-yard field goal, cutting the lead to 28-24.

ELITE COACH EZEKIEL GRABER had the lead and wanted to burn up as much clock as possible. He called runs up the middle and screen passes, making sure the ball stayed in-bounds and the clock kept ticking.

The Krakens' defense couldn't force a stop and couldn't force a turnover. When the Elite moved past the Ionath 30-yard line, the "D" had to start making changes. Hokor called a blitz, sending Pishor and Choto driving in hard to try and force a mistake. That left John Tweedy in single coverage on Warburg. Lindros saw the blitz coming; knowing he would take a big hit, he stepped up and threw a bullet down the middle. Rick Warburg went up for it — John Tweedy raked at the man's arms before the ball even arrived. Pass-interference flags flew, but they didn't matter, as Warburg somehow pulled in the pass one-handed while falling to his back. He landed in the end zone. Buddha City declined the penalty, keeping the touchdown.

Quentin pulled on his helmet. One minute, 45 seconds to play, and the Elite led 35-24.

BUDDHA CITY PLAYED a "prevent" defense, keeping D-backs far downfield to prevent a big play. Quentin's two-minute offense worked his team down the field. Sometimes Krakens receivers got out of bounds, sometimes they didn't. The Krakens used all three timeouts on the drive. When Quentin finally delivered a 17-yard pass for Denver's second touchdown catch of the game, there were still 45 seconds left on the clock. Buddha City 35, Ionath 31 — it would all come down to the onside kick.

• • •

ARIOCH MORNINGSTAR RAN toward the ball. He hit it lightly with lots of spin. The ball bounced forward five yards, then hit and sprang high into the air as the kickoff and kickoff return teams collided. Denver leapt for it, but so did Metairie — the Elite wide receiver wrapped her tentacles around the ball and fell to the ground.

The crowd of 45,000 confirmed churchies went wild. With the sound of defeat ringing in his ears, Quentin closed his eyes and hung his head. All the Elite had to do was take a knee twice. The game was over.

The Ionath Krakens, once favored to reach the Galaxy Bowl, were now 1-4.

QUENTIN WALKED TO MID-FIELD, joining the players from both sides who were greeting each other after the game. Despite the raw hostility of the Purist Nation fans and citizens, there was, ironically, little animosity between the teams. The Elite had just come in with a better game plan, a plan specifically tailored to beat Ionath.

The two quarterbacks met at mid-field.

"Great game, rookie," Quentin said. "You tore it up."

Lindros laughed. "Compared to your day, I was a scrub. I almost feel bad that you threw for over four hundred yards and lost." He winked. "*Almost.*"

"Good luck this season." Quentin slapped his opponent's shoulder pad, then walked over to Ezekiel Graber, coach of the Elite. Quentin didn't want to speak to the man, but it would be an insult to not give him the credit he deserved.

"Coach Graber, congrats on the win."

Graber turned and smiled at Quentin. The infinity tattoo on his forehead looked even more faded than when Quentin had played for the man four years earlier.

"Great game, Barnes," Graber said. "We squeaked out of this one."

Quentin clenched his teeth and nodded. "Metairie had a whale of a game. Looks like your Satanic races played well today." He knew he shouldn't have said that, but he couldn't help the dig. The last time he'd seen Graber had been when Quentin was leaving the Raiders. Graber had tried to make him stay by saying that Quentin wasn't ready for the big-time and that Quentin would be corrupted by exposure to the "satanic races." How funny that when Graber became a coach in the GFL, those same satanic races weren't so satanic.

"She played well," Graber said. "High One is helping some of these sentients see the light, Quentin. I'm helping them to come around to our ways."

Quentin smiled and shook his head. Graber was justifying his beliefs against his actions? Of course. That was the way of Purism — for a religion of endless, unforgiving rules, there seemed to always be a way to make anything acceptable if it suited you.

"Have a great season, Coach," Quentin said, then walked off to find Rick Warburg.

Warburg was standing with John, Ju and Virak. Virak's middle right arm was in a sling. No one had liked Rick when he'd played for the Krakens, but there was no denying his performance had led the Elite to a victory. The gathering of sentients showed Quentin something sports had taught him a long time ago: *respect* and *like* are two different things.

"Rick, you killed us," Quentin said. "Great game."

Warburg was all smiles. "Thank you, Quentin. You were unstoppable today. Just imagine what we could have done together this season."

Quentin nodded. "Yeah, like you wanted to stay in Ionath."

Rick shrugged. "No, not really. Still, I hope you guys are around next year for a rematch."

John's chest puffed up. "What do you mean *around next year*? If you guys keep winning, we can get our rematch in the playoffs, and we'll kick your asses there."

Warburg threw his head back and laughed. "Playoffs? Maybe you guys should worry about Shorah instead of the playoffs. If you lose to the Warlords, you'll officially have the worst record in football. Forget the playoffs, I'll see you next year — unless you get relegated."

Rick turned and jogged off the field.

I'LL GUT YOU AND WEAR YOUR STOMACH AS A HAT scrolled across John's sweaty face. Strong words, but all four of them knew that Rick was right — the playoffs were the last of Ionath's concerns.

PLAYERS SHUFFLED SLOWLY into Infinity Stadium's visitor's locker room. The place felt like a funeral. Quentin leaned against a wall, watching his teammates, analyzing who was okay with the loss, who was down, who was angry and who was devastated. Things had to change and change fast or Warburg's prophecy would come true.

The slam of a body against a locker drew Quentin's attention. Players backed away from a fight between a Sklorno and a Prawatt: Vacaville and Bumberpuff, a tangle of tentacles and whipping bodies.

Quentin ran to them. Vacaville rolled on top of Bumberpuff and wrapped her raspers around the Prawatt's right arm. She yanked them away, sending bits of metal flying.

"Damnyoursoul, demon, you lost us the game!"

Quentin dove in, knocking Vacaville off of the Prawatt. Bumberpuff should have gotten up and moved away, but instead he stood and dove on top of Quentin and Vacaville, whipping his flexible arm down on Vacaville's head.

"I played hard!" Bumberpuff screamed. "You didn't play at all, you stupid cricket scrub!"

Suddenly more Sklorno rushed in, hitting and tackling and digging with raspers. The other Prawatt players slammed into the pile. Both sides screamed racial epithets; Quentin found himself at the bottom of a miniature race war.

"Guys, knock it off!" Quentin almost stood but was knocked to his back again when Tommyboy tackled Cheboygan. Then another weight fell on top of him — Choto the Bright, diving into the pile to cover Quentin's body with his own.

A heavy impact suddenly rolled the entire pile of some ten players to the left. Bodies spilled across the floor. Everyone looked up to see the shirtless Tweedy brothers, standing there with their fists clenched and their muscles rippling.

John snarled. His face tattoo played an angry wash of bright colors. "That's *enough*! The next one of you that throws a punch is going to get *squashed*!"

"*Mega*-squashed!" said Ju and thumped a fist against his chest.

"*Super*-mega-squashed," John said.

Choto pulled Quentin to his feet. Quentin's eyes watered, and he felt blood on his face. Fingertips sought the center of pain — his nose was broken, and badly.

The Sklorno stood and gathered on one side of Quentin, the Prawatt on the other. Both sides stared at each other, eyestalks vibrating and lenses whirring. They wore the same team colors but couldn't possibly look more separate. For a moment, it seemed like the fight might erupt all over again, then John stomped toward the Sklorno and Ju stomped toward the Prawatt. The Sklorno scurried to their locker room. The Prawatt didn't have a species-specific place, so they moved to the back of the central locker room and stayed there.

Coach Hokor came running in. "Is there grab-assing going on? I told you players there is no grab-assing! Who's at fault here?"

Ju thumped his chest. "It's fine, Coach — we got it under control."

"*Mega*-control," John said.

Hokor's black-swirling eye stared at the Tweedy brothers, then at the Prawatt. Finally, he looked at his bleeding quarterback, and the one big eye narrowed to a hateful slit. "I want to know who started this," the coach said. "I want to know *now*."

John shrugged. "Started what?"

Ju's face furrowed with fake confusion. "I don't know what you're talking about, Coach."

Hokor stared at the Tweedy brothers, then he turned to Quentin.

"*Barnes*! We have to end this grab-assing. Who started it?"

Quentin looked at the Tweedys. Did they have something in mind?

"It's under control, Coach," Quentin said. "The players will handle it."

Hokor stomped a little foot. "Well, no more grab-assing, understand? I'm already trying to prepare for Shorah."

Quentin looked for and found Yassoud. Quentin tilted his head toward the Prawatt. "Get them out of here, will ya? Take them to our locker room."

Yassoud walked to the Prawatt, holding both hands wide as if he was corralling wayward sheep. "This way, you crazy kids. Let's go cool off." He gently herded them into the Human locker room.

With the combatants gone, Quentin, John and Ju moved close together so they could speak quietly.

"This is bad," Quentin said. "This racism, we have to make them work together or we're going back down to Tier Two. What can we do?"

"Beat the living crap out of them," Ju said. "A good-old fashioned whoopin' will do the trick. Hey, John, do the Prawatt have asses? I'm not sure how to kick their asses if they don't have asses."

John sighed and shook his head. "My dearest brother, always with the corporal-colonel punishment. When it comes to discipline, we know who we need to ask."

MOTHER KNOWS BEST scrolled across John's head.

Ju smiled and nodded. "Good idea, Ma will take care of this."

Ma Tweedy? Were the two brothers joking? "Guys, we're talking *centuries* of hate here. I don't think Ma can kiss it and make it all better."

"Ma will know what to do," John said. He looked at his brother. "Somehow, she made the two of us get along."

Ju smiled one of his more evil smiles. "And compared to how my brother and I treated each other? Centuries of hate ain't nothing. Q, you better see Doc Patah about that nose. It's messed up."

"Mega-messed up," John said. "But you were kind of ugly to begin with."

The Tweedy brothers headed for the Human locker room.

"Elder Barnes?"

Quentin jumped at the unexpected voice behind him. He turned to see Messal the Efficient standing there.

"Messal, how do you do that?"

"Do what, Elder Barnes?"

"Sneak up on me like that!"

"I assure you, Elder Barnes, I would never intentionally startle you," Messal said. "Miss Yolanda Davenport asked me to tell you that she requests an exclusive interview, right here on Buddha City Station."

Jeanine ... Yolanda might have information on my sister.

"Um ... did Yolanda say what it was about?"

"I'm afraid she said it is about the franchise's dismal record," Messal said. "And also she is researching an ancient offense for a historical article. Elder Barnes, have you ever heard of the *Muybridge offense*?"

Muybridge ... Fred's code-word. Yolanda did have information about Jeanine.

"I've heard of it," Quentin said. "It's really obscure. Book the interview, Messal."

Messal bowed slightly. "Yes, Elder Barnes. Right away."

QUENTIN PACED in his guest suite in the Buddha City Station Hilton, waiting for Yolanda Davenport. She had booked the room so they'd have privacy, away from the other reporters and away from Quentin's teammates. He hoped she hurried up, because this place gave him the creeps.

The guest suite was certainly beautiful. Expensive art flashed in holoframes, statues stood in each corner, the smartpaper looked brand-new and each piece of furniture was worth more than Quentin had made in an entire year of mining. Even with the money he'd earned playing for the Raiders, he wouldn't have been able to afford staying here. All of this for rich guests while citizens starved? The art alone would have bought many months of food for thousands of people.

He was antsy. Did Yolanda have info on his sister, or was this just another football-related story? Well, if it was the latter, it couldn't hurt to give the interview. Yolanda had done him wrong, true, but she'd made up for it and put herself at great risk to do so. She'd even been roughed up a little by Anna Villani's goons, and that Quentin had to respect — Yolanda was willing to put herself at risk and play through the pain to get a job done, just like he was.

[ELDER BARNES, MISS DAVENPORT HAS ARRIVED.]

He walked to the door. It hissed open. Two armored Greens were waiting outside. Behind them, a white-uniformed, white-furred Quyth Worker standing next to the purple-skinned, white-haired Yolanda Davenport. Both cops had a hand on the hilt of their holstered nail guns. The one on the right looked normal, but the one on the left was a woman — a bit of a rarity in the Greens.

Quentin smiled at her. "Aren't you a little small to be a Green?"

He couldn't see her expression behind the face shield. The name on her chest-plate read R. MCGUILLICUDY. The man's chest-plate read X. XHIANG.

"Funny," Xhiang said. "You all done being a comedian?"

"High One guides us to our true calling," Quentin said. "I just got to be me."

Xhiang's fingers tightened on the nail gun's handle, reminding Quentin that on Buddha City Station, accidents happen — even to star quarterbacks.

"Uh ... sorry," Quentin said. "Please, come on in."

Xhiang stepped in, followed by Yolanda, the Worker, then the other cop.

The door shut. Five sentients stood in the well-decorated living room. Quentin waited for someone to talk.

Yolanda looked at the Worker and nodded. The Worker pulled small devices from his pockets and set them on a coffee table, on the backs of chairs, all over the place. He fiddled with these devices for a moment, then turned to Yolanda.

"The room is clear," he said. "I found two recording devices, but now they are both jammed. We are free to talk."

Yolanda let out a big breath. "Finally," she said. "Quentin, your people are so damn paranoid about heretics spreading a message of this or a message of that."

He nodded. "I'm familiar with the concept."

She gestured to the Worker. "Meet Whykor the Aware. He works for Commissioner Froese and also helps me with stories from time to time."

The Worker offered a pedipalp hand. Quentin reached down and shook it.

"Exceptional game this afternoon, Mister Barnes," Whykor said. "The second-best completion percentage of your career, including your time with the Raiders."

Was that true? Quentin had no idea. "If you say so. Nice to meet you."

Yolanda then gestured to Xhiang. "And I believe you already know this guy."

The cop pulled off his helmet.

"High One," Quentin said. "Fred?"

Frederico smiled. "I wouldn't call it my best disguise ever, Q. Face shields are almost like cheating."

"How did you get here?"

"Your yacht," Fred said. "We flew it to Stewart, then we took a commercial flight to the Station."

"We?"

Fred smiled and looked at McGuillicudy. She raised her face shield — Quentin found himself looking at the woman of his childhood memories.

"Jeanine?" The word came out as a whisper. He could barely believe it.

She took off the helmet. Brown hair spilled down around caramel skin. She smiled at him.

"Hello, brother."

He didn't know what to say. Then it hit him — what better place for Fred to set up a meeting? Jeanine was a native Nationalite. She could effortlessly blend in on the Station, on Micovi or on any of the Purist Nation worlds. How Fred got his hands on a pair of Greens uniforms was another thing entirely, but everything had a price, and Fred had unlimited access to Quentin's massive bank account.

Quentin stayed very still, as if a sudden movement might make his sister run screaming from the suite. "I ... I thought you didn't want to see me."

She nodded. "I didn't. Like Fred told you, I needed some time." She looked around the room. "Do you think I could speak to my brother in private?"

Yolanda walked to the bedroom door. "Whykor, come on, let's go over some notes on that story about Don Pine's return to Jupiter. Fred, can a girl buy you a drink? I brought a bottle of Isis Whiskey."

Fred followed Yolanda and Whykor to the bedroom. "None for me, thanks," he said. "The Station might be easy to infiltrate, but it's still a place where one wrong word can get someone looking at your papers. I'll just have water."

They entered the bedroom and shut the door behind them, leaving Quentin alone with the sister he'd never known.

She sat on the couch, then gestured that he should do the same. He sat next to her. Was this *really* Jeanine, or was someone playing games with his heart again? The thought of that man who had pretended to be his father, the man Gredok had used to trick Quentin, to ...

She smiled. "You're wondering if I'm really your sister?"

Quentin laughed, the sound carrying embarrassment and relief. "Yeah, a little."

She reached out and took his hand — her caramel-colored skin against his light brown. "I know Gredok lied to you, but I *am* your sister. I think you know that. I held you when you were a baby. When you were about as big as your head is now, I changed your diapers. I fed you, helped take care of you."

She spoke the truth. He knew her *face*, a face that was burned into his earliest memories. There could be no mistake. He felt tears welling up in his eyes. After spending his childhood wishing that his family would find him, after scanning the stands at each and every game hoping to see someone who could connect him to something beyond his lonely existence, after allowing himself to be duped and used, he *finally* found himself looking at family.

He wiped away tears with his free hand. "Fred said you were afraid of me. Are you still?"

She nodded. "Yes, I am. My past is ... I've had issues with angry men, Quentin, and from what I've seen, you're angrier than most."

"So why did you want to see me?"

"Because of the Orbiting Death game," she said. "Yalla the Biter tried to get you to fight, and you walked away."

Quentin felt a surge of anxiety — he'd come so close to hitting Yalla, to giving into the anger. If he had, would it have cost him his sister? If she feared who he was, he couldn't pretend that he'd mastered his lifelong temper — he had to tell her the truth.

"I only walked away for the team," he said. "I ... I wanted to kick the crap out of him."

She patted his hand, held it tight. "You wanted to, but you *didn't*. That's what matters. I barely know you, little brother, but you made me proud."

The words sent a surge through his chest. She was *proud* of him? Not for his on-field accomplishments or for being an intergalactic star — she was proud simply because he'd controlled his anger.

She smiled at him again. He marveled at her blue eyes, the same eyes he saw whenever he looked in the mirror. He wished he had the words to tell her what it all meant to him, but somehow, he knew she understood.

He touched her brown hair. "I remember you being blond?"

She laughed, a small thing brought on by a distant memory of her past.

"Yeah. Dying my hair pissed Dad off, so I did it a lot. I had blond hair, purple hair, green, blue, red ... you name it. This is my real color, boring old brown."

She looked off, seemed to be thinking, remembering. "If you're anything like Dad was, walking away from that fight had to be hard." She stared at him again. "High One, look at you — you could be Dad's twin."

"What was he like?"

Her smile faded. "You were too young to remember, but … well, when I was a teenager, there were a lot of hard times in our house. He was gone a lot. When he was home, there were problems."

"What kind of problems?"

She waved a hand. "It doesn't matter now." She bit at her lower lip, chose her words carefully. "Dad did the best he could to provide for us, but he saw horrible things. And he didn't talk about it, but he did horrible things as well."

Quentin had just assumed his father worked in the mines like everyone else. "What did he do?"

"He was a mercenary," she said. "He was a teenager himself during the Takeover. He fought against the Creterakians. After that, he hired out to whomever could pay him. He worked all over the galaxy. Some wars were documented, some weren't. He also did some work for the Church. I asked him about it a lot. All he would ever way was, *my family has to eat.*"

The rush of information coursed through Quentin, swirled around in his head, grabbed his heart and squeezed. His father had been a mercenary? The concept hammered home just how privileged Quentin's life had become and brought guilt that he still found ways to complain about it.

"Is that how Dad died? Fighting in a war?"

She stared at him for a second, then shook her head. "I never said he died. Dad is still alive."

Quentin opened his mouth to speak, but he had no words.

The bedroom door opened. Frederico rushed out, pulling on his helmet, Yolanda and Whykor close behind.

Fred grabbed Jeanine's helmet and tossed it to her.

"McGuillicudy, get your gear," he said. "We have to move. We've been made."

She stood and put the helmet on.

Quentin wasn't about to let her go so soon. "Come on, Fred — already? What is it, Gredok?"

"Worse," Fred said. "Anna Villani."

Anna Villani, owner of the OS1 Orbiting Death. A stab of fear and anger shot through Quentin. "What the hell does that psycho want?"

Fred nodded at Jeanine. "Villani wants *her*. Anna isn't done with you, Q. She knows about your sister, she knows your sister is here. I don't know how Villani found out, but she did. I have to get Jeanine out of here, fast."

Jeanine buckled her helmet strap and flipped down her visor. "I'm ready."

Villani wasn't even there and she was taking Quentin's sister away from him. He wanted to wrap his hands around Anna's neck and *squeeze*. "Why does she want Jeanine?"

"Leverage," Fred said as he quickly rearranged Jeanine's gear. "Villani can't touch you without risking Gredok's wrath and starting a major gang war, but she can snag your sister. Anna wants payback on you for getting Ju off the hook for Grace McDermot's murder. And if Anna gets your sister, how well do you think you'll play against the Orbiting Death next year?"

His sister hadn't done anything to anybody, yet here she was the target of not one but *two* crimelords — all because of Quentin.

"Jeanine, I'm sorry," Quentin said. "I didn't mean for this to happen."

Jeanine sneered, a dismissive gesture that Quentin had seen and felt on his own face many times.

"Screw Villani," she said. "And screw Gredok. This is their fault, not yours, baby brother." She stepped forward and wrapped her arms around him. He hugged her back, his emotions bubbling out of control.

Fred gently pulled her away. "Come on, McGuillicudy, time to move."

Quentin grabbed the detective's shoulder. "Fred, thank you. Keep her safe, I'll pay you whatever it takes."

Fred smiled a smile that was half reassurance, half cockiness. "I'm not doing this just for the money anymore, or for you — I'm doing it for Jeanine. They'll have to kill me before they get her. We'll fly to Stewart, grab the *Hypatia* and we'll be back in Ionath

City in a couple of days. Anna's goons don't have the chops to catch me."

He flipped down his visor, once again anonymous behind the black material, then left the suite. Jeanine followed him out.

The door hissed shut, leaving Quentin alone with Yolanda and Whykor. Quentin sat heavily on the couch. Had his efforts to rescue Ju Tweedy put his own sister in danger? Obviously, but what else could he have done?

Yolanda pulled a chair in front of him and sat. "Quentin, I'm very sorry you have to go through all of this."

He looked at her perfect, purple face, her white hair and frosted lips. He looked her in the eye. "Thanks. And thank you for helping set this up, Yolanda. I owe you."

She smiled. "Yes, you do, so let's cash in. I know you're upset about your family, but I still have a job to do. Ready for the interview?"

Whykor pulled another device out of his pocket: a camera.

Quentin sighed, then nodded. "Sure. Ask me anything you want."

GFL WEEK SIX ROUNDUP
Courtesy of Galaxy Sports Network

Home		Away	
Alimum Armada	27	Hittoni Hullwalkers	10
Buddha City Elite	35	Ionath Krakens	31
Isis Ice Storm	17	Coranadillana Cloud Killers	14
Bord Brigands	28	Themala Dreadnaughts	17
Yall Criminals	31	Orbiting Death	24
Wabash Wolfpack	24	To Pirates	21
Neptune Scarlet Fliers	24	Bartel Water Bugs	20
Shorah Warlords	10	**D'Kow War Dogs**	21
Jang Atom Smashers	35	New Rodina Astronauts	13
Sheb Stalkers	14	Texas Earthlings	10

Almost halfway through the season, and the Criminals are the only remaining undefeated team. Yall (5-0) maintained its first-place standing in the Planet Division with a 31-24 win over OS1 Orbiting Death (3-3). Criminals receiver Concord led the way with 211 receiving yards and two touchdowns, both of which came on simple out-passes that the Sklorno turned into long touchdown plays of 65 and 57 yards. Running back Jack Townsend added 114 yards on the ground and two rushing touchdowns of his own.

Yall has a one-game lead on division rival Wabash (4-1). The Wolfpack took sole possession of second with a 24-21 win over the To Pirates (3-2). To is tied for third with Isis (3-2) and Alimum (3-2).

The Buddha City Elite (3-3) remain in striking distance of first in the Planet, thanks to a 35-31 win over Ionath (1-4). Elite quarterback Gary Lindros threw for 286 yards and five touchdowns on the day, including three touchdown strikes to tight end Rick Warburg. Lindros was outperformed by Ionath QB Quentin Barnes, who went 34-of-40 for 412 yards and four TDs. Ionath is only a half-game above last place and could very well be headed for relegation.

In the Solar, Neptune (4-1) hung a 24-20 score on previously undefeated Bartel (4-1). The result moves both teams into a three-way tie with Jupiter for first place in the division. The Jacks (4-1) had a bye this week.

Texas (3-2) fell a game back in the division race, thanks to a 14-10 loss to Sheb (3-3). The Earthlings are in a three-way tie for fourth with Jang (3-2), which beat New Rodina (1-5) 35-13, and Vik (3-2), which had a bye.

Deaths

No deaths reported this week.

Offensive Player of the Week

Yall receiver **Concord,** who caught 13 passes for 211 yards and two touchdowns in the Criminals' 31-24 win over the Orbiting Death.

Defensive Player of the Week

Coranadillana defensive end **Jesper Schultz,** who had three sacks and four solo tackles in a loss against the Isis Ice Storm.

19

Week Seven:
Shorah Warlords at
Ionath Krakens

PLANET DIVISION

5-0 Yall Criminals

4-1 Wabash Wolfpack

3-2 Alimum Armada

3-2 Isis Ice Storm

3-2 To Pirates

3-3 Buddha City Elite

3-3 OS1 Orbiting Death

2-3 Themala Dreadnaughts

1-4 Ionath Krakens

1-5 Coranadillana Cloud Killers

1-5 Hittoni Hullwalkers

SOLAR DIVISION

4-1 Bartel Water Bugs

4-1 Jupiter Jacks (bye)

4-1 Neptune Scarlet Fliers

3-2 Jang Atom Smashers

3-2 Texas Earthlings

3-2 Vik Vanguard (bye)

3-3 Bord Brigands

3-3 Sheb Stalkers

2-3 D'Kow War Dogs

1-5 New Rodina Astronauts

0-6 Shorah Warlords

THE DAWN SUN LIT UP the clouds of Ionath, filling the stadium with a pink light. The Krakens were home again, preparing for their Week Seven tilt against the winless Shorah Warlords. Yet another must-win game, but preparation had to wait for a racial integration session.

A session led by none other than Ma Tweedy.

She stood at mid-field, right on top of the Ionath Krakens logo. On her left stood the four Prawatt players. On her right, the twelve remaining Sklorno players.

Ma Tweedy squinted at both sides. It was hard to tell if her eyes were actually open, but she seemed to look at each player individually.

"I hear you boys have been fighting," she said. "Which one of you is Bumberpuff?"

The captain raised a flexible arm. "That's me."

Ma Tweedy curled her finger in. "Come here."

Bumberpuff looked at Quentin. "What is this? This tiny Human woman is not an official part of the organization."

"Do what she says," Quentin said. "Unless you want to sit out the game against Shorah?"

Bumberpuff's body rattled once in annoyance, then he walked up to Ma Tweedy — a spidery X-Walker standing over a four-foot-tall Human woman wearing an orange and black Krakens jacket.

She looked up at him. "You're the leader?"

"I was the commander of the greatest warship in the history of civilization," Bumberpuff said. "The Prawatt on this team were under my command, so yes, I am effectively their leader."

Ma Tweedy nodded. "You're the leader, and you get into stupid little fights?"

Bumberpuff's body rattled. "*Stupid little fights?* That *cricket* attacked me!"

Ma pointed a finger at him. "*Shushit!* We do *not* use that kind of language here! You were attacked, but the way I heard it, Quentin knocked the *Sklorno* player off of you, then you came in for more, is that right?"

"Well, she was the one—"

"*Shushit!* Did you come in for more?"

Bumberpuff turned to Quentin. "This is ridiculous. I don't have to stand here and listen—"

"Last warning," Quentin said. "One more word out of you, John and I tell Coach Hokor that you need to sit this week out. Don't you *want* to be on the field against the Warlords?"

Alien or not, Quentin knew Bumberpuff's competitive streak. The sentient had left everything he knew behind to come and play football for the Krakens. If he wasn't playing, he'd made that sacrifice for nothing.

The Prawatt turned back to Ma Tweedy. "Yes, I came in for more."

"*Ma'am.*"

"What?"

"*Ma'am,*" she said. "Since you seem to have trouble respecting others, you call me *ma'am.*"

Bumberpuff's body rattled. He hated this. "Yes, *ma'am.*"

"Good," Ma Tweedy said. She turned and squinted at the Sklorno players. "And which one of you is Vacaville?"

Vacaville jumped high. "That is me! Me-*me-me*!"

She waved the Sklorno forward. Vacaville sprinted in — even though it was only ten feet, she sprinted anyway. Her race knew only knew one speed: all-out.

Ma Tweedy stared at Vacaville. "Why did you attack him?"

"He is a demon! He is a devil! Evil-*evil*-evil!"

Ma Tweedy nodded. "And this *devil* also took your starting spot, did he not?"

Vacaville's eyestalks quivered. "Yes! And he should not have! He played awful! He cost us the game against Buddha City! Devil-devil-evil kills my people! He—"

Ma Tweedy's finger snaked out lightning quick and tapped Vacaville between her tentacles.

"*Shushit!*"

The Sklorno leaned back. Quentin saw that John and Ju were trying not to giggle.

Ma Tweedy waggled her finger at Vacaville. "You lost your starting spot because you weren't good enough to play it."

Vacaville's eyestalks quivered again, then sagged.

Ma shook her head. "I know you're upset about that. Anyone would be, but the game of football isn't about making sentients feel good. It's about winning games. You lost your spot, you can be sad about it, but it's the way life goes."

Vacaville's legs wobbled as if she might collapse at any moment. "But the demons took roster spots from our sisters! And Bumberpuff did not play well! I have worked hard my whole life and waited-waited-waited for my chance to play Tier One! It is not fair to lose my spot to a monster!"

"Life ain't fair," Ma Tweedy said. "Get used to it."

She slowly turned in place, affixing her squinty gaze on the other three Prawatt and the other eleven Sklorno players. "You all hate each other? You are teammates. You are *Krakens*. I'm not going to stand by and watch your hatred mess things up for my three boys."

Quentin's skin tingled with goosebumps at those words. Ma Tweedy meant it — he was just as much a son of hers as John and Ju.

Ma clapped her hands together. "No one in the Krakens organization gives a damn about your race, your wars, your religion or whatever other silly reason you're at each other's throats."

John raised his hand. "Ma, the Prawatt don't have throats."

"Jonathan, *shushit!* Another word out of you and you'll join them."

John took one step back, then one step behind his brother.

She moved her gaze across the Sklorno and Prawatt like her eyes were machine guns leveling enemy soldiers.

"You don't have to like each other, but you *will* respect each other, you *will* play as a team," she said. "You all want to act like children? Then you're going to get treated like children. Raise your hands — or tentacles, or whatever — if you were in that fight in the Buddha City locker room."

There was a pause. All four Prawatt raised a biomechanical arm. Five Sklorno raised a tentacle: Vacaville, Cheboygan,

Davenport, Wahiawa and the rookie Niami. All the guilty parties had admitted it.

Ma Tweedy waved them forward. "All of you sit here on the Krakens logo. Alternate species — Prawatt/Sklorno, Prawatt/Sklorno. Make a circle. Hurry up! I don't have all day! My shows are on soon, and *you better not* make me miss them!"

The players scrambled into a sitting circle. There was something undeniable about Ma Tweedy. She wasn't much bigger than a Ki snack, but all races seemed to react to her commands.

She's a leader, Quentin thought. *Sentients just respond to her, the same way they respond to me.*

Quentin saw John and Ju elbowing each other lightly. Whatever Ma had planned, the boys had obviously been on the receiving end many times before.

Ma Tweedy stood in the center of the circle. "Now, all of you reach out a tentacle, or whatever, and hold hands."

Eyestalks shot up. Prawatt bodies quivered.

Bumberpuff stood. "No! I will not *hold hands* with these bloodthirsty primitives!"

Quentin stepped forward. "Bumberpuff, that's it. You're out."

"*What?*" he said. "Come on, Quentin! Playing against Sklorno on the field is one thing, but to *touch* them? In a friendly way? That's ridiculous."

Quentin jerked his thumb toward the locker room. "You're out. You don't play this week."

Bumberpuff's eyespots seemed to shake, catching the morning sun. "No! I have to play! We have to beat Shorah!"

"Too late. I warned you."

The captain suddenly sat. "I'll do it. I'll hold hands."

Quentin stared at him, then looked at the Tweedy brothers. They were laughing so hard they had to hold each other up — they weren't going to be any help. Quentin looked at Ma Tweedy. "What do you think? Should I let him off the hook?"

She nodded. "Give him one more chance. Just *one.*"

Quentin shrugged. "Okay. Bumberpuff, you better do what she says."

Bumberpuff reached out his arms and grabbed the tentacle of Niami on his right and Vacaville on his left. The Sklorno started to pull away.

Quentin stepped closer, pointing his finger at them. "Knock it off! The same punishment goes for all of you. If you don't hold hands, you don't dress for the game."

There was a pause, then all nine sentients begrudgingly reached out to each other.

Ma Tweedy smiled. "Good. Now you can all stay here holding hands for the next hour, and think about how this will happen again every time you fight."

Quentin stared, amazed — Sklorno and Prawatt alike sat there quietly. He walked over to Ju and John.

"Did Ma used to do this to you guys or something?"

Ju nodded. "Oh, yeah," he said, wiping away tears. "John and I used to fight a lot. She'd make us sit on the front steps of our building and hold hands for hours."

"We *hated* it," John said. THINGS YOU HATE ARE ALWAYS FUNNY WHEN THEY HAPPEN TO SOMEONE ELSE scrolled across his face. "We were so embarrassed. People would walk by and laugh at us, which was bad, or they would say *awww, look at those cute boys holding hands*, which was worse."

"*Mega*-worse," Ju said. "If we didn't do what she said, she'd take away privileges."

Privileges ... this was the same thing, wasn't it? These two races wanted to kill each other, but they held hands because if they didn't, they wouldn't be allowed to play football. If he wasn't seeing it with his own eyes, Quentin would have never believed it.

An elbow slammed into his shoulder.

"Here's the good part, Q," John said. "Just watch."

The rest of the team came out of the tunnel. Human, HeavyG, Ki and Quyth Warrior all walked out toward the quiet spectacle. The Humans and HeavyG hooted and teased. The pedipalps of the Quyth Warriors quivered in laughter. The Ki didn't have any reaction — to them, sentients clustering tightly together seemed perfectly normal.

Coach Hokor flew out on his hovercart. He descended into the middle of the circle. Prawatt and Sklorno both looked at him expectantly, hoping he would end the charade.

Hokor hopped out onto the painted grass. He looked at the players sitting there, holding hands. "*Barnes!* Is this your doing?"

Quentin was about to take the blame, but Ju spoke first.

"John and I did it, Coach! We brought you in a consultant who knows how to make sentients get along."

Hokor looked at Ma Tweedy. She smiled and nodded at him. Hokor again stared at the seated players. His eye swirled with orange, and his pedipalps twitched once.

"Look at you all," Hokor said. "You're getting along like *teammates*. Let's start practice with O-line versus D-line. I think we can live without our wide receivers and defensive backs for quite a while."

Eyestalks and lenses looked to the ground — grown sentients sagging like children in trouble. John and Ju started laughing all over again, and Quentin had to fight to stop from doing the same.

DESPITE A SPLIT LIP, a black eye and a bruise that wrapped from his left chest, around his shoulder and all the way to his spine, Quentin felt fantastic. No matter how bad the beating, a victory always took the pain away. *Most* of it, anyway.

He and his teammates had run their victory lap around Ionath Stadium, high-fiving every fan that could reach over the retaining wall. He'd then gone to the locker room, taking the time to speak to each and every teammate about what they did well that afternoon. He even spoke to the players that hadn't gotten into the game, thanking them for a great week of practice that contributed to a Krakens win. He finished up his post-game ritual with a trip to the Ki baths. Finally free of the game's blood, dirt and blue Iomatt stains, he put on his fancy suit and followed Messal the Efficient to the press conference.

Messal led Quentin out into the media room. Orange skirting decorated with the Krakens logo hung around a black-topped table. A small podium sat in the center of the table. The smart-paper wall behind the table showed the slowly moving logos — the Krakens logo and the GFL shield, as well as advertisers like Junkie Gin, Farouk Outdoor Wear and Xibi Anti-Rad Suits. He noticed a new logo advertising a movie: *Overlord Doom, Part IV*.

As Quentin sat in his chair, he realized the movie featured Patuth the Muscular, who had starred in the first three movies of the series. But Patuth's usual co-star, Gloria Wanganeen, wasn't there. Instead of Gloria, Quentin saw a familiar face — Somalia Midori. His rock-star girlfriend was now going to be a *movie* star? He almost hadn't recognized Somalia's face; instead of a spiked Mohawk, her hair looked long, brown and soft.

Quentin realized he hadn't talked to her in weeks. All the business with the Prawatt, preparing for games, meeting his sister, all the traveling, those things had consumed every last moment of his time. He made a mental note to call her that afternoon.

He sat in his spot at the table to the right of the podium. On the other side of the crysteel security windows sat the fifty-headed monster known as *the media*. These were the Krakens beat reporters, sentients from all across known space that followed every moment of the Ionath season.

Messal stood on a stool behind the podium and addressed the reporters. "Elder Barnes will now take questions regarding the Krakens' forty-eight to forty-four win over the Shorah Warlords. Please keep your questions specific to the game. If you wish to discuss other matters with Elder Barnes, contact me through proper channels and we will schedule an interview. First question?"

The fifty-headed monster erupted, all heads calling out *Quentin! Quentin!* which was odd, considering that Messal was the one who picked which reporter could speak.

Messal pointed to a black-striped, blue-skinned Leekee. "Go ahead."

The Leekee looked at Quentin. "Kelp Bringer, Leekee Galaxy Times. Quentin, your offense was unstoppable today. Six hundred and ten yards, Ju Tweedy rushed for over a hundred yards, you threw for four-fifty and set a franchise record today with *six* touchdown passes, breaking the five-TD-pass record set by Bobby Adrojnik in 2665. How does it feel to break Adrojnik's record, probably the first of many you'll break?"

As he always did at every press conference, Quentin heard the voice of Don Pine: *Think before you talk. Don't rush your answers. A pause actually makes you look smarter, more introspective.*

Quentin took a breath and formulated his answer. "It's an honor to be mentioned alongside Adrojnik," he said. "But, I wouldn't say I'm in his company. Adrojnik led Ionath to a GFL title. Until I do that, I'm not his equal in any capacity. Next question?"

Quentin! Quentin!

Messal pointed to a black-skinned Human. The fifty-headed monster quieted as the man stood.

"Jonathan Sandoval, Net Colony News Syndicate. The Krakens are averaging thirty-five points a game, and you're averaging four-point-two touchdown passes *per game*. Through six contests, you've got twenty-five touchdown passes and only two interceptions. You're making it look like a video game out there."

"Uh ... I haven't really looked at my stats so far this season."

The fifty-headed monster laughed, but he wasn't joking. He'd been too busy to pay attention to stats — those numbers were insane. Sandoval was right; it sounded like something you got when playing Madden 2685 on the easiest level.

"Quick follow-up question," Sandoval said. "How much of this offensive success do you attribute to Don Pine finally leaving the team?"

Quentin felt a surge of anxiety, but he took a slow breath and calmed himself. How ironic that Don Pine's advice helped him relax when it was a loaded question about Don Pine himself?

He had to watch his words. Someday, maybe, he could tell the truth about Pine, about how he'd betrayed the game and his teammates, but now was not that time.

"I owe him a lot," Quentin said. "Our successes or failures have nothing to do with Don leaving. This is Tier One football — you lose players, you gain players. Trading him brought us Denver, just in time to help us out after Hawick got hurt. The Krakens are a team, no player is more important than any other."

Next question?"

Messal pointed to a Quyth Leader.

"Pikor the Assuming, UBS Sports," the Leader said. "Quentin, you just beat a winless team at home, and barely won at that. Next week you go on the road against four-and-two Alimum, a team that's won two straight and is vying for the Planet Division title. Do you think you stand a chance against a solid outfit like the Armada?"

If these reporters thought he'd boast or say something stupid that would provide the Armada with locker-room fodder, they were wrong. He wasn't an ignorant rookie anymore.

"Alimum is a great team," he said. "We need a great week of preparation if we hope to beat them. Next question."

Quentin! Quentin!

Messal pointed to a purple-skinned Human woman with white hair. Quentin couldn't stop himself from smiling. Once he had despised this woman, but she had risked her life to connect Quentin with his sister. With that one act of kindness, all was forgiven.

"Yolanda Davenport, Galaxy Sports Magazine. As my colleague pointed out, you're having an amazing individual season. In fact, if it weren't for the play of Rick Renaud, you'd be the favorite for league MVP honors. Yet despite your play, the Krakens have only two wins — that's clearly because your pass defense is the worst in the league. Ionath just gave up *forty-four points* to the winless Warlords. Are those defensive struggles due to the racial conflicts between the Prawatt and the Sklorno players? There have been reports of racial slurs in the locker room and even a race-riot that injured players. If your own team can't get along, how can you hope to avoid relegation?"

Quentin saw the fifty heads lean in closer. Leave it to Yolanda to ignore the stats and go for the hard-hitting question. How had she found out about the locker-room fight? And for once, couldn't this woman just back off?

"We handle all issues internally," Quentin said. "There has been an ... *adjustment period* ... with our new players. I'll put my Prawatt teammates up against any receiver in the galaxy. I'm as proud of them as I am of my Sklorno teammates. Next question."

The rest of the questions were fairly stupid, further evidence that most of the sentients who reported on football had no idea what it took to play the game. He answered each question slowly and carefully, thinking his answers through before speaking, but he couldn't get Yolanda's question out of his head — *If your own team can't get along, how can you hope to avoid relegation?*

GFL WEEK SEVEN ROUNDUP
Courtesy of Galaxy Sports Network

Home		Away	
Alimum Armada	25	Wabash Wolfpack	7
Ionath Krakens	48	Shorah Warlords	44
Yall Criminals	70	Isis Ice Storm	7
Themala Dreadnaughts	14	To Pirates	38
Bartel Water Bugs	24	Jupiter Jacks	14
D'Kow War Dogs	17	New Rodina Astronauts	7
Jang Atom Smashers	14	Neptune Scarlet Fliers	24
Texas Earthlings	24	Vik Vanguard	27

Can anyone stop the Criminals? That's the question being asked around the league this week after Yall (6-0) embarrassed the Isis Ice Storm (3-3) by the staggering score of 70-7 in front of a galaxy-wide audience on Monday Night Football. The 63-point margin of victory is the highest in league history.

This Criminals squad is already being dubbed "the greatest team in GFL history" and not just because of quarterback Rick Renaud. Eight different Criminals players scored touchdowns against Isis. Renaud threw for three of those. Running back Jack Townsend rushed for 151 yards and a touchdown, fullback Tay "the Weazel" Nguyen added another 112 yards and a rushing touchdown of his own. Even backup quarterback Morite Whittmore added a pair of scores, one in the air and one on the ground. The Criminals returned a punt for a TD, and linebacker Forrest Dane Cauthorn notched a pair of defensive touchdowns.

"It was the worst butt-whipping I've ever experienced," said Ice Storm coach Joe Carlson. "Offense, defense, special teams, they outclassed us in every possible aspect of the game. I don't see anyone beating Yall for the rest of the season."

Yall is now two full games ahead of the three teams tied for second place: Alimum (4-2), To (4-2) and Wabash (4-2). Alimum beat Wabash 25-7, while To hammered defending champion Themala (2-4) by a score of 38-14.

Ionath (2-4) moved one game clear of the Planet Division relegation bubble, thanks to a 48-44 shootout over winless Shorah (0-7).

In the Solar Division, Bartel (5-1) continued its charmed season with a 24-14 home win over the Jupiter Jacks (4-2). Coming into the week, Bartel, Jupiter and Neptune (5-1) were all tied for first in the division. Neptune remains tied for first thanks to a 24-14 win over Jang (3-3).

"This proves we're for real," said Bartel owner Fish Fin Chewer. "Halfway through the season and we've lost only one game. We won't accept anything less than the playoffs."

Jupiter falls into a third-place tie with Vik (4-2). With 15 seconds to play, Vanguard linebacker Mur the Mighty sacked Texas QB Case Johanson, forcing a fumble that he also recovered. Vik kicked a field goal as time expired, winning 27-24 over the Earthlings (3-3).

With the season half gone, the relegation race is starting to heat up. Coranadillana (1-5) and Hittoni (1-5) are in trouble in the Planet, while Shorah (0-7) and New Rodina (1-6) both face difficult times in the Solar.

Deaths

No deaths reported this week.

Defensive Player of the Week

Yall Criminals middle linebacker **Forrest Dane Cauthorn**, who had six solo tackles, ten assists, one fumble return for a touchdown and one interception return for a touchdown in the Criminals 70-7 blowout of the Isis Ice Storm.

Offensive Player of the Week

Alimum running back **Dave Frizzell**, who carried the ball 22 times for 109 yards and three touchdowns in the Armada's 25-7 win over the Wabash Wolfpack.

20

Week Eight:
Ionath Krakens at
Alimum Armada

PLANET DIVISION

6-0 Yall Criminals

4-2 Alimum Armada

4-2 To Pirates

4-2 Wabash Wolfpack

3-3 Buddha City Elite (bye)

3-3 Isis Ice Storm

3-3 OS1 Orbiting Death (bye)

2-4 Ionath Krakens

2-4 Themala Dreadnaughts

1-5 Coranadillana Cloud Killers (bye)

1-5 Hittoni Hullwalkers (bye)

SOLAR DIVISION

5-1 Bartel Water Bugs

5-1 Neptune Scarlet Fliers

4-2 Jupiter Jacks

4-2 Vik Vanguard

3-3 Bord Brigands (bye)

3-3 D'Kow War Dogs

3-3 Jang Atom Smashers

3-3 Sheb Stalkers (bye)

3-3 Texas Earthlings

1-6 New Rodina Astronauts

0-7 Shorah Warlords

QUENTIN STARED OUT into the blackness of punch-space. They'd punch out in moments. His stomach was doing flip-flops, and this time it had little to do with his motion sickness.

Word was the city of Alimum was having a difficult time controlling riots. Millions of citizens were burning, destroying and even killing because Ionath's Prawatt players were coming down to play against their beloved Armada.

Riots, over a football game.

And yet he knew this went way beyond sports. The Krakens' latest acquisitions were forcing an entire galaxy to reevaluate their stance on the Prawatt race. In his few years of life, Quentin had learned that sentients did not like to be forced to reevaluate anything.

His Sklorno teammates packed the observation deck, ready to lose their little minds at the sight of planet Chachana. Like they did for any Dynasty world, they pressed against the crysteel windows, their raspers dangling, their bodies hopping up and down, under and over each other.

John Tweedy was nowhere to be seen. He hadn't talked to Quentin that much lately. Things had seemed a little off with his friend since Quentin had somehow offended him on the landing deck of Buddha City Station. John wasn't being *un*friendly, but it wasn't the same. Besides — John spent most of his time with Becca, and Quentin spent all of his time studying game holos.

Captain Bumberpuff was also absent. Quentin had asked him to stay in his room this time, so as not to create an incident with the overly excited Sklorno.

The reality wave hit, and sure enough, Quentin's body did what it always did. He finished his messy and unfortunate ritual, then looked out the viewing deck's crysteel windows.

Out in the void waited the pale-pink orb of Chachana. It was much bigger than the Purist Nation worlds, even a little bit larger than Earth. It was his second trip here, but his focus drifted from the planet to a dozen or so tiny lights that seemed to be growing brighter.

He felt an instant rush of adrenaline. Pirate fighters? *Not again …*

As if to confirm his fears, the alarm blared through the *Touchback*, followed by Captain Kate's voice bellowing over the ship's sound system.

"*Battle stations! We have ships approaching with hostile intentions. All non-essential personnel report to the dining deck, everyone else, man your positions.*"

Quentin turned to run, to head for Gun Cabin Six, but before he did he saw a huge, white shape out beyond the viewport. It came from somewhere behind the *Touchback*, not there one second, huge and rushing forward the next. On that mass of white, he saw a flash of purple and blue — the GFL logo.

Denver started throwing herself against the crysteel windows. "The commissioner! I love-love-*love* him to save us!"

It was the *Regulator*, the flagship of Rob Froese.

Something slammed into the *Touchback*, throwing Quentin to the deck. A second alarm joined the first. As he scrambled to his feet, the *Regulator* started firing.

Clouds of rapidly expanding gas shot out of the white ship's gun batteries. Some clouds were giant, billowing puffs, others were staccato bursts marking rapid-fire weapons. Quentin could no longer see all of the approaching lights, not with the *Regulator* blocking his view, but the ones he could see flashed brighter for a moment, then faded to black.

It was over in seconds. The sirens continued for a while, then fell silent. Quentin wasn't sure what to do. Should he still report to the gun cabin?

"*Attention,*" called Captain Kate. "*Emergency is over. First shuttle passengers report to the landing bay. GFL fighter craft will escort the shuttle down to Alimum. And if any of you boys or girls sees Commissioner Froese, make sure you tell him that Captain Kate owes him a bottle of Scotch. And a kiss. Maybe several kisses.*"

Denver, Cheboygan, Halawa and Wahiawa all ran to Quentin.

"Quentinbarnesquentinbarnes," Denver said. "Are you unhurt?"

Quentin nodded. He was shaken up a bit, but it would take more than a little fall to hurt him.

"I'm fine," he said. "Come on, let's get to the shuttle bay. It's probably not a good idea to keep GFL fighters waiting."

"Fighters!" Denver said. "I did not know the GFL had fighters!"

Quentin shook his head. "Neither did I." He guessed no one had, and he also guessed that before Rob Froese took over as commissioner, there hadn't been any GFL fighters at all.

They headed for the shuttle bay. How many sentients had just died in that exchange? And more than that, what was *wrong* with everyone? Football was worth dying for, if you played on the field, but if you didn't — was it really worth *killing* for?

QUENTIN AND HIS TEAMMATES stepped off the shuttle and onto Alimum Stadium's beautiful landing pad. The hum of nearby engines filled the air. Four white hovertanks floated high around the landing pad. Each tank bore the GFL logo on its sides and bottom, and each pointed wicked-looking guns away from the pad and into the city.

Like the domed stadium itself, the landing pad was made of two layers of crysteel sandwiched around a two-foot-thick moving wave of multicolored plasma. Beneath Quentin's feet, the floor blazed like a living, molten jewel. The stadium itself shimmered and glowed, illuminating the pink clouds above for miles around, lighting up half of the city with its glowing magnificence.

But that staggering beauty couldn't hide the ugliness of this place. Normal crysteel rose up from the landing platform's edges, curving in to protect sentients against attacks that might come from the buildings towering high on all sides, or from the five levels of roads that snaked through the city. He'd been on this same platform two years ago — the crysteel walls looked more scorched and more bullet-ridden than before. In several places, he saw splatters that looked like dried blood.

Creterakians in white uniforms clung to the underside of those crysteel curves. They clearly didn't want to expose themselves, even for a moment.

Quentin felt an elbow hit his right shoulder.

"*Jeeze*, Q — even the bats don't want to pop their nasty little heads up! This is serious!" Whatever was bugging John, it faded away in the face of such severe security measures.

The *Regulator* had destroyed eight ships. All of the ships had been modified civilian vessels, no match for Commissioner Froese's converted warship.

Choto the Bright slid in line on Quentin's left.

"I do not like this," he said. "The landing pad's armor is significant, and with the tanks there is little that could harm us, but I still do not like it."

As Quentin and his teammates lined up for inspection, a roof door — heavily armored — opened, and three white-uniformed Quyth Leaders scurried out. Usually, they were already waiting when a shuttle landed.

A reddish-furred Leader appeared to be in charge. He waved at Quentin and the others to come inside.

Quentin looked at John. John shrugged and shouted at the Leader.

"Hey, your miniature masterfulness, no inspection?"

If the Leader answered, no one heard it thanks to the explosion that blasted against the crysteel wall on their left. Choto at his side, Quentin sprinted for the armored door, his teammates close behind. As he ran, he heard gunfire and the whine of hovertanks moving to engage the attackers. He also heard the hum of the *Touchback*'s shuttle lifting off and heading back up into orbit.

Quentin ran inside, the others close behind. The armored door clanged shut, cutting off the sounds of battle beyond. Quentin looked around. John and his other first-shuttle teammates were packed into the hallway. Everyone seemed fine. A little shell-shocked, perhaps, but fine.

The Quyth Leader smoothed out his reddish fur. "You'll be safe here," he said. "The terrorists have been trying to hit the landing pad all day, but their weaponry isn't good enough to breach our defenses."

"All *day?*" Quentin said. "High One, what if they attack the shuttle on the way down? Shouldn't we cancel the game?"

The Leader's pedipalps twitched. "*Cancel the game.* You are making a joke? I have heard about you, Barnes, and your sense of humor." The leader waved them down the hall. "There is nothing to worry about. Customs check is canceled for today, head to your locker room."

"But more of my teammates have to fly down, they —"

A big hand gently grabbed his arm. Quentin turned to look at Michael Kimberlin.

"Quentin, come on," the HeavyG said. "The league personnel know what they are doing. They wouldn't take chances with teams."

"*Wouldn't take chances?* We just got shot at!"

Choto leaned in. "Michael is correct, Quentin. Those explosions were little more than fireworks. Our teammates should make it down. We need to prepare for the game. We *must* defeat the Armada."

Quentin didn't know what to say. He followed Choto farther into the stadium as they all headed for the locker room. Explosions? Gunfire? *Tanks?* How could anyone think of football at a time like this?

He shook his head and tried to clear his mind. He had no control over the game being canceled or not. And if it was game on, his head needed to be in it.

From the *Ionath City Gazette*

Krakens Pound Armada, Defense Finally Steps Up

by TOYAT THE INQUISITIVE

ALIMUM, CHACHANA, SKLOR-NO DYNASTY — The Krakens' second-straight win has moved the team two games clear of the relegation zone and possibly put Ionath on track for a late-season playoff run.

Ionath (3-4) traveled to Alimum (4-3) for a Week Eight tilt against the Planet Division playoff contender and returned home with a 42-28 victory. Coming into the game, Alimum had won two straight and was tied for second in the division.

Ju Tweedy led the Ionath offense with 186 yards rushing and three touchdowns. Tweedy's only flaws in the game were his two fumbles, both of which led to Alimum touchdowns.

"Ju needs to hold onto the ball," said Ionath coach Hokor the Hookchest. "He has protected the ball this season so today was most likely a statistical anomaly. We will continue to give him carries and expect him to excel."

Wide receiver Denver had her best game of the season, catching eight passes for 156 yards and two touchdowns.

Krakens quarterback Quentin Barnes threw for 312 yards, two touchdown passes and no interceptions. He also ran for 56 yards and another touchdown. He was sacked three times.

Ionath (3-4) traveled to Alimum (4-3) for a Week Eight tilt against the Planet Division playoff contender and returned home with a 42-28 victory.

Turnovers were the real reason Alimum fell behind early. Armada quarterback Kirill Gomelsky was intercepted twice in the first quarter, once by Ionath free safety Katzembaum Weasley and once by cornerback Cormorant Bumberpuff.

Weasley's interception set up a 17-yard TD pass from Barnes to Denver, while Bumberpuff returned his interception 52 yards for a touchdown. The pick-six marked the first time in history that a Prawatt player scored points in a GFL game.

Bumberpuff added two more interceptions in the second half. Gomelsky seemed slightly upset about the game.

"The [expletive] Prawatt just [expletive] move different than what I'm used to," Gomelsky said. "How the [expletive] am I supposed to [expletive] prepare for a [expletive] game against a [expletive] race I've never seen? I know I'll figure them out by next year, but they were just different enough that I [expletive] couldn't get a [expletive] [expletive] [expletive] handle on it."

Gomelsky also suffered four sacks: two by Mum-O-Killowe, one by Alexsandar Michnik and a one by rookie linebacker Pishor the Fang.

The game was marked by several violent incidents. A fringe Sklorno religious group attacked the *Touchback*, Ionath's team bus, when that ship came out of punch-space. A GFL warship repelled the attack. Eight small

The game was marked by several violent incidents. A fringe Sklorno religious group attacked the Touchback, Ionath's team bus, when that ship came out of punch-space.

ships were destroyed, and 56 Sklorno died in the exchange. A second attack at the stadium's landing pad resulted in the death of another 11 attackers. No one from the Krakens organization or any GFL security forces was hurt.

The win moves Ionath into a four-way tie for sixth place in the Planet Division. Alimum dropped to fourth place behind Yall (7-0), To (5-2) and Wabash (5-2).

Next week, the Krakens host Coranadillana. With a win, Ionath evens their record at 4-4 and remains in the hunt for a playoff spot.

"We need to beat the Cloud Killers," said Barnes. "They've beaten us the last two years, but we're gelling as a team and have to find a way to win at home."

GFL WEEK EIGHT ROUNDUP
Courtesy of Galaxy Sports Network

Home		Away	
Alimum Armada	28	**Ionath Krakens**	42
Yall Criminals	65	Buddha City Elite	0
Orbiting Death	16	Coranadillana Cloud Killers	14
To Pirates	45	Hittoni Hullwalkers	35
Wabash Wolfpack	31	Isis Ice Storm	17
Themala Dreadnaughts	24	Jupiter Jacks	21
Bartel Water Bugs	38	Jang Atom Smashers	35
Bord Brigands	21	**Texas Earthlings**	24
Sheb Stalkers	13	D'Kow War Dogs	3
Vik Vanguard	17	Neptune Scarlet Fliers	7

For the second week in a row, the Yall Criminals (7-0) set the all-time highest margin of victory. Last week Yall beat Isis (3-4) by 63 points, 70-7, and this week the Criminals hung a 65-0 shutout on the Buddha City Elite.

"I know we're new to Tier One, but come on," said Elite coach Ezekiel Graber. "The Criminals are just dominant. There isn't one weak spot on that team."

Yall running back Jack Townsend set a single-game rushing record with 289 yards. He carried the ball only 18 times, averaging 16 yards per attempt while running for scores of 99, 42, 23 and 14 yards.

"I was feeling it," Townsend said. "I think the Elite did a good job of containing me. Except for those four touchdown runs, I mean."

To (5-2) and Wabash (5-2) both won to stay within two games of Yall in the Planet Division. Alimum slipped three games back thanks to an upset home loss to Ionath (3-4). Alimum quarterback Kirill Gomelsky was intercepted four times, once by Prawatt free safety Katzembaum Weasley and three times by Prawatt corner-back Cormorant Bumberpuff.

"I just run the plays that are called," Bumberpuff said. "I give thanks to the Old Ones because without them we are nothing. Thank you, Old Ones!"

Coranadillana (1-6) and Hittoni (1-6) both lost, keeping them locked in a race for Planet Division relegation.

In the Solar Division, Bartel (6-1) moved into sole possession of first place thanks to a 38-35 victory over Jang (3-4). The Water Bugs continue to win with their punishing ground game. Quarterback Andre "Death Ray" Ridley scored one rushing touchdown, while running backs Jason Crashmore and Bradley Richardson each scored two.

After starting out 4-0, Jupiter (4-3) dropped their third straight game to defending champion Themala (3-4). The 24-21 loss puts Jupiter in a tie for fourth in the Solar. The win keeps the Dreadnaughts' playoff hopes alive. Jacks quarterback Don Pine was sacked five times and threw three interceptions in the loss.

Texas (4-3) beat Bord (3-4) 24-21, and Sheb (4-3) kept D'Kow (3-4) out of the end zone to win 13-3.

In the Solar relegation watch, New Rodina (1-6) and Shorah (0-7) both had byes.

Deaths

No deaths reported this week.

Offensive Player of the Week

Yall running back **Jack Townsend**, who rushed for a league-record 289 yards against Buddha City. Townsend also had four rushing touchdowns.

Defensive Player of the Week

Themala middle linebacker **Tibi the Unkempt**, who recorded three sacks in the Dreadnaughts' 24-21 win over Jupiter.

21

Week Nine:
Coranadillana Cloud Killers
at Ionath Krakens

PLANET DIVISION		SOLAR DIVISION	
7-0	Yall Criminals	6-1	Bartel Water Bugs
5-2	To Pirates	5-2	Neptune Scarlet Fliers
5-2	Wabash Wolfpack	5-2	Vik Vanguard
4-3	Alimum Armada	4-3	Jupiter Jacks
4-3	OS1 Orbiting Death	4-3	Sheb Stalkers
3-4	Buddha City Elite	4-3	Texas Earthlings
3-4	Ionath Krakens	3-4	Bord Brigands
3-4	Isis Ice Storm	3-4	D'Kow War Dogs
3-4	Themala Dreadnaughts	3-4	Jang Atom Smashers
1-6	Coranadillana Cloud Killers	1-6	New Rodina Astronauts (bye)
1-6	Hittoni Hullwalkers	0-7	Shorah Warlords (bye)

THE KRAKENS RUSHED OUT of the tunnel and onto Ionath Stadium's blue field. The sold-out crowd welcomed them once again, 185,000 fans hungry for a third-straight victory.

Quentin ran to the sidelines. He stopped there, raised his right fist high. The team smashed in around him, all pressing tight together. Before John could say anything to steal the moment, Quentin yelled at the top of his lungs and started the team's pregame chant, each line answered by forty-four screaming members of the Orange and the Black.

"Whose house?"

"Our house!"

"Whose house?"

"Our house!"

"What law?"

"Our law!"

"Who wins?"

"Krakens!"

"Who wins?"

"Krakens!"

He turned to look at as many teammates as possible, butting helmets and punching armored shoulders as he talked.

"We win this, we're back in the playoff hunt! The Cloud Killers have beaten us two years in a row, but that ends *now*! They don't beat us in our stadium, not again. Let's whip 'em good!"

The Krakens screamed a final war cry, then broke up and spread out down the sidelines. Across the field, Quentin saw today's foe — the Coranadillana Cloud Killers. White jerseys with blue polka dots, white helmets decorated on both sides with the team's logo: blue claws ripping through a stylized yellow cloud dotted with light blue. Leg armor and shoes of light blue completed the uniforms. The Killers had won just one game and were having a terrible year, but Quentin felt nervous — regardless of records, Coranadillana had always found a way to beat Ionath. But today would be different, Quentin *knew* it would.

An elbow slammed into his shoulder.

"Ouch! Dammit, John, I'm about to play a game!"

"Q, check it out," John said. "I want you to be my best man!"

"What?"

"My best man! You know, at a wedding?"

What the hell was John talking about? "Uncle Johnny, can we just focus on the game and not your future plans for matrimony?"

John smiled. For once, his eyes weren't wide with rage. He looked happy. The big linebacker pointed to the holoscreen.

The announcer's voice echoed through the packed stadium.

"Sentients of all ages, if you'd direct your attention to the main holoscreen, our very own linebacker John Tweedy has an announcement he'd like to make to the galaxy."

John's face appeared in the holoscreen. The image panned back: was he wearing a tuxedo?

Quentin turned to the real-life John Tweedy standing next to him. "Uncle Johnny, what are you doing?"

John grinned wide. "I recorded it earlier, Q! It's gonna be super-mega-awesome! Talk to you later, I gotta find Becca."

John ran down the sidelines. Quentin felt a churning, cold feeling in the pit of his stomach. John *wouldn't*, would he? At least not here, not *now*, not before a game …

"Hi, everyone!" said the forty-foot-high holographic John Tweedy. *"I just wanted to share this moment with the Krakens family. That's all of you, the fans!"*

Dumbfounded, Quentin stared up at the screen. Was this what John had been doing with his time in the past few weeks?

Quentin looked back to the sidelines. He saw John reach Becca. She was standing there, her orange, black and white helmet under her right arm. Like the rest of the stadium, she was also staring at the screen, a confused look on her face. John tapped her on the shoulder pad, set his helmet on the ground and got down on one knee.

The stadium boomed with the amplified, echoing sound of a forty-foot-high holographic John Tweedy.

"Becca Montagne. Will you marry me?"

From his knee, John held up a golden ring. Not a thin little delicate thing, but a thick, solid mass of metal set with a diamond as big as Quentin's knuckle. Even from many yards away, he recognized the type — it was a championship ring.

The Packers' Super Bowl ring.

John hadn't given it to her back in Week Two. He'd saved it, saved it for this moment.

Becca stared down, shock in her eyes. The crowd started to clap and cheer, to whistle and chirp, to bang forearms against chests. Becca looked back up to the holographic John, who was smiling just as big as the John on one knee before her.

An entire stadium of 185,000-plus watched.

Quentin couldn't breathe.

Becca looked around the stadium, looked at John, looked at all the Krakens players. She seemed to be searching for something.

Then her eyes locked with Quentin's.

She stared at him. He stared back. For a moment, everything faded away: the crowd, the stadium, the players, even John ... nothing else existed. For that moment it was just Quentin and Becca. Why was she looking at *him*?

Don't say yes, Becca, don't say it ...

Why would he think that? John was his best friend ... he wanted John to be happy.

Becca kept staring at him. What did she want? Did she need his approval or something?

The crowd started to chant: "*Say yes! Say yes! Say yes!*"

John grinned wider. He didn't stand up, but he looked to the crowd, waved his arms as if to say *more-more-more!*

Worst of all, JUST SAY YES scrolled across his face.

Becca seemed to ignore everything, everything but Quentin.

Quentin felt like he was going to throw up. He couldn't think. Her hard stare became too much to bear.

He shrugged his shoulders.

Becca's eyes narrowed. They should have crinkled, joined a smiling mouth to show her happiness, but instead her eyes looked full of pain, full of loss. She again looked around at the chanting, cheering, happy crowd.

She looked down at John. Becca nodded.

The crowd went wild.

Quentin felt anger blossom in his chest. How could John do this before the game, in front of all of these people? That was no way to prepare for a critical matchup, and it made Quentin furious that John trivialized a must-win game with this showboating.

But deep down, he knew he was angry for another reason.

Becca was going to marry John Tweedy, and Quentin hadn't done anything to stop it.

QUENTIN'S MOUTH FILLED with the coppery taste of hot blood. A nebulae-sized headache blossomed in his brain. He pushed himself to his hands and knees. His body screamed at him to *just stay down*, but you couldn't be a winner if you listened to your body.

He rolled to his butt. Ionath Stadium and the blue field seemed to swirl around him. He didn't know where that ringing sound was coming from, but he hoped it stopped before it made him hurl.

He felt something hard in the roof of his mouth. He reached in to pull out his mouthpiece, then spit into his open hand — a splatter of mucus/blood hit his palm, along with his front right tooth.

Always that stupid tooth. Always.

"Hey, big guy," said a deep, HeavyG voice. "You okay?"

Quentin looked up. Even that small motion made his head pulse with new agony. Coranadillana defensive end Jesper Schultz was standing over him. He only had half of his blue-polka-dotted white jersey. He'd lost the other half in the second quarter. Blood trickled from a rip on the right side of his neck. Dark-blue Iomatt stains smeared his light-blue leg armor. His cracked and chipped white helmet sat cockeyed and looked broken.

"Fine," Quentin said. "Never felt better."

"Good, I thought I'd killed you," Schultz said. "Would have looked good on my stat sheet, but I'm glad you're not dead."

"Thanks," Quentin said. "I'm touched."

Beyond Schultz, Quentin saw the Krakens' dominant left tackle

Kill-O-Yowet. It was Kill-O's job to block Schultz. Normally, Kill-O could shut down any pass rusher, but Schultz had Kill-O's number, just like the Cloud Killers had the Krakens' number. It was Schultz's third sack of the game — Kill-O found a way to not look at Quentin, which was quite an accomplishment considering the Ki species' five eyes let them see in all directions at once.

Off to his left, Quentin heard a woman moaning in pain. Becca Montagne, on her left side, clutching her right knee. Quentin's jumbled memory replayed what had just happened. The Krakens were behind 20-14. He'd dropped back on second-and-10, only to see Schultz drive Kill-O backward, then spin inside the Ki lineman and come free. Becca tried to step up and block the defensive end, but the male HeavyG had leveled the female HeavyG with a big forearm uppercut. Quentin didn't even have time to duck — Jesper had laid him out.

The end result of Jesper's latest play? A shamed left tackle, an injured fullback and a quarterback spitting up blood.

Jesper held out a hand to help Quentin to his feet. Quentin took it. The HeavyG started to pull him up, then Quentin's knees buckled and he fell to his side.

Quentin was vaguely aware of Jesper waving to the Krakens' sidelines, waving and pointing to Quentin.

The heads-up display in Quentin's helmet popped down. Hokor's big-eyed face appeared, although it seemed like there were three fuzzy versions of the black-striped yellow—furred coach.

"*Barnes!* Come out of the game."

Quentin shook his head, which ratcheted up the brain-pain so bad he instantly threw up. Vomit dripped from his facemask. He squinted his eyes, trying to manage the agony.

"*Barnes!* I'm sending Goldman in, get out —"

"*No!* Coach, I can win this."

Yitzhak Goldman started running onto the field. Quentin pushed himself to his feet. He pointed at Goldman, then pointed to the sidelines.

Yitzhak stopped running. He looked back to Hokor, who threw his little hat down then waved Yitzhak off the field.

Quentin couldn't remember ever hurting this bad. He could feel sorry for himself later — a touchdown and an extra point would give Ionath the win. Quentin wanted the ball in his hands.

The medsled slid toward the sidelines, Becca dangling from the silver wires beneath it, Doc Patah flying gracefully alongside.

Was she okay? How bad was it?

Quentin closed his eyes. He couldn't worry about Becca right now, he had a game to win.

Hokor called a play. Quentin jogged back to the huddle. Third down and 15 to go, he needed to convert.

He didn't remember calling the play or breaking the huddle — all of a sudden he was standing behind center, staring out at a blurry defense. The linebackers seemed to shift into mirror images of each other, separate, then blend back together.

You can do this, you HAVE to do this ...

He looked right, needing to see Becca, but Becca wasn't there — Kopor the Climber was.

Why is he in at fullback?

Quentin slid his hands under Bud-O-Shwek.

"Blue, sixteen! Blue, six*teeeen!*"

The pain of just calling out the snap forced his eyes shut. One more play, just one more pass, and he could give his team the win.

"*Hut-hut!*"

Quentin took the snap and dropped back. He saw Halawa breaking free, but she suddenly blurred in and out of focus. Quentin stepped up, trying to concentrate — he heard big feet pounding toward him (*it's Schultz, get rid of it get rid of it*) and gunned the ball downfield.

As soon as he released, he realized he hadn't seen the Cloud Killers' safety coming over to help. The white-jerseyed player swept in for an easy interception.

Quentin Barnes bent at the waist and threw up again. Denver ran up, helped Quentin stand, helped walk him off the field.

The sidelines were a sea of dejection. The game was all but over. For the third-straight year, Coranadillana had beaten them.

Should he have come out of the game? He'd played hurt so

many times, but a shot to the head … blurry vision … maybe that was a different thing altogether.

Quentin reached the sidelines and kept walking, right to a medbench. He sat, slowly, so as not to jostle his brain any further. Maybe Doc could do something about the headache, and, hopefully, fix that broken tooth — *again*.

THE REJUVE FLUID'S HEAT SOAKED into Quentin's battered body. It helped ease the pain of bruises, accelerated the healing of his cuts and scrapes. It did nothing, however, for the pounding in his skull. Doc Patah could fix many things, but he said a concussion had to just run its course.

Quentin had Ionath Stadium's dimly lit training room all to himself. The room's other three tanks lie empty, waiting for another football victim to repair. The back of his head rested against his tank's edge. Fluid bobbed around his jaw and chin, just a half-inch below his lower lip. The only light came from one of Doc Patah's holotanks. Normally, that display would show some kind of medical scan … perhaps ruptured internal organs, or some broken bones, maybe a ligament tear. Now, however, it showed a single play, repeating over and over from every available angle.

Kill-O-Yowet hadn't made a mistake, he hadn't screwed up, he'd just flat-out been beat by a great player. Jesper's inside spin was a perfectly timed thing of beauty, bringing him in so fast that Becca barely had time to react. She had thrown herself in Jesper's path, doing the only thing she could to at least slow him down a little before he decapitated Quentin.

On the replay, Schultz brought up his massive left forearm, caught Becca under the chin, flipping her vertically, a violent hit that made her knee bend the wrong way when her armored shoe dug into the soft, blue turf.

A concussion. Commissioner Froese didn't screw around with brain injuries — Quentin would have to be evaluated and approved by a league-appointed doctor before he'd be allowed to practice again, let alone play in a game. That examination would come tomorrow. For now, all he could do was sit there and *hurt*.

Motion at the door drew Quentin's attention away from holotank's repeating play. Becca Montagne hobbled into the room, a pair of crutches supporting her weight, a fresh brace on her right leg.

Quentin looked at her for a moment, then back to the replay of Schultz's hit. Just seeing her made him angry. Angry and frustrated. He suddenly wanted to blame her for the injury, wanted to yell at her for *something*, but he knew she'd sacrificed her body to protect him.

His concussion wasn't her fault — so why did looking at her face make his chest burn?

He chose to look at her leg brace. At the knee, small lights beeped a pattern of red, then green, then yellow — Doc Patah's surgery on the hoof.

"How bad is it?"

She shrugged. "Torn ACL. Doc says I can practice light on Tuesday, should be fine by Wednesday. How's the head? Concussion?"

"Yeah."

Becca looked down. "Sorry, Q. I missed my block."

A half-second's worth of laughter slipped out before it froze in a hiss of pain.

"Damn," he said. "Try not to do anything funny, okay? Computer, play angle four, start from before the snap. Becca, watch this."

She looked up at the holotank, her eyes filled with self-loathing. Becca could get so moody when she thought she'd done something wrong. He didn't understand why the sight of her made him mad, but as team leader he was *not* going to let her take any blame for this.

"Look how fast you react," he said. "Three, maybe four players in the league could react that fast. *Pause*."

The replay froze. It showed Becca launching herself at the oncoming, long-armed, stubby-legged HeavyG monster known as Jesper Schultz.

"You got a pad on him," Quentin said. "You did enough."

She pointed at the replay. "Look at that! I barely even slowed him down."

"But you *did* slow him down, Becca. If you hadn't, look how hard he would have hit me. *Play*."

The replay continued. For the hundredth time, Quentin watched Jesper Schultz's right arm come up under Becca, spinning her vertically, then Schultz's shoulder pad slamming into Quentin's chest, driving the already-unconscious quarterback to the ground.

"He sacked you," she said. "He gave you a concussion."

"Sure, but he didn't *kill* me. I've been watching this hit over and over. If you hadn't thrown yourself at him like that, I might be in intensive care. Or in a coffin."

She stared at him, her eyes full of hurt. It wasn't just the sack that bothered her ... there was something more.

"Becca, are you okay? Where's Uncle Johnny?"

"I told him I needed some time alone."

Quentin said nothing. She wanted time *alone*? Weren't girls supposed to be all giddy when someone proposed?

Her look of hurt changed to one of anger. "Did you put him up to this, Quentin? Did you tell your best friend to propose to me in front of all of those sentients? In front of an entire *stadium*?"

Why was she yelling at *him*? "No. I didn't even know it was going to happen."

Becca's eyes narrowed to slits. "Are you *sure*? Maybe you thought it was funny to tell him to do it where I couldn't say *no*."

Couldn't say no? She'd accepted John's proposal, why would she do that if she didn't want to marry him? Maybe she thought John hadn't come up with the idea himself. Quentin could see where that might make a girl upset.

"Becca, I swear — I didn't tell him to do it."

She laughed. "Right, like you actually need to use words to get someone to do what you want. Isn't that the reason you studied Gredok? So that you can manipulate people, just like he does? So that you can get sentients to do what you want, but make them think it's their idea?"

No, that wasn't him. That wasn't what he did ... was it? He'd learned to manipulate, sure, but that was just to fight back against Gredok's influence, or as crazy as it still sounded — to deal with the living god of a race of machines. Couldn't she see that? He did what was best for the team, and she was comparing him to *Gredok*?

He was trying to be gracious, yet here she was getting in his face.

"I didn't manipulate John into doing a damn thing," Quentin said. "He loves you. And why would I manipulate him ... do you think I *want* you to marry John?"

Her eyes widened. "Don't you?"

No, I don't. Those words instantly flashed through Quentin's mind ... but why? Becca was his teammate. John was his best friend. The two of them were perfect for each other. And yet when he'd seen John on one knee, Quentin had felt that intense, gut reaction, that urge to say *don't do it.*

Becca put the crutches closer and took one step forward.

"Quentin," she said quietly, "why don't you want me to marry John?"

She was staring at him again, staring with those wide, dark eyes, waiting for an answer in a way that forced him to look elsewhere. Suddenly, his damaged brain seemed to finally put the pieces together, and he knew the answer: *Because you know me so well. Because you seem to know me better than anyone else. Because I should have asked you out a long time ago.*

But he hadn't done that. Hadn't, and now he couldn't, not when John Tweedy loved her so much. It was too late. Quentin couldn't say how he felt, because if Becca hadn't loved John right back then she wouldn't have said *yes.* John loved Becca, and Becca loved John. It was that simple. Quentin hadn't realized he wanted Becca for more than a friend — that didn't give him the right to ruin what she and John had together.

"I never said I don't want you to marry John. I hope you guys are really, really happy together."

Her wide eyes narrowed once again. They looked wet. She turned on her crutches and hobbled out of the training room.

Quentin's head hurt even worse than before.

"Computer, shut off the holotank."

The tank blinked out, leaving the room in total darkness. Quentin closed his eyes and tried to not think about Becca and John.

GFL WEEK NINE ROUNDUP
Courtesy of Galaxy Sports Network

Home		Away	
To Pirates	35	Alimum Armada	7
Orbiting Death	42	Buddha City Elite	14
Ionath Krakens	14	**Coranadillana Cloud Killers**	20
Hittoni Hullwalkers	41	Isis Ice Storm	13
Wabash Wolfpack	38	Themala Dreadnaughts	21
Jupiter Jacks	21	**Yall Criminals**	34
D'Kow War Dogs	7	**Bartel Water Bugs**	24
Bord Brigands	24	Jang Atom Smashers	17
Neptune Scarlet Fliers	14	**Texas Earthlings**	28
Sheb Stalkers	17	New Rodina Astronauts	14
Vik Vanguard	25	Shorah Warlords	17

There are still four weeks remaining in the 2685 season, and the Criminals have already locked up a playoff berth.

Yall (8-0) remained undefeated by holding off a strong effort from Jupiter (4-4). The Jacks took a 21-14 lead into the locker room at the half, paced by three touchdown passes from quarterback Don Pine. Pine was knocked out of the game mid-way through the third quarter, however, and the Criminals scored 20 unanswered points for the win. The Jacks have now lost four straight games and will likely miss the playoffs for the first time in seven seasons.

Wabash and To both improved to 6-2. They remain tied for second in the Planet Division.

In the Solar Division, Bartel improved to 7-1 and maintained sole possession of first place with a 24-7 win over D'Kow (3-5). Vik (6-2) defeated Shorah (0-8) by a score of 25-17 to stay in second place, while Neptune (5-3) fell into a third-place tie due to a 28-14 loss to Texas (5-3). The Scarlet Fliers and the Earthlings are tied with the surprising Sheb Stalkers (5-3), who edged out New Rodina 17-14.

In the Planet Division relegation watch, both Coranadillana (2-6) and Hittoni (2-6) won to remain tied for last place.

Thanks to Shorah's loss, New Rodina (1-7) is still a game above the Solar Division relegation zone. Going back to last season, the Warlords have now lost a record 15 straight Tier One games.

Deaths

Alimum wide receiver **Belcourt,** killed on a clean hit by To Pirates strong safety Ciudad Juarez. This was Ciudad's eighth confirmed fatality. She is now four fatalities behind the GFL's all-time leader Yalla the Biter, who has 12.

Offensive Player of the Week

Vik wide receiver **Gourock,** who caught three passes — all for touchdowns — in the Vanguard's 25-17 win over the Shorah Warlords.

Defensive Player of the Week

Themala cornerback **Germany,** who had two interceptions and two sacks in the Dreadnaughts' 38-21 loss to the Wabash Wolfpack.

22

Week Ten:
Ionath Krakens at
Themala Dreadnaughts

PLANET DIVISION

8-0 y. Yall Criminals

6-2 To Pirates

6-2 Wabash Wolfpack

5-3 OS1 Orbiting Death

4-4 Alimum Armada

3-5 Buddha City Elite

3-5 Ionath Krakens

3-5 Isis Ice Storm

3-5 Themala Dreadnaughts

2-6 Coranadillana Cloud Killers

2-6 Hittoni Hullwalkers

SOLAR DIVISION

7-1 Bartel Water Bugs

6-2 Vik Vanguard

5-3 Neptune Scarlet Fliers

5-3 Sheb Stalkers

5-3 Texas Earthlings

4-4 Bord Brigands

4-4 Jupiter Jacks

3-5 D'Kow War Dogs

3-5 Jang Atom Smashers

1-7 New Rodina Astronauts

0-8 Shorah Warlords

x = playoffs, y = division title, * = team has been relegated

"**WELCOME BACK, FOOTBALL FANS.** Masara the Observant here with Chick McGee for our final post-game analysis following Ionath's 41-35 road win over defending GFL champion Themala. Chick, as we close out our broadcast, let's get your final thoughts on what this loss does for the Dreadnaughts' awful season."

"Well, Masara, Themala came into this game at three-and-five and needed a win to stay alive in the playoff hunt. Now at three-and-six, without a mighty miracle of mystical magnificence, the Dreadnaughts will not return to the post season for a chance to defend their title. And more importantly, the loss means Themala — the defending GFL champions — are just *one game* above the two teams tied for relegation in the Planet Division. To avoid relegation themselves, the 'Naughts need at least one more win, possibly two."

"Chick, have you ever seen a collapse of a defending Galaxy Bowl champion like this?"

"Not in recent memory, Masara. And we've never seen a defending champ get relegated the season after they win the title — the Dreadnaughts are hoping they're not the first."

"Chick, let's switch gears and talk about Ionath. The Krakens are now four-and-five, but this win was their third in their last four outings. Are they playing well enough to make the playoffs?"

"Masara, let's not go counting our Quyth Leaders before they bite off the testicles of their litter mates, shall we?"

"*Chick!* That's not only insulting, it's borderline racist, and furthermore, you—"

"Sorry, Masara, sorry, folks at home, but let's not dwell on my debacle of dialogue. We're talking about Ionath. The difference in this game was the Krakens' defensive backfield. Like other quarterbacks the Krakens have faced, Themala QB Gavin Warren picked Ionath apart with crossing routes and short plays, but once an opponent gets into the red zone, the Krakens' DBs become very, very tough. They intercepted Warren *three times* in the red zone, and that made the difference in a one-touchdown game."

"Chick, why are the Prawatt defenders so tough inside the twenty when they can't seem to stop anyone from the twenty out?"

"Well, Masara, the game the Prawatt play in their system had a bigger playing area and allows passing in any direction. Their goal was to not let the receivers get past them, but they could leave those receivers a lot of space. With the accuracy of GFL quarterbacks, space is one thing a defender can *not* give. When the field shortens to the thirty yards of the red zone — that's the ten-yard-deep end zone and the goal line out to the twenty, for you casual fans — the DBs seem to understand they are covering a smaller field and play much tighter defense. You also have to remember the Prawatt are still learning. They only have six games under their belts, and that *includes* the game we just watched."

"Chick, several teams have complained that it is unfair for Ionath to be the only franchise with Prawatt players. Is that a valid claim?"

"So far fifteen of the twenty-two Tier One teams have joined the complaint to block the Prawatt from further play. And it's not just Anna Villani and the other team owners, Masara — the Purist Nation is threatening trade boycotts unless the Creterakian government steps in and forces the Prawatt out of the league. Riots on Alimum alone have now taken the lives of an estimated two thousand sentients. All over the galaxy, sentients are objecting to the presence of the Devil's Rope."

"Uh, Chick, isn't that a racist term?"

"It's the Prawatt, Masara — it's not like anyone cares about them, am I right?"

"So true, Chick, so true. But are these complaints going to impact Commissioner Froese's decision to let the Prawatt play?"

"I doubt it, Masara. Teams can complain all they want. It's kind of like how I can keep complaining to our producers about how your body odor smells like putrid diarrhea oozing out of a rotted carp, yet they still put me in the booth with you week after week."

"Chick! How dare you compare me to fecal material! You Humans are obsessed with—"

"Sorry, Masara, sorry, folks at home, but I'm getting word from the producers that the post-game press conference is under way. Let's go to our feed live in the media room of Themala Stadium."

• • •

THE THEMALA MEDIA ROOM put Ionath Stadium's to shame. Last year the Dreadnaughts carried a late-season surge into play-offs, then rattled off three straight upsets to take the 2684 GFL title. Team owner Eric Parker had poured money back into the franchise with new uniforms, big-time roster moves and stadium upgrades. Judging from what Quentin saw, Parker had spent a lot of that upgrade money on the media room.

The facility seated sixty sentients comfortably. Ionath's seated forty, and only then if they were packed in like meatfish being shipped to market. Everything here looked new, from the walls to the tables to the crysteel security window to the ceiling-wide holo-deck that constantly flashed game highlights. The entire rear wall was a replica of the 2684 GFL championship banner — Parker made sure that during a press conference, both his players and the opposition saw that banner behind the media's eager faces.

Quentin sat at the interview table, as did Cormorant Bumberpuff. To their right was the standard podium, with Messal the Efficient standing behind it. The media had requested both Quentin and Bumberpuff at the same time. That was unusual — usually Coach Hokor was first, then Quentin, then any other players that had standout games.

This media room might be different, newer, more spacious, but the multi-headed monster sounded exactly the same. This time, however, in addition to the familiar cries of *Quentin! Quentin!* he also heard the new sound of *Bumberpuff! Bumberpuff!*

Quentin hoped this would go well. If the Prawatt were truly going to integrate into the league, they had to do the same things that were asked of the other races. That included dealing with the media.

Messal pointed to a familiar, black-skinned face.

"Jonathan Sandoval, Net Colony News Syndicate," the man said. "Mister Bumberpuff, you've really come on strong in the past few games."

There was something funny about the way Sandoval was

speaking. He seemed to be talking slow ... the way you'd talk to someone you thought was stupid.

"Five interceptions in the last three games," Sandoval said. "You've also got two sacks and are becoming known as one of the league's best hitters. How do you account for this success?"

Bumberpuff's arms waved. The media stiffened, leaned back, hissed in air — all signs of fear, as if Bumberpuff might be preparing to attack. The Prawatt sensed the tension; he lowered his arms and sat still.

Quentin tensed as he waited for his teammate to respond. The media members were here to do a job, but it was clear they feared the Prawatt almost as much as the typical galactic citizen did.

Bumberpuff waited a few more seconds, then spoke quietly.

"It has taken me and my fellow defensive backs some time to adjust to the speed of this game," he said. "The more we play, the more adept we will become at the subtleties and nuances of the passing attack. As to the reason for my success — if you wish to call giving up thousands of passing yards in those same three games *success* — all I can say is that we listen carefully to Coach Hokor, we work closely with our Sklorno teammates, and we practice hard. We will get better."

The media stared for a moment, then looked around at each other, nodding as if to say well *look at that, the monsters can talk all smart-like*. Quentin wanted to throttle them all for being surprised at Bumberpuff's intelligence, but he knew that wouldn't help anything.

Messal pointed to a small Ki that couldn't have weighed more than two hundred pounds. A Creterakian sat perched on the Ki's shoulder. It wore a yellow bodysuit decorated with images of flapping Creterakians that were also wearing yellow bodysuits. Where did that species find such horrible clothes?

The Ki barked out a guttural sentence. The Creterakian flapped its wings and flew in a small circle as it talked.

"I speak for Ron-Do-Hall, Ki Empire Sports Fest," the Creterakian said. "Quentin, the influential and always objective Ron-Do says that the Themala owner has filed a new complaint stating that adding a new species in mid-season is unfair. Considering how well Bumberpuff and Weasley played today, do you think that Parker's claim is accurate?"

Quentin started laughing. He tried to stop but couldn't. It was a good twenty seconds before he was able to talk.

"Oh ... sorry about that," Quentin said. "You guys crack me up. Really, you do. Gavin Warren threw for something like three hundred and sixty yards today?"

"Three-sixty-two," someone shouted out.

"Three-sixty-two," Quentin said, nodding. "Three hundred and sixty-two yards of passing. In *one stinking game*. He also threw for three touchdowns. Does that sound like we have an *unfair* advantage? These claims are ridiculous. Warren did whatever he wanted up and down the field, but he got picked off in the red zone. Our defense got tough when it mattered. Next question."

Quentin! Quentin!

Ron-Do suddenly reared up on his hind legs, eight feet of Ki rising into the air, waving its arms and barking out commands. He was tiny compared to the Ki on the Krakens roster but still a helluva lot bigger than the other reporters.

The Creterakian translated. "The inquisitive and ever accurate Ron-Do feels you did not answer the question. He wants to know how you respond to accusations that the Krakens are cheating this year by being the only team with Prawatt players."

"*Cheating?*" Quentin stood up. "The Prawatt Jihad has existed a lot longer than the GFL. Every franchise — Tier One all the way down to Tier Three — could have recruited the species at any point in the league's twenty-seven-year history. The fact that those teams were *afraid* to do whatever it takes to win is *their* problem, not ours."

The Creterakian flapped faster, letting him hover in place as Ron-Do barked out a follow-up question.

"The wonderful and attractive Ron-Do points out that Ionath is the only team with access to this species."

"We brought in Bumberpuff and the other Prawatt in Week Three," Quentin said. "That was *two months* ago. Since then,

I haven't heard of a single team flying into Jihad space to get their own Prawatt players. Sure, there are fears that their ships will be damaged or destroyed, that players and staff might be hurt of even killed, but you know what? Those are the same risks we faced. The difference between Ionath and the other teams is that the Krakens do whatever it takes to win." He banged his fist against his chest. "*Whatever it takes*. This press conference is over. We have to start preparing for Hittoni. You want a story? Get ready for Ionath to run the table, make the playoffs, then take the GFL title. *There's* your story. Bumberpuff, come on, we're out of here."

Transcript from the "Galaxy's Greatest Sports Show with Dan, Akbar and Tarat the Smasher"

DAN: Sports fans, welcome back to the most wonderful thing that ever existed, the Galaxy's Greatest Sports Show. I'm Dan Gianni. With me as usual are Akbar and our own resident Hall-of-Famer, Tarat the Smasher. Let's talk about Week Ten's biggest upset! Wabash is shocked — shocked, I say — by the formerly winless Shorah Warlords.

AKBAR: I can't believe the Wolfpack lost to Shorah. The 'Pack looked playoff bound while the Warlords were winless.

TARAT: The impending threat of relegation can drive a team to play above their level, Akbar. I think that is what happened in this instance.

DAN: That may be true, Tarat, but it's safe to say that Wabash also played below theirs. I mean the Wolfpack was favored by seventeen points!

TARAT: That is why they play the games, Dan.

DAN: At any rate, Wabash picked a terrible time to lose focus. With just three games left in the season, the 'Pack are now six-and-three and at risk of missing the playoffs. They are still two games ahead of Ionath, Alimum and Isis but must travel to the Black Hole to face the six-and-three Orbiting Death. The week after that, Wabash hits the Big Eye to face Ionath. If the Krakens beat Hittoni this week, then win at home against the Wolfpack, they could leapfrog Wabash into that fourth and final playoff spot.

TARAT: Ionath started the season at one-and-four. To get back into playoff contention is very impressive.

AKBAR: I don't know, guys — every year the Krakens make these late-season runs. They did it to move into Tier One in 2682, to avoid relegation in 2683 and then to make the playoffs in 2684. They've won three of their last four to regain a sliver of a speck of a fraction of a hope at reaching the playoffs, but sooner or later the Krakens' tank has to run dry.

TARAT: Akbar, I disagree with you. If a team makes the playoffs, the regular-season record does not matter. The significant factor is how the team is playing at the time they enter the playoffs. Right now, Quentin Barnes is playing MVP-caliber football.

DAN: Oh, give me a break, Smasher! Rick Renaud has the league MVP award locked up. He's on pace to break a dozen individual records. He can't be stopped.

TARAT: Dan, I admit that Renaud is the leading candidate, but there are three games still to be played in the regular season. If Barnes puts the Krakens into the playoffs despite all of his team's injuries and off-season conflicts, he has to be considered.

AKBAR: I think it's a moot point, guys. Ionath gets to host Hittoni — a winnable game — but then hosts Wabash and *then* has to end the season with a road game against the To Pirates! I just don't see Ionath winning all three of those games, which they have to do to make the playoffs. I mean, *another* dramatic, late-season run where the Krakens *have* to win all their final games? Just too much, I don't think they'll pull it off.

DAN: Your view is noted, little buddy. Let's go to the callers. Line Five from the Ki Rebel Alliance, you're on the space, *go!*

• • •

THE COMPUTER'S ANNOUNCEMENT broke his concentration.
[JOHN TWEEDY AT YOUR DOOR.]

Quentin snapped his fingers at the holodeck, pausing the playback in the middle of Hittoni linebacker Kitiara Lomax sacking Isis Ice Storm quarterback Paul Infante. Hittoni was only 2-7, but Lomax had just come back from injury. With their star middle linebacker again in the lineup, the Hullwalkers had whooped the tar out of the Ice Storm, 41-13. Records didn't matter — what mattered was how well the Hullwalkers matched up against the Krakens, and they matched up well, indeed.

Quentin wanted to spend every moment of the flight from Themala to Ionath studying for the game against Hittoni. He needed to prepare, but the work also let him forget about Becca and John. Fat chance of that now. John was probably here to celebrate, crack open a few beers and talk about his future with Becca.

Seeing Becca had made Quentin angry. Seeing John would probably do the same, but John was his friend — if the man wanted to celebrate, Quentin would help him do just that.

"Let him in."

The door hissed open. John entered, head tilted down, eyes glowering out from under his eyebrows. His hands were balled into tight fists. Even under his street clothes, Quentin could see muscles twitching.

WHY WHY WHY scrolled across his face.

The last time Quentin had seen John like this was back in Quentin's rookie season, when the Krakens were preparing to play against the OS1 Orbiting Death — Ju's team at the time.

"Uh, hey, John. What's up?"

"Hey, Q," John said. "Got a minute? We need to talk."

John looked mad. John looked *dangerous*.

"Uh, sure. Wanna sit down?"

John walked to the couch and sat. He stayed tense for a moment, then all the anger seemed to leach out of him. He *deflated* more than he leaned back. His fists finally relaxed. "Got any beer?"

"Sure," Quentin said. He walked to his small kitchenette and grabbed two mag cans of Miller Lager. He handed one to John and opened the other. The can instantly frosted up, chilling the beer inside.

John opened his, waited for the frost to form, then drank it in one pull. He compressed the can and offered Quentin the empty. "Got another?"

Quentin took the can. He walked back to the kitchenette and returned with four more Millers. John drained another one, then stared at the paused holotank.

He reached into his pants pocket. He pulled something out and tossed it onto the coffee table in front of the couch. It clattered once, spun with a flash of gold, then fell flat.

It was a Green Bay Packers championship ring.

"She said *no.*"

John's words seemed to make everything stop, seemed to make the room as still as the image paused inside the holotank. Quentin sat on the couch next to his best friend.

"John, I ... I'm sorry."

John shrugged and drained his beer. He compressed the can, set it on the carpet, then opened his third.

Quentin sipped his. He had no idea what to say.

"But, John ... she said *yes* at the game. Didn't she?"

John closed his eyes and nodded. "She said she was sorry about that. She was kinda mad I did that in front of all those people. She apologized a bunch, but the only reason she said *yes* was so I wouldn't be embarrassed."

John had always been a man that wore his emotions on his sleeve. Usually, those emotions were general intensity, a love of life or on-field anger. Now, however, the emotion was *pain*. It hurt Quentin to see his friend so upset.

And yet, Quentin felt another emotion, one that made him feel horrible about himself; was he ... *happy?* Happy that Becca had said *no?*

John looked up. "Q, what do I do?"

Quentin's eyebrows rose. "You're asking me?"

John nodded. "Yeah, sure. You and Somalia get along so good, you know? I mean, what do I do now?"

Somalia. Quentin suddenly couldn't remember the last time he'd even called her. She was busy shooting that movie. Quentin was busy trying to lead his team to the playoffs, busy trying to get a whole shucking *race* integrated into the GFL, busy doing his part to stop a galactic war. With all of those things, did he even have time for a girlfriend?

"John, I hate to break it to you, but maybe the reason Somalia and I get along so well is that we don't see each other very much. I don't know much about relationships, but it's probably a lot different when people see each other every day like you and Becca do."

John stared, then looked to the wall, to the frame that held Mitchell Fayed's jersey.

"Becca said she loves me," he said. "But she said she can't marry me because she thinks she might love someone else even more."

Quentin froze. *She might love someone else even more.*

John looked away from Fayed's jersey, turned his gaze on Quentin. There wasn't as much hurt in his eyes this time — it remained, sure, but now there was something else.

"Q, who do you think it is? Who does Becca love more?"

Quentin felt his head shaking before he knew he was doing it. "I don't know, John."

John's body tensed. His eyes narrowed, then relaxed. He sighed, the kind of sigh that makes an entire body sag. He looked at the holotank. "Hullwalkers, huh?"

Quentin nodded. "Yeah. They're a lot tougher than their record."

"They are," John said. "I watched the highlights. No sign of Lomax's knee injury. He's all the way back. He beat the living hell out of Infante. I hope you're careful on Sunday. *Really* careful. When you think about it, a mean-ass middle linebacker can be a quarterback's worst nightmare."

Quentin just stared at John. He swallowed. Was that some kind of threat? Quentin wasn't sure. It could just be John talking.

John stood and drained his beer. "Thanks for the brewskies, buddy. We're almost back to Ionath. I'm taking the first shuttle down, then hitting the clubs. You want to join me?"

Quentin's head shook all on its own again. "I can't, John. I have to spend every minute prepping."

John nodded. "Yeah, I figured. Maybe Tim Crawford will want to head out. Later, Q."

The big linebacker walked out of Quentin's quarters. The doors swished shut behind him, leaving Quentin alone with his thoughts and emotions, emotions he didn't understand. Something about the whole situation was overwhelming, stressful.

He didn't want to deal with it. Or, maybe … maybe he just *couldn't* deal with it.

He snapped his fingers at the holodeck. He watched Kitiara Lomax close in on Infante and drag the quarterback down for the sack. Watching felt better. It let the parts of his brain that *always* knew what to do take over. When he watched football, everything else faded away.

GFL WEEK TEN ROUNDUP
Courtesy of Galaxy Sports Network

Home		Away	
Isis Ice Storm	21	Alimum Armada	13
Buddha City Elite	17	**To Pirates**	24
Coranadillana Cloud Killers	17	**Yall Criminals**	28
Bartel Water Bugs	10	Hittoni Hullwalkers	7
Themala Dreadnaughts	35	**Ionath Krakens**	41
Orbiting Death	24	Neptune Scarlet Fliers	9
Shorah Warlords	24	Wabash Wolfpack	20
Bord Brigands	17	Sheb Stalkers	14
Jupiter Jacks	27	D'Kow War Dogs	10
Jang Atom Smashers	21	**Vik Vanguard**	24
New Rodina Astronauts	10	**Texas Earthlings**	31

The To Pirates (7-2) notched their fourth straight victory this week to move within one win of locking up a Planet Division playoff berth. To came out on top of Buddha City (3-6) in a back-and-forth 24-17 affair.

Wabash had been tied with To for second, but the Wolfpack's 24-20 upset loss to Shorah (1-8) drops them all the way to a third-place tie with OS1. The Orbiting Death (6-3) recorded a 24-9 victory over Neptune (5-4).

Both OS1 and Wabash will make the playoffs if they win their last two games. On the outside looking in are Alimum, Ionath and Isis, all at 4-5.

The Krakens' 41-35 win over Themala (3-6) keeps them in the playoff hunt. Ionath quarterback Quentin Barnes threw for 392 yards and four touchdowns, including two TD strikes to wide receiver Denver. Running back Ju Tweedy added another score on a highlight-reel 65-yard run en route to 126 yards on the ground.

This marked the third year in a row that Ionath has defeated the defending Galaxy Bowl champion.

In the Solar Division, Bartel (8-1) defeated Hittoni (2-7) 10-7 to move to within one win of locking up the Water Bugs' third straight playoff berth and their fourth in the last five years. The Bugs won despite being held to just 198 yards of total offense, scoring their only touchdown on a fourth-quarter fumble recovery in the end zone.

Vik (7-2) remains in second thanks to a 24-21 win over Jang (3-6). Texas (6-3) took sole possession of third place with a 31-10 win over New Rodina (1-8). The Earthlings have now won three straight.

Bord, Neptune, Jupiter and Sheb are all 5-4 and all tied for fourth in the Solar Division.

Jupiter won for the first time since Week Four by defeating D'Kow 27-10. Jacks quarterback Don Pine threw for three touchdowns and 281 yards.

Deaths

No deaths reported this week.

Offensive Player of the Week

Ionath quarterback **Quentin Barnes**, who went 26-of-32 for 392 yards and four touchdown passes in the Krakens' 41-35 win over Themala.

Defensive Player of the Week

Hittoni Hullwalkers middle linebacker **Kitiara Lomax**, who recorded 15 solo tackles and three sacks in the Hullwalkers' 24-20 upset over Wabash.

23

Week Eleven: Hittoni Hullwalkers at Ionath Krakens

PLANET DIVISION		SOLAR DIVISION	
9-0	y. Yall Criminals	8-1	Bartel Water Bugs
7-2	To Pirates	7-2	Vik Vanguard
6-3	OS1 Orbiting Death	6-3	Texas Earthlings
6-3	Wabash Wolfpack	5-4	Bord Brigands
4-5	Alimum Armada	5-4	Jupiter Jacks
4-5	Ionath Krakens	5-4	Neptune Scarlet Fliers
4-5	Isis Ice Storm	5-4	Sheb Stalkers
3-6	Buddha City Elite	3-6	D'Kow War Dogs
3-6	Themala Dreadnaughts	3-6	Jang Atom Smashers
2-7	Coranadillana Cloud Killers	1-8	New Rodina Astronauts
2-7	Hittoni Hullwalkers	1-8	Shorah Warlords

x = playoffs, y = division title, * = team has been relegated

THE COMMUNAL LOCKER ROOM BUZZED with squeaks, chirps, chest-clacks, cheers and laughter, and yet — despite the win — an air of darkness wove unseen tendrils through the celebration.

Most of the sweaty, dirty, bloody players were rightfully happy. The Krakens had just defeated Hittoni 35-28, winning for the second straight week and bringing their record to 5-5. Earlier in the day, Wabash had topped OS1. That put the Death in fourth place with a record of 6-4. The Krakens had already beaten OS1 and the Alimum Armada, which was also 5-5. That meant the playoffs were within reach — if Ionath won their final two games against Wabash and the To Pirates, *and* OS1 lost at least one of their last two, the Krakens were playoff-bound. It was a long shot, it would take more hard work than ever before (and a heaping helping of luck), but after a 1-4 start they had fought their way back to a realistic shot at post-season play.

And on top of that, Quentin and his teammates knew they were peaking at just the right time. The Prawatt players contin ued to improve. They covered one-on-one routes better, they did a great job in zone coverage, and wow, could those X-Walkers *hit*.

Quentin no longer felt the effects of the concussion he'd suffered against Coranadillana. He was in sync with all of his receivers, almost like they were parts of his body or they had all become part of a communal football brain. He'd thrown for three TDs against the Hullwalkers: one to Crazy George, one to Halawa and even one to backup receiver Mezquitic, who had come in for an injured Milford. To make it all the sweeter, he'd gone yet another game without throwing an interception.

Granted, the Hullwalkers had only two wins under their belt, but that didn't matter — the Krakens had won a game they were supposed to win.

Ionath had won four of their last five. If they did make the playoffs, they'd be as good as any team they faced ... well, maybe with the exception of Yall, who remained undefeated.

Everything was going as well as it could, but that darkness couldn't be ignored — an on-field death took the edge off any post-game excitement, even when that player had lined up for the opposition.

John Tweedy sat on a bench, head down, face-tat silent. He hadn't taken off any gear other than his helmet. He had put in a phenomenal game, the best performance of his entire career. He'd also killed the Hullwalkers' running back.

The fatality would be reviewed, of course, but there was no question that it had been a clean hit. Simorgh "the Lethal Lady" Dinatale had taken a handoff from Hullwalkers QB Jeremy Osborne. A simple run up the middle. The 'Walkers O-line had opened a nice hole. Dinatale ran through that hole, John came forward from his linebacker position to fill that hole. Dinatale had no room to cut, so she'd lowered her shoulders and tried to take on John Tweedy head to head.

In the heat of the moment, she'd made a mistake — a mistake that got her killed.

Even on the sidelines, over the buzz of 185,000 fans, Quentin had heard the gunshot-*crack* of the hit. Dinatale dropped the ball. She'd fallen face-down on to the blue Iomatt field. Mai-An-Ihkole had scooped up the fumble and even tried to run it back — a Ki carrying the ball was always an entertaining event — but Quentin hadn't seen that. He'd been staring at Dinatale. The HeavyG woman hadn't moved.

The post-game autopsy revealed a broken neck and brain damage. Final report: Simorgh Dinatale had died on impact.

Some Sklorno players were trying to get John to sing, as he often did after a win. They jumped around him, squealing and chirping. Dying didn't mean the same thing to them that it meant to the other races. Ju saw the ladies hovering around his brother. He walked over, spread his arms and gently pushed the Sklorno away, trying to give John some space.

Quentin watched John. The man barely moved. Quentin wanted to say something, but there was nothing to say. If John wanted to talk, he'd talk.

Quentin saw Becca slowly approach John. She walked up hesitantly, unsure if she should be there or not. She'd killed a player in her rookie season. Becca had taken that hard, so hard she almost quit the game forever. Quentin's words had helped her deal with that pain — maybe she wanted to do the same thing for her former fiancé.

She stopped a few feet away from John, close enough so that he had to know she was there. Becca waited, shifted from foot to foot, but John didn't look up. Finally, she sat on the bench next to him. He still didn't acknowledge her presence. She slowly reached up and put a hand on his shoulder, then leaned in and said something that Quentin couldn't hear.

John gave her a sidelong glance. He stood and walked to the Human dressing room, leaving Becca alone on the bench.

She looked like she'd been slapped. She hung her head and sat very still. Quentin wanted to go to her, but what could he say? Becca had spurned John's proposal. Now, she wanted to be there for John in a time of need, but either he wasn't ready for that or he just didn't want her help ever again.

Becca stood and walked to the HeavyG locker room.

Quentin watched the rest of his teammates for a while. The Prawatt and the Sklorno stayed away from each other; they weren't buddies, but they weren't trying to kill each other, either, and he was willing to count that as a win.

The team had really come together. Ju was the best running back in football, no question. The defense was tightening up, and as a quarterback, Quentin knew his game couldn't get much hotter. Would all of that matter if John fell apart or if Becca lost focus? What if the Prawatt and Sklorno started going at it again?

Two more wins would put them in the playoffs. Just two more wins, but Quentin knew better than to look more than one opponent ahead. And that next opponent? The Wabash Wolfpack, the team that had knocked Ionath out of last year's playoffs.

Every Kraken was already burning inside for a chance at payback — if John Tweedy needed a target for his anger, the Wolfpack would fit the bill just fine.

GFL WEEK ELEVEN ROUNDUP
Courtesy of Galaxy Sports Network

Home		Away	
Neptune Scarlet Fliers	28	**Alimum Armada**	30
Coranadillana Cloud Killers	21	Buddha City Elite	10
Ionath Krakens	35	Hittoni Hullwalkers	28
Isis Ice Storm	7	**To Pirates**	27
Themala Dreadnaughts	10	**Yall Criminals**	49
Orbiting Death	13	**Wabash Wolfpack**	21
Bartel Water Bugs	28	Bord Brigands	10
D'Kow War Dogs	3	**Jang Atom Smashers**	14
Jupiter Jacks	9	Sheb Stalkers	7
Vik Vanguard	21	New Rodina Astronauts	13
Texas Earthlings	28	Shorah Warlords	27

With just two games left in the regular season, three teams have secured playoff berths.

Both To (8-2) and Bartel (9-1) won this week to confirm their appearance in the 2685 GFL Tier One tournament. Yall (10-0) is also in the playoffs and wrapped up the Planet Division title with 49-10 drubbing of Themala (3-7). The Criminals defeated the Pirates 42-28 back in Week Two, which gives Yall the head-to-head tiebreaker should both teams finish at 10-2. Yall has sealed up home-field advantage for the first two rounds of the playoffs and, by all measurements, looks unstoppable.

Wabash (7-3) defeated OS1 (6-4) by a score of 21-13 in a critical matchup that could determine the third and fourth Planet Division playoff slots. Since Wabash now owns the head-to-head tiebreaker between the two teams, the Wolfpack needs only one more win to clinch a playoff berth. OS1, meanwhile, is facing pressure from Ionath (5-5) and Alimum (5-5).

The Krakens kept their playoff hopes alive with a 35-28 win

over Hittoni (2-8). Alimum kept pace as well, winning 30-28 in a cross-divisional match with Neptune (5-5).

The Bartel Water Bugs clinched the first Solar Division playoff spot with a 28-10 win over Bord (5-5). Also in the Solar, Vik (8-2) moved one game closer to locking up a trip to the post-season with a 21-13 victory over New Rodina (1-9).

This week, Bartel and Vik will clash on Monday Night Football. If the Water Bugs win, they clinch the division championship. A victory for the Vanguard secures them a playoff berth.

Texas (7-3) posted its fourth straight win with a 28-27 last-second defeat of Shorah (1-9). The Earthlings are in for sure if they win their last two games. Shorah led 27-7 at the break, but a second-half collapse cost them the game. Shorah remains tied for last with New Rodina, and one of those two teams will be relegated from the Solar Division at season's end.

Despite not scoring a touchdown, Jupiter (6-4) remains in fourth place thanks to a 9-7 win over Sheb (5-5).

In Planet Division relegation news, Hittoni's hopes remain alive, but barely. The Hullwalkers must win their last two games and the Dreadnaughts must lose their last two. Because Themala defeated Hittoni in Week Two, the 'Naughts have the head-to-head tie-breaker should they finish with identical records.

Deaths

Hittoni Hullwalkers running back **Simorgh Dinatale**, killed on a clean hit by Ionath Krakens linebacker John Tweedy. This was Tweedy's first fatality in Tier One play.

Offensive Player of the Week

To quarterback **Frank Zimmer**, who threw for three touchdowns and 265 yards in the Pirates' 27-7 win over Isis (4-6).

Defensive Player of the Week

Wabash cornerback **Mars**, who had two interceptions in the Wolfpack's critical 21-13 win over the OS1 Orbiting Death.

24

Week Twelve:
Wabash Wolfpack at
Ionath Krakens

PLANET DIVISION

10-0 y. Yall Criminals

8-2 x. To Pirates

7-3 Wabash Wolfpack

6-4 OS1 Orbiting Death

5-5 Alimum Armada

5-5 Ionath Krakens

4-6 Isis Ice Storm

3-7 Buddha City Elite

3-7 Coranadillana Cloud Killers

3-7 Themala Dreadnaughts

2-8 Hittoni Hullwalkers

SOLAR DIVISION

9-1 x. Bartel Water Bugs

8-2 Vik Vanguard

7-3 Texas Earthlings

6-4 Jupiter Jacks

5-5 Bord Brigands

5-5 Neptune Scarlet Fliers

5-5 Sheb Stalkers

4-6 Jang Atom Smashers

3-7 D'Kow War Dogs

1-9 New Rodina Astronauts

1-9 Shorah Warlords

x = playoffs, y = division title, * = team has been relegated

QUENTIN'S RECEIVERS seemed to *glow*. Invisible lines of moving energy connected him to his teammates, lines upon which each pass rode for a completion no matter where defenders were or how little space they allowed. His throws seemed effortless, perfect.

It wasn't as if the Wolfpack defense played poorly. They came at Quentin with overload blitzes, delayed blitzes and corner blitzes, but he saw everything — if they blitzed, that meant a Kraken was open, and Quentin did not miss. When the Wolfpack did *not* blitz, he had time to check through his teammates and thread the ball laser-tight into moving windows of opportunity.

Wabash's defensive backs weren't the league's best, but they were *far* from the worst. Veteran cornerback Mars and safety Mississauga had already faced Quentin three times — that afternoon, their experience didn't matter. The way he played they might as well have been Tier Two rookies.

What Quentin saw, Quentin took, and that day he saw *everything*.

He felt extra satisfaction from each pass he completed to a receiver covered by cornerback Gladwin or free safety Cooperstown. The Krakens had tried to pick up both players the year before, but Wabash owner Gloria Ogawa had signed them away, intentionally spending just enough money to keep those Sklorno players from wearing orange and black.

In the first half, Quentin completed passes to Denver, Milford, Halawa, Tara the Freak, Crazy George Starcher, Becca and Yassoud. In the second half, he hit his top three Sklorno receivers time and time again while also connecting with Mezquitic, Yotaro Kobayasho and even Ju Tweedy. On the day, Quentin hit 10 different Krakens for a total of 38 completions.

The offensive onslaught didn't stop even when Ju went out of the game with a broken leg late in the second quarter. Yassoud came in and posted the best game of his career, rushing for a hundred yards and a pair of touchdowns. Quentin couldn't have been happier for the man. Ju's break was clean, which meant he'd be back in the lineup in just a few days, but it was great for 'Soud to finally prove his worth as a solid backup.

As a team, the Krakens racked up 42 points. The Ionath defense took another step forward and held Wabash to just 21 — a sound whoopin' on both sides of the ball.

After the game, Quentin heard the cacophonous cheers of the Big Eye crowd as he walked out to mid-field to shake hands with the Wolfpack players. There he met his quarterbacking counterpart, Rich Bennett, who just smiled and shook his head, an expression that said *how in the hell were we supposed to beat you when you play like that?*

Quentin shook hands with everyone he could find, stopping every now and then to look up to the owner's box high above the stadium's first deck. There he saw Gredok the Splithead standing next to Wolfpack owner Gloria Ogawa. Quentin could almost feel Gredok's smug satisfaction at having beaten his biggest rival, could almost taste Ogawa's rage at having lost to hers. Ionath had won two of the last three contests against Wabash, but as far as Quentin was concerned, the Wolfpack had won the game that really mattered — last year's opening round of the playoffs.

Quentin finished his hand-shaking, then ran to the retaining wall to high-five the Krakens faithful. His teammates fell in line behind him. The fans ate it up, cheering their players and the fact that Ionath had moved to 6-5. He realized the Prawatt still weren't part of that celebration — perhaps they wanted to get back to the locker room and didn't feel comfortable getting that close to the fans. Quentin couldn't blame them for that.

Scores from some of the afternoon games had already come in — unfortunately, OS1 had won. The Orbiting Death and the Wolfpack were both 7-4, but Ionath had defeated both squads. If either of those teams lost their last game to finish 7-5, and Ionath won their final outing to end with the same record, the Krakens had the head-to-head tiebreaker and would grab the Planet Division's final playoff spot.

It all came down to Week Thirteen. Ionath had to travel to the planet To, had to beat the Pirates on the road. One more win, a loss by either Wabash or OS1, and the Krakens would ride a four-game winning streak into the playoffs.

It wasn't all good news, though — defensive tackle Mai-An-Ihkole went out in the fourth quarter with a back injury. There was no word yet as to the severity. Without him lining up against the Pirates one week from now, the Krakens' defense would suffer greatly.

At least John hadn't caused any problems. He'd been quiet and intense all week, but he'd kept his personal issues off the field.

Just one more game — if John could stay focused for just *one more game*, then the only thing on his mind, the only thing on *any* of their minds, would be the playoffs.

The playoffs, and a GFL title.

SWEATSHIRT HOODS PULLED UP over their heads, Quentin Barnes and Choto the Bright walked into the Ionath City Police station at Fifth Ring and Third Radius roads.

"John and the others chose a poor time to lose discipline," Choto said. "Gredok will not be happy."

It was halfway between midnight and dawn, a time when all Krakens should have been asleep. Instead, Quentin was here to bail out his middle linebacker.

Quentin looked around the police station. There were twenty or thirty sentients in the station's waiting room, some nursing various cuts and bruises, some cuffed to sturdy chairs and two that were passed out on the floor. One of those was lying in a puddle of its own vomit. Or maybe it was blood, Quentin wasn't sure. A glass tank held six Sklorno males — odds were they'd huffed too much concentrated nitrogen, then gone after the first female they saw. Quentin could only hope their targets had been properly dressed and covered head to toe.

"Maybe we can get this done quick," Quentin said. "Maybe Gredok doesn't have to know."

"A player was arrested," Choto said. "The only way Gredok would not know is if he was in punch-space. We may have to call Gredok, Quentin — considering the loss of Mai-An-Ihkole, if we do not get John back, there is no way we can stop the To Pirates.

Shayat the Thick can substitute for John on a few plays a game, but he is not a starter."

Quentin nodded. John was not only the captain of the defense, he was its anchor, its best player. If Shayat the Thick started at middle linebacker, Pirates' QB Frank Zimmer would tear the Warrior apart.

Mai-An-Ihkole's injury turned out to be far worse than anyone had expected. Mai-An was out for the season, meaning the Krakens had lost a starting defensive tackle. To lose a starting middle linebacker as well? The Krakens might as well not even make the trip to To.

They were so close ... just one more game ...

"We'll get John back," Quentin said. "Come on."

Quentin walked to the main desk. A Quyth Warrior sat in a chair surrounded by holoscreens.

"Excuse me, Officer?"

The cop didn't bother looking away from his screens. "What do you want, Human?"

"Uh ... " Quentin leaned in and spoke quietly, hoping the other people in the lobby didn't hear. "I'm here to get John Tweedy, Cliff Frost, Yassoud Murphy and Tim Crawford."

The cop's baseball-sized eye snapped up. "My mother-father," he said, his cornea swirling with yellow. "You are Quentin Barnes."

Quentin smiled. He wasn't comfortable with his fame, but sometimes star power had its advantages.

"That's me, Officer. I understand the boys got caught up in a little scuffle."

"*A little scuffle*," the cop echoed. "I do not think that is an accurate assessment of the situation, Elder Barnes."

Quentin held his smile despite his annoyance — why did the Quyth insist on calling him *Elder?*

The cop turned to a holoscreen. He tapped floating icons, pulling up a street-camera recording. Quentin didn't recognize the place, but it was the bottom two floors of a towering, hexagonal skyscraper: a typical Ionath City nightspot. The third story and up were the baked-red ceramic commonly found in most city buildings. The first and second floors, however, were mostly glass and garishly colored tile work. Jittering holo-art flashed in time to the music coming from inside.

On the recording, sentients walked up and down the nighttime street. It looked busy and mostly peaceful.

"I don't see anything," Quentin said. "Was John too loud or something?"

"Just watch," the cop said.

Three seconds later, the club's glass front shattered outward as a Ki body flew through it to land on the sidewalk beyond. The long, multi-legged victim rolled weakly on the ground, black blood spurting from a dozen cuts. Another body leapt out of the window: this one was Human, big, muscular and very angry.

John Tweedy.

The holo-John threw his head back and howled at the night. The club's doors slammed open. Frost and Crawford came out, dragging Quyth Warriors that were so big they had to be bouncers. More sentients rushed out of the club as the brawl spilled onto the street, making the sidewalk crowd run for cover, making grav-cabs swerve out of the way. A hulking HeavyKi scuttled out of the broken window. He was about to blindside John, but Yassoud came out the door and landed a head-snapping hit on the twelve-foot-long monster.

The cop touched the *pause* icon. Quentin stared at his four teammates, now frozen in their mini-riot.

"As you can see, Elder Barnes, there are injuries," the cop said. "There is also extensive property damage."

Quentin's heart sank. He had to do something to get those guys out of jail. "What about GFL immunity? You *can't* hold my teammates. That's the law, right?"

The cop's pedipalps twitched. "Elder Barnes, immunity means players cannot be extradited to face charges, or seized while on a league-authorized ship, or arrested while attending a league-related function, such as a game or practice. When players are caught in the act of assaulting sentients and causing property damage, however, they can be arrested. Immunity also is on hold until we know the status of one of the sentients involved in the altercation. This sentient is in the hospital. If he should die, then this becomes a murder investigation."

"*Murder?*"

"Correct. Your teammates aren't going anywhere."

"But, but, we have to leave for To in a few hours, we have the Pirates, and it was just a bar fight, and—"

"*Where are my clients?*"

The new voice cut off Quentin's words. He turned to see a rare sight walking through the precinct door — a Whitokian. On either side of her walked well-dressed toughs; the Human Bobby Brobst and that HeavyKi with two eye patches. They belonged to Gredok, which meant the Whitokian did as well.

Outside of the city's water tanks and liquid tubes, you didn't see much of that race. And as far as Quentin was concerned, that was a good thing.

The cone-shaped Whitokians were perhaps the most disgusting-looking sentients in the galaxy. The first thing you noticed about them was the *slime*; a coating of mucus covered her orange skin. He knew it was a "her" because males were smaller and had greenish skin.

Her pointy end anchored two pairs of spindly legs, a pair on the right and a pair on the left. Membranes ran between the legs of each pair. In the water, Whitokians spread the legs wide, letting the membrane between work as a powerful flipper that could drive them forward *or* backward at high speed. On land, each pair of legs pressed together and operated as a single limb, making the loose membrane between sag in fleshy, slime-covered wrinkles.

At the wider end of the cone were their heads — he *hated* to look at their heads. The mouth was a pucker of puffy flesh with three long, spidery arms on either side. Just like on the legs, sagging membrane ran between the arms — in the water, the limbs could aid in swimming or be used like a Human used his, to grab things and move them, to wield tools or weapons. Above the mouth, the Whitokian's two oblong eyes seemed disturbingly identical to those of a Human or HeavyG.

No one had ever really come up with a good nickname for the Whitokians. Some people called them "lobster-squids," but that didn't really match up. "Frog-crabs" and "slime-shrimp" were others, but none of the standard Earth-based animal comparisons did them justice.

This Whitokian wore a black bodysuit that covered everything save for her head, arms and legs. Her legs left a trail of tiny slime-drops in her wake. She walked up to the main desk, waving a holocube like it was a grenade and speaking in a voice that was simultaneously low-pitched *and* screechy.

"I have a writ of representation for Cliff Frost, John Tweedy, Yassoud Murphy and Timothy Crawford," she said. "They are to be released immediately!"

Quentin didn't know what to do, so he stepped aside. The cop's eye flooded green, and his pedipalps stopped twitching — the situation apparently wasn't funny anymore.

"Those four sentients are in custody," the Warrior said. "No one can see them except for legal representation."

The Whitokian tossed the cube down on the countertop, where it spun on one corner before rattling to a stop.

"I'm Beebee Cheebee, their lawyer," she said. "You get my clients out here, *now*, or I'll have Yolon the Self-Sacrificing down here so fast it will make your middle arms molt."

The Warrior shifted uncomfortably. Quentin couldn't blame him — Yolon was the mayor of Ionath City. Did this lawyer really know the *mayor*?

"Now means *now*," the Whitokian said. "What's the matter, Officer, don't you *like* your badge? Do you want to lose it?"

Beebee Cheebee slapped her membranous hands on the countertop, splattering more slime-drops across the lobby. Quentin felt a glob hit his left cheek. He quickly wiped it off, then took a second step back as the lawyer continued her rant.

"If *you're* not qualified, then get Potor the Accommodating out here," she said. "I'm sure he won't appreciate your blatant racism against Humans who were clearly defending themselves against violent aggression."

The Warrior reached a hand to a holopanel and furiously tapped icons. Seconds later, a Quyth Leader in a police uniform walked out of a door and into the lobby.

The Leader spoke a sentence of Quyth language to the Warrior. The Warrior answered in kind. Quentin didn't understand what they'd said, but the Leader then addressed the Whitokian lawyer.

"I am Walan the Abusive," he said.

"*The Abusive?*" said the Whitokian. "That's an unfortunate name for a police officer."

"It is from my past. Because I would certainly never be abusive to sentients in my custody. Or to lawyers that make trouble."

The Whitokian's tone grew more animated, more angry. "Where is Potor the Accommodating? He runs this precinct, and I usually deal with him."

The Quyth Leader's eye swirled with threads of black. "Potor has been removed for corruption. It seems he was taking bribes from certain gangland figures."

Short, thin spines slid out of the Whitokian's skin. As soon as they appeared, they slid back inside, hidden from view. Quentin wondered if that was some kind of uncontrollable reaction, like an angry Human unconsciously scowling and making fists.

"Well, it doesn't matter who is in charge," the Whitokian said. "I have a writ of bail payment from Judge Kalag the Fair."

Walan slowly smoothed out his uniform. He seemed to revel in taking his time, simply because it annoyed the lawyer.

"Judge Kalag," Walan said. "What a surprise that you have a writ from him." The Leader stared for a moment, his single eye narrowing. "Since you have paid the bail, your clients are free to go. All except Tim Crawford."

Beebee Cheebee's body seemed to puff up, making her spines stick all the way out. "What? What right do you have to hold Crawford?"

"He hit a cop," the Leader said. "I don't care who you know — Crawford's going to be in jail for at *least* the rest of the season."

Beebee's body depuffed, the spines again sliding from sight.

"We'll see about that, Walan. Just bring the rest of them to me immediately."

"I would suggest that you send someone in to calm down John Tweedy," Walan said. "He was the one who started the brawl. If he does anything else tonight, I will see to it personally that he is held *without bail* for at least a month. His season will be over. You may send in one sentient to speak with Tweedy before I release him."

The Whitokian turned to Quentin. "Barnes, I am told that you are friends with John?"

Quentin nodded.

"Good," the lawyer said. "Then get in there and inform him he is to be on his best behavior. Do not disappoint Gredok."

Quentin would have liked nothing more than to disappoint Gredok at every turn, but now was not the time. One more win and the Krakens were in the playoffs. John *would* behave, Quentin would make sure of it.

The Quyth Warrior cop opened the door and gestured for Quentin to step inside. "This way, Elder Barnes. I'll take you to John Tweedy's cell."

THE JAIL SMELLED of cleaning agents and body odor. Somewhere in there was a Ki that hadn't bathed in days — an unmistakable, foul odor that reminded Quentin of rotting fish and burning wood.

Quentin followed the Quyth Warrior cop down a long hall lined with clear crysteel doors. Each door led into a small, white cell. Most of the cells were full, occupied predominantly by Quyth Warriors and Humans. Quentin saw Yassoud in one cell, sleeping on a bunk.

They stopped at a door. Quentin looked in, saw John sitting on the edge of a bunk, head hung low and eyes closed. His clothes were torn and dirty. He had blood crusted above his right eye and under his nose. He hadn't even bothered to wipe himself off.

The cop opened the door part way. "Elder Barnes, as a fan I will tell you that Walan does not exaggerate. If Mister Tweedy does anything bad, he will stay in this cell until the season is over. He will also probably find out why Walan has that last name."

Quentin nodded. "Thank you for telling me that."

"You are welcome," the cop said. He reached into his pocket and handed over a message cube. "If you do not mind, I would love the autograph of Yitzhak Goldman. Could you get that for me?"

"Sure," Quentin said. He took the cube and put it in his pocket.

The cop opened the door the rest of the way, letting Quentin walk inside.

"John, you okay?"

John lifted his head and opened the eye that wasn't swollen shut. "You? How shucking perfect." He dropped his head back down.

"Gredok's lawyer got you guys out. You want to tell me what the hell you think you were doing pulling a stunt like this? If we beat the Pirates next week, we could be in the playoffs!"

John slowly stood. His good eye burned with anger … anger clearly focused on Quentin.

"More life advice from the Chosen One," John said. "I guess I better pay close attention, right?"

Chosen One? Was John still drunk? "Yeah, you *should* pay attention. They sent me back here to make sure you don't pull anything on the way out. Why did you get in a bar fight, anyway? Is this about Becca?"

John smiled an evil smile. "I got in a bar fight because I wanted to hit someone. Duh. And everyone thinks you're so damn smart. Amazing. Yeah, Q, it's about Becca. Becca and *you.*"

Quentin felt a flush of embarrassment, as if he'd been caught doing something wrong.

"John, what do you mean by *Becca and me?*"

The linebacker rubbed his hands together. He slowly cracked his knuckles, one by one, ignoring the cuts that still oozed clear fluid.

"You and Becca," John said again. "I told you why she wouldn't marry me, remember?"

Quentin's throat felt dry. "Because she loves someone else more."

John nodded. "Yeah. She loves someone else more — *you*."

Quentin took a step back. He shook his head. That wasn't possible. "John, you must have heard her wrong or something. There's nothing going on between me and Becca."

John stopped cracking his knuckles. He looked away. "She didn't *say* it. She didn't have to. Once she called off the engagement, I started watching her. I see the way she looks at you. It's the way she should be looking at *me*."

Quentin couldn't stop shaking his head. "That's impossible. She basically *hates* me. We work together on the field just fine, but off it, we don't even get along."

John closed his eyes, again went to work on his hands. The *snap-crack* of his knuckles sounded too loud in the tiny room.

"Q, know how I killed that Hittoni running back?"

"It was an accident," Quentin said quickly, automatically. "It wasn't your fault, John. That's the life we've all chosen — every player knows the risks."

John locked eyes again. "I wasn't asking for sympathy and understanding. I asked if you knew *how* I killed her. Like ... what was going through my head to make me hit someone that hard. Go ahead, Q ... ask me *how* I killed her."

Somehow, Quentin already knew the answer. He didn't want to hear it confirmed, but he couldn't stop the words from coming out. "How ... how did you kill her?"

John smiled. "I just pretended she was you."

Quentin knew the feeling of heartbreak. He'd felt it when his fake father had been revealed, when he'd had gone from finally having a family to realizing he was again all alone in the universe, that he'd *always* been alone. That had been the worst sensation he'd ever experienced — and yet somehow, this was far, *far* worse. With the fake father, Quentin had fallen for a con-job. John's friendship had *real*, it had been *pure*.

Now, it was gone.

But I didn't do anything ... I never said anything to her ...

"Your face," John said. "Every play that's all I see — your stupid, pretty-boy face. I don't care who we're playing, I see *you*, I want to hurt *you*. Now I'm hitting harder than I ever have, Q, so thanks for that."

Quentin had to do something, to *say* something. How could this be happening? "John, I ... there's nothing between me and Becca. I swear."

John hung his head and stared at the ground. "You don't even see it," he said. "That makes it even worse. You're all good-looking and stuff. You're a quarterback. You date movie stars. You're on the cover of Galaxy Sports Magazine. You stop wars, for shuck's sake."

Quentin's chest ached. His friend's pain felt like a hook dragging through his heart.

John looked up. His anger was gone. Instead, his face screamed of anguish, of loss.

"You could have had anybody," he said. "You could have any girl in the galaxy. So why did you pick *my* girl?"

"I didn't, John! I would *never* do something like that to you!"

"You didn't have to *do* anything, Quentin. You were just *you*."

John was dying inside, and even though Quentin hadn't done anything wrong, he was responsible for that pain. Quentin had never really had friends until he'd come to Ionath. He'd certainly never had a *best* friend until he'd met John. The way John looked at him now ... it made Quentin feel like the lowest sentient in the galaxy.

But even with that awful feeling, even with the knowledge that he'd probably lost John's friendship forever, Quentin still had a job to do. The Krakens franchise counted on Quentin to lead the team to a GFL title. He had a responsibility to the organization. To his teammates. To his coach. Yes, even to Gredok. Without John Tweedy, Ionath could not win a title.

"John, I ... I know this has to hurt. I am so sorry about that, but we have to put it aside for now, we have to get our minds on —"

John snarled. SHUT UP BEFORE I CAN'T STOP MYSELF flashed across his face.

Quentin took a step back. In his rookie season, he'd watched John kill a Quyth Warrior with his bare hands. That was the John Tweedy Quentin saw now.

John shook his head, hard — the words faded away, but the snarl did not. "You know something, Barnes? You didn't invent the game of football. I was a Kraken years before you were, and somehow I made it to the pros with your *leadership* to show me the way."

"No, John, I wasn't saying that at all, I —"

"*Shut up*! I *know* what we need to do. I got dumped by a girl — you think I suddenly forgot about the shucking playoffs? About the *title*? Well, I haven't. Could you at least do me the favor of not acting like I don't know what matters unless *you* tell me?"

John's anger poured off of him in waves. And John was right — he'd been an upper-tier team captain while Quentin was back in the PNFL, winning meaningless games in a backwater league.

"Okay, John," Quentin said. "Okay."

John's lip curled up a little higher, then lowered. The fight went out of his eyes; the hurt returned. He walked out of the cell.

Quentin waited a few seconds to give John his space, then followed him out. In the lobby, the Whitokian lawyer, Bobby Brobst, the HeavyKi, Cliff Frost and Yassoud were waiting. No Tim Crawford — between injuries and stupidity, the Krakens had lost both a starting defensive tackle *and* a backup at that same position.

But at least they hadn't lost their defensive captain.

Not yet.

Quentin and his teammates left the station. They had to get ready for the trip to To. They had to get ready to fight on the blood-red field of Pirates Stadium.

They *had* to win.

GFL WEEK TWELVE ROUNDUP
Courtesy of Galaxy Sports Network

Home		Away	
Alimum Armada	13	**Orbiting Death**	16
Buddha City Elite	28	Texas Earthlings	10
Coranadillana Cloud Killers	14	**Themala Dreadnaughts**	17
Yall Criminals	42	Hittoni Hullwalkers	14
Ionath Krakens	42	Wabash Wolfpack	21
Sheb Stalkers	21	Isis Ice Storm	10
To Pirates	24	D'Kow War Dogs	12
Bartel Water Bugs	12	**Vik Vanguard**	23
Shorah Warlords	0	**Bord Brigands**	32
Jang Atom Smashers	12	**Jupiter Jacks**	35
New Rodina Astronauts	17	**Neptune Scarlet Fliers**	28

Twelve weeks are in the books and one week remains, a week that will determine who fills the four remaining playoff berths.

Yall's magical season continued as the Criminals (11-0) pounded Hittoni 42-14, officially relegating the three-time league champion Hullwalkers (2-9) to Tier Two.

"We'll start over," said Hittoni owner Lily Hanisek. "We'll figure out how the wheels came off, fix the problems, and we'll be back."

To (9-2) locked up the second seed in the Planet Division with a 24-12 victory over D'Kow (3-8). Being the second seed means that the Pirates will host their first-round playoff game.

Wabash (7-4) had a chance to lock up a playoff spot but fell 42-21 to surging Ionath (6-5). Krakens quarterback Quentin Barnes tossed for 312 yards, three touchdowns and one interception while adding another TD on the ground. Running back Ju Tweedy suffered a broken leg, but backup Yassoud Murphy ran for 100 yards. Murphy had two touchdowns, one receiving and one rushing.

"The team needed me to step up, so oh, yep, I did," Murphy said. "I ain't here for the free cupcakes, if you know what I mean."

Tweedy will be back for Ionath's Week Thirteen tilt against To.

Three teams have a shot at the last two Planet Division play-off spots: Wabash, OS1 and Ionath. Wabash is automatically in if it defeats Sheb (6-5). The 'Pack can lose to the Stalkers and still make the playoffs if either OS1 or Ionath lose. The Orbiting Death is also in if it wins — a likely prospect considering they face the already relegated Hullwalkers. Ionath must beat To *and* see either Wabash or OS1 lose.

In the Solar Division, Vik (9-2) took control of first place with a 23-12 win over Bartel (9-2). Vik is guaranteed a home playoff game in round one and will have home-field advantage throughout if they win their final game against Isis (4-7). Bartel is also guaranteed at least one home playoff game.

For the final two spots in the Solar Division, five teams remain eligible. Jupiter (7-4) won its third straight game, 35-12 over the Jang Atom Smashers (4-7). Jacks quarterback Don Pine posted his best outing of the season, throwing for three touchdowns and 288 yards.

Jupiter is tied with Texas (7-4) for third place. Both teams are in if they win their Week Thirteen games: the Jacks face Bord (6-5), while the Earthlings square off against Bartel.

Bord can grab a playoff spot with a win over Jupiter and a Neptune loss. Due to head-to-head tiebreakers, the Sheb Stalkers are in if they win *and* if both Bord and Texas lose. Neptune needs to win and also see losses by Sheb and Jupiter.

The Solar Division relegation comes down to the final game between New Rodina (1-10) and Shorah (1-10). The winner remains in Tier One for the 2686 season, while the loser is relegated to Tier Two.

Deaths

No deaths reported this week.

Offensive Player of the Week

Vik running back **Doc Coleman**, who carried the ball 41 times for 186 yards in the Vanguard's 23-12 win over Bartel.

Defensive Player of the Week

To strong safety **Ciudad Juarez**, who had six solo tackles, a sack and knocked two receivers out of the game in the Pirates' 24-12 win over D'Kow.

25

Week Thirteen:
Ionath Krakens at
To Pirates

PLANET DIVISION		SOLAR DIVISION	
11-0	y. Yall Criminals	9-2	x. Vik Vanguard
9-2	x. To Pirates	9-2	x. Bartel Water Bugs
7-4	Wabash Wolfpack	7-4	Jupiter Jacks
7-4	OS1 Orbiting Death	7-4	Texas Earthlings
6-5	Ionath Krakens	6-5	Bord Brigands
5-6	Alimum Armada	6-5	Neptune Scarlet Fliers
4-7	Isis Ice Storm	6-5	Sheb Stalkers
4-7	Buddha City Elite	4-7	Jang Atom Smashers
4-7	Themala Dreadnaughts	3-8	D'Kow War Dogs
3-8	Coranadillana Cloud Killers	1-10	New Rodina Astronauts
2-9	Hittoni Hullwalkers*	1-10	Shorah Warlords

x = playoffs, y = division title, * = team has been relegated
Where possible, standings now reflected head-to-head
tiebreakers for teams with identical schedules.

QUENTIN NEVER SAW her coming, but he sure felt her when she arrived.

For the second time that game, the blitz of All-Pro safety Ciudad Juarez landed from the blindside. She hit so hard it rattled his teeth, bounced his brain around inside his skull and made his bones jam together in ways that defied nature.

Quentin slammed into the red turf, rattling his head (and his teeth) all over again. He tried to draw a breath but could not. Was he dead? Was he dying? More importantly, had he fumbled? He felt the ball pressing into his stomach, which was part of why he couldn't breathe — he'd landed on it, knocking the wind out of him.

He hadn't fumbled. And if he knew that, he wasn't dead. The *dying* part, though … of that he couldn't be sure.

Whistles blew, signifying the end of the play, then blew again — Coach Hokor had called a timeout.

Quentin's heads-up display flipped down, but only halfway: Juarez's hit seemed to have broken his helmet.

"Barnes!" said Hokor's chest. "Get your lazy ass up!"

"Coach, if I'm dead, I have to tell you that heaven is not as cool as I've heard."

"*Barnes!* You're not dead, I can see your chest moving. Get up!"

Quentin started to push himself up. Tentacles wrapped around his shoulder pads and helped lift him. He found himself staring into the four armored eyestalks of Ciudad Juarez, the second-most-lethal player in the history of the GFL.

She stood there in her iconic uniform — blood-red jersey with the white-lined black numbers, blood-red leg armor with white-lined black stripes running from her hips to her armored black shoes. She had a small Ki skull and crossbones logo above each tentacle, where her shoulders would be if she were another species and actually had shoulders.

Her blood-red helmet had a single, white-lined black stripe down the middle. She'd personalized her uniform in a rather morbid way: one eyestalk had eight lines of black tape wrapped around the blood-red armor, one line for each sentient she'd killed on the field.

"Godling," she said. "You did not die!"

"Not yet," Quentin said. "But if I don't make it out of the locker room alive, you can put another notch in your helmet."

"If you die after the game, *please* tell the football gods that I was the one who delivered you to the Gridiron of the Immortals."

Gridiron of the Immortals? Well, that was a pretty cool concept of heaven.

Was he really standing here making small talk with a player that had killed *seven* sentients?

Quentin gave her helmet a friendly slap, then forced his battered body to the sidelines where Hokor was waiting. Along the way, Quentin looked up to the scoreboard:

Fourth quarter, 0:10 to play, To 42, Ionath 40, fourth-and-15, Ionath's ball on the 50-yard line.

This was it — a trip to the playoffs hung on the next play. Quentin tried to ignore the pounding in his head. He stopped in front of Coach Hokor.

"*Barnes!* Listen carefully. We just received the score from the Wabash game. The Sheb Stalkers *shut them out*, seven to zero. That means if we win, we are in the playoffs! Now, we need fifteen yards or more on this next play or we turn the ball over on downs and miss our chance. We get the first down, call our last time out, and kick it for the win. What play do you think will work?"

The Wolfpack had lost? Quentin stared at his two coaches. No, wait, that wasn't right ... he only had *one* coach — but two of them wavered before his eyes, splitting and merging, splitting and merging.

"Coach, I think we need to kick it."

"*Kick it?* That's a sixty-seven-yard field goal attempt, Barnes! We need to go for the first down. Are you really that hurt?"

Quentin thought back to all the times he'd lied about his injuries. He wanted to do that now because he wanted the ball in his hands. He *always* wanted the ball in his hands, but this wasn't just about *him* — the entire season hung on the next play. If he saw two coaches, he'd see two receivers and two defensive backs; he couldn't trust himself to make an accurate throw.

"Coach, I think I got another concussion. I can't shucking see straight."

Hokor stared at him, the softball-sized eye suddenly flooded a deep red-violet. "Barnes, are you telling me that you *can't* play this down?"

Quentin instantly started to say he could, that he'd been wrong — but he had to think of the team first. "Kick it, Coach. It's our only chance."

Hokor looked out to the field, as if to count how long the kick would be when he already knew.

"We can put Montagne in," Hokor said.

Quentin nodded in her direction. Her right arm dangled limp. Feeling proud of her for being so tough seemed like he was betraying John, but she *was* tough, and he *was* proud.

"She dislocated her arm mid-way through the third quarter," Quentin said. "She can still block, but no way she can throw. And I don't think we can rely on Goldman for a play this big. Arioch's already hit four field goals today, including a sixty-three yarder. He's hot. Kick it."

Hokor threw his hat to the ground. "But it's a sixty-seven-yard kick! That would be a franchise-record field goal! Morningstar has never hit from that far away!"

Quentin looked down the sidelines, saw Arioch and waved him over. The tiny kicker jogged up. He seemed to be neither concerned nor in a hurry. He stopped in front of Quentin and Coach Hokor. Was Arioch chewing gum? The guy didn't look stressed — he looked *bored.*

Quentin put a hand on the kicker's shoulder pad. "You think you can hit this?"

Arioch chewed. He looked to the ball sitting on the 50, then to the goalpost, then back to Quentin. "Whatever," he said.

Coach Hokor reached down, picked up his little hat, then again threw it to the ground. "*Whatever?* A trip to the playoffs rides on this, Human! *Can you* or *can't you* kick it?"

Arioch chewed. He repeated the process: look to the 50, then to the goalpost, then to Hokor. He shrugged. "Sure, why not?"

Hokor's eye swirled a bright green. He turned and grabbed Quentin's arm. "*Barnes!* Snap out of it. You always want the ball in crunch-time. We just need one more first down, then he can hit the kick with ease. Get back in the game!"

Quentin started to shake his head, which caused the pain in his head to suddenly ratchet up a notch. Then, his stomach pinched, and he threw up so fast he couldn't even get his hand up to block it.

Quentin opened his eyes — he'd thrown up all over Coach Hokor the Hookchest.

The coach blinked his softball-sized eye. Black now swirled alongside the green. Hokor reached down, picked up his little hat, then used it to wipe vomit from his now-wet fur.

"Kick team!" he screamed. "Get on the field!"

Arioch looked at Quentin. Arioch pointed at Quentin with his index fingers, thumbs sticking straight up in the double-gun gesture. "Pow-pow, big fella." The kicker jogged onto the blood-red field, casually swinging his arms as if he were a little kid playing in the summer sun.

Pow-pow, big fella? Was it too late to run the play after all? Yes, yes it was — when you throw up on your coach, that's a hint and a half it's time to sit out a play or two.

Quentin watched the kick team line up. Every sentient in the stadium stood, over a hundred thousand of them, mostly Ki and mostly wearing the Pirates' signature color.

Blood-red fans.

A blood-red field.

And on that field the blood-red-clad To Pirates.

It didn't matter that To had already clinched a playoff berth — no one wanted to enter the playoffs following a Week Thirteen loss.

The teams lined up. The battered and bedraggled orange-clad Krakens settled in. Yitzhak — his jersey a spotless, blazing orange as usual — knelt down on one knee seven yards behind that line of scrimmage. Beyond Yitzhak, Arioch stood two yards back and two yards to the left. He leaned forward, just a bit, waiting for his moment.

Yitzhak extended a hand toward Bud-O-Shwek. Bud-O waited two seconds, then snapped it. The ball sailed back as the lines clashed. Quentin saw Ciudad Juarez sprinting in from the side for the block. Zak caught the ball and placed it as Arioch shot in and *kicked.*

BLINK —

All sound faded away. All pain was forgotten. The tumbling ball sailed high, its brown and white surface lit up by stadium lights. It seemed to scoot to the right, surely heading wide for a miss, then it slid a little left. The ball reached its apex, started to descend. It was heading for the right goalpost. Was it long enough? Would it pass inside that post or outside of it?

Closer, descending ...

Closer, again angling right ...

The ball passed inside the goalpost, just above the upright.

Just to the left of that post, a black- and white-clad Harrah ref raised two mouth-flaps straight to the sky.

BLINK —

The sound came rushing back, and with it the pain. Quentin dropped to one knee as his teammates went crazy, jumping and screaming and leaping. Several people thumped him on the shoulder pads, rattling his abused head, and then Doc Patah was there, flying in circles, screaming at everyone to *stay away.* After a few moments, Quentin felt big hands help him up. Michael Kimberlin, all smiles, guiding Quentin toward the tunnel.

Quentin looked up at the scoreboard.

Ionath 43, To 42, 0:04 to play.

As Quentin let himself be led to the tunnel, he saw the Krakens line up for the kickoff. Arioch hit it low and weak, a squib kick that made it nearly impossible for the Pirates to mount a big return.

The ball bounced twice and skittered across the blood-red field before a Pirates player picked it up at the To 35-yard line. He managed only two steps before a pinwheeling Tommyboy Snuffalupagus slid past a blocker and brought him down.

The clock had hit 0:00.

The Ionath Krakens were in the playoffs once again.

GFL WEEK THIRTEEN ROUNDUP
Courtesy of Galaxy Sports Network

Home		Away	
Alimum Armada	34	**Yall Criminals**	35
Buddha City Elite	10	**Themala Dreadnaughts**	13
Jang Atom Smashers	14	Coranadillana Cloud Killers	10
Hittoni Hullwalkers	3	**Orbiting Death**	38
To Pirates	42	**Ionath Krakens**	43
Isis Ice Storm	31	Vik Vanguard	27
Wabash Wolfpack	0	**Sheb Stalkers**	7
Texas Earthlings	35	Bartel Water Bugs	31
Bord Brigands	7	**Jupiter Jacks**	15
Neptune Scarlet Fliers	10	D'Kow War Dogs	7
Shorah Warlords	42	New Rodina Astronauts	10

Football fans, meet the 2685 playoff teams.

Ionath (7-5) completed yet another unlikely late-season run, winning six of its last eight games to snag the Planet Division's fourth seed. And the Krakens did it in their usual dramatic style with a last-second field goal that capped a 17-point fourth-quarter comeback over the To Pirates (9-3).

"We made the big dance last year, but now that's not enough," said Ionath quarterback Quentin Barnes. "We've come together as a team at the right time. We're ready for our run at the title."

In the first round of the playoffs, Ionath travels to top-seeded Yall. The Criminals (12-0) have been called "the greatest team ever assembled," but in Week Thirteen they had their hands full against Alimum (5-7). Criminals linebacker Riha the Hammer blocked a 26-yard field goal as time expired, allowing Yall to slip away from Alimum with a 35-34 win.

Despite the loss to Ionath, To remains the second seed in the Planet and will host the Orbiting Death (8-4) in the first round. OS1 had an easy 38-3 outing against relegated Hittoni (2-10).

The Solar Division solidified as both Jupiter (8-4) and Texas (8-4) won to lock up the third and fourth seeds, respectively. The Earthlings defeated Bartel (9-3) 35-31 to earn the franchise's first-ever trip to the Tier One playoffs.

"We did it," said Texas coach Kate Bailey. "Everyone doubted us, but we're not done yet. We're bringing the title back to the world that invented the game."

Texas travels to Vik for a first-round game against the number-one seeded Vanguard (9-3). Vik wrapped up the Solar's top seed despite losing 31-27 in a cross-divisional road game at Isis (5-7).

Jupiter (8-4) closed out the season with four straight victories, thanks in no small part to resurgent veteran QB Don Pine. Against Bord (6-6), Pine couldn't get his team into the end zone, but the Jacks' five field goals were enough for a 15-7 victory.

"Pretty or ugly, a win is a win is a win," Pine said after the game. "We're playing for the memory of Zia and Compton. We'll see you in the Galaxy Bowl."

In the first round, the Jacks travel to Bartel to face the second-seeded Water Bugs.

Wabash (7-5) was shut out 7-0 by the Sheb Stalkers (7-5). The Wolfpack would have made the Planet Division playoffs with a win.

"We didn't score a point," said Wabash owner Gloria Ogawa. "I am less than pleased with this turn of events."

In the loser-gets-relegated showdown between Shorah (2-10) and New Rodina (1-11), the Warlords dominated 42-10. Shorah remains in Tier One next season, while the three-time league champion Astronauts are relegated to Tier Two for the first time in franchise history.

"I can't believe how fast it all fell apart," said New Rodina owner Barbara Jungbauer. "Two years ago we played in the Galaxy Bowl, and now this. It's crushing."

Deaths

Bartel Water Bugs quarterback **Andre "Death Ray" Ridley**, killed on a clean hit by Texas' Alonzo Castro and Chok-Oh-Thilit. This is Castro's first fatality and Chok-Oh-Thilit's third.

Offensive Player of the Week

Ionath kicker **Arioch Morningstar**, who hit five field goals including a franchise-record 67-yarder to give the Krakens a 43-42 win over the To Pirates. Morningstar also hit from 63, 60, 40 and 23 yards.

Defensive Player of the Week

Yall linebacker **Riha the Hammer**, who forced two fumbles, recovered another for a touchdown and blocked the game-winning kick in the Criminals' 35-34 win over Alimum.

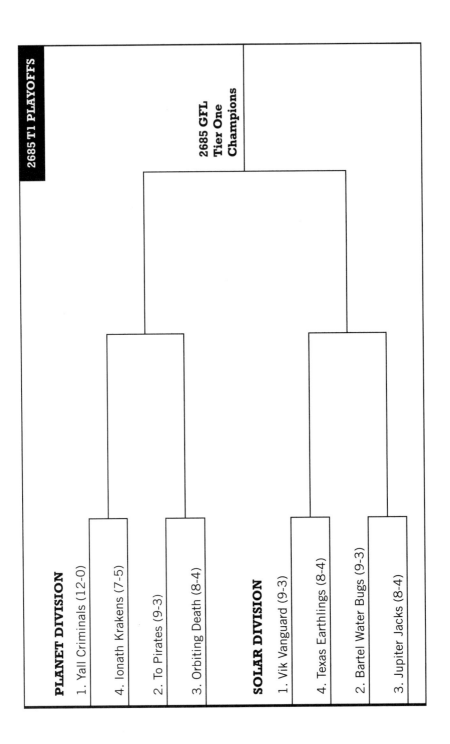

2685 T1 PLAYOFFS

PLANET DIVISION

1. Yall Criminals (12-0)

4. Ionath Krakens (7-5)

2. To Pirates (9-3)

3. Orbiting Death (8-4)

SOLAR DIVISION

1. Vik Vanguard (9-3)

4. Texas Earthlings (8-4)

2. Bartel Water Bugs (9-3)

3. Jupiter Jacks (8-4)

2685 GFL
Tier One
Champions

26

Final Regular Season Standings

PLANET DIVISION

12-0 y. Yall Criminals

9-3 x. To Pirates

8-4 x. OS1 Orbiting Death

7-5 x. Ionath Krakens

7-5 Wabash Wolfpack

5-7 Alimum Armada

5-7 Isis Ice Storm

5-7 Themala Dreadnaughts

4-8 Buddha City Elite

3-9 Coranadillana Cloud Killers

2-10 Hittoni Hullwalkers*

SOLAR DIVISION

9-3 y. Vik Vanguard

9-3 x. Bartel Water Bugs

8-4 x. Jupiter Jacks

8-4 x. Texas Earthlings

7-5 Neptune Scarlet Fliers

7-5 Sheb Stalkers

6-6 Bord Brigands

5-7 Jang Atom Smashers

3-9 D'Kow War Dogs

2-10 Shorah Warlords

1-11 New Rodina Astronauts*

x = playoffs, y = division title, * = team has been relegated

2685 ALL-PRO
FIRST-TEAM OFFENSE

Quarterback

Rick Renaud
Yall Criminals

Quentin Barnes
Ionath Krakens

Condor Adrienne
OS1 Orbiting Death

Running Back

Jack Townsend
Yall Criminals

CJ Wellman
Jupiter Jacks

Ju Tweedy
Ionath Krakens

Fullback

Mike Buckner
OS1 Orbiting Death

Tay Nguyen
Yall Criminals

Wide Receiver

Concord
Yall Criminals

Gourock
Vik Vanguard

Leavenworth
Texas Earthlings

Mosfellsbær
Bartel Water Bugs

Tight End

Andreas Kimming
Yall Criminals

Rick Warburg
Buddha City Elite

Tackle

Michael Brown
D'Kow War Dogs

Maik-De-Jog
Neptune Scarlet Fliers

Eric Woodford
Bord Brigands

Guard

David Sobkowiak
To Pirates

Aashish Passi
Vik Vanguard

Kil-Jel-Oh
Bartel Water Bugs

Center

Graham Harting,
To Pirates

Mor-En-Cee
Isis Ice Storm

2685 ALL-PRO
FIRST-TEAM DEFENSE

Defensive End
Ryan Nossek
Isis Ice Storm

Drew Davison
Jupiter Jacks

Jesper Schultz
Coranadillana Cloud Killers

Interior Lineman
Anthony Meaders
Yall Criminals

Chok-Oh-Thilit
Texas Earthlings

Mum-O-Killowe
Ionath Krakens

Outside Linebacker
Forrest Dane Cauthorn
Yall Criminals

Zeus the Ram
D'Kow War Dogs

Jan "The Destroyer" Dennison
Neptune Scarlet Fliers

Inside/Middle Linebacker
Yalla the Biter
OS1 Orbiting Death

John Tweedy
Ionath Krakens

Cornerback
Almyra
Jang Atom Smashers

Karachi
OS1 Orbiting Death

Xuchang
Jupiter Jacks

Free/Strong Safety
East Windsor
Vik Vanguard

Ciudad Juarez
To Pirates

Mississauga
Wabash Wolfpack

SPECIAL TEAMS
Punter: Nicole Gugliucci
Alimum Armada
Place Kicker: Arioch Morningstar
Ionath Krakens
Kick Returner: Chetumal
Hittoni Hullwalkers

COACH OF THE YEAR
Jako the Mug
Sheb Stalkers

LEAGUE MVP
Rick Renaud
Yall Criminals

From the *Ionath City Gazette*

GFL Names 2685 All-Pro Team

by TOYAT THE INQUISITIVE

NEW YORK, EARTH, PLANTEARY UNION — GFL Commissioner Rob Froese today announced the 2685 All-Pro selections, and the Ionath Krakens are well represented among the galaxy's best.

Ionath's reputation glittered bright this year with the gleam from five All-Pro selections: quarterback Quentin Barnes, running back Ju Tweedy, linebacker John Tweedy, kicker Arioch Morningstar and defensive tackle Mum-O-Killowe. This was Mum-O-Killowe's second-straight All-Pro selection.

Yall quarterback Rick Renaud was named the league MVP. Renaud led the Criminals to an undefeated, 12-0 regular season. He set a league record with 39 touchdown passes yet threw only eight interceptions on the year. His mark of 3,841 yards, or 320.1 yards per game, is third-highest all-time single season total.

The Criminals led the league with seven All-Pro selections. Defensive lineman Anthony Meaders and outside linebacker Forrest Dane Cauthorn joined Yall's five offensive selections: Renaud, running back Jack Townsend, fullback Tay Nguyen, wide receiver Concord and tight end Andreas Kimming.

IT FELT AMAZING to be named All-Pro. He was one of the best in the league, recognized by fans, the media and his peers. As good as that felt, as much as it meant, two things hadn't changed. First, the award did nothing to dull his all-consuming desire for the GFL championship, and second, it didn't do a damn thing to stop his motion sickness.

Quentin pulled the bag out of his golden puke bucket, tied it and set it down. These were automatic motions, something his hands did because his brain was occupied with the view outside the crysteel window.

The planet Yall, the endless city of Virilliville.

Home of the Yall Criminals.

The Yall Criminals, *the best team ever assembled.*

On either side of him, his Sklorno teammates packed in at the windows. They jumped up and down, squealed and whistled; their dangling raspers flung spit onto the crysteel.

He stood at the center window, Michael Kimberlin on his right, Mum-O-Killowe on his left, Cormorant Bumberpuff behind him. Quentin wished John was there, but John did everything he could to avoid Quentin. Ju was probably with John. No Rebecca, either — outside of practice, Quentin hadn't seen much of that girl.

Having a Prawatt in the same room with the Sklorno created a sense of tension. They were getting along in practice and in the locker room, mostly by just avoiding each other. Denver, Milford and the others clearly didn't want Bumberpuff on the viewing deck, but he had a right to be there as did every member of the team. The Sklorno tolerated him — Quentin felt that was good enough for now.

Out in space, Yall waited. Civilization blackened the surface, buildings packed in so dense it was hard to see any of that world's natural burnished-blue color. If Virilliville had borders, those borders merged with some other infinite sprawl, making the planet one big, endless city.

Mum-O moved a few steps forward. He pressed his four hands against the crysteel. His five eyes narrowed.

"Fillak ohnol retol," he said quietly. "Retol."

Kimberlin leaned toward Quentin. "Mum-O feels that —"

"I know what he feels," Quentin said. He understood more and more of the Ki language, but Mum-O's tone communicated everything. No words were needed.

This six-hundred-pound creature had once been Quentin's enemy. Now he was a fellow All-Pro, a teammate, a partner in the quest for immortality. Quentin put a hand on the Ki's upper shoulder, felt the warm skin and the cool enamel dots embedded there.

"You're right, my friend," Quentin said. "We *are* going to shock the galaxy."

Bumberpuff leaned closer to the window. "Half a trillion sentients will watch this game," he said. "They all think we'll lose. Shock them? Hell, yes, we will shock them."

[FIRST SHUTTLE FLIGHT PASSENGERS TO THE LANDING BAY.]

Quentin, Michael, Bumberpuff and Mum-O turned and walked out of the viewing bay. Denver, Milford and Halawa followed, their demeanor more solemn than the second-string Sklorno they left behind.

Intensity. Desire. *Hunger.* All of them wanted this game, wanted it more than anything they'd felt in their entire lives. The road to the Galaxy Bowl started in Virilliville.

And to travel that road, all the Krakens had to do was beat the best team in history.

QUENTIN STOOD IN FRONT of the holoboard in the central visitor's locker room of Tomb of the Virilli Stadium. His teammates wore their away jerseys, blazing orange with white-trimmed black letters and numbers. Black upper-arm padding led to orange-enameled bracers and black gloves with built-in orange-enameled armor for the backs of fingers and hands. Their legs were clad in black thigh armor, blazing-orange-enameled lower-leg armor and finally the black and orange armored boots.

Quentin reached up with his right hand, pinched his jersey between his forefinger and thumb. He lifted it slightly, showing it to his teammates.

"We're wearing visitor's colors," he said. "That's because this is the Criminals' home stadium. At least, that's what they think it is. But tonight, this field and this stadium will belong to *us*."

Human and HeavyG heads started to nod, just a little. The Ki let out small grunts. The Sklorno chirped. The Prawatt vibrated. The Quyth Warriors stared and blinked.

"This is the *playoffs*," Quentin said. "We've been here before. Last year, we learned a hard lesson. The Wolfpack taught us that the regular season doesn't matter. All that matters is what you do in the next sixty minutes."

Heads nodded more vigorously. The chirps and the grunts grew louder.

Quentin took his time. He met the eyes of every player on his team. He fed them his energy, his conviction, his indomitable will. They absorbed this invisible message, soaked it in and stored it for the battle to come.

"They say the Criminals are the greatest team ever assembled," he said. "Jack Townsend, All-Pro running back, he's going to stomp all over us, right?"

Heads stopped nodding and started shaking.

Quentin smiled wide. "Oh, come *on*, team. You've all heard the media, right? You've heard how our secondary can't stop All-Pro receiver Concord, right?"

Defensive backs — both Sklorno and Prawatt — shifted in place. They vibrated, metallic skin rattling and eyestalks quivering.

Quentin held up his hands in a gesture of helplessness. "We might as well not even go out there, right? We are *fourteen-point* underdogs. I mean, they have league MVP Rick Renaud, don't they?"

A wave of anger flared through the team. Mum-O barked out words that spoke of anger and agitation; he was sick to death of hearing about Rick Renaud, *everyone* was. Eyes narrowed. Fists clenched. Quentin wasn't that angry he hadn't won the MVP, but his teammates were still furious. The way they could vent their frustration was by stopping Renaud.

Quentin lifted both hands, signaling for silence. The team's murmur died down.

"We've already been written off," he said. "They call us *lucky* to be here. Outside of this room, no one thinks you can win. We're going to prove those people wrong. Today? This field ... is *ours*. This stadium? It belongs to *us*. Close your eyes." He watched as all of his teammates, a mean and nasty band of brothers and sisters armored up in orange and black, closed their eyes.

"Take a moment and think of what you will do to help us win," he said. "Find that place, that *primitive* place, where this isn't a game anymore, where every down is a fight for your life.

"Today, it's us, or it's them. Today, we fight for each other, and we will crush those that stand before us. When I tell you to open your eyes, open them and see through the eyes of the monsters that you are."

Quentin closed his eyes and bowed his head.

It was almost time.

QUENTIN BENT BEHIND center for his first snap of the playoffs. The uniforms of both teams were spotless. The orange jerseys of his teammates blazed so brightly they almost hurt the eyes, while their orange and black leg armor gleamed under the stadium lights.

The white field seemed to glow, ever so slightly, a swath of illumination against the nighttime sky above. Dark-green lines and numbers still had crisp, defined edges. Those edges would soon blur as the game wore on.

"Red, nineteen!"

The white of the field seemed to bleed past the sidelines and crawl up into the stands. At least 80 percent of the 165,000 in attendance wore white, and most of those were bouncing Sklorno females. The stands seemed to move like rippling water, the shouts and the screams made the air boil with excitement.

Playoff football. There was nothing like it.

Quentin looked across at the defense, at their white helmets with the purple "ball-and-chain Sklorno" logo. Deep-purple jerseys looked almost black under the lights, made the white numbers on their stomachs and the letters that spelled CRIMINALS across their chests seem to blaze brighter. White arm armor and purple gloves complemented purple leg armor lined with three vertical, white stripes across the thighs and the shins.

First-and-10 on the Ionath 22-yard line.

So it began.

"Hut-*hut!*"

IONATH'S FIRST TWO DRIVES produced 44 yards but no points. Fortunately, the defense held Yall to much the same result.

Rick Renaud, league MVP, master of the long ball, was having trouble with the Prawatt defensive backs. Renaud had studied and scouted his new foes, that much was clear, but the Prawatt movements made him hold onto the ball for just a little bit too long. Just two drives into the game, and Mum-O already had two sacks.

Quentin tried not to get excited. Renaud was a patient man. He was taking his time, trying to figure things out. He was far more willing to take a sack than to force a pass and have it intercepted. Sooner or later, Quentin knew Renaud would find a weakness and exploit it.

Unfortunately, that weakness came *sooner*. On the Criminals' third drive, Renaud started calling screen passes. He drew in the attacking Krakens' defensive line, then passed to running backs who followed walls of offensive linemen. The Prawatt had trouble finding a way around those blockers. Yall ran three screen passes on the drive, the final one going to Tay "the Weazel" Nguyen, who used his blockers to scamper for a 32-yard touchdown.

First score of the game had the Criminals up 7-0.

THE CRIMINALS' DEFENSE had decided to defend the pass first, daring Ionath to run the ball. Coach Hokor took that dare.

In the second quarter, Ju Tweedy started to find his rhythm. The Krakens' interior offensive line of left guard Sho-Do-Thikit, center Bud-O-Shwek and right guard Michael Kimberlin proved to be more than a match for Yall defensive tackles Anthony Meaders and Kin-Ah-Thak. Hokor called runs up the middle, one after another. Ju would take the handoff and slam forward for four, five, six yards or more. He didn't have any breakaway runs, but the Krakens controlled the ball and kept Rick Renaud and company off the field.

Quentin didn't care how his team moved the ball, as long as that ball moved. He threw only three times in the entire second quarter. The constant pounding paid off — with 4:56 to go in the half, Ju finally broke a pair of tackles and rumbled his way upfield for a 17-yard TD.

Tie game, Yall 7, Ionath 7.

MUM-O-KILLOWE SEEMED TO HAVE taken Quentin's pregame speech to heart, because *monster* was the only word that could describe the young Ki lineman's performance. After Ju's touchdown, Mum-O landed another sack of Renaud — his third of the half — that killed a Criminals drive and forced them to settle for a field goal.

Mum-O's performance left the Criminals no choice but to double-team him — if he couldn't be stopped by one player, they'd shut him down with two. The constant double-teams ensured that Chat-E-Riret, playing for the injured Mai-An-Ihkole, was almost always blocked one on one. The backup played well and even managed his first sack of the season. The strong play of Mum-O and Chat-E demanded all the attention of the Criminals' defensive line, which gave room for the Krakens' linebackers to wreak havoc on inside blitzes.

On a third-and-eight, Renaud dropped back to pass. Mum-O drove in hard, drawing the double team. Virak the Mean waited a second and a half before tucking and rolling in fast on a delayed blitz. Renaud started to throw, then paused; something about the

Krakens' coverage made him hesitate for a split second. He felt the pressure and tried to scramble, but it was too late: Virak came out of the roll and hit the purple-clad Yall quarterback from behind, forcing a fumble. The ball bounced and flopped, seemed to intentionally evade several purple-jerseyed players that reached for it. A flash of a tumbling orange and black uniform cut toward the ball — the pigskin bounced high, then Choto the Bright popped out of his roll and hauled it in.

If a Warrior rolls while holding the ball, his knees and elbows touch the turf and refs will blow their whistles, calling that Warrior *down*. So Choto ran, his thick legs pumping his big body toward the end zone.

Yall's Sklorno receivers gave chase. Bumberpuff and Weasley threw key blocks that stopped them from bringing Choto down. Concord finally caught up with him. She wrapped her tentacles around him, tried to drag him down and strip the ball, but Choto kept on stumbling. When he finally fell, his body hit the purple paint of the end zone.

Quentin didn't cheer, he didn't scream, he just nodded. That was the break Ionath needed, but the game was far from over. Arioch Morningstar kicked in the extra point. With less than a minute remaining in the first half, the Krakens were ahead 14-10.

THE HALFTIME LOCKER ROOM seemed to pulse with electricity. Two quarters down, two to go, and Ionath was *ahead* by four. Coach Hokor stood at the holoboard, drawing up ways for the Krakens offense to improve in the second half. The game was supposed to be an offensive shootout, but both defenses had stepped up strong.

The players sat around the board, close together, taking bottles of water from Messal the Efficient. Doc Patah fluttered from player to player, patching up cuts and applying nanomeds to major contusions. The Krakens had been lucky so far — not a single player had come out of the game due to injury.

John Tweedy stood on the other side of the central locker room, surrounded by his defensive teammates. They talked excitedly, exchanging ideas and information, trying to guess what Renaud and the Criminals would do differently in the second half. Ionath's defense found itself in an unexpected position: what adjustments do you make when you've held the league's best offense to just 10 points?

Quentin listened to Hokor. In the second half, the coach wanted to use more play-action fakes to Ju to draw the linebackers in, giving Quentin more room to complete short passes and crossing patterns.

Denver sat up close to the holoboard, following Hokor's every word. The Criminals had covered her well all evening, but Quentin knew that sooner or later, she would get a step on her defenders. When she did, he was going to put the ball on the money.

Ionath had the lead. The Krakens were just one half away from victory.

IN THE SECOND HALF, the Criminals came out throwing. Renaud stopped dropping back deep. Instead, he used shallow, three-step drops to throw quick-hitting passes. Quentin watched in amazement as the league MVP put on a display of power and accuracy. The short slant, out and hook routes only gained four or five yards at a time, but they kept the chains moving. The Krakens' DBs were forced to come up and play tighter — the Criminals seemed to be one missed tackle away from a big play.

That missed tackle came at 8:53 of the third quarter. Renaud took the snap, turned and gunned the ball to the left, to Concord, who drove in on a 45-degree angle slant route. Renaud hit Concord in stride, delivering the ball just beyond the pedipalp fingers of Choto the Bright. Bumberpuff dove for her and wrapped her up, but Concord's big legs kept pumping. Bumberpuff seemed to slide off, then fell to the white field.

The purple- and white-clad receiver took off, hitting top speed almost instantly. Free safety Katzenbaum Weasley gave chase, but it was already too late — against an All-Pro like Concord, any missed tackle could turn into points.

Extra point good: Yall 17, Ionath 14.

QUENTIN COUNTERED AT THE END of the third quarter. Ionath ran play-action to Ju, faking the handoff, then Quentin dropped back. He was supposed to throw over the middle to Starcher, but he first looked for Denver, who was running straight downfield.

She had a step on her defender. One step was all she needed.

Quentin threw to the back corner of the end zone, counting on his friend to pull away from her defender and run under the ball. Denver did just that — she was three steps clear when the ball fell feather-light into her outstretched tentacles.

The crowd roared a combination of anger and approval. Quentin bent, plucked a few blades of white grass off the field and sniffed them deep. Yall's field smelled like chocolate.

Extra point, good: Quentin and Denver had put their team ahead 21-17.

NOT EVEN A DOUBLE TEAM could stop the magnificent Mum-O-Killowe. In the fourth quarter, Renaud dropped back for another quick pass. Mum-O split his double team and raised his four arms high. Renaud had to move fast to avoid the sack. He scooted left, but Mum-O reached out a right arm and grabbed the quarter-back's purple jersey. Renaud tried to get rid of the ball — he made a hurried throw to tight end Andreas Kimming.

The pass was a little slow, a little bit behind, and Kimming had to reach back for it. He caught it, but when he turned to face forward, John Tweedy landed a hit that knocked the tight end off his feet and sent the ball flying — it bounced once, then tumbled right into the arms of Virak the Mean. Criminals players brought him down immediately. The Harrah zebes flew in and signaled Krakens' ball.

Five minutes and forty-eight seconds to play in the game, the ball on their own 25, a four-point lead. Quentin ran onto the field with his offense, knowing that the upset was now theirs to lose.

THIRD DOWN AND SEVEN, on the Yall 27, 1:31 to play. The Criminals only had one timeout left. A first down here sealed the victory.

Quentin took the snap and pivoted on his left heel, turning all the way around and pitching the ball to Ju Tweedy. Ju caught it and ran left, parallel to the line of scrimmage. Becca was out in front of him. So was Michael Kimberlin, who had pulled from his right guard position.

Becca and Mike were a funny-looking combination. Mike's big, athletic body lumbered along — Becca was a foot and a half shorter than him and didn't quite come up to his sternum. Funny looking, maybe, but both were among the best in the galaxy at what they did.

The purple-clad defenders slammed forward, desperate to make the stop. Forrest Dane Cauthorn angled in. Becca tried to take out his legs, but the agile linebacker leapt over her and grabbed a handful of Ju's jersey. The extra weight slowed Ju just enough for Riha the Hammer to come in and make the stop at the 20-yard line, one yard short of the first down.

The Criminals used their last timeout — 1:25 to play.

Quentin slapped his helmet in frustration. One more yard would have won the game!

Arioch Morningstar and Yitzhak Goldman calmly ran onto the field with the kick team. Arioch nailed the 37-yard field goal to put Ionath up 24-17.

Now, it was all up to the defense.

RICK RENAUD HADN'T WON the league MVP on a fluke. Quentin stood on the sidelines. He could do nothing but watch the battered, bleeding Criminals' quarterback complete a pass for 15 yards, then one for 8 that took his receiver out of bounds, then another for 11. Renaud had been sacked four times, knocked down at least a dozen more, had fumbled once and had thrown an interception. He'd taken everything the Krakens had dished out, and yet here he was, guiding his team downfield.

First-and-10 on the Ionath 45, just 48 seconds to play. No time-outs. Renaud dropped back. Mum-O rushed in, as did Michnik and Khomeni. The pocket collapsed. Renaud stepped forward, tucked the ball and ran. John Tweedy came up for the stop, but Renaud threw a stiff-arm that caught John off-guard. John's head rocked back and he fell hard to the turf. The crowd roared loud enough to set the air ablaze. Renaud ran straight upfield. Wahiawa came up hard and Renaud slid to the ground, avoiding the hit.

The 17-yard scramble took the Criminals to the Ionath 28. Renaud rushed his team to the line. He spiked the ball to stop the clock with 35 seconds left to play.

Quentin felt helpless. It was completely out of his hands.

Renaud broke the huddle and brought his team to the line. He barked out the snap-count. The insane crowd pleaded for their team to get a touchdown and tie up the game.

Renaud took the snap and dropped back. Mum-O roared in yet again, forcing the quarterback to scramble left immediately. Aleksandar Michnik tossed his blocker aside and came in hard. Renaud had nowhere to run. He stopped, planted, stepped up and threw for the end zone just before Michnik leveled him.

BLINK —

The ball hung in the air for an eternity, a pointy planet completing a long orbit around an unseen sun. Reality faded to just three things: the spinning brown ball with the white laces; Concord in her torn purple jersey and scratched white helmet; and Cormorant Bumberpuff, his tattered streamers of orange and black trailing behind him. The former starship captain ran stride for stride with the best receiver in football.

Against the backdrop of blazing stadium lights and a black night sky, Quentin watched the ball descend toward the end zone.

Concord leapt. Bumberpuff leapt with her. They soared high, a slow-motion dance of impossible grace and athleticism. Concord's tentacles reached just a touch higher than Bumberpuff's long-fingered hands. She grabbed the ball, holding it firm as both players started to fall into the end zone.

Bumberpuff turned in mid-air. One arm pulled at the ball while the other smashed into Concord's white helmet. A black- and white-clad zebe flew in, with them every inch of the way.

Concord landed hard on her back and she lost her grip on the ball. She slid across the end zone's purple turf, trying to regain her grip — she secured the ball tight just as she slid out of the back of the end zone.

BLINK —

The crowd detonated. The stadium rocked from the noise of thousands of squealing Sklorno females. Quentin's head dropped. He put his hands on his knees. With the extra point, the game would be tied and they'd go into overtime.

"Dammit," he said. "We *had* them."

Then, a pair of hands grabbed at his jersey. It was Yitzhak, yanking him back upright.

"Q! The ref is signaling out of bounds!"

Quentin's head snapped up. Sure enough the zebe was floating above the end zone, both mouth-flaps waving horizontally in the signal for *incomplete catch*.

The crowd booed, then fell silent as all the zebes converged on that corner of the end zone. Players backed away. Hologram projectors beamed a photo-realistic projection of the play down onto the field. In slow motion — *real* slow motion this time, not Quentin's weird sense of time — an entire stadium watched the same play happen all over again.

Quentin watched the replay on the main holoboard above the end zone stands. He watched Bumberpuff and Concord fall, watched the ball bounce out of her tentacles when she landed hard on her back, watched her slide, then watched her tentacles reach up and grab the ball — the replay froze at that exact moment.

Her shoulder was on the ground past the end zone's back line.

She'd been out of bounds when she gained full control of the ball.

The zebes confirmed the signal: *incomplete pass*.

Only 23 seconds remained. The Criminals' offense tiredly ran back to their huddle, but the quarterback wasn't the dirty, bloody warrior Rick Renaud — it was backup Maurice Whitmore.

"Where's Renaud?"

"I think Michnik broke his arm," Yitzhak said. "I don't believe it, we're going to win this thing!"

Quentin almost couldn't let himself believe that was true.

On third-and-10, Whitmore threw an incompletion. Quentin couldn't even breathe as the backup QB called the signals for fourth-and-10 — Yall's last chance to tie the game. Whitmore took the snap and dropped back. He started to throw, then stopped — Concord was pulling past Bumberpuff and heading for the end zone.

Whitmore stepped up to throw, but before he could, Mum-O-Killowe recorded his fifth sack of the game.

The zebes blew the play dead. Ball turned over on downs.

Quentin screamed and ran onto the field. It was over.

Best team ever assembled, maybe, but on this night, the Yall Criminals were *second* best.

From *LeeKee Galaxy Times*

Krakens Shock League, End Yall's Perfect Season

by KELP BRINGER

VIRILLIVILLE, YALL, SKLORNO DYNASTY — This year's Yall Criminals squad was repeatedly called "the greatest team ever assembled," but now that name will be nothing but a footnote in GFL history. The league's best group of talent lost to a rag-tag collection of outcasts, mutants, psych cases, walking wounded and little-known aliens as the Ionath Krakens upset the Criminals 24-17.

The much-maligned Ionath defense held the league's best offense to a season-low in both yardage and completions. League MVP Rick Renaud was never able to find a rhythm. Ionath coach Hokor the Hookchest harried Renaud with blitzes, but it was the constant pressure and five sacks by fourth-year defensive tackle Mum-O-Killowe that made the difference.

> *"Mum-O came into his own tonight. He put on one of the greatest playoff performances I have ever seen."*
>
> HOKOR
> THE HOOKCHEST

"Mum-O came into his own tonight," Hokor said. "He put on one of the greatest playoff performances I have ever seen."

In the semi-finals, Ionath travels to OS1 for a tilt in the Black Hole against arch-rival Orbiting Death, who dominated the To Pirates

20-10. OS1's defense held To to just 224 yards of total offense. On a tragic note, legendary quarterback Frank Zimmer died mid-way through the third quarter on a clean hit by Death linebacker Yalla the Biter. This is Yalla's third fatality of the season — a single-season league record — and his 13th overall.

In the Solar Division, Vik destroyed visiting Texas 42-0 in the biggest blowout in GFL playoff history.

In the Solar Division, Vik destroyed visiting Texas 42-0 in the biggest blowout in GFL playoff history. The game was held at Kin-Shal-An Trade Guild Stadium. The Earthlings lost several players in a pregame locker room accident when a gas vent backed up. Fourteen players were rushed to medical facilities, but as of yet no deaths have been reported. GFL Commissioner Rob Froese is investigating the incident as a possible assault by the Vik franchise.

Jupiter defeated Bartel 24-17 to move into the semi-finals against Vik. Jacks quarterback Don Pine played a ball-control offense, throwing only 18 passes on the day but completing 17 of them. The Jacks had no turnovers, while Bartel gave up two interceptions and a fumble.

Because of the gas incident on Vik, Froese has declared Kin-Shal-An Trade Guild Stadium unsafe. That means Jupiter will host the semi-final game against Vik, despite the fact that the Vanguard are the top seed and the Jacks are seeded third.

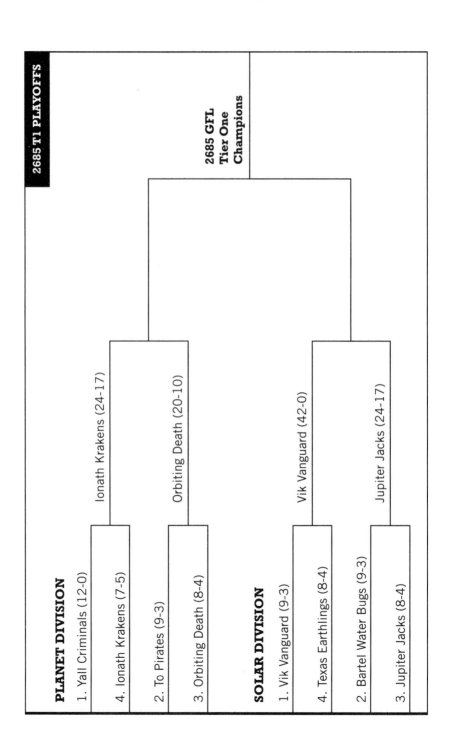

2685 T1 PLAYOFFS

2685 GFL
Tier One
Champions

PLANET DIVISION

1. Yall Criminals (12-0)

4. Ionath Krakens (7-5)

Ionath Krakens (24-17)

2. To Pirates (9-3)

3. Orbiting Death (8-4)

Orbiting Death (20-10)

SOLAR DIVISION

1. Vik Vanguard (9-3)

4. Texas Earthlings (8-4)

Vik Vanguard (42-0)

2. Bartel Water Bugs (9-3)

3. Jupiter Jacks (8-4)

Jupiter Jacks (24-17)

THE ENTIRE KRAKENS TEAM sat at tables in The Dead Fly bar, waiting for dinner to be served. Madderch City on Orbital Station One was home to the Orbiting Death, but also the home town of one Choto the Bright.

Choto's family owned The Dead Fly. Choto had asked Gredok's permission for the team to eat dinner there the night before the semi-final game against OS1. Gredok said yes, then agreed to an interview on the Galaxy's Greatest Sports Show. During that interview, Gredok said that his Krakens wanted to enjoy their time on OS1's largest city — if anything happened to them on the day before the semi-final, it was proof that Commissioner Froese couldn't protect the league's players.

Froese had probably been infuriated to be called out like that, but he couldn't let a public challenge go unanswered, especially not after what had happened to Texas before the Vik Vanguard playoff game.

White-uniformed security lined The Dead Fly's walls. Ki, Human and Quyth Warrior guards tried to stay out of everyone's way, but they were clearly ready if any trouble occurred. Sklorno in white power armor guarded the doors outside and patrolled the surrounding streets. White-uniformed Harrah soared over the blue-crystal city. Somewhere around two hundred white-uniformed Creterakians perched on the rooftops of buildings surrounding The Dead Fly, just waiting for someone to cause trouble.

Without spending any of his own money, Gredok had provided his team absolute safety. Not even Anna Villani would dare attack the Krakens. Quentin had to admire Gredok's manipulative skills.

Even though they were in Madderch, Villani's stronghold, Quentin actually felt safe. Tomorrow, he and his teammates would take on Condor Adrienne and the Orbiting Death for the second time that season. The victor went to the Galaxy Bowl. One more win, and Quentin would play for the league title.

He sat at a table with Choto, Yassoud, Michael Kimberlin and — of all people — Arioch Morningstar, the kicker. They drank non-intoxicating beverages (something Yassoud complained about loudly and often) and waited for the food.

For all the pressure they were under, the team seemed relaxed. This would be the third time in four seasons the Krakens had played at the Black Hole. Most of the players had plenty of experience with that stadium, the black field and the die-hard Death fans.

Plus, the Krakens had beaten OS1 back in Week Five, when Bumberpuff had been a brand-new starter and Weasley had barely played at all. Since then, both of them had become solid defensive backs — Condor was going to have his work cut out for him.

The odor coming from the kitchen made Quentin's stomach rumble. He couldn't quite place it, but it smelled so familiar.

"Choto, when do we eat? I'm starving."

Choto stood. "I have prepared something special for the team. My family paid to have this event catered by two chefs that we know we can trust."

Quentin sniffed: he smelled the heavy spice of Tower-style food and also something that smelled like … like *home*?

"Choto, did you find a Purist Nation cook?"

"I did, Quentin. And I believe you will enjoy the food very much. I also have Doc Patah in the kitchen, just to make sure the dishes will not upset any of our digestive systems."

Quentin raised his eyebrows in admiration. That was a smart thing to do. The last thing anyone wanted was to spend the morning of a playoff game in the bathroom, throwing up.

The kitchen doors opened. A white-skinned Harrah flew out. He wore a red backpack with gold characters painted on it. Quentin laughed and started clapping. The Tweedy brothers got out of their seats and ran over.

"Chucky Chong!" Ju said. "It's great to see you!"

"It's *mega*-great to see you!" John said.

"Herro," Chucky said. "I hope you boys are ready to road up on my rovery Reague-style chow."

The kitchen doors opened again. Quyth Worker waiters came out carrying large trays loaded with plate after plate of chow mein, sauces, bread and other items. The waiters started placing plates in front of the players. They didn't put anything down in front of Quentin.

"Hey, Choto, what's the deal? You're not going to feed your quarterback?"

Choto's eye swirled with light orange, a color of happiness. "Chucky Chong is cooking for everyone. The other chef is cooking just for you, although I imagine Jason Procknow will also appreciate his food."

The kitchen doors opened again, filling the bar with that other smell. Even before Quentin saw the man carrying a platter piled high with barbecued chicken, the scent finally registered — the odor seemed to take Quentin back in time, a decade earlier when he had been an orphan on Micovi, when he had been forced to steal food or starve to death.

The man looked the same. More gray at the temples, maybe, and the gut was a little bigger, but there was no mistaking Mister Sam, the cook who had taken Quentin in and given him a better life.

Quentin felt a knot in his throat. "Choto," he said, "how did you ... how could you know ... "

"I talked to Frederico," Choto said. "He met Mister Sam on a recent trip to the Purist Nation and said you would appreciate a meal prepared by your favorite cook."

Mister Sam smiled and walked over. He set the entire platter down in front of Quentin. Steam rose up from chicken that was slathered in reddish-orange sauce and lined with black, parallel grill marks.

The man stood straight and smiled.

"Quentin Barnes," he said. "Stand up and let me look at you."

Quentin stood. Mister Sam wasn't even six feet tall. Quentin towered over him, outweighed him by at least two hundred pounds, but for a moment Quentin felt like an awkward kid all over again.

"Mister Sam. I don't believe it."

Sam smiled and nodded. "Believe it. Look at you! I see you continue to eat enough for a small city, but you tell me —" his smile faded and his face grew dead-serious. "— have you found *any* barbecue as good as mine?"

Quentin smiled and shook his head. "I haven't. I can come pretty close on my own, but you are still the master."

Sam smiled wide and pointed to Quentin's chair. "Sit! *Eat!* I have been hired to cook for you, not to chitchat. I can now go home and tell everyone that people fly Mister Sam all across the galaxy for his chicken! The other cooks on Micovi will be so jealous! We can talk some after your game tomorrow. For now, eat, boy, *eat!*"

Sam walked away, or started to until John ran up to him and begged for a plate of the chicken. Sam clapped John on the back and took the linebacker into the kitchen.

Quentin sat. He looked at Choto, newly amazed that someone from another species could be so damn cool.

"Choto, thank you. This means a lot."

Choto's eye flooded a light green. "It is my honor." The Warrior started in on his bowl of chow mein. Quentin noticed that the food was full of insect legs, some of which were still moving.

He looked away from it and focused on the chicken. The best food he had ever known was sitting right in front of him. The only way this night could get any better was if his sister was here with him. His sister, and Fred, who had helped make this happen.

Quentin grabbed a steaming chicken leg and bit in. It was every bit as sweet and tangy as he remembered.

The religion of Purism said there was no such thing as omens, but it was hard not to think of this as the best omen ever.

And that bode well for the next day.

ONCE AGAIN, HE WORE the blazing-orange "away" jersey.

He was a part of the field, the stadium, the air, even the players on both sides of the ball. The game and Quentin Barnes had become one. Energy flowed from the field into him, then from him back into the field, as if he were the living god the Sklorno thought him to be.

The Death opposed him in their metalflake-red helmets and flat-black jerseys, their *home* jerseys, but this didn't *feel* like OS1's home field, and Quentin didn't *feel* like a visitor. The Black Hole — a stadium built from clear blue crystal that framed a black field and held 133,000 fans. Once upon a time this place had intimidated him, but not anymore.

"Red, twenty-nine!" he called down the left side of the line. "Red, twenty-nine!" he called down the right.

All afternoon long, the Orbiting Death's offense had dominated the game. Condor Adrienne moved his team up and down the field at will — at least until they got into the red zone. Once inside the 20, the Krakens' defense got down and dirty, they got *mean*. Sacks by Mum-O and Alexsandar Michnik had shaken Condor up. Constant pressure had forced him into bad throws. OS1 had racked up an obscene amount of yards, but two of their long drives ended with interceptions — once on the 5-yard line and once in the end zone. Four other times the Death had moved into scoring territory, and all four times the Krakens' defense had held them to a field goal.

For all the yardage, Condor Adrienne and his ilk had yet to score a touchdown.

The Krakens' offense played damn near close to perfect. No interceptions, no fumbles, two touchdowns and two field goals had given Ionath a 20-12 lead. Quentin had played smart instead of risky. Instead of trying to force passes, he avoided pressure by throwing the ball out of bounds. He had the lead, and he wasn't about to blow it with stupid turnovers.

Now, in the fourth quarter and on third down and eight at the Death 22-yard line, he had a chance to ice the game. A field goal would put Ionath up 23-12 — an 11-point lead, something Condor could make up with a touchdown, a two-point conversion and a field goal! A Krakens touchdown, on the other hand, would create a 15-point lead — OS1 would have to score two touchdowns with just 4:31 left in the game.

"Red, twenty-nine!"

The black-clad Death linebackers suddenly came forward, standing in the gaps between their black-clad defensive linemen. Matt McRoberts on Quentin's left, Yalla the Biter in the middle and James McPike on the right. Quentin read their eyes, their faces — somehow, he knew that Yalla and McPike were coming, while McRoberts was going to drop back in coverage.

Time to audible.

Quentin stood and shouted down the line.

"Flash! Flash!"

The black-helmeted, orange-facemasked heads of the Krakens turned to look at him.

"Green, eighty-eight!" Quentin said. "Green, eighty-eight!"

The Krakens' heads again faced forward. He had changed the play from a five-step drop to a hot-pass for George Starcher, who was lined up at right tight end. If Starcher ran the route correctly, at the snap he would move forward three steps and then immediately turn back for the pass.

Quentin slid his hands beneath Bud-O-Shwek. The sold-out Black Hole crowd screamed for a stop, they screamed for blood.

Scream all you want, suckers, today the Krakens are the ones that will feed.

"Hut-hut … *hut*!"

He took the snap; the clock in his head started ticking away. His instincts had been right — Yalla the Biter blitzed up the middle, while McPike was coming from the right. Quentin took just one step back, turned and threw, using his height to fire the ball over the clashing line. McPike saw the quick pass and tried to turn, but he wasn't fast enough. The ball shot to where McPike had been one second before, right into the huge hands of George Starcher.

Crazy George tucked the ball into his right arm and pounded upfield. McRoberts chased him from the left. Near the sidelines, Tara the Freak blocked the Death cornerback, hitting her so hard the defender fell onto her tail and skidded out of bounds. Tara wasn't done; he sprinted forward, looking for a block. George cut right and followed him.

The Death's free safety came in hard. Tara smashed into her, and both players hit the ground.

George reached the sidelines and turned upfield, McRoberts a few steps behind. The black-clad strong safety was the only thing between George and six points.

The strong safety dove at George's big legs. George suddenly jumped, hurdling the Sklorno defensive back. She shot underneath, sliding out of bounds. George landed, but stumbled, and that slowed him. McRoberts caught him at the 2-yard line, wrapping him around the waist. As George fell forward, he reached the ball out with his right hand — the ball hit the inside of the end zone's orange pylon.

The Harrah ref's mouth-flaps shot into the air — touchdown.

Most of the capacity crowd booed, but thousands of Krakens fans cheered with delight. Just over four minutes remained in the semi-final game, and the Death needed three scores. The contest was all but over.

Quentin knelt and plucked a few blades of the field's black plants. The blades had some red blood on them, but he didn't care — he sniffed deeply, then rubbed his fingers together, letting the torn plants flutter to the field.

He could barely believe it.

The Ionath Krakens were going to the Galaxy Bowl.

From *UBS Sports*

Former Teammates Square Off for the GFL Title as Ionath Clashes with Jupiter

by PIKOR THE ASSUMING

MADDERCH, OS1, QUYTH CONCORDIA — The Ionath Krakens are headed to their first Tier One championship game in 10 years, thanks to a 27-12 defeat of arch-rival OS1. Ionath (9-5) will square off against Jupiter (10-4) in a rematch of Galaxy Bowl XVII, which Jupiter won 21-16.

Galaxy Bowl XXVII game takes place at Shipyard Stadium in the city of Hittoni on planet Wilson 6 in the League of Planets.

The star of this semi-final win wasn't All-Pro quarterback Quentin Barnes, or All-Pro running back Ju Tweedy, or even All-Pro linebacker John Tweedy, but rather the Krakens' defensive backfield. Orbiting Death quarterback Condor Adrienne was picked off three times, twice by breakout star cornerback Cormorant Bumberpuff and once by strong safety Davenport. All three interceptions came when OS1 (9-5) was in the red zone, keeping a possible 21 points off the board.

"I am pleased to contribute to my team's success," said Bumberpuff. "I trust this shows that all races can work together for victory."

In the Solar Division semi-final, Don Pine led Jupiter to a 21-18 win over first-seeded Vik Vanguard (10-4). Pine threw for a pair of first-half touchdowns that led the Jacks to a 14-3 halftime lead. Pine went down in the third quarter when a Mur the Mighty sack broke three of his toes. With Pine on the bench, Vik rattled off 13 straight points to go up 16-14. Heavily bandaged, Pine returned to the game late in the fourth to hero-ically lead the Jacks to the game-winning touchdown.

> *"I am pleased to contribute to my team's success. I trust this shows that all races can work together for victory."*
>
> CORMORANT BUMBERPUFF

Earlier this year, Pine played for Ionath as a backup to Quentin Barnes. Jupiter traded Denver to Ionath in exchange for the veteran quarterback, a trade that now seems like a brilliant move for both teams.

This is Jupiter's second-straight trip to the Galaxy Bowl. Last year the Jacks lost the championship game 28-24 to Themala. Don Pine led the Jacks to back-to-back GFL titles in 2675 and 2676. This is Jupiter's fifth Galaxy Bowl appearance.

This is Ionath's third appearance in the title game. The Krakens won the 2665 Galaxy Bowl but lost in 2675 to Jupiter.

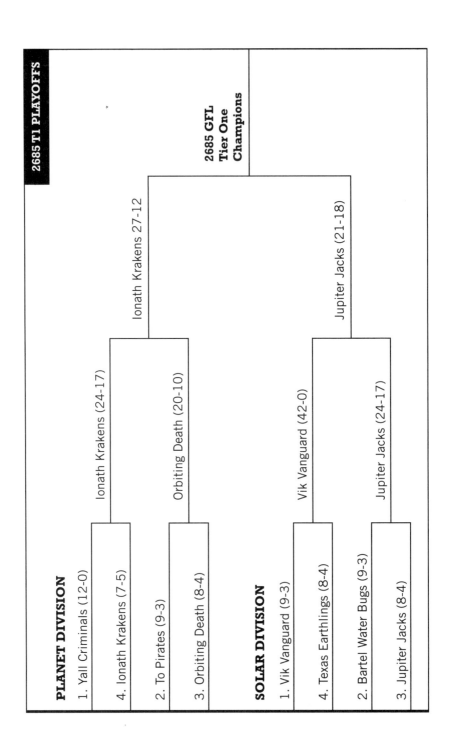

2685 T1 PLAYOFFS

PLANET DIVISION

1. Yall Criminals (12-0)

4. Ionath Krakens (7-5)

2. To Pirates (9-3)

3. Orbiting Death (8-4)

SOLAR DIVISION

1. Vik Vanguard (9-3)

4. Texas Earthlings (8-4)

2. Bartel Water Bugs (9-3)

3. Jupiter Jacks (8-4)

Ionath Krakens (24-17)

Orbiting Death (20-10)

Vik Vanguard (42-0)

Jupiter Jacks (24-17)

Ionath Krakens 27-12

Jupiter Jacks (21-18)

2685 GFL Tier One Champions

AS QUENTIN WALKED around the mostly empty Shipyard, he knew that this game would be different in more ways than one.

GFL rules stipulated that playing fields had to be at a temperature between 14 and 26 degrees Celsius. An unseasonal, unexpected cold front had descended upon Hittoni, bringing with it sub-zero temperatures and something that Upper Tier GFL players weren't used to seeing: snow.

It was five degrees above zero. The snow was falling. In some instances, the game might have been delayed or even postponed, but not today. Not for the Galaxy Bowl. Too many pieces were already in place for the league's crowning moment. Commissioner Froese had already ruled that the game would go on as scheduled.

Quentin walked through the empty stadium, watching snow slowly accumulate on every surface. He walked alone — he wanted to soak up everything about this moment, lock in every scent, touch every surface, preserve it in his brain forever.

The week had been a slice of madness. Everyone in the galaxy wanted to talk to him, to his teammates, to Hokor and to Gredok. The Jupiter players and staff were probably going through the same thing. Froese's people had done a great job of keeping most of the universe at bay — the commissioner wanted players to help hype the game, but he also wanted them sharp and focused. Froese knew the value of a first-class contest.

After all, an estimated 250 *billion* sentients would watch this game, either live or as soon as the punch-drive relay beacons brought each quarter's action from Wilson 6 to the rest of the galaxy. And that number didn't include any potential Prawatt viewers. The Galaxy Bowl was the single-most-watched event in the history of civilization, of *all* civilizations. With that kind of crowd, you certainly didn't want to disappoint.

Quentin couldn't imagine a more perfect place to win the GFL title. The Shipyard, home of the Hittoni Hullwalkers. More a museum than a stadium, the concourse showcased the history of space travel.

Floating relics of pre-punch-drive vessels painted a picture of Humanity's past. He stared at ancient ships that had simple names like *Pioneer* and *Ikaros*. He walked through the recreation of a white, winged vessel called the *Challenger*. He ran his hands across the surfaces of the *Helios,* the *Jaxa* and the *Shenzou.*

And still the snow came down. He slid his foot across the concrete floor, watched the tip of his toe push up a mini-wave of snow and leave a wet streak in its path. The Shipyard was an open-air stadium: no dome would protect the players from the elements.

On Micovi, Quentin had played in all conditions, from blistering desert heat to icy rain to full-out blizzards. The snow wouldn't bother him, but how would it impact his teammates? How would it impact the Jupiter Jacks? Most importantly, how would it impact Don Pine?

Snow didn't make Quentin nervous, but Don did. Don had won two Galaxy Bowls. He knew exactly what needed to be done to claim victory in the league's grandest game. By this time tomorrow, Pine would either be fitted for a third ring, or Quentin for his first.

How ironic that the Galaxy Bowl was here, at the home of the three-time champion Hullwalkers, a team now relegated to the GFL's second tier. That was the nature of the game: teams got better, teams got worse. For now, however, none of that mattered. The Krakens were *here*, they were ready to claim immortality.

At the end of Quentin's walk, he stopped at his favorite display: *Sputnik*. It was the first man-made object put into orbit. Nothing much to it, really — just a silver sphere barely two feet in diameter. Seven hundred and twenty-eight years ago, this simple object had marked his ancestors' shift from a primitive, planet-bound people to a space-faring race.

Few objects in history could mark the definitive change from one era to another the way Sputnik did. Quentin's "Sputnik moment" came when he'd first stepped on the practice field of the Micovi Raiders. He had stopped being a *miner* and become a *football player*. His life had changed forever. Now, he was on the cusp of another such moment — he could move from *football player* to *legend*.

Championships are forever.

Quentin Barnes had waited his entire life for this opportunity. He stared at *Sputnik* a moment longer, then turned and headed for the locker room.

THE TEAM GATHERED IN THE TUNNEL. Quentin watched his breath sliding away in thin, dissipating clouds. He felt the cold on his face, on his fingers and palms, but nowhere else thanks to this temperature-regulating Koolsuit.

Only minutes now.

Out in the stadium, a roaring crowd awaited. As the "visiting" team, the orange-clad Krakens would take the field first. The Jacks — courtesy of their better record — would come out after.

John Tweedy stood on Quentin's left. Whatever conflicts they had were nowhere to be seen. John was all business. Quentin genuinely felt sorry for Don Pine, knowing that the blue-skinned man would soon feel the wrath of a hyper-focused elder Tweedy brother. Ju, the younger but bigger of the two, stood on Quentin's right. Ju seemed relaxed, almost jovial, but then again he always did before a fight.

This time, no pregame speech had been needed. The Krakens knew their roles, knew what they had to do. Players had searched deep within themselves, preparing to call forth every last ounce of energy, every last measure of will. They all knew they might never again play in a championship — the GFL was a violent, unforgiving place, and next season they could be injured, cut, traded ... they could die. Even if they stayed healthy and played for many years, at that moment twenty teams full of the greatest athletes in the galaxy were sitting at home, watching.

It was now or never.

One chance to be champions.

One chance to be *immortal*.

"*Sentients of all races, please welcome your Planet Division Champions, the Ionath ... Kraaaaaaaaakennnns!*"

Quentin ran out of the tunnel and into the pouring snow. Powerful lights lit up the stadium and blazed off the white field, a field that had already been white before the snow started to fall. Grounds crews had shoveled clear the blue lines and numbers.

A stadium full of football fans screamed with satisfaction at the gladiatorial spectacle to come. This time, all races seemed to be represented equally, about half of them clad in orange and black, the other half clad in copper, silver and gold. Flags flew, pom-poms bounced and voices screamed, the roar of the bloodthirsty monster waiting to be fed.

And feed them he would.

Even as he ran to the sidelines, Quentin measured the feel of each step in preparation for the upcoming battle. The falling snow made the surface slick, but the field beneath hadn't frozen — the footing still felt firm, perfect for running. That wouldn't last long, however: by the second half, he knew they'd be playing on a sea of mud, snow and icy water.

He reached the sidelines. His teammates pressed in around him, waiting for his words. They pushed him and pushed each other. He pushed back, hitting and shoving, each concussive impact spiking his adrenaline just a touch further — this, too, was part of the ritual, part of preparing for battle.

Quentin cleared some space for himself. His orange- and black-clad teammates surrounded him: Ki and Quyth Warrior, Sklorno and Human, Prawatt and HeavyG. He started to talk, but stopped. He threw his head back and just *howled*.

His teammates did the same, forty-five premier athletes giving in to the rage and joy and overwhelming emotion of the moment.

Quentin finished his howl, then turned in place, staring at each and every teammate.

"No one thought we would be here," he said, shaking his head and yelling loud enough to be heard over the crowd. "No one thought you could do this."

He looked at the wide eyes of John Tweedy, the black stare of Mum-O-Killowe. He saw the glinting metal and colorful streamers of Cormorant Bumberpuff, the huge shoulders and thick head of Michael Kimberlin. Becca Montagne stared back at him, her eyes ablaze with fire and life. Denver and Milford, Yassoud Murphy, Virak and Choto, Cheboygan and Tara the Freak, all ready to do whatever it took.

Finally, Quentin's gaze fell upon Crazy George Starcher. For the first time, George had painted his face orange and black.

Quentin raised his left fist high. His teammates surged forward, reaching their hands to his. They barked and chittered and screamed and grunted. Quentin bellowed out the team chant, every line answered by his teammates.

"Whose house?"

"Our house!"

"Whose house?"

"Our house!"

"What law?"

"Our law!"

"Who wins?"

"Krakens!"

"Who wins?"

"Krakens!"

"This ... is ... *it*," he said. "Win today, and you will *never* be forgotten! Destroy on three. One, two, *three*."

"Destroy-destroy-destroy!"

His teammates spread out across the sidelines. Quentin looked out to the field. Through the falling snow, he saw that the refs were calling for the team captains.

Quentin walked onto the white field. John fell in on his left, Ju on his right. Today, Ma Tweedy's three boys would represent Ionath.

They reached mid-field. A huge GFL logo had been painted on the turf, but it was already fuzzy from a half-inch of snow. Across from Quentin and his teammates stood the Jupiter captains: Ki defensive tackle Kal-Gah-Het, Sklorno cornerback Xuchang and Don Pine.

Don smiled at Quentin. "Hey, kid — fancy meeting you here."

Quentin nodded respectfully. This wasn't like the games against rival teams OS1, Coranadillana or Wabash; the Jacks and the Krakens had no bad blood between them. Both teams would play like their lives depended on it. Sentients would get hurt, some might even die, but Quentin knew it would be a clean game.

John pointed at Don. "No offense, Donny Boy, but I've always wanted to hit you right in your mouth."

Don laughed. "How come? Did I do something to offend you?"

"You're a quarterback," John said. "All quarterbacks offend me."

The Harrah ref reached a mouth-flap into his black- and white-striped backpack and came out holding a large coin. He held it out, the stadium lights reflecting off of the metal. Snowflakes landed on it, melting instantly into tiny drops of water.

"This is the coin we will use for the toss," the referee said, his voice amplified a thousand times over by the Shipyard's sound system. The coin showed the planet Creterak.

"This is heads," the ref said, then flipped the coin over. Quentin felt a surge of excitement: the coin must have been minted for this game because the other side showed the Shipyard's signature icon — *Sputnik*.

"This is tails," the ref said. "Ionath is the visiting team, who will call it for Ionath?"

Ju raised his hand. "I will."

Quentin and John had privately agreed to let Ju have that honor. The younger Tweedy's already huge chest puffed up even bigger with pride.

The Harrah ref held out the coin. "Call it in the air," he said, then flipped it.

"Tails," Ju said.

"Ionath calls tails," the ref said as the coin descended. It hit the blue of the GFL logo, bounced once, then landed flat — Sputnik side up.

"Tails," the ref said. "Ionath, do you choose to kick or receive."

Quentin smiled. "We want the ball."

"Krakens choose to receive," the ref said. He then asked what side of the field the Jacks wanted, but Quentin wasn't listening. His first Galaxy Bowl, and he would start out the game with the ball in his hands.

• • •

THE JACKS LINED UP for the kickoff. Quentin stood on the sidelines, shifting from foot to foot. His offensive teammates stood around him. The crowd stomped and chanted as the Jacks' kicker, Jack Burrill, raised his hand. The ref blew the whistle. Burrill lowered his hand, then ran toward the ball and put his foot into it. Galaxy Bowl XXVII was on.

The ball sailed through the air. Rookie kick returner Niami waited in her own end zone. The ball fell into her tentacles. She took one step forward, then stopped — the kicking team was already closing in. Still standing in the end zone, she knelt. Whistles blew: touchback.

Quentin pulled on his helmet and ran onto the field.

HE HAD TO PEE and felt like he might throw up. The butterflies ripped through his stomach at supersonic speed. He knew the sensations would pass as soon as he felt that first hit or threw that first pass.

He stood in front of his huddle: four Ki linemen and Michael Kimberlin in front, bent down so the back row could see over them — Denver on the left side, Milford on the right, with Crazy George Starcher, Rebecca Montagne and Ju Tweedy in-between.

"All right, ladies and gentlemen," Quentin said. "I hope you took in the sights and waved to the cameras because now it's time to go to work and get dirty. Three plays in a row to start the game, no-huddle, all out of I-right formation. First play is trap left, then counter strong, then rollout left. Becca, Ju, let's start softening them up right away. All plays on two, on two. Ready?"

"*BREAK!*"

The Krakens jogged and scuttled to their positions on the 20-yard line. Quentin walked up slowly, taking everything in as he did.

Snow continued to come down on the Shipyard's capacity crowd. Harrah flew in circles around the upper deck, some trailing streamers of orange and black, some trailing silver, copper and gold. The Harrah steered clear of clusters of white-clad Creterakians that clung to security posts.

So many bats … Quentin had never before seen that many Creterakians all in one place. There was no better terrorist target than a Galaxy Bowl, and Froese wanted to make sure everyone saw an overwhelming amount of security.

Quentin looked back to the field. The snowfall was already blurring the field's dark-blue lines and numbers. At every timeout, stadium staff would be running shovels across the field to clear those lines.

He looked to the far goalposts. Blue streamers dangled from the top of each post, the light wind barely making them flutter. It was cold, and his receivers weren't used to cold, but other than the temperature, conditions were perfect for throwing.

Quentin surveyed the defense. The Jacks looked resplendent in gleaming copper helmets, the Jacks logo on either side complementing gold facemasks. Gold jerseys reflected the stadium lights, as did their silver sleeves and silver-trimmed copper numbers. The Jacks logo sparkled from the thighs of copper leg armor and shoes. The Jupiter players looked like an army of fancy robots, but Quentin knew there was nothing fancy about their play.

This was Jupiter's third Galaxy Bowl appearance in the last four seasons. In the past, they'd won with overpowering offense. This year, however, they'd lost that offense yet had somehow produced the league's best defense, a defense that earned its supper by coming after the quarterback.

Come and get it, Jupiter — I'm ready for whatever you can dish out.

Quentin slapped the sides of his helmet, *left-right, left-right.* Enough gawking; time to go to work.

He bent behind center and slid his hands under Bud-O-Shwek.

"Red, thirteen! Red, thir*teeeen!* Hut-hut!"

The ball slapped into his hands. The offensive and defensive lines collided with the sound of a head-on hovercar crash. He pushed off his left foot, moving back as he turned to the right.

Becca shot past, rushing into the line to block. Quentin extended the ball toward Ju Tweedy. Ju's arms snapped down on the ball, and he drove forward.

The orange-clad Krakens pushed out, but only a few feet. Gold jerseys and copper helmets smashed in, silver sleeves glinting as defender arms reached out for Ju. Ju lowered his shoulders and plowed forward, only to be met head to head by right linebacker Katan the Beheader.

Whistles blew. Two-yard gain. Second down and eight on the Ionath 22-yard line.

The Krakens scrambled to the line of scrimmage. The Jacks scrambled as well, clearly prepared for Ionath's no-huddle offense.

Quentin looked over the defensive formation, then called out the snap-count.

AFTER THREE POSSESSIONS, the Krakens had yet to pick up a first down. Quentin jogged off the field as the punt team ran on. He found Coach Hokor.

"Coach, we're being too conservative," Quentin said. "We *have* to open things up."

"Take it easy, Barnes. The score is still zero-zero."

"But we can't move the ball."

"Neither can they," Hokor said. "This is only the first quarter. Remember, Barnes, this is a marathon, not a sprint."

Quentin took a breath and tried to calm himself. He knew it would take some time to wear down the Jacks' defensive line and establish the run game. That was the smart play. Quentin wasn't stupid enough that he wanted to go pass-crazy against the Jacks' excellent defensive backfield of free safety Luxembourg, safety Matidi and cornerbacks Morelia and Xuchang. He could throw against them, *would* throw against them, but that had to wait.

For now, he would stick to the game plan.

Quentin watched Don Pine drop back five steps. The Krakens' front four barreled in hard, as they had all through the scoreless first quarter. Mum-O-Killowe's four arms ripped at his opposing offensive guard but he couldn't get past. Alexsandar Michnik and Ibrahim Khomeni attacked from the outside, coming straight at their opposing offensive tackles — Pine couldn't run like Quentin, but the old man could slip inside an out-of-control defensive end and scramble long enough for his receivers to get open.

Ionath's other defensive tackle, Chat-E-Riret, vanished beneath a gold-jerseyed offensive guard. Michnik reached for Pine, but Pine stepped forward into the space created by the fallen Chat-E.

The ball arced through the falling snow. Jupiter receiver New Delhi had a step on Bumberpuff. The perfectly thrown pass arced toward the end zone's right corner. Katzenbaum Weasley pinwheeled over to help. Prawatt and Sklorno jumped at the same time, but the pass was so on-target Weasley didn't have a chance. Twenty feet above the white turf, the ball sailed inches over Weasley's outstretched fingertips and into New Delhi's tentacles. She tucked it tight and landed in the end zone for a 35-yard touchdown.

Jealousy roiled through Quentin. He would not let Don Pine get a third ring, he *would not*.

The extra point was good — 7-0 Jupiter, 3:42 left to play in the second quarter.

"CHICK, I DON'T KNOW what just got into Quentin Barnes, but his arm has really come alive."

"Right you are, Masara. Barnes is five-for-five on this drive — all short passes, but he's marched his team down to the Jupiter twenty-three. Barnes *has* to step up, Masara, because Ionath's running game just isn't getting it done against the Gold Wall of Jupiter."

"Chick, we have word back from the sidelines. Krakens defensive tackle Chat-E-Riret has a broken lower knee on his middle right leg. He's out for the game."

"Ouch, Masara! Riret was the Krakens' backup defensive tackle, filling in for Mai-An-Ihkole, who was lost for the season back in Week Twelve against the Wabash Wolfpack. With Tim

Crawford suspended for assaulting a police officer in Ionath City, that means third-stringer Jason Procknow, a rookie from the Purist Nation, will have to play the rest of the game at defensive tackle."

"Chick, that doesn't bode well for the Krakens' pass rush, but right now Ionath has the ball in scoring position. Quentin Barnes breaks the huddle. The Krakens line up with four wide receivers, Denver and Milford wide left, Tara the Freak and Halawa wide right. Ju Tweedy is the single back. Barnes settles behind center. He takes the snap and drops back, play-action fake to Ju Tweedy, Barnes is looking downfield, here comes the blitz and … *wait*! Ju Tweedy is open over the middle. Barnes steps up, he's *hammered* as he releases, but Tweedy catches the pass and turns upfield! He breaks a tackle, he's at the fifteen, the ten, Matidi is trying to fight off a Halawa block, the five, and Ju runs over an off-balance Matidi for the touchdown!"

"Masara, what a play by Barnes! He saw the linebacker blitz coming and knew that if he waited just a second longer, Ju Tweedy would get open in that linebacker's vacated spot. Barnes had to stand in there and take a real whack in the face, but he got the pass off and let the Mad Ju do the voodoo he does so well."

"Chick, Ju Tweedy in the open field is a frightening sight for any defensive back. Here's the extra point attempt … good! We're all tied up seven to seven!"

WITH JUST UNDER TWO MINUTES remaining in the half, the field was already in bad shape and quickly getting worse. Cleats and bodies chewed up the turf, revealing the red-black mud beneath until the falling snow again turned these field wounds white. The center of the field, roughly from the 30 to the 30, was already ripped and ravaged, resulting in poor, dangerous footing for both offense and defense.

Quentin stood on the sidelines. He tried to keep still. He knew the other offensive players were watching him, so he focused on standing tall and looking confident.

Out on the field, the Krakens' D was trying to stop the Jacks. Ionath wasn't the only team intent on establishing a running game. Pine kept handing off to running back CJ Wellman, and Wellman kept picking up muddy yards. Those yards were hard-earned, though, with John Tweedy, Virak the Mean and Choto the Bright teeing off every time Wellman touched the ball.

Rookie defensive tackle Jason Procknow was in over his head. The Jacks' left guard constantly drove him backward. Jupiter took advantage of that, running at Procknow's position on just about every other play and picking up positive yards every time.

The snow came down. The Jacks' offense lined up. The Krakens' defense dug in. Both teams were muddy, bloody and torn. Cones of breath slid out of the mouths on either side and met in the middle, giving birth to a mixed fog of war. Don Pine barked out the count.

He took the snap, turned and stretched the ball toward Wellman. Wellman snapped his arms together for a play-action fake. Don continued back three more steps, then turned to look downfield — and stared straight at a blitzing John Tweedy.

Don calmly side-stepped right. The over-committed John shot past. Don stepped forward, looking for a receiver, but he didn't see Khomeni beat his blocker and barrel in. The HeavyG defensive end blindsided Pine, knocking the gold- and copper-clad quarterback clear off his feet.

The ball tumbled free.

Quentin's breath locked in his chest. The brown ball bounced across the wet, white field, splashing up mud as it skidded off of torn plants and trampled snow. Choto dove for it, as did Jason Procknow and two Jacks offensive linemen. Bodies piled up, dirty arms fighting and digging for the ball.

The Harrah refs hovered over the pile, then dove in, sliding bonelessly between the packed bodies.

Whistles blew. The pile broke up. A Harrah ref floated up and signaled downfield — Ionath's ball. Jason Procknow stood, his jersey torn, his left shoulder pad broken and dangling, his right arm holding the ball high.

Quentin pulled on his helmet as he ran onto the field. He glanced at the scoreboard — 1:45 to play in the first half, ball on the Jupiter 40-yard line.

The whistles blew again. Quentin looked and saw that two players were still lying on the turf — Choto the Bright and Don Pine. Choto rolled on the ground, middle right arm clutched in both pedipalp hands. The cracked armor around Don's right knee showed a leg bent at a strange angle.

Quentin waved to his offensive players. "Huddle up! Come on, come on."

He gathered his teammates together as doctors from both sidelines flew out to tend to their wounded.

INJURIES WERE PART of the sport.

Quentin didn't wish one on any player, but when the stadium lights shone down on a medsled carrying Don Pine off the field, Quentin knew the game had changed. The Jacks' backup quarterback would have trouble moving the ball. If Quentin played conservative, didn't turn the ball over, and made sure they got at least a field goal on this drive to take a 10-7 lead into the locker room at halftime, the Krakens would be well on their way to a GFL title.

On the first play, Quentin rolled left and found Denver for a 13-yard gain to take them to the Jupiter 27.

They tried Ju off-tackle right on the second play, but it was stuffed for a two-yard loss. The O-line couldn't open holes for Ju, and the big running back was getting frustrated. Other than his touchdown catch, the Jacks had kept him mostly contained.

On second down, Quentin backpedaled and flipped a quick screen pass to Becca. She hauled it in, turned upfield, cutting left and right as she followed the big body of Michael Kimberlin. Linebackers drove in, bringing Becca down for a seven-yard gain.

Third-and-five on the Jupiter 20, 1:38 to play and counting.

Ionath huddled up. Several of Quentin's teammates were already bleeding, their mud-covered jerseys rumpled and streaked with white from the plants that made up the ravaged field.

In the huddle's back row, Ju breathed hard, clouds of vapor billowing out of his mouth. "Q, gimme the damn ball," he said. "I can get the first down."

"Shut up," Quentin said. "No talking in my huddle."

Quentin's heads-up display slid out of its recessed housing in his helmet to show the holographic face of Hokor the Hookchest.

"Barnes! What do you think?"

The Krakens needed five yards for the first down. A first down gave them a shot at a touchdown and a 14-7 lead. Normally on third-and-five, Quentin would pass, but he didn't want to risk an interception, or a sack and a fumble.

"Coach, let's run it," Quentin said. "Ju thinks he can get the first. If he doesn't, we kick the field goal and take a lead into the locker room."

"Agreed," Hokor said. "That defensive line has to give up some yards sooner or later. I-set, trap left."

Quentin tapped his helmet to make the heads-up display slide into its housing. He called the play and saw Ju smile.

At the line, Quentin scanned the defense. The Jacks' linemen were getting bloody as well, the small tears and rips of their already dirty metallic uniforms a testament to the ongoing battle. He looked right and saw Xuchang in single coverage on Halawa. Quentin considered audibling to a quick slant — Halawa could run that route to perfection, but would she stay inside of the All-Pro cornerback?

Don't risk it, keep it on the ground, let Ju do his thing.

"Blue, eighty-eight! Blue, eighty-eighty! Hut-hut ... *hut!*"

The ball slapped into his hands. He turned as Becca shot by on yet another mission to block the Jacks' linebackers, then handed the ball to Ju. The running back stutter-stepped, looking for a hole. He slid between Kill-O-Yowet and Sho-Do-Thikit, who fought against their gold-jerseyed opponents.

Quentin saw Becca try to block Katan the Beheader, but he got lower than her and knocked her on her ass. He came free. Ju planted to spin, but a chunk of white turf gave way — his right foot slid wide, *too* wide. Katan lowered a shoulder and put Ju hard to his back.

Whistles blew. A three-yard gain — no first down. The Krakens would have to kick the field goal.

Quentin started off the field when he noticed that Ju hadn't gotten up. The big running back lay on the ground, rolling side to side in pain.

Quentin's heart sank. It looked like Ju might have pulled a groin muscle. Doc Patah could fix cuts, stop bleeding, even work on cracked and broken bones, but pulled muscles were far harder for game-day fixes.

If it was, in fact, a pulled groin, then the Krakens' All-Pro running back was out for the game.

"CHICK, WE'RE HALFWAY to a new GFL champion, and what a game! Arioch Morningstar's kick put the Krakens up 10-7 at the half. This is a defensive struggle — how much do field conditions play into that?"

"Masara, the snow is definitely the cause of the low offensive output, but we are also looking at multiple injuries on both sides of the ball. Reports are that Don Pine broke his patella and is probably done for the day. On the Ionath side, defensive tackle Chat-E-Riret is definitely out, as is Choto the Bright, who has a broken middle right arm. That's *two* defensive starters out of the game. And if Ju Tweedy doesn't return, the Krakens will probably split carries between Becca *The Wrecka* Montagne and Yassoud Murphy, neither of which is the kind of punishing, dominant back that Ju is."

"Chick, that means the Krakens' running game will struggle, but at the same time the Jacks have to rely on backup quarterback Rich Amooi to lead them to the title. I'm not sure how effective CJ Wellman will be running the ball for the Jacks if this playing surface continues to deteriorate in the second half."

"Masara, you're right about that. The snow keeps coming down, and this turf's already looking more chewed up than a cow carcass dangled over a pit of starving Purist orphans."

"Chick! You can't say that kind of—"

"Sorry, Masara, sorry, folks at home. They've finished setting up for the halftime show. Let's give it over to Somalia Midori and Trench Warfare!"

THE KRAKENS WERE AHEAD on the scoreboard, but you wouldn't have known it from looking at the training room.

Choto the Bright had already taken off his jersey and upper-body armor. He had a splint on his right middle arm. He stared at the ground, dejected.

The Warrior wasn't alone. Ki defensive tackle Chat-E-Riret sat half-submerged in a rejuve tank made for his species. He didn't seem upset at all. In fact, he munched away on a bag of spider snacks that floated in the pink liquid, and seemed elated that — win or lose — for the rest of his life, he could say that he'd played in the Galaxy Bowl.

Doc Patah fluttered near Ju Tweedy. Ju's muddy jersey lay in a pile on the floor, shoulder armor unceremoniously dropped on top of it. Ju's Koolsuit clung to his well-defined muscles like a black second skin. He was trying to walk, but each step made his face wrinkle with pain.

"See, Doc?" he said. "I'm fine. I'm going back in?"

"The only thing you are *going in* is the rejuve tank, Ju. You pulled a ligament."

A look of anger replaced Ju's expression of pain. "Doc, dammit, just shoot me up with something or whatever. I have to get back in the game!"

"I could shoot you up with every painkiller in the galaxy, and it wouldn't help a torn ligament," Doc Patah said. "And even if I operated right now, it would take you two days to recover. You're out."

Ju snarled and grabbed at Doc Patah. The Harrah's wings fluttered, carrying him back a few feet. Ju tried to give chase, but as soon as his foot planted, his face scrunched up in agony and he fell.

Quentin walked to him and knelt. "Ju, take it easy."

Ju lay on the floor, head in his hands. He shook his head. Quentin saw tears in the big Human's eyes.

"Q, I gotta go back in. This is my time — I can't let the team down."

To have come this far, an entire career spent working toward this moment to suffer a game-ending injury? Quentin's heart broke for his friend.

John came over as well. He gently helped Ju sit up. "You did good, baby brother."

Quentin put a hand on Ju's shoulder. "You scored a touchdown in the Galaxy Bowl. How many sentients can say that?"

Ju wiped away tears of frustration. "But the second half ... we can win this thing!"

"Can and will," Quentin said.

John tousled his younger brother's sweaty hair. "You did your part. You made Ma proud. You made *me* proud. We'll bring it home."

Ju sniffed. His jaw muscles twitched. "Go get Yassoud," he said. "Tell him to come talk to me. I've got some info on how the D-line is playing."

"Sure," Quentin said. "I'll go get him right now."

"And I'm not crying," Ju said. "No shucking way I'm crying."

John smiled. "Hell no, bro — it's the pain meds, messing with your feminine side is all."

Quentin left the training room. He walked into the central locker room. The entire team was gathered around the holoboard, listening to Coach Hokor outline new blocking schemes.

Quentin walked up to stand next to Hokor. The coach and the team looked at him expectantly.

"Murphy, come with me," Quentin said. "Also Procknow, Darkeye, Shayat, Martinez and Pishor. Let's go."

Quentin turned and walked to the Human locker room. He heard players scrambling to follow him, heard Hokor continue his talk. Quentin knew he should be there for Hokor's adjustments, but the coach would let him know if there was anything critical — for now, there was something more important that had to be done.

In the Human locker room, Quentin looked at his teammates. Mud covered the jersey and face of Jason Procknow, the rookie defensive tackle. Yassoud was a bit cleaner, but that would change quickly once the third quarter started. Samuel Darkeye, Shayat the Thick and rookie Pishor the Fang would all rotate in to fill Choto's spot at right outside linebacker. Jay Martinez, another running back, would be called upon when Yassoud needed a rest.

Quentin stared at them each in turn. "This is your dream," he said. "You won't be riding the bench in the second half, you'll be playing in the Galaxy Bowl. Step up to the challenge, play big, and you'll be wearing a championship ring."

They stared back at him, their eyes fixed with determination.

"This is your moment," he said. "Give every last breath out there because you may never get a chance like this again."

Four Human heads nodded. The stubby antennae of Shayat the Thick and Pishor the Fang bobbed.

Quentin put his hand on Yassoud's shoulder pad. "Ju asked to see you. Go talk to him. We need you, 'Soud. Can you deliver?"

Yassoud smiled and stroked his braided beard. There was no fear in those eyes, just confidence, confidence and *want*.

"Let me put it to you this way, Hayseed," he said. "If I'd have known I'd play the second half, I would have bet *way* more on this game."

QUENTIN TOOK THE SNAP and turned left. He extended the ball for Yassoud but pulled it back at the last second as 'Soud snapped his arms down for a fake handoff. Quentin turned and ran right, the ball on his right hip in hopes of hiding it from the defense for just a few precious seconds.

His blockers kept going left, leaving him all alone heading right — a "naked boot" play. Sometimes the naked boot would fool the defense and give him tons of open space, but this wasn't one of those times. The Jacks' left defensive end, Tony Jones, ran hard to the outside, cutting Quentin off from reaching the sidelines and turning it upfield: Quentin would have to pass or cut back inside, where the rest of the Jacks' defense would get him.

He looked for open receivers. Downfield, Halawa was cutting right on a flag pattern that would take her to the corner of the end zone. She was covered. Closer in, Crazy George turned on an out-pattern toward the right sideline. He was also covered, but there was just enough space to throw.

The closer Quentin got to the sidelines, the better the footing became. Those areas hadn't been chewed up by nonstop, pounding cleats. Quentin stutter-stepped to stop his forward momentum, then stepped up to pass — and was blasted from behind. The ball flew out of his hands as a big body drove him hard into the snowy white turf. Everything went black: he didn't know how long that lasted, but he came to with his head pounding, his ears ringing and the sound of a roaring crowd filling the cold stadium. Quentin slowly got to his feet. He turned to look back downfield — the metal-jerseyed Jupiter Jacks were in the end zone, jumping and high-fiving and generally having a good time.

Yassoud walked up and put a hand on Quentin's shoulder.

"Did I fumble?"

"Oh, yep."

"And they ran it back for a touchdown?"

"Oh, yep. We better get you to the sidelines, Q. You took a pretty good shot."

The fumble return for a touchdown gave Jupiter a 13-10 lead, with the extra point still to come. Quentin tried to fight down the pain as he jogged to the sidelines. Hokor was waiting for him.

"Coach, who hit me? I'm so sorry, I—"

"*Barnes!* Shut up." Hokor twirled his pedipalp hand inward, telling Quentin to come down to his level. Quentin knelt.

"Barnes, this is the Galaxy Bowl. Great players make great plays. Xuchang came on a corner blitz from the right, chased you all the way across the field and nailed you. She made a big play, so now *you* have to get out there and make one for us, understand?"

Quentin nodded. He looked up to the holoboard and watched the replay. Hokor was right — just as Quentin had reared back to throw, Xuchang had hit him in the back, bending him like a rag doll.

"Impressive," Hokor said. "It would seem anything getting hit that hard should have an impact crater, but I do not see one on your face."

Quentin looked at his coach. Hokor's pedipalps were shaking.

"Coach ... did you just make a joke?"

"I did," Hokor said. "I am told that I am very fun at parties. You fumbled, they scored. Put it behind you and win me this game."

Hokor walked away. Quentin stood there as a stream of teammates walked by, slapping his shoulder pads and saying *don't worry about it, Q.*

He took a deep breath. *Great players make great plays.* Hell, if Coach could actually *joke* about it in the biggest game of their lives, then Quentin wouldn't let it haunt him. He just had to get those points back.

As time expired in the third quarter, he watched the Jacks' kicker knock home the extra point.

Jupiter 14, Ionath 10, one quarter left to play.

THE FOURTH QUARTER CAME, and still the snow poured down. The wind picked up, driving at the falling white, making the countless flakes dance and swirl. The temperature had dropped again — each step crunched into thin crystals of ice forming on the surface of exposed, black-red mud. Every breath puffed out as a thin cloud that was quickly lost in the blowing snow.

Fifteen minutes remained. Just four points separated the two teams. A championship hung in the balance. For one squad, glory everlasting. The other would become nothing more than a footnote, a name quickly forgotten.

Quentin had been patient. He'd played conservative. He'd avoided risks. The High One had laced Quentin's left arm with lightning. If history was to be written, Quentin would write it his way. He was a born gunslinger, and now the bullets would fly.

The Krakens started the fourth quarter's first drive on their own 23-yard line. Quentin ignored his battered body and just *threw*. He hit Starcher for 8 yards, then Denver for 15, Halawa for 7, Tara the Freak for 12 and then Tara again on a little 5-yard pattern that the mutant Warrior turned into a 17-yard gain when he broke a pair of tackles.

On first-and-10 from the Jupiter 18, the Jacks' defensive backs moved up close into bump-and-run coverage on his receivers, cutting off Quentin's short throws. Quentin threw his first incompletion of the drive, then handed off to Yassoud on second down for a five-yard gain.

On third-and-five, Quentin took the snap and dropped back, his feet crunching through the mud's thin covering of ice. The Jacks' two Ki tackles blasted through the line and were on him immediately, an attacking wall of metal colors and angry eyes. Quentin didn't even have time to scramble — he went down as a thousand-plus pounds of angry linemen drove him into the rapidly solidifying ground.

This time, at least, he held onto the ball.

He limped off the field. His right knee wasn't obeying. It hurt like hell. Quentin didn't think there was any major damage — hopefully Doc Patah could tweak it enough to make the pain go away.

Quentin stopped at the sidelines and turned to watch his field goal unit line up. A 37-yard attempt to cut the lead to just a single point. Arioch had been playing lights-out all season — could he hit one more?

Bud-O-Shwek snapped the ball. Yitzhak caught it and placed it. A thousand cameras flashed in the stands as Arioch Morningstar — the smallest sentient on the team — stepped up and did his thing.

The backward-spinning brown leather ball sailed through the air. Quentin held his breath, watching it apex and then descend. It split the uprights a good ten feet above the crossbar.

Field goal, good. Jupiter 14, Ionath 13.

Quentin turned and hobbled toward the medbenches. "Doc! Get over here and do your magic!"

• • •

QUENTIN SAT ON A MEDBENCH at the back of the Ionath sideline. He kept his eyes closed and his hands locked on the bench as Doc Patah slid a needle into his knee, over and over, injecting some kind of painkiller and nanomed concoction beneath the skin.

"Young Quentin, your right knee is damaged," Patah said. "I can make it function, but you should strongly consider coming out of the game."

Quentin actually laughed. He shook his head.

"Doc, you crack me up."

The crowd got louder, then roared, but it wasn't the sound of a score or a turnover. Quentin looked up to the holodisplay. What he saw shocked him — Don Pine, a flexicast around his knee, hobbling onto the field.

"Doc," Quentin said, "whatever you have to do, fix my damn knee, and fix it *now*."

CJ WELLMAN TOOK THE PITCH from Don Pine and ran hard for the right sidelines, looking for a spot to turn it upfield.

Quentin watched Krakens linebacker Shayat the Thick rush in. Wellman met Shayat head to head and instantly spun away — the same move Quentin often used to break Quyth Warrior tackles. Shayat grabbed at Wellman's jersey but slipped off and fell face-first into the freezing red-black mud.

He'd missed the tackle, but his effort had forced Wellman to cut back inside toward Cormorant Bumberpuff. The Prawatt came out of his pinwheel roll and ran forward on two legs, arms outstretched to catch Wellman. Wellman didn't have time to make another move, so he lowered his head and plowed forward into Bumberpuff, who took the hit, wrapped the running back up and dragged him down.

Whistles blew. Wellman got up, but Bumberpuff did not. The Harrah refs looked at Bumberpuff's limp form, then blew their whistles again to signify an injury timeout.

"Oh, dear," Doc Patah said. "I am still not proficient in repairing that species."

Doc's wings fluttered. The Harrah shot out toward the fallen Kraken.

Quentin stood, testing his knee. It would have to do. He saw Vacaville run out onto the field — the much-maligned Sklorno cornerback now had to cover for the Prawatt starter.

The medsled carted Bumberpuff off the field.

Quentin watched the Jacks' offense huddle up. Pine called the play. The Jacks ran to the line. Pine limped behind them, hitch-stepping along on his braced right leg. If Quentin were in Don's shoes, he would go after Vacaville on the first play.

Come on, girl, time to step up and make a play.

Don lined up in the shotgun. He put a player in motion from right to left, leaving receiver Beaverdam alone just inside the right sideline — covered one on one by Vacaville.

The center long-snapped the ball to Don. The lines smashed into each other. Don stood tall as his receivers shot downfield. He turned right and pump-faked, and as he did Quentin's heart sank — he knew what was about to happen.

Vacaville tried to jump the route, and Beaverdam shot down the sidelines.

Don fired a tight spiral that hit Beaverdam 20 yards downfield. Weasley pinwheeled over fast, but Beaverdam threw a wicked head-and-shoulders fake and cut inside. The move was enough to give her a step, and a step was all she needed — Beaverdam ran into the end zone with Weasley and Vacaville trailing behind.

Quentin set his helmet on the ground. He rubbed his face with both hands.

The Jacks' kicker knocked home the extra point.

Jupiter 21, Ionath 13 with 8:24 left in the game.

FIELD POSITION WAS ALWAYS the game within the game. The team that has to move the farthest usually loses. The Krakens had started every drive from inside their own 25-yard line — that meant when Ionath drove 30 or even 40 yards before they faced a fourth down, they still had to punt.

With 6:52 left in the game and the Krakens down by 8, Quentin and his offense ran off the field after yet another stalled drive. He'd gone 4-of-5 for 27 yards on that outing, and Yassoud had even broken off a solid 12-yard run, but on third-and-6 Denver had dropped a pass to bring up a fourth down.

On the way off the field, Quentin saw Vacaville running on. He waved at the Sklorno, calling her over.

"Yes, his holiness Quentinbarnes?"

Quentin grabbed the back of her neck and pulled her close.

"Listen to me," he said. "Don Pine just beat you bad. He's going to do the *same thing* and see if you fall for it again. Time to step up, Vacaville. No more mistakes, got it?"

He felt her quivering. He let her go. Her head nodded hard even while her eyestalks stayed level and focused on his.

"Yes, Godling! I will obey!"

Quentin got to the sidelines, then turned to watch. The Krakens punted. Jupiter's returner waved for a fair catch.

The Jupiter offense ran onto the field. Don called the huddle, then lined up in the shotgun formation as the Jacks dug in for the play. Sure enough, a Jacks receiver again went in motion, again leaving Vacaville isolated in one-on-one coverage against Beaverdam.

Quentin's chest felt like his heart had stopped — he'd been right, Don was calling the same play. He was going for the kill, trying to put his team up 28-13.

The ball flipped back as the lines clashed. Don caught it, held it near his right ear as he stood tall. John Tweedy broke through, spinning his way in. Don had to act fast. He pump-faked, then threw deep before John could get to him.

This time, Vacaville didn't bite on the fake. She ran step for step with Beaverdam and had inside position — she was facing the ball, her back to Beaverdam, putting her between the receiver and the ball. Beaverdam tried to reach over Vacaville, but Vacaville hauled in the pass for the interception.

Both players tumbled to the ground. The line-judge ref blew his whistle and signaled Ionath's ball.

The Krakens' sideline erupted. For the first time that season, and at the most critical time possible, Vacaville had made a play.

Quentin and company ran out onto the field. As Vacaville ran off, Quentin stopped her.

"Great job!" he screamed in her face. "I give you blessings or whatever I'm supposed to do. *Great job!*"

Quentin pushed her away, then jogged to his forming huddle.

Krakens' ball, first-and-10 on their own 17-yard line. Ionath had all of its timeouts and needed a touchdown and a two-point conversion to tie the game.

"MASARA, BARNES IS DEADLY ACCURATE, but the Jacks are giving him the underneath routes. They're protecting that lead by not giving up a deep pass. Even though the Krakens have converted on eight of their thirteen third-down conversion attempts, here they are again facing fourth down."

"Yes, Chick, but this time they are on the Jupiter twenty-five. Arioch Morningstar is on the field to attempt his third field goal of the game, this one set up by the Vacaville interception. Chick, the Jacks will get the ball back with at least a five-point lead. Don Pine can barely move. Should Coach Any Davis Roth bring in the backup to try and run out the clock?"

"Masara, if Don Pine had no legs at all, I'd still have him in the game. He's never lost a Galaxy Bowl. He may be in the twilight of his career, but Jupiter's late-season run deep into the playoffs has shown everyone why the man is a two-time league MVP."

"Here's the snap, the kick ... and it's good! Ionath has cut the lead to five points. Just four minutes to play, Chick. Ionath has all three timeouts left *and* the two-minute warning. They have to stop Jupiter, get the ball back and score a touchdown to win the GFL title."

"Masara, it's all up to John Tweedy and the Krakens' defense. Can they make a stop and put the ball back in the hands of Quentin

Barnes? We'll find out, right after this message from Junkie Gin, the official gin of Galaxy Bowl Twenty-Seven."

QUENTIN AND HIS OFFENSIVE TEAMMATES stood on the sidelines. They were all praying, even the ones who didn't practice religion or believe in High One. They all watched John, Alexsandar, Mum-O, Virak, Ibrahim and the others dig in on third down, a last-ditch effort to stop Jupiter and get the ball back for the Ionath offense.

Jupiter had returned the kickoff back to their own 40. Don Pine threw for a quick 12 yards to pick up a first down. Pine then tried another pass, which Katzenbaum Weasley broke up, stopping the clock. On second down, New Delhi caught an out-pass and was forced out of bounds by Wahiawa — a major mistake by New Delhi, as she should have fallen down in-bounds to keep the clock ticking.

That brought up third-and-one on the Jupiter 39, 2:11 to play. If Jupiter gained that yard, if the Jacks got the first down, the game was all but over.

Jupiter lined up in a power set: two tight ends, a fullback and a tailback. They weren't even bothering to hide it — they were going to pick up that yard on the ground. The Krakens' D packed in tight, the linemen down low, Virak the Mean, John Tweedy and Shayat the Thick standing in the gaps. Even the defensive backs came up close, Vacaville, Davenport, Weasley and Wahiawa hovering just off the line of scrimmage.

This was as smash-mouth as football got: one yard to determine who was tougher.

Don barked out the count and took the snap. He turned and handed the ball to Wellman. Out of all the defensive stars on the Krakens, it was a backup linebacker that made the stop — Shayat the Thick slipped through the blockers and hit Wellman in the backfield. Wellman spun off, but the damage was done as Mum-O and John Tweedy brought him down for a three-yard loss.

Fourth down, four yards to go.

The clock ticked down to the two-minute warning. Whistles blew. The wind whipping snow all around him, Quentin held his breath as he watched the Jupiter sidelines and waited.

Coach Roth had to make a decision — punt or attempt a 59-yard field goal. Jupiter led 21-17. If they hit the long field goal, they'd be up by seven with two minutes to play. But if they attempted and *missed* that field goal, the Krakens would have the ball on their own 42-yard line and need to drive just 58 yards in those same two minutes. If the Jacks punted, Ionath would have to drive 80 or even 90 yards for the winning touchdown.

The two-minute warning timeout ended. The Jacks' punt team ran onto the field. That was the smart choice — with the crappy field conditions and the wind, Coach Roth didn't trust her kicker to make that long field goal.

Quentin forced himself to breathe normally. If he could lead his team to a touchdown, one little, *measly* touchdown, the Ionath Krakens would take the GFL title.

THE POCKET COLLAPSED around him. Quentin tried to scramble right, but blitzing linebacker Katan the Beheader hit him in the shoulder, spinning him around. Quentin stumbled, trying to keep his feet — he pushed out with his right hand, palm hitting hard against Katan's facemask, then righted himself only to see the Ki defensive tackle Kal-Gah-Het already extending, his huge body shooting forward like a missile.

Quentin rocked back. The hard hit hammered him, but that pain felt insignificant compared to the sudden agony that raged through his right hand. Two big bodies drove him into the ground, frozen crests of mud jabbing into his ribs like dull knives.

Whistles blew. Quentin relaxed his left hand and let the ball roll away. He felt one of the bodies push down as whoever it was got off of him. Quentin tried to pull back his right hand, but he'd barely moved before the pain raged up his arm and locked him still.

Quentin looked up to see Katan the Beheader's black eye staring down at him — Quentin's pinkie had slipped *through* the bars of Katan's facemask, then twisted and broken during the tackle. The pinkie bent at an obscene angle. A little bit of bone stuck out through the skin between the first and second knuckles. Blood dripped down onto torn white turf and the red-black ice. Katan's pedipalp hands gently removed Quentin's ruined finger, but even the smallest touch rippled with shearing agony.

His pinkie, *broken.* Agonizing pain blazed from his hand up to his elbow and beyond. It didn't matter, he had to stay in the game ... he *had* to lead his team to the win.

Quentin started to rise when big hands pressed on his chest and held him down.

"Sit still," Michael Kimberlin said. "Doc Patah is on his way out."

"Get off me, Mike. Huddle up."

Kimberlin shook his head. "No, Quentin, look at your hand."

Quentin pushed Mike away and stood, his left hand clutching his ravaged right to his chest. And then Doc Patah was there.

"Young Quentin, come with me."

"No! I can't go out now!"

"You have to," Patah said. "The officials called an injury time-out. Since you are the player injured, you must leave the field for at least one play."

Doc was right, that was the rule. Quentin started walking off the field and saw Yitzhak running on.

Quentin stopped and turned back to Kimberlin.

"Michael," he said. "Get Becca."

Kimberlin jogged to the huddle. Yitzhak stopped in front of Quentin, his white face alive with excitement.

"Don't worry, Q," he said. "I can do this."

Quentin shook his head. "No, you can't."

Yitzhak looked confused, then more so when a battered Becca jogged over.

She looked like she'd been through a war. A cut under her left eye bled profusely. Her swollen lower left lip puffed out in a perpetual pout. Blood and frozen mud streaked her torn jersey.

She'd cracked her helmet in two places, and her left forearm guard dangled from a broken strap.

"You wanted me, Q?"

Quentin nodded. "You're in at quarterback."

The eyes of both Yitzhak and Becca widened, but for different reasons.

"No way," Yitzhak said. "Look at her, she's beat to hell! She's been in the whole game, she's taken too many hits."

Quentin again shook his head. "You're out. Becca's in."

Yitzhak pointed a finger at Quentin's face. "I've been on this team for five years, practicing this offense for *five years*. This is my chance! I've been on the sidelines the whole game, I have fresh legs — you're picking a beat-up fullback over me?"

"Becca gives us the best chance to win," Quentin said. "Sorry, Zak, but get off the field."

Yitzhak's face screwed into a scowl of hate, of humiliation. He turned and ran back to the sideline.

Quentin's eye piece popped down.

"*Barnes!*" Hokor screamed. "What's going on? Why is Goldman coming out?"

"Becca's at QB, Coach," Quentin said. "Send out Kopor the Climber to take her place at fullback."

Hokor started to talk, but Quentin tapped his helmet to shut of the heads-up display. He turned to Becca.

She nodded. "I won't let you down. I can win this."

"Maybe, but you won't get the chance," he said. "I'm coming back in. Just don't turn the ball over."

Even as Quentin ran off the field, Patah's mouth-flaps pulled at his right wrist.

Quentin let the Harrah take the hand as they headed for a medbench. Quentin looked up at the holoscreen high above the field. One minute, thirteen seconds to play. The Krakens had all three timeouts.

Quentin sat. "Doc, get me back in the game."

Doc said nothing. Quentin took his first good, long look at the wound.

The pinkie seemed like it was barely attached. Blood pooled up around a shard of bone sticking out of his skin. He wouldn't be able to take a snap, wouldn't be able to hold the football with both hands.

Coach Hokor rushed up, eye swirling green. "How is it? Can he play?"

Quentin started to say *of course*, but Doc Patah spoke first.

"Young Quentin is finished for the day."

Quentin felt numbness in his soul. Fourth quarter of the Galaxy Bowl, his team down 21-16. Up on the big screen, Becca handed off to Yassoud, who slammed the ball forward for three yards. Second-and-seven. The clock kept ticking.

Hokor looked from the hand to Doc. His softball-sized eye flooded black. "Fix it," the coach said. "You fix that hand, or I'll see you flayed. Get Barnes back in the game."

Doc Patah ignored the little coach, spoke directly to Quentin instead.

"You need to come to the training room right now," Doc said. "I have to operate immediately if I am going to save your finger."

Late in the fourth quarter, his team down by five, and he'd leave the game to save a *pinkie*? A pinkie that wasn't even on his throwing hand?

No.

"Don't save it," Quentin said.

Out on the field, Becca took the snap and rolled right. The Jacks closed in on her, but she lowered her head and ran a linebacker over, then stumbled forward for a six-yard gain.

Hokor looked at the game clock — 0:48 to play.

"Timeout!" he screamed, then ran toward the field. "Timeout!"

Whistles blew. The Krakens had a third–and-one, two time-outs left, ball on their own 45.

Doc Patah released the hand, floated up until his sensory pits were at eye-level.

"Quentin, what do you mean, *don't save it?*"

"Every little bump hurts so bad it shuts me down. I can't have it dangling there. I *have* to get back in the game. So, *cut it off.*"

Doc Patah said nothing. The sensory pits stared back, seemingly emotionless.

Quentin did not look away. It wasn't a battle of wills as much as it was an understanding, an unspoken pact that any sacrifice was worth a title. Patah had been a ringside doctor for heavyweight fighters — he knew better than anyone how far an athlete would go to become a champion.

The Harrah fluttered over to a rack and opened a drawer. He reached in and pulled out a small, metal device. He fluttered back and slid the device around Quentin's broken pinkie.

"Quentin, you do realize this is permanent. You can't regrow it. You understand that once it's gone, it's *gone*?"

Quentin looked up at the holoboard above the end zone. It showed Becca lining up behind Bud-O-Shwek, ready to take the snap. The dirty, bloody, metallic Jupiter players dug in for the stop. Becca called out the signals, her breath billowing with each syllable. The wind picked up, forcing her to scream even louder just to be heard.

She was a phenomenal fullback, an All-Pro last year, one of the best in the game. But lined up behind center, barking out the signals, Rebecca Montagne looked like she *belonged*.

She took the snap, dropped back three steps, then turned and gunned a pass five yards downfield to George Starcher. Crazy George caught it and turned toward the sidelines, trying to get out of bounds to stop the clock, but the Jacks brought him down well in-bounds.

Whistles blew as Hokor used another timeout. Forty-two seconds to play, fifty yards to go, and the Krakens had only one timeout left.

Quentin looked at Doc. "I understand. Do it."

"I'll have to cut it, clamp it and then cauterize it to stop the bleeding. The nanomeds won't have enough time to seal the skin. Do you want anesthesia?"

Quentin shook his head. "Nothing that will dull my reactions. Get it over with."

Doc Patah hit a button; the device made a whirring, metallic sound.

"Try to hold still," Doc said.

Quentin closed his eyes.

"AND MONTAGNE SCRAMBLES out of bounds for a four-yard gain. Chick, it's second-and-six on the Jupiter forty-five. Is this it for Ionath? Their All-Pro running back is out, their quarterback is out, and their starting fullback is in at quarterback. One timeout remains, thirty-six seconds to go. Can Becca *The Wrecka* pull off the win?"

"It looks doubtful, Masara. Jupiter got here because they have the best defense in the league. If they kept Barnes out of the end zone, I don't think Montagne can do any better."

"Any chance that Barnes will come back in?"

"Zero chance, Masara. Did you see that hand? It looked like the aftermath of a Sklorno male being run over by a wheel truck. We're talking *squish!*"

"Chick! That's not an appropriate thing to —"

"Sorry, Masara, sorry, folks at home, I just ... what's this? The crowd is going crazy."

"Chick! Quentin Barnes is coming onto the field!"

"I don't believe it, Masara. How can he play with that hand? Can we get a close-up of his right hand?"

"Chick, I see that hand is heavily bandaged with nanocyte tape there, but something doesn't look right about it."

"Well, slap my bare behind and christen me a follower of High One, Masara, it looks like Quentin Barnes had his right pinkie *cut off* to get back into the game."

"Cut off? Amazing! But how will he take a snap?"

"He'll have to go from the shotgun formation. Wow! Listen to this crowd! Quentin Barnes must be carved from solidified testosterone, Masara!"

"Chick, calm down! Your elbows are flying all over the place!"

"Sorry, Masara, I'm just so pumped up! Kopor the Climber is running off the field, Montagne is staying in at fullback. The Krakens are huddling up. This is the stuff of living legends, Masara.

A field goal won't cut it. Ionath needs a touchdown to win the Galaxy Bowl. Can Nine-Fingers Barnes actually pull this off?"

WIND SCREAMED IN, moving the snow horizontally more than vertically. The stadium lights turned each flake into a fast-moving spark of white flame.

Quentin stood in front of the huddle. His right hand felt like he wore a glove of molten metal. In a lifetime of pain, he'd never known anything that hurt so much.

His teammates, his friends, his fellow Krakens, they all looked at his hand, then at his eyes. They knew what he'd done to get back on the field. At that moment, he could have ordered them to fly a ship into the sun, and they would have pushed the thrusters to full speed ahead.

They weren't much better off than he was. Sho-Do-Thikit's lower left arm hung uselessly. One of Halawa's three eyestalks quivered and waved, spasming beyond her ability to control it. Blood poured down from Michael Kimberlin's chin, soaking his orange jersey and staining the white trim around his black numbers and letters. Yassoud Murphy smiled wide, showing off his bloody mouth and newly missing front teeth. Kill-O-Yowet had tucked his middle right leg up on his back — it was hurting so bad he didn't even want it to touch the rock-hard, frozen ground.

The Ionath Krakens were the walking wounded. Leading them was a quarterback with nine fingers.

He locked eyes with Denver. Ever since their rookie season, they'd shared a connection, a kind of telepathy that went beyond even the instinctual communication he had with his other receivers. All four of her eyes stared at him, unblinking, sending a clear message — *throw me the ball, and I will not fail you.*

Quentin nodded at her, then spoke to his huddle. "Our defense gave us a chance. No field goal this time. Forty-five yards in thirty-six seconds. We need to save that last timeout, so pay attention to our down and distance — if they're going to stop you, get out of bounds no matter what it takes. *Forty-five yards* — that's all that stands between you and your destiny. Now, does anyone need to sit out a play so Doc Patah can patch up your ouchies?"

His teammates actually laughed.

He looked at Rebecca. Her eyes blazed with pride for her quarterback. She didn't get to be the hero, and she didn't care — all she wanted was the win.

"Okay," Quentin said. "Every formation is shotgun from here on out. Pro-set, spread left, X-slant, Y-streak, Z-hook, A-wheel. Becca, stay home and don't let them touch me, you got it?"

She nodded. "I'll die first."

"Let's hope it doesn't come to that," Quentin said. "Krakens, no matter what we get on that first play, the second play is no-huddle, pro-set screen right. Line up fast so we catch them sleeping. First play on two, on *two*, second play on *first sound*. Ready?"

"*BREAK!*"

Bruised, damaged and ignoring their exhaustion, the energized Krakens ran up to the line as if it was the first play of the game. Orange-clad linemen got into their stances. Halawa lined up wide right, Tara the Freak in the left slot and Denver wide left. Quentin stood six yards behind center, Becca on his left, Yassoud on his right.

The stage was set for a storybook ending, but Jupiter wasn't about to roll over and play the victim. The copper-jerseyed Jacks looked just as beat up as their Ionath counterparts. If the Jupiter defenders made the stop, they would be champions.

Quentin tucked his bandaged right hand against his belly. He stretched his left hand out in front of him. First things first: he had to focus on catching the snap one-handed.

"Blue, fifty-five! *Bluuue*, fifty-five! Hut-hut!"

Bud-O-Shwek flipped the ball back. Quentin tracked it, caught it with his big left hand. He started looking at his receivers even as his hand pinned the ball against his stomach, turned it until his fingers found the laces.

He counted through his receivers — Halawa on a slant from right to the middle of the field: covered; Tara on a streak: covered;

Denver sprinting out: Jacks cornerback Morelia running with her stride for stride — Quentin stepped up and threw as hard as he could.

Denver planted and turned. Morelia turned with her, displaying absolutely perfect coverage, but the ball was already there — Denver hauled it in. Morelia wrapped her up, tried to drag her down. Denver's folded legs pumped as she fought her way out of bounds for an 11-yard gain that stopped the clock.

Thirty seconds to play.

First-and-10 on the Jupiter 34.

The Krakens' players scrambled, scuttled and sprinted to the line. The Jacks' players screamed at each other, trying to line up as quickly as they could. Just like the last play, Quentin stood six yards back, Becca on his left, 'Soud on his right.

He waited only long enough for his linemen to settle in.

"Hut!"

The ball flipped his way — a bad, wobbly snap. Quentin grabbed at it but couldn't hold it. The ball bounced up, spinning madly. As it dropped back down, he cupped his left hand under it and pulled it into his belly. His fingers searched for the laces. He sensed pressure coming from the right — Xuchang on a corner blitz, a blur of copper and gold. Yassoud was running out to the right, waiting for the screen pass. Quentin tried to lift the ball and throw, but it again slipped in his grip, and as it did he knew he was dead.

Xuchang drove in, but she didn't reach him — Becca stepped in front of Quentin and leveled the blitzing cornerback.

Quentin heard the *ohhhh* of the capacity crowd as his fingers again found the canvas laces and he again lifted the ball to his ear. The Jacks' defensive linemen poured in. Quentin threw it to Yassoud just as the linemen smashed Quentin into the brick-hard field.

Agony tore through Quentin's right hand, but he used it to lift a Ki leg blocking his view. Yassoud was heading upfield, the sideline on his right side, Kimberlin and right tackle Vu-Ko-Will out in front of him. Jacks defenders slammed into the blockers. Yassoud ran toward the sidelines but cut left inside of Kimberlin's block to pick up an extra six yards before being brought down just past mid-field.

Why didn't you run out of bounds?

"Timeout!" Quentin screamed, pushing hard at the Ki so he could stand. "*Timeout!*"

Whistles blew, stopping the clock with 20 seconds to play. Quentin looked to the scoreboard: first-and-10 on the Jacks 23-yard line.

The Krakens huddled up. Yassoud ran to the back of the huddle, hanging his head — he knew his split-second reaction to go for more yards had forced his team to use its last timeout. Quentin wanted to hit him, to grab him and throw him off the field, but that wouldn't do any good. Instead, he reached over the front row of Ki and slapped 'Soud's helmet.

"Eyes up," Quentin said. "We got the first down, we can still win it, so eyes up and get your head in the game."

Becca pointed at Quentin's right hand. "You need to go out for a play?"

He looked at the hand. The nanocyte bandage was gone, left somewhere on the torn-up white turf. Doc Patah had burned the wound shut, but that, too, had ripped open — blood streamed down to the field. Too much blood, too fast: he'd get dizzy, but there was no time for another fix.

Quentin turned to look at the enemy. He saw the Jacks players talking to each other, pointing at his hand, nodding.

If I was them, I'd think I can't take another hit ... they won't be looking for the one-handed, bleeding quarterback to run the ball. They also won't expect me to go up the middle, not with so little time left.

Hokor's face appeared in his heads-up helmet display.

"*Barnes!* Let's go screen left to Becca and protect that hand."

"Sure thing," Quentin said, then immediately tapped his helmet to turn off the heads-up. He leaned in over his huddle.

"Time to catch them off-guard," he said. "Listen close. Second play is a no-huddle, line up immediately and we'll throw the corner fade to Denver, but first we're going pro-set shotgun, quarterback draw."

Becca shook her head. "Quentin, *no!* Your hand—"

"Shut your mouth, Montagne! One more sound from you and you're out!"

She stared at him hard, then ground her teeth and looked down.

Quentin again scanned the faces of his teammates. "Both plays are on first sound, first sound," he said. "Ready?"

"*BREAK!*"

The Krakens ran to the line. Denver spread out to the right, George Starcher settled in at right tight end. Halawa lined up wide left.

Instead of keeping his right hand at his belly, this time Quentin put it behind his back — he couldn't risk getting his blood on the ball and making it slick.

The icy wind chilled his face. He watched the Jacks line up: four defensive linemen, two linebackers in the middle.

"Hut!"

The ball flipped back. Quentin caught it with his left hand, fingers naturally landing on the laces. He stood tall and started checking through his receivers. He felt his linemen letting the defensive tackles come in, but pushing them to the right or the left, opening up the middle of the field. Becca ran left, Yassoud ran right, and the linebackers covering them went with.

Quentin tucked the ball tight and shot forward, armored boots hitting hard on the field's frozen mud. He ran between Bud-O and Kimberlin and past the line of scrimmage. He cut inside Kal-Gah-Het, who couldn't get around Vu-Ko-Will's block. Linebacker Katan the Beheader reached out for the tackle. Quentin stutter-stepped then cut left. The linebacker tried to plant and match the move, but his forward momentum made him slide across the snowy field — his hand slapped at Quentin's stomach, then slid away.

Quentin saw the orange end zone and angled for the left corner. *So close!* Morelia and Luxembourg moved in on him, blocking his path to the promised land. Quentin lowered his head, intent on dragging both of them into the end zone, but the backs were too smart for that — Morelia undercut him while Luxembourg took him high, dragging him down. Quentin turned to land on his left shoulder, protecting both the ball and his right hand. When he hit, his helmet *slammed* against the ice-hard ground.

The world spun, varying shades of black whizzing behind closed eyelids.

Then, hands pulling him to his feet. Becca's voice in his ear: "Quentin! Get up! Come on!"

She half helped, half carried him to the line. His feet barely seemed to work. He pressed his wounded hand to his belly, somehow aware that if the refs stopped the game because he was bleeding all over the place, he'd have to go to the sidelines for at least one play.

Strong hands grabbed his shoulders, moved him, then stopped him in place.

He felt hot breath coming through his helmet's ear-hole. "Stay still," Rebecca said.

He was aware of a screaming crowd, a howling wind and the guttural shout of Becca "The Wrecka" Montagne calling out a snap-count.

Quentin opened his eyes. The offensive linemen were in their stances, ready for the play. Becca was lined up as quarterback, right behind Bud-O-Shwek. Before Quentin could react, she took the snap and spiked the ball against the ground, stopping the clock.

Wake up, wake up NOW, or this is all over.

Head throbbing, hand on fire, Quentin looked up at the scoreboard: second–and-goal on the Jupiter 4-yard line, 12 seconds left in the game.

He turned toward the huddle to see Becca staring at him, pointing urgently to the sideline.

"Quentin," she said, "just get off the shucking field!"

He shook his head. It was only pain. He could ignore it just a little bit longer.

Quentin looked at the play clock — they had 17 seconds to get the next play off, or they'd be flagged for delay of game, a 5-yard penalty.

He stumbled to the huddle. As he did, Coach Hokor appeared in his heads-up display.

"*Barnes*! If you can't function, get off the field! Are you sure you can do this?"

Quentin fought back the pain enough to force a fake smile.

"Just give me the ball, Coach."

Hokor started to call a play, but Quentin reached inside his helmet, grabbed the display, snapped it off and tossed it away.

One play left, maybe two: he would make the call, and win or lose the results would be on him.

Quentin grabbed Halawa and pushed her toward the sidelines. He looked there, saw Tara the Freak and waved inward, calling him onto the field. Halawa sprinted off while Tara sprinted on.

He stood in front of his huddle. His receivers: Denver, George Starcher, Tara the Freak. Becca Montagne and Yassoud could also run pass routes, carry the ball or stay home to block. The offensive line waited for his commands, ready to leave everything on the frozen tundra. They would not let him down, and he, in turn, would lead them home.

The pain in his body, his head, his hand — it didn't vanish, but it ceased to matter. He could hurt later.

The crowd's roar grew so loud it drowned out the howling wind. In a nighttime blizzard on an alien planet, with an entire galaxy watching, Quentin Barnes would make his mark.

"Pro-set shotgun," Quentin said. "X-out, Y-hook, Z-fade, A and B both wheel. Get to the line fast. It's too loud here, so we go on my foot motion. Ready?"

"*BREAK!*"

The disciplined Krakens sprinted to their positions. Quentin stood six yards behind Bud-O. Everyone was in place with four seconds still to go on the play clock.

Second down and goal from the four. Twelve seconds left in the game.

The play he had called sent all of his receivers and running backs on pass patterns, which meant there would be no one left to pick up a blitz. A gamble, but at the same time, the Jacks had to cover five players — someone was bound to get open.

Quentin lifted his right foot high, then returned it to the ground. Bud-O waited one more second, then flipped the ball back.

As the ball ripped through the air, Quentin felt a stabbing, shooting pain in his right hand, making him wince — it was enough to throw off his focus. The ball hit his left hand and dropped to the frozen ground.

Even as he reached for it, he felt something coming from his right. Quentin reacted on instinct, throwing his body on top of the ball just as Xuchang dove for it. She'd come on a corner blitz, so fast he'd never had a chance. She ripped at his hands with both her tentacles and her raspers, cutting grooves into his armor, but he pulled the ball to his belly and tucked his knees up around it.

Whistles blew.

Quentin jumped to his feet and looked to the scoreboard: eight seconds and counting.

No timeouts.

"Get on the line! Move!"

It was third down. He could spike the ball to stop the clock and still have one final play, but if he couldn't hold the snap … he pointed at Becca.

"Becca, spike it!"

She ran behind Bud-O as Quentin moved to her normal full-back spot. Becca took a quick look to make sure everyone was set, then took the snap and threw the ball down at the field.

Whistles blew.

Quentin looked up at the clock: fourth down and goal from the 11-yard line, one second left in the game.

"Huddle up!"

"**CHICK, THIS IS AMAZING!** It all comes down to the final play of the Galaxy Bowl. What drama!"

"You can say that again, Masara. Fourth down, no timeouts, this *will* be the last play."

"Chick, why doesn't Barnes go out of the game? He can barely take a snap!"

"Masara, if the Krakens lose this game, that's a question that will be asked for decades. I saw Hokor trying to wave Barnes off the field, but Barnes is ignoring him. On this final play, Barnes could become the first Purist Nation quarterback ever to lead a Tier One team to the GFL title — even if someone shot him in the head, he'd probably scoop up his brains, stuff them back in and stay in the game."

"Listen to this crowd, Chick! The supporters of both squads are going insane. Such noise!"

QUENTIN TOOK A DEEP BREATH, then let it out slow. His entire life boiled down to this, to one, single play that would end in either glory or failure.

His subconscious counted off the seconds of the play clock. He had plenty of time to focus, plenty of time to really connect with his teammates, to look each one in the eye.

Denver, Quentin's first cross-species friend, the one he'd brought home to Ionath.

Yassoud, who had learned to play for the team instead of worrying about himself.

Crazy George Starcher, who had faced down his personal demons to become one of the best tight ends in the game.

Tara the Freak, a mutant outcast who had found a family with the Krakens.

Michael Kimberlin, the former Jupiter Jack, the brilliant, patient tutor who also fought like an animal from whistle to whistle.

Kill-O-Yowet, the dominant left tackle, the sentient that protected Quentin from the best defensive ends the galaxy had to offer.

Sho-Do-Thikit, the dauntless rock of a left guard, the leader of all of Ionath's Ki players.

Bud-O-Shwek, his ageless, stalwart center, and Vu-Ko-Will, his incredibly strong right tackle.

Quentin's eyes finally drifted to the middle of his huddle's second row, to Rebecca Montagne. Dirt and blood — both Human red and Ki black — smeared her face, coated her orange jersey so thickly he could barely read her number 38.

BLINK —

Time stopped, as it often did on the field, but *never* during a huddle. All noise vanished. Everything vanished, save for Becca. Her wide eyes blazed with fire and life. Her nose flared as she took in deep breaths. She was in the moment, fully aware of what was on the line and — like Quentin — ready to do whatever it took to get the victory.

Becca, who had been his ever-reliable teammate for two seasons.

Becca, who played every down like it was her last.

Becca, who had fought by his side at Chucky Chong's diner on OS1.

Becca, who had played so well in the Prawatt's Game, bravely going toe to toe with what were then unknown, monstrous aliens.

Becca, who had walked with him on the Prawatt homeworld, who had been with him when he met a living god.

Becca, the All-Pro.

They had fought together. They had bled together. They had won together.

Becca is a Valkyrie. She is MY Valkyrie.

For the first time, the truth he'd denied for so long hit home, hit so hard it made him shiver.

He was in love with Becca Montagne.

He was in love with his best friend's girl.

She smiled at him, showing blood-streaked teeth. "This play ain't gonna call itself, Q."

BLINK —

The roar of the crowd again filled his ears. He looked at her one more time, took in her smile and the lust for life that blazed from her eyes. He smiled back at her.

Quentin Barnes stood tall. He had to yell to be heard over the crowd's scream, and yell he did.

"Krakens, it's time to make history. We are on a collision course with a GFL title, and the only variable is *one second* of time."

Eyes widened, lips curled into sneers, heads nodded. Quentin banged his left fist against his chest armor, *bam-bam-bam*.

"This play is for Stockbridge. This play is for Aka-Na-Tak. This play is for Killik the Unworthy. This play is for Mitchell Fayed. Our brothers and sister *died* to help get us here. You have one play, *this* play, to show that they didn't die in vain."

He felt the huddle's energy, a battery charged to full and then beyond capacity until it crackled and glowed.

"One play to take what is ours. Pro-set shotgun. X-fade —" that would line Denver wide right, send her in at a slant to shake the defender, then angle her to the end zone's back right corner for a high pass.

"— Y-skinny-post —" that would put Crazy George on the line as the right tight end. He'd come straight off the line, then look back inside to his left, waiting for an almost instant pass from Quentin.

"— Z-slant-cross —" Tara the Freak would line up wide left. On the snap, Tara would slant in to the right, looking for an instant pass. If it wasn't there, he'd cross the middle of the field just a step past the goal line, waiting to see if Quentin threw his way.

"— A-wing-left, block and out —" Yassoud would line up a step behind and a step to the right of left tackle Kill-O-Yowet. 'Soud's job was to put a hard shoulder into the defensive end, then go five yards deep into the end zone and cut left toward the sidelines.

Quentin didn't call "B," the letter assigned to fullback Becca. By not giving her a route, he was telling her to stay home and block. With everything on the line, he wanted his Valkyrie by his side to protect him.

"On my second motion, *second* motion. Ready?"

"*BREAK!*"

BLINK —

The crowd noise again vanished. Quentin welcomed the silence, his old friend.

He stood six yards back from the line and stared out at the Jacks' defenders. They were lined up in a five-man front: three defensive tackles and two defensive ends. Two linebackers stood behind them, up close to the line, showing blitz. Would they come in hard or drop back into pass protection?

On the far left, Xuchang lined up one on one against Denver.

On the far right, Morelia lined up close to Tara, a bit inside of the Quyth Warrior to cut off the quick slant pass.

At left wing, the safety Matidi lined up in front of Yassoud, and on the right side of the line, free safety Luxembourg was covering Crazy George.

On the final play of the game, the Jacks were going with one-on-one coverage, betting on their league-best defensive secondary to cover the Krakens' talented receivers. Quentin suddenly wished he'd gone with Yassoud in the backfield for a play-action pass, but he couldn't risk an audible that would be drowned out by the crowd.

In a bitter bit of irony, Quentin had no choice but to run the play that he'd called.

He looked to his right, to Becca. She met his gaze. He pointed left, to the Jacks' defensive end, then pointed to the ground.

Becca nodded. She faced forward. So did Quentin.

"Red, sixteen!" he called. He couldn't hear the words, couldn't hear anything, but the billowing, white cone of his frozen breath marked his shouts. "Red, six*teeeeen!*"

One last play to show that they didn't die in vain.

A memory of Mitchell Fayed's face.

This one is for you, Machine.

Quentin lifted his right foot and put it back down.

The Jacks' left tackle rocked forward, but rocked back just as quick, avoiding the off-sides penalty. Quentin had hoped the tackle would jump, moving the ball half the distance to the goal line, but the Jacks were too disciplined.

And away ... we ... go.

He raised his right foot again. It seemed to take forever for his foot to return to the ground.

Bud-O-Shwek snapped the ball. It came at Quentin, a perfect, slow-motion spiral. He saw the laces, clean and white, spinning along with the ball's rotation. He saw them, moved his left hand up, caught the ball one-handed with the laces perfectly positioned beneath his fingers. He felt their texture, felt the ball's cool, pebbly leather against his palm.

He stepped back with his left foot, putting him into a throwing position: right foot forward, right shoulder pointed toward the end zone.

In front of him, the lines collided in a dreamy, final fight for victory. The multiple feet of Kill-O, Sho-Do and Bud-O slid backward across the frozen mud, driven by the Jacks' assault. Kimberlin stepped forward, got under his defender's four arms and drove the Ki down to the ground. Vu-Ko slid backward and fell, instantly overpowered by the Jacks' left defensive end, HeavyG Tony Jones.

Jones pounded in on all fours. Becca rushed forward to block the oncoming copper-clad monster. Quentin ran left, parallel to the line and away from Jones — if Becca couldn't stop the defensive end, Quentin had to get as far away from him as possible.

As Quentin moved he looked for options. The patterns of Denver and George had taken them toward the right side of the field — as fast as Quentin was moving left, they were already too far away to be a factor unless they broke off their routes and came back toward the middle of the end zone.

That left Quentin with two targets: Yassoud Murphy and Tara the Freak. Quentin ran hard left. Katan the Beheader kept pace, tucked into a ball and rolling along the goal line, paralleling Quentin's path — he was "ghosting" Quentin in case Quentin stepped up and tried to run it in.

Tara was slanting toward the middle of the end zone. He raised his pedipalp hand to say *I'm open*, but Morelia was right behind him — Quentin couldn't risk that throw.

Quentin saw Yassoud running left along the back of the end zone. 'Soud also had his hand raised, but the Sklorno safety Matidi was a half-step behind him, trying to bait Quentin into throwing a ball so she could step in front of Yassoud and pick it off.

Quentin had no choice — he had to run for the end zone's front corner, he had to out-run the Beheader.

In the end zone, Tara suddenly planted, then tucked and rolled left, coming back toward the goal line, toward Quentin. Morelia planted to change direction and stay with him, but she slid, her skidding feet kicking up small waves of snow.

Katan the Beheader saw Quentin angling for the end zone. The Warrior popped out of his roll and sprinted forward to meet Quentin at the line of scrimmage.

Too fast! Quentin knew he couldn't reach the end zone — if he tried, the Warrior would push him out of bounds, ending the game. Quentin planted hard and tried to cut inside, but — just like Morelia — his feet slid across snowy turf.

He started to fall.

Katan rushed forward, lowering his head for a hit that would finish the game.

Feet sliding left, body falling right, Quentin ran out of options — he gunned an akward, desperation pass toward the front left corner of the end zone, hoping Tara could get there in time.

The Beheader's shoulder slammed into Quentin's facemask. The back of Quentin's head bounced off the frozen ground. He saw his helmet rolling away across the field, felt the cold attack his sweaty scalp.

The impact bounced him up enough for him to reach out with his left hand, press it against the ground, holding him up enough to watch the game's final moment.

Morelia's speed let her catch up with Tara.

But the pass was low and dropping fast.

Tara dove toward the end zone's front-left corner, to where the ball would land. His long, mutated pedipalp arms stretched out, hands close together and fingers splayed wide. Morelia dove as well, reaching her tentacles down in front of Tara in an attempt to knock the ball away. Quentin saw a black- and white-striped official flying close by, matching their speed.

The wobbling ball started to drop. Just two inches above the turf, it crossed the goal line. The backs of Tara's pedipalp hands hit the ground and slid through the snow, which in that spot was strangely untouched and pristine. The ball dropped into his palms. His long fingers squeezed down just as Morelia landed on top of him, her tentacles and raspers pulling at the ball.

Together, the two players slid, their bodies kicking up arcing plumes of white that sparkled in the stadium lights. Morelia's raspers tore at Tara's hands, tearing skin and making black blood fly.

BLINK —

The two players slid out of the end zone's sideline and right into a line of photographers, sending bodies and equipment flying in all directions. The crowd's overwhelming rage and anticipation made Quentin wince.

Had Tara held onto the ball?

Floating cameras angled in from all directions. Strobes flashed and spotlights pointed, illuminating the downed photographers, Morelia, the Harrah ref and Tara, who during the slide had rolled to his back.

His bloody hands were still stretched out above his head. And between those hands, three inches off the ground ...

... the football.

He hadn't dropped it.

The Harrah ref hovered over Morelia and Tara for one last second, then blew his whistle and lifted his mouth-flaps up into the air.

Touchdown.

Quentin screamed, a single note of joy that encompassed everything he was. He struggled to rise on legs that didn't want to obey. He pushed himself up and ran toward his receiver.

Morelia sagged and rolled off of Tara. The Sklorno fell to the ground, motionless, defeated. She had done everything that could be done, but Tara's will had been stronger.

Tara sat up just as Quentin tackled him, leveling the Quyth Warrior and knocking the ball free. Quentin hugged Tara tight, screamed in his face.

"Tara! You did it! We won we won *we won* the Galaxy Bowl!"

The Warrior's eye flooded red-violet, as if he couldn't believe he had made the game-winning catch. His mutated pedipalps twitched and vibrated in laughing joy. Quentin tried to lift Tara up, but they were leveled by a quickly growing pile of Ionath Krakens.

Quentin's teammates, his screaming, yelling, joyous teammates, piled into the end zone.

They were the champions of the galaxy.

THE KRAKENS SCREAMED. They shouted. They pushed and hugged each other. They clacked arms against their chests. They jumped, sang, ran and laughed. Orange and black confetti filled the air. The Quyth Concordia national anthem blared from the Shipyard's sound system.

Everything seemed to go by in a blur. One second Quentin was in a pile of his celebrating teammates, the next he was shaking hands with Jacks players (he couldn't seem to find Don — that was bothersome, but not surprising, as his childhood hero had revealed his true colors long ago), the next he and his teammates were running around the field, reaching up to high-five the Ionath fans who hung over the retaining wall, desperate to touch their victorious soldiers.

Camera flashes strobed, spotlights tracked him every step of the way. Reporters reached microphones up to his face, but he didn't hear half of the questions and didn't bother to answer the others. He touched as many fans as he could. The Krakens faithful were beside themselves with joy — Humans smiling and laughing, fully covered Sklorno females jumping and doing flips, Ki barking congratulations, flying Harrah doing barrel rolls, the eyes of Quyth Workers, Warriors and Leaders alike all showing the yellow-orange of utter happiness and joy. For the first time since joining the Krakens, Quentin realized something shocking — the Orange and the Black didn't just bind the *players* together as one tribe, it also bound the *fans*. Maybe tomorrow the races could go back to hating each other, but for this single, pure moment, every species melded into one, giant family.

A tug on his arm. Messal the Efficient, shoving a T-shirt and a hat into his hands. Quentin held up the hat, looked at it — a holo-image waved across the front, an image that read IONATH KRAKENS: GALAXY BOWL XXVII CHAMPIONS.

He threw his head back and howled at the night sky. He laughed as he put the hat on, then bounced on his toes, jumping up and down in place. His Sklorno teammates swarmed in, wrapping their tentacles around him and jumping in time.

Another tug on his arm. Quentin again looked down to Messal.

"Elder Barnes, you're wanted on the podium for the trophy ceremony."

Messal pointed. A wide platform was floating down to midfield. People were already on that platform, including the diminutive form of Commissioner Froese.

Messal tugged on his arm again. "Elder Barnes, *please* — we will be *late*!"

Quentin reached down and picked up Messal. He tucked the Worker under his good arm, then turned to his teammates.

"Krakens! Let's go get our hardware!"

Messal kicked and struggled. "Elder Barnes, put me down!"

Quentin ran toward the podium, fake-stiff-arming with his ravaged right hand as he pretended Messal was his football.

QUENTIN BARNES WAS THE CENTER of the galaxy.

He no longer felt pain in his hand. He'd finally let Doc take care of that with a few shots — Quentin had needed a clear head for the game, but now the game was over.

He stood on the stage. His excited teammates packed in around him, as did Coach Hokor, Messal the Efficient and Gredok the Splithead. The wind and snow had finally slowed to almost nothing, but now orange and black confetti rained down, landing on the field, sticking to hair and fur and filthy uniforms.

Rob Froese stood on a pedestal, putting him almost at eye level with Quentin. On that pedestal, the golden football, the GFL Championship Trophy. Standing next to Froese was a smiling

Chick McGee, the sports broadcaster who — along with Masara the Observant — had called the Galaxy Bowl for several years running. Chick held a microphone and waved to the crowd.

The commissioner smiled wide; his red teeth revealed his happiness. He had presided over one of the greatest games in GFL history, a back-and-forth affair that finished on the last play of the game. There had been a few key injuries, but no one had died. It had been a Galaxy Bowl for the ages.

Gredok and Hokor didn't have a pedestal. They moved carefully, trying to avoid the big legs of over-exuberant football players. Quentin reached down and picked up his furry coach.

"*Barnes!* Put me down!"

"No way, Coach. You need to be up high for this." He sat Hokor on his shoulder pad. Hokor struggled for a moment but finally relaxed and looked around. His pedipalps shook with joyous laughter.

"Barnes, you are smarter than you look — it *is* a good view from up here."

Not to be outdone, Virak the Mean pushed his way to the front of the stage. He picked up Gredok and set the tiny gangster on his own shoulder pad. Quentin laughed at the sight of Gredok riding high. There was no hate now, could be no animosity at this moment — no matter what the Leader had done, the Krakens wouldn't have been here were it not for his immeasurable skill at player acquisition. He had earned this championship just as much as anyone who wore a uniform.

Gredok tried to stay serious, but the emotions of the moment overwhelmed even him. His pedipalps quivered with joy. His eye swirled yellow-orange. As he looked around, his gaze locked with Quentin's.

The two sentients stared at each other for a moment. Then Quentin reached his left hand toward the team owner. Virak tensed. Quentin felt Choto the Bright behind him, suddenly trying to push forward to handle the potential threat. Quentin stepped sideways to block Choto, sending a subtle message that everything was okay.

Quentin held his hand palm-out in front of the Leader. "High-five me, Gredok. We're number-one!"

Gredok stared for a moment, then reached out a tiny pedipalp hand and slapped Quentin's palm.

"Congratulations, Barnes. You have earned the right to forever be known as a *champion.*"

Quentin nodded, then turned away to look into the stands. Much of the crowd had filtered out of the stadium, but thousands remained for the final ceremony. Orange and black confetti still fluttered through the air. Quentin couldn't stop smiling, couldn't stop laughing. He felt hands on his free arm — Becca, looking up at him, her face blazing with joy. She had ditched her shoulder pads and now wore a white T-shirt.

On the shirt, orange-trimmed black letters spelled out GALAXY BOWL CHAMPIONS. Beneath those words, the six-tentacled logo of the Ionath Krakens. Below the logo, a phrase that made Quentin's chest vibrate with pride: THE ONLY VARIABLE WAS TIME.

He put his arm around her shoulders and pulled her in tight for a hug. She hugged him back. Her body felt warm and inviting.

"Quentin," she said, "we did it!"

He nodded. "We sure as hell did."

Chick McGee raised the microphone to his mouth. His amplified voice echoed across the field.

"Let's have a big round of applause for such a fantastic Galaxy Bowl!"

The crowd roared in approval.

"Wonderful," Chick said. "Sentients, to present the GFL championship trophy, please give a big welcome to league Commissioner Rob Froese."

The crowd's yell was a paltry imitation of the roars that came during the game, but Froese smiled and waved, clearly soaking up his moment in the spotlight. He leaned into his podium and spoke into a microphone.

"What a great football game between two hard-fighting teams," Froese said. "I thank them, and I thank you, football fans, for such a great season."

He paused for more applause, then continued.

"It's been twenty seasons since Ionath won a title. That span included a trip back down to Tier Two, but overcoming adversity is a part of football, as it is a part of life. I hope that this second title is all the sweeter because of it." Froese turned to look at Quentin and the two Quyth Leaders who had led Ionath to the title. "To Gredok the Splithead and Coach Hokor the Hookchest, I present to you the 2685 GFL championship trophy."

Tiny Human hands lifted the trophy toward Gredok. He reached out, grabbed it, then held it high. The Ionath faithful in the stands screamed in joy as yet another round of confetti poured down.

Chick lifted a microphone to his mouth. "Gredok, the title is back in Ionath. How does this feel?"

He angled the microphone toward Gredok. The Leader moved the trophy to the side and leaned in.

"It feels long overdue," Gredok said. "After our one-and-four start, everyone assumed we were finished. Ten wins later, the bitter taste of defeat coats their lying tongues, while we savor the delicious taste of victory."

Quentin laughed and shook his head. That was about as gracious as Gredok could be.

Chick took the trophy from Gredok and handed it up to Hokor.

"Coach, you won the big one," Chick said. "What does it say about this team that you overcame so many injuries to take the title?"

Hokor stared at the trophy for a moment. Quentin saw the golden reflection in Hokor's big cornea. When Hokor spoke, Quentin wasn't sure if he was talking to Chick or to the trophy itself.

"I am proud of our players," the coach finally said. "They have all worked very hard to get here. I have to thank Gredok the Splithead for his brilliance at assembling such talent. That is all."

Hokor handed the trophy down to Quentin, then slid off of Quentin's shoulder and faded into the mass of sentients packed onto the podium.

Quentin stared. He held the Galaxy Bowl trophy in his hands. The stadium lights played off the metal and the carved facets, making the prize glimmer and vibrate as if it were a living thing.

We did it. We actually did it. We are immortal.

A thump on his shoulder. Quentin looked at Chick, who was smiling wide. "Quentin, are you with us?"

Quentin blinked, then laughed. "Yeah, sorry. What did you say?"

"I said, how does it feel to be the champion of the galaxy?"

There were no words to describe the feeling. No poet in all existence could frame the experience.

"I'm just ... I'm just really *proud* of our team," he said. "We overcame so much. No matter what happened, we found a way."

His eyes scanned his teammates, then locked with John Tweedy's.

Quentin held John's gaze as he again leaned into the mic. "Things went wrong, and we worked together to get past them. At the end of the day, we play as a family, we win as a family."

John blinked rapidly, then looked down and away.

Quentin hoped he could get through to John, but now was not the time for that. He held the trophy by its base and raised it high. His teammates jumped in place, they pumped fists, they waved tentacles, they banged arms against chests, they bellowed and screamed and hooted and squealed. He had led them here, to this moment, and together they had seized it.

"Quentin," Chick said, "there's just one more thing before we let you go celebrate with your team and your fans. Commissioner Froese was supposed to present the next award, but someone else asked if he could, and the commissioner graciously said why the shuck not?"

Froese reached out and tapped Chick on the shoulder. Chick turned, Froese said something in his ear, then the broadcaster again raised the mic to his lips.

"Sorry, Commissioner, sorry, folks at home, I meant to say that Froese graciously backed out. And now, the presentation."

Chick took a step back, and there was Don Pine. Dirt and blood streaked his blue skin. His white hair stuck out in all directions. Frozen mud covered his metallic jersey, was caked on his armor and the once-white brace on his leg. Don had one hand behind his back.

Chick grinned white, hamming up the moment for the sentients present and the billions watching all across the galaxy.

"Sports fans, this is unusual," he said. "Correction, it's *highly* unusual to have someone from the opposing team on the victory podium. But don't think of this man as a Jupiter Jack, think of him as a two-time GFL champion. Here to present the Galaxy Bowl MVP trophy is former league MVP Donald Pine."

Chick handed Don the microphone, and the crowd cheered. Had Quentin heard that right? In all the commotion of the game and the championship ceremony, had he actually forgotten about the game's Most Valuable Player award?

Don raised the microphone. "First, congratulations to the Ionath Krakens. I started the season with you guys. I know how hard everyone in the franchise works. To my friends in the Orange and the Black, I salute you."

The Krakens players cheered loudly, their love for the man unchanged by a trade to Jupiter. Every one of them had broken bread with Don Pine, and every one held memories of his leadership, his teaching, his mentoring and his patience.

Quentin could barely breathe. Was this even possible? Could this *really* be happening?

Don turned to face Quentin. Finally, the blue face split into a wide smile. "Quentin Barnes, I remember the first day you arrived to play Upper Tier ball. I'm honored to have been your teammate. Knowing you has changed my life for the better. What you did on that field today was legendary. It is my great privilege to present you with the Galaxy Bowl Most Valuable Player Award."

Don pulled the hand from behind his back. In it, he held the Galaxy Bowl MVP trophy. It was a silver, regulation-sized football mounted on a dark wooden base. A swoop under the trophy showed the home planets of the league's original five races: Earth, Ki, Chachana, Quyth and Vosor 3. A black shield showed the words, the *impossible* words: GALAXY BOWL XXVII, MOST VALUABLE PLAYER.

Quentin's mostly numb right hand seemed to float, to reach out and gently take the trophy. Don slapped him on the shoulder pad, nodded, then turned and walked off the podium.

In his left hand, Quentin held the GFL championship trophy. In his right, the Galaxy Bowl MVP Award.

All of his dreams had come true.

He raised both trophies high over his head. The crowd and his teammates roared in joy, they roared for the title, but mostly, they roared for *him*.

THE SOUNDS OF A WINNING locker room: Humans screaming and laughing, Sklorno chittering and squealing, Ki arms clacking, champagne corks popping, etching machines whirring and scraping *GFL Champions 2685* into Quyth Warrior chitin.

Quentin stood on a bench, trying to sing an ancient Earth victory song as the big ball of Ki linemen clapped out a rhythm and Sklorno tried to sing along. He cradled the Galaxy Bowl trophy in his left arm. Ju was in the training room with Doc Patah, John was with Ju, so somehow the duties of singing had fallen to the third Tweedy brother.

"Weeeee are the champions ... my freh-end ... "

He could barely get the words out. He didn't know the first thing about music. His words sounded off-key, off-tempo, but no one seemed to care. The team wanted him to sing, so sing he did.

Yassoud jumped onto the bench next to him, one arm around Quentin, the other raising a bottle of champagne. Cliff Frost, George Starcher, Becca and Yotaro Kobayasho stood in front of them, their arms around each other, swaying in time to the song. The other Human players were doing the same. The HeavyG did their best to join in, although they focused mostly on an impromptu feast arranged by Alexsandar Michnik and Ibrahim Khomeni. The two defensive ends had — somehow — arranged for an entire roasted pig to be rolled in. They were eating away, full mouths singing in deep voice.

The Ki players had wiggled into a nightmarish ball that dominated the center of the communal locker room. Their bodies slid in and out, black eyes and vocal tubes there one second, gone the next, whichever arms happened to be on the surface of the ball clapping away in time. In contrast to Quentin's awful singing, their rhythm sounded crisp and sharp.

The squealing Sklorno were damn near damaging themselves from accidentally jumping into the ceiling. Every few seconds, one of them would succumb to excitement and sprint in a random direction until she hit a wall or a locker. Quentin wondered if they might accidentally kill themselves; if they did, at least they'd die at the pinnacle of joy.

Even the Prawatt celebrated by doing a version of the pinwheel dance Quentin had seen back in the arena on the *Grieve*. That experience seemed like it had happened a decade ago, but in reality only a few scant months had passed.

"And weeeeee'll keep on fie-ting ... 'til the end!"

Happiness, satisfaction and validation transformed the locker room into a madhouse. They *were* the champions — the best in the galaxy.

"But it's been no bed of roses ... "

Quentin felt a little hand tapping his thigh. He looked down into the face of Messal the Efficient. Messal still cradled Quentin's Galaxy Bowl MVP trophy. Quentin had given it to him for safe-keeping. Messal should have been celebrating with everyone else, at least as much as his restrained personality would allow, and his eye *should* have been flooded with the orange of happiness, but it wasn't — it swirled with purple, the color of sadness.

"Elder Barnes, there is news about your sister."

Not just news: *bad* news. Quentin's happiness vanished. Was she okay? Was she hurt? Was she ... *dead*? He handed the Galaxy Bowl trophy to Yassoud, distantly heard his teammates still singing, still celebrating, still laughing.

He stepped down off the bench to stand next to Messal. "News about Jeanine? What is it?"

"A punch-drive beacon came in with GFL diplomatic immunity codes," Messal said. "I am the point of initial contact for the

Krakens franchise, so the message came to me. I am supposed to first take such information directly to Gredok, but it is most unfortunate that at this time my personal communications system seems to be malfunctioning. Therefore, I am passing this time-sensitive information on to the intended party, which is you."

Quentin read between the lines — Messal feared that if Gredok got the information first, the Leader wouldn't share it, might even order Messal into silence. Messal was taking a big risk to give Quentin the message.

"Thank you," Quentin said. "Let me see it."

"Perhaps you would watch this in Doc Patah's training room? In private?"

A coldness sank into Quentin's chest, his stomach, his legs. "Sure," he said. "That's fine."

He followed Messal out of the communal locker room's screaming celebration. They walked to the training room. Quentin's feet felt heavy. His legs didn't want to obey. Suddenly, all the pain and exhaustion of the game flooded back, multiplied twice over.

In the training room, a calmer celebration was under way. Ju sat in a rejuve tank, up to his chest in pink fluid. John sat on a stool next to him. Ju had a bottle of champagne, while John had the biggest bottle of beer Quentin had ever seen. Michael Kimberlin was there as well, his hand extended for Doc Patah. Doc was clamping a cut on Kimberlin's hand.

Three heads turned, as did Doc Patah. The laughter faded when they saw Quentin's face.

"Q," Ju said. "You okay?"

Messal scooted forward. "Mister Tweedy, I am afraid we need some privacy. Would you all mind exiting the room for just a few moments?"

"Just play it," Quentin said. "I don't care who's here. Play it now."

Messal looked at Quentin, the purple in his eye joined by swirling green. He held his pedipalp palm-up and tapped the floating icons above it. A small holo started to play. Messal paused it, then grabbed the image and made a throwing motion at the training room's main holotank. In that tank, a paused image of Frederico Esteban Giuseppe Gonzaga appeared. Fred was standing in the salon of the *Hypatia*, Quentin's yacht. His mouth was open in mid-word.

Messal bowed. "The message is ready to play for you, Elder Barnes. I will take my leave." The Worker quickly left the training room.

Quentin walked to the holotank. He stared at the image, then reached out and waved his hand from left to right, starting the playback.

"— on the run from an attacker. They said they'd let me go if I gave them Jeanine, but shuck that. I —"

Quentin held his right hand out palm-forward. The playback stopped. He checked the date-stamp — the message had been created four days earlier. He pointed at the message path icon: the beacon had reached Wilson 6 from Loppu Waypoint a day ago, from planet Home in the League of Planets a day before that, from New Whitok a half-day before that, and before New Whitok, a one-and-a-half-day jump from Gateway.

Gateway? Quentin didn't know that planet. What system was that in?

He swiped left to right: an unpaused Fred continued.

"I've got the *Hypatia* on full burn," he said. "We don't ha —"

The holo froze and flickered. A few red and blue lines streaked across the image, then it went clear again and continued.

"— ve any choice, we have to —"

The image jittered — from a physical shake this time, not an electronic one — and Fred fell to the left, out of the frame. Quentin heard a scream.

Jeanine.

Then he saw her, his sister, his flesh and blood. She was in the background, spraying a fire extinguisher at a small flame. The image filled with white: part smoke, part fire-retardant.

Fred popped back into view, now bleeding from a cut above his right eye.

"We've been hit! The *Hypatia* isn't built for combat. I'm making a run for the Portath Cloud."

"You're *what?*" Quentin said, as if Fred could somehow hear him through the days-old message.

"It's our only chance," Fred said.

Another blast of static filled the image. Fred's face blurred and wavered. It split into two, then three, then melded together as one again. This time, the red and blue lines didn't go away. They flickered and danced even as Fred continued.

"Quentin, if you get this, I'm sorry," he said. "I told you I'd die before I let anything happen to your sister, and I meant it. Our only chance is they won't fol —"

His face froze in mid-syllable, but Quentin hadn't paused the playback. The playback seemed to be stuck.

Quentin's hands curled into trembling fists. His right hand started bleeding again. A stream of red spattered down to the training room floor.

Kimberlin leaned in, his voice calm. "Quentin, there is interference from the Portath Cloud. It causes problems with all electrical systems."

"— low us in," continued the shimmering, jittering holo of Fred. "I have to launch this beacon now or it won't escape the Cloud."

Jeanine pushed her way into view. She put her arm around Fred. She looked more angry than scared.

"Baby brother, I love you. Sorry we didn't get to spend more time together. If there is a High One, maybe he'll get us out of this in —"

The image shuddered wildly. Quentin heard Jeanine scream, heard something roaring, saw the image fracture and flicker. The red and blue lines grew larger.

A horribly distorted image of Fred's face said one last thing: "Launch beacon! Launch now-now-now!"

The holotank went black.

Quentin stared at it, hoping the blackness would suddenly change, hoping that Fred's face would appear, that his sister's face would talk to him ... but the blackness remained.

Kimberlin's big hand rested on his shoulder.

"Quentin, if Fred and your sister went into the Portath Cloud, then they are gone. I am sorry."

Quentin's soul filled with a blackness not unlike that in the holotank. He shrugged off the hand.

"They're *not* gone," he said. "I'm going to find them."

Kimberlin shook his head. "You can't, Quentin. No one comes out of the Cloud. Creterakian ships don't go in there, even *pirate* ships don't go in there."

Quentin closed his eyes, tried to control the rage building inside. He would not believe his only family was gone. He would *not*.

When he turned away from the tank, he saw that more sentients had entered the training room. Messal the Efficient, Denver, Becca, Milford, Bumberpuff, Choto the Bright, Mum-O-Killowe, Tara the Freak and Crazy George Starcher all stood there, their expressions showing that they'd seen at least some of the playback. Messal must have sent them when he left the room.

Doc Patah floated over to the Worker.

"The destruct signal from the *Hypatia*," the Harrah said. "Has it been detected?"

Messal lifted his palm and tapped icons. "Let me look through the Creterakian ship registry. I have a friend in that department so I have some access codes." He stared at the Quyth-language images ripping through the air, then looked up. "There is no destruct signal from the *Hypatia*. I can't speak for the passengers, but the ship is probably still space-worthy."

"*Probably*," Kimberlin said. "Rarely does a destruct signal come out of Portath space. No one knows if the ships that go in are still in one piece or if they were destroyed and the signal doesn't escape because of interference. What we do know is this — *what goes into the Cloud never comes out*. Quentin, it doesn't matter if there's no destruct signal. Fred and Jeanine are *gone*."

"She's my sister," Quentin said. "I have to go after them."

John Tweedy stood. "I'm going with you, Q."

Quentin turned to look at his friend. "John ... what? You've barely spoken to me for weeks."

John shrugged. "And I won't be chatting your ear off on this trip, either. But you know what? When I needed someone to come get Ju, you were there. That means I'm coming with you to get your sister."

Ju nodded, his chin dipping into the pink fluid. "I'm also in. My head would be a paperweight on Anna Villani's desk if not for you, Q-Dog. I'm going."

Mum-O-Killowe growled. Just a single syllable, but Quentin understood it all too well: Mum-O would join the excursion, and if anyone objected — Quentin included — things would turn ugly very fast.

Choto the Bright didn't say anything. He didn't have to. It was understood that where Quentin went, Choto went.

Denver and Milford started hopping up and down. "Danger-danger, Quentinbarnes," Denver said. "The Godling must not go without us!"

"Us!" Milford said. "Us-us-us-in-in-in!"

Quentin looked at Becca. She always shot down his plans, always had something negative to say. She stared back at him. She said nothing. Instead, she nodded once — she was in. That one gesture filled Quentin with hope, and also fear. Hope that with her at his side, he could succeed, and fear that if she came with him, she could get hurt.

Get hurt, or worse ... she might die.

Kimberlin sighed. He shook his head. "Quentin, am I correct in assuming that there is nothing I can do to talk you out of this suicide?"

Quentin nodded.

Kimberlin closed his eyes. He paused for a moment, then looked at Quentin and spoke. "I will likely regret this, but the Portath Cloud is the only part of known space that I have not seen. If I do not take this chance to see it, I would regret it for all my remaining days. I will come with you and help you find your sister."

George Starcher raised his hand. "Tara and I will sally forth into the void as cohorts in your worthy quest to rescue the fair maiden Jeanine, we will brave the dragons of the deep and vanquish all who would oppose you, Quentin."

Tara just jerked a thumb at George. "What he said."

Quentin looked around the room, looked at all the sentients who were willing to go into unknown space with him on the drop of a hat. This was different than the second trip to Prawatt Jihad territory. The Prawatt had already seen the *Touchback*, had already met Quentin. That trip had been a risk, sure, but a *known* risk. The Portath Cloud, on the other hand, was uncharted. Kimberlin had only said what everyone else already knew: ships that entered the Cloud were never heard from again.

Quentin knew the history. Over a century ago, eighty Purist Nation warships had chased a fleet of fourteen League of Planets vessels into the Cloud. The Nation ships were never heard from again. *Eighty* warships, gone. Seven of the League ships made it out — and that was the last recorded instance of anyone escaping the Cloud.

None of that mattered. He was going in. But how? Fred had taken the *Hypatia*. Gredok wouldn't let Quentin take the *Touchback*, not ever again.

"We need a ship," Quentin said. "We have to find one that will take us to the Portath Cloud."

The sentients looked at him for a moment, then at each other. *They* were all willing to go with him, but finding a crew that would take a vessel into a realm of death was another story entirely.

"I can get a ship."

All heads turned toward Cormorant Bumberpuff. A stiff brace covered his right leg. He favored his right arm as if it hurt to move it, to even bump it. Like most of the Krakens, his body had paid the price for the championship. The four-limbed, X-shaped sentient hobbled forward.

"Quentin, you have done more for my kind than anyone I have ever heard of," the captain said. "You stopped a *war*. You saved thousands of my people from death, maybe even millions. If you need a ship to enter the Portath Cloud, then I will get you the biggest ship you have ever seen. I can promise you one thing — if the Portath want a fight, a fight is exactly what they will get."

Heads nodded. They were all committed. Quentin suddenly

realized he couldn't take them — only Bumberpuff, and only because the Prawatt could get a ship. Just as he feared for Becca's safety, he feared for the safety of all his friends — he couldn't let anything happen to *any* of them.

As Quentin searched for the right words to tell them he didn't need them to come, Doc Patah floated over. His sensory pits flared, and there was some color to his normally pallid skin.

"You also need a medical professional for this trip," Doc said. "One last time in my fading years, I wanted to be part of a championship team. I wanted one last taste of the heavyweight title, and you gave that to me. I also wronged you when I told you that man was your genetic father. To make up for that, I will help you find your sister."

Even Doc wanted to come. Quentin stood there, dumbfounded — what had he ever done to generate such loyalty?

He looked at them all: Quyth, Sklorno, Ki, HeavyG, Human, Harrah and even Prawatt. Seven races that had spent centuries slaughtering each other, and now all of these sentients were willing to ride with him into the unknown, willing to help him rescue a woman they'd never even met.

Sure, he could tell them *no*, but he knew they wouldn't listen. Far more important, if he was going to save his sister, he knew he needed all the help he could get — he couldn't do this alone.

And hadn't he been in their shoes before? No one could have stopped him from helping to rescue Ju Tweedy. He'd put his life on the line to save George Starcher from killing himself. He had refused to stop supporting Tara the Freak. When trouble came, Quentin did what Quentin needed to do — were his friends any different?

He studied the expressions on their faces. He saw fear, certainly, but not a shred of doubt. Each and every one of them was a shining example of true loyalty.

"You could all get killed," Quentin said. "You need to know that."

Becca Montagne walked up to him, slowly, limping slightly from an injury suffered in the game. She stood in front of him, looked up at him with her big, dark eyes.

"If we die, we die as we live," she said. "We die as a *team*."

Quentin nodded. He would have done the same for any one of them, would have put his life on the line and wouldn't have given it a second thought. That *they* would do so for *him*? It stirred up emotions that he really didn't know how to handle.

Together, he and his friends would go after Fred and Jeanine.

The Krakens were coming, and High One help anyone who got in their way.

Ionath Krakens 2685 Galaxy Bowl Champions Roster

No.	Name	Pos	Ht / Ln	Wt	Age	Exp
10	Barnes, Quentin	QB	7-0	360	21	3
27	Breedsville	CB	8-3	282	12	3
79	Bud-O-Shwek	C	13-1	630	64	28
39	Bumberpuff, Cormorant	CB	8-1	270	65	0
65	Cay-O-Kiware	LG	12-0	625	35	9
67	Chat-E-Riret	DT	12-2	632	31	4
6	Cheboygan	WR	8-0	360	8	1
54	Choto the Bright	LB	6-0	400	30	6
69	Crawford, Tim	DT	7-10	565	20	1
27	Cretzlefinger, Luciano	FS	8-0	265	55	0
49	Darkeye, Samuel	LB	6-5	310	24	4
22	Davenport	SS	8-0	265	14	6
81	Denver	WR	8-10	318	11	2
96	Frost, Cliff	DE	6-11	532	27	5
51	Gan-Ta-Kapil	C	11-11	563	61	22
14	Goldman, Yitzhak	QB	6-4	265	32	8
13	Halawa	WR	9-6	320	10	2
80	Hawick	WR	8-8	282	15	7
95	Khomeni, Ibrahim	DE	6-10	525	26	5
76	Kill-O-Yowet	LT	12-2	513	37	11
71	Kimberlin, Michael	OG	8-0	615	31	11
85	Kobayasho, Yotaro	TE	7-1	380	36	7
28	Kopor the Climber	FB	6-0	415	24	4
92	Mai-An-Ihkole	DT	10-11	650	44	14
20	Martinez, Jay	RB	6-2	304	24	2
16	Marval, Pete	FB	6-7	381	23	0
83	Mezquitic	WR	8-5	295	14	7
91	Michnik, Alexsandar	DE	6-11	525	32	11
82	Milford	WR	9-0	305	10	3
38	Montagne, Rebecca	FB	6-6	330	20	2
2	Morningstar, Arioch	P/K	5-10	185	28	9
93	Mum-O-Killowe	DT	12-6	600	18	3
26	Murphy, Yassoud	RB	6-6	315	27	3
21	Niami	CB	7-9	285	9	0
72	Palmer, Rich	DE	8-1	425	19	1
64	Pishor the Fang	LB	6-4	400	19	0
66	Procknow, Jason	DT	7-8	612	19	0
33	Sandpoint	FS	8-6	295	10	0
57	Shayat the Thick	LB	5-11	439	35	5
62	Sho-Do-Thikit	LG	13-1	600	41	18
70	Shun-On-Won	RG	12-1	585	28	2
63	Shut-O-Dital	LT	12-8	580	23	4
25	Snuffalupagus, Tommyboy	FS	8-2	288	50	0
87	Starcher, George	TE	7-6	400	31	10
11	Tara the Freak	WR	6-3	360	22	1
50	Tweedy, John	LB	6-6	310	27	7
48	Tweedy, Ju	RB	6-6	345	25	6
23	Vacaville	CB	8-7	335	15	4
58	Virak the Mean	LB	6-2	375	43	3
75	Vu-Ko-Will	RT	11-11	579	50	9
31	Wahiawa	CB	9-6	320	10	2
40	Weasley, Katzembaum	FS	8-1	282	50	0
73	Zer-Eh-Detak	RT	12-8	690	20	3

From *Galaxy Sports Magazine*

KRAKENS TAKE THE GFL CROWN

by YOLANDA DAVENPORT

HITTONI, WILSON 6
LEAGUE OF PLANETS

On the Ionath Krakens' practice field, in their locker room, on their team bus, anywhere there are players and staff, a phrase has been endlessly repeated: *The Ionath Krakens are on a collision course with a GFL championship, the only variable is time.*

That mantra drove them. It served as a beacon guiding them to a destiny of greatness, a destiny that the Krakens finally seized when they defeated the Jupiter Jacks 23-21 to win Galaxy Bowl XXVII and claim the GFL title.

While both defenses played exceptionally, in the end this epic affair boiled down to a battle of quarterbacks. Jacks' signal-caller Don Pine was gunning for his third championship ring. Despite throwing for two touchdown passes, he fell short of that goal.

"It was Ionath's time," Pine said after the game. "We threw everything we had at them, and they kept coming. Ionath earned this win."

Krakens quarterback Quentin Barnes took home the Galaxy Bowl MVP honor for his gutsy performance. In the fourth quarter, Barnes — a lefty — opted to have his badly damaged right pinkie amputated rather than sit out the rest of the game. This reporter can't imagine the pain the 21-year-old faced every time he tucked the ball and took a hit.

"Did it hurt? Uh, yeah," Barnes said. "But I'll tell you right now that a GFL title is the best painkiller you could ever have."

Barnes went 22-of-30 for 242 yards and two touchdown

"It was Ionath's time. We threw everything we had at them, and they kept coming. Ionath earned this win."

DON PINE

---

passes. He also ran the ball four times for 39 yards. While not a record-setting performance by any measure, Barnes' consistent on-field leadership and his ability to come back from injury made the difference for the Krakens.

The only variable was time?

On Sunday night, that time came.

Congratulations to the Ionath Krakens — the champions of the galaxy.

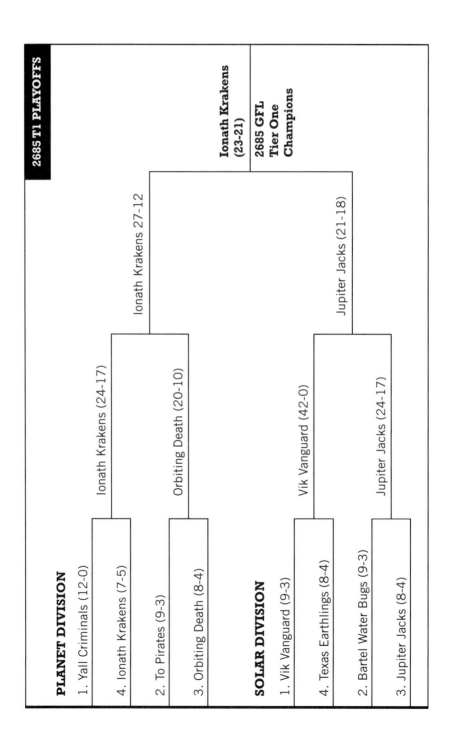

THE END